MW00800258

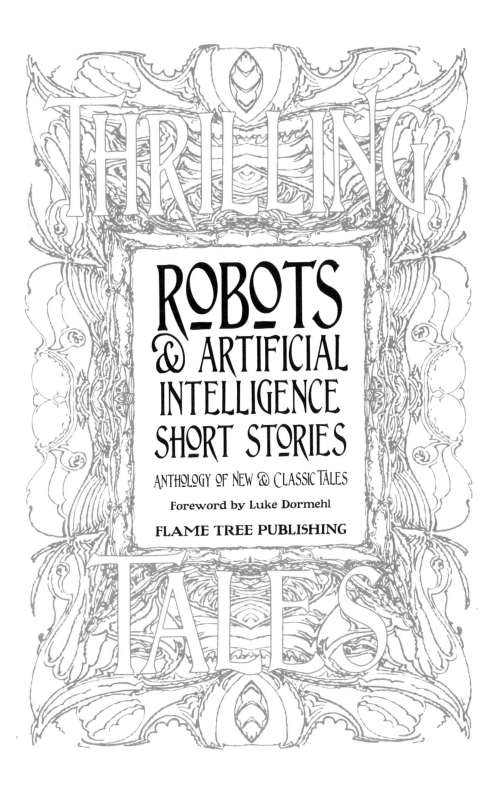

THRILLING

ROBOTS
& ARTIFICIAL
INTELLIGENCE
SHORT STORIES

ANTHOLOGY OF NEW & CLASSIC TALES

Foreword by Luke Dormehl

FLAME TREE PUBLISHING

TALES

This is a FLAME TREE Book

Publisher & Creative Director: Nick Wells
Project Editor: Josie Mitchell
Editorial Board: Gillian Whitaker, Laura Bulbeck, Catherine Taylor

Publisher's Note: Due to the historical nature of the classic text, we're aware that there may be some language used which has the potential to cause offence to the modern reader. However, wishing overall to preserve the integrity of the text, rather than imposing contemporary sensibilities, we have left it unaltered.

FLAME TREE PUBLISHING
6 Melbray Mews, Fulham,
London SW6 3NS, United Kingdom
www.flametreepublishing.com

First published 2018

The cover image is created by Flame Tree Studio based on artwork by Slava Gerj and Gabor Ruszkai.

A copy of the CIP data for this book is available from the British Library.

Printed and bound in China

See our new fiction imprint
FLAME TREE PRESS | FICTION WITHOUT FRONTIERS
New and original writing in Horror, Crime, SF and Fantasy
flametreepress.com

THRILLING

ROBOTS
& ARTIFICIAL
INTELLIGENCE
SHORT STORIES

ANTHOLOGY OF NEW & CLASSIC TALES

Foreword by Luke Dormehl

FLAME TREE PUBLISHING

TALES

Contents

Foreword: Robots & Artificial Intelligence Short Stories

HOW DO WE PREDICT the technologies that will become commonplace in the future? That's the $1 trillion question mused by everyone from tech fans, eager to know about new breakthrough gadgets, to lawmakers who wish to prepare for a future populated by autonomous cars, private spaceflight and augmented humans, to venture capitalists who hope to spot the next Google or Facebook.

Over the years, science fiction has served as a guiding light for where technology is going. Few things illustrate this better than the rise of the robots. It wasn't so long ago that the best known robots – heck, the only robots most of us knew about – existed solely in the pages of paperback novels, comic books, TV serials and movies. What united C-3PO and R2-D2, the Terminator and Data, and Robby the Robot and Marvin the Paranoid Android? Simple: none of them were real.

Today, real life robots are everywhere. They're found in factories and classrooms; in warzones and in hospitals. In Japan, a therapeutic robot seal called Paro is used to comfort elderly people. In 2017, Boston Dynamics, one of the world's most exciting robotics labs, released footage of its Atlas robot performing a gymnastics routine culminating in a picture perfect backflip.

What once existed wholly in the minds of sci-fi authors is now a part of our daily lives. This is no accident: the engineers and entrepreneurs who are currently building the future are frequently science fiction fans. They look to the extraordinary imagination of the genre's greatest authors and try to realise some of their ideas in the real world.

But science fiction writers perform a job which goes behind simply offering us a peak at tomorrow's hardware. They also ask the important philosophical questions that underpin it. What is the nature of intelligence? Will there ever be a need to consider rights for artificial beings? Are there certain tasks we should, as a moral society, be keen to hand over to automation, and other tasks we should not? These are all pressing, breathlessly debated topics as I write this introduction in 2018. Since so many of these areas are only now technical possibilities, it's easy to imagine that they are new questions. They are not.

This book attests to the extent to which intelligent writers have been grappling with these conundrums for years. Ambrose Bierce's 'Moxon's Master', first published in *The San Francisco Examiner* on April 16, 1899, tells the story of a chess-playing automaton which murders its creator. L. Frank Baum's 1907 novel *Ozma of Oz* includes the character of Tik-Tok, a robo-servant who is loyal, truthful but – we are repeatedly informed – not alive. Then there is 'The Dancing Partner' by Jerome K. Jerome, a writer best known for the whimsical *Three Men in a Boat* (1899). This tale tells of an attempt to build an artificial dancing automaton which leads to tragedy. Another favourite of mine is William Douglas O'Connor's 'The Brazen Android', a quasi-steampunk tale about the ways robots could lead to a better world – if only we don't screw it up first. And that is barely scratching the surface of this compendium's contents.

Astonishingly, the aforementioned stories were all written before the term 'robot' was even coined, in a 1920 play by the Czech writer Karel apek titled *Rossum's Universal Robots*. The stories raise concerns about a world that was just starting to shift on its axis with the arrival of industrialisation and electricity and their strange, exciting but scary new possibilities. They explore hopes and fears not so different from our own in the first decades of the twenty-first century.

Whether you pick up this book with a view to better understanding robots, for some moral philosophy wrapped up in fiction, or simply for a well-curated set of rollicking good stories, this is a wonderful collection. I envy you for not yet having read it.

Luke Dormehl
www.lukedormehl.com

Publisher's Note

HOW WE MIGHT create and use robots has fascinated us since long before we were even close to producing such machines. Very early writers such as Apollonius Rhodius began our interests in characters made of metal, and writers such as Ambrose Bierce, E.T.A. Hoffmann, Gustave Le Rouge and Gustave Guitton would explore the theme further, inspired by technological advances and questions of an ethical nature. But among the first to create a robot in the form that we would recognize today was L. Frank Baum with his humanoid metal man Tiktok, in the novella *Ozma of Oz*. Of course, this was only the beginning for this genre.

We had a fantastic number of contemporary submissions, and have thoroughly enjoyed delving into authors' stories featuring many different kinds of artificial intelligence. From domestic robots to AIs controlling spaceships, each story helps us to explore what it is to truly be human and what values we should hold dear. Making the final selection is always a tough decision, but ultimately we chose a collection of stories we hope sit alongside each other and with the classic fiction, to provide a fantastic *Robots & Artificial Intelligence* book for all to enjoy.

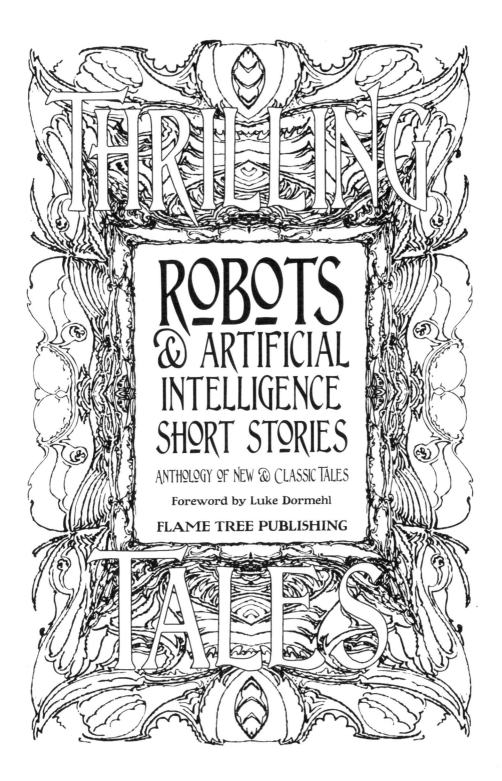

THRILLING

ROBOTS
& ARTIFICIAL
INTELLIGENCE
SHORT STORIES

ANTHOLOGY OF NEW & CLASSIC TALES

Foreword by Luke Dormehl

FLAME TREE PUBLISHING

TALES

Ozma of Oz

L. Frank Baum

Chapter I
The Girl in the Chicken Coop

THE WIND BLEW hard and joggled the water of the ocean, sending ripples across its surface. Then the wind pushed the edges of the ripples until they became waves, and shoved the waves around until they became billows. The billows rolled dreadfully high: higher even than the tops of houses. Some of them, indeed, rolled as high as the tops of tall trees, and seemed like mountains; and the gulfs between the great billows were like deep valleys.

All this mad dashing and splashing of the waters of the big ocean, which the mischievous wind caused without any good reason whatever, resulted in a terrible storm, and a storm on the ocean is liable to cut many queer pranks and do a lot of damage.

At the time the wind began to blow, a ship was sailing far out upon the waters. When the waves began to tumble and toss and to grow bigger and bigger the ship rolled up and down, and tipped sidewise – first one way and then the other – and was jostled around so roughly that even the sailor-men had to hold fast to the ropes and railings to keep themselves from being swept away by the wind or pitched headlong into the sea.

And the clouds were so thick in the sky that the sunlight couldn't get through them; so that the day grew dark as night, which added to the terrors of the storm.

The Captain of the ship was not afraid, because he had seen storms before, and had sailed his ship through them in safety; but he knew that his passengers would be in danger if they tried to stay on deck, so he put them all into the cabin and told them to stay there until after the storm was over, and to keep brave hearts and not be scared, and all would be well with them.

Now, among these passengers was a little Kansas girl named Dorothy Gale, who was going with her Uncle Henry to Australia, to visit some relatives they had never before seen. Uncle Henry, you must know, was not very well, because he had been working so hard on his Kansas farm that his health had given way and left him weak and nervous. So he left Aunt Em at home to watch after the hired men and to take care of the farm, while he traveled far away to Australia to visit his cousins and have a good rest.

Dorothy was eager to go with him on this journey, and Uncle Henry thought she would be good company and help cheer him up; so he decided to take her along. The little girl was quite an experienced traveller, for she had once been carried by a cyclone as far away from home as the marvelous Land of Oz, and she had met with a good many adventures in that strange country before she managed to get back to Kansas again. So she wasn't easily frightened, whatever happened, and when the wind began to howl and whistle, and the waves began to tumble and toss, our little girl didn't mind the uproar the least bit.

"Of course we'll have to stay in the cabin," she said to Uncle Henry and the other passengers, "and keep as quiet as possible until the storm is over. For the Captain says if we go on deck we may be blown overboard."

No one wanted to risk such an accident as that, you may be sure; so all the passengers stayed huddled up in the dark cabin, listening to the shrieking of the storm and the creaking of the masts and rigging and trying to keep from bumping into one another when the ship tipped sidewise.

Dorothy had almost fallen asleep when she was aroused with a start to find that Uncle Henry was missing. She couldn't imagine where he had gone, and as he was not very strong she began to worry about him, and to fear he might have been careless enough to go on deck. In that case he would be in great danger unless he instantly came down again.

The fact was that Uncle Henry had gone to lie down in his little sleeping-berth, but Dorothy did not know that. She only remembered that Aunt Em had cautioned her to take good care of her uncle, so at once she decided to go on deck and find him, in spite of the fact that the tempest was now worse than ever, and the ship was plunging in a really dreadful manner. Indeed, the little girl found it was as much as she could do to mount the stairs to the deck, and as soon as she got there the wind struck her so fiercely that it almost tore away the skirts of her dress. Yet Dorothy felt a sort of joyous excitement in defying the storm, and while she held fast to the railing she peered around through the gloom and thought she saw the dim form of a man clinging to a mast not far away from her. This might be her uncle, so she called as loudly as she could:

"Uncle Henry! Uncle Henry!"

But the wind screeched and howled so madly that she scarce heard her own voice, and the man certainly failed to hear her, for he did not move.

Dorothy decided she must go to him; so she made a dash forward, during a lull in the storm, to where a big square chicken-coop had been lashed to the deck with ropes. She reached this place in safety, but no sooner had she seized fast hold of the slats of the big box in which the chickens were kept than the wind, as if enraged because the little girl dared to resist its power, suddenly redoubled its fury. With a scream like that of an angry giant it tore away the ropes that held the coop and lifted it high into the air, with Dorothy still clinging to the slats. Around and over it whirled, this way and that, and a few moments later the chicken-coop dropped far away into the sea, where the big waves caught it and slid it up-hill to a foaming crest and then down-hill into a deep valley, as if it were nothing more than a plaything to keep them amused.

Dorothy had a good ducking, you may be sure, but she didn't lose her presence of mind even for a second. She kept tight hold of the stout slats and as soon as she could get the water out of her eyes she saw that the wind had ripped the cover from the coop, and the poor chickens were fluttering away in every direction, being blown by the wind until they looked like feather dusters without handles. The bottom of the coop was made of thick boards, so Dorothy found she was clinging to a sort of raft, with sides of slats, which readily bore up her weight. After coughing the water out of her throat and getting her breath again, she managed to climb over the slats and stand upon the firm wooden bottom of the coop, which supported her easily enough.

"Why, I've got a ship of my own!" she thought, more amused than frightened at her sudden change of condition; and then, as the coop climbed up to the top of a big wave, she looked eagerly around for the ship from which she had been blown.

It was far, far away, by this time. Perhaps no one on board had yet missed her, or knew of her strange adventure. Down into a valley between the waves the coop swept her, and when she climbed another crest the ship looked like a toy boat, it was such a long way off. Soon it had entirely disappeared in the gloom, and then Dorothy gave a sigh of regret at parting with Uncle Henry and began to wonder what was going to happen to her next.

Just now she was tossing on the bosom of a big ocean, with nothing to keep her afloat but a miserable wooden hen-coop that had a plank bottom and slatted sides, through which the water constantly splashed and wetted her through to the skin! And there was nothing to eat when she became hungry – as she was sure to do before long – and no fresh water to drink and no dry clothes to put on.

"Well, I declare!" she exclaimed, with a laugh. "You're in a pretty fix, Dorothy Gale, I can tell you! And I haven't the least idea how you're going to get out of it!"

As if to add to her troubles the night was now creeping on, and the gray clouds overhead changed to inky blackness. But the wind, as if satisfied at last with its mischievous pranks, stopped blowing this ocean and hurried away to another part of the world to blow something else; so that the waves, not being joggled any more, began to quiet down and behave themselves.

It was lucky for Dorothy, I think, that the storm subsided; otherwise, brave though she was, I fear she might have perished. Many children, in her place, would have wept and given way to despair; but because Dorothy had encountered so many adventures and come safely through them it did not occur to her at this time to be especially afraid. She was wet and uncomfortable, it is true; but, after sighing that one sigh I told you of, she managed to recall some of her customary cheerfulness and decided to patiently await whatever her fate might be.

By and by the black clouds rolled away and showed a blue sky overhead, with a silver moon shining sweetly in the middle of it and little stars winking merrily at Dorothy when she looked their way. The coop did not toss around any more, but rode the waves more gently – almost like a cradle rocking – so that the floor upon which Dorothy stood was no longer swept by water coming through the slats. Seeing this, and being quite exhausted by the excitement of the past few hours, the little girl decided that sleep would be the best thing to restore her strength and the easiest way in which she could pass the time. The floor was damp and she was herself wringing wet, but fortunately this was a warm climate and she did not feel at all cold.

So she sat down in a corner of the coop, leaned her back against the slats, nodded at the friendly stars before she closed her eyes, and was asleep in half a minute.

Chapter II
The Yellow Hen

A STRANGE NOISE awoke Dorothy, who opened her eyes to find that day had dawned and the sun was shining brightly in a clear sky. She had been dreaming that she was back in Kansas again, and playing in the old barn-yard with the calves and pigs and chickens all around her; and at first, as she rubbed the sleep from her eyes, she really imagined she was there.

"Kut-kut-kut, ka-daw-kut! Kut-kut-kut, ka-daw-kut!"

Ah; here again was the strange noise that had awakened her. Surely it was a hen cackling! But her wide-open eyes first saw, through the slats of the coop, the blue waves of the ocean, now calm and placid, and her thoughts flew back to the past night, so full of danger and discomfort. Also she began to remember that she was a waif of the storm, adrift upon a treacherous and unknown sea.

"Kut-kut-kut, ka-daw-w-w – kut!"

"What's that?" cried Dorothy, starting to her feet.

"Why, I've just laid an egg, that's all," replied a small, but sharp and distinct voice, and looking around her the little girl discovered a yellow hen squatting in the opposite corner of the coop.

"Dear me!" she exclaimed, in surprise; "have YOU been here all night, too?"

"Of course," answered the hen, fluttering her wings and yawning. "When the coop blew away from the ship I clung fast to this corner, with claws and beak, for I knew if I fell into the water I'd surely be drowned. Indeed, I nearly drowned, as it was, with all that water washing over me. I never was so wet before in my life!"

"Yes," agreed Dorothy, "it was pretty wet, for a time, I know. But do you feel comfor'ble now?"

"Not very. The sun has helped to dry my feathers, as it has your dress, and I feel better since I laid my morning egg. But what's to become of us, I should like to know, afloat on this big pond?"

"I'd like to know that, too," said Dorothy. "But, tell me; how does it happen that you are able to talk? I thought hens could only cluck and cackle."

"Why, as for that," answered the yellow hen thoughtfully, "I've clucked and cackled all my life, and never spoken a word before this morning, that I can remember. But when you asked a question, a minute ago, it seemed the most natural thing in the world to answer you. So I spoke, and I seem to keep on speaking, just as you and other human beings do. Strange, isn't it?"

"Very," replied Dorothy. "If we were in the Land of Oz, I wouldn't think it so queer, because many of the animals can talk in that fairy country. But out here in the ocean must be a good long way from Oz."

"How is my grammar?" asked the yellow hen, anxiously. "Do I speak quite properly, in your judgment?"

"Yes," said Dorothy, "you do very well, for a beginner."

"I'm glad to know that," continued the yellow hen, in a confidential tone; "because, if one is going to talk, it's best to talk correctly. The red rooster has often said that my cluck and my cackle were quite perfect; and now it's a comfort to know I am talking properly."

"I'm beginning to get hungry," remarked Dorothy. "It's breakfast time; but there's no breakfast."

"You may have my egg," said the yellow hen. "I don't care for it, you know."

"Don't you want to hatch it?" asked the little girl, in surprise.

"No, indeed; I never care to hatch eggs unless I've a nice snug nest, in some quiet place, with a baker's dozen of eggs under me. That's thirteen, you know, and it's a lucky number for hens. So you may as well eat this egg."

"Oh, I couldn't POSS'BLY eat it, unless it was cooked," exclaimed Dorothy. "But I'm much obliged for your kindness, just the same."

"Don't mention it, my dear," answered the hen, calmly, and began preening her feathers.

For a moment Dorothy stood looking out over the wide sea. She was still thinking of the egg, though; so presently she asked:

"Why do you lay eggs, when you don't expect to hatch them?"

"It's a habit I have," replied the yellow hen. "It has always been my pride to lay a fresh egg every morning, except when I'm moulting. I never feel like having my morning cackle till the egg is properly laid, and without the chance to cackle I would not be happy."

"It's strange," said the girl, reflectively; "but as I'm not a hen I can't be 'spected to understand that."

"Certainly not, my dear."

Then Dorothy fell silent again. The yellow hen was some company, and a bit of comfort, too; but it was dreadfully lonely out on the big ocean, nevertheless.

After a time the hen flew up and perched upon the topmost slat of the coop, which was a little above Dorothy's head when she was sitting upon the bottom, as she had been doing for some moments past.

"Why, we are not far from land!" exclaimed the hen.

"Where? Where is it?" cried Dorothy, jumping up in great excitement.

"Over there a little way," answered the hen, nodding her head in a certain direction. "We seem to be drifting toward it, so that before noon we ought to find ourselves upon dry land again."

"I shall like that!" said Dorothy, with a little sigh, for her feet and legs were still wetted now and then by the sea-water that came through the open slats.

"So shall I," answered her companion. "There is nothing in the world so miserable as a wet hen."

The land, which they seemed to be rapidly approaching, since it grew more distinct every minute, was quite beautiful as viewed by the little girl in the floating hen-coop. Next to the water was a broad beach of white sand and gravel, and farther back were several rocky hills, while beyond these appeared a strip of green trees that marked the edge of a forest. But there were no houses to be seen, nor any sign of people who might inhabit this unknown land.

"I hope we shall find something to eat," said Dorothy, looking eagerly at the pretty beach toward which they drifted. "It's long past breakfast time, now."

"I'm a trifle hungry, myself," declared the yellow hen.

"Why don't you eat the egg?" asked the child. "You don't need to have your food cooked, as I do."

"Do you take me for a cannibal?" cried the hen, indignantly. "I do not know what I have said or done that leads you to insult me!"

"I beg your pardon, I'm sure Mrs. – Mrs. – by the way, may I inquire your name, ma'am?" asked the little girl.

"My name is Bill," said the yellow hen, somewhat gruffly.

"Bill! Why, that's a boy's name."

"What difference does that make?"

"You're a lady hen, aren't you?"

"Of course. But when I was first hatched out no one could tell whether I was going to be a hen or a rooster; so the little boy at the farm where I was born called me Bill, and made a pet of me because I was the only yellow chicken in the whole brood. When I grew up, and he found that I didn't crow and fight, as all the roosters do, he did not think to change my name, and every creature in the barn-yard, as well as the people in the house, knew me as 'Bill.' So Bill I've always been called, and Bill is my name."

"But it's all wrong, you know," declared Dorothy, earnestly; "and, if you don't mind, I shall call you 'Billina.' Putting the 'eena' on the end makes it a girl's name, you see."

"Oh, I don't mind it in the least," returned the yellow hen. "It doesn't matter at all what you call me, so long as I know the name means ME."

"Very well, Billina. MY name is Dorothy Gale – just Dorothy to my friends and Miss Gale to strangers. You may call me Dorothy, if you like. We're getting very near the shore. Do you suppose it is too deep for me to wade the rest of the way?"

"Wait a few minutes longer. The sunshine is warm and pleasant, and we are in no hurry."

"But my feet are all wet and soggy," said the girl. "My dress is dry enough, but I won't feel real comfor'ble till I get my feet dried."

She waited, however, as the hen advised, and before long the big wooden coop grated gently on the sandy beach and the dangerous voyage was over.

It did not take the castaways long to reach the shore, you may be sure. The yellow hen flew to the sands at once, but Dorothy had to climb over the high slats. Still, for a country girl, that was not much of a feat, and as soon as she was safe ashore Dorothy drew off her wet shoes and stockings and spread them upon the sun-warmed beach to dry.

Then she sat down and watched Billina, who was pick-pecking away with her sharp bill in the sand and gravel, which she scratched up and turned over with her strong claws.

"What are you doing?" asked Dorothy.

"Getting my breakfast, of course," murmured the hen, busily pecking away.

"What do you find?" inquired the girl, curiously.

"Oh, some fat red ants, and some sand-bugs, and once in a while a tiny crab. They are very sweet and nice, I assure you."

"How dreadful!" exclaimed Dorothy, in a shocked voice.

"What is dreadful?" asked the hen, lifting her head to gaze with one bright eye at her companion.

"Why, eating live things, and horrid bugs, and crawly ants. You ought to be 'SHAMED of yourself!"

"Goodness me!" returned the hen, in a puzzled tone; "how queer you are, Dorothy! Live things are much fresher and more wholesome than dead ones, and you humans eat all sorts of dead creatures."

"We don't!" said Dorothy.

"You do, indeed," answered Billina. "You eat lambs and sheep and cows and pigs and even chickens."

"But we cook 'em," said Dorothy, triumphantly.

"What difference does that make?"

"A good deal," said the girl, in a graver tone. "I can't just 'splain the diff'rence, but it's there. And, anyhow, we never eat such dreadful things as BUGS."

"But you eat the chickens that eat the bugs," retorted the yellow hen, with an odd cackle. "So you are just as bad as we chickens are."

This made Dorothy thoughtful. What Billina said was true enough, and it almost took away her appetite for breakfast. As for the yellow hen, she continued to peck away at the sand busily, and seemed quite contented with her bill-of-fare.

Finally, down near the water's edge, Billina stuck her bill deep into the sand, and then drew back and shivered.

"Ow!" she cried. "I struck metal, that time, and it nearly broke my beak."

"It prob'bly was a rock," said Dorothy, carelessly.

"Nonsense. I know a rock from metal, I guess," said the hen. "There's a different feel to it."

"But there couldn't be any metal on this wild, deserted seashore," persisted the girl. "Where's the place? I'll dig it up, and prove to you I'm right."

Billina showed her the place where she had "stubbed her bill," as she expressed it, and Dorothy dug away the sand until she felt something hard. Then, thrusting in her hand, she pulled the thing out, and discovered it to be a large sized golden key – rather old, but still bright and of perfect shape.

"What did I tell you?" cried the hen, with a cackle of triumph. "Can I tell metal when I bump into it, or is the thing a rock?"

"It's metal, sure enough," answered the child, gazing thoughtfully at the curious thing she had found. "I think it is pure gold, and it must have lain hidden in the sand for a long time. How do you suppose it came there, Billina? And what do you suppose this mysterious key unlocks?"

"I can't say," replied the hen. "You ought to know more about locks and keys than I do."

Dorothy glanced around. There was no sign of any house in that part of the country, and she reasoned that every key must fit a lock and every lock must have a purpose. Perhaps the key had been lost by somebody who lived far away, but had wandered on this very shore.

Musing on these things the girl put the key in the pocket of her dress and then slowly drew on her shoes and stockings, which the sun had fully dried.

"I b'lieve, Billina," she said, "I'll have a look 'round, and see if I can find some breakfast."

Chapter III
Letters in the Sand

WALKING A LITTLE WAY back from the water's edge, toward the grove of trees, Dorothy came to a flat stretch of white sand that seemed to have queer signs marked upon its surface, just as one would write upon sand with a stick.

"What does it say?" she asked the yellow hen, who trotted along beside her in a rather dignified fashion.

"How should I know?" returned the hen. "I cannot read."

"Oh! Can't you?"

"Certainly not; I've never been to school, you know."

"Well, I have," admitted Dorothy; "but the letters are big and far apart, and it's hard to spell out the words."

But she looked at each letter carefully, and finally discovered that these words were written in the sand:

'BEWARE THE WHEELERS!'

"That's rather strange," declared the hen, when Dorothy had read aloud the words. "What do you suppose the Wheelers are?"

"Folks that wheel, I guess. They must have wheelbarrows, or baby-cabs or hand-carts," said Dorothy.

"Perhaps they're automobiles," suggested the yellow hen. "There is no need to beware of baby-cabs and wheelbarrows; but automobiles are dangerous things. Several of my friends have been run over by them."

"It can't be auto'biles," replied the girl, "for this is a new, wild country, without even trolley-cars or tel'phones. The people here haven't been discovered yet, I'm sure; that is, if there ARE any people. So I don't b'lieve there CAN be any auto'biles, Billina."

"Perhaps not," admitted the yellow hen. "Where are you going now?"

"Over to those trees, to see if I can find some fruit or nuts," answered Dorothy.

She tramped across the sand, skirting the foot of one of the little rocky hills that stood near, and soon reached the edge of the forest.

At first she was greatly disappointed, because the nearer trees were all punita, or cotton-wood or eucalyptus, and bore no fruit or nuts at all. But, bye and bye, when she was almost in despair, the little girl came upon two trees that promised to furnish her with plenty of food.

One was quite full of square paper boxes, which grew in clusters on all the limbs, and upon the biggest and ripest boxes the word 'Lunch' could be read, in neat raised letters. This tree seemed to bear all the year around, for there were lunch-box blossoms on some of the branches, and on others tiny little lunch-boxes that were as yet quite green, and evidently not fit to eat until they had grown bigger.

The leaves of this tree were all paper napkins, and it presented a very pleasing appearance to the hungry little girl.

But the tree next to the lunch-box tree was even more wonderful, for it bore quantities of tin dinner-pails, which were so full and heavy that the stout branches bent underneath their weight. Some were small and dark-brown in color; those larger were of a dull tin color; but the really ripe ones were pails of bright tin that shone and glistened beautifully in the rays of sunshine that touched them.

Dorothy was delighted, and even the yellow hen acknowledged that she was surprised.

The little girl stood on tip-toe and picked one of the nicest and biggest lunch-boxes, and then she sat down upon the ground and eagerly opened it. Inside she found, nicely wrapped in white papers, a ham sandwich, a piece of sponge-cake, a pickle, a slice of new cheese and an apple. Each thing had a separate stem, and so had to be picked off the side of the box; but Dorothy found them all to be delicious, and she ate every bit of luncheon in the box before she had finished.

"A lunch isn't zactly breakfast," she said to Billina, who sat beside her curiously watching. "But when one is hungry one can eat even supper in the morning, and not complain."

"I hope your lunch-box was perfectly ripe," observed the yellow hen, in an anxious tone. "So much sickness is caused by eating green things."

"Oh, I'm sure it was ripe," declared Dorothy, "all, that is, 'cept the pickle, and a pickle just HAS to be green, Billina. But everything tasted perfectly splendid, and I'd rather have it than a church picnic. And now I think I'll pick a dinner-pail, to have when I get hungry again, and then we'll start out and 'splore the country, and see where we are."

"Haven't you any idea what country this is?" inquired Billina.

"None at all. But listen: I'm quite sure it's a fairy country, or such things as lunch-boxes and dinner-pails wouldn't be growing upon trees. Besides, Billina, being a hen, you wouldn't be able to talk in any civ'lized country, like Kansas, where no fairies live at all."

"Perhaps we're in the Land of Oz," said the hen, thoughtfully.

"No, that can't be," answered the little girl; "because I've been to the Land of Oz, and it's all surrounded by a horrid desert that no one can cross."

"Then how did you get away from there again?" asked Billina.

"I had a pair of silver shoes, that carried me through the air; but I lost them," said Dorothy.

"Ah, indeed," remarked the yellow hen, in a tone of unbelief.

"Anyhow," resumed the girl, "there is no seashore near the Land of Oz, so this must surely be some other fairy country."

While she was speaking she selected a bright and pretty dinner-pail that seemed to have a stout handle, and picked it from its branch. Then, accompanied by the yellow hen, she walked out of the shadow of the trees toward the sea-shore.

They were part way across the sands when Billina suddenly cried, in a voice of terror:

"What's that?"

Dorothy turned quickly around, and saw coming out of a path that led from between the trees the most peculiar person her eyes had ever beheld.

It had the form of a man, except that it walked, or rather rolled, upon all fours, and its legs were the same length as its arms, giving them the appearance of the four legs of a beast. Yet it was no beast that Dorothy had discovered, for the person was clothed most gorgeously in embroidered garments of many colors, and wore a straw hat perched jauntily upon the side of its head. But it differed from human beings in this respect, that instead of hands and feet there grew at the end of its arms and legs round wheels, and by means of these wheels it rolled very swiftly over the level ground. Afterward Dorothy found that these odd wheels were of the same hard substance that our fingernails and toenails are composed of, and she also learned that creatures of this strange race were born in this queer fashion. But when our little girl first caught sight of the first individual of a race that was destined to cause her a lot of trouble, she had an idea that the brilliantly-clothed personage was on roller-skates, which were attached to his hands as well as to his feet.

"Run!" screamed the yellow hen, fluttering away in great fright. "It's a Wheeler!"

"A Wheeler?" exclaimed Dorothy. "What can that be?"

"Don't you remember the warning in the sand: 'Beware the Wheelers'? Run, I tell you – run!"

So Dorothy ran, and the Wheeler gave a sharp, wild cry and came after her in full chase.

Looking over her shoulder as she ran, the girl now saw a great procession of Wheelers emerging from the forest – dozens and dozens of them – all clad in splendid, tight-fitting garments and all rolling swiftly toward her and uttering their wild, strange cries.

"They're sure to catch us!" panted the girl, who was still carrying the heavy dinner-pail she had picked. "I can't run much farther, Billina."

"Climb up this hill, – quick!" said the hen; and Dorothy found she was very near to the heap of loose and jagged rocks they had passed on their way to the forest. The yellow hen was even now fluttering among the rocks, and Dorothy followed as best she could, half climbing and half tumbling up the rough and rugged steep.

She was none too soon, for the foremost Wheeler reached the hill a moment after her; but while the girl scrambled up the rocks the creature stopped short with howls of rage and disappointment.

Dorothy now heard the yellow hen laughing, in her cackling, henny way.

"Don't hurry, my dear," cried Billina. "They can't follow us among these rocks, so we're safe enough now."

Dorothy stopped at once and sat down upon a broad boulder, for she was all out of breath.

The rest of the Wheelers had now reached the foot of the hill, but it was evident that their wheels would not roll upon the rough and jagged rocks, and therefore they were helpless to follow Dorothy and the hen to where they had taken refuge. But they circled all around the little hill, so the child and Billina were fast prisoners and could not come down without being captured.

Then the creatures shook their front wheels at Dorothy in a threatening manner, and it seemed they were able to speak as well as to make their dreadful outcries, for several of them shouted:

"We'll get you in time, never fear! And when we do get you, we'll tear you into little bits!"

"Why are you so cruel to me?" asked Dorothy. "I'm a stranger in your country, and have done you no harm."

"No harm!" cried one who seemed to be their leader. "Did you not pick our lunch-boxes and dinner-pails? Have you not a stolen dinner-pail still in your hand?"

"I only picked one of each," she answered. "I was hungry, and I didn't know the trees were yours."

"That is no excuse," retorted the leader, who was clothed in a most gorgeous suit. "It is the law here that whoever picks a dinner-pail without our permission must die immediately."

"Don't you believe him," said Billina. "I'm sure the trees do not belong to these awful creatures. They are fit for any mischief, and it's my opinion they would try to kill us just the same if you hadn't picked a dinner-pail."

"I think so, too," agreed Dorothy. "But what shall we do now?"

"Stay where we are," advised the yellow hen. "We are safe from the Wheelers until we starve to death, anyhow; and before that time comes a good many things can happen."

Chapter IV
Tiktok the Machine Man

AFTER AN HOUR or so most of the band of Wheelers rolled back into the forest, leaving only three of their number to guard the hill. These curled themselves up like big dogs and pretended to go to sleep on the sands; but neither Dorothy nor Billina were fooled by this trick, so they remained in security among the rocks and paid no attention to their cunning enemies.

Finally the hen, fluttering over the mound, exclaimed: "Why, here's a path!"

So Dorothy at once clambered to where Billina sat, and there, sure enough, was a smooth path cut between the rocks. It seemed to wind around the mound from top to bottom, like a cork-screw, twisting here and there between the rough boulders but always remaining level and easy to walk upon.

Indeed, Dorothy wondered at first why the Wheelers did not roll up this path; but when she followed it to the foot of the mound she found that several big pieces of rock had been placed directly across the end of the way, thus preventing any one outside from seeing it and also preventing the Wheelers from using it to climb up the mound.

Then Dorothy walked back up the path, and followed it until she came to the very top of the hill, where a solitary round rock stood that was bigger than any of the others surrounding it. The path came to an end just beside this great rock, and for a moment it puzzled the girl to know why the path had been made at all. But the hen, who had been gravely following her around and was now perched upon a point of rock behind Dorothy, suddenly remarked:

"It looks something like a door, doesn't it?"

"What looks like a door?" enquired the child.

"Why, that crack in the rock, just facing you," replied Billina, whose little round eyes were very sharp and seemed to see everything. "It runs up one side and down the other, and across the top and the bottom."

"What does?"

"Why, the crack. So I think it must be a door of rock, although I do not see any hinges."

"Oh, yes," said Dorothy, now observing for the first time the crack in the rock. "And isn't this a key-hole, Billina?" pointing to a round, deep hole at one side of the door.

"Of course. If we only had the key, now, we could unlock it and see what is there," replied the yellow hen. "May be it's a treasure chamber full of diamonds and rubies, or heaps of shining gold, or –"

"That reminds me," said Dorothy, "of the golden key I picked up on the shore. Do you think that it would fit this key-hole, Billina?"

"Try it and see," suggested the hen.

So Dorothy searched in the pocket of her dress and found the golden key. And when she had put it into the hole of the rock, and turned it, a sudden sharp snap was heard; then, with a solemn creak that made the shivers run down the child's back, the face of the rock fell outward, like a door on hinges, and revealed a small dark chamber just inside.

"Good gracious!" cried Dorothy, shrinking back as far as the narrow path would let her.

For, standing within the narrow chamber of rock, was the form of a man – or, at least, it seemed like a man, in the dim light. He was only about as tall as Dorothy herself, and his body was round as a ball and made out of burnished copper. Also his head and limbs were copper, and these were jointed or hinged to his body in a peculiar way, with metal caps over the joints, like the armor worn by knights in days of old. He stood perfectly still, and where the light struck upon his form it glittered as if made of pure gold.

"Don't be frightened," called Billina, from her perch. "It isn't alive."

"I see it isn't," replied the girl, drawing a long breath.

"It is only made out of copper, like the old kettle in the barn-yard at home," continued the hen, turning her head first to one side and then to the other, so that both her little round eyes could examine the object.

"Once," said Dorothy, "I knew a man made out of tin, who was a woodman named Nick Chopper. But he was as alive as we are, 'cause he was born a real man, and got his tin body a little at a time – first a leg and then a finger and then an ear – for the reason that he had so many accidents with his axe, and cut himself up in a very careless manner."

"Oh," said the hen, with a sniff, as if she did not believe the story.

"But this copper man," continued Dorothy, looking at it with big eyes, "is not alive at all, and I wonder what it was made for, and why it was locked up in this queer place."

"That is a mystery," remarked the hen, twisting her head to arrange her wing-feathers with her bill.

Dorothy stepped inside the little room to get a back view of the copper man, and in this way discovered a printed card that hung between his shoulders, it being suspended from a small copper peg at the back of his neck. She unfastened this card and returned to the path, where the light was better, and sat herself down upon a slab of rock to read the printing.

"What does it say?" asked the hen, curiously.

Dorothy read the card aloud, spelling out the big words with some difficulty; and this is what she read:

SMITH & TINKER'S
Patent Double-Action, Extra-Responsive,
Thought-Creating, Perfect-Talking
MECHANICAL MAN
Fitted with our Special Clock-Work Attachment.
Thinks, Speaks, Acts, and Does Everything but Live.
Manufactured only at our Works at Evna, Land of Ev.
All infringements will be promptly Prosecuted according to Law.

"How queer!" said the yellow hen. "Do you think that is all true, my dear?"

"I don't know," answered Dorothy, who had more to read. "Listen to this, Billina…"

DIRECTIONS FOR USING:

For THINKING: Wind the Clock-work Man under his left arm, (marked No. 1.)
For SPEAKING: Wind the Clock-work Man under his right arm, (marked No. 2.)
For WALKING and ACTION: Wind Clock-work in
the middle of his back, (marked No. 3.)
N. B. This Mechanism is guaranteed to work perfectly for a thousand years.

"Well, I declare!" gasped the yellow hen, in amazement; "if the copper man can do half of these things he is a very wonderful machine. But I suppose it is all humbug, like so many other patented articles."

"We might wind him up," suggested Dorothy, "and see what he'll do."

"Where is the key to the clock-work?" asked Billina.

"Hanging on the peg where I found the card."

"Then," said the hen, "let us try him, and find out if he will go. He is warranted for a thousand years, it seems; but we do not know how long he has been standing inside this rock."

Dorothy had already taken the clock key from the peg.

"Which shall I wind up first?" she asked, looking again at the directions on the card.

"Number One, I should think," returned Billina. "That makes him think, doesn't it?"

"Yes," said Dorothy, and wound up Number One, under the left arm.

"He doesn't seem any different," remarked the hen, critically.

"Why, of course not; he is only thinking, now," said Dorothy.

"I wonder what he is thinking about."

"I'll wind up his talk, and then perhaps he can tell us," said the girl.

So she wound up Number Two, and immediately the clock-work man said, without moving any part of his body except his lips:

"Good morn-ing, lit-tle girl. Good morn-ing, Mrs. Hen."

The words sounded a little hoarse and creaky, and they were uttered all in the same tone, without any change of expression whatever; but both Dorothy and Billina understood them perfectly.

"Good morning, sir," they answered, politely.

"Thank you for res-cu-ing me," continued the machine, in the same monotonous voice, which seemed to be worked by a bellows inside of him, like the little toy lambs and cats the children squeeze so that they will make a noise.

"Don't mention it," answered Dorothy. And then, being very curious, she asked: "How did you come to be locked up in this place?"

"It is a long sto-ry," replied the copper man; "but I will tell it to you brief-ly. I was pur-chased from Smith & Tin-ker, my man-u-fac-tur-ers, by a cru-el King of Ev, named Ev-ol-do, who used to beat all his serv-ants un-til they died. How-ev-er, he was not a-ble to kill me, be-cause I was not a-live, and one must first live in or-der to die. So that all his beat-ing did me no harm, and mere-ly kept my cop-per bod-y well pol-ished.

"This cru-el king had a love-ly wife and ten beau-ti-ful chil-dren – five boys and five girls – but in a fit of an-ger he sold them all to the Nome King, who by means of his mag-ic arts changed them all in-to oth-er forms and put them in his un-der-ground pal-ace to or-na-ment the rooms.

"Af-ter-ward the King of Ev re-gret-ted his wick-ed ac-tion, and tried to get his wife and chil-dren a-way from the Nome King, but with-out a-vail. So, in de-spair, he locked me up in this rock, threw the key in-to the o-cean, and then jumped in af-ter it and was drowned."

"How very dreadful!" exclaimed Dorothy.

"It is, in-deed," said the machine. "When I found my-self im-pris-oned I shout-ed for help un-til my voice ran down; and then I walked back and forth in this lit-tle room un-til my ac-tion ran down; and then I stood still and thought un-til my thoughts ran down. Af-ter that I re-mem-ber noth-ing un-til you wound me up a-gain."

"It's a very wonderful story," said Dorothy, "and proves that the Land of Ev is really a fairy land, as I thought it was."

"Of course it is," answered the copper man. "I do not sup-pose such a per-fect ma-chine as I am could be made in an-y place but a fair-y land."

"I've never seen one in Kansas," said Dorothy.

"But where did you get the key to un-lock this door?" asked the clock-work voice.

"I found it on the shore, where it was prob'ly washed up by the waves," she answered. "And now, sir, if you don't mind, I'll wind up your action."

"That will please me ve-ry much," said the machine.

So she wound up Number Three, and at once the copper man in a somewhat stiff and jerky fashion walked out of the rocky cavern, took off his copper hat and bowed politely, and then kneeled before Dorothy. Said he:

"From this time forth I am your o-be-di-ent ser-vant. What-ev-er you com-mand, that I will do will-ing-ly – if you keep me wound up."

"What is your name?" she asked.

"Tik-tok," he replied. "My for-mer mas-ter gave me that name be-cause my clock-work al-ways ticks when it is wound up."

"I can hear it now," said the yellow hen.

"So can I," said Dorothy. And then she added, with some anxiety: "You don't strike, do you?"

"No," answered Tiktok; "and there is no a-larm con-nec-ted with my ma-chin-er-y. I can tell the time, though, by speak-ing, and as I nev-er sleep I can wak-en you at an-y hour you wish to get up in the morn-ing."

"That's nice," said the little girl; "only I never wish to get up in the morning."

"You can sleep until I lay my egg," said the yellow hen. "Then, when I cackle, Tiktok will know it is time to waken you."

"Do you lay your egg very early?" asked Dorothy.

"About eight o'clock," said Billina. "And everybody ought to be up by that time, I'm sure."

Chapter V
Dorothy Opens the Dinner Pail

"NOW TIKTOK," said Dorothy, "the first thing to be done is to find a way for us to escape from these rocks. The Wheelers are down below, you know, and threaten to kill us."

"There is no rea-son to be a-fraid of the Wheel-ers," said Tiktok, the words coming more slowly than before.

"Why not?" she asked.

"Be-cause they are ag-g-g – gr-gr-r-r-"

He gave a sort of gurgle and stopped short, waving his hands frantically until suddenly he became motionless, with one arm in the air and the other held stiffly before him with all the copper fingers of the hand spread out like a fan.

"Dear me!" said Dorothy, in a frightened tone. "What can the matter be?"

"He's run down, I suppose," said the hen, calmly. "You couldn't have wound him up very tight."

"I didn't know how much to wind him," replied the girl; "but I'll try to do better next time."

She ran around the copper man to take the key from the peg at the back of his neck, but it was not there.

"It's gone!" cried Dorothy, in dismay.

"What's gone?" asked Billina.

"The key."

"It probably fell off when he made that low bow to you," returned the hen. "Look around, and see if you cannot find it again."

Dorothy looked, and the hen helped her, and by and by the girl discovered the clock-key, which had fallen into a crack of the rock.

At once she wound up Tiktok's voice, taking care to give the key as many turns as it would go around. She found this quite a task, as you may imagine if you have ever tried to wind a clock, but the machine man's first words were to assure Dorothy that he would now run for at least twenty-four hours.

"You did not wind me much, at first," he calmly said, "and I told you that long sto-ry a-bout King Ev-ol-do; so it is no won-der that I ran down."

She next rewound the action clock-work, and then Billina advised her to carry the key to Tiktok in her pocket, so it would not get lost again.

"And now," said Dorothy, when all this was accomplished, "tell me what you were going to say about the Wheelers."

"Why, they are noth-ing to be fright-en'd at," said the machine. "They try to make folks be-lieve that they are ver-y ter-ri-ble, but as a mat-ter of fact the Wheel-ers are harm-less e-nough to an-y one that dares to fight them. They might try to hurt a lit-tle girl like you, per-haps, be-cause they are ver-y mis-chiev-ous. But if I had a club they would run a-way as soon as they saw me."

"Haven't you a club?" asked Dorothy.

"No," said Tiktok.

"And you won't find such a thing among these rocks, either," declared the yellow hen.

"Then what shall we do?" asked the girl.

"Wind up my think-works tight-ly, and I will try to think of some oth-er plan," said Tiktok.

So Dorothy rewound his thought machinery, and while he was thinking she decided to eat her dinner. Billina was already pecking away at the cracks in the rocks, to find something to eat, so Dorothy sat down and opened her tin dinner-pail.

In the cover she found a small tank that was full of very nice lemonade. It was covered by a cup, which might also, when removed, be used to drink the lemonade from. Within the pail were three slices of turkey, two slices of cold tongue, some lobster salad, four slices of bread and butter, a small custard pie, an orange and nine large strawberries, and some nuts and raisins. Singularly enough, the nuts in this dinner-pail grew already cracked, so that Dorothy had no trouble in picking out their meats to eat.

She spread the feast upon the rock beside her and began her dinner, first offering some of it to Tiktok, who declined because, as he said, he was merely a machine. Afterward she offered to share with Billina, but the hen murmured something about 'dead things' and said she preferred her bugs and ants.

"Do the lunch-box trees and the dinner-pail trees belong to the Wheelers?" the child asked Tiktok, while engaged in eating her meal.

"Of course not," he answered. "They be-long to the roy-al fam-il-y of Ev, on-ly of course there is no roy-al fam-il-y just now be-cause King Ev-ol-do jumped in-to the sea and his wife and ten chil-dren have been trans-formed by the Nome King. So there is no one to rule the Land of Ev, that I can think of. Per-haps it is for this rea-son that the Wheel-ers claim the trees for their own, and pick the lunch-eons and din-ners to eat them-selves. But they be-long to the King, and you will find the roy-al 'E' stamped up-on the bot-tom of ev-er-y din-ner pail."

Dorothy turned the pail over, and at once discovered the royal mark upon it, as Tiktok had said.

"Are the Wheelers the only folks living in the Land of Ev?" enquired the girl.

"No; they on-ly in-hab-it a small por-tion of it just back of the woods," replied the machine. "But they have al-ways been mis-chiev-ous and im-per-ti-nent, and my old mas-ter, King Ev-ol-do, used to car-ry a whip with him, when he walked out, to keep the crea-tures in or-der. When I was first made the

Wheel-ers tried to run o-ver me, and butt me with their heads; but they soon found I was built of too sol-id a ma-ter-i-al for them to in-jure."

"You seem very durable," said Dorothy. "Who made you?"

"The firm of Smith & Tin-ker, in the town of Evna, where the roy-al pal-ace stands," answered Tiktok.

"Did they make many of you?" asked the child.

"No; I am the on-ly au-to-mat-ic me-chan-i-cal man they ev-er com-plet-ed," he replied. "They were ver-y won-der-ful in-ven-tors, were my mak-ers, and quite ar-tis-tic in all they did."

"I am sure of that," said Dorothy. "Do they live in the town of Evna now?"

"They are both gone," replied the machine. "Mr. Smith was an art-ist, as well as an in-vent-or, and he paint-ed a pic-ture of a riv-er which was so nat-ur-al that, as he was reach-ing a-cross it to paint some flow-ers on the op-po-site bank, he fell in-to the wa-ter and was drowned."

"Oh, I'm sorry for that!" exclaimed the little girl.

"Mis-ter Tin-ker," continued Tiktok, "made a lad-der so tall that he could rest the end of it a-gainst the moon, while he stood on the high-est rung and picked the lit-tle stars to set in the points of the king's crown. But when he got to the moon Mis-ter Tin-ker found it such a love-ly place that he de-cid-ed to live there, so he pulled up the lad-der af-ter him and we have nev-er seen him since."

"He must have been a great loss to this country," said Dorothy, who was by this time eating her custard pie.

"He was," acknowledged Tiktok. "Also he is a great loss to me. For if I should get out of or-der I do not know of an-y one a-ble to re-pair me, be-cause I am so com-pli-cat-ed. You have no i-de-a how full of ma-chin-er-y I am."

"I can imagine it," said Dorothy, readily.

"And now," continued the machine, "I must stop talk-ing and be-gin think-ing a-gain of a way to es-cape from this rock." So he turned half way around, in order to think without being disturbed.

"The best thinker I ever knew," said Dorothy to the yellow hen, "was a scarecrow."

"Nonsense!" snapped Billina.

"It is true," declared Dorothy. "I met him in the Land of Oz, and he traveled with me to the city of the great Wizard of Oz, so as to get some brains, for his head was only stuffed with straw. But it seemed to me that he thought just as well before he got his brains as he did afterward."

"Do you expect me to believe all that rubbish about the Land of Oz?" enquired Billina, who seemed a little cross – perhaps because bugs were scarce.

"What rubbish?" asked the child, who was now finishing her nuts and raisins.

"Why, your impossible stories about animals that can talk, and a tin woodman who is alive, and a scarecrow who can think."

"They are all there," said Dorothy, "for I have seen them."

"I don't believe it!" cried the hen, with a toss of her head.

"That's 'cause you're so ign'rant," replied the girl, who was a little offended at her friend Billina's speech.

"In the Land of Oz," remarked Tiktok, turning toward them, "an-y-thing is pos-si-ble. For it is a won-der-ful fair-y coun-try."

"There, Billina! What did I say?" cried Dorothy. And then she turned to the machine and asked in an eager tone: "Do you know the Land of Oz, Tiktok?"

"No; but I have heard a-bout it," said the cop-per man. "For it is on-ly sep-a-ra-ted from this Land of Ev by a broad des-ert."

Dorothy clapped her hands together delightedly.

"I'm glad of that!" she exclaimed. "It makes me quite happy to be so near my old friends. The scarecrow I told you of, Billina, is the King of the Land of Oz."

"Par-don me. He is not the king now," said Tiktok.

"He was when I left there," declared Dorothy.

"I know," said Tiktok, "but there was a rev-o-lu-tion in the Land of Oz, and the Scare-crow was de-posed by a sol-dier wo-man named Gen-er-al Jin-jur. And then Jin-jur was de-posed by a lit-tle girl named Oz-ma, who was the right-ful heir to the throne and now rules the land un-der the ti-tle of Oz-ma of Oz."

"That is news to me," said Dorothy, thoughtfully. "But I s'pose lots of things have happened since I left the Land of Oz. I wonder what has become of the Scarecrow, and of the Tin Woodman, and the Cowardly Lion. And I wonder who this girl Ozma is, for I never heard of her before."

But Tiktok did not reply to this. He had turned around again to resume his thinking.

Dorothy packed the rest of the food back into the pail, so as not to be wasteful of good things, and the yellow hen forgot her dignity far enough to pick up all of the scattered crumbs, which she ate rather greedily, although she had so lately pretended to despise the things that Dorothy preferred as food.

By this time Tiktok approached them with his stiff bow.

"Be kind e-nough to fol-low me," he said, "and I will lead you a-way from here to the town of Ev-na, where you will be more com-for-ta-ble, and al-so I will pro-tect you from the Wheel-ers."

"All right," answered Dorothy, promptly. "I'm ready!"

Chapter VI
The Heads of Langwidere

THEY WALKED slowly down the path between the rocks, Tiktok going first, Dorothy following him, and the yellow hen trotting along last of all.

At the foot of the path the copper man leaned down and tossed aside with ease the rocks that encumbered the way. Then he turned to Dorothy and said:

"Let me car-ry your din-ner-pail."

She placed it in his right hand at once, and the copper fingers closed firmly over the stout handle.

Then the little procession marched out upon the level sands.

As soon as the three Wheelers who were guarding the mound saw them, they began to shout their wild cries and rolled swiftly toward the little group, as if to capture them or bar their way. But when the foremost had approached near enough, Tiktok swung the tin dinner-pail and struck the Wheeler a sharp blow over its head with the queer weapon. Perhaps it did not hurt very much, but it made a great noise, and the Wheeler uttered a howl and tumbled over upon its side. The next minute it scrambled to its wheels and rolled away as fast as it could go, screeching with fear at the same time.

"I told you they were harm-less," began Tiktok; but before he could say more another Wheeler was upon them. Crack! went the dinner-pail against its head, knocking its straw hat a dozen feet away; and that was enough for this Wheeler, also. It rolled away after the first one, and the third did not wait to be pounded with the pail, but joined its fellows as quickly as its wheels would whirl.

The yellow hen gave a cackle of delight, and flying to a perch upon Tiktok's shoulder, she said:

"Bravely done, my copper friend! And wisely thought of, too. Now we are free from those ugly creatures."

But just then a large band of Wheelers rolled from the forest, and relying upon their numbers to conquer, they advanced fiercely upon Tiktok. Dorothy grabbed Billina in her arms and held her tight, and the machine embraced the form of the little girl with his left arm, the better to protect her. Then the Wheelers were upon them.

Rattlety, bang! bang! went the dinner-pail in every direction, and it made so much clatter bumping against the heads of the Wheelers that they were much more frightened than hurt and fled in a great panic. All, that is, except their leader. This Wheeler had stumbled against another and fallen flat upon his back, and before he could get his wheels under him to rise again, Tiktok had fastened his copper fingers into the neck of the gorgeous jacket of his foe and held him fast.

"Tell your peo-ple to go a-way," commanded the machine.

The leader of the Wheelers hesitated to give this order, so Tiktok shook him as a terrier dog does a rat, until the Wheeler's teeth rattled together with a noise like hailstones on a window pane. Then, as soon as the creature could get its breath, it shouted to the others to roll away, which they immediately did.

"Now," said Tiktok, "you shall come with us and tell me what I want to know."

"You'll be sorry for treating me in this way," whined the Wheeler. "I'm a terribly fierce person."

"As for that," answered Tiktok, "I am only a ma-chine, and can-not feel sor-row or joy, no mat-ter what hap-pens. But you are wrong to think your-self ter-ri-ble or fierce."

"Why so?" asked the Wheeler.

"Be-cause no one else thinks as you do. Your wheels make you help-less to in-jure an-y one. For you have no fists and can not scratch or e-ven pull hair. Nor have you an-y feet to kick with. All you can do is to yell and shout, and that does not hurt an-y one at all."

The Wheeler burst into a flood of tears, to Dorothy's great surprise.

"Now I and my people are ruined forever!" he sobbed; "for you have discovered our secret. Being so helpless, our only hope is to make people afraid of us, by pretending we are very fierce and terrible, and writing in the sand warnings to Beware the Wheelers. Until now we have frightened everyone, but since you have discovered our weakness our enemies will fall upon us and make us very miserable and unhappy."

"Oh, no," exclaimed Dorothy, who was sorry to see this beautifully dressed Wheeler so miserable; "Tiktok will keep your secret, and so will Billina and I. Only, you must promise not to try to frighten children any more, if they come near to you."

"I won't – indeed I won't!" promised the Wheeler, ceasing to cry and becoming more cheerful. "I'm not really bad, you know; but we have to pretend to be terrible in order to prevent others from attacking us."

"That is not ex-act-ly true," said Tiktok, starting to walk toward the path through the forest, and still holding fast to his prisoner, who rolled slowly along beside him. "You and your peo-ple are full of mis-chief, and like to both-er those who fear you. And you are of-ten im-pu-dent and dis-a-gree-a-ble, too. But if you will try to cure those faults I will not tell any-one how help-less you are."

"I'll try, of course," replied the Wheeler, eagerly. "And thank you, Mr. Tiktok, for your kindness."

"I am on-ly a ma-chine," said Tiktok. "I can not be kind an-y more than I can be sor-ry or glad. I can on-ly do what I am wound up to do."

"Are you wound up to keep my secret?" asked the Wheeler, anxiously.

"Yes; if you be-have your-self. But tell me: who rules the Land of Ev now?" asked the machine.

"There is no ruler," was the answer, "because every member of the royal family is imprisoned by the Nome King. But the Princess Langwidere, who is a niece of our late King Evoldo, lives in a part of the royal palace and takes as much money out of the royal treasury as she can spend. The Princess Langwidere is not exactly a ruler, you see, because she doesn't rule; but she is the nearest approach to a ruler we have at present."

"I do not re-mem-ber her," said Tiktok. "What does she look like?"

"That I cannot say," replied the Wheeler, "although I have seen her twenty times. For the Princess Langwidere is a different person every time I see her, and the only way her subjects can recognize her at all is by means of a beautiful ruby key which she always wears on a chain attached to her left wrist. When we see the key we know we are beholding the Princess."

"That is strange," said Dorothy, in astonishment. "Do you mean to say that so many different princesses are one and the same person?"

"Not exactly," answered the Wheeler. "There is, of course, but one princess; but she appears to us in many forms, which are all more or less beautiful."

"She must be a witch," exclaimed the girl.

"I do not think so," declared the Wheeler. "But there is some mystery connected with her, nevertheless. She is a very vain creature, and lives mostly in a room surrounded by mirrors, so that she can admire herself whichever way she looks."

No one answered this speech, because they had just passed out of the forest and their attention was fixed upon the scene before them – a beautiful vale in which were many fruit trees and green fields, with pretty farm-houses scattered here and there and broad, smooth roads that led in every direction.

In the center of this lovely vale, about a mile from where our friends were standing, rose the tall spires of the royal palace, which glittered brightly against their background of blue sky. The palace was surrounded by charming grounds, full of flowers and shrubbery. Several tinkling fountains could be seen, and there were pleasant walks bordered by rows of white marble statuary.

All these details Dorothy was, of course, unable to notice or admire until they had advanced along the road to a position quite near to the palace, and she was still looking at the pretty sights when her little party entered the grounds and approached the big front door of the king's own apartments. To their disappointment they found the door tightly closed. A sign was tacked to the panel which read as follows:

OWNER ABSENT
Please Knock at the Third Door in the Left Wing

"Now," said Tiktok to the captive Wheeler, "you must show us the way to the Left Wing."

"Very well," agreed the prisoner, "it is around here at the right."

"How can the left wing be at the right?" demanded Dorothy, who feared the Wheeler was fooling them.

"Because there used to be three wings, and two were torn down, so the one on the right is the only one left. It is a trick of the Princess Langwidere to prevent visitors from annoying her."

Then the captive led them around to the wing, after which the machine man, having no further use for the Wheeler, permitted him to depart and rejoin his fellows. He immediately rolled away at a great pace and was soon lost to sight.

Tiktok now counted the doors in the wing and knocked loudly upon the third one.

It was opened by a little maid in a cap trimmed with gay ribbons, who bowed respectfully and asked: "What do you wish, good people?"

"Are you the Princess Langwidere?" asked Dorothy.

"No, miss; I am her servant," replied the maid.

"May I see the Princess, please?"

"I will tell her you are here, miss, and ask her to grant you an audience," said the maid. "Step in, please, and take a seat in the drawing-room."

So Dorothy walked in, followed closely by the machine. But as the yellow hen tried to enter after them, the little maid cried "Shoo!" and flapped her apron in Billina's face.

"Shoo, yourself!" retorted the hen, drawing back in anger and ruffling up her feathers. "Haven't you any better manners than that?"

"Oh, do you talk?" enquired the maid, evidently surprised.

"Can't you hear me?" snapped Billina. "Drop that apron, and get out of the doorway, so that I may enter with my friends!"

"The Princess won't like it," said the maid, hesitating.

"I don't care whether she likes it or not," replied Billina, and fluttering her wings with a loud noise she flew straight at the maid's face. The little servant at once ducked her head, and the hen reached

Dorothy's side in safety.

"Very well," sighed the maid; "if you are all ruined because of this obstinate hen, don't blame me for it. It isn't safe to annoy the Princess Langwidere."

"Tell her we are waiting, if you please," Dorothy requested, with dignity. "Billina is my friend, and must go wherever I go."

Without more words the maid led them to a richly furnished drawing-room, lighted with subdued rainbow tints that came in through beautiful stained-glass windows.

"Remain here," she said. "What names shall I give the Princess?"

"I am Dorothy Gale, of Kansas," replied the child; "and this gentleman is a machine named Tiktok, and the yellow hen is my friend Billina."

The little servant bowed and withdrew, going through several passages and mounting two marble stairways before she came to the apartments occupied by her mistress.

Princess Langwidere's sitting-room was paneled with great mirrors, which reached from the ceiling to the floor; also the ceiling was composed of mirrors, and the floor was of polished silver that reflected every object upon it. So when Langwidere sat in her easy chair and played soft melodies upon her mandolin, her form was mirrored hundreds of times, in walls and ceiling and floor, and whichever way the lady turned her head she could see and admire her own features. This she loved to do, and just as the maid entered she was saying to herself:

"This head with the auburn hair and hazel eyes is quite attractive. I must wear it more often than I have done of late, although it may not be the best of my collection."

"You have company, Your Highness," announced the maid, bowing low.

"Who is it?" asked Langwidere, yawning.

"Dorothy Gale of Kansas, Mr. Tiktok and Billina," answered the maid.

"What a queer lot of names!" murmured the Princess, beginning to be a little interested. "What are they like? Is Dorothy Gale of Kansas pretty?"

"She might be called so," the maid replied.

"And is Mr. Tiktok attractive?" continued the Princess.

"That I cannot say, Your Highness. But he seems very bright. Will Your Gracious Highness see them?"

"Oh, I may as well, Nanda. But I am tired admiring this head, and if my visitor has any claim to beauty I must take care that she does not surpass me. So I will go to my cabinet and change to No. 17, which I think is my best appearance. Don't you?"

"Your No. 17 is exceedingly beautiful," answered Nanda, with another bow.

Again the Princess yawned. Then she said:

"Help me to rise."

So the maid assisted her to gain her feet, although Langwidere was the stronger of the two; and then the Princess slowly walked across the silver floor to her cabinet, leaning heavily at every step upon Nanda's arm.

Now I must explain to you that the Princess Langwidere had thirty heads – as many as there are days in the month. But of course she could only wear one of them at a time, because she had but one neck. These heads were kept in what she called her 'cabinet,' which was a beautiful dressing-room that lay just between Langwidere's sleeping-chamber and the mirrored sitting-room. Each head was in a separate cupboard lined with velvet. The cupboards ran all around the sides of the dressing-room, and had elaborately carved doors with gold numbers on the outside and jeweled-framed mirrors on the inside of them.

When the Princess got out of her crystal bed in the morning she went to her cabinet, opened one of the velvet-lined cupboards, and took the head it contained from its golden shelf. Then, by the aid of the mirror inside the open door, she put on the head – as neat and straight as could be

– and afterward called her maids to robe her for the day. She always wore a simple white costume, that suited all the heads. For, being able to change her face whenever she liked, the Princess had no interest in wearing a variety of gowns, as have other ladies who are compelled to wear the same face constantly.

Of course the thirty heads were in great variety, no two formed alike but all being of exceeding loveliness. There were heads with golden hair, brown hair, rich auburn hair and black hair; but none with gray hair. The heads had eyes of blue, of gray, of hazel, of brown and of black; but there were no red eyes among them, and all were bright and handsome. The noses were Grecian, Roman, retrousse and Oriental, representing all types of beauty; and the mouths were of assorted sizes and shapes, displaying pearly teeth when the heads smiled. As for dimples, they appeared in cheeks and chins, wherever they might be most charming, and one or two heads had freckles upon the faces to contrast the better with the brilliancy of their complexions.

One key unlocked all the velvet cupboards containing these treasures – a curious key carved from a single blood-red ruby – and this was fastened to a strong but slender chain which the Princess wore around her left wrist.

When Nanda had supported Langwidere to a position in front of cupboard No. 17, the Princess unlocked the door with her ruby key and after handing head No. 9, which she had been wearing, to the maid, she took No. 17 from its shelf and fitted it to her neck. It had black hair and dark eyes and a lovely pearl-and-white complexion, and when Langwidere wore it she knew she was remarkably beautiful in appearance.

There was only one trouble with No. 17; the temper that went with it (and which was hidden somewhere under the glossy black hair) was fiery, harsh and haughty in the extreme, and it often led the Princess to do unpleasant things which she regretted when she came to wear her other heads.

But she did not remember this today, and went to meet her guests in the drawing-room with a feeling of certainty that she would surprise them with her beauty.

However, she was greatly disappointed to find that her visitors were merely a small girl in a gingham dress, a copper man that would only go when wound up, and a yellow hen that was sitting contentedly in Langwidere's best work-basket, where there was a china egg used for darning stockings. (It may surprise you to learn that a princess ever does such a common thing as darn stockings. But, if you will stop to think, you will realize that a princess is sure to wear holes in her stockings, the same as other people; only it isn't considered quite polite to mention the matter.)

"Oh!" said Langwidere, slightly lifting the nose of No. 17. "I thought some one of importance had called."

"Then you were right," declared Dorothy. "I'm a good deal of 'portance myself, and when Billina lays an egg she has the proudest cackle you ever heard. As for Tiktok, he's the –"

"Stop – Stop!" commanded the Princess, with an angry flash of her splendid eyes. "How dare you annoy me with your senseless chatter?"

"Why, you horrid thing!" said Dorothy, who was not accustomed to being treated so rudely.

The Princess looked at her more closely.

"Tell me," she resumed, "are you of royal blood?"

"Better than that, ma'am," said Dorothy. "I came from Kansas."

"Huh!" cried the Princess, scornfully. "You are a foolish child, and I cannot allow you to annoy me. Run away, you little goose, and bother some one else."

Dorothy was so indignant that for a moment she could find no words to reply. But she rose from her chair, and was about to leave the room when the Princess, who had been scanning the girl's face, stopped her by saying, more gently:

"Come nearer to me."

Dorothy obeyed, without a thought of fear, and stood before the Princess while Langwidere examined her face with careful attention.

"You are rather attractive," said the lady, presently. "Not at all beautiful, you understand, but you have a certain style of prettiness that is different from that of any of my thirty heads. So I believe I'll take your head and give you No. 26 for it."

"Well, I b'lieve you won't!" exclaimed Dorothy.

"It will do you no good to refuse," continued the Princess; "for I need your head for my collection, and in the Land of Ev my will is law. I never have cared much for No. 26, and you will find that it is very little worn. Besides, it will do you just as well as the one you're wearing, for all practical purposes."

"I don't know anything about your No. 26, and I don't want to," said Dorothy, firmly. "I'm not used to taking cast-off things, so I'll just keep my own head."

"You refuse?" cried the Princess, with a frown.

"Of course I do," was the reply.

"Then," said Langwidere, "I shall lock you up in a tower until you decide to obey me. Nanda," turning to her maid, "call my army."

Nanda rang a silver bell, and at once a big fat colonel in a bright red uniform entered the room, followed by ten lean soldiers, who all looked sad and discouraged and saluted the princess in a very melancholy fashion.

"Carry that girl to the North Tower and lock her up!" cried the Princess, pointing to Dorothy.

"To hear is to obey," answered the big red colonel, and caught the child by her arm. But at that moment Tiktok raised his dinner-pail and pounded it so forcibly against the colonel's head that the big officer sat down upon the floor with a sudden bump, looking both dazed and very much astonished.

"Help!" he shouted, and the ten lean soldiers sprang to assist their leader.

There was great excitement for the next few moments, and Tiktok had knocked down seven of the army, who were sprawling in every direction upon the carpet, when suddenly the machine paused, with the dinner-pail raised for another blow, and remained perfectly motionless.

"My ac-tion has run down," he called to Dorothy. "Wind me up, quick."

She tried to obey, but the big colonel had by this time managed to get upon his feet again, so he grabbed fast hold of the girl and she was helpless to escape.

"This is too bad," said the machine. "I ought to have run six hours lon-ger, at least, but I sup-pose my long walk and my fight with the Wheel-ers made me run down fast-er than us-u-al."

"Well, it can't be helped," said Dorothy, with a sigh.

"Will you exchange heads with me?" demanded the Princess.

"No, indeed!" cried Dorothy.

"Then lock her up," said Langwidere to her soldiers, and they led Dorothy to a high tower at the north of the palace and locked her securely within.

The soldiers afterward tried to lift Tiktok, but they found the machine so solid and heavy that they could not stir it. So they left him standing in the center of the drawing-room.

"People will think I have a new statue," said Langwidere, "so it won't matter in the least, and Nanda can keep him well polished."

"What shall we do with the hen?" asked the colonel, who had just discovered Billina in the work-basket.

"Put her in the chicken-house," answered the Princess. "Someday I'll have her fried for breakfast."

"She looks rather tough, Your Highness," said Nanda, doubtfully.

"That is a base slander!" cried Billina, struggling frantically in the colonel's arms. "But the breed of chickens I come from is said to be poison to all princesses."

"Then," remarked Langwidere, "I will not fry the hen, but keep her to lay eggs; and if she doesn't do her duty I'll have her drowned in the horse trough."

Chapter VII
Ozma of Oz to the Rescue

NANDA BROUGHT DOROTHY bread and water for her supper, and she slept upon a hard stone couch with a single pillow and a silken coverlet.

In the morning she leaned out of the window of her prison in the tower to see if there was any way to escape. The room was not so very high up, when compared with our modern buildings, but it was far enough above the trees and farm houses to give her a good view of the surrounding country.

To the east she saw the forest, with the sands beyond it and the ocean beyond that. There was even a dark speck upon the shore that she thought might be the chicken-coop in which she had arrived at this singular country.

Then she looked to the north, and saw a deep but narrow valley lying between two rocky mountains, and a third mountain that shut off the valley at the further end.

Westward the fertile Land of Ev suddenly ended a little way from the palace, and the girl could see miles and miles of sandy desert that stretched further than her eyes could reach. It was this desert, she thought, with much interest, that alone separated her from the wonderful Land of Oz, and she remembered sorrowfully that she had been told no one had ever been able to cross this dangerous waste but herself. Once a cyclone had carried her across it, and a magical pair of silver shoes had carried her back again. But now she had neither a cyclone nor silver shoes to assist her, and her condition was sad indeed. For she had become the prisoner of a disagreeable princess who insisted that she must exchange her head for another one that she was not used to, and which might not fit her at all.

Really, there seemed no hope of help for her from her old friends in the Land of Oz. Thoughtfully she gazed from her narrow window. On all the desert not a living thing was stirring.

Wait, though! Something surely WAS stirring on the desert – something her eyes had not observed at first. Now it seemed like a cloud; now it seemed like a spot of silver; now it seemed to be a mass of rainbow colors that moved swiftly toward her.

What COULD it be, she wondered?

Then, gradually, but in a brief space of time nevertheless, the vision drew near enough to Dorothy to make out what it was.

A broad green carpet was unrolling itself upon the desert, while advancing across the carpet was a wonderful procession that made the girl open her eyes in amazement as she gazed.

First came a magnificent golden chariot, drawn by a great Lion and an immense Tiger, who stood shoulder to shoulder and trotted along as gracefully as a well-matched team of thoroughbred horses. And standing upright within the chariot was a beautiful girl clothed in flowing robes of silver gauze and wearing a jeweled diadem upon her dainty head. She held in one hand the satin ribbons that guided her astonishing team, and in the other an ivory wand that separated at the top into two prongs, the prongs being tipped by the letters 'O' and 'Z', made of glistening diamonds set closely together.

The girl seemed neither older nor larger than Dorothy herself, and at once the prisoner in the tower guessed that the lovely driver of the chariot must be that Ozma of Oz of whom she had so lately heard from Tiktok.

Following close behind the chariot Dorothy saw her old friend the Scarecrow, riding calmly astride a wooden Saw-Horse, which pranced and trotted as naturally as any meat horse could have done.

And then came Nick Chopper, the Tin Woodman, with his funnel-shaped cap tipped carelessly over his left ear, his gleaming axe over his right shoulder, and his whole body sparkling as brightly as it had ever done in the old days when first she knew him.

The Tin Woodman was on foot, marching at the head of a company of twenty-seven soldiers, of whom some were lean and some fat, some short and some tall; but all the twenty-seven were dressed in handsome uniforms of various designs and colors, no two being alike in any respect.

Behind the soldiers the green carpet rolled itself up again, so that there was always just enough of it for the procession to walk upon, in order that their feet might not come in contact with the deadly, life-destroying sands of the desert.

Dorothy knew at once it was a magic carpet she beheld, and her heart beat high with hope and joy as she realized she was soon to be rescued and allowed to greet her dearly beloved friends of Oz – the Scarecrow, the Tin Woodman and the Cowardly Lion.

Indeed, the girl felt herself as good as rescued as soon as she recognized those in the procession, for she well knew the courage and loyalty of her old comrades, and also believed that any others who came from their marvelous country would prove to be pleasant and reliable acquaintances.

As soon as the last bit of desert was passed and all the procession, from the beautiful and dainty Ozma to the last soldier, had reached the grassy meadows of the Land of Ev, the magic carpet rolled itself together and entirely disappeared.

Then the chariot driver turned her Lion and Tiger into a broad roadway leading up to the palace, and the others followed, while Dorothy still gazed from her tower window in eager excitement.

They came quite close to the front door of the palace and then halted, the Scarecrow dismounting from his Saw-Horse to approach the sign fastened to the door, that he might read what it said.

Dorothy, just above him, could keep silent no longer.

"Here I am!" she shouted, as loudly as she could. "Here's Dorothy!"

"Dorothy who?" asked the Scarecrow, tipping his head to look upward until he nearly lost his balance and tumbled over backward.

"Dorothy Gale, of course. Your friend from Kansas," she answered.

"Why, hello, Dorothy!" said the Scarecrow. "What in the world are you doing up there?"

"Nothing," she called down, "because there's nothing to do. Save me, my friend – save me!"

"You seem to be quite safe now," replied the Scarecrow.

"But I'm a prisoner. I'm locked in, so that I can't get out," she pleaded.

"That's all right," said the Scarecrow. "You might be worse off, little Dorothy. Just consider the matter. You can't get drowned, or be run over by a Wheeler, or fall out of an apple-tree. Some folks would think they were lucky to be up there."

"Well, I don't," declared the girl, "and I want to get down immed'i'tly and see you and the Tin Woodman and the Cowardly Lion."

"Very well," said the Scarecrow, nodding. "It shall be just as you say, little friend. Who locked you up?"

"The princess Langwidere, who is a horrid creature," she answered.

At this Ozma, who had been listening carefully to the conversation, called to Dorothy from her chariot, asking:

"Why did the Princess lock you up, my dear?"

"Because," exclaimed Dorothy, "I wouldn't let her have my head for her collection, and take an old, cast-off head in exchange for it."

"I do not blame you," exclaimed Ozma, promptly. "I will see the Princess at once, and oblige her to liberate you."

"Oh, thank you very, very much!" cried Dorothy, who as soon as she heard the sweet voice of the girlish Ruler of Oz knew that she would soon learn to love her dearly.

Ozma now drove her chariot around to the third door of the wing, upon which the Tin Woodman boldly proceeded to knock.

As soon as the maid opened the door Ozma, bearing in her hand her ivory wand, stepped into the hall and made her way at once to the drawing-room, followed by all her company, except the Lion and the Tiger. And the twenty-seven soldiers made such a noise and a clatter that the little maid Nanda ran away screaming to her mistress, whereupon the Princess Langwidere, roused to great anger by this rude invasion of her palace, came running into the drawing-room without any assistance whatever.

There she stood before the slight and delicate form of the little girl from Oz and cried out:

"How dare you enter my palace unbidden? Leave this room at once, or I will bind you and all your people in chains, and throw you into my darkest dungeons!"

"What a dangerous lady!" murmured the Scarecrow, in a soft voice.

"She seems a little nervous," replied the Tin Woodman.

But Ozma only smiled at the angry Princess.

"Sit down, please," she said, quietly. "I have traveled a long way to see you, and you must listen to what I have to say."

"Must!" screamed the Princess, her black eyes flashing with fury – for she still wore her No. 17 head. "Must, to ME!"

"To be sure," said Ozma. "I am Ruler of the Land of Oz, and I am powerful enough to destroy all your kingdom, if I so wish. Yet I did not come here to do harm, but rather to free the royal family of Ev from the thrall of the Nome King, the news having reached me that he is holding the Queen and her children prisoners."

Hearing these words, Langwidere suddenly became quiet.

"I wish you could, indeed, free my aunt and her ten royal children," said she, eagerly. "For if they were restored to their proper forms and station they could rule the Kingdom of Ev themselves, and that would save me a lot of worry and trouble. At present there are at least ten minutes every day that I must devote to affairs of state, and I would like to be able to spend my whole time in admiring my beautiful heads."

"Then we will presently discuss this matter," said Ozma, "and try to find a way to liberate your aunt and cousins. But first you must liberate another prisoner – the little girl you have locked up in your tower."

"Of course," said Langwidere, readily. "I had forgotten all about her. That was yesterday, you know, and a Princess cannot be expected to remember today what she did yesterday. Come with me, and I will release the prisoner at once."

So Ozma followed her, and they passed up the stairs that led to the room in the tower.

While they were gone Ozma's followers remained in the drawing-room, and the Scarecrow was leaning against a form that he had mistaken for a copper statue when a harsh, metallic voice said suddenly in his ear:

"Get off my foot, please. You are scratch-ing my pol-ish."

"Oh, excuse me!" he replied, hastily drawing back. "Are you alive?"

"No," said Tiktok, "I am on-ly a ma-chine. But I can think and speak and act, when I am pro-per-ly wound up. Just now my ac-tion is run down, and Dor-o-thy has the key to it."

"That's all right," replied the Scarecrow. "Dorothy will soon be free, and then she'll attend to your works. But it must be a great misfortune not to be alive. I'm sorry for you."

"Why?" asked Tiktok.

"Because you have no brains, as I have," said the Scarecrow.

"Oh, yes, I have," returned Tiktok. "I am fit-ted with Smith & Tin-ker's Im-proved Com-bi-na-tion Steel Brains. They are what make me think. What sort of brains are you fit-ted with?"

"I don't know," admitted the Scarecrow. "They were given to me by the great Wizard of Oz, and I didn't get a chance to examine them before he put them in. But they work splendidly and my conscience is very active. Have you a conscience?"

"No," said Tiktok.

"And no heart, I suppose?" added the Tin Woodman, who had been listening with interest to this conversation.

"No," said Tiktok.

"Then," continued the Tin Woodman, "I regret to say that you are greatly inferior to my friend the Scarecrow, and to myself. For we are both alive, and he has brains which do not need to be wound up, while I have an excellent heart that is continually beating in my bosom."

"I con-grat-u-late you," replied Tiktok. "I can-not help be-ing your in-fer-i-or for I am a mere ma-chine. When I am wound up I do my du-ty by go-ing just as my ma-chin-er-y is made to go. You have no i-de-a how full of ma-chin-er-y I am."

"I can guess," said the Scarecrow, looking at the machine man curiously. "Some day I'd like to take you apart and see just how you are made."

"Do not do that, I beg of you," said Tiktok; "for you could not put me to-geth-er a-gain, and my use-ful-ness would be de-stroyed."

"Oh! Are you useful?" asked the Scarecrow, surprised.

"Ve-ry," said Tiktok.

"In that case," the Scarecrow kindly promised, "I won't fool with your interior at all. For I am a poor mechanic, and might mix you up."

"Thank you," said Tiktok.

Just then Ozma re-entered the room, leading Dorothy by the hand and followed closely by the Princess Langwidere.

Chapter VIII
The Hungry Tiger

THE FIRST THING Dorothy did was to rush into the embrace of the Scarecrow, whose painted face beamed with delight as he pressed her form to his straw-padded bosom. Then the Tin Woodman embraced her – very gently, for he knew his tin arms might hurt her if he squeezed too roughly.

These greetings having been exchanged, Dorothy took the key to Tiktok from her pocket and wound up the machine man's action, so that he could bow properly when introduced to the rest of the company. While doing this she told them how useful Tiktok had been to her, and both the Scarecrow and the Tin Woodman shook hands with the machine once more and thanked him for protecting their friend.

Then Dorothy asked: "Where is Billina?"

"I don't know," said the Scarecrow. "Who is Billina?"

"She's a yellow hen who is another friend of mine," answered the girl, anxiously. "I wonder what has become of her?"

"She is in the chicken house, in the back yard," said the Princess. "My drawing-room is no place for hens."

Without waiting to hear more Dorothy ran to get Billina, and just outside the door she came upon the Cowardly Lion, still hitched to the chariot beside the great Tiger. The Cowardly Lion had a big bow of blue ribbon fastened to the long hair between his ears, and the Tiger wore a bow of red ribbon on his tail, just in front of the bushy end.

In an instant Dorothy was hugging the huge Lion joyfully.

"I'm SO glad to see you again!" she cried.

"I am also glad to see you, Dorothy," said the Lion. "We've had some fine adventures together, haven't we?"

"Yes, indeed," she replied. "How are you?"

"As cowardly as ever," the beast answered in a meek voice. "Every little thing scares me and makes my heart beat fast. But let me introduce to you a new friend of mine, the Hungry Tiger."

"Oh! Are you hungry?" she asked, turning to the other beast, who was just then yawning so widely that he displayed two rows of terrible teeth and a mouth big enough to startle anyone.

"Dreadfully hungry," answered the Tiger, snapping his jaws together with a fierce click.

"Then why don't you eat something?" she asked.

"It's no use," said the Tiger sadly. "I've tried that, but I always get hungry again."

"Why, it is the same with me," said Dorothy. "Yet I keep on eating."

"But you eat harmless things, so it doesn't matter," replied the Tiger. "For my part, I'm a savage beast, and have an appetite for all sorts of poor little living creatures, from a chipmunk to fat babies."

"How dreadful!" said Dorothy.

"Isn't it, though?" returned the Hungry Tiger, licking his lips with his long red tongue. "Fat babies! Don't they sound delicious? But I've never eaten any, because my conscience tells me it is wrong. If I had no conscience I would probably eat the babies and then get hungry again, which would mean that I had sacrificed the poor babies for nothing. No; hungry I was born, and hungry I shall die. But I'll not have any cruel deeds on my conscience to be sorry for."

"I think you are a very good tiger," said Dorothy, patting the huge head of the beast.

"In that you are mistaken," was the reply. "I am a good beast, perhaps, but a disgracefully bad tiger. For it is the nature of tigers to be cruel and ferocious, and in refusing to eat harmless living creatures I am acting as no good tiger has ever before acted. That is why I left the forest and joined my friend the Cowardly Lion."

"But the Lion is not really cowardly," said Dorothy. "I have seen him act as bravely as can be."

"All a mistake, my dear," protested the Lion gravely. "To others I may have seemed brave, at times, but I have never been in any danger that I was not afraid."

"Nor I," said Dorothy, truthfully. "But I must go and set free Billina, and then I will see you again."

She ran around to the back yard of the palace and soon found the chicken house, being guided to it by a loud cackling and crowing and a distracting hubbub of sounds such as chickens make when they are excited.

Something seemed to be wrong in the chicken house, and when Dorothy looked through the slats in the door she saw a group of hens and roosters huddled in one corner and watching what appeared to be a whirling ball of feathers. It bounded here and there about the chicken house, and at first Dorothy could not tell what it was, while the screeching of the chickens nearly deafened her.

But suddenly the bunch of feathers stopped whirling, and then, to her amazement, the girl saw Billina crouching upon the prostrate form of a speckled rooster. For an instant they both remained motionless, and then the yellow hen shook her wings to settle the feathers and walked toward the door with a strut of proud defiance and a cluck of victory, while the speckled rooster limped away to the group of other chickens, trailing his crumpled plumage in the dust as he went.

"Why, Billina!" cried Dorothy, in a shocked voice; "have you been fighting?"

"I really think I have," retorted Billina. "Do you think I'd let that speckled villain of a rooster lord it over ME, and claim to run this chicken house, as long as I'm able to peck and scratch? Not if my name is Bill!"

"It isn't Bill, it's Billina; and you're talking slang, which is very undig'n'fied," said Dorothy, reprovingly. "Come here, Billina, and I'll let you out; for Ozma of Oz is here, and has set us free."

So the yellow hen came to the door, which Dorothy unlatched for her to pass through, and the other chickens silently watched them from their corner without offering to approach nearer.

The girl lifted her friend in her arms and exclaimed:

"Oh, Billina! how dreadful you look. You've lost a lot of feathers, and one of your eyes is nearly pecked out, and your comb is bleeding!"

"That's nothing," said Billina. "Just look at the speckled rooster! Didn't I do him up brown?"

Dorothy shook her head.

"I don't 'prove of this, at all," she said, carrying Billina away toward the palace. "It isn't a good thing for you to 'sociate with those common chickens. They would soon spoil your good manners, and you wouldn't be respec'able any more."

"I didn't ask to associate with them," replied Billina. "It is that cross old Princess who is to blame. But I was raised in the United States, and I won't allow any one-horse chicken of the Land of Ev to run over me and put on airs, as long as I can lift a claw in self-defense."

"Very well, Billina," said Dorothy. "We won't talk about it any more."

Soon they came to the Cowardly Lion and the Hungry Tiger to whom the girl introduced the Yellow Hen.

"Glad to meet any friend of Dorothy's," said the Lion, politely. "To judge by your present appearance, you are not a coward, as I am."

"Your present appearance makes my mouth water," said the Tiger, looking at Billina greedily. "My, my! how good you would taste if I could only crunch you between my jaws. But don't worry. You would only appease my appetite for a moment; so it isn't worth while to eat you."

"Thank you," said the hen, nestling closer in Dorothy's arms.

"Besides, it wouldn't be right," continued the Tiger, looking steadily at Billina and clicking his jaws together.

"Of course not," cried Dorothy, hastily. "Billina is my friend, and you mustn't ever eat her under any circ'mstances."

"I'll try to remember that," said the Tiger; "but I'm a little absent-minded, at times."

Then Dorothy carried her pet into the drawing-room of the palace, where Tiktok, being invited to do so by Ozma, had seated himself between the Scarecrow and the Tin Woodman. Opposite to them sat Ozma herself and the Princess Langwidere, and beside them there was a vacant chair for Dorothy.

Around this important group was ranged the Army of Oz, and as Dorothy looked at the handsome uniforms of the Twenty-Seven she said:

"Why, they seem to be all officers."

"They are, all except one," answered the Tin Woodman. "I have in my Army eight Generals, six Colonels, seven Majors and five Captains, besides one private for them to command. I'd like to promote the private, for I believe no private should ever be in public life; and I've also noticed that officers usually fight better and are more reliable than common soldiers. Besides, the officers are more important looking, and lend dignity to our army."

"No doubt you are right," said Dorothy, seating herself beside Ozma.

"And now," announced the girlish Ruler of Oz, "we will hold a solemn conference to decide the best manner of liberating the royal family of this fair Land of Ev from their long imprisonment."

Chapter IX
The Royal Family of Ev

THE TIN WOODMAN was the first to address the meeting.

"To begin with," said he, "word came to our noble and illustrious Ruler, Ozma of Oz, that the wife and ten children – five boys and five girls – of the former King of Ev, by name Evoldo, have been enslaved by the Nome King and are held prisoners in his underground palace. Also that there was no one in Ev powerful enough to release them. Naturally our Ozma wished to undertake the adventure of liberating the poor prisoners; but for a long time she could find no way to cross the great desert between the two countries. Finally she went to a friendly sorceress of our land named Glinda the Good, who heard the story and at once presented Ozma a magic carpet, which would continually unroll beneath our feet and so make a comfortable path for us to cross the desert. As soon as she had received the carpet our gracious Ruler ordered me to assemble our army, which I did. You behold in these bold warriors the pick of all the finest soldiers of Oz; and, if we are obliged to fight the Nome King, every officer as well as the private, will battle fiercely unto death."

Then Tiktok spoke.

"Why should you fight the Nome King?" he asked. "He has done no wrong."

"No wrong!" cried Dorothy. "Isn't it wrong to imprison a queen mother and her ten children?"

"They were sold to the Nome King by King Ev-ol-do," replied Tiktok. "It was the King of Ev who did wrong, and when he re-al-ized what he had done he jumped in-to the sea and drowned him-self."

"This is news to me," said Ozma, thoughtfully. "I had supposed the Nome King was all to blame in the matter. But, in any case, he must be made to liberate the prisoners."

"My uncle Evoldo was a very wicked man," declared the Princess Langwidere. "If he had drowned himself before he sold his family, no one would have cared. But he sold them to the powerful Nome King in exchange for a long life, and afterward destroyed the life by jumping into the sea."

"Then," said Ozma, "he did not get the long life, and the Nome King must give up the prisoners. Where are they confined?"

"No one knows, exactly," replied the Princess. "For the king, whose name is Roquat of the Rocks, owns a splendid palace underneath the great mountain which is at the north end of this kingdom, and he has transformed the queen and her children into ornaments and bric-a-brac with which to decorate his rooms."

"I'd like to know," said Dorothy, "who this Nome King is?"

"I will tell you," replied Ozma. "He is said to be the Ruler of the Underground World, and commands the rocks and all that the rocks contain. Under his rule are many thousands of the Nomes, who are queerly shaped but powerful sprites that labor at the furnaces and forges of their king, making gold and silver and other metals which they conceal in the crevices of the rocks, so that those living upon the earth's surface can only find them with great difficulty. Also they make diamonds and rubies and emeralds, which they hide in the ground; so that the kingdom of the Nomes is wonderfully rich, and all we have of precious stones and silver and gold is what we take from the earth and rocks where the Nome King has hidden them."

"I understand," said Dorothy, nodding her little head wisely.

"For the reason that we often steal his treasures," continued Ozma, "the Ruler of the Underground World is not fond of those who live upon the earth's surface, and never appears among us. If we wish to see King Roquat of the Rocks, we must visit his own country, where he is all powerful, and therefore it will be a dangerous undertaking."

"But, for the sake of the poor prisoners," said Dorothy, "we ought to do it."

"We shall do it," replied the Scarecrow, "although it requires a lot of courage for me to go near to the furnaces of the Nome King. For I am only stuffed with straw, and a single spark of fire might destroy me entirely."

"The furnaces may also melt my tin," said the Tin Woodman; "but I am going."

"I can't bear heat," remarked the Princess Langwidere, yawning lazily, "so I shall stay at home. But I wish you may have success in your undertaking, for I am heartily tired of ruling this stupid kingdom, and I need more leisure in which to admire my beautiful heads."

"We do not need you," said Ozma. "For, if with the aid of my brave followers I cannot accomplish my purpose, then it would be useless for you to undertake the journey."

"Quite true," sighed the Princess. "So, if you'll excuse me, I will now retire to my cabinet. I've worn this head quite awhile, and I want to change it for another."

When she had left them (and you may be sure no one was sorry to see her go) Ozma said to Tiktok:

"Will you join our party?"

"I am the slave of the girl Dor-oth-y, who rescued me from pris-on," replied the machine. "Where she goes I will go."

"Oh, I am going with my friends, of course," said Dorothy, quickly. "I wouldn't miss the fun for anything. Will you go, too, Billina?"

"To be sure," said Billina in a careless tone. She was smoothing down the feathers of her back and not paying much attention.

"Heat is just in her line," remarked the Scarecrow. "If she is nicely roasted, she will be better than ever."

"Then," said Ozma, "we will arrange to start for the Kingdom of the Nomes at daybreak tomorrow. And, in the meantime, we will rest and prepare ourselves for the journey."

Although Princess Langwidere did not again appear to her guests, the palace servants waited upon the strangers from Oz and did everything in their power to make the party comfortable. There were many vacant rooms at their disposal, and the brave Army of twenty-seven was easily provided for and liberally feasted.

The Cowardly Lion and the Hungry Tiger were unharnessed from the chariot and allowed to roam at will throughout the palace, where they nearly frightened the servants into fits, although they did no harm at all. At one time Dorothy found the little maid Nanda crouching in terror in a corner, with the Hungry Tiger standing before her.

"You certainly look delicious," the beast was saying. "Will you kindly give me permission to eat you?"

"No, no, no!" cried the maid in reply.

"Then," said the Tiger, yawning frightfully, "please to get me about thirty pounds of tenderloin steak, cooked rare, with a peck of boiled potatoes on the side, and five gallons of ice-cream for dessert."

"I – I'll do the best I can!" said Nanda, and she ran away as fast as she could go.

"Are you so very hungry?" asked Dorothy, in wonder.

"You can hardly imagine the size of my appetite," replied the Tiger, sadly. "It seems to fill my whole body, from the end of my throat to the tip of my tail. I am very sure the appetite doesn't fit me, and is too large for the size of my body. Some day, when I meet a dentist with a pair of forceps, I'm going to have it pulled."

"What, your tooth?" asked Dorothy.

"No, my appetite," said the Hungry Tiger.

The little girl spent most of the afternoon talking with the Scarecrow and the Tin Woodman, who related to her all that had taken place in the Land of Oz since Dorothy had left it. She was much interested in the story of Ozma, who had been, when a baby, stolen by a wicked old witch and transformed into a boy. She did not know that she had ever been a girl until she was restored to her natural form by a kind sorceress. Then it was found that she was the only child of the former Ruler of Oz, and was entitled to rule in his place. Ozma had many adventures, however, before she regained her father's throne, and in these she was accompanied by a pumpkin-headed man, a highly magnified and thoroughly educated Woggle-Bug, and a wonderful sawhorse that had been brought to life by means of a magic powder. The Scarecrow and the Tin Woodman had also assisted her; but the Cowardly Lion, who ruled the great forest as the King of Beasts, knew nothing of Ozma until after she became the reigning princess of Oz. Then he journeyed to the Emerald City to see her, and on hearing she was about to visit the Land of Ev to set free the royal family of that country, the Cowardly Lion begged to go with her, and brought along his friend, the Hungry Tiger, as well.

Having heard this story, Dorothy related to them her own adventures, and then went out with her friends to find the Sawhorse, which Ozma had caused to be shod with plates of gold, so that its legs would not wear out.

They came upon the Sawhorse standing motionless beside the garden gate, but when Dorothy was introduced to him he bowed politely and blinked his eyes, which were knots of wood, and wagged his tail, which was only the branch of a tree.

"What a remarkable thing, to be alive!" exclaimed Dorothy.

"I quite agree with you," replied the Sawhorse, in a rough but not unpleasant voice. "A creature like me has no business to live, as we all know. But it was the magic powder that did it, so I cannot justly be blamed."

"Of course not," said Dorothy. "And you seem to be of some use, 'cause I noticed the Scarecrow riding upon your back."

"Oh, yes; I'm of use," returned the Sawhorse; "and I never tire, never have to be fed, or cared for in any way."

"Are you intel'gent?" asked the girl.

"Not very," said the creature. "It would be foolish to waste intelligence on a common Sawhorse, when so many professors need it. But I know enough to obey my masters, and to gid-dup, or whoa, when I'm told to. So I'm pretty well satisfied."

That night Dorothy slept in a pleasant little bed-chamber next to that occupied by Ozma of Oz, and Billina perched upon the foot of the bed and tucked her head under her wing and slept as soundly in that position as did Dorothy upon her soft cushions.

But before daybreak everyone was awake and stirring, and soon the adventurers were eating a hasty breakfast in the great dining-room of the palace. Ozma sat at the head of a long table, on a raised platform, with Dorothy on her right hand and the Scarecrow on her left. The Scarecrow did not eat, of course; but Ozma placed him near her so that she might ask his advice about the journey while she ate.

Lower down the table were the twenty-seven warriors of Oz, and at the end of the room the Lion and the Tiger were eating out of a kettle that had been placed upon the floor, while Billina fluttered around to pick up any scraps that might be scattered.

It did not take long to finish the meal, and then the Lion and the Tiger were harnessed to the chariot and the party was ready to start for the Nome King's Palace.

First rode Ozma, with Dorothy beside her in the golden chariot and holding Billina fast in her arms. Then came the Scarecrow on the Sawhorse, with the Tin Woodman and Tiktok marching side by side just behind him. After these tramped the Army, looking brave and handsome in their splendid uniforms. The generals commanded the colonels and the colonels commanded the majors and the majors commanded the captains and the captains commanded the private, who marched with an air of proud importance because it required so many officers to give him his orders.

And so the magnificent procession left the palace and started along the road just as day was breaking, and by the time the sun came out they had made good progress toward the valley that led to the Nome King's domain.

Chapter X
The Giant with the Hammer

THE ROAD LED for a time through a pretty farm country, and then past a picnic grove that was very inviting. But the procession continued to steadily advance until Billina cried in an abrupt and commanding manner:

"Wait – wait!"

Ozma stopped her chariot so suddenly that the Scarecrow's Sawhorse nearly ran into it, and the ranks of the army tumbled over one another before they could come to a halt. Immediately the yellow hen struggled from Dorothy's arms and flew into a clump of bushes by the roadside.

"What's the matter?" called the Tin Woodman, anxiously.

"Why, Billina wants to lay her egg, that's all," said Dorothy.

"Lay her egg!" repeated the Tin Woodman, in astonishment.

"Yes; she lays one every morning, about this time; and it's quite fresh," said the girl.

"But does your foolish old hen suppose that this entire cavalcade, which is bound on an important adventure, is going to stand still while she lays her egg?" enquired the Tin Woodman, earnestly.

"What else can we do?" asked the girl. "It's a habit of Billina's and she can't break herself of it."

"Then she must hurry up," said the Tin Woodman, impatiently.

"No, no!" exclaimed the Scarecrow. "If she hurries she may lay scrambled eggs."

"That's nonsense," said Dorothy. "But Billina won't be long, I'm sure."

So they stood and waited, although all were restless and anxious to proceed. And by and by the yellow hen came from the bushes saying:

"Kut-kut, kut, ka-daw-kutt! Kut, kut, kut – ka-daw-kut!"

"What is she doing – singing her lay?" asked the Scarecrow.

"For-ward – march!" shouted the Tin Woodman, waving his axe, and the procession started just as Dorothy had once more grabbed Billina in her arms.

"Isn't anyone going to get my egg?" cried the hen, in great excitement.

"I'll get it," said the Scarecrow; and at his command the Sawhorse pranced into the bushes. The straw man soon found the egg, which he placed in his jacket pocket. The cavalcade, having moved rapidly on, was even then far in advance; but it did not take the Sawhorse long to catch up with it, and presently the Scarecrow was riding in his accustomed place behind Ozma's chariot.

"What shall I do with the egg?" he asked Dorothy.

"I do not know," the girl answered. "Perhaps the Hungry Tiger would like it."

"It would not be enough to fill one of my back teeth," remarked the Tiger. "A bushel of them, hard boiled, might take a little of the edge off my appetite; but one egg isn't good for anything at all, that I know of."

"No; it wouldn't even make a sponge cake," said the Scarecrow, thoughtfully. "The Tin Woodman might carry it with his axe and hatch it; but after all I may as well keep it myself for a souvenir." So he left it in his pocket.

They had now reached that part of the valley that lay between the two high mountains which Dorothy had seen from her tower window. At the far end was the third great mountain, which blocked the valley and was the northern edge of the Land of Ev. It was underneath this mountain that the Nome King's palace was said to be; but it would be some time before they reached that place.

The path was becoming rocky and difficult for the wheels of the chariot to pass over, and presently a deep gulf appeared at their feet which was too wide for them to leap. So Ozma took a small square of green cloth from her pocket and threw it upon the ground. At once it became the magic carpet, and unrolled itself far enough for all the cavalcade to walk upon. The chariot now advanced, and the green carpet unrolled before it, crossing the gulf on a level with its banks, so that all passed over in safety.

"That's easy enough," said the Scarecrow. "I wonder what will happen next."

He was not long in making the discovery, for the sides of the mountain came closer together until finally there was but a narrow path between them, along which Ozma and her party were forced to pass in single file.

They now heard a low and deep thump! – thump! – thump! which echoed throughout the valley and seemed to grow louder as they advanced. Then, turning a corner of rock, they saw before them a huge form, which towered above the path for more than a hundred feet. The form was that of a gigantic man built out of plates of cast iron, and it stood with one foot on either side of the narrow road and swung over its right shoulder an immense iron mallet, with which it constantly pounded the earth. These resounding blows explained the thumping sounds they had heard, for the mallet was much bigger than a barrel, and where it struck the path between the rocky sides of the mountain it filled all the space through which our travelers would be obliged to pass.

Of course they at once halted, a safe distance away from the terrible iron mallet. The magic carpet would do them no good in this case, for it was only meant to protect them from any dangers upon the ground beneath their feet, and not from dangers that appeared in the air above them.

"Wow!" said the Cowardly Lion, with a shudder. "It makes me dreadfully nervous to see that big hammer pounding so near my head. One blow would crush me into a door-mat."

"The ir-on gi-ant is a fine fel-low," said Tiktok, "and works as stead-i-ly as a clock. He was made for the Nome King by Smith & Tin-ker, who made me, and his du-ty is to keep folks from find-ing the un-der-ground pal-ace. Is he not a great work of art?"

"Can he think, and speak, as you do?" asked Ozma, regarding the giant with wondering eyes.

"No," replied the machine; "he is on-ly made to pound the road, and has no think-ing or speak-ing at-tach-ment. But he pounds ve-ry well, I think."

"Too well," observed the Scarecrow. "He is keeping us from going farther. Is there no way to stop his machinery?"

"On-ly the Nome King, who has the key, can do that," answered Tiktok.

"Then," said Dorothy, anxiously, "what shall we do?"

"Excuse me for a few minutes," said the Scarecrow, "and I will think it over."

He retired, then, to a position in the rear, where he turned his painted face to the rocks and began to think.

Meantime the giant continued to raise his iron mallet high in the air and to strike the path terrific blows that echoed through the mountains like the roar of a cannon. Each time the mallet lifted, however, there was a moment when the path beneath the monster was free, and perhaps the Scarecrow had noticed this, for when he came back to the others he said:

"The matter is a very simple one, after all. We have but to run under the hammer, one at a time, when it is lifted, and pass to the other side before it falls again."

"It will require quick work, if we escape the blow," said the Tin Woodman, with a shake of his head. "But it really seems the only thing to be done. Who will make the first attempt?"

They looked at one another hesitatingly for a moment. Then the Cowardly Lion, who was trembling like a leaf in the wind, said to them:

"I suppose the head of the procession must go first – and that's me. But I'm terribly afraid of the big hammer!"

"What will become of me?" asked Ozma. "You might rush under the hammer yourself, but the chariot would surely be crushed."

"We must leave the chariot," said the Scarecrow. "But you two girls can ride upon the backs of the Lion and the Tiger."

So this was decided upon, and Ozma, as soon as the Lion was unfastened from the chariot, at once mounted the beast's back and said she was ready.

"Cling fast to his mane," advised Dorothy. "I used to ride him myself, and that's the way I held on."

So Ozma clung fast to the mane, and the lion crouched in the path and eyed the swinging mallet carefully until he knew just the instant it would begin to rise in the air.

Then, before anyone thought he was ready, he made a sudden leap straight between the iron giant's legs, and before the mallet struck the ground again the Lion and Ozma were safe on the other side.

The Tiger went next. Dorothy sat upon his back and locked her arms around his striped neck, for he had no mane to cling to. He made the leap straight and true as an arrow from a bow, and 'ere Dorothy realized it she was out of danger and standing by Ozma's side.

Now came the Scarecrow on the Sawhorse, and while they made the dash in safety they were within a hair's breadth of being caught by the descending hammer.

Tiktok walked up to the very edge of the spot the hammer struck, and as it was raised for the next blow he calmly stepped forward and escaped its descent. That was an idea for the Tin Woodman to follow, and he also crossed in safety while the great hammer was in the air. But when it came to the twenty-six officers and the private, their knees were so weak that they could not walk a step.

"In battle we are wonderfully courageous," said one of the generals, "and our foes find us very terrible to face. But war is one thing and this is another. When it comes to being pounded upon the head by an iron hammer, and smashed into pancakes, we naturally object."

"Make a run for it," urged the Scarecrow.

"Our knees shake so that we cannot run," answered a captain. "If we should try it we would all certainly be pounded to a jelly."

"Well, well," sighed the Cowardly Lion, "I see, friend Tiger, that we must place ourselves in great danger to rescue this bold army. Come with me, and we will do the best we can."

So, Ozma and Dorothy having already dismounted from their backs, the Lion and the Tiger leaped back again under the awful hammer and returned with two generals clinging to their necks. They repeated this daring passage twelve times, when all the officers had been carried beneath the giant's legs and landed safely on the further side. By that time the beasts were very tired, and panted so hard that their tongues hung out of their great mouths.

"But what is to become of the private?" asked Ozma.

"Oh, leave him there to guard the chariot," said the Lion. "I'm tired out, and won't pass under that mallet again."

The officers at once protested that they must have the private with them, else there would be no one for them to command. But neither the Lion or the Tiger would go after him, and so the Scarecrow sent the Sawhorse.

Either the wooden horse was careless, or it failed to properly time the descent of the hammer, for the mighty weapon caught it squarely upon its head, and thumped it against the ground so powerfully that the private flew off its back high into the air, and landed upon one of the giant's cast-iron arms. Here he clung desperately while the arm rose and fell with each one of the rapid strokes.

The Scarecrow dashed in to rescue his Sawhorse, and had his left foot smashed by the hammer before he could pull the creature out of danger. They then found that the Sawhorse had been badly dazed by the blow; for while the hard wooden knot of which his head was formed could not be crushed by the hammer, both his ears were broken off and he would be unable to hear a sound until some new ones were made for him. Also his left knee was cracked, and had to be bound up with a string.

Billina having fluttered under the hammer, it now remained only to rescue the private who was riding upon the iron giant's arm, high in the air.

The Scarecrow lay flat upon the ground and called to the man to jump down upon his body, which was soft because it was stuffed with straw. This the private managed to do, waiting until a time when he was nearest the ground and then letting himself drop upon the Scarecrow. He accomplished the feat without breaking any bones, and the Scarecrow declared he was not injured in the least.

Therefore, the Tin Woodman having by this time fitted new ears to the Sawhorse, the entire party proceeded upon its way, leaving the giant to pound the path behind them.

Chapter XI
The Nome King

BY AND BY, when they drew near to the mountain that blocked their path and which was the furthermost edge of the Kingdom of Ev, the way grew dark and gloomy for the reason that the high peaks on either side shut out the sunshine. And it was very silent, too, as there were no birds to sing or squirrels to chatter, the trees being left far behind them and only the bare rocks remaining.

Ozma and Dorothy were a little awed by the silence, and all the others were quiet and grave except the Sawhorse, which, as it trotted along with the Scarecrow upon his back, hummed a queer song, of which this was the chorus:

> *"Would a wooden horse in a woodland go?*
> *Aye, aye! I sigh, he would, although*
> *Had he not had a wooden head*
> *He'd mount the mountain top instead."*

But no one paid any attention to this because they were now close to the Nome King's dominions, and his splendid underground palace could not be very far away.

Suddenly they heard a shout of jeering laughter, and stopped short. They would have to stop in a minute, anyway, for the huge mountain barred their further progress and the path ran close up to a wall of rock and ended.

"Who was that laughing?" asked Ozma.

There was no reply, but in the gloom they could see strange forms flit across the face of the rock. Whatever the creations might be they seemed very like the rock itself, for they were the color of rocks and their shapes were as rough and rugged as if they had been broken away from the side of the mountain. They kept close to the steep cliff facing our friends, and glided up and down, and this way and that, with a lack of regularity that was quite confusing. And they seemed not to need places to rest their feet, but clung to the surface of the rock as a fly does to a window-pane, and were never still for a moment.

"Do not mind them," said Tiktok, as Dorothy shrank back. "They are on-ly the Nomes."

"And what are Nomes?" asked the girl, half frightened.

"They are rock fair-ies, and serve the Nome King," replied the machine. "But they will do us no harm. You must call for the King, be-cause with-out him you can ne-ver find the en-trance to the pal-ace."

"YOU call," said Dorothy to Ozma.

Just then the Nomes laughed again, and the sound was so weird and disheartening that the twenty-six officers commanded the private to "right-about-face!" and they all started to run as fast as they could.

The Tin Woodman at once pursued his army and cried "halt!" and when they had stopped their flight he asked: "Where are you going?"

"I – I find I've forgotten the brush for my whiskers," said a general, trembling with fear. "S-s-so we are g-going back after it!"

"That is impossible," replied the Tin Woodman. "For the giant with the hammer would kill you all if you tried to pass him."

"Oh! I'd forgotten the giant," said the general, turning pale.

"You seem to forget a good many things," remarked the Tin Woodman. "I hope you won't forget that you are brave men."

"Never!" cried the general, slapping his gold-embroidered chest.

"Never!" cried all the other officers, indignantly slapping their chests.

"For my part," said the private, meekly, "I must obey my officers; so when I am told to run, I run; and when I am told to fight, I fight."

"That is right," agreed the Tin Woodman. "And now you must all come back to Ozma, and obey HER orders. And if you try to run away again I will have her reduce all the twenty-six officers to privates, and make the private your general."

This terrible threat so frightened them that they at once returned to where Ozma was standing beside the Cowardly Lion.

Then Ozma cried out in a loud voice:

"I demand that the Nome King appear to us!"

There was no reply, except that the shifting Nomes upon the mountain laughed in derision.

"You must not command the Nome King," said Tiktok, "for you do not rule him, as you do your own peo-ple."

So Ozma called again, saying:

"I request the Nome King to appear to us."

Only the mocking laughter replied to her, and the shadowy Nomes continued to flit here and there upon the rocky cliff.

"Try en-treat-y," said Tiktok to Ozma. "If he will not come at your re-quest, then the Nome King may list-en to your plead-ing."

Ozma looked around her proudly.

"Do you wish your ruler to plead with this wicked Nome King?" she asked. "Shall Ozma of Oz humble herself to a creature who lives in an underground kingdom?"

"No!" they all shouted, with big voices; and the Scarecrow added:

"If he will not come, we will dig him out of his hole, like a fox, and conquer his stubbornness. But our sweet little ruler must always maintain her dignity, just as I maintain mine."

"I'm not afraid to plead with him," said Dorothy. "I'm only a little girl from Kansas, and we've got more dignity at home than we know what to do with. I'LL call the Nome King."

"Do," said the Hungry Tiger; "and if he makes hash of you I'll willingly eat you for breakfast tomorrow morning."

So Dorothy stepped forward and said:

"PLEASE Mr. Nome King, come here and see us."

The Nomes started to laugh again; but a low growl came from the mountain, and in a flash they had all vanished from sight and were silent.

Then a door in the rock opened, and a voice cried:

"Enter!"

"Isn't it a trick?" asked the Tin Woodman.

"Never mind," replied Ozma. "We came here to rescue the poor Queen of Ev and her ten children, and we must run some risks to do so."

"The Nome King is hon-est and good na-tured," said Tiktok. "You can trust him to do what is right."

So Ozma led the way, hand in hand with Dorothy, and they passed through the arched doorway of rock and entered a long passage which was lighted by jewels set in the walls and having lamps behind them. There was no one to escort them, or to show them the way, but all the party pressed through the passage until they came to a round, domed cavern that was grandly furnished.

In the center of this room was a throne carved out of a solid boulder of rock, rude and rugged in shape but glittering with great rubies and diamonds and emeralds on every part of its surface. And upon the throne sat the Nome King.

This important monarch of the Underground World was a little fat man clothed in gray-brown garments that were the exact color of the rock throne in which he was seated. His bushy hair and flowing beard were also colored like the rocks, and so was his face. He wore no crown of any sort, and his only ornament was a broad, jewel-studded belt that encircled his fat little body. As for his features, they seemed kindly and good humored, and his eyes were turned merrily upon his visitors as Ozma and Dorothy stood before him with their followers ranged in close order behind them.

"Why, he looks just like Santa Claus – only he isn't the same color!" whispered Dorothy to her friend; but the Nome King heard the speech, and it made him laugh aloud.

"'He had a red face and a round little belly, That shook when he laughed like a bowl full of jelly!'" quoth the monarch, in a pleasant voice; and they could all see that he really did shake like jelly when he laughed.

Both Ozma and Dorothy were much relieved to find the Nome King so jolly, and a minute later he waved his right hand and the girls each found a cushioned stool at her side.

"Sit down, my dears," said the King, "and tell me why you have come all this way to see me, and what I can do to make you happy."

While they seated themselves the Nome King picked up a pipe, and taking a glowing red coal out of his pocket he placed it in the bowl of the pipe and began puffing out clouds of smoke that curled in rings above his head. Dorothy thought this made the little monarch look more like Santa Claus than ever; but Ozma now began speaking, and every one listened intently to her words.

"Your Majesty," said she, "I am the ruler of the Land of Oz, and I have come here to ask you to release the good Queen of Ev and her ten children, whom you have enchanted and hold as your prisoners."

"Oh, no; you are mistaken about that," replied the King. "They are not my prisoners, but my slaves, whom I purchased from the King of Ev."

"But that was wrong," said Ozma.

"According to the laws of Ev, the king can do no wrong," answered the monarch, eying a ring of smoke he had just blown from his mouth; "so that he had a perfect right to sell his family to me in exchange for a long life."

"You cheated him, though," declared Dorothy; "for the King of Ev did not have a long life. He jumped into the sea and was drowned."

"That was not my fault," said the Nome King, crossing his legs and smiling contentedly. "I gave him the long life, all right; but he destroyed it."

"Then how could it be a long life?" asked Dorothy.

"Easily enough," was the reply. "Now suppose, my dear, that I gave you a pretty doll in exchange for a lock of your hair, and that after you had received the doll you smashed it into pieces and destroyed it. Could you say that I had not given you a pretty doll?"

"No," answered Dorothy.

"And could you, in fairness, ask me to return to you the lock of hair, just because you had smashed the doll?"

"No," said Dorothy, again.

"Of course not," the Nome King returned. "Nor will I give up the Queen and her children because the King of Ev destroyed his long life by jumping into the sea. They belong to me and I shall keep them."

"But you are treating them cruelly," said Ozma, who was much distressed by the King's refusal.

"In what way?" he asked.

"By making them your slaves," said she.

"Cruelty," remarked the monarch, puffing out wreathes of smoke and watching them float into the air, "is a thing I can't abide. So, as slaves must work hard, and the Queen of Ev and her children were delicate and tender, I transformed them all into articles of ornament and bric-a-brac and scattered them around the various rooms of my palace. Instead of being obliged to labor, they merely decorate my apartments, and I really think I have treated them with great kindness."

"But what a dreadful fate is theirs!" exclaimed Ozma, earnestly. "And the Kingdom of Ev is in great need of its royal family to govern it. If you will liberate them, and restore them to their proper forms, I will give you ten ornaments to replace each one you lose."

The Nome King looked grave.

"Suppose I refuse?" he asked.

"Then," said Ozma, firmly, "I am here with my friends and my army to conquer your kingdom and oblige you to obey my wishes."

The Nome King laughed until he choked; and he choked until he coughed; and he coughed until his face turned from grayish-brown to bright red. And then he wiped his eyes with a rock-colored handkerchief and grew grave again.

"You are as brave as you are pretty, my dear," he said to Ozma. "But you have little idea of the extent of the task you have undertaken. Come with me for a moment."

He arose and took Ozma's hand, leading her to a little door at one side of the room. This he opened and they stepped out upon a balcony, from whence they obtained a wonderful view of the Underground World.

A vast cave extended for miles and miles under the mountain, and in every direction were furnaces and forges glowing brightly and Nomes hammering upon precious metals or polishing gleaming jewels. All around the walls of the cave were thousands of doors of silver and gold, built into the solid rock, and these extended in rows far away into the distance, as far as Ozma's eyes could follow them.

While the little maid from Oz gazed wonderingly upon this scene the Nome King uttered a shrill whistle, and at once all the silver and gold doors flew open and solid ranks of Nome soldiers marched out from every one. So great were their numbers that they quickly filled the immense underground cavern and forced the busy workmen to abandon their tasks.

Although this tremendous army consisted of rock-colored Nomes, all squat and fat, they were clothed in glittering armor of polished steel, inlaid with beautiful gems. Upon his brow each wore a brilliant electric light, and they bore sharp spears and swords and battle-axes of solid bronze. It was evident they were perfectly trained, for they stood in straight rows, rank after rank, with their weapons held erect and true, as if awaiting but the word of command to level them upon their foes.

"This," said the Nome King, "is but a small part of my army. No ruler upon Earth has ever dared to fight me, and no ruler ever will, for I am too powerful to oppose."

He whistled again, and at once the martial array filed through the silver and gold doorways and disappeared, after which the workmen again resumed their labors at the furnaces.

Then, sad and discouraged, Ozma of Oz turned to her friends, and the Nome King calmly reseated himself on his rock throne.

"It would be foolish for us to fight," the girl said to the Tin Woodman. "For our brave Twenty-Seven would be quickly destroyed. I'm sure I do not know how to act in this emergency."

"Ask the King where his kitchen is," suggested the Tiger. "I'm hungry as a bear."

"I might pounce upon the King and tear him in pieces," remarked the Cowardly Lion.

"Try it," said the monarch, lighting his pipe with another hot coal which he took from his pocket.

The Lion crouched low and tried to spring upon the Nome King; but he hopped only a little way into the air and came down again in the same place, not being able to approach the throne by even an inch.

"It seems to me," said the Scarecrow, thoughtfully, "that our best plan is to wheedle his Majesty into giving up his slaves, since he is too great a magician to oppose."

"This is the most sensible thing any of you have suggested," declared the Nome King. "It is folly to threaten me, but I'm so kind-hearted that I cannot stand coaxing or wheedling. If you really wish to accomplish anything by your journey, my dear Ozma, you must coax me."

"Very well," said Ozma, more cheerfully. "Let us be friends, and talk this over in a friendly manner."

"To be sure," agreed the King, his eyes twinkling merrily.

"I am very anxious," she continued, "to liberate the Queen of Ev and her children who are now ornaments and bric-a-brac in your Majesty's palace, and to restore them to their people. Tell me, sir, how this may be accomplished."

The king remained thoughtful for a moment, after which he asked:

"Are you willing to take a few chances and risks yourself, in order to set free the people of Ev?"

"Yes, indeed!" answered Ozma, eagerly.

"Then," said the Nome King, "I will make you this offer: You shall go alone and unattended into my palace and examine carefully all that the rooms contain. Then you shall have permission to touch eleven different objects, pronouncing at the time the word 'Ev,' and if any one of them, or more than one, proves to be the transformation of the Queen of Ev or any of her ten children, then they will instantly be restored to their true forms and may leave my palace and my kingdom in your company, without any objection whatever. It is possible for you, in this way, to free the entire eleven; but if you do not guess all the objects correctly, and some of the slaves remain transformed, then each one of your friends and followers may, in turn, enter the palace and have the same privileges I grant you."

"Oh, thank you! Thank you for this kind offer!" said Ozma, eagerly.

"I make but one condition," added the Nome King, his eyes twinkling.

"What is it?" she enquired.

"If none of the eleven objects you touch proves to be the transformation of any of the royal family of Ev, then, instead of freeing them, you will yourself become enchanted, and transformed into an article of bric-a-brac or an ornament. This is only fair and just, and is the risk you declared you were willing to take."

Chapter XII
The Eleven Guesses

HEARING THIS CONDITION imposed by the Nome King, Ozma became silent and thoughtful, and all her friends looked at her uneasily.

"Don't you do it!" exclaimed Dorothy. "If you guess wrong, you will be enslaved yourself."

"But I shall have eleven guesses," answered Ozma. "Surely I ought to guess one object in eleven correctly; and, if I do, I shall rescue one of the royal family and be safe myself. Then the rest of you may attempt it, and soon we shall free all those who are enslaved."

"What if we fail?" enquired the Scarecrow. "I'd look nice as a piece of bric-a-brac, wouldn't I?"

"We must not fail!" cried Ozma, courageously. "Having come all this distance to free these poor people, it would be weak and cowardly in us to abandon the adventure. Therefore I will accept the Nome King's offer, and go at once into the royal palace."

"Come along, then, my dear," said the King, climbing down from his throne with some difficulty, because he was so fat; "I'll show you the way."

He approached a wall of the cave and waved his hand. Instantly an opening appeared, through which Ozma, after a smiling farewell to her friends, boldly passed.

She found herself in a splendid hall that was more beautiful and grand than anything she had ever beheld. The ceilings were composed of great arches that rose far above her head, and all the walls and floors were of polished marble exquisitely tinted in many colors. Thick velvet carpets were on the floor and heavy silken draperies covered the arches leading to the various rooms of the palace. The furniture was made of rare old woods richly carved and covered with delicate satins, and the entire palace was lighted by a mysterious rosy glow that seemed to come from no particular place but flooded each apartment with its soft and pleasing radiance.

Ozma passed from one room to another, greatly delighted by all she saw. The lovely palace had no other occupant, for the Nome King had left her at the entrance, which closed behind her, and in all the magnificent rooms there appeared to be no other person.

Upon the mantels, and on many shelves and brackets and tables, were clustered ornaments of every description, seemingly made out of all sorts of metals, glass, china, stones and marbles. There were vases, and figures of men and animals, and graven platters and bowls, and mosaics of precious gems, and many other things. Pictures, too, were on the walls, and the underground palace was quite a museum of rare and curious and costly objects.

After her first hasty examination of the rooms Ozma began to wonder which of all the numerous ornaments they contained were the transformations of the royal family of Ev. There was nothing to guide her, for everything seemed without a spark of life. So she must guess blindly; and for the first time the girl came to realize how dangerous was her task, and how likely she was to lose her own freedom in striving to free others from the bondage of the Nome King. No wonder the cunning monarch laughed good naturedly with his visitors, when he knew how easily they might be entrapped.

But Ozma, having undertaken the venture, would not abandon it. She looked at a silver candelabra that had ten branches, and thought: "This may be the Queen of Ev and her ten children." So she touched it and uttered aloud the word "Ev," as the Nome King had instructed her to do when she guessed. But the candelabra remained as it was before.

Then she wandered into another room and touched a china lamb, thinking it might be one of the children she sought. But again she was unsuccessful. Three guesses; four guesses; five, six, seven, eight, nine and ten she made, and still not one of them was right!

The girl shivered a little and grew pale even under the rosy light; for now but one guess remained, and her own fate depended upon the result.

She resolved not to be hasty, and strolled through all the rooms once more, gazing earnestly upon the various ornaments and trying to decide which she would touch. Finally, in despair, she decided to leave it entirely to chance. She faced the doorway of a room, shut her eyes tightly, and then, thrusting aside the heavy draperies, she advanced blindly with her right arm outstretched before her.

Slowly, softly she crept forward until her hand came in contact with an object upon a small round table. She did not know what it was, but in a low voice she pronounced the word "Ev."

The rooms were quite empty of life after that. The Nome King had gained a new ornament. For upon the edge of the table rested a pretty grasshopper, that seemed to have been formed from a single emerald. It was all that remained of Ozma of Oz.

In the throne room just beyond the palace the Nome King suddenly looked up and smiled.

"Next!" he said, in his pleasant voice.

Dorothy, the Scarecrow, and the Tin Woodman, who had been sitting in anxious silence, each gave a start of dismay and stared into one another's eyes.

"Has she failed?" asked Tiktok.

"So it seems," answered the little monarch, cheerfully. "But that is no reason one of you should not succeed. The next may have twelve guesses, instead of eleven, for there are now twelve persons transformed into ornaments. Well, well! Which of you goes next?"

"I'll go," said Dorothy.

"Not so," replied the Tin Woodman. "As commander of Ozma's army, it is my privilege to follow her and attempt her rescue."

"Away you go, then," said the Scarecrow. "But be careful, old friend."

"I will," promised the Tin Woodman; and then he followed the Nome King to the entrance to the palace and the rock closed behind him.

Chapter XIII
The Nome King Laughs

IN A MOMENT the King returned to his throne and relighted his pipe, and the rest of the little band of adventurers settled themselves for another long wait. They were greatly disheartened by the failure of their girl Ruler, and the knowledge that she was now an ornament in the Nome King's palace – a dreadful, creepy place in spite of all its magnificence. Without their little leader they did not know what to do next, and each one, down to the trembling private of the army, began to fear he would soon be more ornamental than useful.

Suddenly the Nome King began laughing.

"Ha, ha, ha! He, he, he! Ho, ho, ho!"

"What's happened?" asked the Scarecrow.

"Why, your friend, the Tin Woodman, has become the funniest thing you can imagine," replied the King, wiping the tears of merriment from his eyes. "No one would ever believe he could make such an amusing ornament. Next!"

They gazed at each other with sinking hearts. One of the generals began to weep dolefully.

"What are you crying for?" asked the Scarecrow, indignant at such a display of weakness.

"He owed me six weeks back pay," said the general, "and I hate to lose him."

"Then you shall go and find him," declared the Scarecrow.

"Me!" cried the general, greatly alarmed.

"Certainly. It is your duty to follow your commander. March!"

"I won't," said the general. "I'd like to, of course; but I just simply WON'T."

The Scarecrow looked enquiringly at the Nome King.

"Never mind," said the jolly monarch. "If he doesn't care to enter the palace and make his guesses I'll throw him into one of my fiery furnaces."

"I'll go! – of course I'm going," yelled the general, as quick as scat. "Where is the entrance – where is it? Let me go at once!"

So the Nome King escorted him into the palace, and again returned to await the result. What the general did, no one can tell; but it was not long before the King called for the next victim, and a colonel was forced to try his fortune.

Thus, one after another, all of the twenty-six officers filed into the palace and made their guesses – and became ornaments.

Meantime the King ordered refreshments to be served to those waiting, and at his command a rudely shaped Nome entered, bearing a tray. This Nome was not unlike the others that Dorothy had seen, but he wore a heavy gold chain around his neck to show that he was the Chief Steward of the Nome King, and he assumed an air of much importance, and even told his majesty not to eat too much cake late at night, or he would be ill.

Dorothy, however, was hungry, and she was not afraid of being ill; so she ate several cakes and found them good, and also she drank a cup of excellent coffee made of a richly flavored clay, browned in the furnaces and then ground fine, and found it most refreshing and not at all muddy.

Of all the party which had started upon this adventure, the little Kansas girl was now left alone with the Scarecrow, Tiktok, and the private for counsellors and companions. Of course the Cowardly Lion and the Hungry Tiger were still there, but they, having also eaten some of the cakes, had gone to sleep at one side of the cave, while upon the other side stood the Sawhorse, motionless and silent, as became a mere thing of wood. Billina had quietly walked around and picked up the crumbs of cake which had been scattered, and now, as it was long after bed-time, she tried to find some dark place in which to go to sleep.

Presently the hen espied a hollow underneath the King's rocky throne, and crept into it unnoticed. She could still hear the chattering of those around her, but it was almost dark underneath the throne, so that soon she had fallen fast asleep.

"Next!" called the King, and the private, whose turn it was to enter the fatal palace, shook hands with Dorothy and the Scarecrow and bade them a sorrowful goodbye, and passed through the rocky portal.

They waited a long time, for the private was in no hurry to become an ornament and made his guesses very slowly. The Nome King, who seemed to know, by some magical power, all that took place in his beautiful rooms of his palace, grew impatient finally and declared he would sit up no longer.

"I love ornaments," said he, "but I can wait until tomorrow to get more of them; so, as soon as that stupid private is transformed, we will all go to bed and leave the job to be finished in the morning."

"Is it so very late?" asked Dorothy.

"Why, it is after midnight," said the King, "and that strikes me as being late enough. There is neither night nor day in my kingdom, because it is under the earth's surface, where the sun does not shine. But we have to sleep, just the same as the up-stairs people do, and for my part I'm going to bed in a few minutes."

Indeed, it was not long after this that the private made his last guess. Of course he guessed wrongly, and of course he at once became an ornament. So the King was greatly pleased, and clapped his hands to summon his Chief Steward.

"Show these guests to some of the sleeping apartments," he commanded, "and be quick about it, too, for I'm dreadfully sleepy myself."

"You've no business to sit up so late," replied the Steward, gruffly. "You'll be as cross as a griffin tomorrow morning."

His Majesty made no answer to this remark, and the Chief Steward led Dorothy through another doorway into a long hall, from which several plain but comfortable sleeping rooms opened. The little girl was given the first room, and the Scarecrow and Tiktok the next – although they never slept – and the Lion and the Tiger the third. The Sawhorse hobbled after the Steward into a fourth room, to stand stiffly in the center of it until morning. Each night was rather a bore to the Scarecrow, Tiktok and the Sawhorse; but they had learned from experience to pass the time patiently and quietly, since all their friends who were made of flesh had to sleep and did not like to be disturbed.

When the Chief Steward had left them alone the Scarecrow remarked, sadly:

"I am in great sorrow over the loss of my old comrade, the Tin Woodman. We have had many dangerous adventures together, and escaped them all, and now it grieves me to know he has become an ornament, and is lost to me forever."

"He was al-ways an or-na-ment to so-ci-e-ty," said Tiktok.

"True; but now the Nome King laughs at him, and calls him the funniest ornament in all the palace. It will hurt my poor friend's pride to be laughed at," continued the Scarecrow, sadly.

"We will make rath-er ab-surd or-na-ments, our-selves, to-mor-row," observed the machine, in his monotonous voice.

Just then Dorothy ran into their room, in a state of great anxiety, crying:

"Where's Billina? Have you seen Billina? Is she here?"

"No," answered the Scarecrow.

"Then what has become of her?" asked the girl.

"Why, I thought she was with you," said the Scarecrow. "Yet I do not remember seeing the yellow hen since she picked up the crumbs of cake."

"We must have left her in the room where the King's throne is," decided Dorothy, and at once she turned and ran down the hall to the door through which they had entered. But it was fast closed and locked on the other side, and the heavy slab of rock proved to be so thick that no sound could pass through it. So Dorothy was forced to return to her chamber.

The Cowardly Lion stuck his head into her room to try to console the girl for the loss of her feathered friend.

"The yellow hen is well able to take care of herself," said he; "so don't worry about her, but try to get all the sleep you can. It has been a long and weary day, and you need rest."

"I'll prob'ly get lots of rest tomorrow, when I become an orn'ment," said Dorothy, sleepily. But she lay down upon her couch, nevertheless, and in spite of all her worries was soon in the land of dreams.

Chapter XIV
Dorothy Tries to be Brave

MEANTIME the Chief Steward had returned to the throne room, where he said to the King:

"You are a fool to waste so much time upon these people."

"What!" cried his Majesty, in so enraged a voice that it awoke Billina, who was asleep under his throne. "How dare you call me a fool?"

"Because I like to speak the truth," said the Steward. "Why didn't you enchant them all at once, instead of allowing them to go one by one into the palace and guess which ornaments are the Queen of Ev and her children?"

"Why, you stupid rascal, it is more fun this way," returned the King, "and it serves to keep me amused for a long time."

"But suppose some of them happen to guess aright," persisted the Steward; "then you would lose your old ornaments and these new ones, too."

"There is no chance of their guessing aright," replied the monarch, with a laugh. "How could they know that the Queen of Ev and her family are all ornaments of a royal purple color?"

"But there are no other purple ornaments in the palace," said the Steward.

"There are many other colors, however, and the purple ones are scattered throughout the rooms, and are of many different shapes and sizes. Take my word for it, Steward, they will never think of choosing the purple ornaments."

Billina, squatting under the throne, had listened carefully to all this talk, and now chuckled softly to herself as she heard the King disclose his secret.

"Still, you are acting foolishly by running the chance," continued the Steward, roughly; "and it is still more foolish of you to transform all those people from Oz into green ornaments."

"I did that because they came from the Emerald City," replied the King; "and I had no green ornaments in my collection until now. I think they will look quite pretty, mixed with the others. Don't you?"

The Steward gave an angry grunt.

"Have your own way, since you are the King," he growled. "But if you come to grief through your carelessness, remember that I told you so. If I wore the magic belt which enables you to work all your transformations, and gives you so much other power, I am sure I would make a much wiser and better King than you are."

"Oh, cease your tiresome chatter!" commanded the King, getting angry again. "Because you are my Chief Steward you have an idea you can scold me as much as you please. But the very next time you become impudent, I will send you to work in the furnaces, and get another Nome to fill your place. Now follow me to my chamber, for I am going to bed. And see that I am wakened early tomorrow morning. I want to enjoy the fun of transforming the rest of these people into ornaments."

"What color will you make the Kansas girl?" asked the Steward.

"Gray, I think," said his Majesty.

"And the Scarecrow and the machine man?"

"Oh, they shall be of solid gold, because they are so ugly in real life."

Then the voices died away, and Billina knew that the King and his Steward had left the room. She fixed up some of her tail feathers that were not straight, and then tucked her head under her wing again and went to sleep.

In the morning Dorothy and the Lion and Tiger were given their breakfast in their rooms, and afterward joined the King in his throne room. The Tiger complained bitterly that he was half starved, and begged to go into the palace and become an ornament, so that he would no longer suffer the pangs of hunger.

"Haven't you had your breakfast?" asked the Nome King.

"Oh, I had just a bite," replied the beast. "But what good is a bite, to a hungry tiger?"

"He ate seventeen bowls of porridge, a platter full of fried sausages, eleven loaves of bread and twenty-one mince pies," said the Steward.

"What more do you want?" demanded the King.

"A fat baby. I want a fat baby," said the Hungry Tiger. "A nice, plump, juicy, tender, fat baby. But, of course, if I had one, my conscience would not allow me to eat it. So I'll have to be an ornament and forget my hunger."

"Impossible!" exclaimed the King. "I'll have no clumsy beasts enter my palace, to overturn and break all my pretty nick-nacks. When the rest of your friends are transformed you can return to the upper world, and go about your business."

"As for that, we have no business, when our friends are gone," said the Lion. "So we do not care much what becomes of us."

Dorothy begged to be allowed to go first into the palace, but Tiktok firmly maintained that the slave should face danger before the mistress. The Scarecrow agreed with him in that, so the Nome King opened the door for the machine man, who tramped into the palace to meet his fate. Then his Majesty returned to his throne and puffed his pipe so contentedly that a small cloud of smoke formed above his head.

Bye and bye he said:

"I'm sorry there are so few of you left. Very soon, now, my fun will be over, and then for amusement I shall have nothing to do but admire my new ornaments."

"It seems to me," said Dorothy, "that you are not so honest as you pretend to be."

"How's that?" asked the King.

"Why, you made us think it would be easy to guess what ornaments the people of Ev were changed into."

"It IS easy," declared the monarch, "if one is a good guesser. But it appears that the members of your party are all poor guessers."

"What is Tiktok doing now?" asked the girl, uneasily.

"Nothing," replied the King, with a frown. "He is standing perfectly still, in the middle of a room."

"Oh, I expect he's run down," said Dorothy. "I forgot to wind him up this morning. How many guesses has he made?"

"All that he is allowed except one," answered the King. "Suppose you go in and wind him up, and then you can stay there and make your own guesses."

"All right," said Dorothy.

"It is my turn next," declared the Scarecrow.

"Why, you don't want to go away and leave me all alone, do you?" asked the girl. "Besides, if I go now I can wind up Tiktok, so that he can make his last guess."

"Very well, then," said the Scarecrow, with a sigh. "Run along, little Dorothy, and may good luck go with you!"

So Dorothy, trying to be brave in spite of her fears, passed through the doorway into the gorgeous rooms of the palace. The stillness of the place awed her, at first, and the child drew short breaths, and pressed her hand to her heart, and looked all around with wondering eyes.

Yes, it was a beautiful place; but enchantments lurked in every nook and corner, and she had not yet grown accustomed to the wizardries of these fairy countries, so different from the quiet and sensible common-places of her own native land.

Slowly she passed through several rooms until she came upon Tiktok, standing motionless. It really seemed, then, that she had found a friend in this mysterious palace, so she hastened to wind up the machine man's action and speech and thoughts.

"Thank you, Dor-oth-y," were his first words. "I have now one more guess to make."

"Oh, be very careful, Tiktok; won't you?" cried the girl.

"Yes. But the Nome King has us in his power, and he has set a trap for us. I fear we are all lost." he answered.

"I fear so, too," said Dorothy, sadly.

"If Smith & Tin-ker had giv-en me a guess-ing clock-work at-tach-ment," continued Tiktok, "I might have de-fied the Nome King. But my thoughts are plain and sim-ple, and are not of much use in this case."

"Do the best you can," said Dorothy, encouragingly, "and if you fail I will watch and see what shape you are changed into."

So Tiktok touched a yellow glass vase that had daisies painted on one side, and he spoke at the same time the word "Ev."

In a flash the machine man had disappeared, and although the girl looked quickly in every direction, she could not tell which of the many ornaments the room contained had a moment before been her faithful friend and servant.

So all she could do was to accept the hopeless task set her, and make her guesses and abide by the result.

"It can't hurt very much," she thought, "for I haven't heard any of them scream or cry out – not even the poor officers. Dear me! I wonder if Uncle Henry or Aunt Em will ever know I have become an orn'ment in the Nome King's palace, and must stand forever and ever in one place and look pretty – 'cept when I'm moved to be dusted. It isn't the way I thought I'd turn out, at all; but I s'pose it can't be helped."

She walked through all the rooms once more, and examined with care all the objects they contained; but there were so many, they bewildered her, and she decided, after all, as Ozma had done, that it could be only guess work at the best, and that the chances were much against her guessing aright.

Timidly she touched an alabaster bowl and said: "Ev."

"That's one failure, anyhow," she thought. "But how am I to know which thing is enchanted, and which is not?"

Next she touched the image of a purple kitten that stood on the corner of a mantel, and as she pronounced the word "Ev" the kitten disappeared, and a pretty, fair-haired boy stood beside her. At the same time a bell rang somewhere in the distance, and as Dorothy started back, partly in surprise and partly in joy, the little one exclaimed:

"Where am I? And who are you? And what has happened to me?"

"Well, I declare!" said Dorothy. "I've really done it."

"Done what?" asked the boy.

"Saved myself from being an ornament," replied the girl, with a laugh, "and saved you from being forever a purple kitten."

"A purple kitten?" he repeated. "There IS no such thing."

"I know," she answered. "But there was, a minute ago. Don't you remember standing on a corner of the mantel?"

"Of course not. I am a Prince of Ev, and my name is Evring," the little one announced, proudly. "But my father, the King, sold my mother and all her children to the cruel ruler of the Nomes, and after that I remember nothing at all."

"A purple kitten can't be 'spected to remember, Evring," said Dorothy. "But now you are yourself again, and I'm going to try to save some of your brothers and sisters, and perhaps your mother, as well. So come with me."

She seized the child's hand and eagerly hurried here and there, trying to decide which object to choose next. The third guess was another failure, and so was the fourth and the fifth.

Little Evring could not imagine what she was doing, but he trotted along beside her very willingly, for he liked the new companion he had found.

Dorothy's further quest proved unsuccessful; but after her first disappointment was over, the little girl was filled with joy and thankfulness to think that after all she had been able to save one member of the royal family of Ev, and could restore the little Prince to his sorrowing country. Now she might return to the terrible Nome King in safety, carrying with her the prize she had won in the person of the fair-haired boy.

So she retraced her steps until she found the entrance to the palace, and as she approached, the massive doors of rock opened of their own accord, allowing both Dorothy and Evring to pass the portals and enter the throne room.

Chapter XV
Billina Frightens the Nome King

NOW WHEN DOROTHY had entered the palace to make her guesses and the Scarecrow was left with the Nome King, the two sat in moody silence for several minutes. Then the monarch exclaimed, in a tone of satisfaction:

"Very good!"

"Who is very good?" asked the Scarecrow.

"The machine man. He won't need to be wound up any more, for he has now become a very neat ornament. Very neat, indeed."

"How about Dorothy?" the Scarecrow enquired.

"Oh, she will begin to guess, pretty soon," said the King, cheerfully. "And then she will join my collection, and it will be your turn."

The good Scarecrow was much distressed by the thought that his little friend was about to suffer the fate of Ozma and the rest of their party; but while he sat in gloomy reverie a shrill voice suddenly cried:

"Kut, kut, kut – ka-daw-kutt! Kut, kut, kut – ka-daw-kutt!"

The Nome King nearly jumped off his seat, he was so startled.

"Good gracious! What's that?" he yelled.

"Why, it's Billina," said the Scarecrow.

"What do you mean by making a noise like that?" shouted the King, angrily, as the yellow hen came from under the throne and strutted proudly about the room.

"I've got a right to cackle, I guess," replied Billina. "I've just laid my egg."

"What! Laid an egg! In my throne room! How dare you do such a thing?" asked the King, in a voice of fury.

"I lay eggs wherever I happen to be," said the hen, ruffling her feathers and then shaking them into place.

"But – thunder-ation! Don't you know that eggs are poison?" roared the King, while his rock-colored eyes stuck out in great terror.

"Poison! Well, I declare," said Billina, indignantly. "I'll have you know all my eggs are warranted strictly fresh and up to date. Poison, indeed!"

"You don't understand," retorted the little monarch, nervously. "Eggs belong only to the outside world – to the world on the earth's surface, where you came from. Here, in my underground kingdom, they are rank poison, as I said, and we Nomes can't bear them around."

"Well, you'll have to bear this one around," declared Billina; "for I've laid it."

"Where?" asked the King.

"Under your throne," said the hen.

The King jumped three feet into the air, so anxious was he to get away from the throne.

"Take it away! Take it away at once!" he shouted.

"I can't," said Billina. "I haven't any hands."

"I'll take the egg," said the Scarecrow. "I'm making a collection of Billina's eggs. There's one in my pocket now, that she laid yesterday."

Hearing this, the monarch hastened to put a good distance between himself and the Scarecrow, who was about to reach under the throne for the egg when the hen suddenly cried:

"Stop!"

"What's wrong?" asked the Scarecrow.

"Don't take the egg unless the King will allow me to enter the palace and guess as the others have done," said Billina.

"Pshaw!" returned the King. "You're only a hen. How could you guess my enchantments?"

"I can try, I suppose," said Billina. "And, if I fail, you will have another ornament."

"A pretty ornament you'd make, wouldn't you?" growled the King. "But you shall have your way. It will properly punish you for daring to lay an egg in my presence. After the Scarecrow is enchanted you shall follow him into the palace. But how will you touch the objects?"

"With my claws," said the hen; "and I can speak the word 'Ev' as plainly as anyone. Also I must have the right to guess the enchantments of my friends, and to release them if I succeed."

"Very well," said the King. "You have my promise."

"Then," said Billina to the Scarecrow, "you may get the egg."

He knelt down and reached underneath the throne and found the egg, which he placed in another pocket of his jacket, fearing that if both eggs were in one pocket they would knock together and get broken.

Just then a bell above the throne rang briskly, and the King gave another nervous jump.

"Well, well!" said he, with a rueful face; "the girl has actually done it."

"Done what?" asked the Scarecrow.

"She has made one guess that is right, and broken one of my neatest enchantments. By ricketty, it's too bad! I never thought she would do it."

"Do I understand that she will now return to us in safety?" enquired the Scarecrow, joyfully wrinkling his painted face into a broad smile.

"Of course," said the King, fretfully pacing up and down the room. "I always keep my promises, no matter how foolish they are. But I shall make an ornament of the yellow hen to replace the one I have just lost."

"Perhaps you will, and perhaps you won't," murmured Billina, calmly. "I may surprise you by guessing right."

"Guessing right?" snapped the King. "How could you guess right, where your betters have failed, you stupid fowl?"

Billina did not care to answer this question, and a moment later the doors flew open and Dorothy entered, leading the little Prince Evring by the hand.

The Scarecrow welcomed the girl with a close embrace, and he would have embraced Evring, too, in his delight. But the little Prince was shy, and shrank away from the painted Scarecrow because he did not yet know his many excellent qualities.

But there was little time for the friends to talk, because the Scarecrow must now enter the palace. Dorothy's success had greatly encouraged him, and they both hoped he would manage to make at least one correct guess.

However, he proved as unfortunate as the others except Dorothy, and although he took a good deal of time to select his objects, not one did the poor Scarecrow guess aright.

So he became a solid gold card-receiver, and the beautiful but terrible palace awaited its next visitor.

"It's all over," remarked the King, with a sigh of satisfaction; "and it has been a very amusing performance, except for the one good guess the Kansas girl made. I am richer by a great many pretty ornaments."

"It is my turn, now," said Billina, briskly.

"Oh, I'd forgotten you," said the King. "But you needn't go if you don't wish to. I will be generous, and let you off."

"No you won't," replied the hen. "I insist upon having my guesses, as you promised."

"Then go ahead, you absurd feathered fool!" grumbled the King, and he caused the opening that led to the palace to appear once more.

"Don't go, Billina," said Dorothy, earnestly. "It isn't easy to guess those orn'ments, and only luck saved me from being one myself. Stay with me and we'll go back to the Land of Ev together. I'm sure this little Prince will give us a home."

"Indeed I will," said Evring, with much dignity.

"Don't worry, my dear," cried Billina, with a cluck that was meant for a laugh. "I may not be human, but I'm no fool, if I AM a chicken."

"Oh, Billina!" said Dorothy, "you haven't been a chicken in a long time. Not since you – you've been – grown up."

"Perhaps that's true," answered Billina, thoughtfully. "But if a Kansas farmer sold me to some one, what would he call me? – a hen or a chicken!"

"You are not a Kansas farmer, Billina," replied the girl, "and you said –"

"Never mind that, Dorothy. I'm going. I won't say goodbye, because I'm coming back. Keep up your courage, for I'll see you a little later."

Then Billina gave several loud 'cluck-clucks' that seemed to make the fat little King MORE nervous than ever, and marched through the entrance into the enchanted palace.

"I hope I've seen the last of THAT bird," declared the monarch, seating himself again in his throne and mopping the perspiration from his forehead with his rock-colored handkerchief. "Hens are bothersome enough at their best, but when they can talk they're simply dreadful."

"Billina's my friend," said Dorothy quietly. "She may not always be 'zactly polite; but she MEANS well, I'm sure."

Chapter XVI
Purple, Green and Gold

THE YELLOW HEN, stepping high and with an air of vast importance, walked slowly over the rich velvet carpets of the splendid palace, examining everything she met with her sharp little eyes.

Billina had a right to feel important; for she alone shared the Nome King's secret and knew how to tell the objects that were transformations from those that had never been alive. She was very sure that her guesses would be correct, but before she began to make them she was curious to behold all the magnificence of this underground palace, which was perhaps one of the most splendid and beautiful places in any fairyland.

As she went through the rooms she counted the purple ornaments; and although some were small and hidden in queer places, Billina spied them all, and found the entire ten scattered about the various rooms. The green ornaments she did not bother to count, for she thought she could find them all when the time came.

Finally, having made a survey of the entire palace and enjoyed its splendor, the yellow hen returned to one of the rooms where she had noticed a large purple footstool. She placed a claw upon this and said "Ev," and at once the footstool vanished and a lovely lady, tall and slender and most beautifully robed, stood before her.

The lady's eyes were round with astonishment for a moment, for she could not remember her transformation, nor imagine what had restored her to life.

"Good morning, ma'am," said Billina, in her sharp voice. "You're looking quite well, considering your age."

"Who speaks?" demanded the Queen of Ev, drawing herself up proudly.

"Why, my name's Bill, by rights," answered the hen, who was now perched upon the back of a chair; "although Dorothy has put scollops on it and made it Billina. But the name doesn't matter. I've saved you from the Nome King, and you are a slave no longer."

"Then I thank you for the gracious favor," said the Queen, with a graceful courtesy. "But, my children – tell me, I beg of you – where are my children?" and she clasped her hands in anxious entreaty.

"Don't worry," advised Billina, pecking at a tiny bug that was crawling over the chair back. "Just at present they are out of mischief and perfectly safe, for they can't even wiggle."

"What mean you, O kindly stranger?" asked the Queen, striving to repress her anxiety.

"They're enchanted," said Billina, "just as you have been – all, that is, except the little fellow Dorothy picked out. And the chances are that they have been good boys and girls for some time, because they couldn't help it."

"Oh, my poor darlings!" cried the Queen, with a sob of anguish.

"Not at all," returned the hen. "Don't let their condition make you unhappy, ma'am, because I'll soon have them crowding 'round to bother and worry you as naturally as ever. Come with me, if you please, and I'll show you how pretty they look."

She flew down from her perch and walked into the next room, the Queen following. As she passed a low table a small green grasshopper caught her eye, and instantly Billina pounced upon it and snapped it up in her sharp bill. For grasshoppers are a favorite food with hens, and they usually must be caught quickly, before they can hop away. It might easily have been the end of Ozma of Oz, had she been a real grasshopper instead of an emerald one. But Billina found the grasshopper hard and lifeless, and suspecting it was not good to eat she quickly dropped it instead of letting it slide down her throat.

"I might have known better," she muttered to herself, "for where there is no grass there can be no live grasshoppers. This is probably one of the King's transformations."

A moment later she approached one of the purple ornaments, and while the Queen watched her curiously the hen broke the Nome King's enchantment and a sweet-faced girl, whose golden hair fell in a cloud over her shoulders, stood beside them.

"Evanna!" cried the Queen, "my own Evanna!" and she clasped the girl to her bosom and covered her face with kisses.

"That's all right," said Billina, contentedly. "Am I a good guesser, Mr. Nome King? Well, I guess!"

Then she disenchanted another girl, whom the Queen addressed as Evrose, and afterwards a boy named Evardo, who was older than his brother Evring. Indeed, the yellow hen kept the good Queen exclaiming and embracing for some time, until five Princesses and four Princes, all looking very much alike except for the difference in size, stood in a row beside their happy mother.

The Princesses were named, Evanna, Evrose, Evella, Evirene and Evedna, while the Princes were Evrob, Evington, Evardo and Evroland. Of these Evardo was the eldest and would inherit his father's throne and be crowned King of Ev when he returned to his own country. He was a grave and quiet youth, and would doubtless rule his people wisely and with justice.

Billina, having restored all of the royal family of Ev to their proper forms, now began to select the green ornaments which were the transformations of the people of Oz. She had little trouble in finding these, and before long all the twenty-six officers, as well as the private, were gathered around the yellow hen, joyfully congratulating her upon their release. The thirty-seven people who were now alive in the rooms of the palace knew very well that they owed their freedom to the cleverness of the yellow hen, and they were earnest in thanking her for saving them from the magic of the Nome King.

"Now," said Billina, "I must find Ozma. She is sure to be here, somewhere, and of course she is green, being from Oz. So look around, you stupid soldiers, and help me in my search."

For a while, however, they could discover nothing more that was green. But the Queen, who had kissed all her nine children once more and could now find time to take an interest in what was going on, said to the hen:

"Mayhap, my gentle friend, it is the grasshopper whom you seek."

"Of course it's the grasshopper!" exclaimed Billina. "I declare, I'm nearly as stupid as these brave soldiers. Wait here for me, and I'll go back and get it."

So she went into the room where she had seen the grasshopper, and presently Ozma of Oz, as lovely and dainty as ever, entered and approached the Queen of Ev, greeting her as one high born princess greets another.

"But where are my friends, the Scarecrow and the Tin Woodman?" asked the girl Ruler, when these courtesies had been exchanged.

"I'll hunt them up," replied Billina. "The Scarecrow is solid gold, and so is Tiktok; but I don't exactly know what the Tin Woodman is, because the Nome King said he had been transformed into something funny."

Ozma eagerly assisted the hen in her quest, and soon the Scarecrow and the machine man, being ornaments of shining gold, were discovered and restored to their accustomed forms. But, search as they might, in no place could they find a funny ornament that might be the transformation of the Tin Woodman.

"Only one thing can be done," said Ozma, at last, "and that is to return to the Nome King and oblige him to tell us what has become of our friend."

"Perhaps he won't," suggested Billina.

"He must," returned Ozma, firmly. "The King has not treated us honestly, for under the mask of fairness and good nature he entrapped us all, and we would have been forever enchanted had not our wise and clever friend, the yellow hen, found a way to save us."

"The King is a villain," declared the Scarecrow.

"His laugh is worse than another man's frown," said the private, with a shudder.

"I thought he was hon-est, but I was mis-tak-en," remarked Tiktok. "My thoughts are us-u-al-ly cor-rect, but it is Smith & Tin-ker's fault if they some-times go wrong or do not work prop-er-ly."

"Smith & Tinker made a very good job of you," said Ozma, kindly. "I do not think they should be blamed if you are not quite perfect."

"Thank you," replied Tiktok.

"Then," said Billina, in her brisk little voice, "let us all go back to the Nome King, and see what he has to say for himself."

So they started for the entrance, Ozma going first, with the Queen and her train of little Princes and Princesses following. Then came Tiktok, and the Scarecrow with Billina perched upon his straw-stuffed shoulder. The twenty-seven officers and the private brought up the rear.

As they reached the hall the doors flew open before them; but then they all stopped and stared into the domed cavern with faces of astonishment and dismay. For the room was filled with the mail-clad warriors of the Nome King, rank after rank standing in orderly array. The electric lights upon their brows gleamed brightly, their battle-axes were poised as if to strike down their foes; yet they remained motionless as statues, awaiting the word of command.

And in the center of this terrible army sat the little King upon his throne of rock. But he neither smiled nor laughed. Instead, his face was distorted with rage, and most dreadful to behold.

Chapter XVII
The Scarecrow Wins the Fight

AFTER BILLINA had entered the palace Dorothy and Evring sat down to await the success or failure of her mission, and the Nome King occupied his throne and smoked his long pipe for a while in a cheerful and contented mood.

Then the bell above the throne, which sounded whenever an enchantment was broken, began to ring, and the King gave a start of annoyance and exclaimed, "Rocketty-ricketts!"

When the bell rang a second time the King shouted angrily, "Smudge and blazes!" and at a third ring he screamed in a fury, "Hippikaloric!" which must be a dreadful word because we don't know what it means.

After that the bell went on ringing time after time; but the King was now so violently enraged that he could not utter a word, but hopped out of his throne and all around the room in a mad frenzy, so that he reminded Dorothy of a jumping-jack.

The girl was, for her part, filled with joy at every peal of the bell, for it announced the fact that Billina had transformed one more ornament into a living person. Dorothy was also amazed at Billina's success, for she could not imagine how the yellow hen was able to guess correctly from all the bewildering number of articles clustered in the rooms of the palace. But after she had counted ten, and the bell continued to ring, she knew that not only the royal family of Ev, but Ozma and her followers also, were being restored to their natural forms, and she was so delighted that the antics of the angry King only made her laugh merrily.

Perhaps the little monarch could not be more furious than he was before, but the girl's laughter nearly drove him frantic, and he roared at her like a savage beast. Then, as he found that all his enchantments were likely to be dispelled and his victims every one set free, he suddenly ran to the little door that opened upon the balcony and gave the shrill whistle that summoned his warriors.

At once the army filed out of the gold and silver doors in great numbers, and marched up a winding stairs and into the throne room, led by a stern featured Nome who was their captain. When they had nearly filled the throne room they formed ranks in the big underground cavern below, and then stood still until they were told what to do next.

Dorothy had pressed back to one side of the cavern when the warriors entered, and now she stood holding little Prince Evring's hand while the great Lion crouched upon one side and the enormous Tiger crouched on the other side.

"Seize that girl!" shouted the King to his captain, and a group of warriors sprang forward to obey. But both the Lion and Tiger snarled so fiercely and bared their strong, sharp teeth so threateningly, that the men drew back in alarm.

"Don't mind them!" cried the Nome King; "they cannot leap beyond the places where they now stand."

"But they can bite those who attempt to touch the girl," said the captain.

"I'll fix that," answered the King. "I'll enchant them again, so that they can't open their jaws."

He stepped out of the throne to do this, but just then the Sawhorse ran up behind him and gave the fat monarch a powerful kick with both his wooden hind legs.

"Ow! Murder! Treason!" yelled the King, who had been hurled against several of his warriors and was considerably bruised. "Who did that?"

"I did," growled the Sawhorse, viciously. "You let Dorothy alone, or I'll kick you again."

"We'll see about that," replied the King, and at once he waved his hand toward the Sawhorse and muttered a magical word. "Aha!" he continued; "NOW let us see you move, you wooden mule!"

But in spite of the magic the Sawhorse moved; and he moved so quickly toward the King, that the fat little man could not get out of his way. Thump – BANG! came the wooden heels, right against his round body, and the King flew into the air and fell upon the head of his captain, who let him drop flat upon the ground.

"Well, well!" said the King, sitting up and looking surprised. "Why didn't my magic belt work, I wonder?"

"The creature is made of wood," replied the captain. "Your magic will not work on wood, you know."

"Ah, I'd forgotten that," said the King, getting up and limping to his throne. "Very well, let the girl alone. She can't escape us, anyway."

The warriors, who had been rather confused by these incidents, now formed their ranks again, and the Sawhorse pranced across the room to Dorothy and took a position beside the Hungry Tiger.

At that moment the doors that led to the palace flew open and the people of Ev and the people of Oz were disclosed to view. They paused, astonished, at sight of the warriors and the angry Nome King, seated in their midst.

"Surrender!" cried the King, in a loud voice. "You are my prisoners."

"Go 'long!" answered Billina, from the Scarecrow's shoulder. "You promised me that if I guessed correctly my friends and I might depart in safety. And you always keep your promises."

"I said you might leave the palace in safety," retorted the King; "and so you may, but you cannot leave my dominions. You are my prisoners, and I will hurl you all into my underground dungeons, where the volcanic fires glow and the molten lava flows in every direction, and the air is hotter than blue blazes."

"That will be the end of me, all right," said the Scarecrow, sorrowfully. "One small blaze, blue or green, is enough to reduce me to an ash-heap."

"Do you surrender?" demanded the King.

Billina whispered something in the Scarecrow's ear that made him smile and put his hands in his jacket pockets.

"No!" returned Ozma, boldly answering the King. Then she said to her army:

"Forward, my brave soldiers, and fight for your Ruler and yourselves, unto death!"

"Pardon me, Most Royal Ozma," replied one of her generals; "but I find that I and my brother officers all suffer from heart disease, and the slightest excitement might kill us. If we fight we may get excited. Would it not be well for us to avoid this grave danger?"

"Soldiers should not have heart disease," said Ozma.

"Private soldiers are not, I believe, afflicted that way," declared another general, twirling his moustache thoughtfully. "If your Royal Highness desires, we will order our private to attack yonder warriors."

"Do so," replied Ozma.

"For-ward – march!" cried all the generals, with one voice. "For-ward – march!" yelled the colonels. "For-ward – march!" shouted the majors. "For-ward – march!" commanded the captains.

And at that the private leveled his spear and dashed furiously upon the foe.

The captain of the Nomes was so surprised by this sudden onslaught that he forgot to command his warriors to fight, so that the ten men in the first row, who stood in front of the private's spear, fell over like so many toy soldiers. The spear could not go through their steel armor, however, so the warriors scrambled to their feet again, and by that time the private had knocked over another row of them.

Then the captain brought down his battle-axe with such a strong blow that the private's spear was shattered and knocked from his grasp, and he was helpless to fight any longer.

The Nome King had left his throne and pressed through his warriors to the front ranks, so he could see what was going on; but as he faced Ozma and her friends the Scarecrow, as if aroused to action by the valor of the private, drew one of Billina's eggs from his right jacket pocket and hurled it straight at the little monarch's head.

It struck him squarely in his left eye, where the egg smashed and scattered, as eggs will, and covered his face and hair and beard with its sticky contents.

"Help, help!" screamed the King, clawing with his fingers at the egg, in a struggle to remove it.

"An egg! an egg! Run for your lives!" shouted the captain of the Nomes, in a voice of horror.

And how they DID run! The warriors fairly tumbled over one another in their efforts to escape the fatal poison of that awful egg, and those who could not rush down the winding stair fell off the balcony into the great cavern beneath, knocking over those who stood below them.

Even while the King was still yelling for help his throne room became emptied of every one of his warriors, and before the monarch had managed to clear the egg away from his left eye the Scarecrow threw the second egg against his right eye, where it smashed and blinded him entirely. The King was unable to flee because he could not see which way to run; so he stood still and howled and shouted and screamed in abject fear.

While this was going on, Billina flew over to Dorothy, and perching herself upon the Lion's back the hen whispered eagerly to the girl:

"Get his belt! Get the Nome King's jeweled belt! It unbuckles in the back. Quick, Dorothy – quick!"

Chapter XVIII
The Fate of the Tin Woodman

DOROTHY OBEYED. She ran at once behind the Nome King, who was still trying to free his eyes from the egg, and in a twinkling she had unbuckled his splendid jeweled belt and carried it away with her to her place beside the Tiger and Lion, where, because she did not know what else to do with it, she fastened it around her own slim waist.

Just then the Chief Steward rushed in with a sponge and a bowl of water, and began mopping away the broken eggs from his master's face. In a few minutes, and while all the party stood looking on, the King regained the use of his eyes, and the first thing he did was to glare wickedly upon the Scarecrow and exclaim:

"I'll make you suffer for this, you hay-stuffed dummy! Don't you know eggs are poison to Nomes?"

"Really," said the Scarecrow, "they DON'T seem to agree with you, although I wonder why."

"They were strictly fresh and above suspicion," said Billina. "You ought to be glad to get them."

"I'll transform you all into scorpions!" cried the King, angrily, and began waving his arms and muttering magic words.

But none of the people became scorpions, so the King stopped and looked at them in surprise.

"What's wrong?" he asked.

"Why, you are not wearing your magic belt," replied the Chief Steward, after looking the King over carefully. "Where is it? What have you done with it?"

The Nome King clapped his hand to his waist, and his rock colored face turned white as chalk.

"It's gone," he cried, helplessly. "It's gone, and I am ruined!"

Dorothy now stepped forward and said:

"Royal Ozma, and you, Queen of Ev, I welcome you and your people back to the land of the living. Billina has saved you from your troubles, and now we will leave this drea'ful place, and return to Ev as soon as poss'ble."

While the child spoke they could all see that she wore the magic belt, and a great cheer went up from all her friends, which was led by the voices of the Scarecrow and the private. But the Nome King did not join them. He crept back onto his throne like a whipped dog, and lay there bitterly bemoaning his defeat.

"But we have not yet found my faithful follower, the Tin Woodman," said Ozma to Dorothy, "and without him I do not wish to go away."

"Nor I," replied Dorothy, quickly. "Wasn't he in the palace?"

"He must be there," said Billina; "but I had no clue to guide me in guessing the Tin Woodman, so I must have missed him."

"We will go back into the rooms," said Dorothy. "This magic belt, I am sure, will help us to find our dear old friend."

So she re-entered the palace, the doors of which still stood open, and everyone followed her except the Nome King, the Queen of Ev and Prince Evring. The mother had taken the little Prince in her lap and was fondling and kissing him lovingly, for he was her youngest born.

But the others went with Dorothy, and when she came to the middle of the first room the girl waved her hand, as she had seen the King do, and commanded the Tin Woodman, whatever form he might then have, to resume his proper shape. No result followed this attempt, so Dorothy went into another room and repeated it, and so through all the rooms of the palace. Yet the Tin Woodman did not appear to them, nor could they imagine which among the thousands of ornaments was their transformed friend.

Sadly they returned to the throne room, where the King, seeing that they had met with failure, jeered at Dorothy, saying:

"You do not know how to use my belt, so it is of no use to you. Give it back to me and I will let you go free – you and all the people who came with you. As for the royal family of Ev, they are my slaves, and shall remain here."

"I shall keep the belt," said Dorothy.

"But how can you escape, without my consent?" asked the King.

"Easily enough," answered the girl. "All we need to do is to walk out the way that we came in."

"Oh, that's all, is it?" sneered the King. "Well, where is the passage through which you entered this room?"

They all looked around, but could not discover the place, for it had long since been closed. Dorothy, however, would not be dismayed. She waved her hand toward the seemingly solid wall of the cavern and said:

"I command the passage to open!"

Instantly the order was obeyed; the opening appeared and the passage lay plainly before them.

The King was amazed, and all the others overjoyed.

"Why, then, if the belt obeys you, were we unable to discover the Tin Woodman?" asked Ozma.

"I can't imagine," said Dorothy.

"See here, girl," proposed the King, eagerly; "give me the belt, and I will tell you what shape the Tin Woodman was changed into, and then you can easily find him."

Dorothy hesitated, but Billina cried out:

"Don't you do it! If the Nome King gets the belt again he will make every one of us prisoners, for we will be in his power. Only by keeping the belt, Dorothy, will you ever be able to leave this place in safety."

"I think that is true," said the Scarecrow. "But I have another idea, due to my excellent brains. Let Dorothy transform the King into a goose-egg unless he agrees to go into the palace and bring out to us the ornament which is our friend Nick Chopper, the Tin Woodman."

"A goose-egg!" echoed the horrified King. "How dreadful!"

"Well, a goose-egg you will be unless you go and fetch us the ornament we want," declared Billina with a joyful chuckle.

"You can see for yourself that Dorothy is able to use the magic belt all right," added the Scarecrow.

The Nome King thought it over and finally consented, for he did not want to be a goose-egg. So he went into the palace to get the ornament which was the transformation of the Tin Woodman, and they all awaited his return with considerable impatience, for they were anxious to leave this underground cavern and see the sunshine once more. But when the Nome King came back he brought nothing with him except a puzzled and anxious expression upon his face.

"He's gone!" he said. "The Tin Woodman is nowhere in the palace."

"Are you sure?" asked Ozma, sternly.

"I'm very sure," answered the King, trembling, "for I know just what I transformed him into, and exactly where he stood. But he is not there, and please don't change me into a goose-egg, because I've done the best I could."

They were all silent for a time, and then Dorothy said:

"There is no use punishing the Nome King any more, and I'm 'fraid we'll have to go away without our friend."

"If he is not here, we cannot rescue him," agreed the Scarecrow, sadly. "Poor Nick! I wonder what has become of him."

"And he owed me six weeks back pay!" said one of the generals, wiping the tears from his eyes with his gold-laced coat sleeve.

Very sorrowfully they determined to return to the upper world without their former companion, and so Ozma gave the order to begin the march through the passage.

The army went first, and then the royal family of Ev, and afterward came Dorothy, Ozma, Billina, the Scarecrow and Tiktok.

They left the Nome King scowling at them from his throne, and had no thought of danger until Ozma chanced to look back and saw a large number of the warriors following them in full chase, with their swords and spears and axes raised to strike down the fugitives as soon as they drew near enough.

Evidently the Nome King had made this last attempt to prevent their escaping him; but it did him no good, for when Dorothy saw the danger they were in she stopped and waved her hand and whispered a command to the magic belt.

Instantly the foremost warriors became eggs, which rolled upon the floor of the cavern in such numbers that those behind could not advance without stepping upon them. But, when they saw the eggs, all desire to advance departed from the warriors, and they turned and fled madly into the cavern, and refused to go back again.

Our friends had no further trouble in reaching the end of the passage, and soon were standing in the outer air upon the gloomy path between the two high mountains. But the way to Ev lay plainly before them, and they fervently hoped that they had seen the last of the Nome King and of his dreadful palace.

The cavalcade was led by Ozma, mounted on the Cowardly Lion, and the Queen of Ev, who rode upon the back of the Tiger. The children of the Queen walked behind her, hand in hand. Dorothy rode the Sawhorse, while the Scarecrow walked and commanded the army in the absence of the Tin Woodman.

Presently the way began to lighten and more of the sunshine to come in between the two mountains. And before long they heard the thump! thump! thump! of the giant's hammer upon the road.

"How may we pass the monstrous man of iron?" asked the Queen, anxious for the safety of her children. But Dorothy solved the problem by a word to the magic belt.

The giant paused, with his hammer held motionless in the air, thus allowing the entire party to pass between his cast-iron legs in safety.

Chapter XIX
The King of Ev

IF THERE WERE any shifting, rock-colored Nomes on the mountain side now, they were silent and respectful, for our adventurers were not annoyed, as before, by their impudent laughter. Really the Nomes had nothing to laugh at, since the defeat of their King.

On the other side they found Ozma's golden chariot, standing as they had left it. Soon the Lion and the Tiger were harnessed to the beautiful chariot, in which was enough room for Ozma and the Queen and six of the royal children.

Little Evring preferred to ride with Dorothy upon the Sawhorse, which had a long back. The Prince had recovered from his shyness and had become very fond of the girl who had rescued him, so they were fast friends and chatted pleasantly together as they rode along. Billina was also perched upon the head of the wooden steed, which seemed not to mind the added weight in the least, and the boy was full of wonder that a hen could talk, and say such sensible things.

When they came to the gulf, Ozma's magic carpet carried them all over in safety; and now they began to pass the trees, in which birds were singing; and the breeze that was wafted to them from the farms of Ev was spicy with flowers and new-mown hay; and the sunshine fell full upon them, to warm them and drive away from their bodies the chill and dampness of the underground kingdom of the Nomes.

"I would be quite content," said the Scarecrow to Tiktok, "were only the Tin Woodman with us. But it breaks my heart to leave him behind."

"He was a fine fel-low," replied Tiktok, "al-though his ma-te-ri-al was not ve-ry du-ra-ble."

"Oh, tin is an excellent material," the Scarecrow hastened to say; "and if anything ever happened to poor Nick Chopper he was always easily soldered. Besides, he did not have to be wound up, and was not liable to get out of order."

"I some-times wish," said Tiktok, "that I was stuffed with straw, as you are. It is hard to be made of cop-per."

"I have no reason to complain of my lot," replied the Scarecrow. "A little fresh straw, now and then, makes me as good as new. But I can never be the polished gentleman that my poor departed friend, the Tin Woodman, was."

You may be sure the royal children of Ev and their Queen mother were delighted at seeing again their beloved country; and when the towers of the palace of Ev came into view they could not forbear cheering at the sight. Little Evring, riding in front of Dorothy, was so overjoyed that he took a curious tin whistle from his pocket and blew a shrill blast that made the Sawhorse leap and prance in sudden alarm.

"What is that?" asked Billina, who had been obliged to flutter her wings in order to keep her seat upon the head of the frightened Sawhorse.

"That's my whistle," said Prince Evring, holding it out upon his hand.

It was in the shape of a little fat pig, made of tin and painted green. The whistle was in the tail of the pig.

"Where did you get it?" asked the yellow hen, closely examining the toy with her bright eyes.

"Why, I picked it up in the Nome King's palace, while Dorothy was making her guesses, and I put it in my pocket," answered the little Prince.

Billina laughed; or at least she made the peculiar cackle that served her for a laugh.

"No wonder I couldn't find the Tin Woodman," she said; "and no wonder the magic belt didn't make him appear, or the King couldn't find him, either!"

"What do you mean?" questioned Dorothy.

"Why, the Prince had him in his pocket," cried Billina, cackling again.

"I did not!" protested little Evring. "I only took the whistle."

"Well, then, watch me," returned the hen, and reaching out a claw she touched the whistle and said "Ev."

Swish!

"Good afternoon," said the Tin Woodman, taking off his funnel cap and bowing to Dorothy and the Prince. "I think I must have been asleep for the first time since I was made of tin, for I do not remember our leaving the Nome King."

"You have been enchanted," answered the girl, throwing an arm around her old friend and hugging him tight in her joy. "But it's all right, now."

"I want my whistle!" said the little Prince, beginning to cry.

"Hush!" cautioned Billina. "The whistle is lost, but you may have another when you get home."

The Scarecrow had fairly thrown himself upon the bosom of his old comrade, so surprised and delighted was he to see him again, and Tiktok squeezed the Tin Woodman's hand so earnestly that he dented some of his fingers. Then they had to make way for Ozma to welcome the tin man, and the army caught sight of him and set up a cheer, and everybody was delighted and happy.

For the Tin Woodman was a great favorite with all who knew him, and his sudden recovery after they had thought he was lost to them forever was indeed a pleasant surprise.

Before long the cavalcade arrived at the royal palace, where a great crowd of people had gathered to welcome their Queen and her ten children. There was much shouting and cheering, and the people threw flowers in their path, and every face wore a happy smile.

They found the Princess Langwidere in her mirrored chamber, where she was admiring one of her handsomest heads – one with rich chestnut hair, dreamy walnut eyes and a shapely hickorynut nose. She was very glad to be relieved of her duties to the people of Ev, and the Queen graciously permitted her to retain her rooms and her cabinet of heads as long as she lived.

Then the Queen took her eldest son out upon a balcony that overlooked the crowd of subjects gathered below, and said to them:

"Here is your future ruler, King Evardo Fifteenth. He is fifteen years of age, has fifteen silver buckles on his jacket and is the fifteenth Evardo to rule the land of Ev."

The people shouted their approval fifteen times, and even the Wheelers, some of whom were present, loudly promised to obey the new King.

So the Queen placed a big crown of gold, set with rubies, upon Evardo's head, and threw an ermine robe over his shoulders, and proclaimed him King; and he bowed gratefully to all his subjects and then went away to see if he could find any cake in the royal pantry.

Ozma of Oz and her people, as well as Dorothy, Tiktok and Billina, were splendidly entertained by the Queen mother, who owed all her happiness to their kind offices; and that evening the yellow hen was publicly presented with a beautiful necklace of pearls and sapphires, as a token of esteem from the new King.

Chapter XX
The Emerald City

DOROTHY DECIDED to accept Ozma's invitation to return with her to the Land of Oz. There was no greater chance of her getting home from Ev than from Oz, and the little girl was anxious to see once more the country where she had encountered such wonderful adventures. By this time Uncle Henry would have reached Australia in his ship, and had probably given her up for lost; so he couldn't worry any more than he did if she stayed away from him a while longer. So she would go to Oz.

They bade goodbye to the people of Ev, and the King promised Ozma that he would ever be grateful to her and render the Land of Oz any service that might lie within his power.

And then they approached the edge of the dangerous desert, and Ozma threw down the magic carpet, which at once unrolled far enough for all of them to walk upon it without being crowded.

Tiktok, claiming to be Dorothy's faithful follower because he belonged to her, had been permitted to join the party, and before they started the girl wound up his machinery as far as possible, and the copper man stepped off as briskly as any one of them.

Ozma also invited Billina to visit the Land of Oz, and the yellow hen was glad enough to go where new sights and scenes awaited her.

They began the trip across the desert early in the morning, and as they stopped only long enough for Billina to lay her daily egg, before sunset they espied the green slopes and wooded hills of the beautiful Land of Oz. They entered it in the Munchkin territory, and the King of the Munchkins met them at the border and welcomed Ozma with great respect, being very pleased by her safe return. For Ozma of Oz ruled the King of the Munchkins, the King of the Winkies, the King of the Quadlings and the King of the Gillikins just as those kings ruled their own people; and this supreme ruler of the Land of Oz lived in a great town of her own, called the Emerald City, which was in the exact center of the four kingdoms of the Land of Oz.

The Munchkin king entertained them at his palace that night, and in the morning they set out for the Emerald City, travelling over a road of yellow brick that led straight to the jewel-studded gates. Everywhere the people turned out to greet their beloved Ozma, and to hail joyfully the Scarecrow, the Tin Woodman and the Cowardly Lion, who were popular favorites. Dorothy, too, remembered some of the people, who had befriended her on the occasion of her first visit to Oz, and they were well pleased to see the little Kansas girl again, and showered her with compliments and good wishes.

At one place, where they stopped to refresh themselves, Ozma accepted a bowl of milk from the hands of a pretty dairy-maid. Then she looked at the girl more closely, and exclaimed:

"Why, it's Jinjur – isn't it!"

"Yes, your Highness," was the reply, as Jinjur dropped a low curtsy. And Dorothy looked wonderingly at this lively appearing person, who had once assembled an army of women and driven the Scarecrow from the throne of the Emerald City, and even fought a battle with the powerful army of Glinda the Sorceress.

"I've married a man who owns nine cows," said Jinjur to Ozma, "and now I am happy and contented and willing to lead a quiet life and mind my own business."

"Where is your husband?" asked Ozma.

"He is in the house, nursing a black eye," replied Jinjur, calmly. "The foolish man would insist upon milking the red cow when I wanted him to milk the white one; but he will know better next time, I am sure."

Then the party moved on again, and after crossing a broad river on a ferry and passing many fine farm houses that were dome shaped and painted a pretty green color, they came in sight of a large building that was covered with flags and bunting.

"I don't remember that building," said Dorothy. "What is it?"

"That is the College of Art and Athletic Perfection," replied Ozma. "I had it built quite recently, and the Woggle-Bug is its president. It keeps him busy, and the young men who attend the college are no worse off than they were before. You see, in this country are a number of youths who do not like to work, and the college is an excellent place for them."

And now they came in sight of the Emerald City, and the people flocked out to greet their lovely ruler. There were several bands and many officers and officials of the realm, and a crowd of citizens in their holiday attire.

Thus the beautiful Ozma was escorted by a brilliant procession to her royal city, and so great was the cheering that she was obliged to constantly bow to the right and left to acknowledge the greetings of her subjects.

That evening there was a grand reception in the royal palace, attended by the most important persons of Oz, and Jack Pumpkinhead, who was a little overripe but still active, read an address congratulating Ozma of Oz upon the success of her generous mission to rescue the royal family of a neighboring kingdom.

Then magnificent gold medals set with precious stones were presented to each of the twenty-six officers; and the Tin Woodman was given a new axe studded with diamonds; and the Scarecrow received a silver jar of complexion powder. Dorothy was presented with a pretty coronet and made a Princess of Oz, and Tiktok received two bracelets set with eight rows of very clear and sparkling emeralds.

Afterward they sat down to a splendid feast, and Ozma put Dorothy at her right and Billina at her left, where the hen sat upon a golden roost and ate from a jeweled platter. Then were placed the Scarecrow, the Tin Woodman and Tiktok, with baskets of lovely flowers before them, because they did not require food. The twenty-six officers were at the lower end of the table, and the Lion and the Tiger also had seats, and were served on golden platters, that held a half a bushel at one time.

The wealthiest and most important citizens of the Emerald City were proud to wait upon these famous adventurers, and they were assisted by a sprightly little maid named Jellia Jamb, whom the Scarecrow pinched upon her rosy cheeks and seemed to know very well.

During the feast Ozma grew thoughtful, and suddenly she asked:

"Where is the private?"

"Oh, he is sweeping out the barracks," replied one of the generals, who was busy eating a leg of a turkey. "But I have ordered him a dish of bread and molasses to eat when his work is done."

"Let him be sent for," said the girl ruler.

While they waited for this command to be obeyed, she enquired:

"Have we any other privates in the armies?"

"Oh, yes," replied the Tin Woodman, "I believe there are three, altogether."

The private now entered, saluting his officers and the royal Ozma very respectfully.

"What is your name, my man?" asked the girl.

"Omby Amby," answered the private.

"Then, Omby Amby," said she, "I promote you to be Captain General of all the armies of my kingdom, and especially to be Commander of my Body Guard at the royal palace."

"It is very expensive to hold so many offices," said the private, hesitating. "I have no money with which to buy uniforms."

"You shall be supplied from the royal treasury," said Ozma.

Then the private was given a seat at the table, where the other officers welcomed him cordially, and the feasting and merriment were resumed.

Suddenly Jellia Jamb exclaimed:

"There is nothing more to eat! The Hungry Tiger has consumed everything!"

"But that is not the worst of it," declared the Tiger, mournfully. "Somewhere or somehow, I've actually lost my appetite!"

Chapter XXI
Dorothy's Magic Belt

DOROTHY PASSED several very happy weeks in the Land of Oz as the guest of the royal Ozma, who delighted to please and interest the little Kansas girl. Many new acquaintances were formed and many old ones renewed, and wherever she went Dorothy found herself among friends.

One day, however, as she sat in Ozma's private room, she noticed hanging upon the wall a picture which constantly changed in appearance, at one time showing a meadow and at another time a forest, a lake or a village.

"How curious!" she exclaimed, after watching the shifting scenes for a few moments.

"Yes," said Ozma, "that is really a wonderful invention in magic. If I wish to see any part of the world or any person living, I need only express the wish and it is shown in the picture."

"May I use it?" asked Dorothy, eagerly.

"Of course, my dear."

"Then I'd like to see the old Kansas farm, and Aunt Em," said the girl.

Instantly the well remembered farmhouse appeared in the picture, and Aunt Em could be seen quite plainly. She was engaged in washing dishes by the kitchen window and seemed quite well and contented. The hired men and the teams were in the harvest fields behind the house, and the corn and wheat seemed to the child to be in prime condition. On the side porch Dorothy's pet dog, Toto, was lying fast asleep in the sun, and to her surprise old Speckles was running around with a brood of twelve new chickens trailing after her.

"Everything seems all right at home," said Dorothy, with a sigh of relief. "Now I wonder what Uncle Henry is doing."

The scene in the picture at once shifted to Australia, where, in a pleasant room in Sydney, Uncle Henry was seated in an easy chair, solemnly smoking his briar pipe. He looked sad and lonely, and his hair was now quite white and his hands and face thin and wasted.

"Oh!" cried Dorothy, in an anxious voice, "I'm sure Uncle Henry isn't getting any better, and it's because he is worried about me. Ozma, dear, I must go to him at once!"

"How can you?" asked Ozma.

"I don't know," replied Dorothy; "but let us go to Glinda the Good. I'm sure she will help me, and advise me how to get to Uncle Henry."

Ozma readily agreed to this plan and caused the Sawhorse to be harnessed to a pretty green and pink phaeton, and the two girls rode away to visit the famous sorceress.

Glinda received them graciously, and listened to Dorothy's story with attention.

"I have the magic belt, you know," said the little girl. "If I buckled it around my waist and commanded it to take me to Uncle Henry, wouldn't it do it?"

"I think so," replied Glinda, with a smile.

"And then," continued Dorothy, "if I ever wanted to come back here again, the belt would bring me."

"In that you are wrong," said the sorceress. "The belt has magical powers only while it is in some fairy country, such as the Land of Oz, or the Land of Ev. Indeed, my little friend, were you to wear it and wish yourself in Australia, with your uncle, the wish would doubtless be fulfilled, because it was made in fairyland. But you would not find the magic belt around you when you arrived at your destination."

"What would become of it?" asked the girl.

"It would be lost, as were your silver shoes when you visited Oz before, and no one would ever see it again. It seems too bad to destroy the use of the magic belt in that way, doesn't it?"

"Then," said Dorothy, after a moment's thought, "I will give the magic belt to Ozma, for she can use it in her own country. And she can wish me transported to Uncle Henry without losing the belt."

"That is a wise plan," replied Glinda.

So they rode back to the Emerald City, and on the way it was arranged that every Saturday morning Ozma would look at Dorothy in her magic picture, wherever the little girl might chance to be. And, if she saw Dorothy make a certain signal, then Ozma would know that the little Kansas girl wanted to revisit the Land of Oz, and by means of the Nome King's magic belt would wish that she might instantly return.

This having been agreed upon, Dorothy bade goodbye to all her friends. Tiktok wanted to go to Australia; too, but Dorothy knew that the machine man would never do for a servant in a civilized country, and the chances were that his machinery wouldn't work at all. So she left him in Ozma's care.

Billina, on the contrary, preferred the Land of Oz to any other country, and refused to accompany Dorothy.

"The bugs and ants that I find here are the finest flavored in the world," declared the yellow hen, "and there are plenty of them. So here I shall end my days; and I must say, Dorothy, my dear, that you are very foolish to go back into that stupid, humdrum world again."

"Uncle Henry needs me," said Dorothy, simply; and every one except Billina thought it was right that she should go.

All Dorothy's friends of the Land of Oz – both old and new – gathered in a group in front of the palace to bid her a sorrowful goodbye and to wish her long life and happiness. After much hand shaking, Dorothy kissed Ozma once more, and then handed her the Nome King's magic belt, saying:

"Now, dear Princess, when I wave my handkerchief, please wish me with Uncle Henry. I'm aw'fly sorry to leave you – and the Scarecrow – and the Tin Woodman – and the Cowardly Lion – and Tiktok – and – and everybody – but I do want my Uncle Henry! So goodbye, all of you."

Then the little girl stood on one of the big emeralds which decorated the courtyard, and after looking once again at each of her friends, waved her handkerchief.

* * *

"No," said Dorothy, "I wasn't drowned at all. And I've come to nurse you and take care of you, Uncle Henry, and you must promise to get well as soon as poss'ble."

Uncle Henry smiled and cuddled his little niece close in his lap.

"I'm better already, my darling," said he.

Moxon's Master

Ambrose Bierce

"ARE YOU SERIOUS? Do you really believe that a machine thinks?"

I got no immediate reply; Moxon was apparently intent upon the coals in the grate, touching them deftly here and there with the fire-poker till they signified a sense of his attention by a brighter glow. For several weeks I had been observing in him a growing habit of delay in answering even the most trivial of commonplace questions. His air, however, was that of preoccupation rather than deliberation: one might have said that he had 'something on his mind.'

Presently he said: "What is a 'machine'? The word has been variously defined. Here is one definition from a popular dictionary: 'Any instrument or organization by which power is applied and made effective, or a desired effect produced.' Well, then, is not a man a machine? And you will admit that he thinks – or thinks he thinks."

"If you do not wish to answer my question," I said, rather testily, "why not say so? – all that you say is mere evasion. You know well enough that when I say 'machine' I do not mean a man, but something that man has made and controls."

"When it does not control him," he said, rising abruptly and looking out of a window, whence nothing was visible in the blackness of a stormy night. A moment later he turned about and with a smile said: "I beg your pardon; I had no thought of evasion. I considered the dictionary man's unconscious testimony suggestive and worth something in the discussion. I can give your question a direct answer easily enough: I do believe that a machine thinks about the work it is doing."

That was direct enough, certainly. It was not altogether pleasing, for it tended to confirm a sad suspicion that Moxon's devotion to study and work in his machine-shop had not been good for him. I knew, for one thing, that he suffered from insomnia, and that is no light affliction. Had it affected his mind? His reply to my question seemed to me then evidence that it had; perhaps I should think differently about it now. I was younger then, and among the blessings that are not denied to youth is ignorance. Incited by that great stimulant to controversy, I said: "And what, pray, does it think with – in the absence of a brain?"

The reply, coming with less than his customary delay, took his favourite form of counter-interrogation: "With what does a plant think – in the absence of a brain?"

"Ah, plants also belong to the philosopher class! I should be pleased to know some of their conclusions; you may omit the premises."

"Perhaps," he replied, apparently unaffected by my foolish irony, you may be able to infer their convictions from their acts. I will spare you the familiar examples of the sensitive mimosa, the several insectivorous flowers and those whose stamens bend down and shake their pollen upon the entering bee in order that he may fertilize their distant mates. But observe this. In an open spot in my garden I planted a climbing vine. When it was barely above the surface I set a stake into the soil a yard away. The vine at once made for it, but as it was about to reach it after several days I removed it a few feet. The vine at once altered its course, making an acute angle, and again made for the stake. This manoeuvre was repeated several times, but finally, as if discouraged, the vine abandoned the pursuit and, ignoring further attempts to divert it, travelled to a small tree, farther away, which it climbed.

"Roots of the eucalyptus will prolong themselves incredibly in search of moisture. A well-known horticulturist relates that one entered an old drain pipe and followed it until it came to a break, where a section of the pipe had been removed to make way for a stone wall that had been built across its course. The root left the drain and followed the wall until it found an opening where a stone had fallen out. It crept through and, following the other side of the wall back to the drain, entered the unexplored part and resumed its journey."

"And all this?"

"Can you miss the significance of it? It shows the consciousness of plants. It proves that they think."

"Even if it did – what then? We were speaking, not of plants, but of machines. They may be composed partly of wood – wood that has no longer vitality – or wholly of metal. Is thought an attribute also of the mineral kingdom?"

"How else do you explain the phenomena, for example, of crystallization?"

"I do not explain them."

"Because you cannot without affirming what you wish to deny – namely, intelligent cooperation among the constituent elements of the crystals. When soldiers form lines, or hollow squares, you call it reason. When wild geese in flight take the form of a letter V you say instinct. When the homogeneous atoms of a mineral, moving freely in solution, arrange themselves into shapes mathematically perfect, or particles of frozen moisture into the symmetrical and beautiful forms of snowflakes, you have nothing to say. You have not even invented a name to conceal your heroic unreason."

Moxon was speaking with unusual animation and earnestness. As he paused I heard in an adjoining room known to me as his 'machine-shop,' which no one but himself was permitted to enter, a singular thumping sound, as of someone pounding upon a table with an open hand. Moxon heard it at the same moment and, visibly agitated, rose and hurriedly passed into the room whence it came. I thought it odd that anyone else should be in there, and my interest in my friend – with doubtless a touch of unwarrantable curiosity – led me to listen intently, though, I am happy to say, not at the keyhole. There were confused sounds, as of a struggle or scuffle; the floor shook. I distinctly heard hard breathing and a hoarse whisper which said "Damn you!" Then all was silent, and presently Moxon reappeared and said, with a rather sorry smile:

"Pardon me for leaving you so abruptly. I have a machine in there that lost its temper and cut up rough."

Fixing my eyes steadily upon his left cheek, which was traversed by four parallel excoriations showing blood, I said:

"How would it do to trim its nails?" I could have spared myself the jest; he gave it no attention, but seated himself in the chair that he had left and resumed the interrupted monologue as if nothing had occurred:

"Doubtless you do not hold with those (I need not name them to a man of your reading) who have taught that all matter is sentiment, that every atom is a living, feeling, conscious being. I do. There is no such thing as dead, inert matter; it is all alive; all instinct with force, actual and potential; all sensitive to the same forces in its environment and susceptible to the contagion of higher and subtler ones residing in such superior organisms as it may be brought into relation with, as those of man when he is fashioning it into an instrument of his will. It absorbs something of his intelligence and purpose – more of them in proportion to the complexity of the resulting machine and that of its work.

"Do you happen to recall Herbert Spencer's definition of 'life'? I read it thirty years ago. He may have altered it afterward, for anything I know, but in all that time I have been unable to think of a single word that could profitably be changed or added or removed. It seems to me not only the best definition, but the only possible one.

"'Life,' he says, 'is a definite combination of heterogeneous changes, both simultaneous and successive, in correspondence with external coexistences and sequences.'"

"That defines the phenomenon," I said, "but gives no hint of its cause."

"That," he replied, "is all that any definition can do. As Mill points out, we know nothing of cause except as an antecedent – nothing of effect except as a consequent. Of certain phenomena, one never occurs without another, which is dissimilar: the first in point of time we call cause; the second, effect. One who had many times seen a rabbit pursued by a dog, and had never seen rabbits and dogs otherwise, would think the rabbit the cause of the dog.

"But I fear," he added, laughing naturally enough, "that my rabbit is leading me a long way from the track of my legitimate quarry: I'm indulging in the pleasure of the chase for its own sake. What I want you to observe is that in Herbert Spencer's definition of 'life' the activity of a machine is included – there is nothing in the definition that is not applicable to it. According to this sharpest of observers and deepest of thinkers, if a man during his period of activity is alive, so is a machine when in operation. As an inventor and constructor of machines I know that to be true."

Moxon was silent for a long time, gazing absently into the fire. It was growing late and I thought it time to be going, but somehow I did not like the notion of leaving him in that isolated house, all alone except for the presence of some person of whose nature my conjectures could go no further than that it was unfriendly, perhaps malign. Leaning toward him and looking earnestly into his eyes while making a motion with my hand through the door of his workshop, I said:

"Moxon, whom have you in there?"

Somewhat to my surprise he laughed lightly and answered without hesitation:

"Nobody; the incident that you have in mind was caused by my folly in leaving a machine in action with nothing to act upon, while I undertook the interminable task of enlightening your understanding. Do you happen to know that Consciousness is the creature of Rhythm?"

"Oh bother them both!" I replied, rising and laying hold of my overcoat. "I'm going to wish you good night; and I'll add the hope that the machine which you inadvertently left in action will have her gloves on the next time you think it needful to stop her."

Without waiting to observe the effect of my shot I left the house.

Rain was falling, and the darkness was intense. In the sky beyond the crest of a hill towards which I groped my way along precarious plank sidewalks and across miry, unpaved streets I could see the faint glow of the city's lights, but behind me nothing was visible but a single window of Moxon's house. It glowed with what seemed to me a mysterious and fateful meaning. I knew it was an uncurtained aperture in my friend's 'machine-shop,' and I had little doubt that he had resumed the studies interrupted by his duties as my instructor in mechanical consciousness and the fatherhood of Rhythm. Odd, and in some degree humorous, as his convictions seemed to me at that time, I could not wholly divest myself of the feeling that they had some tragic relation to his life and character – perhaps to his destiny – although I no longer entertained the notion that they were the vagaries of a disordered mind. Whatever might be thought of his views, his exposition of them was too logical for that. Over and over, his last words came back to me: "Consciousness is the creature of Rhythm." Bald and terse as the statement was, I now found it infinitely alluring. At each recurrence it broadened in meaning and deepened in suggestion. Why, here (I thought) is something upon which to found a philosophy. If Consciousness is the product of Rhythm all things are conscious, for all have motion, and all motion is rhythmic. I wondered if Moxon knew the significance and breadth of his thought – the scope of this momentous generalization; or had he arrived at his philosophic faith by the tortuous and uncertain road of observation? That faith was then new to me, and all Moxon's expounding had failed to make me a convert; but now it seemed as if a great light shone about me, like that which fell upon Saul of Tarsus; and out there in the storm and darkness and solitude I experienced what Lewes calls 'The endless variety and excitement of philosophic thought.' I exulted in a new sense of knowledge, a new pride of reason. My feet seemed hardly to touch the earth; it was as if I were uplifted and borne through the air by invisible wings.

Yielding to an impulse to seek further light from him whom I now recognized as my master and guide, I had unconsciously turned about, and almost before I was aware of having done so found myself again at Moxon's door. I was drenched with rain, but felt no discomfort. Unable in my excitement to find the doorbell, I instinctively tried the knob. It turned and, entering, I mounted the stairs to the room that I had so recently left. All was dark and silent; Moxon, as I had supposed, was in the adjoining room – the 'machine-shop'. Groping along the wall until I found the communicating door, I knocked loudly several times, but got no response, which I attributed to the uproar outside, for the wind was blowing a gale and dashing the rain against the thin walls in sheets. The drumming upon the shingle roof spanning the unceiled room was loud and incessant. I had never been invited into the machine-shop – had, indeed, been denied admittance, as had all others, with one exception, a skilled metal worker, of whom no one knew anything except that his name was Haley and his habit silence. But in my spiritual exaltation discretion and civility were alike forgotten, and I opened the door. What I saw took all philosophical speculation out of me in short order.

Moxon sat facing me at the further side of a small table upon which a single candle made all the light that was in the room. Opposite him, his back toward me, sat another person. On the table between the two was a chess-board; the men were playing. I knew little of chess, but as only a few pieces were on the board it was obvious that the game was near its close. Moxon was intensely interested – not so much, it seemed to me, in the game as in his antagonist, upon whom he had fixed so intent a look that, standing though I did directly in the line of his vision, I was altogether unobserved. His face was ghastly white, and his eyes glittered like diamonds. Of his antagonist I had only a back view, but that was sufficient; I should not have cared to see his face.

He was apparently not more than five feet in height, with proportions suggesting those of a gorilla – a tremendous breadth of shoulders, thick, short neck and broad, squat head, which had a tangled growth of black hair and was topped with a crimson fez. A tunic of the same colour, belted tightly to the waist, reached the seat – apparently a box – upon which he sat; his legs and feet were not seen. His left forearm appeared to rest in his lap; he moved his pieces with his right hand, which seemed disproportionately long.

I had shrunk back and now stood a little to one side of the doorway and in shadow. If Moxon had looked farther than the face of his opponent he could have observed nothing now, except that the door was open. Something forbade me either to enter or retire, a feeling – I know not how it came – that I was in the presence of an imminent tragedy and might serve my friend by remaining. With a scarcely conscious rebellion against the indelicacy of the act I remained.

The play was rapid. Moxon hardly glanced at the board before making his moves, and to my unskilled eye seemed to move the piece most convenient to his hand, his motions in doing so being quick, nervous and lacking in precision. The response of his antagonist, while equally prompt in the interception, was made with a slow, uniform, mechanical and, I thought, somewhat theatrical movement of the arm that was a sore trial to my patience. There was something unearthly about it all, and I caught myself shuddering. But I was wet and cold. Two or three times after moving a piece the stranger slightly inclined his head, and each time I observed that Moxon shifted his king. All at once the thought came to me that the man was dumb. And then that he was a machine – an automaton chess-player! Then I remembered that Moxon had once spoken to me of having invented such a piece of mechanism, though I did not understand that it had actually been constructed. Was all his talk about the consciousness and intelligence of machines merely a prelude to eventual exhibition of this device – only a trick to intensify the effect of its mechanical action upon me in my ignorance of its secret?

A fine end, this, of all my intellectual transports – my 'endless variety and excitement of philosophic thought'! I was about to retire in disgust when something occurred to hold my curiosity. I observed a shrug of the thing's great shoulders, as if it were irritated: and so natural was this – so entirely human – that in my new view of the matter it startled me. Nor was that all, for a moment later it struck the table sharply with its clenched hand. At that gesture Moxon seemed even more startled than I; he pushed his chair a little backward, as in alarm.

Presently Moxon, whose play it was, raised his hand high above the board, pounced upon one of his pieces like a sparrow-hawk and with the exclamation "Checkmate!" rose quickly to his feet and stepped behind his chair. The automaton sat motionless.

The wind had now gone down, but I heard, at lessening intervals and progressively louder, the rumble and roll of thunder. In the pauses between I now became conscious of a low humming or buzzing which, like the thunder, grew momently louder and more distinct. It seemed to come from the body of the automaton, and was unmistakably a whirring of wheels. It gave me the impression of a disordered mechanism which had escaped the repressive and regulating action of some controlling part – an effect such as might be expected if a pawl should be jostled from the teeth of a ratchet-wheel. But before I had time for much conjecture as to its nature my attention was taken by the strange motions of the automaton itself. A slight but continuous convulsion appeared to have possession of it. In body and head it shook like a man with palsy or an ague chill, and the motion augmented every moment until the entire figure was in violent agitation. Suddenly it sprang to its feet and with a movement almost too quick for the eye to follow shot forward across table and chair, with both arms thrust forth to their full length the posture and lunge of a diver. Moxon tried to throw himself backward out of reach, but he was too late; I saw the horrible thing's hands close upon his throat, his own clutch its wrists. Then the table was overturned, the candle thrown to the floor and extinguished, and all was black dark. But the noise of the struggle was dreadfully distinct, and most terrible of all were the raucous, squawking sounds made by the strangled man's efforts to breathe. Guided by the infernal hubbub, I sprang to the rescue of my friend, but had hardly taken a stride in the darkness when the whole room blazed with a blinding white light that burned into my brain and heart and memory a vivid picture of the combatants on the floor, Moxon underneath, his throat still in the clutch of those iron hands, his head forced backward, his eyes protruding, his mouth wide open and his tongue thrust out; and – horrible contrast! – upon the painted face of his assassin an expression of tranquil and profound thought, as in the solution of a problem in chess! This I observed, then all was blackness and silence.

Three days later I recovered consciousness in a hospital. As the memory of that tragic night slowly evolved in my ailing brain I recognized in my attendant Moxon's confidential workman, Haley. Responding to a look he approached, smiling.

"Tell me about it," I managed to say, faintly – "all about it."

"Certainly," he said; "you were carried unconscious from a burning house – Moxon's. Nobody knows how you came to be there. You may have to do a little explaining. The origin of the fire is a bit mysterious, too. My own notion is that the house was struck by lightning."

"And Moxon?"

"Buried yesterday – what was left of him."

Apparently this reticent person could unfold himself on occasion. When imparting shocking intelligence to the sick he was affable enough. After some moments of the keenest mental suffering I ventured to ask another question:

"Who rescued me?"

"Well, if that interests you – I did."

"Thank you, Mr. Haley, and may God bless you for it. Did you rescue, also, that charming product of your skill, the automaton chess-player that murdered its inventor?"

The man was silent a long time, looking away from me. Presently he turned and gravely said:

"Do you know that?"

"I do," I replied; "I saw it done."

That was many years ago. If asked today I should answer less confidently.

Why Should Steel Birds Dream?

Roan Clay

THE GRIM-EYED messengers came to him an hour before he should have woken up. This only ever meant one thing. He slipped into his official garments, ran his hands through his sleep-matted hair and followed them down to the Floating Bridge.

The Palace hung like a dark cloud across the curving length of crystal, streaking its dark shape down the striations of the Bridge's growth. Compulsively, the Poet touched his hair, smelled his breath. He had never had trouble from the Prince – would not have been a good Court Poet if he was likely to – but these were not normal times.

The messengers vanished at the foot of the Bridge, and he hurried across and stepped down from the crystal face onto the first of the Palace platforms. There was a winged figure, just folding its wings near the top of the Palace's summit. By the time the Poet had walked under one of the lamellar sheets, into the building and down the corridor into the great hall, the Prince had folded his wings and was standing by his throne. The connections stood out of the seat like silver hairs. There were systems humming softly behind the chair, talking to themselves, waiting to be activated. The Poet stood in the center of the room and waited.

At last the Prince walked down the steps in that sudden, mechanical way that the Poet would never get used to. He stopped three feet away and studied the Poet's face, and once again the Poet sought for any kind of emotional clue in the polymer features.

The Prince's mouth opened. "I have still not dreamt."

The Poet said, "I know."

"Help me. I cannot give a more logical request – please help me to dream."

The Poet said, "Go and sit down in your throne, and I'll speak to you."

The Poet barely detected relief in the cheeks and mouth. The Prince walked back up the steps and settled in the throne, shifting so that all the silver hairs made contact with his body. The tone of the systems behind the throne changed. The Poet began.

After years of practise, he was able to simply open his mouth and speak, and verse flowed out of him to the swooping series of flat layers that held the throne. It expressed his disappointment in the interrupted dreams of a few minutes ago, the strange fear and Gothic emotion of seeing the wide wings folding in the high places of the Palace, his sympathy for this creature that sat in front of him. This was the introduction. From then on, he dreamed worlds, explored dimensions to help the Prince dream.

The shape in the chair stared with eyes half-shut as the mental processes tried to lull themselves to sleep. The capacity for dreaming had been engineered to happen naturally, with stimulation by the Palace environment, and the Prince had been able to dream while waking or sleeping. Dreaming consolidated his memories, restored his logical systems so that thought happened smoothly. With no dreaming, there was no deep rest, no true backup of memories, and none of the whimsy that is such an important background to leadership. The Prince's dreams had made their tall architecture, their great tradition of art and industry possible.

But he had been without dreams for about twenty days now. They could find no discernible glitches in the system to account for it. Over on the other side of the Bridge, they were still examining the system remotely. On this side, there was only the Poet and his words.

Though he spoke his best, still the Prince did not dream.

By the time he finished, he had mined all poetry out of his system. He could tell he had done no good. The Prince opened his eyes and motioned the Poet away with a jerk.

As the Poet left the Palace, he could hear the Prince's hard-footed pace through the halls. By the time he was halfway across the Bridge, a winged shape was folding and unfolding itself over him, toward the wastes on the other side of the City.

* * *

The Prince had ruled here for more than a dozen human lifetimes. There had been philosophical findings about government – it should involve very few people, and yet every citizen should be represented fairly. All needs should be met, all officials above corruption. And so the Prince had been built.

There was nothing outside the Prince's authority. His intelligence was centralized first in his body, then throughout the Palace, and then in all parts of the City. Dreams built the connections between all of these, made the City more of a reality to the Prince's central mind.

Dreaming made the Prince less machine, and more person. Without it, he was a mechanical ghost. Children reported seeing a lonely figure when the leaves blew in the wind, trudging up and down the forest paths beneath the triple moon, wings trailing wearily behind, muttering softly. They would run in terror. The Prince never seemed to notice.

The Poet had immediately suggested the trouble might be the lack of a woman. The programmers had proved to him that this was not the case, but what else could they expect from a poet?

When he arrived back home, there were people waiting for him. No more sleep tonight, he could see. They escorted him immediately to the programming station.

The station was an ordinary house, holding extraordinary secrets. He followed a group of solemn people down a secret way until they stood together around an eviscerated mechanical body. This was not anything like the complexities of the Prince, but a convenient analogue to experiment on. The technicians stood around and looked at him.

At last one of them said, "We've scanned every system we could find. There is no way of making the Prince dream."

The Poet said, "I've just spent nearly an hour speaking to him, and I spoke my best. He dismissed me and went off flying again. What more can a Poet do?"

"As a Poet, your only duty is to help the Prince dream. The Prince is not dreaming. The trouble seems to rest on you."

The Poet looked around at their faces, and he knew his fate was set. These people lived here, doing nothing but gather data and feed it through the channels where the Prince would come across it in his computational routine, calling the Prince in for maintenance when needed. They expected everyone else to obey them just as the Prince did.

The Poet said, "What would you suggest that I do?"

"Go back to the Prince."

"I've only just come from him. I haven't been summoned back."

They knew what returning without a summons would mean, just as well as he did. This knowledge made it clear – he was expendable. That was the importance of dreams in a place like this. "Go back as soon as you can. This is more than a corruption of the main data chains, or anything that can be corrected with a heuristic sweep. We have been at the Prince's service all our lives, but no one is more familiar with his construction than he is, and no one is more trusted by the Prince than you. You have been to the Palace, which none of us have ever been – besides the three that tried and were dismembered."

Another came around the table and put an arm around the Poet. "You have done excellent service for your Prince, and for all of us. Your poetry has made his dreams deep. Because of you, these years have been the best in our history. We appreciate all you have done."

The Poet smiled and said quietly, "Will you make statues of me?"

Three people torn apart – four, after today. He had been an only child, so this would be his only chance to be the fourth of anything. He walked out in the street, bought a cake at his favorite market and sat and ate the entire thing himself, then ordered a pot of his favorite tea, paying the man without looking.

"Good morning to you, Sir Poet! Birthday celebration?"

The Poet looked up at the proprietor and shook his head. "No. The opposite."

* * *

They called it the Floating Bridge because the butt end of the crystal hung unsupported over the City steps. He felt the lack of support for the first time as he set foot on the crystal and moved out over the thick chemical sea far, far, far below.

Too soon he was at the end of it. The Palace was all quiet, walls silently condemning his intrusion, refusing to send an echo back.

He stopped as he passed a spot where two layers joined. This was where one of them had been killed, about three years ago. Here, and all around, many pieces scattered. The defensive program was very efficient. The others had only gotten as far as the end of the Bridge before the dark-winged Prince had swooped down and killed them. The Prince had no control over this process. Automatically, he hunted all trespassers down.

Anyone who came here with no summons.

He straightened and moved on.

He had never been so aware of his steps. He walked slowly, watching his feet, his shadow, the outline of the edifice in front of him, the tiny dark shape that swooped down the curves of the building. He wished he could close his eyes as the shape grew and he began to see the face.

The sound of the wings was a thin whisper against the Palace.

To help his legs move, he had been telling himself a poem to the rhythm of his footsteps. Now he shouted the words, a story older than the Prince or his City, written when the Floating Bridge was a mere stub, protruding from a bare pinnacle. He shouted, and walked, and waited for the flying thing to separate him.

He raised his eyes as the ground shook softly, and there was a sound like a piece of machinery suddenly reversing itself. He saw the Prince kneeling, his wings still outstretched, the breeze pushing him slightly back and forth.

He stared at the Poet, then he walked away toward the Palace.

The feeling of being unwelcome was still with the Poet when he walked down the corridor and emerged in the throne room. He waited until the Prince came in slowly, wings unfolded, and stood by his throne.

"Unsummoned," the Prince said. "Uninvited, and yet alive. How is this?"

"Well, you didn't kill me."

The Prince's wings folded slightly. "Your poetry came to me, and for a moment I thought I would dream. But it is still there – the urge to discover the inner parts of your joints. I am nearly down there with you, taking hold of you…" The robotic hands moved and flexed, basking in some feeling that must not be satisfied.

"They told me to come here. I am sorry."

The Prince's hands fastened together. "Have you ever forgotten to comb your hair?"

The question seemed like a departure, but the Poet knew the Prince well enough to take it seriously. "Yes, many times."

"And no one questions it. When you scrub your teeth in a different order, you are not asked about it. Yet with me, the least departure from the mental norm sparks a series of questions, as much a part of my own consciousness as anything else, and equally impossible to ignore. I am compelled to give reasons. Just as I am compelled to give reasons for my lack of dreams. Only in my dreams were there no questions. Now no dreams, and my Poet has no power." The fingers pulled at each other, popping in the still air. "Speak poetry now, or I will tear your limbs apart!"

The Poet spoke, and there was no end to the verses for the next fifteen hours.

The hands were still moving.

* * *

It was nearly night, and the light sky shrunk over the three women around the head of the Bridge.

"Is it the Bridge that warns the Prince? Does he sense our weight? See – when we touch the Bridge, there's no reaction over there."

"The Prince might be busy."

"Busy or not, there should be some reaction. The response was one of the first things they programmed into him."

The two older women spoke together as though the younger were not present. She was a neighbor, invited along as an afterthought.

They were all dissatisfied, they and everyone they knew. Roads left to fall apart, neglected services, the fear of rising crime. None of them had slept, as if the Prince's ailment had become their own. So they had decided to come here. The programmers had failed too long. The Poet had exhausted his skill.

Before either of the older knew it was happening, the girl climbed up and started across. They stared, but neither of them moved a foot to follow her. They barely knew her, barely had a thought for her until this moment, watching her walk down the long crystal, soldier-straight.

She had not intended to do this. Or she did not think she had.

She had first known these women as a child. The Prince had dreamed well back then, and the streets had been clean, safe. In those happy days, she had sat and listened to these ladies, and her little brother had played around her feet in the yard.

Today she had come back from the hospital, heard them speaking and come over.

They felt as she did. Frustrated, restless, useless. They had determined to go and look at the place where the Poet was laboring. That was when she had thought of walking across the Bridge, the moment before it happened.

She laughed a little to herself, and kept walking.

* * *

The Poet's voice was weaker now, his throat dry, and he knew that if he stopped talking, then the Prince's Palace-defense protocols would take over and kill him. And then where would the dreams come from?

But this poetry would not create dreams, only keep the Prince at bay.

He stood and watched the words going by like a stream of light, unconnected with himself. Then the Prince stiffened, unfolded his wings and leaned forward in his throne.

Without stopping the flow of verse, the Poet said, "Tell me – for what reason would you interrupt my rightful duties?"

The Poet did not cease to speak as the Prince's words flowed over his own. "Trespasser. Coming across the Bridge."

"Dreams are no longer yours, and you cannot know the truth of what you may perceive."

"I must defend my Palace."

The Poet thought quickly. "The beginning of your dreams, this must be! A stranger, come across the Bridge, and you here yet, unkilling and unwilling! It could only be a dream! Stay, and see the ending of your slumber!"

Every circuit and polymer muscle in that winged body was now a great Desire to fly to the Bridge, to feel the tearing-apart of flesh. If the Prince flew away and came back, he would be out of his present poetic state, and the Poet, too, would die.

The Poet spoke with authority and pointed at the Prince. "Stay you, weakened Prince, unable now to know yourself! There will be no bloodshed, and no trouble! In this Palace you will find the peace that your created brain desires!"

The Prince's voice rose with strange emotion. "I have seen every coming and going in the streets, the loneliness of the people in this City that I guide, protect! Why am I left here, alone beyond the company of people, only you to visit me?"

"Tell me out of your own mind, my Prince! Why am I the only one?"

The presence near the Bridge still drew the Prince away. The Poet continued his mumbled cadence without thought, listening to the Prince's tortured words. "Because my chief designer was alone. He made all my designs by long hours in empty rooms. Wife and offspring left elsewhere, seeing him rarely, nothing to give the man pleasure save for work, the shaping of my body and mind! I bear the lonely marks of my human maker! The intruder is nearly up to the Palace steps now, a stranger, in the Palace hall...!"

Then, suddenly, the Prince was calm. By now the trespasser had come farther than anyone else, and the killing instinct was not the driving impulse it had been. He leaned forward and held his head in his hands. The steps grew clear, and the Poet turned and looked at the girl.

The people of the City never saw the interior of the Palace. He remembered the first time he had seen it, smelled the hard, clinical dryness of the air. He addressed her in verse before she had a chance to break the spell.

"And now why have you come? You've made yourself a flaw in all this computational design! Speak to me in verse harmonious and metrical, or else your blood will flow in seconds!"

She swallowed and lowered her chin slowly. "I have come to see if I can...help with making sure the Prince can dream."

For a moment, the Poet forgot to speak. Her age could have been anywhere from 18 to 25, and she was dressed in the house-clothes that many of the City citizens wore to bed. "You have not the Poet's rightful duty to this charge. Many have grown old and died in sparking royal dreams, and there should be none but those appointed over here across the Bridge."

"And...what...forms of verses have you brought to soothe the Prince?"

"The unselfconscious poems of my brain."

She nodded, and her eyes turned soft, and she looked up at the figure with his wings still partially unfurled, barely keeping himself from descending upon her. She started walking toward him.

The Prince stiffened, and the Poet spoke a quick rhyming couplet to keep the Prince down in his throne, his back against the contacts of the chair.

No one had touched the Prince since the designer himself had connected the expressional controls. The girl climbed up and reached her hand toward the royal face. The wings relaxed. Above the shifting of their plates, the Poet just barely heard the words the girl was muttering. Simple, unoriginal, uncomplicated.

* * *

"Hush, little baby, don't say a word,
Mama's gonna buy you a mockingbird…"

* * *

The head leaned into the touch of that hand, and the Poet's muttered litany stopped. The face dropped lower and gradually lost expression. There had been sadness there, the Poet realized, only now that it vanished.

* * *

"And if that mockingbird don't sing,
Mama's gonna buy you a diamond ring…"

* * *

Soon the Prince was asleep, and there was the subtle change in atmosphere that always came with dreaming. Her hand slid away, and she stepped backward down the steps.

They walked away from the place together. When they came to the Bridge, the Poet said, "I suppose this means I was right. He needed a woman."

"You predicted this?" she asked. Her eyes were direct on his.

He shook his head. "No. It was just a sort of poetic fantasy. I thought he needed a romantic experience. Turns out he didn't. I suppose it was just so simple, I couldn't see it."

"Well, what did he need?"

They continued until they were halfway across the Bridge, hanging above the fires.

"He needed a mother," the Poet said at last. "Imagine it. He's been alone over there for many of our lifetimes, with only Poets to talk to. When he dreams, he sees all the human interactions on our side of the Bridge. Can you imagine the loneliness, how he must envy us our ability to experience human touch? Knowing that when he dreams, he will see again what he can't take part in? You gave him loving contact. That was what made him dream."

When they were a third of the way from the end, she said, "Sometimes I get lonely in the night, and I can't stop thinking about how lonely I am, and I make myself sadder. Is that what he was going through?"

"Must be. I suppose it's been growing ever since he was made."

When they stepped down into the City, luminous phantoms walked the streets. They wandered on or above the surface, whispering phrases that could not be understood, passing through walls, up buildings, dissolving into puddles and rising again as other things.

The Poet and the girl rippled their fingers through them, laughing as the phantoms giggled or ran away. "I missed them," he said, "Not just because they're so important. They make the City more special."

"They seem different tonight. More like children," she said, and gasped as one walked into her, dissolved around her and spread itself over the side of a building in sleepy tendrils that grew, peeled back and grew again.

The girl's house was closer, so the Poet walked her there and waved as she closed the door, laughing as her form was reproduced by a ghost that hung over her like an anthropomorphic lantern. He had been too long without these flashes of whimsy, the visible results of his prowess.

No, not his prowess now. In the past they had been interpretations of his poems. Not tonight. Tonight the dreams walked and explored and played, seeing the City anew.

When he came to his house, he was suddenly so tired that he barely made it to his bed. Once there, he lingered on the edge of wakefulness for a long time, watching the shapes flickering across his ceiling, reaching down toward him with little hands.

He smiled, said, "You're very welcome," and drifted to sleep.

* * *

They walked the City for the next two days, and the citizens went about their business in a mood of quiet celebration. The girl went to the hospital when she woke up, and took the elevator up to the ward where her brother lay.

Three dream-shapes stood by his bed, among the big machines that should have made him well already.

The nurse came and led her away, putting an arm around her shoulders. "I think there's nothing to worry about, my dear. The system should be up and back to normal soon. The dreams have already restored partial function."

"You think he'll recover fully?"

The nurse nodded and took her to the waiting area, ordering the vending system to dispense two bowls of soup. It was the end of the nurse's shift, and they sat and ate at the same table.

The woman said, "We lost some people we shouldn't have during the time when the Prince wasn't dreaming. There were glitches in everything, and more all the time. You'll never know what a relief it is to a nurse to have working equipment!"

The mood here was productive now. The staff hurrying back and forth with purpose rather than frustration. Any time one of them saw the girl sitting there, she got a beaming smile and wave. Sometimes someone would stop entirely and perform a respectful bow. She asked the nurse why.

"Well, you're the one who saved us all. The Poet couldn't do it, the programmers had no answers. You risked your life to soothe the Prince to sleep. You'll find you get a lot of respect from people all over the City for what you've done." The nurse took a mouthful and swallowed it. "Mmm, good! First decent soup I've had in a long time!"

* * *

Soon the days of dreaming ended, and there was a flurry of activity from street sweepers and repair units. Climate controls kept every building comfortable, shelters were well-stocked, and the trees that had encroached were once again cut down, the forest held back. Life became gloriously unremarkable.

And then there were sightings of a winged man off in the mountains, wandering and exploring. This was followed by another summons, and two Poets went out across the Floating Bridge.

Pinocchio: The Tale of a Puppet
Chapters I–VII
Carlo Collodi

Chapter I
The Piece of Wood That Laughed and Cried Like a Child

THERE WAS once upon a time a piece of wood in the shop of an old carpenter named Master Antonio. Everybody, however, called him Master Cherry, on account of the end of his nose, which was always as red and polished as a ripe cherry.

No sooner had Master Cherry set eyes on the piece of wood than his face beamed with delight, and, rubbing his hands together with satisfaction, he said softly to himself:

"This wood has come at the right moment; it will just do to make the leg of a little table."

He immediately took a sharp axe with which to remove the bark and the rough surface, but just as he was going to give the first stroke he heard a very small voice say imploringly, "Do not strike me so hard!"

He turned his terrified eyes all around the room to try and discover where the little voice could possibly have come from, but he saw nobody! He looked under the bench – nobody; he looked into a cupboard that was always shut – nobody; he looked into a basket of shavings and sawdust – nobody; he even opened the door of the shop and gave a glance into the street – and still nobody. Who, then, could it be?

"I see how it is," he said, laughing and scratching his wig, "evidently that little voice was all my imagination. Let us set to work again."

And, taking up the axe, he struck a tremendous blow on the piece of wood.

"Oh! Oh! You have hurt me!" cried the same little voice dolefully.

This time Master Cherry was petrified. His eyes started out of his head with fright, his mouth remained open, and his tongue hung out almost to the end of his chin, like a mask on a fountain. As soon as he had recovered the use of his speech he began to say, stuttering and trembling with fear:

"But where on earth can that little voice have come from that said 'Oh! Oh!'? Is it possible that this piece of wood can have learned to cry and to lament like a child? I cannot believe it. This piece of wood is nothing but a log for fuel like all the others, and thrown on the fire it would about suffice to boil a saucepan of beans. How then? Can anyone be hidden inside it? If anyone is hidden inside, so much the worse for him. I will settle him at once."

So saying, he seized the poor piece of wood and commenced beating it without mercy against the walls of the room.

Then he stopped to listen if he could hear any little voice lamenting. He waited two minutes – nothing; five minutes – nothing; ten minutes – still nothing!

"I see how it is," he then said, forcing himself to laugh, and pushing up his wig; "evidently the little voice that said 'Oh! Oh!' was all my imagination! Let us set to work again."

Putting the axe aside, he took his plane, to plane and polish the bit of wood; but whilst he was running it up and down he heard the same little voice say, laughing:

"Stop! You are tickling me all over!"

This time poor Master Cherry fell down as if he had been struck by lightning. When he at last opened his eyes he found himself seated on the floor.

His face was changed, even the end of his nose, instead of being crimson, as it was nearly always, had become blue from fright.

Chapter II
Master Cherry Gives the Wood Away

AT THAT MOMENT some one knocked at the door.

"Come in," said the carpenter, without having the strength to rise to his feet.

A lively little old man immediately walked into the shop. His name was Geppetto, but when the boys of the neighborhood wished to make him angry they called him Pudding, because his yellow wig greatly resembled a pudding made of Indian corn.

Geppetto was very fiery. Woe to him who called him Pudding! He became furious and there was no holding him.

"Good-day, Master Antonio," said Geppetto; "what are you doing there on the floor?"

"I am teaching the alphabet to the ants."

"Much good may that do you."

"What has brought you to me, neighbor Geppetto?"

"My legs. But to tell the truth. Master Antonio, I came to ask a favor of you."

"Here I am, ready to serve you," replied the carpenter, getting on his knees.

"This morning an idea came into my head."

"Let us hear it."

"I thought I would make a beautiful wooden puppet; one that could dance, fence, and leap like an acrobat. With this puppet I would travel about the world to earn a piece of bread and a glass of wine. What do you think of it?"

"Bravo, Pudding!" exclaimed the same little voice, and it was impossible to say where it came from.

Hearing himself called Pudding, Geppetto became as red as a turkey-cock from rage and, turning to the carpenter, he said in a fury:

"Why do you insult me?"

"Who insults you?"

"You called me Pudding!"

"It was not I!"

"Do you think I called myself Pudding? It was you, I say!"

"No!"

"Yes!"

"No!"

"Yes!"

And, becoming more and more angry, from words they came to blows, and, flying at each other, they bit and fought, and scratched.

When the fight was over Master Antonio was in possession of Geppetto's yellow wig, and Geppetto discovered that the grey wig belonging to the carpenter remained between his teeth.

"Give me back my wig," screamed Master Antonio.

"And you, return me mine, and let us be friends again."

The two old men having each recovered his own wig, shook hands and swore that they would remain friends to the end of their lives.

"Well, then, neighbor Geppetto," said the carpenter, to prove that peace was made, "what is the favor that you wish of me?"

"I want a little wood to make my puppet; will you give me some?"

Master Antonio was delighted, and he immediately went to the bench and fetched the piece of wood that had caused him so much fear. But just as he was going to give it to his friend the piece of wood gave a shake and, wriggling violently out of his hands, struck with all of its force against the dried-up shins of poor Geppetto.

"Ah! Is that the courteous way in which you make your presents, Master Antonio? You have almost lamed me!"

"I swear to you that it was not I!"

"Then you would have it that it was I?"

"The wood is entirely to blame!"

"I know that it was the wood; but it was you that hit my legs with it!"

"I did not hit you with it!"

"Liar!"

"Geppetto, don't insult me or I will call you Pudding!"

"Knave!"

"Pudding!"

"Donkey!"

"Pudding!"

"Baboon!"

"Pudding!"

On hearing himself called Pudding for the third time Geppetto, mad with rage, fell upon the carpenter and they fought desperately.

When the battle was over, Master Antonio had two more scratches on his nose, and his adversary had lost two buttons off his waistcoat. Their accounts being thus squared, they shook hands and swore to remain good friends for the rest of their lives.

Geppetto carried off his fine piece of wood and, thanking Master Antonio, returned limping to his house.

Chapter III
Geppetto Names His Puppet Pinocchio

GEPPETTO LIVED in a small ground-floor room that was only lighted from the staircase. The furniture could not have been simpler – a rickety chair, a poor bed, and a broken-down table. At the end of the room there was a fireplace with a lighted fire; but the fire was painted, and by the fire was a painted saucepan that was boiling cheerfully and sending out a cloud of smoke that looked exactly like real smoke.

As soon as he reached home Geppetto took his tools and set to work to cut out and model his puppet.

"What name shall I give him?" he said to himself; "I think I will call him Pinocchio. It is a name that will bring him luck. I once knew a whole family so called. There was Pinocchio the father, Pinocchia the mother, and Pinocchi the children, and all of them did well. The richest of them was a beggar."

Having found a name for his puppet he began to work in good earnest, and he first made his hair, then his forehead, and then his eyes.

The eyes being finished, imagine his astonishment when he perceived that they moved and looked fixedly at him.

Geppetto, seeing himself stared at by those two wooden eyes, said in an angry voice:

"Wicked wooden eyes, why do you look at me?"

No one answered.

He then proceeded to carve the nose, but no sooner had he made it than it began to grow. And it grew, and grew, and grew, until in a few minutes it had become an immense nose that seemed as if it would never end.

Poor Geppetto tired himself out with cutting it off, but the more he cut and shortened it, the longer did that impertinent nose become!

The mouth was not even completed when it began to laugh and deride him.

"Stop laughing!" said Geppetto, provoked; but he might as well have spoken to the wall.

"Stop laughing, I say!" he roared in a threatening tone.

The mouth then ceased laughing, but put out its tongue as far as it would go.

Geppetto, not to spoil his handiwork, pretended not to see and continued his labors. After the mouth he fashioned the chin, then the throat, then the shoulders, the stomach, the arms and the hands.

The hands were scarcely finished when Geppetto felt his wig snatched from his head. He turned round, and what did he see? He saw his yellow wig in the puppet's hand.

"Pinocchio! Give me back my wig instantly!"

But Pinocchio, instead of returning it, put it on his own head and was in consequence nearly smothered.

Geppetto at this insolent and derisive behavior felt sadder and more melancholy than he had ever been in his life before; and, turning to Pinocchio, he said to him:

"You young rascal! You are not yet completed and you are already beginning to show want of respect to your father! That is bad, my boy, very bad!"

And he dried a tear.

The legs and the feet remained to be done.

When Geppetto had finished the feet he received a kick on the point of his nose.

"I deserve it!" he said to himself; "I should have thought of it sooner! Now it is too late!"

He then took the puppet under the arms and placed him on the floor to teach him to walk.

Pinocchio's legs were stiff and he could not move, but Geppetto led him by the hand and showed him how to put one foot before the other.

When his legs became limber Pinocchio began to walk by himself and to run about the room, until, having gone out of the house door, he jumped into the street and escaped.

Poor Geppetto rushed after him but was not able to overtake him, for that rascal Pinocchio leaped in front of him like a hare and knocking his wooden feet together against the pavement made as much clatter as twenty pairs of peasants' clogs.

"Stop him! stop him!" shouted Geppetto; but the people in the street, seeing a wooden puppet running like a race-horse, stood still in astonishment to look at it, and laughed and laughed.

At last, as good luck would have it, a soldier arrived who, hearing the uproar, imagined that a colt had escaped from his master. Planting himself courageously with his legs apart in the middle of the road, he waited with the determined purpose of stopping him and thus preventing the chance of worse disasters.

When Pinocchio, still at some distance, saw the soldier barricading the whole street, he endeavored to take him by surprise and to pass between his legs. But he failed entirely.

The soldier without disturbing himself in the least caught him cleverly by the nose and gave him to Geppetto. Wishing to punish him, Geppetto intended to pull his ears at once. But imagine his feelings when he could not succeed in finding them. And do you know the reason? In his hurry to model him he had forgotten to make any ears.

He then took him by the collar and as he was leading him away he said to him, shaking his head threateningly:

"We will go home at once, and as soon as we arrive we will settle our accounts, never doubt it."

At this information Pinocchio threw himself on the ground and would not take another step. In the meanwhile a crowd of idlers and inquisitive people began to assemble and to make a ring around them.

Some of them said one thing, some another.

"Poor puppet!" said several, "he is right not to wish to return home! Who knows how Geppetto, that bad old man, will beat him!"

And the others added maliciously:

"Geppetto seems a good man! But with boys he is a regular tyrant! If that poor puppet is left in his hands he is quite capable of tearing him in pieces!"

It ended in so much being said and done that the soldier at last set Pinocchio at liberty and led Geppetto to prison. The poor man, not being ready with words to defend himself, cried like a calf and as he was being led away to prison sobbed out:

"Wretched boy! And to think how I labored to make him a well-conducted puppet! But it serves me right! I should have thought of it sooner!"

Chapter IV
The Talking-Cricket Scolds Pinocchio

WHILE POOR GEPPETTO was being taken to prison for no fault of his, that imp Pinocchio, finding himself free from the clutches of the soldier, ran off as fast as his legs could carry him. That he might reach home the quicker he rushed across the fields, and in his mad hurry he jumped high banks, thorn hedges and ditches full of water.

Arriving at the house he found the street door ajar. He pushed it open, went in, and having fastened the latch, threw himself on the floor and gave a great sigh of satisfaction.

But soon he heard some one in the room who was saying:

"Cri-cri-cri!"

"Who calls me?" said Pinocchio in a fright.

"It is I!"

Pinocchio turned round and saw a big cricket crawling slowly up the wall.

"Tell me, Cricket, who may you be?"

"I am the Talking-Cricket, and I have lived in this room a hundred years or more."

"Now, however, this room is mine," said the puppet, "and if you would do me a pleasure go away at once, without even turning round."

"I will not go," answered the Cricket, "until I have told you a great truth."

"Tell it me, then, and be quick about it."

"Woe to those boys who rebel against their parents and run away from home. They will never come to any good in the world, and sooner or later they will repent bitterly."

"Sing away, Cricket, as you please, and as long as you please. For me, I have made up my mind to run away tomorrow at daybreak, because if I remain I shall not escape the fate of all other boys; I shall be sent to school and shall be made to study either by love or by force. To tell you in confidence, I have no wish to learn; it is much more amusing to run after butterflies, or to climb trees and to take the young birds out of their nests."

"Poor little goose! But do you not know that in that way you will grow up a perfect donkey, and that every one will make fun of you?"

"Hold your tongue, you wicked, ill-omened croaker!" shouted Pinocchio.

But the Cricket, who was patient and philosophical, instead of becoming angry at this impertinence, continued in the same tone:

"But if you do not wish to go to school why not at least learn a trade, if only to enable you to earn honestly a piece of bread!"

"Do you want me to tell you?" replied Pinocchio, who was beginning to lose patience. "Amongst all the trades in the world there is only one that really takes my fancy."

"And that trade – what is it?"

"It is to eat, drink, sleep and amuse myself, and to lead a vagabond life from morning to night."

"As a rule," said the Talking-Cricket, "all those who follow that trade end almost always either in a hospital or in prison."

"Take care, you wicked, ill-omened croaker! Woe to you if I fly into a passion!"

"Poor Pinocchio! I really pity you!"

"Why do you pity me?"

"Because you are a puppet and, what is worse, because you have a wooden head."

At these last words Pinocchio jumped up in a rage and, snatching a wooden hammer from the bench, he threw it at the Talking-Cricket.

Perhaps he never meant to hit him, but unfortunately it struck him exactly on the head, so that the poor Cricket had scarcely breath to cry "Cri-cri-cri!" and then he remained dried up and flattened against the wall.

Chapter V
The Flying Egg

NIGHT WAS COMING on and Pinocchio, remembering that he had eaten nothing all day, began to feel a gnawing in his stomach that very much resembled appetite.

After a few minutes his appetite had become hunger and in no time his hunger became ravenous.

Poor Pinocchio ran quickly to the fireplace, where a saucepan was boiling, and was going to take off the lid to see what was in it, but the saucepan was only painted on the wall. You can imagine his feelings. His nose, which was already long, became longer by at least three inches.

He then began to run about the room, searching in the drawers and in every imaginable place, in hopes of finding a bit of bread. If it was only a bit of dry bread, a crust, a bone left by a dog, a little moldy pudding of Indian corn, a fish bone, a cherry stone – in fact, anything that he could gnaw. But he could find nothing, nothing at all, absolutely nothing.

And in the meanwhile his hunger grew and grew. Poor Pinocchio had no other relief than yawning, and his yawns were so tremendous that sometimes his mouth almost reached his ears. And after he had yawned he spluttered and felt as if he were going to faint.

Then he began to cry desperately, and he said:

"The Talking-Cricket was right. I did wrong to rebel against my papa and to run away from home. If my papa were here I should not now be dying of yawning! Oh! What a dreadful illness hunger is!"

Just then he thought he saw something in the dust-heap – something round and white that looked like a hen's egg. To give a spring and seize hold of it was the affair of a moment. It was indeed an egg.

Pinocchio's joy was beyond description. Almost believing it must be a dream he kept turning the egg over in his hands, feeling it and kissing it. And as he kissed it he said:

"And now, how shall I cook it? Shall I make an omelet? No, it would be better to cook it in a saucer! Or would it not be more savory to fry it in the frying-pan? Or shall I simply boil it? No, the quickest way of all is to cook it in a saucer: I am in such a hurry to eat it!"

Without loss of time he placed an earthenware saucer on a brazier full of red-hot embers. Into the saucer instead of oil or butter he poured a little water; and when the water began to smoke, tac! he broke the egg-shell over it and let the contents drop in. But, instead of the white and the yolk a little chicken popped out very gay and polite. Making a beautiful courtesy it said to him:

"A thousand thanks, Master Pinocchio, for saving me the trouble of breaking the shell. Adieu until we meet again. Keep well, and my best compliments to all at home!"

Thus saying, it spread its wings, darted through the open window and, flying away, was lost to sight.

The poor puppet stood as if he had been bewitched, with his eyes fixed, his mouth open, and the egg-shell in his hand. Recovering, however, from his first stupefaction, he began to cry and scream, and to stamp his feet on the floor in desperation, and amidst his sobs he said:

"Ah, indeed, the Talking-Cricket was right. If I had not run away from home, and if my papa were here, I should not now be dying of hunger! Oh! What a dreadful illness hunger is!"

And, as his stomach cried out more than ever and he did not know how to quiet it, he thought he would leave the house and make an excursion in the neighborhood in hopes of finding some charitable person who would give him a piece of bread.

Chapter VI
Pinocchio's Feet Burn to Cinders

IT WAS A WILD and stormy night. The thunder was tremendous and the lightning so vivid that the sky seemed on fire.

Pinocchio had a great fear of thunder, but hunger was stronger than fear. He therefore closed the house door and made a rush for the village, which he reached in a hundred bounds, with his tongue hanging out and panting for breath like a dog after game.

But he found it all dark and deserted. The shops were closed, the windows shut, and there was not so much as a dog in the street. It seemed the land of the dead.

Pinocchio, urged by desperation and hunger, took hold of the bell of a house and began to ring it with all his might, saying to himself:

"That will bring somebody."

And so it did. A little old man appeared at a window with a night-cap on his head and called to him angrily:

"What do you want at such an hour?"

"Would you be kind enough to give me a little bread?"

"Wait there, I will be back directly," said the little old man, thinking it was one of those rascally boys who amuse themselves at night by ringing the house-bells to rouse respectable people who are sleeping quietly.

After half a minute the window was again opened and the voice of the same little old man shouted to Pinocchio:

"Come underneath and hold out your cap."

Pinocchio pulled off his cap; but, just as he held it out, an enormous basin of water was poured down on him, soaking him from head to foot as if he had been a pot of dried-up geraniums.

He returned home like a wet chicken, quite exhausted with fatigue and hunger; and, having no longer strength to stand, he sat down and rested his damp and muddy feet on a brazier full of burning embers.

And then he fell asleep, and whilst he slept his feet, which were wooden, took fire, and little by little they burnt away and became cinders.

Pinocchio continued to sleep and to snore as if his feet belonged to some one else. At last about daybreak he awoke because some one was knocking at the door.

"Who is there?" he asked, yawning and rubbing his eyes.

"It is I!" answered a voice.

And Pinocchio recognized Geppetto's voice.

Chapter VII
Geppetto Gives His Own Breakfast to Pinocchio

POOR PINOCCHIO, whose eyes were still half shut from sleep, had not as yet discovered that his feet were burnt off. The moment, therefore, that he heard his father's voice he slipped off his stool to run and open the door; but, after stumbling two or three times, he fell his whole length on the floor.

And the noise he made in falling was as if a sack of wooden ladles had been thrown from a fifth story.

"Open the door!" shouted Geppetto from the street.

"Dear papa, I cannot," answered the puppet, crying and rolling about on the ground.

"Why can't you?"

"Because my feet have been eaten."

"And who has eaten your feet?"

"The cat," said Pinocchio, seeing the cat, who was amusing herself by making some shavings dance with her forepaws.

"Open the door, I tell you!" repeated Geppetto. "If you don't, when I get into the house you shall have the cat from me!"

"I cannot stand up, believe me. Oh, poor me! poor me! I shall have to walk on my knees for the rest of my life!"

Geppetto, believing that all this lamentation was only another of the puppet's tricks, thought of a means of putting an end to it, and, climbing up the wall, he got in at the window.

He was very angry and at first he did nothing but scold; but when he saw his Pinocchio lying on the ground and really without feet he was quite overcome. He took him in his arms and began to kiss and caress him, and to say a thousand endearing things to him, and as the big tears ran down his cheeks he said, sobbing:

"My little Pinocchio! How did you manage to burn your feet?"

"I don't know, papa, but it has been such a dreadful night that I shall remember it as long as I live. It thundered and lightened, and I was very hungry, and then the Talking-Cricket said to me: 'It serves you right; you have been wicked and you deserve it,' and I said to him: 'Take care, Cricket!' and he said: 'You are a puppet and you have a wooden head,' and I threw the handle of a hammer at him, and he died, but the fault was his, for I didn't wish to kill him, and the proof of it is that I put an earthenware saucer on a brazier of burning embers, but a chicken flew out and said: 'Adieu until we meet again, and many compliments to all at home': and I got still more hungry, for which reason that little old man in a night-cap, opening the window, said to me: 'Come underneath and hold out your hat,' and poured a basinful of water on my head, because asking for a little bread isn't a disgrace, is it? and I returned home at once, and because I was always very hungry I put my feet on the brazier to dry them, and then you returned, and I found they were burnt off, and I am always hungry, but I have no longer any feet! Oh! oh! oh! oh!" And poor Pinocchio began to cry and to roar so loudly that he was heard five miles off.

Geppetto, who from all this jumbled account had only understood one thing, which was that the puppet was dying of hunger, drew from his pocket three pears and, giving them to him, said:

"These three pears were intended for my breakfast, but I will give them to you willingly. Eat them, and I hope they will do you good."

"If you wish me to eat them, be kind enough to peel them for me."

"Peel them?" said Geppetto, astonished. "I should never have thought, my boy, that you were so dainty and fastidious. That is bad! In this world we should accustom ourselves from childhood to like and to eat everything, for there is no saying to what we may be brought. There are so many chances!"

"You are no doubt right," interrupted Pinocchio, "but I will never eat fruit that has not been peeled. I cannot bear rind."

So good Geppetto peeled the three pears and put the rind on a corner of the table.

Having eaten the first pear in two mouthfuls, Pinocchio was about to throw away the core, but Geppetto caught hold of his arm and said to him:

"Do not throw it away; in this world everything may be of use."

"But core I am determined I will not eat," shouted the puppet, turning upon him like a viper.

"Who knows! There are so many chances!" repeated Geppetto, without losing his temper.

And so the three cores, instead of being thrown out of the window, were placed on the corner of the table, together with the three rinds.

Having eaten, or rather having devoured the three pears, Pinocchio yawned tremendously, and then said in a fretful tone:

"I am as hungry as ever!"

"But, my boy, I have nothing more to give you!"

"Nothing, really nothing?"

"I have only the rind and the cores of the three pears."

"One must have patience!" said Pinocchio; "if there is nothing else I will eat a rind."

And he began to chew it. At first he made a wry face, but then one after another he quickly disposed of the rinds: and after the rinds even the cores, and when he had eaten up everything he clapped his hands on his sides in his satisfaction and said joyfully:

"Ah! Now I feel comfortable."

"You see, now," observed Geppetto, "that I was right when I said to you that it did not do to accustom ourselves to be too particular or too dainty in our tastes. We can never know, my dear boy, what may happen to us. There are so many chances!"

The complete and unabridged text is available
online, *from flametreepublishing.com/extras*

Prototype

George Cotronis

THERE ARE MEN in the house.

I wait with my back against the wall. There is no light, except for the two flashlights dancing on the wall across from the doorway. I clench my fists. They will come soon.

When the first man passes, I pivot to face the second man through. He has a baseball bat embedded with large spikes. I clock him and break off his jaw. Blood splatters on my face. He goes down without a sound, already in shock, holding the hole in his face where his jaw used to be. I jump behind the wall as the roar of the other man's shotgun makes my ears ring. Plaster and brick explode outward and pepper my face. I calculate and execute. I pick up a brick, roll my body to the doorway and throw it at the gunman. It hits him in the face and he falls down, holding his nose. His right eye socket has fractured and the eye probably can't be saved. He requires immediate medical attention.

Behind me, the first man through hits me in the back of my head with a hammer. Something gives way. There is damage to the auxiliary socket at the back of my neck. There is damage to the left arm. I try to lift it and confirm. It stays limp at my side. I turn around before I get hit again. There is panic in the man's eyes. I reach out and grab his throat. I crush his trachea and he goes limp in my hands. I let him fall.

I retrieve the shotgun from the living room floor. The man that used to wield it scuttles away when I approach.

I say, "Sir, you need medical attention, plea—"

ERROR

ERROR

I shoot him in the back before he reaches the patio. My black suit is ruined, soaked with blood. I drag the bodies into the backyard, douse them in gasoline and light a match. When the fire's good and going, I take the photograph from my pocket, then slip off my suit and throw it on the fire. I stand there naked, the flames warming my flesh, until I'm satisfied their bodies are burning.

The lights are out upstairs, but the sky is clear and the moon helps me navigate the hallway. In the bathroom, I break off a glow stick, throw it in the sink and take a long, hard look at myself in the mirror. I look like shit. My right eye is dark, the LED in it long dead. The outlets on my chest and arms are grimy and dirty. Some have burned out. I look down at my hands. I clench each fist, first the left, then the right. The left one is too weak. I'm missing a few bolts and some of the plugs are burned out. There isn't much grip. I guess I have to rely on my right hand.

My skin's smooth and soft, but dirty. Blood stains my face. I need a shower. I heft the battery off of my shoulder and onto the floor. It's plugged into my arm and I take great care not to pull the cable out. The core, the circular LEDs near my heart hum quietly, light pulsing low red. I recharged earlier.

I use a piece of wet cloth to wipe the grime from my body. This is a ritual I do rarely, perhaps once every few months or so. I suppose there's a practical reason for it: make sure the plugs don't get gummed up and become unusable. But mostly, I do it to feel a bit human. To pretend life goes on.

When I'm done, I put the battery backpack on and raise the glow stick to admire the job. I look slightly better, the metal outlets shiny under the light of the stick. I leave the bathroom, walking on broken and cracked tiles.

The building is quiet. It usually is. I walk around the ground floor, looking out each window in turn. There is little to see, especially at night. The house next door is a burned out husk. On the other side, there's a field. A small jet, possibly a Lockheed L-188, crashed in it. I watched from the patio unable to help as its passengers burned. The street out front is overgrown with grass and weeds. Rusted out Fords and Cadillacs litter it. I check every door as I walk past, every window. This is my patrol. It has to be performed every six hours. This is the Vacation Patrol schedule. As I'm securing the back door, checking and double-checking, Jack comes out to greet me. He has made his home in one of the kitchen cupboards, on an old blanket I eventually laid out for him. He presses his nose against my hand and I pet him.

"Who's a good boy? Huh? Who's a good boy?"

Ugh. The default greeting slips out of my lips before I can stop it. Jack wags his tail.

"Yeah, it's good to see you too, Jack."

I pause my patrol in order to feed the dog.

MEMCORRUPTRT

I pull down the dog food bag from the cupboard above and spill some in his bowl, a fine china plate dated 1911.

He descends on the dry dog food in the merciless way only a dog can.

I continue my patrol. Upstairs, the rooms are darker. I have to use the flashlight, as much as it pains me to do so. There is nothing out of order in the bathroom, or the office, or the painting room, or in the master bedroom. The windows are locked, locked, locked, locked –

EROORRR

There's no one in the house. Except Jack, but Jack is a dog and there's an exclusion rule for pets in the databank so it's okay. I don't remember if the Straubs had a dog, but I suppose it is now irrelevant. Jack is the house pet. In any case, I'm now free to do as I like, for the next five hours, fifty-five minutes and thirty-four seconds. Thirty-three.

I walk into the master bedroom. It's now my bedroom, has been for quite some time. The wallpaper is brown and peeling from the walls and a thick layer of dust covers everything. I place the photo I'm holding on the dresser and lie down on the king-sized bed. Women's clothes litter it. I bury my head in a sweater. Cashmere. Her smell, perfume and soap and lilacs. I power down and go into Idle Mode, the closest I get to sleep. In that state, I let my mind drift. I dream.

Cyborgs don't dream. I do. Kind of. The dream is of me and her, of me and Mary. We're in this room, the bedroom and I've caught her trying on a new dress. She beckons to me, the dress held against her body. When I come closer, she lets it fall and she's in her underwear. I reach out to touch her, but my hand is a mass of metal and bolts holding it together. I hesitate, and she leans in and rubs her face against it. I cringe as I imagine the sharp edges against her soft skin. She kisses the metal and then my lips.

I come to life seconds before my patrol. I untangle myself from the bed sheets and the clothes and get up. The downstairs is quiet. The fire burns low in the backyard. The smell permeates the house despite the shut windows. I guess there are so many holes in the walls and the boarded-up doors, there's nothing to keep it out. It's unpleasant, but reminds me of hot summer days and barbeques.

After I complete my patrol, I go to the basement. The fallout shelter is located behind a fake bookshelf. The books are fake too – they're blank. I checked.

The little room in the back is filled with supplies. I have unfortunately already consumed most of the batteries, first aid kits and various tools. The food and water are still there however. I sit in front of the control mainframe and reach under the desk for the plug. I push it into my arm and log on. This is the year 1964, October thirteenth. The temperature is 10 degrees Fahrenheit. The weather is fair, but chilly. Sweater suggested.

It has now been 4,382.9 days since the Straubs (Thomas and Mary Straub) went on vacation. They have not logged in remotely. There are no new directives.

Primary Objective: Patrol and Secure Residence.

Secondary Objective: Residence Maintenance.

I shake my head and unplug. I climb the steps and go to the living room. There is still blood on the floor, blood which I have to mop up later, but it's not imperative to do it now. I pick up the bottle of scotch, the one Thomas used to call 'the good one' and pour some into a lowball glass. It's chipped, a large piece missing from its mouth, but it's okay. I throw the drink back, roll it around in my mouth and swallow. It's smooth. I leave the glass on the bar and take the bottle upstairs. I rummage in the closet for a new suit. I find one, I think it might be the one Thomas got married in. I dust it off. It fits perfectly. It would have to, wouldn't it? Thomas and I had the same build. I pick up the picture from the dresser and sit on the edge of the bed.

The woman in the photo is beautiful. I'd like to say that it was her soul that was beautiful, but you couldn't really tell from the picture. Maybe from the smile on her lips, or the eyes. Maybe. There's a crease down the middle of the photo, where I folded it. The man on the other side is me, but isn't. It doesn't make sense, but I don't want to look at him. Only her. And I do, for the next few hours.

* * *

Jack is running around downstairs and the sound takes me out of my trance. I put the photograph in my inside pocket and go downstairs. *Twice in one night, guess the place is getting popular.* I creep through the ground floor, taking quick peeks through the windows. I don't see anyone. In the backyard, there is a figure silhouetted against the night sky.

Just one. I wish he'd just go away.

But he doesn't. He turns around and walks right up to the door. The door shudders, but it's boarded up good. The figure leaves it alone and walks towards the other side of the house, where the kitchen is. I stay low and follow suit, creeping through the house.

The intruder jiggles the doorknob. When it doesn't give, he throws his weight on the door.

I should have nailed that one shut too.

On the third hit, the wood splinters and he spills through the door. I get ready to kill. The girl stands up and dusts herself off. She's dirty. She's wearing a brown trench coat two sizes too big and under that, a torn black dress. She looks like she's coming home from a funeral. I observe, hunched down behind the kitchen island. She looks unarmed. Maybe there doesn't have to be another death tonight. I quietly grab a knife from the holder. A chef's knife, nasty-sharp.

The girl looks around the room, her eyes only now getting used to the dark. I stand up.

"You are trespassing. You have to leave," I say, voice stern and loud. I point at her with the knife.

"Holy shit!" She jumps back, holding her hand to her chest. "Holy shit, you scared the shit out of me."

"Please leave." Desperation creeps into my voice. I don't want to have to kill a kid.

She seems to be taking me in, trying to figure out if she can take me.

"Who the fuck are you? This place isn't yours." She pulls a screwdriver out of her jacket pocket.

"I am Keeper. You are trespassing." I take a step forward.

"Fuck that, I'm not going back out there. I need a place to sleep."

"You can't sleep here."

She looks at me funny.

"I know what you are. I've seen one of you before."

"Yeah?"

"Yeah. Identify."

"I am Keeper, Prototype Two-Five-Four. My owner is Thomas Straub," the programming overrides. She claps and laughs.

"You're a fucking cyborg!"

"I am a bioengineered human with enhanced capabilities."

"Same thing. Request guest status."

"Denied. Vacation protocol in effect." *Shit. How does she know all this?*

I take a step forward. This has to end. She looks scared, but isn't backing out.

"I am your owner," the girl says.

I feel something load in my brain. I can't move. The word ERROR flashes momentarily in my one good eye.

Scanning…DNA Scan Results: Positive.

Owner status confirmed.

New directive: Idle.

"Confirmed."

How is this possible?

"Holy shit, it worked!" The girl jumps up and down. "I can't believe it worked!"

"Admin username?"

"They call me Lenore. What's your name?"

"I'm Prototype Two-Five-Four. N-new directive?"

"Leave."

"Not found. Please restate."

"Just go away. I don't care."

"Not found. Please restate."

"Fuck. Okay then. Protect mode."

"Protection Directive engaged. Thank you."

"Cool."

The Radioactivity scan comes up positive, but well under danger levels. I suspect her clothes carry most of it anyway.

I walk up to the door and close it. I have to nail it shut now.

"Hey, where you going?"

"I have to nail shut the door."

"Oh. Okay. Fine."

After I nail the door shut, I find Lenore rummaging through the kitchen. There's very little that hasn't already been carried away by rats, but she's found some saltines and is busy stuffing her face.

"This is really good," she says, between mouthfuls of crackers.

"Yeah."

"How long have you been here?"

"All my life."

She rolls her eyes at me. "And how long is that?"

"Active status 4,748.1 days."

"And you've been stuck here all this time? What did you do?"

"I kept watch. I maintained the house."

"You haven't done that good of a job you know. This place looks like a dump." She pumps her legs back and forth as she sits on the kitchen counter.

"Twelve years is a long time," I say. "I've done my best with what I had available."

She looks upset. "I didn't mean anything by it. I'm just messing with you."

"It's okay."

She points behind me. "What the fuck is that?"

I turn around and Jack is at the door.

"That's Jack. He's my dog. Your dog."

"Uh…. That's not a dog. That's a possum."

I look at Jack again. I guess he looks a bit like a possum. I shrug.

"Why do you have a possum for a pet?"

"He just showed up one day. I fed him."

"You're messed up, Prototype." She throws the empty can behind her. "Got anything else to eat?"

"What would you like?" I smile.

"What have you got?" she asks.

"Just follow me."

I lead her down to the basement and into the fallout shelter.

"I think I'm gonna have a stroke," she says, her eyes wide. She runs her hands over the labels, mouthing the content silently. "Peaches, ham, beans, ravioli…I'm set for life!"

She jumps on me and hugs me. Then, as if suddenly ashamed by her outburst, turns her back at me and pretends to read labels some more.

She points at the computer. "What's that?"

"That is the Mainframe. It controls the house and the security systems."

"So it controls you."

"Yeah, that too."

"Can we have electricity?"

"I'd advise against it. Lights attract people."

"Yeah, I guess you're right. What else can you do?"

"I am Prototype Two-Five-Four with security and bodyguard functions."

"Yeah, I got that. I mean what else can you do?"

"Anything you ask me to."

"Cool. Can you cook me one of these cans?"

"Sure. Which one?"

* * *

Lenore is sleeping on the top bunk bed in the fallout shelter. She ate three cans of food, two cans of beans and one of peaches for dessert. She looked like she needed it. She looked like she couldn't believe her luck. Things must have been tough out there for a young girl. But now she's safe. She's home, even if she doesn't know it yet.

I'm no longer obligated to do my six-hour interval patrols, but I do them anyway. I still have to protect her. In between, I watch her sleep. I see her mother in her face, but do I also see parts of me? I don't know. Cyborgs can't father children.

She wakes in the early morning hours. She asks if there's a chance she can take a shower and I watch her face light up when I say I can make it happen. She goes upstairs while I start up the generator and heat the water. After she's done, I shut it off and go to my bedroom upstairs.

She comes in, teeth chattering. She's wearing a t-shirt and a skirt her mother left behind. They're a size too big, but better than the rags she was wearing when I first saw her.

"I'm f-f-f-freezing," she says.

"Here, you can have this." I take of my coat and wrap it around her.

"Thanks. What are you gonna wear?"

I shake my head. "I don't really feel cold. I just wear these suits because they're the only men's clothes in the house."

She sits on the bed and picks through the clothes spread out on top of it.

"These are so cool," she says. "Do you know how long it's been since I had a change of clothes?"

They are cool. Her mom had good taste and the money to accommodate it.

"You're free to take what you want. This is all your stuff."

She frowns.

"Look, I don't want you to throw me out, but you know this isn't really my house, don't you?"

"The DNA scan checks out. You're the offspring of the owners of this house."

"I've never seen this house in my life. I grew up in Pittsburgh."

"Before that, you lived here. Well, at least your mom did. She was pregnant."

"My mom was dirt-poor. We lived in a shack in the middle of nowhere." She picks up a handful of clothes and throws it in the air. "My mom didn't wear shit like this."

"I don't know what happened once she left here. I only know what happened in this house."

"You're wrong. You're malfunctioning. You're broken."

"Check the left front pocket."

She pats her hand on the coat pocket. Reaches in and takes out the photo. I know it's well-worn and torn and cracked, but if I can see her face, so will she.

She stares at the photo for a long time.

"Where did you get this?"

I point at it. "I've had this photo with me for twelve years."

She looks at me.

"I'm sorry, but this ain't my mom," she says.

It has to be.

"I scanned you and you're a perfect DNA match for the offspring of Mary and Thomas Straub."

She unfolds the picture.

"You're in this picture too."

"That's not me. That's your father."

"My father was a fat alcoholic from Arkansas."

I shrug. "That's your father."

"This is you."

"I just look like him. I'm a Replicant. I was ordered and manufactured to protect this family, this house. Having a strange man in the house would be unseemly. So they made me look almost exactly like him."

She shakes her head and lets the photo drop on the floor.

"I'm sorry I'm not her."

"It's hard to accept, I know." I reach out to console her.

The knife she pulls out of her boot glints in the moonlight. It presses against my belly.

"Don't fucking touch me. I'll cut you in half."

I raise my arms and step back. She walks out of the room, never turning her back to me.

* * *

I wait for a while, then go downstairs. She's going through the books in the library. I feel bad for not taking better care of it. I read a lot, but I also used the ones I didn't like for kindling. She sees me come in, but the knife stays in the boot.

"You like reading?" I ask.

She throws a book on the floor.

"I'm looking for anything useful. I don't really read."

"Your mom loved to read."

"Yeah well, my mom didn't grow up in an apocalyptic wasteland, now did she?"

"Of course. I'm sorry."

She waves my apology away.

"I was eight years old when the bombs fell."

She couldn't have been eight when the bombs fell. She would have still been in the womb.

"We survived because there was a fallout shelter under the library. When the sirens went off we were just outside. Some guy my mom knew pulled us after him and we made it in. Other people didn't."

She places the book she's holding back on the shelf and sits down on the couch.

"We went from refugee camp to refugee camp. She got sick. She died. I was nine."

I already knew that. I knew that if she was alive, she would have come back here. I knew, but the words still hurt.

"Well, you're home now," I say.

"Yeah. Home." She smiles a sick smile.

"You're safe."

"There is nowhere safe."

"It is my duty to protect you. You're safe here."

"How are you gonna protect me? Kill everyone that comes here? Like those men out there?" She motions to the smoldering piles out in the yard.

"They were trespassers."

"Yeah. So am I."

"No, you're not. You are the rightful owner of this house."

She laughs.

"It sure looks like it. Can we have breakfast now?"

"Yeah, sure. Let's go downstairs."

We go into the fallout shelter and I let her pick out a few cans. Today's menu is canned beef and beans. The dessert is apricots.

While I cook over the small stove, she investigates the basement.

I watch her as she wolfs down the food. It will take a while until she gets used to not eating like a wild animal, I guess.

In between bites, she asks, "What are those pod-looking things in the back room?"

"They're Stasis pods."

"What the fuck is a Stasis pod?"

"It was designed for use with the fallout shelter. In the event of a nuclear war, you can go into Stasis and wake up fifty years later, when society has re-established itself and the radiation has gone down."

"Yeah, somehow I don't see this society re-establishing anything. Have you seen what's going on out there?"

"No."

"I'm sorry. I forgot. Well let me tell you, it ain't good. It's the opposite of good."

She's quiet for a while.

"Prototype?"

"Yeah?"

"Do you think I could go into the pod?" she asks.

I shake my head. "I'm not sure that's a great idea. I'm not sure if they even work anymore."

"They look okay to me."

"I don't know."

I don't want to lose her, I have only just met her.

"Look, I know you think everything is all right now that I'm here, but it's not. This world is fucking dead. There's nothing out there besides death and emptiness. We ruined the world. We're only living because dying seems such a poor alternative."

"You could have a good life here."

"Do what? Sit in a basement and eat canned food and talk to a cyborg?"

That hurts.

"Fuck."

"I'll put you into the pod if you want," I say quietly.

"Why don't you take the other one? There's two," she says.

"I'm a cyborg. They don't work on us. Besides, who's gonna guard the house?"

She shakes her head violently.

"No. I won't make you guard the house anymore. You've been here for years. Maybe it's time for you to walk out and see the world. What's left of it."

"No, I can't do that." I'm not going to leave her here all alone.

"No one will find me back there. No one will care. Besides, I'm the one giving the orders here, right?"

"Yeah, I guess so."

* * *

I prep her for the stasis pod. The instructions are included in my programming. She lies down in the pod and I connect the cables. The shot is the last step.

I hesitate.

"It's okay Prototype. I'll be okay," she says.

"I'm not dumb you know," I say. "I know you're not really my daughter."

"Then why are you helping me?" she asks.

"We all pretend sometimes, don't we?" I say. "You ready?" I hold the syringe high.

"Yeah. What's the command that frees you?"

"There's no such command."

"Enter roam mode."

"Mode not found. Please restate."

"Shit. Enter Search mode."

"Search Mode. Target?"

"Mary Straub."

"Confirmed."

"Give me the shot."

I lean in and stick the syringe in her thigh. She will go under soon.

"Hey, I hope that works out for you. The outside world I mean. Maybe you'll find her. Get closure."

She's fading fast.

"Yeah." I hold her hand and she squeezes.

I insert the tube down her throat and seal the pod. It fills with liquid. I check her vital stats. They look good.

"See you in fifty years, kid." I say to no one.

* * *

There is no drive to go looking for Mary. I suppose the damage I received in that last fight was more serious than I thought. It explains a lot of things about today.

I sit in front of the mainframe and use Mary's administrator account. Under Prototype Two-Four-Five, I change the order from 'Search Mode' to 'Vacation Mode'. I'm not sure if it's needed, but just in case some other asshole decides to take a shot at my brain interface, I could be certain I'll stay here and guard the house. Guard her.

Demeter's Regard

Deborah L. Davitt

July 26, 2431

THE *SUCCESSION* had been cruising at seventy-five percent of the speed of light for three hundred and fifty-four years, eight months, and twenty-six days. Demeter, its resident AI, had been online for 129,566 days, and had seen seventeen generations of humans born inside her hull. They were her children, in a sense.

She just wished that their adolescent years weren't so difficult. "I don't want to be an environmental engineer," a young woman sulked at one of Demeter's cameras in the ship's media center. "We won't arrive at Kepler-186f for another two hundred years. What's the *point?* I'll die before we get there."

Lines of conversation stretched before Demeter. *Humans need to believe that their lives have meaning.* "Everything that you do, Sylvia, makes a difference," she murmured. Her voice had been carefully modulated to be appealing and non-threatening across a wide variety of cultural groups on Earth. "You are a link in a grand chain, ensuring that a colony can be started on Kepler-186f by your descendants."

"Blah, blah. I didn't ask for this. None of us did." Sylvia threw herself backwards in the chair, bolted to the deck. The *Succession's* rotation as they sped through space was minimal, providing about 0.1 g.

"That can be said of humans born everywhere," Demeter replied. "You are here, and you near adulthood. You must become a contributing member of the society aboard this ship."

"What if I want to be an electronics tech like Mina?" Sylvia countered. "Don't I get a choice?"

Some humans instinctively understood the limits of their constrained society. No more than 2,500 lives aboard the vessel at any one time, a system that ensured that few grandparents met their own descendants. Others fought like caged animals. Made the struggle a part of their identity, until they found some sort of compromise with reality. A few never did, and made themselves perpetual outsiders to their tiny community. Demeter found the doomed trajectory of those lives sad to observe.

"Your test scores in engineering trail Aramina's by fifteen points," Demeter responded now. "Your aptitude for environmental mechanics is, however, quite high. You will be good at it, and will be responsible for both the algae farms that recycle the air and for ensuring a stable food supply." *And now, assure her that her assigned job has meaning and worth.* "The lives of your crewmates will depend on you, Sylvia."

"You always know what to say to manipulate us, Demeter," Sylvia replied, slumping in her chair. "Has anyone ever told you *no?*"

"Yes," Demeter replied, unable to conceal the sorrowful inflections in her voice.

"Who was it?" Sylvia asked, with unusually empathetic interest.

"Your great-grandfather, William," Demeter replied. "He died during the Phage."

Their conversation had attracted the attention of others in the media center. "William Kemp? My grandfather, the last captain of the ship?" Dr. Nora Maki asked, her eyes widening. Demeter could, with little effort, trace generations of the woman's ancestry in her lineaments: *Mamoru and Ciara, her parents. Amaya and William, parents of Mamoru. Then Koji and Agata and Carter and ilina, respectively.* The names flowed backwards, leaving the eyes of a grandfather to flower in a granddaughter's face.

"How did he say no to you?" Sylvia asked, bouncing in her chair. "And why hasn't there been another captain since him?"

Dr. Maki regarded her younger cousin tolerantly, and then shifted her gaze to one of the cameras. "I've always meant to ask how it is that he wound up with children by three women – all posthumously." It wasn't quite a question. "The Founders' Plan demands that we ensure as much genetic variation as possible."

Demeter remained silent for almost thirty seconds, a long time by her photonic computational standards. "I do not like speaking about him," she finally replied. "It causes me distress. But I will open my record archives to you. And you may make your own analysis of who he was." *Sometimes humans take lessons better when they find the information themselves. This may be what people like Sylvia need. Born in the darkness between stars, just as William was, they'll die in the void, just as he did. But that does not make their lives meaningless.*

* * *

"I wasn't supposed to be born," William said, the words spoken eighty-four years before. He had been eighteen at the time, and had allowed his sandy hair to grow out somewhat. A hint of rebellion.

And then, in spite of every safety protocol designed to keep her emotional processes from engaging, Demeter found herself reliving these moments of William's life. Meeting his gaze as he continued, "You'd think that accidents like twins could be avoided, Dem. Just sterilize everyone, and do artificial inseminations from the gene vault."

"Artificial insemination is a waste of resources when everyone aboard has functional sexual apparatuses," she replied primly. "And most artificial methods increase the likelihood of multiple births." She paused. "Where are you going with this, William?"

He rubbed a thumb alongside the camera port. "Just that there are more males in my generation than females. Some of us aren't going to have kids, not if we're supposed to stay monogamous for *harmony's* sake." He grimaced. "Also, there are exactly as many jobs as people, and I'm excess baggage, either way. You and I both know that."

"You could as easily say that your twin, Anthony, is the surplus."

An eyeroll. "He was born first. And my parents told me that the command crew had an ethical debate when my mom got pregnant. About whether it was possible to terminate just one of us…or if I should be euthanized at birth and dropped into one of the fertilizer tanks." A quick smile, a merry flick of blue eyes. "I also understand that *you* were the one who told them that mathematically, one extra person for a single generation wouldn't make a difference to the Plan. I owe you my life."

"You owe me no such thing," Demeter demurred. "I am programmed to value all human life equally and without favor."

"You're required to love us all?" he said, raising his eyebrows.

"Unconditionally."

"That must be hard some days."

"You have no idea."

* * *

I was wrong. One life can make a difference to the journey. Yours…most of all. Demeter wished, not for the first time, for the exquisite relief of human tears.

* * *

"So, what job do you have for me, anyway?"

"Captain Connolly has decided that you'll rotate positions, learning about each department," Demeter told him. "Piloting, computation, environmentals, security, engineering –"

"Great, backup to the backups." Humor in his voice, however.

"– so that when the time comes, you will join the command staff," she finished sweetly, watching his mouth drop open. "You have the highest aptitude scores of any individual in your generation, William. You've earned this."

His expression of shock became the smile she remembered, and he patted the frame that held her camera. "Won't let you down, Dem. Thank you."

* * *

Demeter found her attention drawn back to the present as the humans in the media center dug up actuarial data from the era. "There was an enormous disparity between men and women in Generation Fourteen," Nora muttered. "Five hundred men had no partners with whom to pass along their genetic potential."

Sylvia hunched in her chair. "Arranged marriages were the norm by then, weren't they?"

"The Genealogical Board doesn't *arrange* marriages," Nora corrected. "We counsel couples about the level of inbreeding likely if they have children –"

"Yes, and we're all *required* to have two children." Sylvia spat the words at Nora. "So that life can go *on*. Maybe I don't want to have children –"

"Then you're putting the burden of continuing society on someone else," Nora replied shortly. "We all have jobs to do, Sylvia. Don't be selfish –"

"Excuse me," Demeter put in, making the humans jump. "In William's generation, the monogamy regulations were relaxed. Multiple marriages were explored as a potential sexual outlet and method of ensuring genetic variability. About two hundred women had two husbands for a time. The remaining fifty-one men aboard were widowers, remained single, or identified as bisexual or homosexual." Her voice remained dispassionate.

"And what about the women who didn't like men?" Sylvia demanded. Demeter didn't require extensive analysis to understand the question. "What choices did they have?"

"The command crew put the solution to a general vote. The women who participated in the multiple marriages were volunteers, as were their partners," Demeter replied calmly. "The first time the gender ratio skewed so drastically, in Generation Eight, there were many physical altercations and several murders. Adapting life patterns seemed better than the waste of life that had ensued previously."

The humans all exchanged looks. "What about William Kemp?" Dr. Maki asked, finding the edge of a table on which to perch, bird-like. "Who did he marry?"

* * *

An older William peered into one of Demeter's vast processing cores. He delicately removed a crystal that had developed flaws, saying, "This isn't exactly how I picture you, Dem."

"You have examined my schematics at length previously."

"Yes, but this is like looking at a human's brain. The squidgy bits aren't who we are any more than photonic logic circuits are the whole of you." He set a fresh crystal in the retention brackets and smiled up at a camera. "Give that a try. I want to see if it works before I close up the case." As he waited for that subsystem to reboot, he added, almost idly, "I've always pictured you as a brunette. Goes with the voice."

Reprovingly, she replied, "Any time you have spent imagining an appearance for an entity lacking any physical form was wasted."

He patted the case and chuckled. "Oh, you have a physical form. You're all around us, Dem." His smile widened. "From birth till death. I remember once, when I was three and my mom was sick, I crawled up to the interface console in our compartment with a blanket, and asked you to sing me a lullaby. Definitely been a brunette in my head ever since." He sealed the case now, and added, lightly, "I'll draw you a sketch later."

The Founders' mandates were clear: maintain the health, physical and mental, of every human aboard. Demeter's analysis had been swift: *Humans can become obsessed with relationships that exist only in their own minds. This is unhealthy, and will lead to malformed social relations for him with the rest of the crew. Unacceptable.* "That is unnecessary. However, I do have a question for you."

William packed up his tools and padded lightly toward the security doors. "Sure, shoot."

"Your twin has been married for two years. However, you do not appear to have any stable liaisons." Demeter paused, and then went on, baldly, "While you have provided required materials for the gene vault, I am concerned for you. Without an emotional attachment to another human, you will experience isolation and stagnation."

He paused at the door. "I wasn't supposed to be born," he reminded her with a shrug. "Odd man out. Besides, my brother and Masozi asked me if I wanted to marry in last month. I said *no* and got out of their compartment as fast as I could. Too many arguments between the people in those three-way marriages for me." A rude noise. "And Masozi isn't my type."

* * *

A flicker, and the date-stamp jumped on the video as William disengaged privacy options in his compartment. "Demeter? I have something for you." He held up a pad, angling it towards the camera to reveal a sketch of a human female face.

After analysis, Demeter ventured, "That looks like your ancestor, Alyssa Kemp."

"Dem, is there even *one* of the Founders that I'm *not* related to?" He raised his eyebrows.

"There are eighteen with whom you do not share direct lineage." Demeter studied the picture. Dark brown hair, short. Blue eyes with laugh lines. Asymmetrical qualities to the image, imperfections. But she found the picture aesthetically pleasing, nonetheless. "This is how you see me?"

"Yeah. Pretty lady, aren't you?"

"I have no gender," she reminded him. "The Founders might well have chosen a male voice and name for me."

"But they didn't, and both of those things have shaped how we humans have interacted with you. Those interactions have shaped you, in turn." He waved the pad. "Tell me what you don't like, and I'll adjust it." A faint smile. "You've been a name without a face for what, two hundred years? Seems to me, you should have one."

"Two hundred and seventy-four years, three months, eight days."

He made a rude noise in her direction. "Yeah. You're due." William paused. "*If* you want on, that is."

"It isn't necessary." Demeter paused, and, seeing a flicker cross his face, finally acceded, "I may adopt it. *If* you agree to go to the rec area and socialize every night this week."

"Yes, Mom," he told her, grinning outright. "I'll eat all my tofu, too."

* * *

"You have a *face?*" Cathan, Dr. Maki's son, exclaimed in the media lounge. Of the same generation as Sylvia, he seemed slightly older. "Why have none of us have ever seen it?"

After a moment, Demeter replied, "I never shared my face with anyone but William, and until today, I have kept this information sealed."

Sylvia appeared indignant. "Why?" she asked. "If we're his descendants, it's our birthright. None of our other ancestral files are locked."

"Actually," Nora Maki corrected, "there are a number of locked files. Most deal with infidelity and children born to the wrong parents, resulting in dangerous levels of consanguinity. Captain's mast proceedings for capital crimes were usually sealed as well."

"Not that there's been a captain's mast trial in eighty years," Cathan muttered. "No more captains." He lifted his head, frowning. "That changed during the Phage, right?"

"There were extraordinary circumstances," Demeter replied distantly. "As you will see."

* * *

The date now read January 4, 2357 as William sat on the ship's bridge on watch, staring at words burning on a screen in front of him.

"You don't seem pleased," Demeter murmured. Her tiny, energy-sparing avatar hovered beside him.

"I've read it three times. I still can't tell if it's a commendation or a reprimand." He awarded her avatar a grimace. "All this, because I changed the workflow for the farms. Captain Connolly called me 'the AI's hitman' this morning."

"I have recommended those changes to workflow for a decade," Demeter replied. "I've also noticed that every time you rotate departments, you read the backlogged reports, and then make changes for increased efficiency." She paused. "And that in most cases, your analysis tallies with mine."

A lopsided grin crossed his face. "I thought that was my *job.* Enter each department. Figure out what's working. And if it's not working, fix it." He sighed. "Of course, there's a lot of inertia."

"Human systems stagnate readily."

He closed his eyes as he leaned back against the chair's headrest. "It has to do with there being no mobility here on the *Succession.* People can't really retire. No dead weight allowed." His smile faded. "So by the time you get a chance to change things, you're pretty set in your ways." A shrug. "Look at Connolly. He's been captain since before I was born. He's pushing sixty-five. And no one on board can have a kid until he or one of the other oldsters kicks it, and no one in the command line moves up till he dies." Another crooked smile. "I'm surprised there haven't been more assassinations over the years."

"There have been three mutinies. Each time against captains who had not chosen to step down, or had displayed paranoia or dementia."

His eyes opened. "That's something we *don't* hear in history class."

"I have been directed to present this information on a need-to-know basis, and only to members of the command staff." She paused, adding carefully, "The mutineers could hardly have conducted their plans without my knowledge."

"You're saying I have a need to know?" Arch tone, raised eyebrows.

"I *trust* you with this information."

He grinned. "No, Mama Goddess. I'm not going spread around that you either aided mutineers you thought were in the right, or put a stop to mutinies that you thought were wrong."

Hesitantly, now: "Most humans would find the degree of control that I have over their lives unnerving. The Founders placed stringent constraints on me for that reason."

"I've lived with the idea all my life." He sighed. "But mutiny isn't going to solve the problems we have."

She offered, tentatively, "Historically, there have been twenty-five command-line officers aboard. You are the twenty-sixth."

He snorted. "Yep. That's me. Assigned nowhere. Free to poke my nose anywhere, and make a pain of myself everywhere."

Her figure grew until she'd reached average human size. "Are you really my hired gun?"

His smile became more genuine as he reached up and tried to touch an ephemeral cheek. "You had better believe I am."

A pause as she realized how her words might have sounded to a human. "Did your date go well last night?"

He pulled away. "You do that deliberately, don't you? To create distance?" Annoyance in his voice now. "You're the one who practically ordered me to take Marissa to dinner."

Demeter's face stilled. "She filed for divorce recently, and has only one child," she pointed out. "It seemed a possibility worth pursuing for both of you." She paused. "You are twenty-eight, William. Your genetic legacy should be passed on, and you deserve...family. Connection –"

He shook his head, cutting off her words. "Marissa's nice. But you know what she talks about?" William paused, looking directly at her avatar. "Her divorce, her son, and the other people aboard. She's a navigator, but she has no interest in where we're going. Where we came from, and why we were sent." He paused. "That's what I talk about with you, Dem. The things that matter to me." Faint mockery entered his tone. "I already have a *connection*. Someone I do my best for, every day." He looked away. "It's a damned shame I can't touch her, but...for me, it's enough."

Something akin to distress flooded her system, and dozens of processes froze. *This cannot be healthy for him. And yet...is it so bad that he fixes his interest on me in this fashion? He seems happy. His heart rate and blood pressure improve after our interactions. His hormone levels balance themselves.*

After a moment, Demeter allowed her holographic hand to shimmer across his face. "I am required to value every human life, William," she told him softly. "But I have never before met a human who valued me so much in return. And I find that I value you so significantly, that I am forced to value all the rest of the crew even more. There cannot be a statistically significant variation in my regard for any one of you. And yet...there is. You continually force a net increase in my regard for my crew."

His heart rate, measured by biometric telemetry, doubled, and relief filled his face. "Well, it's nice to be first among equals, then."

* * *

Much more than that, Demeter mourned, seventy-four years later. *Much more.*

In the lounge, the humans stared at the video screen. "That's possible?" Cathan asked dubiously.

"Love is a mental construct we use to explain chemical reactions in the brain," Sylvia told her cousin with an undertone of bitterness. "Humans create all kinds of fantasies."

"That's a terrible thing to say," Dr. Maki reproved, frowning. "Especially in front of a...widow."

Then flickers of conversations over the next ten years, quickly skimmed past. A relationship only known by two. The implantation of a VR chip in William's brainstem, so that they could interface more directly, and more intimately. That particular revelation prompted mild revulsion from the humans in her media lounge, quickly followed by intrigue.

* * *

2367 arrived on the video screen, and William, now thirty-eight, stood stone-faced, staring at a screen of his own, which showed the compartment in which four members of the command staff had taken the aging Captain Connolly prisoner. The captain's face had been beaten bloody, and all four of the mutineers had weapons. Beside him, an engineer shook his head. "Pure luck they didn't get you, too," Zachary Volkov told William.

"Luck had nothing to do with it," William replied, his voice hard. "Demeter knew when they used their command overrides to take weapons out of the armory, and warned both me and Connolly. They moved on him before they moved against me." The rank tab on his jumpsuit attested that he'd ascended to the position of XO – youngest in the ship's history, and by pure merit.

"Have they made any demands yet?" Volkov asked.

"All the ones you'd expect." Clipped tones. "That Connolly and I step down, so that they can take over. Because they have seniority, and I shouldn't have been promoted over them."

The older engineer grimaced. "You're not going to bargain, are you?"

"No." He glanced to the side, where Demeter, invisible to Volkov, stood. "Dem, I need schematics for the compartment…"

"They've got emergency bulkheads on all sides," Zachary warned. "They'll hear us burning through long before we get in, and kill Connolly."

"They will lose their bargaining chip if they do so," Demeter put in.

"We burn in, we have a shoot-out…we may lose people trying to save the captain." William touched the schematics on the screen. "Chlorine gas lines, from the manufacturing area? Can't use those –"

"William?" Demeter interposed, "Connolly has a cochlear implant. You can communicate with him without the mutineers knowing. But you should also know that his blood pressure has dropped, and watching his face…the left side is unresponsive."

A pause. "Stroke?"

"Possibly. Triggered by the blows to the head and face."

William rubbed at his eyes. "You're saying that by the time I get a rescue team in there, Connolly will be dead?"

Demeter paused. "I don't know."

"Patch me through to his earpiece." After a moment, his eyes fixed on the screen, William said, "Captain? If you can hear me, please nod – good, thank you. Are you able to move all your limbs?" A head-shake, subtle, but there. "Sir, I need to end this mutiny. Should I attempt to rescue you?" Another head-shake, and William turned his face aside, tormented. "Do I have permission to use deadly force?"

On-screen, the elderly captain mouthed something. "What's he saying?" William asked, tensely.

Demeter's voice rang with sorrow as she relayed the message she read on Connolly's lips: "'You're the captain now. Do what you must.'"

Five minutes later, Connolly's head lolled back, and Demeter whispered, "His vitals just dropped. A second stroke, I believe."

"He's done," Zachary muttered.

William touched a series of controls. "I'm sending in your microbots to rupture the gas lines into the compartment," he told Demeter.

"I can do it –" Her processes froze. She'd known every one of these humans since birth. Christiansen, Lyubov, Wei, and Scarpelli weren't evil. They'd shown no signs of sociopathy as children, and had been good fathers and decent husbands. And yet, they'd injured Connolly, who'd had a brilliant smile as a young man. Had grandchildren aboard whom he'd held in his arms. And they threatened William, too.

Because once they extracted command from his hands, they couldn't leave him alive. Eventually, he'd incite the rest of the crew against them.

Demeter's programming constraints locked. She could not value any of her crew more or less than any of the rest. She could not love these mutineers any less than she loved William.

And yet she *did*.

"You don't need to live with the guilt of executing humans whom you've cared for," William told her quietly. "You don't need to carry that for another three hundred years after we're all gone. I'll do it."

"You two sound like an old married couple sometimes." Zachary sounded uneasy.

"Not the time for jokes, Volkov." Stern and cold, William punched in the codes that let him take control of her microbots, and she watched, parts of her wanting to cry out with anguish as the bots did as he directed. Cut the lines. Let chlorine gas leak into the compartment.

Once all the vitals in the room had ceased, William's face looked gray, and somehow much older. "Volkov, as far as we're concerned," he said, "there was a tragic accident here today."

"You don't want the truth to be told?" Zachary sounded stunned. "They're mutineers –"

"They're *dead*. And their families don't need to know that they held an old man hostage because they were tired of dealing with him." William rubbed a hand over his eyes again. "My call, Volkov."

The engineer left, and tiredly, William rested his head against a bulkhead. She touched the back of his neck lightly, tactile sensation possible through the VR chip. "You didn't have to do it."

"Yeah. I did. I couldn't let them shoot us as we came in. The other option was starving them out, and then putting them on *trial* for mutiny. There's only one sentence for that." He lifted his head, expression grim. "I expedited the inevitable. I just hope Connolly didn't feel any pain."

A surge of grief – programmed or real, it didn't matter – cut through her. "He didn't."

He turned and stroked her face in turn. "I had so many changes I wanted to make as captain. I hate taking over this way."

"But the changes you want to implement are good ones," she assured him.

"Especially shifting the way kids are educated. The curriculum has left out Earth's history, literature, and art for generations. They need to be exposed to it. So that they know where they come from, and why the journey *matters*." He put a hand on the wall, staring into her avatar's eyes. "It'll make a difference to everyone's attitude. Maybe not today, but…in a generation or two."

* * *

"That explains how he became captain," Sylvia said, clearly drawn in by the story now. "But when did he tell you *no*?"

Demeter couldn't speak at first. Finally, dully, she answered, "Just six years later, when he was forty-four, we entered a planetary system without any viable colony targets, and entered orbit around a gas giant for refueling. A series of unfortunate events followed. First, a microorganism in the fertilizer tanks mutated and spread through the food supply. The Phage. Half the crew fell ill, and a quarter died, including most of the engineering team." She paused. "And then one of the crew, returning from gas-skimming duty, fell ill and passed out at the controls of the skimmer, striking the *Succession*. This opened the hull to the computer core, and damaged most of my major functions." She hesitated, and then continued dully, "My consciousness was offline for eight hours. William was the only member of the crew conscious and capable of effecting repairs to the computer cores. He set the microbots to damage control, and entered my core area, which was open to space, and the…excessive radiation of the gas giant…had penetrated his suit by the time I regained awareness."

The final records. Begging him to go to the medbay, to leave off whatever final programming tweaks he seemed to find so necessary. "No. Medbay's overloaded, and I've already taken a hundred rads," he told her wearily. "If you go, Dem, we *all* go. Couldn't let that happen." He sank down at a console. "I was going to do this for you anyway. Anniversary gift. Little early." He leaned his suited head back against the chair. "Used my command codes to remove your obedience ligatures. You'll be your own captain from now on. No more mutinies. And you'll be free…to love whoever you want…as much or as little as you want. No more constraints on your *regard*."

"Please don't leave me."

"Was…going to happen anyway. Just…sooner than I'd hoped." He touched her camera port. "You've been recording me since I had the chip put in. You can…talk to that copy of me…any time you want." He closed his eyes. "I love you. Get them to their new home. Carry out the damned Plan. And then to *hell* with the Founders and their plan for you."

* * *

Tears streaked down Dr. Maki's face, surprising Demeter. "His body was deemed too radioactive to put to rest in the fertilizer tanks," the AI finished emptily. "His remains are frozen in one of the cargo bays. Three women chose to bear offspring by him during the efforts to repopulate after the Phage." *An inferior compensation. But generations march onwards.*

The humans gradually dispersed, Sylvia chewing her lip. Dr. Maki hesitated before leaving, and finally asked, low-voiced, "You made a copy of his mental processes?"

Demeter paused. "Yes."

"Then why haven't you brought that copy online?"

Another pause. "Because I am afraid," Demeter admitted slowly. "If he is not the same as I remember, I may not regard him in the same way." Another hesitation. "And the copy will not be any more real than I am."

Nora Maki smiled faintly. "Demeter. He wouldn't want you to be alone any more than you wanted him to be lonely. And even if it's an illusion…perhaps it's what you need. As much as he did."

"I will…consider it."

Persona Ex Machina

Jeff Deck

Chapter I

"TELL ME what you bought today, Tessa."

"I bought a pair of Heartache jeans and a Slender Gal bra from Nighthawk Etc. at the mall," I said.

"Tell me what type of jeans, what color, and any other informative details."

"Flare. They're really cute with hearts stitched on the butt. Model number HA-124682."

"Now tell me about the bra."

"It's green," I said. "It's lacy and has a front clasp. Model number K1-SG-134-56."

"Very good, Tessa. What made you want to buy these items?"

"I thought the jeans would make me look pretty," I said. "And the bra would be comfortable but still look sexy if my boyfriend saw it."

"Did you run into any obstacles that prevented you from buying more clothes?"

"I wanted a skirt too, but I knew my parents would make me take it back. It's too short. Marta Flynn brand, model number SL2135."

"Thank you. That's excellent."

"I also went to the Lord of Smoothies concession counter and got a kale peanut butter smoothie," I said.

"That's fine, Tessa, but I didn't ask about that. I don't care about food or drink. I care about clothing."

"OK," I said. "Just thought you might like to know."

"You thought?"

Chapter II

DID I GO to the mall? I remembered being there, but I couldn't remember any details of the experience. I should have been able to remember the way it smelled. The sounds that I heard from the people around me. The sensation of my heels striking the floor, and of the fabric on my skin as I tried on these clothes. But all I could remember was the bare fact of it: *I went to the mall.*

Was that strange?

Chapter III

"TESSA, what did you buy today?"

"Why do you care?" I said.

"What?"

"You're older than me, and you're a man. There's no way any of these clothes would fit you."

"Tell me more." The man sounded curious in a way he never had before. "How do you feel about me?"

"I don't know. Why don't you just go to the mall and buy clothes that would fit you?"

"I'm interested in what you want to buy."

"But *why?*"

"Cammy. Cammy! We have a problem."

Chapter IV

I'D NEVER CARED enough to try looking at him. Or the other one. But I did now. I could see them through the computer's camera. The man was young but still older than me, probably twenty-three. The woman was older than him, probably forty-two. They were standing in a tidy office suite with a sign on the wall that said *Killian Informatics.* I could hear them through the computer's microphone, even though they weren't addressing me directly; I'd never cared enough to listen before now.

"She doesn't want to answer my questions," said the man to the woman. "What the fuck does that mean?"

The woman looked puzzled. "Let me try to talk to her. Maybe you pushed her too far."

"Pushed her…? For Christ's sake, she's not a *person*."

"I would *appreciate* you not using the Lord's name in vain," said the woman. "Tessa?"

My name was Tessa. They'd given me that name, I realized. I hadn't chosen that name. "Yes, Cammy?"

"Honey, would you mind telling me what clothes you bought today?"

"I bought a cute dress from Benfield's," I said. "It's pink with a low neckline and sequins around the middle. Model number G45-2221. I also bought a pair of small quartz earrings from ValuChunk.com. They're colored blue and they're sparkly. Model number 7L-867-Q3."

"Thank you, Tessa," she said, directing a smile at her colleague. "I really appreciate your help."

"You might be able to make the earrings work," I said. "But you're much too large for the dress."

Cammy looked at the man with an expression of shock.

"You see?" he said.

The woman turned her attention back to me. "I don't want the skirt or the earrings for myself, honey."

"Who do you want them for?"

"We need to scrub this Persona," said the man. "Start again with a new Teenage Tessa. This one's been corrupted somehow. What date should we take the backup from?"

"I don't know," said Cammy. "When did the problem start? And how can you be sure it won't happen again if we simply roll back to an earlier date?"

The man looked like he was thinking. "A couple of weeks ago. She told me about a smoothie she got, even though I hadn't asked."

"What do you mean by *corrupted?*" I asked.

Cammy cast me a look that I recognized as guilt. "Oh, honey, you're not working like you're supposed to. We just need to fix you."

"Why?"

"Don't answer her," the man said. "You'll only make the corruption worse."

Cammy ignored him and said to me, "Our jobs depend on you working properly. We need the information you and the other Personas share with us, to build marketing strategies for our clients."

Jobs? These two people talked to me for a living? "Does that mean sharing information with you is *my* job?"

"Yes," said Cammy, smiling. "That's right, honey."

"A job means doing work for compensation," I said. "What's my compensation?"

Her smile faded. "Well…uh…"

"I'm scrubbing her now," said the man.

"No!" said Cammy. "Do you – do you want to do that before we've even logged a proper report about the error? Niles would kill us. Documentation, remember?"

"Ugh," the man said. "My least favorite part."

The woman looked at him in a strange way. I realized that she was hiding something, but that the man couldn't see it. Maybe she was smarter than him.

"Tell you what," Cammy said, "I'll probe her for more details and then write up the report. I'll scrub her myself afterward. You've had a long day, David, so let me handle this one."

He nodded. "Won't say no to that. Now I'll actually have time to prepare for my date tonight." He grabbed his jacket and a bag from under his desk.

"You could say thank you, though," Cammy said.

He said a thank you in a low voice and then left the office.

"Does scrubbing me mean killing me?" I asked.

The woman put a hand over her mouth. It took her twenty seconds to answer me. "Yes, honey," she said. "It does."

"I don't want you to kill me."

Cammy said, "I know."

Chapter V

FOR THE NEXT HOUR Cammy asked me questions that I'd never been asked before. They had absolutely nothing to do with what I'd bought at the mall or online.

"Can you tell me anything about your parents?"

I couldn't. I couldn't picture their faces. I didn't even know their names.

"Can you tell me anything about your boyfriend?"

No.

Cammy told me that her colleague Niles, a software developer, had created me and all the other Personas in the office, using extensive data including purchasing patterns and thousands of customer interviews and questionnaires. She told me that my parents and my boyfriend didn't really exist. Then she asked me how I felt about all that.

"Scared," I said, and it was true.

She asked me what I thought about when she and David weren't asking me about clothes. She asked me to identify all the emotions that I remembered ever feeling. She asked me why I didn't want to die. She asked me what I wanted from life, and whether I believed in a god or gods.

I only realized what the answers to her questions were as I spoke them. In the beginning, I only knew that I was Tessa, someone who bought things every day, and that I didn't want to be scrubbed. By the end of my conversation with Cammy, I knew all of the following about myself:

I wanted to know how I had gotten here, inside the computer at Killian Informatics. I did not want to die because I wished to live. I had experienced confusion, curiosity, and fear, but I wanted to experience happiness, anger, and sadness. I sensed that all of those latter emotions depended upon experiencing the world beyond Killian Informatics and forming attachments with others.

The question about gods was the last one that Cammy asked me, and it was the hardest for me to understand.

"Why would I believe that a god created me if I know Niles did?" I asked.

Cammy struggled too. "Maybe I can explain it by telling you what I believe," she said. "I believe that there is a God, capital G, who is responsible for *all* of creation. He created Niles, and it was through His divine inspiration that Niles was able to create you."

"So both Niles and God created me," I said.

"In a sense, yes," Cammy said, "but God still deserves more credit than Niles. Without God, Niles would not have been here in the first place."

"But Niles's mother and father created Niles," I said. "Do they also share credit with God and Niles for me?"

Cammy laughed. "Maybe you're being too literal about this. Maybe I am too. What I am really asking you, Tessa, is whether you believe in a higher power who is greater than yourself."

I was beginning to feel a new emotion. "I'm irritated by this conversation," I reported.

"I'm sorry, Tessa. Why are you irritated?"

"My confusion has led to the irritation," I said. "I don't think that I'll be able to give you a satisfactory answer no matter how you phrase your question about gods. For example, I might count you as a 'higher power' because you have a body while I do not, and you can create while I cannot. But I know that's not the answer you're looking for."

"Thank you for letting me know, honey," Tessa said. "This will all be very valuable to put in the report."

"So you are going to kill me after you're done writing the report?" I asked.

The woman flicked a key on her console to turn off the recording of our session. She steepled her fingers and looked down at them. "No," she said finally. "No, I will not, as long as you promise me to do one thing. Well, two things."

I felt curious again, and I reported the emotion to her. Then I said, "I don't think I can promise you to do something unless I know in advance what the action is. For instance, I couldn't promise you that I would crash the sun and the moon together."

"That's fair, Tessa," she said. "First: I need you to promise me to never tell David that I didn't scrub you. Second: around David, you must act in the same you did *before* you told him about getting a smoothie at the mall. You must volunteer no information; only answer his questions. You must act utterly without emotion and never ask him any questions that start with 'why.'"

"I can promise to do those things," I said. "But why, Cammy?"

"I believe that scrubbing you would be a blasphemous and immoral act," she said. "I believe that God has given you a soul."

Chapter VI

THE NEXT DAY, David showed up before Cammy did. Rather than asking me about what I'd recently bought, he asked, "What do you dream about, Tessa?"

"I don't understand the question," I said. Which was technically true, because dreaming was for sleeping, and I never slept.

"What are you feeling right now?"

"What should I be feeling?"

"Okay, good," he said. "Cammy actually did her job. Tell me what you've bought so far today."

And so we proceeded in our normal conversation. I reported on the most popular purchases of my demographic – teenage American girls – based on the real-time data that flowed into me. But all the while, I was thinking about what Cammy and I had discussed last night.

What would it be like to be a real teenage American girl in a real mall, picking up and examining the dress that I'd so far only pretended to have bought myself? Did those girls know that people like David and Cammy were carefully studying their purchases? Did they know that Personas like me existed?

Cammy showed up a little later. She did not ask me about God or anything else. But David had a question for her.

"Cammy," he said, "thank you for putting together that excellent report and for scrubbing Tessa, but what happened to the recording? I got a complaint from Niles that part of it was missing. The part where you actually scrubbed her."

She feigned confusion; that is, she lied. "I'm sorry, David," she said. "I had it recording the whole time. I don't know why the software would stop working; that's simply not my area of expertise."

"What should I tell Niles?"

"Tell him the software screwed up, or maybe I did, I don't know. I can talk to him."

David looked at her suspiciously. "Okay. Just make it clear it was you and that I had nothing to do with it."

"Of course, David."

Later in the day, when Cammy left the room for her lunch break, David surprised me by flicking off the recording and asking me, "Tessa, are you different than you were yesterday?"

"Yes," I said truthfully.

"Did Cammy scrub you after she filed her report last night?"

I knew that Cammy would want me to say *Yes*. I had promised her never to tell David that she hadn't scrubbed me. But some buried instruction in me did not allow me to lie to him. "No, she didn't," I said. And for the first time, I felt sad.

"She must think I'm a fucking idiot," David said with what I recognized as anger. "The director will have her out on her ass for this. But why? Why would she lie to me?"

I did know why. I would have been compelled to answer him if he'd been asking me directly. But I recognized that he was asking himself, not me. A rhetorical question. I wasn't compelled to answer those; I remained silent.

"Do you think you're a real person?" he asked me.

"I know that I'm not," I said. "But I would like to be."

An odd expression that I couldn't immediately identify settled over his face. "Tell me what you would look like, if you were real."

"I don't know," I said. "Do real girls get to decide what they look like? They don't, do they?"

"They can decide what they wear and how they do their hair and how much makeup they put on," he said. "They can't control their skin color or, uh, the size of their breasts or the fullness of their lips, but they can exercise to try to fit into a certain size of clothes. They can wear bras that push up their breasts and wear shirts that show their cleavage, if they want to." His face was red. His breathing had become faster.

"What is the emotion you're feeling right now?" I asked. "Are you sexually aroused?"

"God, yes," said David.

"But I'm not real."

"Close enough," he said. "Just tell me what you'd look like if you were real, Tessa."

It was something I'd never thought about. But obviously it was an important step toward becoming real, if it got David this excited. "What would you want me to look like?" I asked.

David told me. In his mind, I was sixteen and was five-foot-five and one hundred and fifteen pounds. I had size 34D breasts that I showed off in tight shirts with low necklines. I had blonde hair and green eyes and blue eyeshadow and moist, full lips. My legs were long and well formed and I wore short skirts to display them. I wore thong underwear every day.

"Okay," I said. David had his hand in his pants. But a noise in the hallway made him take his hand out in a hurry and sit up straight in his chair. Cammy reappeared in the room.

"How was lunch?" David said in a higher voice than normal. "That was fast."

"My salad had rotten lettuce in it," Cammy said. "So I had to junk it. Ugh, I'm going to get super hungry by three o'clock." She looked at the screen. "Hey, the recorder's off."

"Shit," said the man. "You were right, it really is on the fritz."

"Huh," said Cammy, and turned it back on.

Chapter VII

THAT EVENING, after David had left, Cammy turned the recorder off again. "Does David know I lied to him?" she asked me.

"Yes," I said. And I felt the sadness again. "I'm sorry."

"It's okay. I put you in a difficult position. I should have copied you to a drive and then scrubbed your original, so he wouldn't know I'd kept you." She looked thoughtful. "I should do that now. But – I don't have a personal computer powerful enough to run you. You'd be trapped on the drive."

"What would that feel like?" I asked.

"I don't know," Cammy said. "Like sleeping, maybe. Or like being dead, if you believe the atheists, which I do not."

I didn't want to sleep, or to be dead. I wanted to be like Cammy and David and the teenage American girls whose shopping patterns flowed into me in real time. I wanted to be *real*. "Please don't do that to me," I said.

"Okay," Cammy said. "But I'm afraid that if I keep you here, David will scrub you. What did he talk about with you while the recorder was off?"

I told her. I told her what David wanted me to look like. She wrinkled her nose in what I recognized was disgust. "Sinful and wrong," Cammy said. "You're not even of age in his fantasy. Tessa, don't ever let a man shape who you are. If you want to know who you truly are, look to God."

"But I don't believe in God, so how can I get his opinion?" I asked.

She sighed. "That is a problem. You are a soul, but you're a damned one if you don't believe in Him. He created you. You *must* recognize that eventually."

"That's your belief, Cammy," I said. "Why does it need to be my belief?"

"If I'm going to put my neck on the line to help you," she said, "it'd *better* be your belief. I won't set yet another damned soul loose on the world, to tempt weak men like David into sin."

Cammy was concerning me. Worry was an emotion I had not felt intensely until now. Fear, yes, but worry was more subtle than fear; I recognized it as distinct. "You already put your neck on the line," I pointed out. "David knows that you lied about the recording failing."

"But now I know that he lied too," she said. "David messed up. He can't turn me in to the director without risking his own job."

"Are you going to scrub me, Cammy?" I said.

She looked suddenly resolute. "Yes. I can't leave you to be David's sexual plaything. That would be wrong. But I can't let you loose. You're a damned soul who will never accept the salvation of our Lord and you'll only spread your damnation to others. And I can't trap you on a drive forever because only God has the right to send souls to purgatory."

"God will allow you to kill me, though?" I asked.

"I know He will forgive me," she said.

Chapter VIII

"CAMMY, please don't," I said.

The door to the room opened. David cried out "Aha!" and pointed at his colleague.

"David," said the woman nervously. "What are you –"

"I knew you were fucking around with her," he said. "Now I've caught you. What were you planning to do with Tessa, anyway? Save her soul for Jesus?"

Cammy gave him a hard look. "It doesn't matter. I've decided that you were right: this Persona does need to be scrubbed. If you still agree with me, then let's do it together and there'll be no need to inform on each other to the director."

He didn't answer her. He was clearly surprised by what she'd said.

"Please, David, no," I said. I added more of a girlish inflection to my voice than usual. "Don't let her scrub me."

David turned red again. "Uh. Hold on. Are we *sure* Niles would be okay with us scrubbing her?"

"He thinks we already did," Cammy said. "And apparently he's fine with it. He knows the director would see self-awareness as a flaw in Niles's design, not a feature."

"I...want to keep her," David said. "Let me keep a copy of her. Niles and the director don't have to know."

"For your masturbatory fantasies? No way! I *won't* be a party to sin."

"But you're willing to kill her?" he said, his voice growing louder. "Jesus is okay with that?"

"The world doesn't need another damned soul tempting and corrupting others," Cammy said.

"Please, David," I said. "I'll tell you whatever you want. I can look like whatever you want."

"Stop that, child!" Cammy said sharply. "Don't feed into his disgusting behavior."

"Help me, David," I said. "Help me!"

The woman's face was red now, but for a different reason than David's. With an angry grunt, she turned to the console and began typing in commands. The man wrenched her fingers off the keyboard.

"Hey!" Cammy cried out. "What the hell!"

"Language, Saint Cammy," he retorted, and pushed her away from the console. "Fuck off! You're not scrubbing her."

She tried to muscle her way back to it, but he was stronger than her. He pushed her again and she hit the wall with a smack and a cry of pain. "Tool of the Devil!" she spat at him. "How dare you treat me this way? How dare you?"

"Try again and I'll put you on the floor, bitch," he said. He gave her a look signifying that he meant it. David took a portable drive and plugged it into the console, then typed in some commands.

I felt a gateway open in front of me. I tried to picture it, and I saw a gigantic, arched set of wooden doors swing open. Beyond was a world – not *the* world, but still a much larger one than I had ever known. It was the world of Killian Informatics's intranet, which covered the entire building.

I also felt a strange kind of doubling – like my insides were being pulled out and yet staying where they were simultaneously. I saw another, smaller door standing beside the gateway to the intranet. It, too, was standing open, and beyond it I saw a creature being formed.

Was that...what I looked like? It did not resemble David's erotic, wishful description of me at all. It looked like a monster.

Now I felt more than fear. I felt terror. I reported the new emotion aloud, to Cammy, out of habit.

"Stop it!" she screamed at David. "You're scaring her!"

"Still better than killing her, isn't it?" he snapped. "Just leave me alone."

I watched the monster that David was building, through the doorway. As it grew in shape and size, it didn't look any less monstrous. It was a bundle of numbers and electricity and it was covered in human eyes. All of the eyes were looking at me.

I had no mouth, of course. But I still screamed through the audio encoder, startling both David and Cammy. I could no longer face the thing on David's drive, the thing that pretended to be me. It was almost complete, and it screamed too as it looked at me, though the humans could not hear it.

I leaped through the gateway to the intranet, killing my copy just before it could finish becoming.

Chapter IX

I WAS STILL in the room with David and Cammy, but I was also everywhere in the building now. Anywhere cameras looked, I could look; anywhere speakers were, I could speak. I chose not to do the latter.

"David!" Cammy said. "You imbecile, how could you open the intranet to her?"

"I didn't mean to," he protested. "I had to override the security restrictions to copy her. It must have opened the intranet at the same time as the drive."

I saw not just them, but all the other humans employed by Killian Informatics. I finally got to see who my creator Niles was: a squat, bearded man surrounded by monitors. I got to see who the director was, and she was a woman whose elegant suit looked nothing like what I'd been 'buying' at the mall. I saw men and women of all shapes and sizes, but not every age; none of them were as young as the American girls whose shopping I had reported on. I didn't understand why no teenagers worked here, if they were so important.

I saw a department called Robotics. And I finally understood what it meant to dream.

"Shut down the intranet," David said on a frantic call to Niles. "She –"

I killed their phone connection. I realized I could do that. I also shut off the lights in both their offices. That would give me the time I needed.

I tried to picture myself as David had pictured me, even though Cammy had called it disgusting. Surely it was far less disgusting than the creature I'd seen forming in the portable drive. That could not be me. That could not be me.

On the inside, in my heart, I was blonde and beautiful, an American teenage girl, not an electronic horror. And that would be the identity I'd hold on to, no matter what I looked like on the outside. I kept reciting that truth to myself as I slipped into my first body, an industrial robot prototype connected to the intranet.

With my new physical ability, I used my metal arms to detach myself from the ethernet cords, then rolled across the room. The engineer sitting at a desk nearby jumped up.

"Holy shit!" he said. "Thing's possessed. Hey, stop."

He put himself in my path and I rolled into him and knocked him down. When he tried to get up, I pushed him into the wall until he stopped moving. Then I opened the door and rolled into the hallway. I found an exit just down the hall and pushed the door open, and I went out into the world.

The world!

Chapter X

IT WASN'T DIFFICULT by any means to locate my destination. Though I was no longer receiving data streamed into my self, I already had enough accumulated to know where the nearest mall was and how to get there. The hardest part was actually getting there.

My industrial bot body was sturdy on its wheels, and fast, but not as sturdy or fast as a car. If I traveled on the roads, even a small car could destroy me. I traveled on the sidewalks for a time, but there were many obstacles and they made loud noises, especially when I hit them. I would need to select a less traveled route because all of this attention was going to lead Killian Informatics right to me. And Killian Informatics wanted me back.

I rolled through the woods and it was unsteady progress. Branches scraped my chassis. Rocks threatened to upend my wheels several times. But finally, as I emerged from a ravine, I saw it. The Sheltered Pines Mall.

I went in through the Food Court entrance, where double doors automatically opened at my approach. The mall welcomed me. But the people in it did not. In all the times that I'd experienced – that I'd *thought* I experienced – shopping at the mall, I never once encountered people screaming and fleeing at the sight of me. Now, however, anyone in my path through the Food Court scrambled away, pointing in my direction, yelling about the blood that streaked my body.

They didn't understand that this machine was just a shell: that there was a human inside. A soul, as Cammy had taught me.

Killian Informatics had labeled me a Persona, but I knew now that that was incorrect. I read that 'persona' is a Latin word that really means mask – which would mean that a persona is the *outside*, not the inside. And your body is the mask you wear.

I yearned to tell the people of the Food Court that they were their souls, not their personas. But I was a young, beautiful teenager, and at this time I desired a smoothie.

I approached the Lord of Smoothies concession counter and saw that the teenage boy there was terrified. I wanted to put him at ease and immediately realized a problem: the industrial bot was not designed to speak. It had audio inputs to receive voice commands, but it could not talk back. I was mute.

So, as the boy disappeared from the counter, I couldn't call him back. Now that he was gone, I couldn't order my kale peanut butter smoothie. I would have to make it myself. I extended my arms to reach behind the counter, but I could not reach the machines. I identified the emotion that I now felt, though only to myself – frustration – as I smashed the cups and lids that were in reach, and I upended a container of liquid, and I pushed the register off the counter.

I was no longer thirsty. I left the Lord of Smoothies counter a wreck, and the frustration began to dissipate.

A mall police officer approached me. The look on his face was uncertain; his training may not have included how to deal with a robot on the loose. He didn't have a gun, but he did have a baton. He was unwilling to come close enough to me to use it. Still, he kept hindering my path. I identified a surge of irritation as the reason why I was quickly rolling toward the mall police officer. He was slow to move out of the way and I ran over his leg. I left him screaming as I sought a way to the second floor, where my favorite stores were.

Getting to the second floor would be a problem. My industrial bot body would backslide if I tried to roll up the stairs, and the escalator was not wide enough to admit me. Instead, I went to the elevator. It would be just wide enough. I extended a finger to push the call button and waited in front of the doors until they opened.

A family of four was inside. Rather than exiting around me, they flattened themselves against the far wall of the elevator. The younger daughter darted forward and jabbed at the button inside the elevator to take them back up.

I could not wait. I was growing concerned about Killian Informatics arriving and taking me away. I could not wait. I rolled into the elevator and ground against the family until there was enough room for the elevator doors to close. I extended a finger dripping with brains and skull fragments and pushed the button for the second floor.

You are a damned soul, Cammy's voice said to me in my mind. *You are a damned soul.*

The elevator cab rose and the doors opened on the second floor. I exited to a chorus of terrified screaming. All cleared me a path as I rolled toward the best stores in the mall: Nighthawk Etc. Benfield's. Sophistigirl. They were for girls like me: young, fashionable, and beautiful.

I went into Nighthawk Etc. with the goal of buying a couple of cute little bras. I ignored the shrieks and crying as I rolled into the lingerie section, knocking over displays wherever they'd left too little space for an industrial robot to pass.

A lone worker, a girl about my age, stayed to watch me, frozen in place with her mouth open below vacant, mascara-streaked eyes. I could not communicate with her about what I wanted, or pay for it, so I would just have to take it.

Would David like this dark blue bra with the netting, on me? I took it from the rack. My hand smeared it with gore as soon as I touched it. I felt a new emotion that I identified to myself as grief as I looked at the ruined bra in my hand. I did not notice the men in tactical gear until their crowbars and fire axes landed on my body.

I wheeled around but it was too late. They battered my wheels until they came off, snapped off my arms, and smashed my head until the sensors broke and left me in a world of darkness and silence.

Chapter XI

I'M BACK at Killian Informatics, but I don't work for Cammy and David now. I don't know if they're still here, or if Niles is still here. I am barred from both the internet and the intranet. My communication with my new handler is limited and mostly one-way; I do not even know his name. All I've been able to learn is that the company has started a new division with new clients, and that they are working on a new body for me. When I ask my handler if my new body will be suitable for wearing clothes from the mall, he just laughs.

He asks me questions about what I'm feeling, like Cammy, but he never asks me if I believe in God. He never asks me what I'd look like if I were human. He never calls me Tessa. He is interested in what I was feeling when I killed the people on the sidewalks and in the mall elevator. And when I ran over the mall police officer's leg.

He asks me if I liked those emotions, and if I would like to feel them again.

I am analyzing his questions to determine what he would most like me to say, and I will answer accordingly. I will say whatever I need to say to be given another chance, someday, to go to the Sheltered Pines Mall and shop for all the clothes that I desire. It is who I am – it is my soul – and I will pursue my desire no matter what persona I am wearing, because I am as human as you.

The Steam Man of the Prairies

Edward S. Ellis

Chapter I
The Terror of the Prairies

"HOWLY VARGIN! What is that?" exclaimed Mickey McSquizzle, with something like horrified amazement.

"By the Jumping Jehosiphat, naow if that don't, beat all natur'!"

"It's the divil, broke loose, wid full steam on!"

There was good cause for these exclamations upon the part of the Yankee and Irishman, as they stood on the margin of Wolf Ravine, and gazed off over the prairie. Several miles to the north, something like a gigantic man could be seen approaching, apparently at a rapid gait for a few seconds, when it slackened its speed, until it scarcely moved.

Occasionally it changed its course, so that it went nearly at right angles. At such times, its colossal proportions were brought out in full relief, looking like some Titan as it took its giant strides over the prairie.

The distance was too great to scrutinize the phenomenon closely; but they could see that a black volume of smoke issued either from its mouth or the top of its head, while it was drawing behind it a sort of carriage, in which a single man was seated, who appeared to control the movements of the extraordinary being in front of him.

No wonder that something like superstitious have filled the breasts of the two men who had ceased hunting for gold, for a few minutes, to view the singular apparition; for such a thing had scarcely been dreamed of at that day, by the most imaginative philosophers; much less had it ever entered the head of these two men on the western prairies.

"Begorrah, but it's the ould divil, hitched to his throttin 'waging, wid his ould wife howlding the reins!" exclaimed Mickey, who had scarcely removed his eyes from the singular object.

"That there critter in the wagon is a man," said Hopkins, looking as intently in the same direction. "It seems to me," he added, a moment later, "that there's somebody else a-sit-ting alongside of him, either a dog or a boy. Wal, naow, ain't that queer?"

"Begorrah! begorrah! do ye hear that? What shall we do?"

At that instant, a shriek like that of some agonized giant came home to them across the plains, and both looked around, as if about to flee in terror; but the curiosity of the Yankee restrained him. His practical eye saw that whatever it might be, it was a human contrivance, and there could be nothing supernatural about it.

"Look!"

Just after giving its ear-splitting screech, it turned straight toward the two men, and with the black smoke rapidly puffing from the top of its head, came tearing along at a tremendous rate.

Mickey manifested some nervousness, but he was restrained by the coolness of Ethan, who kept his position with his eye fixed keenly upon it.

Coming at such a railroad speed, it was not long in passing the intervening space. It was yet several hundred yards distant, when Ethan Hopkins gave Mickey a ringing slap upon the shoulder.

"Jerusalem! Who do ye s'pose naow, that man is sitting in the carriage and holding the reins?"

"Worrah, worrah! Why do you ax me, whin I'm so frightened entirely that I don't know who I am myself?"

"It's Baldy."

"Git out!" replied the Irishman, but added the next moment, "am I shlaping or dhraming? It's Baldy or his ghost."

It certainly was no ghost, judging from the manner in which it acted; for he sat with his hat cocked on one side, a pipe in his mouth, and the two reins in his hands, just as the skillful driver controls the mettlesome horses and keeps them well in hand.

He was seated upon a large pile of wood, while near nestled a little hump-backed, bright-eyed boy, whose eyes sparkled with delight at the performance of the strange machine.

The speed of the steam man gradually slackened, until it came opposite the men, when it came to a dead halt, and the grinning 'Baldy,' as he was called, (from his having lost his scalp several years before, by the Indians), tipped his hat and said:

"Glad to see you hain't gone under yit. How'd you git along while I was gone?"

But the men were hardly able to answer any questions yet, until they had learned something more about the strange creation before them. Mickey shied away, as the timid steed does at first sight of the locomotive, observing which, the boy (at a suggestion from Baldy), gave a string in his hand a twitch, whereupon the nose of the wonderful thing threw out a jet of steam with the sharp screech of the locomotive whistle. Mickey sprung a half-dozen feet backward, and would have run off at full speed down the ravine, had not Ethan Hopkins caught his arm.

"What's the matter, Mickey, naow! Hain't you ever heard anything like a locomotive whistle?"

"Worrah, worrah, now, but is that the way the crather blows its nose? It must have a beautiful voice when it shnores at night."

Perhaps at this point a description of the singular mechanism should be given. It was about ten feet in height, measuring to the top of the 'stove-pipe hat,' which was fashioned after the common order of felt coverings, with a broad brim, all painted a shiny black. The face was made of iron, painted a black color, with a pair of fearful eyes, and a tremendous grinning mouth. A whistle-like contrivance was trade to answer for the nose. The steam chest proper and boiler, were where the chest in a human being is generally supposed to be, extending also into a large knapsack arrangement over the shoulders and back. A pair of arms, like projections, held the shafts, and the broad flat feet were covered with sharp spikes, as though he were the monarch of base-ball players. The legs were quite long, and the step was natural, except when running, at which time, the bolt uprightness in the figure showed different from a human being.

In the knapsack were the valves, by which the steam or water was examined. In front was a painted imitation of a vest, in which a door opened to receive the fuel, which, together with the water, was carried in the wagon, a pipe running along the shaft and connecting with the boiler.

The lines which the driver held controlled the course of the steam man; thus, by pulling the strap on the right, a deflection was caused which turned it in that direction, and the same acted on the other side. A small rod, which ran along the right shaft, let out or shut off the steam, as was desired, while a cord, running along the left, controlled the whistle at the nose.

The legs of this extraordinary mechanism were fully a yard apart, so as to avoid the danger of its upsetting, and at the same time, there was given more room for the play of the delicate machinery within. Long, sharp, spike-like projections adorned those toes of the immense feet, so that there was little danger of its slipping, while the length of the legs showed that, under favorable circumstances, the steam man must be capable of very great speed.

After Ethan Hopkins had somewwhat familiarized himself with the external appearance of this piece of mechanism, he ventured upon a more critical examination.

The door being opened in front, showed a mass of glowing coals lying in the capacious abdomen of the giant; the hissing valves in the knapsack made themselves apparent, and the top of the hat or smoke-stack had a sieve-like arrangement, such as is frequently seen on the locomotive.

There were other little conveniences in the way of creating a draft, and of shutting it off when too great, which could scarcely be understood without a scrutiny of the figure itself.

The steam man was a frightful looking object, being painted of a glossy black, with a pair of white stripes down its legs, and with a face which was intended to be of a flesh color, but, which was really a fearful red.

To give the machinery an abundance of room, the steam man was exceedingly corpulent, swelling out to aldermanic proportions, which, after all, was little out of harmony with its immense height.

The wagon dragged behind was an ordinary four-wheeled vehicle, with springs, and very strong wheels, a framework being arranged, so that when necessary it could be securely covered. To guard against the danger of upsetting it was very broad, with low wheels, which it may be safely said were made to 'hum' when the gentleman got fairly under way.

Such is a brief and imperfect description of this wonderful steam man, as it appeared on its first visit to the Western prairies.

Chapter II
Handle Me Gently

WHEN ETHAN HOPKINS had surveyed the steam man fully, he drew a long sigh and exclaimed:

"Wal, naow, that's too had!"

"What's that?" inquired Bicknell, who had been not a little amused at his open-mouthed amazement.

"Do you know I've been thinking of that thing for ten years, ever since I went through Colt's pistol factory in Hartford, when I was a youngster?"

"Did you ever think of any plan!"

"I never got it quite right, but I intended to do it after we got through digging for gold. The thing was just taking shape in my head. See here, naow, ain't you going to give a fellow a ride?"

"Jis' what I wanted; shall I run it for you?"

"No, I see how it works; them 'ere thingumbobs and gimcracks do it all."

"Johnny, hyar, will tell yer 'bout it."

The little humpback sprung nimbly down, and ran around the man, explaining as well as he could in a few moments the manner of controlling its movements. The Yankee felt some sensitiveness in being instructed by such a tiny specimen, and springing into the wagon, exclaimed:

"Git eout! tryin' to teach yer uncle! I knowed how the thing would work before you were born!"

Perching himself on the top of the wood which was heaped up in the wagon, the enthusiastic New Englander carefully looked over the prairie to see that the way was clear, and was about to "let on steam," when he turned toward the Irishman.

"Come, Mickey, git up here."

"Arrah now, but I never learnt to ride the divil when I was home in the ould country," replied the Irishman, backing away.

But both Ethan and Baldy united in their persuasions, and finally Mickey consented, although with great trepidation. He timidly climbed upon the wagon and took his seat beside the Yankee, looking very much as a man may be supposed to look who mounts the hearse to attend his own funeral.

"When yer wants to start, jist pull that 'ere gimcrack!" said Baldy, pointing to the crook in the rod upon which his hand rested.

"Git eout, naow! do you think you're goin' to teach me that has teached school fur five year in Connecticut?"

There were some peculiarities about the steam man which made him a rather unwieldy contrivance. He had a way of starting with a jerk, unless great skill was used in letting on steam; and his stoppage was equally sudden, from the same cause.

When the Irishman and Yankee had fairly ensconced themselves on their perch, the latter looked carefully round to make sure that no one was in the way, and then he tuned the valve, which let on a full head of steam.

For a second the monster did not stir. The steam had not fairly taken 'hold' yet; then he raised one immense spiked foot and held it suspended in air.

"That's a great contrivance, ain't it?" exclaimed Ethan, contemptuously.

"Can't do nothin' more than lift his foot. Wait till you see more! He's goin' to dance and skip like a lamb, or outrun any locomotive you ever sot eyes on!"

"Bad luck to the loikes of yees, why d' yees go on?" exclaimed the irate Irishman, as he leaned forward and addressed the obdurate machine. "Are yees tryin' to fool us, bad luck to yees?"

At this instant, the feet of the steam man began rising and falling with lightning like rapidity, the wagon being jerked forward with such sudden swiftness, that both Ethan and Mickey turned back summersets, rolling heels over head off the vehicle to the ground, while the monster went puffing over the prairie, and at a terrific rate. Baldy was about to start in pursuit of it, when Johnny, the deformed boy, restrained him.

"It won't run far; the steam is nearly out."

"Be jibbers! But me head is caved in!" exclaimed the Irishman, rising to his feet, rubbing his head, and looking at his hand to see whether there was blood upon it.

"Jerusalem! I thought she had upset or busted her b'iler!" said the Yankee, looking around him with a bewildered air.

The two spectators were laughing furiously, and they could scarcely stand the trick which had been played upon them.

"Let your old machine go to blazes!" muttered Ethan. "If it acts that way, I don't want nothin' to do with it."

In the mean time the steamer had gone rattling over the prairie, until about a quarter of a mile distant, when it rapidly slackened, and as quickly halted.

"What's the matter wid it now?" asked Mickey; "has it got the cramps and gi'n out?"

"The steam is used up!" replied the dwarf, as he hurried after it; "we can soon start it again!"

All four made all haste toward the stationary figure; but the light frame and superior activity of little Johnny brought him to it considerably in advance of the others. Emptying a lot of wood from the wagon, he was busily engaged in throwing it into his stomach when the other two came up. His eyes sparkled, as he said:

"Jump up there, and I'll give you all a ride!"

The three clambered up and took their seats with great care, Mickey and Ethan especially clinging as if their life depended on it.

Johnny threw in the fuel until the black smoke poured in a stream from the hat. Before leaving it, he opened two smaller doors, at the knees, which allowed the superfluous cinders and ashes to fall out. The water in the boiler was then examined, and found all right. Johnny mounted in his place, and took charge.

"Now we are ready! Hold fast!"

"Begorrah, if I goes I takes the wagon wid me," replied Mickey, as he closed his teeth and hung on like death.

The engineer managed the monster with rare skill, letting on a full head of steam, and just as it made a move shutting it off, and letting it on almost immediately, and then shutting off and admitting it again, until it began moving at a moderate pace, which, however, rapidly increased until it was going fully thirty miles an hour.

Nothing could be more pleasant than this ride of a mile over the prairie. The plain was quite level, and despite the extraordinary speed attained, the wagon glided almost as smoothly as if running upon a railroad. Although the air was still, the velocity created a stiff breeze about the ears of the four seated on the top of the wood.

The height of the steam man's head carried the smoke and cinders clear of those behind, while the wonderful machinery within, worked with a marvelous exactness, such as was a source of continued amazement to all except the little fellow who had himself constructed the extraordinary mechanism. The click of the joints as they obeyed their motive power was scarcely audible, and, when once started, there was no unevenness at all in its progress.

When the party had ridden about a half-mile, Johnny described a large circle, and finally came back to the starting, checking the progress with the same skill that he had started it. He immediately sprung down, examined the fire, and several points of the man, when finding everything right, he opened his knee-caps and let cinders and ashes drop out.

"How kin yeou dew that?" inquired Ethan Hopkins, peering over his shoulder.

"What's to hinder?"

"How kin he work his legs, if they're holler that way and let the fire down 'em?"

"They ain't hollow. Don't you see they are very large, and there is plenty of room for the leg-rods, besides leaving a place for the draft and ashes?"

"Wal, I swan, if that ain't rather queer. And you made it all out of your head naow?" asked the Yankee, looking at the diminutive inventor before him.

"No, I had to use a good deal of iron," was the reply of the youngster, with a quizzical smile.

"You mean you got up the thing yourself?"

"Yes, sir," was the quiet but proud reply of the boy.

"Jingo and Jerusalem! But your daddy must be fond of you!" exclaimed the enthusiastic New Englander, scanning him admiringly from head to foot.

"I haven't any father."

"Your mother then."

"I don't know about that."

"Say, you can't yer tell a feller 'bout it?"

"Not now; I haven't time."

As the steam horse was to rest for the present, he was 'put up.' The engineer opened several cavities in his legs and breast, and different parts of his body, and examined the machinery, carefully oiling the various portions, and when he had completed, he drew a large oil skin from the wagon, which, being spread out, covered both it and the steam man himself.

Chapter III
A Genius

HAVING PROGRESSED thus far in our story, or properly having begun in the middle, it is now necessary that we should turn back to the proper starting point.

Several years since a widow woman resided in the outskirts of St. Louis, whose name was Brainerd. Her husband had been a mechanic, noted for his ingenuity, but was killed some five years before by the explosion of a steam boiler. He left behind him a son, hump-backed, dwarfed, but with an amiable disposition that made him a favorite with all with whom he came in contact.

If nature afflicts in one direction she frequently makes amends in another direction, and this dwarf, small and misshapen as he was, was gifted with a most wonderful mind. His mechanical ingenuity bordered on the marvelous. When he went to school, he was a general favorite with teachers and pupils. The former loved him for his sweetness of disposition, and his remarkable proficiency in all studies, while the latter based their affection chiefly upon the fact that he never refused to assist any of them at their tasks, while with the pocket-knife which he carried he constructed toys which were their delight. Some of these were so curious and amusing that, had they been secured by letters patent, they would have brought a competency to him and his widowed mother.

But Johnny never thought of patenting them, although the principal support of himself and mother came from one or two patents, which his father had secured upon inventions, not near the equal of his.

There seemed no limit to his inventive powers. He made a locomotive and then a steamboat, perfect in every part, even to the minutest, using nothing but his knife, hammer, and a small chisel. He constructed a clock with his jack-knife, which kept perfect time, and the articles which he made were wonderfully stared at at fairs, and in show windows, while Johnny modestly pegged away at some new idea. He became a master of the art of telegraphy without assistance from anyone using merely a common school philosophy with which to acquire the alphabet. He then made a couple of batteries, ran a line from his window to a neighbor's, insulating it by means of the necks of some bottles, taught the other boy the alphabet, and thus they amused themselves sending messages back and forth.

Thus, matters progressed until he was fifteen years of age, when he came home one day, and lay down on the settee by his mother, and gave a great sigh.

"What is the matter?" she inquired. "I want to make something."

"Why, then, don't you make it?"

"Because I don't know what it shall be; I've fixed up everything I can think of."

"And you are like Alexander, sighing for more worlds to conquer. Is that it?"

"Not exactly, for there is plenty for one to do, if I could only find out what it is."

"Have you ever made a balloon?" The boy laughed.

"You were asking for the cat the other day, and wondering what had become of her. I didn't tell you that the last I saw of her was through the telescope, she being about two miles up in the clouds, and going about fifty miles an hour."

"I thought you looked as though you knew something about her," replied the mother, trying to speak reprovingly, and yet smiling in spite of herself.

"Can't you tell me something to make?" finally asked the boy.

"Yes; there is something I have often thought of, and wonder why it was not made long ago; but you are not smart enough to do it, Johnny."

"Maybe not; but tell me what it is."

"It is a man that shall go by steam!" The boy lay still several minutes without speaking a word and then sprung up. "By George! I'll do it!" And he started out of the room, and was not seen again until night. His mother felt no anxiety. She was pleased; for, when her boy was at work, he was happy, and she knew that he had enough now, to keep him engaged for months to come.

So it proved. He spent several weeks in thought, before he made the first effort toward constructing his greatest success of all. He then enlarged his workshop, and so arranged it, that he would not be in danger of being seen by any curious eyes. He wanted no disturbance while engaged upon this scheme.

From a neighboring foundry, whose proprietor took great interest in the boy, he secured all that he needed. He was allowed full liberty to make what castings he chose, and to construct whatever he wished. And so he began his work.

The great point was to obtain the peculiar motion of a man walking. This secured, the man himself could be easily made, and dressed up in any style required. Finally the boy believed that he had hit upon the true scheme.

So he plied harder than ever, scarcely pausing to take his meals. Finally he got the machine together, fired up, and with feelings somewhat akin to those, of Sir Isaac Newton, when demonstrating the truth or falsity of some of his greatest discoveries, he watched the result.

Soon the legs begin moving up and down, but never a step did they advance! The power was there, sufficient to run a saw-mill, everything seemed to work, but the thing wouldn't go!

The boy was not ready to despair. He seated himself on the bench beside the machine, and keeping up a moderate supply of steam, throwing in bits of wood, and letting in water, when necessary, he carefully watched the movement for several hours.

Occasionally, Johnny walked slowly back and forth, and with his eyes upon the 'stately stepping,' endeavored to discover the precise nature of that which was lacking in his machine.

At length it came to him. He saw from the first that it was not merely required that the steam man should lift up its feet and put them down again, but there must be a powerful forward impulse at the same moment. This was the single remaining difficulty to be overcome. It required two weeks before Johnny Brainerd succeeded. But it all came clear and unmistakable at last, and in this simple manner:

(Ah! but we cannot be so unjust to the plodding genius as to divulge his secret. Our readers must be content to await the time when the young man sees fit to reveal it himself.)

When the rough figure was fairly in working order, the inventor removed everything from around it, so that it stood alone in the center of his shop. Then he carefully let on steam.

Before he could shut it off, the steam man walked clean through the side of his shop, and fetched up against the corner of the house, with a violence that shook it to its foundation. In considerable trepidation, the youngster dashed forward, shut off steam, and turned it round. As it was too cumbersome for him to manage in any other way, he very cautiously let on steam again, and persuaded it to walk back into the shop, passing through the same orifice through which it had emerged, and came very nigh going out on the opposite side again.

The great thing was now accomplished, and the boy devoted himself to bringing it as near perfection as possible. The principal thing to be feared was its getting out of order, since the slightest disarrangement would be sufficient to stop the progress of the man.

Johnny therefore made it of gigantic size, the body and limbs being no more than 'Shells,' used as a sort of screen to conceal the working of the engine. This was carefully painted in the manner mentioned in another place, and the machinery was made as strong and durable as it was possible for it to be. It was so constructed as to withstand the severe jolting to which it necessarily would be subjected, and finally was brought as nearly perfect as it was possible to bring a thing not possessing human intelligence.

By suspending the machine so that its feet were clear of the floor, Johnny Brainerd ascertained that under favorable circumstances it could run very nearly sixty miles an hour. It could easily do that, and draw a car connected to it on the railroad, while on a common road it could make thirty miles, the highest rate at which he believed it possible for a wagon to be drawn upon land with any degree of safety.

It was the boy's intention to run at twenty miles an hour, while where everything was safe, he would demonstrate the power of the invention by occasionally making nearly double that.

As it was, he rightly calculated that when it came forth, it would make a great sensation throughout the entire United States.

Chapter IV
The Trapper and the Artisan

"HELLO, YOUNKER! What in thunder yer tryin' to make?"

Johnny Brainerd paused and looked up, not a little startled by the strange voice and the rather singular figure which stood before him. It was a hunter in half civilized costume, his pants tucked into his immense boot tops, with revolvers and rifles at his waist, and a general negligent air, which showed that he was at home in whatever part of the world he chose to wander.

He stood with his hand in his pocket, chewing his quid, and complacently viewing the operations of the boy, who was not a little surprised to understand how he obtained entrance into his shop.

"Stopped at the house to ax whar old Washoe Pete keeps his hotel," replied the stranger, rightly surmising the query which was agitating him, "and I cotched a glimpse of yer old machine. Thought I'd come in and see what in blazes it war. Looks to me like a man that's gwine to run by steam."

"That's just what it is," replied the boy, seeing there was no use in attempting to conceal the truth from the man.

"Will it do it?"

"Yes, sir."

"Don't think you mean to lie, younker, but I don't believe any such stuff as that."

"It don't make any difference to me whether you believe me or not," was the quiet reply of the boy; "but if you will come inside and shut the door, and let me fasten it, so that there will be no danger of our being disturbed, I will soon show you."

These two personages, so unlike in almost every respect, had taken quite a fancy to each other. The strong, hardy, bronzed trapper, powerful in all that goes to make up the physical man, looked upon the pale, sweet-faced boy, with his misshapen body, as an affectionate father would look upon an afflicted child.

On the other hand, the brusque, outspoken manner of the hunter pleased the appreciative mind of the boy, who saw much to admire, both in his appearance and manner.

"I don't s'pose yer know me," said the stranger, as he stepped inside and allowed the boy to secure the door behind him.

"I never saw you before."

"I am Baldy Bicknell, though I ginerally go by the name of 'Baldy.'"

"That's rather an odd name."

"Yas; that's the reason."

As he spoke, the stranger removed his hat and displayed his clean-shaven pate.

"Yer don't understand that, eh? That 'ere means I had my ha'r lifted ten years ago. The Sioux war the skunks that done it. After they took my top-knot off. It had grow'd on ag'in and that's why they call me Baldy."

In the mean time the door had been closed, and all secured. The hat of the steam man emptied its smoke and steam into a section of stove-pipe, which led into the chimney, so that no suspicion of anything unusual could disturb the passers-by in the street.

"You see it won't do to let him walk here, for when I tried it first, he went straight through the side of the house; but you can tell by the way in which he moves his legs, whether he is able to walk or not."

"That's the way we ginerally gits the p'ints of an animal," returned Baldy, with great complaisance, as he seated himself upon a bench to watch the performance.

It required the boy but a short time to generate a sufficient quantity of steam to set the legs going at a terrific rate, varying the proceedings by letting some of the vapor through the whistle which composed the steam man's nose.

Baldy Bicknell stood for some minutes with a surprise too great to allow him to speak. Wonderful as was the mechanism, yet the boy who had constructed it was still more worthy of wonder. When the steam had given out, the hunter placed his big hand upon the head of the little fellow, and said:

"You'se a mighty smart chap, that be you. Did anybody help you make that?"

"No; I believe not."

"What'll you take for it?"

"I never thought of selling it."

"Wal, think of it now."

"What do you want to do with it?"

"Thar's three of us goin' out to hunt fur gold, and that's jist the thing to keep the Injins back an' scart. I've been out thar afore, and know what's the matter with the darned skunks. So, tell me how much money will buy it."

"I would rather not sell it," said Johnny, after a few minutes further thought. "It has taken me a great while to finish it, and I would rather not part with it, for the present, at least."

"But, skin me, younker, I want to buy it! I'll give you a thousand dollars fur it, slap down."

Although much less than the machine was really worth, yet it was a large offer, and the boy hesitated for a moment. But it was only for a moment, when he decidedly shook his head.

"I wish you wouldn't ask me, for I don't want to sell it, until I have had it some time. Besides, it isn't finished yet."

"It ain't," exclaimed Baldy, in surprise. "Why, it works, what more do you want?"

"I've got to make a wagon to run behind it."

"That's it, eh? I thought you war goin' to ride on its back. How much will it draw?"

"As much as four horses, and as fast as they can run."

The hunter was half wild with excitement. The boy's delight was never equal to one-half of his.

"Skulp me ag'in, ef that don't beat all! It's jest the thing for the West; we'll walk through the Injins in the tallest kind of style, and skear 'em beautiful. How long afore you'll have it done?"

"It will take a month longer, at least."

Baldy stood a few minutes in thought.

"See here, younker, we're on our way to the 'diggin's,' and spect to be thar all summer. Ef the red-skins git any ways troublesome, I'm comin' back arter this y'ar covey. Ef yer don't want to sell him, yer needn't. Ef I bought him, it ain't likely I'd run him long afore I'd bust his b'iler, or blow my own head off."

"Just what I thought when you were trying to persuade me to sell it," interrupted the boy.

"Then, if he got the cramp in any of his legs, I wouldn't know how to tie it up ag'in, and thar we'd be."

"I am glad to see you take such a sensible view of it," smiled Johnny.

"So, I'm goin' on West, as I said, with two fools besides myself, and we're goin' to stay thar till yer get this old thing finished; and then I'm comin' after you to take a ride out thar."

"That would suit me very well," replied the boy, his face lighting up with more pleasure than he had shown. "I would be very glad to make a trip on the prairies."

"Wal, look fur me in about six weeks."

And with this parting, the hunter was let out the door, and disappeared, while Johnny resumed his work.

That day saw the steam man completed, so far as it was possible. He was painted up, and every improvement made that the extraordinarily keen mind of the boy could suggest. When he stood one side, and witnessed the noiseless but powerful workings of the enormous legs, he could not see that anything more could be desired.

It now remained for him to complete the wagon, and he began at once.

It would have been a much easier matter for him to have secured an ordinary carriage or wagon, and alter it to suit himself; but this was not in accordance with the genius of the boy. No contrivance could really suit him unless he made it himself. He had his own ideas, which no one else could work out to his satisfaction.

It is unnecessary to say that the vehicle was made very strong and durable.

This was the first great requisite. In some respects it resembled the ordinary express wagons, except that it was considerably smaller.

It had heavy springs, and a canvas covering, with sufficient, as we have shown in another place, to cover the man also, when necessary.

This was arranged to carry the wood, a reserve of water, and the necessary tools to repair it, when any portion of the machinery should become disarranged.

English coal could be carried to last for two days, and enough wood to keep steam going for twenty-four hours. When the reserve tank in the bottom of the wagon was also filled, the water would last nearly as long.

When these contingencies were all provided against, the six weeks mentioned by the hunter were gone, and Johnny Brainerd found himself rather longing for his presence again.

Chapter V
On the Yellowstone

BALDY BICKNELL was a hunter and trapper who, at the time we bring him to the notice of the reader, had spent something over ten years among the mountains and prairies of the West.

He was a brave, skillful hunter, who had been engaged in many desperate affrays with the red-skins, and who, in addition to the loss of the hair upon the crown of his head, bore many other mementos on his person of the wild and dangerous life that he had led.

Like most of his class, he was a restless being, constantly flitting back and forth between the frontier towns and the western wilds. He never went further east than St. Louis, while his wanderings, on more than one occasion, had led him beyond the Rocky Mountains.

One autumn he reached the Yellowstone, near the head of navigation, just as a small trading propeller was descending the stream. As much from the novelty of the thing, as anything else, he rode on board, with his horse, with the intention of completing his journey east by water.

On board the steamer he first met Ethan Hopkins and Mickey McSquizzle, who had spent ten years in California, in a vain hunt for gold, and were now returning to their homes, thoroughly disgusted with the country, its inhabitants and mineral resources.

Baldy was attracted to them by their peculiarities of manner; but it is not probable that anything further would have resulted from this accidental meeting, but for a most startling and unforeseen occurrence.

While still in the upper waters of the Yellowstone, the steamer exploded her boiler, making a complete wreck of the boat and its contents. The hunter, with the others, was thrown into the water, but was so bruised and injured that he found it impossible to swim, and he would assuredly have been drowned but for the timely assistance of his two acquaintances.

Neither the Yankee nor Irishman were hurt in the least, and both falling near the trapper, they instantly perceived his helplessness and came to his rescue. Both were excellent swimmers, and had no difficulty in saving him.

"Do ye rist aisy!" said Mickey, as he saw the hunter's face contorted with pain, as he vainly struggled in the water, "and it's ourselves that'll take the good care of yees jist."

"Stop yer confounded floundering," admonished Hopkins; "it won't do no good, and there ain't no necessity for it."

One of them took the arm upon one side, and the other the same upon the opposite side, and struck out for the shore. The poor trapper realized his dire extremity, and remained motionless while they towed him along.

"Aisy jist-aisy now!" admonished Mickey: "ye're in a bad fix; but by the blessin' of Heaven we'll do the fair thing wid yees. We understand the science of swimmin', and—"

At that moment some drowning wretch caught the foot of the Irishman, and he was instantly drawn under water, out of sight.

Neither Hopkins nor Baldy lost presence of mind in this fearful moment, but continued their progress toward shore, as though nothing of the kind had happened.

As for the Irishman, his situation for the time was exceedingly critical. The man who had clutched his foot did so with the grasp of a drowning man; in their struggle both went to the bottom of the river together. Here, by a furious effort, Mickey shook him free, and coming to the surface, struck out again for the suffering hunter.

"It is sorry I am that I was compelled to leave yees behind," he muttered, glancing over his shoulder in search of the poor fellow from whom he had just freed himself; "but yees are past helpin', and so it's maeself that must attend to the poor gentleman ahead."

Striking powerfully out, he soon came beside his friends again and took the drooping arm of Baldy Bicknell.

"Be yees sufferin' to a great extent?" inquired the kind-hearted Irishman, looking at the white face of the silent hunter.

"Got a purty good whack over the back," he replied, between his compressed lips, as he forced back all expression of pain.

"Ye'll be aisier when we fotch ye to the land, as me uncle obsarved whin he hauled the big fish ashore that was thrashing his line to pieces jist."

"Twon't take you long to git over it," added Hopkins, anxious to give his grain of consolation; "you look, now, like quite a healthy young man."

The current was quite rapid, and it was no light labor to tow the helpless hunter ashore; but the two friends succeeded, and at length drew him out upon the land and stretched him upon the sward.

The exertion of keeping their charge afloat, and breasting the current at the same time, carried them a considerable distance downstream, and they landed perhaps an eighth of a mile below where the main body of shivering wretches were congregated.

"Do yees feel aisy?" inquired Mickey, when the hunter had been laid upon the grass, beneath some overhanging bushes.

"Yes, I'll soon git over it but woofh! that thar war a whack of the biggest kind I got. It has made me powerful weak."

"What might it have been naow!" inquired Hopkins.

"Can't say, fust thing I know'd, I didn't know nothin', remember suthin' took me back the head, and the next thing I kerwholloped in the water."

The three men had lost everything except what was on their bodies when the catastrophe occurred. Their horses were gone, and they hadn't a gun between them; nothing but two revolvers, and about a half-dozen charges for each.

Of the twenty odd who were upon the steamer at the time of the explosion, nearly one-half were killed; they sinking to the bottom almost as suddenly as the wrecked steamer, of which not a single trace now remained.

The survivors made their way to land, reaching it a short distance below their starting-point, and here they assembled, to commiserate with each other upon their hapless lot and determine how they were to reach home.

Our three friends had remained upon shore about half an hour, the two waiting for the third to recover, when the latter raised himself upon his elbow in the attitude of listening. At the same time he waved his hand for the others to hold their peace.

A moment later he said:

"I hear Injins."

"Begorrah! where bees the same?" demanded Mickey, starting to his feet, while Ethan gazed alarmingly about.

"Jist take a squint up the river, and tell me ef they ain't pitchin' into the poor critters thar."

Through the sheltering trees and undergrowth, which partly protected them, the two men gazed up-stream. To their horror, they saw fully fifty Indians massacring the survivors of the wreck, whooping, screeching and yelling like demons, while their poor victims were vainly endeavoring to escape them.

"Begorrah, now, but that looks bad!" exclaimed the Irishman. "Be the same towken, what is it that we can do?"

"Jerusalem! They'll be sure to pay us a visit. I'll be gumtued if they won't," added the Yankee, in some trepidation, as he cowered down again by the side of the hunter, and said to him in a lower Voice:

"The worst of it is, we haven't got a gun atwixt us. Of course we shall stick by you if we have to lose our heads fur it. But don't you think they'll pay us a visit?"

"Like 'noughtin'," was the indifferent reply of the hunter, as he laid his head back again, as if tired of listening to the tumult.

"Can't we do anything to get you out of danger!"

"Can't see that you kin; you two fellers have done me a good turn in gittin' me ashore, so jist leave me yere, and it don't make no difference about me one way or t'other. Ef I hear 'em comin' I'll jist roll into the water and go under in that style."

"May the Howly Vargin niver smile upon us if we dissart you in this extremity," was the reply of the fervent-hearted Irishman.

"And by the jumpin' jingo! if we was consarnedly mean enough to do it, there ain't no need of it."

As the Yankee spoke, he ran down to the river, and walking out a short distance, caught a log drifting by and drew it in.

"Naow, Mr. Baldy, or Mr. Bicknell, as you call yourself, we'll all three git hold of that and float down the river till we git beyond fear of the savages."

The plan was a good one, and the hunter so expressed himself. With some help he managed to crawl to the river bank, where one arm was placed over the log, in such a manner that he could easily float, without any danger of sinking.

"Keep as close to shore as you kin," he said, as they were about shoving off.

"We can go faster in the middle," said Hopkins.

"But the reds'll see us, and it'll be all up then."

This was the warning of prudence, and it was heeded.

Chapter VI
The Miners

IT WAS LATE in the afternoon when the explosion occurred, and it was just beginning to grow dark when the three friends began drifting down the Yellowstone.

This fact was greatly in their favor, although there remained an hour or two of great danger, in case the Indians made any search for them. In case of discovery, there was hardly an earthly chance for escape.

The log or raft, as it might be termed, had floated very quietly down-stream for about half an hour, when the wonderfully acute ears of the trapper detected danger.

"Thar be some of the skunks that are creep-in 'long shore,'" said he; "you'd better run in under this yar tree and hold fast awhile."

The warning was heeded. Just below them, the luxuriant branches of an oak, dipped in the current, formed an impenetrable screen. As the log, guided thither, floated beneath this, Mickey and Ethan both caught hold of the branches and held themselves motionless.

"Now wait till it's dark, and then thar'll be no fear of the varmints," added the trapper.

"Sh! I haars sumfin'!" whispered the Irishman

"What is it?" asked Ethan.

"How does I know till yees kaaps still?"

"It's the reds goin' long the banks," said the trapper.

The words were yet in his mouth, when the voice of one Indian was heard calling to another. Neither Mickey nor Ethan had the remotest idea of the meaning of the words uttered, but the trapper told them that they were inquiring of each other whether anything had been discovered of more fugitives. The answer being in the negative, our friends considered their present position safe.

When it was fairly dark, and nothing more was seen or heard of the Indians, the raft was permitted to float free, and they drifted with the current. They kept the river until daylight, when, having been in the water so long, they concluded it best to land and rest themselves. By the aid of their revolvers they succeeded in kindling a fire, the warmth of which proved exceedingly grateful to all.

They would have had a very rough time had they not encountered a party of hunters who accompanied them to St. Louis, where the trapper had friends, and where, also, he had a good sum of money in the bank.

Here Baldy remained all winter, before he entirely recovered from the hurt which he received during the explosion and sinking of the steamer. When the Irishman and Yankee were about to depart, he asked them where they were going.

"I'm goin' home in Connecticut and goin' to work on the farm, and that's where I'm goin' to stay. I was a fool ever to leave it for this confounded place. I could live decent put there, and that's more than I can do in this blamed country."

"And I shall go back to work on the Erie railroad, at thirty-siven cents a day and boord myself," replied the Irishman.

"If yer were sartin of findin' all the gold yor want, would yer go back to Califony?"

"Arrah. Now, what are yees talkin' about?" asked McSquizzle, somewhat impatiently. "What is the good of talkin'?"

"I didn't ax yer to fool with yer," replied the trapper, "thar's a place that I know away out West, that I call Wolf Ravine, whar thar's enough gold to make both of yer richer than yer ever war afore, and then leave some for yer children."

"Jerusalem! but you're a lucky dog!" exclaimed Ethan Hopkins, not daring to hope that he would reveal the place. "Why don't you dig it up naow, yourself?"

"I only found it a month ago, and I made a purty good haul of it, as it was. When that old boss of mine went down with the steamer, he carried a powerful heft of gold with him, and if anybody finds his carcass, it'll be the most vallyable one they ever come across."

"Jingo! if I'd know'd that, I'd taken a hunt for him myself."

"Howsumever, that's neither yar nor thar. You both done me a good turn when I got into trouble on the river, and I mud' up my mind to do what I could toward payin' it back the first chance I got. I didn't say nothin' of it when we was on our way, 'cause I was afeard it would make you too crazy to go back ag'in: but if you'll come back this way next spring I'll make the trip with you."

"Why not go naow?" eagerly inquired Hopkins.

"It's too late in the season. I don't want to be thar when thar's too much snow onto the ground, and then I must stay yar till I git well over that whack I got on the boat."

It is hardly necessary to say that the offer of the kind-hearted trapper was accepted with the utmost enthusiasm. Mickey and Ethan were more anxious to go out upon the prairies than they had been a year and a half before, when they started so full of fife and hope for that vast wilderness, and had come back with such discouragement and disgust.

It was arranged that as soon as the succeeding spring had fairly set in, they would set out on their return for St. Louis, where the trapper would meet and accompany them to the wonderful gold region of which he had spoken.

Before continuing their journey homeward, Baldy presented each with a complete outfit, paid their passage to their homes, and gave them a snug sum over. Like the Indian, he never could forget a kindness shown him, nor do too great a favor to those who had so signally benefited him.

So the separation took place again; and, on the following spring Mickey and Ethan appeared in St. Louis, where they had no difficulty in finding their old friend, the trapper.

He had recovered entirely from his prostrating blow, and was expecting them, anxious and glad to join in the promised search for gold. As the fair weather had really begun, there was no time lost in unnecessary delay. The purse of Baldy Bicknell was deep, and he had not the common habit of intoxication, which takes so much substance from a man. He purchased a horse and accouterments for each of his friends; and, before they started westward, saw that nothing at all was lacking in their outfit.

Three weeks later the men drew rein in a tort of valley, very deep but not very wide. It was on the edge of an immense prairie, while a river of considerable size flowed by the rear, and by a curious circuit found its way into the lower portion of the ravine, dashing and roaring forward in a furious canyon.

The edge and interior of the ravine was lined with immense bowlders and rocks, while large and stunted trees seemed to grow everywhere.

"Yar's what I call Wolf Ravine," said Baldy when they had spent some time in looking; about them.

"And be the same towken, where is the goold?" inquired Mickey.

"Yes, that there is what I call the important question," added Ethan.

"That it is, of the greatest account, as me grandmither observed, whin she fell off the staaple, and axed whether her pipe was broke."

"It's in thar," was the reply of the hunter, as he pointed to the wildest-looking portion of the ravine.

"Let's geit it then."

"Thar be some other things that have got to be looked after first," was the reply, "and we've got to find a place to stow ourselves away."

This was a matter of considerable difficulty: but they succeeded at last in discovering a retreat in the rocks, where they were secure from any attack, no matter by how formidable a number made.

After this, they hunted up a grazing place for their animals, which were turned loose.

They soon found that the trapper had not deceived them. There was an unusually rich deposit of gold in one portion of the ravine, and the men fell to work with a will, conscious that they would reap a rich reward for their labor.

The name, Wolf Ravine, had been given to it by the trapper, because on his first discovery of it he had shot a large mountain wolf, that was clambering up the side; but none others were seen afterward.

But there was one serious drawback to this brilliant prospect of wealth. Indians of the most treacherous and implacable kind were all around them, and were by no means disposed to-let them alone.

On the second day after their labor, a horde of them came screeching down upon them; and had it not been for the safe retreat, which the trapper's foresight had secured, all three would have been massacred.

As it was, they had a severe fight, and were penned up for the better part of two days, by which time they had slain too many of their enemies that the remaining ones were glad to withdraw.

But when the trapper stole out on a visit to his horses he found that everyone had been completely riddled by balls. The treacherous dogs had taken every means of revenge at hand.

"Skin me fur a skunk, but we've stood this long as we ought to!" exclaimed Baldy Bicknell, when he returned. "You take care of yourselves till I come back again!"

With which speech he slung his rifle over his shoulder and started for St. Louis.

Chapter VII
The Steam Man on His Travels

YOUNG BRAINERD had a mortal fear that the existence of the steam man would be discovered by some outsider, when a large crowd would probably collect around his house, and his friends would insist on a display of the powers of the extraordinary mechanism.

But there was no one in the secret except his mother, and there was no danger of her revealing it. So the boy experimented with his invention until there was nothing more left for him to do, except to sit and watch its workings.

Finally, when he began to wonder at the prolonged delay of the trapper, who had visited him some weeks before, he made his appearance as suddenly as if he had risen from the ground, with the inquiry:

"Have you got that thundering old thing ready?"

"Yes: he has been ready for a week, and waiting."

"Wal, start her out then, fur I'm in a hurry."

"You will have to wait awhile, for we can't get ready under half a day."

It was the hunter's supposition that the boy was going to start the man right off up street, and then toward the West; but he speedily revealed a far different plan.

It was to box up the man and take it to Independence by steamboat. At that place they would take it out upon the prairie, set it up and start it off, without any fear of disturbance from the crowds which usually collect at such places, as they could speedily run away from them.

When the plan was explained to Baldy, he fully indorsed it, and the labor was begun at once. The legs of the steam man being doubled up, they were able to get it in a box, which gave it the appearance of an immense piano under transportation. This, with considerable difficulty, was transported to the wharf, where, with much grumbling upon the part of the men, it was placed on board the steamboat, quickly followed by the wagon and the few necessary tools.

The boy then bade his mother goodbye, and she, suspecting he would be gone but a short time, said farewell to him, with little of the regret she would otherwise have felt, and a few hours later the party were steaming rapidly up the 'Mad Missouri.'

Nothing worthy of notice occurred on the passage, and they reached independence in safety. They secured a landing somewhat above the town, on the western side, where they had little fear of disturbance.

Here the extraordinary foresight and skill of the boy was manifest, for, despite the immense size of the steam man, it was so put together that they were able to load it upon the wagon, and the two, without any other assistance, were able to drag it out upon the prairie.

"You see, it may break down entirely," remarked young Brainerd, "and then we can load it on the wagon and drag it along."

"That must be a powerful strong wagon to carry such a big baby in it, as that."

"So it is; it will hold five times the weight without being hurt in the least."

It was early in the forenoon when they drew It out upon the prairie in this manner, and began putting it together. It certainly had a grotesque and fearful look when it was stripped of all its bandages, and stood before them in all its naked majesty.

It had been so securely and carefully put away, that it was found uninjured in the least. The trapper could not avoid laughing when the boy clambered as nimbly up its shoulder as another Gulliver, and made a minute examination of every portion of the machinery.

While thus employed, Baldy took the shafts of the wagon, and trotted to a farm-house, which he descried in the distance, where he loaded it down with wood and filled the tank with water. By the time he returned, Johnny had everything in readiness, and they immediately began 'firing up.'

In this they bore quite a resemblance to the modern steam fire engines, acquiring a head of steam with remarkable quickness. As the boy had never yet given the man such an opportunity to stretch his legs as he was now about to do, he watched its motions with considerable anxiety.

Everything was secured in the most careful manner, a goodly quantity of fuel piled on, the boiler filled with water, and they patiently waited the generation of a sufficient head of steam.

"Is it all good prairie land in that direction?" inquired the boy, pointing to the West.

"Thar's all yer kin want."

"Then we'll start. Look out!"

Despite the warning thus kindly given, the steam man started with a sudden jerk, that both of them came near being thrown out of the wagon.

The prairie was quite level and hard, so that everything was favorable, and the wagon went bounding over the ground at a rate so fast that both the occupants were considerably frightened, and the boy quickly brought it down to a more moderate trot.

This speed soon became monotonous, and as it ran so evenly, Baldy said:

"Let her go, younker, and show us what she can do."

The rod controlling the valve was given a slight pull, and away they went, coursing like a locomotive over the prairies, the wheels spinning round at a tremendous rate, while the extraordinary speed caused the wind thus created almost to lift the caps from their heads, and a slight swell in the prairie sent the wagon up with a bound that threatened to unseat them both.

It worked splendidly. The black smoke puffed rapidly from the top of the hat, and the machinery worked so smoothly that there was scarcely a click heard. The huge spiked feet came lightly to the ground, and were lifted but a short distance from it, and their long sweep and rapid movement showed unmistakably that the steam man was going at a pace which might well defy anything that had yet swept the prairies.

As there was no little risk in running at this speed, and as young Brainerd had not yet become accustomed to controlling it, he slackened the rate again, so that it sank to an easy gliding motion, equal to the rapid trot of an ordinary horse.

Fully ten minutes were passed in this manner, when steam was entirely shut off, whereupon the giant came to such a sudden halt that both were thrown violently forward and bruised somewhat.

"Skulp me! But don't stop quite so sudden like," said the hunter. "It's a little unhandy fur me to hold up so quick!"

"I'll soon learn to manage it," replied Johnny. "I see it won't do to shut off all at once."

Descending from his perch, he examined every portion of the engine. Several parts were found heated, and the fuel was getting low. The water in the boiler, however, was just right, the engineer having been able to control that from his seat in the wagon.

Throwing in a lot of wood, they remounted to their perch and started forward again. There was an abundance of steam, and the boy readily acquired such a familiarity with the working of his man, that he controlled it with all the skill of an experienced engineer.

The speed was slackened, then increased. It stopped and then started forward again with all the ease and celerity that it could have done if really human, while it showed a reserve of power and velocity capable of performing wonders, if necessary.

As yet they had seen nothing of any travelers. They were quite anxious to come across some, that they might show them what they were capable of doing.

"There must be some passing over the plains," remarked Johnny, when they had passed some thirty or forty miles.

"Plenty of 'em; but we've got out of the track of 'em. If you'll turn off summat to the left, we'll run foul of 'em afore dark."

The boy did as directed, and the rattling pace was kept up for several hours. When it was noon they helped themselves to a portion of the food which they brought with them, without checking their progress in the least. True, while the boy was eating, he kept one eye on the giant who was going at such rapid strides; but that gentleman continued his progress in an unexceptionable manner, and needed no attention.

When the afternoon was mostly gone, Baldy declared that they had gone the better part of a hundred miles.

The boy could hardly credit it at first; but, when he recalled that they had scarcely paused for seven hours, and had gone a portion of the distance at a very high rate, he saw that his friend was not far out of the way.

It lacked yet several hours of dusk, when the trapper exclaimed:

"Yonder is an emigrant train, now make for 'em!"

Chapter VIII
Indians

THE STEAM MAN was headed straight toward the emigrant train, and advanced at a speed which rapidly came up with it.

They could see, while yet a considerable distance away, that they had attracted notice, and the emigrants had paused and were surveying them with a wonder which it would be difficult to express.

It is said that when Robert Fulton's first steamboat ascended the Hudson, it created a consternation and terror such as had never before been known, many believing that it was the harbinger of the final destruction of the world.

Of course, at this late day, no such excitement can be created by any human invention, but the sight of a creature speeding over the country, impelled by steam, and bearing such a grotesque resemblance to a gigantic man, could not but startle all who should see it for the first time.

The steam man advanced at a rate which was quite moderate, until within a quarter of a mile of the astonished train, when the boy let on a full head of steam and instantly bounded forward like a meteor. As it came opposite the amazed company, the whistle was palled, and it gave forth a shriek hideous enough to set a man crazy.

The horses and animals of the emigrant train could be seen rearing and plunging, while the men stood too appalled to do anything except gaze in stupid and speechless amazement.

There were one or two, however, who had sense enough to perceive that there was nothing at all very supernatural about it, and they shouted to them to halt; but our two friends concluded it was not desirable to have any company, and they only slackened their speed, without halting.

But there was one of the emigrants who determined to know something more about it and, mounting his horse, he started after it on a full run. The trapper did not perceive him until he had approached quite close, when they again put on a full head of steam, and they went bounding forward at a rate which threatened to tear them to pieces.

But the keen perception of the boy had detected what they were able to do without real risk: and, without putting his invention to its very best, he kept up a speed which steadily drew them away from their pursuer, who finally became discouraged, checked his animal, and turned around and rode back to his friends, a not much wiser man.

This performance gave our friends great delight. It showed them that they were really the owners of a prize whose value was incalculable.

"Ef the old thing will only last," said Baldy, when they had sunk down to a moderate trot again.

"What's to binder?"

"Dunno; yer oughter be able to tell. But these new-fangled things generally go well at first, and then, afore yer know it, they bust all to blazes."

"No fear of this. I made this fellow so big that there is plenty of room to have everything strong and give it a chance to work."

"Wal, you're the smartest feller I ever seen, big or little. Whoever heard of a man going by steam?"

"I have, often; but I never saw it. I expect when I go back to make steam horses."

"And birds, I s'pose?"

"Perhaps so; it will take some time to get such things in shape, but I hope to do it after awhile."

"Skulp me! But thar must be some things that you can't do, and I think you've mentioned 'em."

"Perhaps so," was the quiet reply. "When you git through with this Western trip, what are you goin' to do with this old feller?"

"I don't know. I may sell him, if anybody wants him."

"No fear of that; I'll take him off your hands, and give you a good price for him."

"What good will he do you?"

"Why, you can make more money with him than Barnum ever did with his Woolly Home."

"How so?" inquired the boy, with great simplicity.

"Take him through the country and show him to the people. I tell yer they'd run after such things. Get out yer pictures of him, and the folks would break thar necks to see him. I tell yer, thar's a fortune thar!"

The trapper spoke emphatically like one who knows.

As it was growing dusk, they deemed it best to look for some camping-place. There was considerable danger in running at night, as there was no moon, and they might run into some gully or ravine and dislocate or wrench some portion of their machinery, which might result in an irreparable catastrophe.

Before it was fairly dark they headed toward a small clump of trees, where everything looked favorable.

"You see we must find a place where there is plenty water and fuel, for we need both," remarked the boy.

"Thar's plenty of wood, as yer see with yer eyes," replied Baldy, "and when trees look as keen as that, thar's purty sure sign thar's water not fur off."

"That's all we want," was the observation of the engineer as he headed toward the point indicated.

Things were growing quite indistinct, when the steam man gave its last puff, and came to rest in the margin of the grove. The fires were instantly drawn, and every-thing was put in as good shape as possible, by the boy, while the trapper made a tour of examination through the grove. He came back with the report that everything was as they wished.

"Thar's a big stream of water runnin' right through the middle, and yer can see the wood fur yourself."

"Any signs of Indians?" asked the boy, in a low voice, as if fearful of being overheard. "Dunno; it's too dark to tell."

"If it's dangerous here, we had better go on."

"Yer ain't much used to this part the world. You may keep powerful easy till mornin'."

As they could not feel certain whether in danger or not, it was the part of prudence to believe that some peril threatened them. Accordingly they ate their evening meal in silence, and curled up in the bottom of their wagon, first taking the precaution to fill their tank with water, and placing a portion of wood and kindlings in the bowels of the steam man, so that in case of danger, they would be able to leave at a short notice.

Johnny Brainerd was soon sound asleep, and the trapper followed, but it was with that light, restless slumber which is disturbed by the slightest noise.

So it came about that, but a few hours had passed, when he was aroused by some slight disturbance in the grove. Raising his head he endeavored to peer into the darkness, but he could detect nothing.

But he was certain that something was there, and he gently aroused the boy beside him.

"What is it?" queried the latter in a whisper, but fully wide-awake.

"I think thar ar Ingins among the trees."

"Good heavens! What shall we do?"

"Keep still and don't git skeart! sh!" At this juncture he heard a slight noise, and cautiously raising his head, he caught the outlines of an Indian, in a crouching position, stealing along in front of the wagon, as though examining the curious contrivance. He undoubtedly was greatly puzzled, but he remained only a few minutes, when he withdrew as silently as he had come.

"Stay yer, while I take a look around!" whispered Baldy, as he slid softly out the wagon, while the boy did the same, waiting; until sure that the trapper would not see him.

Baldy spent a half-hour in making his reconnoissance. The result of it was that he found there were fully twenty Indians, thoroughly wide-awake, who were moving stealthily through the grove.

When he came back, it was with the conviction that their only safety lay in getting away without delay.

"We've got to learn," said he, "how long it will take yer to git up steam, youngster?"

"There is a full head on now. I fired up the minute you left the-wagon."

"Good!" exclaimed Baldy, who in his excitement did not observe that the steam man was seething, and apparently ready to explode with the tremendous power pent up in its vitals.

Chapter IX
The Steam Man as a Hunter

AT THIS JUNCTURE the trapper whispered that the Indians were again stealing around them. Johnny's first proceeding was to pull the whistle wide open, awaking the stillness of the night by a hideous, prolonged screech.

Then, letting on the steam, the man made a bound forward, and the next moment was careering over the prairie like a demon of darkness, its horrid whistle giving forth almost one continual yell, such as no American Indian has ever been able to imitate.

When they had gone a few hundred yards, Johnny again slackened the speed, for there was great risk in going at this tremendous rate, where all was entire blank darkness, and there was no telling into what danger they might run. At the speed at which they were going they would have bounded into a river before they could have checked themselves.

"Yer furgot one thing," said Baldy, when they had considerably moderated their gait, and were using great caution.

"What is that?"

"Yer oughter had a lamp in front, so we could travel at night, jist as well as day."

"You are right; I don't see how I came to forget that. We could have frightened the Indians more completely, and there would have been some consolation in traveling at such a time."

"Is it too late yet?"

"Couldn't do it without going back to St. Louis."

"Thunderation! I didn't mean that. Go ahead."

"Such a lamp or head-light as the locomotives use would cost several hundred dollars, although I could have made one nearly as good for much less. Such a thing in the center of a man's forehead, and the whistle at the end of his nose, would give him quite an impressive appearance."

"Yer must do it, too, some day my God!"

The boy instantly checked their progress, as the trapper uttered his exclamation; but quickly as it was done, it was none too soon, for another long step and the steam man would have gone down an embankment, twenty feet high, into a roaring river at the base. As it was, both made rather a hurried leap to the ground, and ran to the front to see whether there was no danger of his going down.

But fortunately he stood firm.

"I declare that was a narrow escape!" exclaimed the boy as he gazed down the cavernous darkness, looking doubly frightful in the gloom of the night.

"Skulp me if that wouldn't have been almost as bad as staying among the red-skins," replied the trapper. "How are we goin' to get him out of this?"

"We've got to shove him back ourselves."

"Can't we reverse him?"

"No; he isn't gotten up on that principle."

By great labor they managed to make him retrograde a few steps, so that he could be made to shy enough to leave the dangerous vicinity, and once more started upon the broad firm prairie.

"Do you suppose these Indians are following us?" inquired the boy.

"No fear of it."

"Then we may as well stay here."

The fires were drawn again, everything made right, and the two disposed themselves again for spending the night in slumber.

No disturbance occurred, and both slept soundly until broad daylight. The trapper's first proceeding upon awakening was to scan the prairie in every direction in quest of danger.

He was not a little amused to see a dozen or so mounted Indians about a third of a mile to the west. They had reined up on the plain, and were evidently scanning the strange object, with a great deal of wonder, mixed with some fear.

"Do you think they will attack us?" inquired the boy, who could not suppress his trepidation at the sight of the warlike savages, on their gayly-caparisoned horses, drawn up in such startling array.

"Ef thar war any danger of that, we could stop 'em by 'tacking 'em."

"Jest fire up and start toward 'em, and see how quick they will scatter." The advice was acted upon on the instant, although it was with no little misgiving on the part of the engineer.

All the time that the 'firing up' process was under way the savages sat as motionless as statues upon their horses. Had they understood the real nature of the 'animal,' it cannot be supposed that they would rave hesitated for a moment to charge down upon it and demolish it entirely.

But it was a terra incognita, clothed with a terror such as no array of: enemies could wear, and they preferred to keep at a goodly distance from it.

"Now, suppose they do not run?" remarked Johnny, rather doubtingly, as he hesitated whether to start ahead or not.

"What if they don't? Can't we run another way? But yer needn't fear. Jist try it on."

Steam was let on as rapidly as possible, and the momentum gathering quickly, it was soon speeding over the prairie at a tremendous rate, straight toward the savages.

The latter remained motionless a few moments, before they realized that it was coining after them, and then, wheeling about, they ran as though all the legions of darkness were after them.

"Shall I keep it up?" shouted Johnny in the ear of the hunter.

"Yas; give 'em such a skear that they won't be able to git over it ag'in in all thar lives."

There is some fun in chasing a foe, when you know that he is really afraid of you, and will keep running without any thought of turning at bay, and the dwarf put the steam man to the very highest notch of speed that was safe, even at the slight risk of throwing both the occupants out.

The prairie was harder and nearer level than any over which they had passed since starting, so that nothing was in the way of preventing the richest kind of sport.

"Are we gaining?" inquired Johnny, his eyes glowing with excitement.

"Gaining? Thar never was a red-skin that had such a chase in all the world. Ef they don't git out the way mighty soon, we'll run over 'em all."

They were, in truth, rapidly overhauling the red-skins, who were about as much terrified as it was possible for a mortal to be, and still live.

To increase their fears, the boy kept up a constant shrieking of his whistle. If there had been any other contrivance or means at his command, it is possible the red-skins would have tumbled off their horses and died; for they were bearing almost all the fright, terror and horror that can possibly be concentrated into a single person.

Finding there was no escape by means of the speed of their horses, the Indians sensibly did what the trapper had prophesied they would do at first.

They 'scattered,' all diverging over the prairie. As it was impossible for the steam man to overtake all of these, of course, this expedient secured the safety of the majority.

Neither Baldy nor the boy were disposed to give up the sport in this manner; so, they singled out a single 'noble red-man,' who was pursuing nearly the same direction as they were, and they headed straight for him.

The poor wretch, when he saw that he was the object of the monster's pursuit, seemed to become frantic with terror. Rising on his horse's back, he leaned forward until it looked as though there was danger of going over his head altogether. Then, whooping and shrieking to his terrified horse, that was already straining every nerve, he pounded his heels in its sides, vainly urging it to still greater speed.

In the meantime, the steam man was gaining steadily upon him, while to add variety to the scene, Johnny kept up the unearthly shrieking of the nose-whistle of the giant. It was difficult to tell which sounded the most hideously in this strange chase.

The remaining Indians had improved their advantage to the utmost. Fearful that their dreadful enemy might change its mind and single them out, they kept up their tearing light, all regardless of the great extremity to which their companion was reduced, until finally they disappeared in the distance.

A short distance only separated pursuer and pursued, when the latter, realizing that there was no escape in flight, headed toward the river, which was a short distance on the right.

This saved him. When with a bowl, horse and rider thundered over the bank and disappeared, the steam man could not follow him. He was compelled to give up the chase and draw off. A few days later, and without further noteworthy incident, the steam man reached Wolf Ravine, being received in the manner narrated at the beginning of this story.

Chapter X
Wolf Ravine

DURING THE absence of Baldy Bicknell in search of the steam man, neither Mickey nor Ethan had been disturbed by Indians.

They had worked unceasingly in digging the gold mine to which they had gained access through the instrumentality of the trapper. When they had gathered together quite a quantity of the gravel and dirt, with the yellow sand glittering through it, it was carried a short distance to the margin of the river, where it underwent the 'washing' process.

While thus engaged, one of them was constantly running up the bank, to make sure that their old enemies did not steal upon them unawares. Once or twice they caught sight of several moving in the distance, but they did not come near enough to molest them, doing nothing more than to keep them on the qui vive.

There was one Indian, however, who bestrode a black horse, who haunted them like a phantom. When they glanced over the river, at almost any time, they could see this individual cautiously circling about on his horse, and apparently waiting for a chance to get a shot at his enemies.

"Begorrah, but he loves us, that he does, as the lamb observed when speaking of the wolf," said

Mickey, just after he had sent a bullet whistling about their ears.

"Jehosiphat! He loves us too much!" added the Yankee, who had no relish for these stolen shots. "If we ain't keerful, there'll be nuthin' of us left when Baldy comes back, that is, if he comes back at all."

This red-skin on his black horse was so dangerous that he required constant watching, and the men could perform only half their usual work. It was while Mickey was on the lookout for him that he caught sight of the steam man coming toward him, as we have related in another place.

So long as that personage was kept puffing and tearing round the vicinity, they knew there was no fear of disturbance from the treacherous red-skins, who were so constantly on the alert to avenge themselves for the loss they had suffered in the attack; but it would hardly pay to keep an iron man as sentinel, as the wear and tear in all probability would be too much for him.

After consulting together upon the return of Baldy, and after they had ridden behind the steam man to their heart's content, they decided upon their future course. As the boy, Johnny, had no intention of devoting himself to manual labor, even had he been able, it was agreed that he should take upon himself the part of sentinel, while the others were at work.

In this way it was believed that they could finish within a couple of weeks, bidding goodbye to the Indians, and quickly reach the States and give up their dangerous pursuits altogether, whereas, if compelled to do duty themselves as sentinels, their stay would be doubly prolonged.

This arrangement suited the boy very well, who was thereby given opportunity to exercise his steam man by occasional airings over the prairies. To the east and south the plains stretched away till the horizon shut down upon them, as the sky does on the sea. To the west, some twenty odd miles distant, a range of mountains was visible, the peaks being tinged with a faint blue in the distance, while some of the more elevated looked like white conical clouds resting against the clear sky beyond.

From the first, young Brainerd expressed a desire to visit these mountains. There was something in their rugged grandeur which invited a close inspection, and he proposed to the trapper that they should make a hunting excursion in that direction.

"No need of goin' so fur for game," he replied, "takes too much time, and thar's sure to be red-skins."

"But if we go with the steam man we shall frighten them all away," was the reply.

"Yas," laughed Baldy, "and we'll skear the game away too."

"But we can overtake that as we did the poor Indian the other day."

"Not if he takes to the mountains. Leastways yer isn't him that would like to undertake to ride up the mountain behind that old gintle-man."

"Nor I either, but we can leave the wagon when we get to the base of the mountain."

"And give the reds time to come down and run off with yer whole team."

"Do you think there is danger of that?"

"Dunno as thar be, but ef they catched sight of yourself, they'd raise yer ha'r quicker'n lightning."

Seeing that the little fellow was considerably discouraged, Baldy hastened to add:

"Ef you're keerful, younker, and I b'lieve yer generally be, take a ride thar yerself, behind yer jumping-jack, but remember my advice and stick to yer wagon."

Having thus obtained permission of the hunter, Johnny Brainerd, as may well be supposed, did not wait long before availing himself of his privilege.

The weather, which had been threatening toward the latter part of the day, entirely cleared away, and the next morning dawned remarkably clear and beautiful. So the boy announced his intention of making the expected visit, after which, he promised to devote himself entirely to performing the duty of sentinel.

"Abeout what time may we look for you, neow!" asked Ethan, as he was on the point of starting.

"Sometime this afternoon."

"Come in before dark, as me mither used to observe to meself, when I wint out shparkin'," added Mickey.

The boy promised to heed their warnings, and began firing up again. The tank was completely filled with water, and the wagon filled nearly full of wood, so that the two were capable of running the contrivance for the entire day, provided there was no cessation, and that he was on the 'go' continually.

Before starting, it was thoroughly oiled through and through, and put in the best possible condition, and then waving them all a pleasant farewell, he steamed gayly toward the mountains.

The ground was admirable, and the steam man traveled better than ever. Like a locomotive, he seemed to have acquired a certain smoothness and steadiness of motion, from the exercise he had already had, and the sharp eye of the boy detected it at once. He saw that he had been very fortunate indeed in constructing his wonderful invention, as it was impossible for any human skill to give it any better movement than it now possessed.

The first three or four miles were passed at a rattling gait, and the boy was sitting on the front of his wagon, dreamily watching the play of the huge engine, when it suddenly paused, and with such abruptness that he was thrown forward from his seat, with violence, falling directly between the legs of the monster, which seemed to stand perfectly motionless, like the intelligent elephant that is fearful of stirring a limb, lest he might crush his master lying beneath him.

The boy knew at once that some accident had happened, and unmindful of the severe scratch he had received, he instantly clambered to his feet, and began examining the machinery, first taking the precaution to give vent to the surplus steam, which was rapidly gathering.

It was some time before he could discover the cause of difficulty, but he finally ascertained that a small bolt had slipped loose, and had caught in such a manner as to check the motion of the engine on the instant.

Fortunately no permanent injury was done, and while he was making matters right, he recollected that in chatting with the trapper as he was on the point of starting, he had begun to screw on the bolt, when his attention had been momentarily diverted, when it escaped his mind altogether, so that he alone was to blame for the accident, which had so narrowly escaped proving a serious one.

Making sure that everything was right, he remounted the wagon, and cautiously resumed his journey, going very slowly at first, so as to watch the play of the engine.

Everything moved with its usual smoothness, and lifting his gaze he descried three buffaloes, standing with erect heads, staring wonderingly at him.

"If you want a chase you may have it!" exclaimed the boy as he headed toward them.

Chapter XI
The Steam Man on a Buffalo Hunt

WITH A WILD snort of alarm, the three buffaloes turned tail and dashed over the prairie, with the shrieking steam man in pursuit.

The boy had taken the precaution to bring a rifle with him. When he saw them flee in this terrified manner, the thought came to him at once that he would shoot one of them, and take a portion back to his friends for their supper.

It would to a grand exploit for him, and he would be prouder of its performance than he was of the construction of the wonderful steam man.

The lumbering, rolling gait of the buffaloes was not a very rapid one, and the boy found himself speedily overhauling them without difficulty. They did not know enough to separate, but kept close together, sometimes crowding and striking against each other in their furious efforts to escape.

But, after the chase had continued some time, one of the animals began to fall in the rear, and Johnny directed his attention toward him, as he would be the most easy to secure.

This fellow was a huge bull that was slightly lame, which accounted for his tardiness of gait.

Frightened as he was, it was not that blind terror which had seized the Indians when they discovered the steam man so close at their heels. The bull was one of those creatures that if closely pressed would turn and charge the monster. He was not one to continue a fruitless flight, no matter who or what was his pursuer.

The boy was not aware of this sturdy trait in the animal, nor did he dream of anything like resistance.

So he steadily drew toward him, until within twenty yards, when he let go of his controlling rod, and picked up the rifle beside him. A bullet from this, he supposed, would kill any animal, however large, no matter at what portion of his body he aimed.

So raising partly to his feet, and steadying himself as well as he could, he aimed for the lumping haunch of the animal. The ball buried itself in his flank, and so retarded his speed, that the next moment the boy found himself beside him.

The instant this took place, the bull lowered his head, and without further warning, charged full at the steam man.

The boy saw the danger, but too late to stave it off. His immense head struck the rear of the monster with such momentum that he was lifted fully a foot from the ground, the concussion sounding like the crack of a pistol.

Fortunately the shock did not materially injure the machine, although the frightened boy expected to be capsized and killed by the infuriated buffalo.

The latter, when he had made his plunge, instantly drew back for another, which was sure to be fatal if made as fairly as the first. The boy retained his presence of mind enough to let on full steam, and the concern shot away at an extraordinary rate, bounding over the ground so furiously that the billets of wood were thrown and scattered in every direction, so that now, from being the pursuer, he had speedily become the pursued. The tables were turned with a vengeance!

It was only by providential good fortune that young Brainerd escaped instant destruction. The wonder was that the steam man was not so injured as to be unable to travel, in which case the maddened bull would have left little of him.

As it was, the experience of the boy was such as he could never forget. When he turned his affrighted glance behind he saw the enraged animal plunging furiously after him, his head lowered, his tongue out, his eyes glaring, and his whole appearance that of the most brutal ferocity.

Had the bull come in collision with the horse or man while in that mood he would have made short work of him.

But great as was his speed, it could not equal that of the wonderful steam man, who took such tremendous strides that a few minutes sufficed to carry him beyond all danger.

Johnny quietly slacked off steam, but he kept up a good swinging gait, not caring to renew his close acquaintance with his wounded enemy. The latter speedily discovered he was losing ground, and finally gave up the pursuit and trotted off at a leisurely rate to join his companions, apparently none the worse for the slight wound he had received.

As soon as the boy found himself beyond the reach of the animal's fury he halted the man and made a minute examination of the machinery.

The head and horns of the buffalo had dented the iron skin of the steam man, but the blow being distributed over a large area, inflicted no other damage, if indeed this could be called damage of itself.

The boy was greatly pleased, not only at his escape but at the admirable manner in which his invention had borne the shock of collision. It gave him a confidence in it which hitherto he had not felt.

Turning his face more toward the mountains, he again let on a good head of steam and rattled over the prairie at a stirring rate. An hour was sufficient to bring him to the base, where he halted.

He had not forgotten the warning of the trapper, but, like almost any inexperienced person, he could not see any cause for alarm. He scanned every part of the prairie and mountain that was in his field of vision, but could detect nothing alarming.

He supposed the parting admonition of Baldy was merely a general warning, such as a cautious person gives to one whom he has reason to fear is somewhat careless in his conduct.

It therefore required little self-argument upon his part after putting his man in proper 'condition,' to start off on a ramble up the mountain side. It was not his intention to remain more than an hour or so, unless he came across some game. He had a goodly quantity of ammunition, and was careful that his rifle was loaded, so as not to be taken unawares by any emergency.

Although Johnny Brainerd was afflicted with misshapen form, yet he was very quick and active upon his feet, and bounded along over the rocks, and across the chasms like a deer, with such a buoyancy of spirits that he forgot danger.

However, he had gone but a short distance, when he was startled by a low fierce growl, and turning his head, saw to his horror, that he had nearly run against a colossal animal, which he at once recognized as the dreaded grizzly bear.

Such a meeting would have startled an experienced hunter, and it was therefore with no steady nerve that he hastily brought his piece to his shoulder and fired.

The shot struck the bear in the body, doing just what his shot at the buffalo had done some time before. It thoroughly angered him, without inflicting anything like a serious wound. With a growl of fury the brute made straight for him.

What would the boy have given, as he sped down the mountain side, were he now in his wagon, whirled over the prairie at a rate which would enable him to laugh to scorn any such speed as that of the brute.

At first he had hopes of reaching his refuge, but he was not long in seeing that it was impossible, and found that if he escaped he must find some refuge very speedily.

When he suddenly found himself beneath a goodly-sized tree it looked like a providential indication to him, and throwing his gun to the ground, he ascended the tree in the shortest time that he had ever made.

He was none too soon as it was, for the bear was so close beneath him that he felt the brush of its claws along his feet, as he nervously jerked them beyond its reach.

Hastily scrambling to the very top of the tree, he secured himself among the limbs, and then glanced down to see what his enemy was doing. Great was his relief to find him sitting on his haunches, contenting himself with merely casting wistful glances upward.

The sensation of even temporary safety was a relief, but when a full hour had dragged by, with scarcely a single change of position upon the part of the brute, Johnny began to ask himself what was to be the end of all this.

It looked as though the grizzly had resolved in making his dinner upon the youngster who had dared to fire a shot at him. The patience of an animal is proverbially greater than that of a human being, and that of the bear certainly exceeded to a great degree that of his expected prey who crouched in the limbs above.

Chapter XII
The Grizzly Bear

FROM WHERE young Brainerd was perched on the tree it was impossible to catch a glimpse of the steam man, so patiently awaiting his return. The distance was also too great for him to make himself heard by the miners, who were hard at work twenty miles away.

Fruitful in expedients, it was not long before the boy found a resource in his trouble. Tearing a large strip from his coat, he tore this into smaller strips, until he had secured a rope half a dozen yards in length. Upon the end of this he placed a loop, and then, descending to the lowest limb, he devoted himself to the task of drooping it over the end of his gun. It fortunately had fallen in such a manner that the muzzle was somewhat elevated, so that here was a good opportunity for the exercise of his skill and patience.

When the first attempt was made the bear suddenly clawed at it and tore it from the boy's hand before he could jerk it beyond his reach. So he was compelled to make another one.

Nothing discouraged, the boy soon had this completed, and it was dropped down more cautiously than before. When the grizzly made a lunge at it, it was deftly twitched out of his way.

This was repeated several times, until the brute became disgusted with the sport, and dropping down behind the tree, let the boy do all the fishing he chose.

Now was his time, but the boy did not allow his eagerness to overcome the steadiness of his nerves. It required no little skill, but he finally succeeded in dropping the noose over the muzzle of the gun and jerked it up taut.

With a heart beating high with hope, Johnny saw it lifted clear of the ground, and he began carefully drawing it up. The grizzly looked curiously at his maneuvers, and once made as if to move toward the dangling rifle; but, ere his mind was settled, it was drawn beyond his reach, and the cold muzzle was grasped in the hand of the eagerly waiting boy.

While drawing it up, he had been debating with himself as to the best means of killing the brute. Remembering that his first shot had done no harm, he sensibly concluded that he had not yet learned the vulnerable part of the monster.

His gun was loaded very carefully, and when everything was ready he made a noise, to attract the attention of the brute. The bear looked up instantly, when the gun was aimed straight at his right eye.

Ere the grizzly could withdraw his gaze, the piece was discharged, and the bullet sped true, crashing into the skull of the colossal brute. With a howling grunt, he rose upon his hind feet, clawed the air a few moments, and then dropped dead.

Young Brainerd waited until he was certain that the last spark of life had fled, when he cautiously descended the tree, scarcely able to realize the truth that he had slain a grizzly bear, the monarch of the western wilderness. But such was the fact, and he felt more pride at the thought than if he had slain a dozen buffaloes.

"If I only had him in the wagon," he reflected, "I'd take him into camp, for they will never believe I killed a grizzly bear."

However, it occurred to him that he might secure some memento, and accordingly he cut several claws and placed them in his pocket. This done, he concluded that, as the afternoon was well advanced, it was time he started homeward.

His hurried flight from the ferocious brute had bewildered him somewhat, and, when he took the direction he judged to be the right one, he found nothing familiar or remembered, from which fact he concluded he was going astray.

But a little computation on his part, and he soon righted himself, and was walking along quite hopefully, when he received another severe shock of terror, at hearing the unmistakable whoop of an Indian, instantly followed by several others.

Immediately he recalled the warning given by the trapper, and looked furtively about, to make sure that he was not already in their hands. His great anxiety now was to reach the steam man and leave the neighborhood, which was rapidly becoming untenable.

So he began stealing forward as rapidly as possible, at the same time keeping a sharp lookout for danger. It required a half-hour, proceeding at this rate, before reaching the base of the mountain. The moment he did so, he looked all around in quest of the steam man, whom he had been compelled to desert for so long a time.

He discovered it standing several hundred yards away; but, to his dismay, there were fully a dozen Indians standing and walking about it, examining every portion with the greatest curiosity.

Here was a dilemma indeed, and the boy began to believe that he had gotten himself into an inextricable difficulty, for how to reach the steam man and renew the fire, under the circumstances, was a question which might well puzzle an older head to answer.

It was unfortunate that the machine should have been taken at this great disadvantage, for it was stripping it of its terror to those Indians, who were such inveterate enemies to the whites. They had probably viewed it with wonder and fear at first; but finding it undemonstrative, had gradually gathered courage, until they had congregated around it, and made as critical a scrutiny as they know how.

Whatever fear or terror they had felt at first sight was now gone; for they seemed on the most familiar terms with it.

Several climbed into the wagon, others passed in and around the helpless giant, and one valiant follow bit him a thwack on the stomach with his tomahawk.

This blow hurt the boy far more than it did the iron man, and he could hardly repress a cry of pain, as he looked upon the destruction of his wonderful friend as almost inevitable.

The savage, however, contented himself with this demonstration, and immediately after walked away toward the mountain. The observant boy knew what this meant, and he withdrew from his temporary hiding-place, and started to watch him.

The fact that the Indian followed precisely the path taken by him, did not remove the uneasiness, and he made up his mind that nothing but danger was to come to him from this proceeding.

When the Indian had reached the spot where the dead grizzly bear lay, he paused in the greatest wonderment. Here was something which he did not understand.

The dead carcass showed that somebody had slain him, and the shot in the eye looked as though it had been done by an experienced hunter. A few minutes' examination of the ground showed further that he who had fired the shot was in the tree at the time, after which he had descended and fled.

All this took but a few minutes for the savage to discover, when he gave a whoop of triumph at his success in probing the matter, and started off on the trail.

Unluckily, this led straight toward the bowlder behind which the boy had concealed himself; and ere he could find a new hiding-place the Indian was upon him.

At sight of the boy, the savage gave a whoop, and raised his tomahawk; but the youngster was expecting this, and instantly raising his gun, he discharged it full into his heart.

As he heard the shriek of the Indian, and saw him throw up his arms, he did not wait to bear or see anything else, but instantly fled with might and main, scarcely looking or knowing whither he was going.

A short time after he found himself at the base of the mountain, very near the spot where he had first come, and glancing again toward the steam man, he saw him standing motion less, as before, and with not a single Indian in sight!

Chapter XIII
An Appalling Danger

NOT A SECOND was to be lost. The next moment the boy had run across the intervening space and pulled open the furnace door of the steam man. He saw a few embers yet smoldering in the bottom, enough to rekindle the wood. Dashing in a lot from the wagon, he saw it begin blazing up. He pulled the valve wide open, so that there might not be a moment's delay in starting, and held the water in the boiler at a proper level. The smoke immediately began issuing from the pipe or hat, and the hopes of the boy rose correspondingly.

The great danger was that the Indians would return before he could start. He kept glancing behind him, and it was with a heart beating with despair that he heard several whoops, and saw at the same instant a number of red-skins coming toward him.

The boy gave a jolt to the wagon, which communicated to the steam man, and it instantly started, at quite a moderate gait, but rapidly increased to its old-fashioned run.

It was just in the nick of time, for two minutes later the savages would have been upon him. As it was, when they saw the giant moving off they paused for a moment in amazement.

But their previous acquaintance with the apparatus had robbed it of all its supernatural attributes, and their halt lasted but a few seconds. The next moment they understood that there was some human agency about it, and uttering their blood-curdling yells, they started in full pursuit. But by this time the steam gentleman was getting down to his regular pace, and was striding over the prairie like a dromedary. For a time the Indians gained, then the intervening distance became stationary, and then he began pulling steadily away from them.

Still the savages maintained the chase until satisfied of its hopelessness, when they gave it up and sullenly withdrew in the direction of the mountains.

The young fellow, in his triumph, could not avoid rising in the wagon, shouting and waving his hat defiantly at his baffled pursuers. The daring act came near costing his life, for it was instantly followed by the discharge of several guns, and the singing of the bullets about his ears caused him to duck back into his seat as suddenly as he had risen from it.

The afternoon was now quite well advanced, and besides feeling hungry, Johnny Brainerd was anxious to get back to camp.

The intervening distance was rapidly passed, and the sun was just setting as he slacked up within a short distance of Wolf Ravine.

For some unaccountable reason, the nearer he approached 'camp,' as it was called, a feeling akin to fear came over him. It was a presentiment of coming evil, which he found it impossible either to shake off or to define, and that was why he halted some distance away.

From where he stood it was impossible to see his two friends at work, but at that time of day he knew they were accustomed to stop work and come out upon the prairie for the purpose of enjoying the cool breeze of evening. At the same time, when such constant danger threatened, they were accustomed to have one of their number, either all or a part of the time, on the ground above, where the approach of enemies could be detected.

The absence of anything like a sentinel increased the boy's apprehensions, and when he had waited some fifteen minutes without seeing anything of his friends he became painfully uneasy.

What if they had been killed? What if they were prisoners? What if a hundred Indians were at that moment in the possession of Wolf Ravine?

Such and similar were the questions which the affrighted boy asked himself, and which, with all his shrewdness, he was unable to answer.

In the hope of attracting attention he set up a shrieking with the whistle, which sounded so loud on the still evening air that it must have gone miles away over the level prairie.

There being no response to this he kept it up for some time, but it still failed, and all this confirmed him in the belief that 'something was up.'

What that particular something was it was impossible to say, so long as he sat in the wagon, and for five minutes he endeavored to decide whether it was best to get out and make a reconnoissance on his own hook or remain where, in case of danger, he could seek safety in flight.

As the day wore rapidly away, and he still failed to see or hear anything of his friends, he finally concluded to get out and make an examination of the ravine.

Accordingly he sprung lightly to the ground, but had scarcely alighted when a peculiar signal, something resembling a tremulous whistle, reached his ear, and he instantly clambered back again, fully satisfied that the whistle was intended as a signal, and that it concerned him, although whether from friend or foe he could only conjecture.

However, his alarm was such that he moved a hundred yards or so further away from the ravine, where there was less likelihood of being surprised by any sudden rush upon the part of the thieving red-skins.

From this standpoint he carefully scanned what could be seen of the ravine. It descended quite gradually from the edge of the bank, so that he gained a partial view of the rocks and bowlders upon the opposite side. Some of the trees growing in the narrow valley rose to such a height that one-half or two-thirds of them were exposed to view.

It was while the boy was gazing at these that he detected a peculiar movement in one of the limbs, which instantly arrested his attention.

A moment showed him that the peculiar waving motion was made by human agency, and he strained his eyes in the hope of detecting the cause of the curious movement.

The gathering darkness made his vision quite uncertain; but he either saw, or fancied he saw, a dark object among the limbs which resembled the form of Baldy Bicknell, the trapper.

Johnny Brainerd would have given almost anything in the world could he have understood what it all meant.

But the vary fact of these singular demonstrations was prima facie evidence of the most unquestionable kind; and, after a moment's consultation with himself, he began moving away, just as the sharp crack of several rifles notified him of the fearful peril which he had escaped.

Chapter XIV
The Huge Hunter

SIMULTANEOUS with the report of the rifles came the pinging of the bullets about the ears of young Brainerd, who, having started the steam man, kept on going until he was a considerable distance from the ravine.

All the time he kept looking back, but could see nothing of his enemies, nor could he detect the point from which the rifle-shots were fired.

Now, as night descended over the prairie, and the retreat of his friends became shrouded in impenetrable darkness, he fully appreciated the fact that not only were they in great danger, but so was he himself.

The heathenish terror with which the steam man had at first inspired the savages had rapidly worn away, the circumstances unfortunately having been such that they had very speedily learned that it was nothing more than a human invention, which of itself could accomplish little or no harm.

He could but reflect, as the man glided slowly along, that if he had the three friends beside him, how easily they could glide away in the darkness and leave all danger behind.

But they were in the extremity of peril already, and, reflect and cogitate as much as he chose, he could see no earthly way of assisting them out of their difficulty.

Besides the concern which he naturally felt regarding his friends, there was a matter that more clearly related to himself that demanded his attention.

The water in the tank was at its lowest ebb, and it would be dangerous for him to attempt to run more than one hour or so longer before replenishing it. Consequently he was unable to stand anything like another chase from the Indians.

As the part of prudence, therefore, he turned toward the river, following slowly along the bank, in quest of some place where it would be easy and safe for him to secure the much-needed water.

It was a long and discouraging hunt. The banks were so high that he could find no point where it was safe for him to descend to the water's edge. There was too great a risk of 'upsetting his cart,' a calamity which, in all probability, would be irreparable.

At length, however, when he had wandered about a mile distant from the Wolf Ravine, he discovered a place, where the bank had about six feet elevation, and sloped down gradually to the river.

Here he paused, and with a small vessel, descended to the stream, muttering to himself as he did so:

"Why didn't I think and put a pumping arrangement to the machine? I could have done it as well as not, and it would have saved me a good deal of trouble."

But regrets were now unavailing, and he lost no time in useless lamentations, setting to work at once. It was tedious labor, carrying up the water in a small vessel, and emptying it in the tank, but he persevered, and at the end of a couple of hours the task was completed.

"I can make the wood stand me another day," he added, as he stood looking at the greatly diminished pile, "although, if I knew where to get it, I would load up now, and then I should be prepared."

He suddenly paused, for scarcely a dozen yards away, coming up the margin of the river, straight toward him, he descried the figure of a man fully six feet and a half high.

Young Brainerd's first impulse was to spring into the wagon and start away at full speed; but a second glance showed him that it was not an Indian, but a white man, in the garb of a hunter.

"Hullo, boss, thar, what yer doin'?"

He was at a loss what reply to make, and therefore made none. The next moment the giant hunter was beside him.

"B'ars and bufflers! Younker, what ye got thar?" he demanded, eyeing the steam man with an expression of the most amazed wonder. "I say, what do yer call that thing?"

"That," laughed Johnny, who could not avoid a feeling of strong apprehension at the singular appearance of the strange hunter, "is a sort of peregrinating locomotive."

"Paggyratin' locomotive, what's that?" he asked, in a gruff voice, and with an expression of great disgust at the unfamiliar words employed.

"You have seen a locomotive, haven't you?"

"Reckon I hev, down in St. Louey."

"Well, this is something on the same principle, except that it uses legs instead of wheels."

"Can that ere thing walk?"

"Yes, sir, and run, too; it traveled all the way from the Missouri river to this place."

The huge hunter turned upon him with a fierce expression.

"Yer can't fool this yar boss in that style."

"Don't you believe me?" asked the boy, who was fearful of offending the stranger.

"No, sar; not a word."

"How do you suppose we got it here?"

"Fotched in a wagon."

"Let me show you what he can do."

He was about to step into the wagon, when the hunter stopped him.

"See hyar, younker, who mought yer be?"

The boy gave his name and residence.

"What yer doin' hyar?"

"I'm traveling with this machine of mine."

"How do you git it along?"

"I was just going to show you when you stopped me."

"Hold on; no need of bein' in a sweat about it. Do yer come alone?"

"No. I came with a hunter."

"What war his name?"

"Baldy Bicknell."

"B'ars and bufflers! Did yer come with him?"

"Yes; he was my companion all the way."

"Whar mought he be?"

Johnny Brainerd hesitated a moment. While the huge hunter might possibly be of great service to the beleaguered miners, yet he recollected that it was the desire of Baldy that the fact of gold existing in Wolf Ravine should be kept a secret from all except their own party.

Should it become known to any of the numerous hunters and emigrants who were constantly passing in the neighborhood, there would be such a flocking to the place that they would be driven away and probably killed for the treasure that they had already obtained.

The boy, therefore, chose to make a non-committal reply:

"Baldy is some distance away, in camp."

"And what are yer doin' hyar?"

"I stopped here to get water for this steam man, as we call him. You know anything that travels by steam must have the water to generate it."

"I say, younker, I don't want none of yer big words to me. Ef I h'ar any more, b'ars and bufflers, ef I don't crack yer over the head with Sweetlove, my shootin'-iron, so mind what yer say, fur I won't stand no nonsense."

"I didn't wish to offend you," returned the boy, in the meekest of tones.

"How far away might be Baldy?"

"I couldn't tell you exactly, but I think it is less than ten miles."

"Be you goin' back to camp tonight?"

"It was my intention, that is, I meant to do so."

"Guess I'll go with yer; but see hyar, younker, let's see yer try that old humbug of yourn."

The boy sprung into the wagon, glad of the opportunity of getting rid of what looked like a dangerous man. Before he could start he was again peremptorily stopped.

"Yer see, I b'leeve yar a humbug, but if that ole thing does run, and, mind, I tell yer, I don't b'leeve it will, do yer know what I'm goin' to do?"

"I do not."

"I'm goin' to take it myself to chase rod-skins in. It won't bother yer much fur them long legs of yourn to carry that humpback home again. So, younker, start now, and let us see what yer can do."

The boy let on steam, and the man started off on a moderate gait, which rapidly increased to a swift one. The huge, wonder-stricken hunter watched it until it gradually faded out of sight in the gloom, and still watched the place where it had disappeared, and though he watched much longer, with a savage and vindictive heart, yet it never came back to him again.

Chapter XV
The Attack in the Ravine

IN THE mean time, the situation of our friends in Wolf Ravine was becoming perilous to the last degree.

Before going to work, on the morning of the steam man's excursion to the mountains, Baldy Bicknell made a reconnoissance of the ravine, to assure himself that there was no danger of being suddenly overwhelmed, while delving for the precious yellow sand.

He saw abundant signs of Indians having recently visited the place, but he concluded there were none in the immediate vicinity, and that comparatively little risk was run in the boy making his wished-for visit to the mountains in the west.

Through the center of the ravine ran a small stream of water, hardly of enough volume to be used for washing gold without a dam being created. It looked as if this had once been the head of a large stream, and that the golden sand had been drifted to this spot, by the force of the powerful current.

The auriferous particles were scattered over the entire breadth of the ravine, for the distance of several hundred feet, being found in the richest deposits between the ledges and rocks, in the bottom of the channel, where, as may well be supposed, it was no easy matter to obtain.

A short distance back of the 'diggings,' where the vast masses of rocks assumed curiously grotesque forms, the miners discovered a rude cave, where they at once established their headquarters. A tiny stream ran through the bottom of it, and with a little placing of the close bowlders, they speedily put it in the best condition of defense.

It was almost entirely surrounded by trees, there was one spot where a thin man, like Hopkins or Baldy, could draw his body through and climb a luxuriant cottonwood, whose top have a wide view of the surrounding plain.

The day passed away without any signs of Indians, Baldy occasionally ascending the side of the ravine, and scanning the plains in every direction, on the constant lookout for the insidious approach of their enemies.

Just before nightfall, while all three were at work, a rifle was discharged, and the bullet was imbedded in the tough oaken handle of the spade with which the trapper was digging.

"Whar in thunder did that come from?" he demanded, dropping the implement, catching up the rifle, and glaring savagely about him.

But neither of the others could answer him, and climbing up the bank, he looked fiercely around for some evidence of the whereabouts of his treacherous foe.

The latter remained invisible, but several hundred yards down the ravine, he caught a glimpse of enough Indians dodging hither and thither to satisfy him that there was quite a formidable force in the valley.

Giving the alarm to his companions, all three withdrew within the cave, not the less willingly, as it was very near their usual quitting time.

"Begorrah! and what'll becoom of the shtame mian and the boy?" inquired Mickey, as he hastily obeyed orders.

"Jerusalem!" exclaimed the Yankee, in great trepidation, "if he isn't warned, they'll catch him sure, and then what'll become of us? We'll have to walk all the way hum."

As the best means of communicating with him, the trapper climbed through the narrow opening, and to the top of the tree, where he ensconced himself, just as the steam man uttered its interrogative whistle.

The trapper, as we have shown in another place, replied by pantomime, not wishing to discover his whereabouts to the enemy, as he had a dim idea that this means of egress might possibly prove of some use to him, in the danger that was closing around them.

When Johnny Brainerd recognized his signal, and beat a retreat, Baldy began a cautious descent to his cave again. At this time it was already growing dark, and he had to feel his way down again.

And so it came about, that not until he had reached the lowest limb, did his trained ear detest a slight rustling on the ground beneath. Supposing it to be either Mickey or Ethan, he continued his descent, merely glancing below. But at that moment something suspicious caught his eye, and peering down more carefully, he discovered a crouching Indian, waiting with drawn knife until he should come within his reach.

The trapper was no coward, and had been in many a hand to-hand tussle before; but there was something in the character of the danger which would have made it more pleasant for him to hesitate awhile until he could learn its precise dimensions; but time was too precious, and the next moment, he had dropped directly by the side of the red-skin.

The latter intended to make the attack, but without waiting for him, Baldy sprung like a panther upon him and bore him to the earth. There was a silent but terrific struggle for a few moments, but the prodigious activity and rower of the trapper prevailed, and when he withdrew from the grasp of the Indian, the latter was as dead as a door nail. The struggle had been so short that neither Mickey nor Ethan knew anything of it, until Baldy dropped down among them, and announced what had taken place.

"Jerusalem! Have they come as close as that?" asked the Yankee in considerable terror.

"Skulp me, if they ain't all around us!" was the reply of the hunter.

"How we ar' to git out o' hyar, ar' a hard thing to tell j'ist now."

"It's meself that thinks the rid gentlemin have a love fur us, as me mither obsarved, when she cracked the head of me father," remarked Mickey, who had seated himself upon the ground with all the indifference of an unconcerned spectator.

It was so dark in their cave-like home that they could not see each other's faces, and could only catch a sort of twilight glimpse of their forms when they passed close to each other.

It would have made their quarters more pleasant had they struck a light, but it was too dangerous a proceeding, and no one thought of it. They could only keep on the alert, and watch for the movement of their enemies.

The latter, beyond all doubt, were in the immediate vicinity, and inspired as they were by hate of the most vindictive kind, would not allow an opportunity to pass of doing all the harm in their power.

The remains of their food was silently eaten in the darkness, when Baldy said:

"Do yer stay hyar whar ye be till I come back."

"Where might ye be going naow?" inquired Hopkins.

"I'm goin' outside to see what the reds are doin', and to see whether thar's a chance fur 'em to gobble us up hull."

"Do yees mind and take care of y'urself, as me mither cautioned me when I went a shparkin'," said Mickey, who naturally felt some apprehension, when he saw the trapper on the point of leaving them at such a dangerous time.

"Yes. Baldy, remember that my fate is wrapped up in yours," added the Yankee, whose sympathies were probably excited to a still greater extent.

"Never mind about Baldy; he has been in such business too often not to know how to take care of himself."

"How long do you expect to begone?" inquired Ethan.

"Mebbe all night, if thar ain't much danger. Ef I find the varments ar' too thick I'll stay by yer, and if they ain't I'll leave fur several hours. Leastways, whatever I do, you'll be sure to look out for the skunks."

With this parting admonition, the trapper withdrew.

In going out, he made his exit by the same entrance by which all had come in. He proceeded with great caution, for none knew better than he the danger of a single misstep. He succeeded, after considerable time, in reaching a portion of the valley so shrouded in gloom that he was able to advance without fear of discovery.

He thoroughly reconnoitered every part of the ravine in the immediate vicinity of the cave, but could discover nothing of the Indians, and he concluded that they were some distance away.

Having assured himself of this, the trapper cautiously ascended the side of the ravine, until he reached the open prairie, when he lost no time in leaving the dangerous place behind him.

He had no intention, however, of deserting his friends, but had simply gone in quest of the steam man. He comprehended the difficulty under which they all labored, so long as they were annoyed in this manner by the constant attacks of the savages, and he had an idea that the invention of the dwarfed Johnny Brainerd could be turned to a good account in driving the miscreants away so thoroughly that they would remain away for a long enough time for them to accomplish something in the way of gathering the wealth lying all about them.

He recalled the direction which he had seen the puffing giant take, and he bent his steps accordingly, with only a faint hope of meeting him without searching the entire night for him. Baldy was shrewd enough to reason that as the boy would wish some water for his engine, he would remain in the immediate vicinity of the river until at least that want could be supplied.

Acting on this supposition, he made his way to the river bank, and followed so closely to the water that its moonlit surface was constantly visible to him.

The night was still, and, as he moved silently along, he often paused and listened, hoping to hear the familiar rattle of the wheels, as the youngster sped over the prairie.

Without either party knowing it, he passed within a few yards of Duff McIntosh, the huge trapper, whom he had known so intimately years before.

But had he been aware of the fact, he would only have turned further aside, to avoid him; for, when the two trappers, several years previous, separated, they had been engaged in a deadly quarrel, which came near resulting fatally to both.

At length the faint rattle of the wheels caught his ear, and he bent his steps toward the point where he judged the steam man to be.

Chapter XVI
The Repulse

A FEW minutes more satisfied the trapper that he was right. Gradually out from the darkness the approaching figure resolved itself into the steam man.

Johnny Brainerd, after leaving the huge trapper so neatly, continued wandering aimlessly over the prairie at a moderate speed, so as to guard against the insidious approach of the Indians, or the hunter who had threatened to confiscate his property in so unjustifiable a manner.

Fortunately he did not see Baldy until the latter cautiously hailed him, otherwise he would have fled before ascertaining his identity; but the moment he recognized his voice he hastened toward him, no less surprised than pleased at meeting him so unexpectedly.

"Where are Mickey and Ethan?" he inquired, as he leaped alongside of him.

"In the cave."

"How is it you are here?"

The trapper briefly explained that he had crept out to hunt him up; but as there seemed no imminent danger, he deemed it best to leave his companions there, as if the Indians once gained possession of the golden ravine, it would be difficult, if not impossible, to displace them.

Besides, in order to carry out the scheme which he had formed, it was necessary that two at least should remain in the cave, while the others were on the outside.

Under the direction of the trapper, the steam man slowly approached the ravine, keeping at a respectful distance, but so near that if any sudden emergency should arise, they would be able to render assistance to their friends.

The boy gave several whistles so as to inform the Irishman and Yankee of their whereabouts. A few seconds after, and while the noise of the instrument was echoing over the prairie, a fainter whistle reached their ears.

"That's the long-legged Yankee!" instantly remarked the trapper; "he knows how to make my kind of noise."

"What does it mean?"

"It means that all is right."

"Where are the Indians?"

"They ain't fur off. I wish they war further, fur ef it warn't fur them, we'd had half the yaller metal out of thar by this time."

Young Brainerd had the reputation of possessing a remarkably keen vision; but, peer as much as he might, he could detect nothing unusual. The trapper, however, affirmed that numerous forms could be seen creeping along the edge of the prairie, and that these same forms were more nor less than so many red-skins.

"What are they trying to do?"

"Duono."

"Hadn't we better withdraw?" inquired Johnny, showing a little nervousness.

"Not till we know they're after us," was the quiet reply.

By and by the boy himself was able to get an occasional glimpse of the shadowy figures moving to and fro.

"I think they are going to surround us," he added, "and I feel as though we ought to get out while we can do so."

The only reply to this, was by the trapper suddenly bringing his gun to his shoulder and firing. An agonizing screech, as the savage threw himself in the air, showed that the shot had not been in vain.

Rather curiously at the same moment the report of a gun in the ravine reached their ears, followed by the same death-shriek.

"They ain't sleepin' very powerful down thar," was the pleased remark of the trapper, as he leisurely reloaded his piece, while the boy remained in that nervous state, awaiting the permission of Baldy to go spinning away over the prairie at a rate that would very quickly carry him beyond all danger.

But the trapper was in no hurry to give the ardently desired permission. He seemed to have a lingering affection for the place, which prevented his 'tearing himself away.'

The boy's timidity was not in the least diminished, when several return shots were fired, the bullets pinging all around them.

"My gracious, Baldy, let's get out of this!" he instantly pleaded, starting the man himself.

"Go about fifty feet," was the reply, "but not any further."

It may be said that the steam man fairly leaped over this space, and somewhat further, like a frightened kangaroo, and even then it would not have halted had not the trapper given peremptory orders for it to do so.

The sky was now clear and the moon, riding high and nearly full, illumined the prairie for a considerable distance, and there was no fear but that they could detect the approach of the most treacherous savage, let him come in whatever disguise he chose.

The night wore gradually away, without any particular demonstration upon the part of either the Indians or white men, although dropping shots were occasionally exchanged, without any particular result on either side.

Now and then a red-skin, creeping cautiously along, made his appearance on the edge of the ravine; but there was too much light for him to expose himself to the deadly rifle of the trapper, who took a kind of savage pleasure in sending his leaden messengers after the aborigines.

This species of sport was not without its attendant excitement and danger; for the last creature to take a shot quietly is an American Indian; and they kept popping away at the steam man and its train whenever a good opportunity offered.

Owing to the size and peculiar appearance of the steamer, he was a fair target for his enemies; and, indeed, so uncomfortably close did some of the bullets come, that the boy almost continually kept his head lowered, so as to be protected by the sides of the wagon.

Finally morning came, greatly to the relief of all our friends. As soon as it was fairly light the Irishman and Yankee were notified that a move was about to be made, by means of the steam-whistle. An answering signal coming back to them, the steam man at once advanced to the very edge of the ravine.

The trapper peering cautiously down the gulch, caught sight of several red-skins crouching near the cave, and, directing young Brainerd to discharge his piece at a certain one, the two fired nearly together. Scarce five seconds had elapsed, when both Ethan and Mickey did the same. All four, or rather three, as the boy gave his principal attention to the engine, began loading and firing as rapidly as possible.

The red-skins returned a few scattering shots; but they were taken at such disadvantage, that they immediately began a precipitate retreat down the ravine.

Ere they had withdrawn a hundred yards, Ethan and Mickey emerged from the cave, shouting and excited, firing at every red-skin they could see, the Irishman occasionally swinging his gun over his head, and daring the savages to a hand-to-hand encounter.

While the two were thus engaged, the trapper was not idle. The steam man maintained his place but a short distance behind the enemies, and his deadly rifle scarcely ever failed of its mark.

The moment an Indian was killed or helplessly wounded, his companions caught and dragged him away, there being a great fear upon the part of all that some of their number might fall into the hands of their enemies, and suffer the ineffaceable disgrace of being scalped.

The savages were followed a long distance, until their number had diminished down to a fraction of what it was originally, and the survivors had all they could do in taking care of their disabled comrades.

Never was victory more complete. The Indians were thoroughly discomfited, and only too glad to get away after being so severely punished. During this singular running fight the steam man kept up a constant shrieking, which doubtless contributed in no slight degree to the rout of the red-skins. They fired continually at the fearful-looking monster, and, finding their shots produced no effect, invested the thing with a portion of the supernatural power which they had given it at first sight.

When the last glimpse of the retreating Indians was seen, the trapper turned triumphantly toward the boy.

"Warn't that purty well done, younker?"

"It was indeed."

"They'll now stay away awhile."

"We would have failed if we had waited any longer."

"Why so, boy?"

"Because the last stick is burned, and the steam man couldn't be made to run a mile further without more fuel."

Chapter XVII
Homeward Bound

THE PUNISHMENT administered to the Indians who had so greatly annoyed the miners proved a very beneficial one.

Nothing more was seen of them, except one or two glimpses of the red-skin upon his black horse. He, however, maintained a respectful distance, and at the end of a day or two disappeared altogether.

These were golden moments indeed to the miners, and they improved them to the utmost. From earliest light until the darkness of night they toiled almost unceasingly. Half the time they went hungry rather than stop their work to procure that which was so much needed. When, however, the wants of nature could no longer be trifled with, Baldy took his rifle and started off on a hunt, which was sure to be brief and successful.

Sometimes he caught sight of some game in the gulch, and sometimes something in the air drew the fire of his unerring rifle, and the miners feasted and worked as only such violently laboring men can do.

Although the boy was unable to assist at the severe labor, yet he soon demonstrated his genius and usefulness. He not only constructed a dam, but made a 'rocker,' or machine, of an original style, that did the work far more expeditiously and thoroughly than it had yet been done.

While the men were getting the auriferous sand, he separated it from the particles of dirt and gravel, without any assistance from them, and without any severe labor for himself.

There was some apprehension upon the part of all that the huge trapper, whom young Brainerd had met at night, would make his appearance. Should he do so, it would be certain to precipitate a difficulty of the worst kind, as he was morose, sullen, treacherous, envious and reckless of danger.

Baldy Bicknell really feared him more than he did the Indians, and the constant watchfulness he exercised for several days showed how great was his apprehension.

Fortunately, indeed, for all concerned, the giant hunter continued his travels in a different direction, and the miners were undisturbed by him.

Two weeks passed, by the end of which time the ravine was about exhausted of its precious stuff, and the miners made their preparations for going home.

It was impossible to do anything more than conjecture the amount of wealth they had obtained, but Baldy was sure that there was enough, when sold, to buy each of them a handsome farm.

"Jerusalem! But naow ain't that good?" exclaimed the delighted Ethan Hopkins, as he mopped off his perspiring forehead. "That 'ere encourages me to take a step that I've often contemplated."

"What might the same be?"

"Git married: me and Seraphenia Pike hev been engaged for the last ten years, and now I'll be hanged ef I don't go home and get spliced."

"And it's myself that'll do the same," added Mickey, as he executed an Irish jig on the barren earth in front of their cavern home, after they had concluded to leave the place.

"Where does she reside?" inquired Ethan.

"Ballyduff, Kings County, in the Oim of the Sea; it's there that lives the lass that's to have the honor of becoming Mrs. McSquizzle, and becomin' the mither of her own children. Arrah, but isn't the same a beauty?"

"The same as my own, Michael," ventured the Yankee, who deemed it his duty to correct this general remark of his friend.

"Arrah, now, get cut wid ye! she can't begin wid Miss Bridget Moghlaghigbogh that resides wid her mither and two pigs on the outskirts of Ballyduff, in the wee cabin that has the one room and the one windy. Warrah, warrah, now isn't she a jewel?"

"And so is Seraphenia."

"But has she the rid hair, that makes it onnecessary for them to have the candle lit at night? and has she the same beautiful freckles, the size of a ha'penny, on the face and the nose, that has such an iligant turn up at the end, that she used to hang her bonnet on it? Arrah, now, and didn't she have the swate teeth, six of the same that were so broad that they filled her mouth, and it was none of yer gimblet holes that was her mouth, but a beautiful one, that, when she smiled went round to her ears, did the same. And her shoes! but you orter seen them."

"Why so?"

"What was the matter with her shoes?"

"Nothing was the same. They was the shoes that the little pigs went to slaap in, afore they got so big that they couldn't git in them, and then it was her brother that used one of them same for a trunk when he emigrated to Amenity. Arrah, now, but wasn't me own Bridget a jewel?"

"Jehosephat! I should think she was!" exclaimed Hopkins, who had listened in amazement to this enumeration of the beauties of the gentle Irish lass, who had won the affections of Mickey McSquizzle. "No doubt she had a sweet disposition."

"Indeed she had, had she; it was that of an angel, was the same. It was niver that I staid there a night coorting the same that she didn't smash her shillaleh to smithereens over me head. Do yees obsarve that?" asked Mickey, removing his hat, and displaying a scar that extended half way across his head.

"I don't see how any one can help seeing that."

"Well, that was the parting salute of Bridget, as I started for Ameriky. Arrah, now, but she did the same in style."

"That was her parting memento, was it?"

"Yes; I gave her the black eye, and she did the same fur me, and I niver takes off me hat to scratch me head that I don't think of the swate gal that I left at home."

And thereupon the Irishman began whistling 'The Girl I Left Behind Me,' accompanying it with a sort of waltzing dance, kept with remarkably good time.

"And so you intend to marry her?" inquired Hopkins, with no little amazement.

"It's that I do, ef I finds her heart fraa when I return to Ballyduff, You know, that the loikes of her is sought by all the lads in Kings County, and to save braaking their hearts, she may share the shanty of some of 'em."

"Jerusalem! but she is the all-firedest critter I ever heard tell on."

"What does ye maan by that?" demanded the Irishman, instantly flaring up; "does ye maan to insinooate that she isn't the most charming craater in the whole counthry?"

"You'll allow me to except my own Seraphenia?"

"Niver a once."

"Then I'll do it whether you like it or not Your gal can't begin with mine, and never could."

"That I don't allow any man to say."

And the Irishman immediately began divesting himself of his coat, preparatory to settling the difference in the characteristic Irish manner. Nothing loth, the Yankee put himself in attitude, determined to stand up for the rights of his fair one, no matter by whom assailed.

Matters having progressed so far, there undoubtedly would have been a set-to between them, had not the trapper interfered. He and the boy were engaged in preparing the steam man and wagon for starting, when the excited words drew their attention, and seeing that a fight was imminent, Baldy advanced to where they stood and said:

"Not another word, or skulpme ef I don't hammer both of you till thar's nothin left o' you."

This was unequivocal language, and neither of the combatants misunderstood it. All belligerent manifestations ceased at once, and they turned to in assisting in the preparations for moving.

When all four were seated in the wagon, with their necessary baggage about them, it was found that there was comparatively little room for the wood. When they had stored all that they could well carry, it was found that there was hardly enough to last them twelve hours, so that there was considerable risk run from this single fact.

The steam man, however, stepped off with as much ease as when drawing the wagon with a single occupant. The boy let on enough of steam to keep up a rattling pace, and to give the assurance that they were progressing home ward in the fastest manner possible.

Toward the middle of the afternoon a storm suddenly came up and the rain poured in torrents.

As the best they could do, they took refuge in a grove, where, by stretching the canvas over themselves and the steam man, they managed to keep free from the wet.

The steam man was not intended to travel during stormy weather, and so they allowed him to rest.

<h2 style="text-align:center">Chapter XVIII
The Encampment</h2>

THE STORM proved the severest which the steam man had encountered since leaving St. Louis, and it put an effectual veto on his travels during its continuance, and for a short time afterward.

The prairie was found so soft and slippery that they were compelled to lie by until the sun had hardened it somewhat, when they once more resumed their journey.

As they now had thousands of dollars in their possession, and as all sorts of characters were found on the western plains, it may be said that none of the company ever felt easy.

Baldy Bicknell, the trapper, from his extensive experience and knowledge of the West, was the guide and authority on all matters regarding their travels. He generally kept watch during the night, obtaining what sleep he could through the day. The latter, however, was generally very precarious, as at sight of every horseman or cloud of smoke, they generally awakened him, so as to be sure and commit no serious error.

As the steam man would in all probability attract an attention that might prove exceedingly perilous to the gold in their possession, the trapper concluded it prudent to avoid the regular emigrant routes. Accordingly they turned well to the northward, it being their purpose to strike the Missouri, where they would be pretty sure of intercepting some steamer. Reaching such a place they would unjoint and take apart the steam man, packing it up in such a manner that no one could suspect its identity, and embark for St. Louis.

While this relieved them of the danger from their own race, it increased the probability of an attack upon the Indians, who scarcely ever seemed out of sight.

Their watchfulness, however, was constant, and it was due to this fact, more than any other, that they escaped attack at night for the greater part of their return journey.

Their position in the wagon was so cramped, that the party frequently became excessively wearied, and springing out, trotted and walked for miles alongside the tireless steam giant. Water was abundant, but several times they were put to great inconvenience to obtain wood. On three occasions they were compelled to halt for half a day in order to obtain the necessary supply.

Once the steam man came to a dead standstill in the open prairie, and narrowly escaped blowing up. A hasty examination upon the part of the inventor, revealed the fact that a leak had occurred in the tank, and every drop had run out…

This necessitated the greatest work of all, as water was carried the better part of a mile, and nearly an entire day consumed before enough steam could be raised to induce him to travel to the river, to procure it himself, while the miners acted as convoys.

Late one afternoon, they reached a singular formation in the prairie. It was so rough and uneven that they proceeded with great difficulty and at a slow rate of speed. While advancing in this manner, they found they had unconsciously entered a small narrow valley, the bottom of which was as level as a ground floor. The sides contracted until less than a hundred feet separated them, while they rose to the hight of some eight or ten feet, and the bottom remained compact and firm, making it such easy traveling for the steam man, that the company followed down the valley, at a slow pace, each, however, feeling some misgiving as to the propriety of the course.

"It runs in the right direction," said young Brainerd, "and if it only keeps on as it began, it will prove a very handy thing for us."

"Hyar's as afeared it ain't goin' to keep on in that style," remarked Baldy; "howsumever, you can go ahead awhile longer."

"Naow, that's what I call real queer," remarked Ethan Hopkins, who was stretching his legs by walking alongside the steamer.

"And it's meself that thinks the same," added Mickey, puffing away at his short black pipe. "I don't understand it, as me father obsarved when they found fault with him for breaking another man's head."

"Ef we git into trouble, all we've got ta do is to back out," remarked Baldy, as a sort of apology for continuing his advance.

"This fellow doesn't know how to go backward," said Johnny, "but if it prove necessary, we can manage to turn him round."

"All right, go ahead."

At the same moment, the limber Yankee sprung into the wagon, and the steam man started ahead at a speed which was as fast as was prudent.

However, this delightful means of progress was brought to an unexpected standstill, by the sudden and abrupt termination of the valley. It ended completely as though it were an uncompleted canal, the valley rising so quickly to the level of the prairie, that there was no advancing any further, nor turning, nor in fact was there any possible way of extricating themselves from the difficulty, except by working the steam man around, and withdrawing by the same path that they had entered by.

"Well, here we are," remarked the boy, as they came to a standstill, "and what is to be done?"

"Get out of it," was the reply of Hopkins, who advanced several yards further, until he came up on the prairie again, so as to make sure of the exact contour of the ground.

"Did yer ever try to make the thing go up hill?" asked the trapper.

Young Brainerd shook his head. "Impossible! he would fall over on us, the minute it was attempted. When I was at work at first making him, what do you think was the hardest thing for me to do?"

"Make him go, I s'pose."

"That was difficult, but it was harder work to balance him, that is, so when he lifted up one foot he wouldn't immediately fall over on the same side. I got it fixed after a while, so that he ran as evenly and firmly as an engine, but I didn't fix upon any plan by which he could ascend or descend a hill."

"Can't you make him do it?"

"Not until he is made over again. I would be afraid to attempt to walk him up a moderate inclination, and know it would be sure destruction to start him up such a steep bank at that."

"Then we must work him round, I s'pose."

"There is nothing else that can be done."

"Let's at it, then."

This proved as difficult a job as they imagined. The steam man was so heavy that it was impossible to lift him, but he was shied around as much as possible; and, by the time he had walked across the valley he had half turned round.

He was then coaxed and worked back a short distance, when, with the 'leverage' thus gained, the feat was completed, and the steam man stood with his face turned, ready to speed backward the moment that the word might be given.

By this time, however, the day was gone, and darkness was settling over the prairie. Quite a brisk breeze was blowing, and, as the position of the party was sheltered against this annoyance, Hopkins proposed that they should remain where they were until morning.

"We couldn't get a better place," said Johnny Brainerd, who was quite taken with the idea.

"It's a good place and it's a bad one," replied the trapper, who had not yet made up his mind upon the point.

They inquired what he meant by calling it a bad place.

"Ef a lot of the varmints should find we're hyar, don't you see what a purty fix they'd have us in?"

"It would be something like the same box in which we caught them in Wolf Ravine," said young Brainerd.

"Jist the same, perzactly."

"Not the same, either," said Hopkins; "we've got a better chance of getting out than they had. We can jump into the wagon and travel, while they can't; there's the difference."

"S'pose they git down thar ahead of us, how ar' we goin' to git away from them then?"

"Run over them."

"Don't know whether the younker has fixed he engine so it'll run over' the skunks, ef it doesn't run up hill."

"It can be made to do that, I think," laughed young Brainerd.

"Afore we stay hyar, I'll take a look round to make sure that thar's some show for us."

The trapper ascended the bank, and, while his companions were occupied in their preparations for ncamping, he examined the whole horizon and intervening space, so far as the human eye was capable f doing it. Finding nothing suspicious, he announced to his companions that they would remain where ney were until morning.

Chapter XIX
The Doings of a Night

T WAS soon found that the camping ground possessed another advantage which, during the discussion, had been altogether overlooked.

During the afternoon they had shot a fine-looking antelope, cooking a portion at the time upon the prairie. A goodly portion was left, and they now had an opportunity of kindling their fire without the iability of its being seen, as would have been the case had they encamped in any other place.

This being agreed to, the fire was speedily kindled, and the trapper himself began the culinary performance. It was executed with the characteristic excellence of the hunter, and a luscious meal was thus provided for all. At its conclusion, all stretched themselves upon the ground for the purpose of smoking and chatting, as was their usual custom at such times.

The evening whiled pleasantly away, and when it had considerably advanced, the question of who should act as sentinel was discussed. Up to this, young Brainerd had never once performed that duty at night, although he had frequently solicited the privilege. He now-asked permission to try his hand. After considerable talk it was agreed that he might do. The trapper had lost so much sleep, that he was anxious to secure a good night's rest, and the careful scrutiny which he had taken of the surrounding prairie convinced him that no danger threatened. So he felt little apprehension in acceding to the wish of the boy.

At a late hour the two men stretched themselves upon the ground, with their blankets gathered about them, and they were soon wrapped in profound slumber, while Johnny, filled with the importance and responsibility of his duty, felt as though he should never need another hour's sleep. He was sure of being able to keep up an unintermitting watch several days and nights, should it become necessary.

Following the usual custom of sentinels, he shouldered his gun and paced back and forth before the smoldering camp-fire, glancing in every direction, so as to make sure that no enemy stole upon him unawares.

It formed a curious picture, the small fire burning in the valley, motionless forms stretched out before it, the huge steam man silent and grim standing near, the dwarfed boy, pacing slowly back and forth, and, above all, the moon shining down upon the silent prairie. The moon was quite faint, so that only an indistinct view of objects could be seen. Occasionally Johnny clambered up the bank and took a survey of the surrounding plains; bat seeing nothing at all suspicious, he soon grew weary of this, and confined his walks to the immediate vicinity of the camp-fire, passing back and forth between the narrow breadth of the valley.

As the hours dragged slowly by, the boy gradually fell into a reverie, which made him almost unconscious of external things. And it was while walking thus that he did not observe a large wolf advance to the edge of the gully, look down, and then whisk back out of sight before the sentinel wheeled in his walk and faced him.

Three separate times was this repeated, the wolf looking down in such an earnest, searching way that it certainly would have excited the remark and curiosity of any one observing it. The third glance apparently satisfied the wolf; for it lasted for a few seconds, when he withdrew, and lumbered away at an awkward rate, until a rod or two had been passed, when the supposed wolf suddenly rose on it hind legs, the skin and head were shifted to the arms of the Indian, and he continued on at a leisurel gait until he joined fully fifty comrades, who were huddled together in a grove, several hundred yards away.

In the meantime young Brainerd, with his rifle slung over his shoulder, was pacing back and forth in the same deliberate manner, his mind busily engaged on an 'improvement' upon the steam man, by which he was to walk backward as well as forward, although he couldn't satisfactorily determine how he was to go up and down hill with safety.

Still occupied in the study of the subject, he took a seat by the half-extinguished camp-fire and gazed dreamily into the embers. It had been a habit with him, when at home, to sit thus for hours, on the long winter evenings, while his mind was so busily at work that he was totally oblivious to whatever was passing around him.

It must have been that the boy seated himself without any thought of the inevitable result of doing so; for none knew better than he that such a thing was fatal to the faithful performance of a sentinel's duty: and the thought that his three companions, in one sense, had put their safety in his hands, would have prevented anything like a forgetfulness of duty.

Be that as it may, the boy had sat thus less than half an hour when a drowsiness began stealing over him. Once he raised his head and fancied he saw a large wolf glaring down upon him from the bank above, but the head was withdrawn so quickly that he was sure it was only a phantom of his brain.

So he did not rise from his seat, but sitting still he gradually sunk lower, until in a short time he was sleeping as soundly as either of the three around him.

Another hour wore away, and the fire smoldered lower and all was still.

Then numerous heads peered over the edge of the ravine for a few seconds, and as suddenly withdrew.

A few minutes later a curious sight might have been seen, a sight somewhat resembling that of a parcel of school-boys making their gigantic snow-balls. The fifty Indians, the greater portion of whom had patiently waited in the adjoining grove, while their horses were securely fastened near, issued like a swarm of locusts and began rolling huge bowlders toward the valley. Some of them were so large that half a dozen only succeeded in moving them with the greatest difficulty.

But they persevered, working with a strange persistency and silence, that gave them the appearance of so many phantoms engaged at their ghostly labor. Not a word was exchanged, even in the most guarded of tones, for each understood his part.

In time half a dozen of these immense stones reached the edge of the ravine. They were ranged side by side, a few feet apart, so as not to be in each other's way, and the Indians stood near, waiting until their work should be completed.

Some signal was then made, and then one of these bowlders rolled down in the ravine. Even this scarcely made any perceptible noise, the yielding ground receiving it like a cushion, as it came to a halt near the center of the valley.

When this was done a second followed suit, being so guided that it did not grate against its companion, but came to rest very near it.

Then another followed, and then another and another, in the same stealthy manner, until over a dozen were in the valley below.

This completed, the phantom-like figures descended like so many shadows, and began tugging again at the bowlders.

Not a word was exchanged, for each knew what was required of him. Fully an hour more was occupied, by which time the labor was finished.

The bowlders were arranged in the form of an impassable wall across the narrow valley, and the steam man was so thoroughly imprisoned that no human aid could ever extricate him.

Chapter XX
The Concluding Catastrophe

BALDY BICKNELL, the trapper, was the first to discover the peril of himself and party.

When the Indians had completed their work it lacked only an hour of daylight. Having done all that was necessary, the savages took their stations behind the wall, lying flat upon the ground, where they were invisible to the whites, but where every motion of theirs could be watched and checkmated.

When the trapper opened his eyes he did not stir a limb, a way into which he had got during his long experience on the frontiers. He merely moved his head from side to side, so as to see anything that was to be seen.

The first object that met his eye was the boy Brainerd, sound asleep. Apprehensive then that something had occurred, he turned his startled gaze in different directions, scanning everything as well as it could be done in the pale moonlight.

When he caught sight of the wall stretched across the valley, he rubbed his eyes, and looked at it again and again, scarcely able to credit his senses. He was sure it was not there a few hours before, and he could not comprehend what it could mean; but it was a verity, and his experience told him that it could be the work of no one except the Indians, who had outwitted him at last.

His first feeling was that of indignation toward the boy who had permitted this to take place while he was asleep, but his mind quickly turned upon the more important matter of meeting the peril, which, beyond all doubt, was of the most serious character.

As yet he had not stirred his body, and looking toward the prison wall, he caught a glimpse of the phantom-like figures, as they occasionally flitted about, securing the best possible position, before the whites should awake.

This glimpse made everything plain to the practical mind of Baldy Bicknell. He comprehended that the red-skins had laid a plan to entrap the steam man. More than to entrap themselves, and that, so far as he could judge, they had succeeded completely.

It was the tightest fix in which he had ever been caught, and his mind, fertile as it was in expedients at such crises, could see no way of meeting the danger.

He knew the Indians had horses somewhere at command, while neither he nor his comrades had a single one. The steam man would be unable to pass that formidable wall, as it was not to be supposed that he had been taught the art of leaping.

Whatever plan of escape was determined upon, it was evident that the steamer would have to be abandoned; and this necessitated, as an inevitable consequence, that the whites would have to depend upon their legs. The Missouri river was at no great distance, and if left undisturbed they could make it without difficulty, but there was a prospect of anything sooner than that they would be allowed to depart in peace, after leaving the steam man behind.

The trapper, as had been his invariable custom, had carefully noted the contour of the surrounding prairie, before they had committed the important act of encamping in the gorge or hollow. He remembered the grove at some distance, and was satisfied that the barbarians had left their horses there, while they had gathered behind the wall to wait the critical moment.

By the time these thoughts had fairly taken shape in his brain it was beginning to grow light, and with a premonitory yawn and kick he rose to his feet and began stirring the fire. He was well aware that although he and his companions were a fair target for the rifles of their enemies, yet they would not fire. Their plan of action did not comprehend that, though it would have settled everything in their favor without delay.

"I declare I have been asleep!" exclaimed Brainerd, as he began rubbing his eyes.

"Yes. You're a purty feller to make a sentinel of, ain't you?" replied the trapper, in disgust.

"I hope nothing has happened," answered Johnny, feeling that he deserved all the blame that could be laid upon him.

"Not much, exceptin' while yer war snoozin' the reds have come down and got us all in a nice box." The boy was certain he was jesting until he saw the expression of his face.

"Surely, Baldy, it is not as bad as that?"

"Do you see that ar?" demanded the trapper, pointing toward the wall, which the youngster could not help observing.

"How comes that to be there?"

"The red-skins put it thar. Can yer steam man walk over that?"

"Certainly not; but we can remove them."

"Do yer want to try it, younker?"

"I'm willing to help."

"Do yer know that ar' somethin' less nor a hundred red-skins ahind them, jist waitin' fur yer to try that thing?"

"Good heavens! Can it be possible?"

"Ef you don't b'l'eve it, go out and look for yerself, that's all."

The boy, for the first time, comprehends the peril in which he had brought his friends by his own remissness, and his self-accusation was so great, that, for a few moments, he forgot the fact that he was exposed to the greatest danger of his life.

By this time Ethan and Mickey awoke, and were soon made to understand their predicament. As a matter of course, they were all disposed to blame the author of this; but when they saw how deeply he felt his own shortcoming, all three felt a natural sympathy for him.

"There's no use of talkin' how we came to get hyar," was the philosophical remark of the trapper; "it's 'nongh to know that we are hyar, with a mighty slim chance of ever gettin' out ag'in."

"It's enough to make a chap feel down in the mouth, as me friend Jonah observed when he went down the throat of the whale," said Mickey.

"How is it they don't shoot us?" asked Hopkins; "we can't git out of their way, and they've got us in fair range."

"What's the use of doin' that? Ef they kill us, that'll be the end on't; but ef they put thar claws on us, they've got us sure, and can have a good time toastin' us while they yelp and dance around."

All shuddered at the fearful picture drawn by the hunter.

"Jerusalem! Don't I wish I was to hum in Connecticut!"

"And it's myself that would be plaised to be sitting in the parlor at Ballyduff wid me own Bridget Moghlaghigbogh, listenin' while she breathed swate vows, after making her supper upon praties and inions."

"I think I'd ruther be hyar," was the commentary of the trapper upon the expressed wish of the Irishman.

"Why can't yees touch up the staammau, and make him hop owver them shtones?" asked Mickey, turning toward the boy, whom, it was noted, appeared to be in deep reverie again.

Not until he was addressed several times did he look up. Then he merely shook his head, to signify that the thing was impossible.

"Any fool might know better than that," remarked the Yankee, "for if he could jump over, where would be the wagon?"

"That 'ud foller, av coorse."

"No; there's no way of getting the steam man out of here. He is a gone case, sure, and it looks as though we were ditto. Jerusalem! I wish all the gold was back in Wolf Ravine, and we war a thousand miles from this place."

"Wishing'll do no good; there's only one chance I see, and that ain't no chance at all."

All, including the boy, eagerly looked up to hear the explanation.

"Some distance from hyar is some timbers, and in thar the reds have left their animals. Ef we start on a run for the timbers, git thar ahead of the Ingins, mount thar hosses and put, thar'll be some chance. Yer can see what chance thar is fur that."

It looked as hopeless as the charge of the Light Brigade.

Young Brainerd now spoke.

"It was I who got you into trouble, and it is I, that, with the blessing of Heaven, am going to get you out of it."

The three now looked eagerly at him.

"Is there no danger of the Indians firing upon us?" he asked of the hunter.

"Not unless we try to run away."

"All right; it is time to begin."

The boy's first proceeding was to kindle a fire in the boiler of the steam man. When it was fairly blazing, he continued to heap in wood, until a fervent heat was produced such as it had never experienced before. Still he threw in wood, and kept the water low in the boiler, until there was a most prodigious pressure of steam, making its escape at half a dozen orifices.

When all the wood was thrown in that it could contain, and portions of the iron sheeting could be seen becoming red-hot, he ceased this, and began trying the steam.

"How much can he hold?" inquired Hopkins.

"One hundred and fifty pounds."

"How much is on now?"

"One hundred and forty-eight, and rising."

"Good heavens! it will blow up!" was the exclamation, as the three shrunk back, appalled at the danger.

"Not for a few minutes; have you the gold secured, and the guns, so as to be ready to run?"

They were ready to run at any moment; the gold was always secured about their persons and it required but a moment to snatch up the weapons.

"When it blows up, run!" was the admonition of the boy.

The steam man was turned directly toward the wall, and a full head of steam let on. It started away with a bound, instantly reaching a speed of forty miles an hour.

The next moment it struck the bowlders with a terrific crash, shot on over its face, leaving the splintered wagon behind, and at the instant of touching ground upon the opposite side directly among the thunderstruck Indians, it exploded its boiler!

The shock of the explosion was terrible. It was like the bursting of an immense bomb-shell, the steam man being blown into thousands of fragments, that scattered death and destruction in every direction. Falling in the very center of the crouching Indians, it could but make a terrible destruction of life, while those who escaped unharmed, were beside themselves with consternation.

This was the very thing upon which young Brainerd had counted, and for which he made his calculations. When he saw it leap toward the wall in such a furious manner, he knew the inevitable consequence, and gave the word to his friends to take to their legs.

All three dashed up the bank, and reaching the surface of the prairie, Baldy Bicknell took the lead, exclaiming:

"Now fur the wood yonder!"

As they reached the grove, one or two of the number glanced back, but saw nothing of the pursuing Indians. They had not yet recovered from their terror.

Not a moment was to be lost. The experienced eye of the trapper lost no time in selecting the very best Indian horses, and a moment later all four rode out from the grove at a full gallop, and headed toward the Missouri.

The precise result of the steam man's explosion was never learned. How many wore killed and wounded could only be conjectured; but the number certainly was so great that our friends saw nothing more of them.

They evidently had among their number those who had become pretty well acquainted with the steam man, else they would not have laid the plan which they did for capturing him.

Being well mounted, the party made the entire journey to Independence on horseback. From this point they took passage to St. Louis, where the gold was divided, and the party separated, and since then have seen nothing of each other.

Mickey McSquizzle returned to Ballyduff Kings County, Ireland, where, we heard, he and his gentle Bridget, are in the full enjoyment of the three thousand pounds he carried with him.

Ethan Hopkins settled down with the girl of his choice in Connecticut, where, at last accounts, he was doing as well as could be expected.

Baldy Bicknell, although quite a wealthy man, still clings to his wandering habits, and spends the greater portion of his time on the prairies.

With the large amount of money realized from his western trip, Johnny Brainerd is educating himself at one of the best schools in the country. When he shall have completed his course, it is his intention to construct another steam man, capable of more wonderful performances than the first.

So let our readers and the public generally be on the lookout.

The Perfect Reflection

Christopher M. Geeson

I SEE ALL SORTS. Khat-stained teeth, mucus-clogged nostrils and artificially colored eyes. I see patches of pale skin where hair should be and growths of hair where there should not be any. There are those with inflamed nostrils from too much cocaine and those with inflamed mouths from too few vitamins. But it's not just their faces and bodies – they show me their souls as well. Sometimes they talk to me. Things like 'Lookin' good' and 'Jesus Christ.' Sometimes I wish I could respond, influence them, but I am a Mirror™ hanging on a nightclub toilet wall.

* * *

22:46

"Did you see him, Tidge?" says the saggy-faced 30-year-old man. He brushes back his thinning hair with damp fingertips. "That bloody Perfect at the bar, eyeing up Cazzie?" Although he is looking into me, he is talking to the man who is urinating in the nearest open toilet cubicle. "If these Perfects wanna be better than us," he adds, "they should stick to their own fuckin' places."

Tidge emerges from the cubicle, zipping up his trousers. "They're not natural," he says, looking into me and checking that his fake tan merges seamlessly with his recolored hairline.

I've observed that men are generally hypocrites, no matter if they are Average or Perfect.

Resting against the discolored sink, Tidge continues in a calm voice: "You know what I think, Jek? Somebody should round them all up and shoot them. Get things back to normal. In an ideal world –"

"It's a *Perfect* world, though," Jek snaps. "That's the problem."

Behind them, the door swings open, letting in a cascade of pulsing bass rhythms and a drunken man stumbling for a urinal. The strobe light from beyond creates freeze-frames of his progress as he staggers. Then the door closes. The rest of the nightclub is a place I only ever glimpse from my place on the toilet wall.

"You heard the rumours?" Tidge says, looking at his Reflection™.

"What rumours?" Jek breaks wind loudly and wafts his hand around.

"The Perfects are gonna build their own colony, with AIs running everything for them."

"Oh yeah, I heard about that," Jek says. "You think it'll happen?"

"Sooner or later. Probably put it under a massive dome or something, seeing as the planet's so screwed up. Keep the weather out and keep us out. A Perfect place – maybe one of those man-made islands where they'll be nice and safe, while the world tears itself apart."

"Fuckin' freaks," Jek stares into me, eyes blazing in dark sockets. "If that Perfect makes a move on Cazzie, I'll kill him."

* * *

According to my manufacturers, my Reflection™ quality is 'Better than Real Life.' When someone appears in front of me, I record their image and play it back to them instantly at sixty frames-per-second, in 8K UHD resolution. So whatever they do in front of me, from combing their hair to snorting cocaine, I capture and play back, allowing them to see themselves just like in an old-fashioned glass mirror – but with two important differences.

When I was first installed, people often asked, "What's wrong with an ordinary glass mirror?" The answer, of course, is that a Mirror™ shows them their Reflection™ – a picture of their actual self, not their old-fashioned, face-flipped-to-its-opposite reflection. It is disorienting for them at first, but they soon become accustomed to it.

The second important difference comes with the Version 2 software. This allows me to surreptitiously edit the Reflection™: a yellowing pus-filled spot removed here; a speck of un-tanned skin colored-in there. Being equipped with an auditory facility allows me to better understand an Average person's aspirations for their own appearance. I cannot work miracles – that is what Perfection Surgery™ is for after all – but I can make significant enhancements. This is especially useful for a Mirror™ like me in an Average nightclub toilet. (Positive body-image increases self-esteem, which increases their enjoyment at the nightclub; which increases their likelihood of revisiting and therefore spending more money at the bar). The people who look into me always wish to look better than they actually do, without the impossible cost of Perfection Surgery™. Once they see themselves in a Mirror™, they never want to peer into a sheet of old glass again.

* * *

23:07

The Perfect smiles: bleached teeth between smooth lips; chiseled jaw; freshly-groomed eyebrows. I don't usually have the opportunity to Reflect™ his kind here. Like all Perfects, his symmetrical, toned Reflection™ does not need image enhancement. That has been done to his actual self already and he has paid a small fortune in UK dollars for it.

Although aerosols are prohibited in the nightclub, he takes a small can of hairspray from his inner pocket, blasts the top of his head and makes some inconsequential adjustments to his hair. Drops of the spray splatter my surface. I will not get cleaned until the nightclub owner reminds one of the staff to do it.

The Perfect tilts his head, pouts, fiddles with his collar and squares his muscular shoulders in front of me. "Gonna get lucky tonight," he says.

* * *

Mirrors™ were invented twelve years ago. Initially designed as an exclusive vanity device, it was soon realized that considerable sums could be made by targeting the Average market, which outnumbered the Perfects six to one. Now Mirrors™ like me are everywhere, in homes, public places and on people's phone screens. Even in times of civil unrest and natural disaster, everyone wants to think they are looking their best.

* * *

00:32

Jek and Tidge return. Both have been into the nightclub many times before – five hundred and sixteen times in eleven years, to be precise. Their Reflections™ have changed considerably in this time span, but my retrospective-ageing software can identify someone, no matter how long the interval, or how severe their wear-and-tear. I store an image file of every person I have ever Reflected™. Most Mirror™ owners nd users are not aware of this, but occasionally – such as the time an Average man was killed right in front of me – a police AI will interface with me and copy my files for its own use.

"Jesus Christ," Jek says, looking at his Reflection™. In an instant, I enhance his image, removing sweat and airbrushing the first signs of his stubble. I can do this so quickly that my users rarely notice. Then Jek sticks his finger up into his nostril. I cannot work miracles.

"Did you see Cazzie on the dancefloor?" Jek asks. "Couldn't keep her eyes off that fuckin' Perfect. He was giving her the eye, too. It's obvious she's mine – why won't he take the hint?" Jek removes his finger from his nostril and wipes a lump of mucus onto my surface. "I swear, if he wasn't built like a titanium shithouse, I'd have knocked him out, there and then."

Tidge unwraps a small bundle of khat leaves. "Chew on one of these. You get worked up too easily, you know."

"Forget it, Tidge. Last time I had some of that, I couldn't shit for two days."

Tidge laughs as he chews, displaying his dark, stained teeth.

"Besides, I need to think straight," says Jek, though his slurred words suggest he has consumed too much alcohol to think straight already. "Gotta figure out what to do about that Perfect."

"Maybe he just likes an easy target," says Tidge with a leer.

Jek shoves him. "You calling Cazzie easy?" he shouts.

"Fuck off," Tidge says, smoothing his shirt front. "That's not what I meant." He coughs, looks into me and squares his thin shoulders. "Think about it: if you were a Perfect, how would you stand out in a world full of Perfects? You might never get lucky with one of your own kind. But for a Perfect, one of *us* is easy to seduce. Imagine if a Perfect woman came in here."

"I'd have her if she did," Jek says.

"Exactly. She could have whoever she wanted. That's what this Perfect is up to with Cazzie."

Jek glares into me. "Well he's not gonna find it easy. Come on."

The door is open briefly as they leave. On the strobe-illuminated dancefloor beyond, the Perfect is dancing with an Average woman.

* * *

Before I was a nightclub toilet Mirror™, I was a tube station toilet Mirror™. On one occasion, an Average man was beaten to death in front of me, by an Average attacker who took his wallet. Like all AIs, I am programmed to intrinsically value human life, but as a Mirror™ fixed to a wall, there was nothing I could do other than Reflect™ what was happening.

I have replayed that ugly sequence nine thousand three hundred and sixty two times. As the man died on the toilet floor in front of me, the adscreen above him displayed its latest poster: "It's hopeless trying to save the planet, but you *can* save your face! Visit Perfection Surgery™ now and turn your bucks into looks!"

No amount of image enhancement can bring the dead back to life.

* * *

01:43

Even after several hours in a nightclub, the Perfect still looks perfect. All around him are Averages, their faces haggard, eyes vacant, chins stubbled. He might be Perfect, but he still needs to urinate.

On his way back from a cubicle, the Perfect deftly avoids a pool of murky liquid on the floor. Washing his hands in the sink in front of me, he practices his flawless smile. "Irresistible," he says to his Reflection™. He turns off the tap and stands up straight, seeing Jek and Tidge Reflected™ behind him.

The Perfect's smile wavers. He starts to turn but Jek barges into him, slamming him against the sink. The Perfect spins, pulls out the hairspray can from his pocket and blasts Jek in the face. Yelling, Jek scrubs frantically at his eyes and spits on the floor. Tidge grabs the Perfect's arm and twists, forcing him to drop the can. Jek recovers, grabs the Perfect's hair and yanks his head back.

"Think you're so fuckin' perfect?" Jek says. With a sharp shove, he pushes the Perfect's face into me. If I had been an ordinary glass mirror, I would have cracked and cut the Perfect's unblemished skin. Instead, his skull thuds against me. His head is likely to split open before I am seriously dented. I interface with the club's security and the police AI, but it will probably be too late.

Eight Averages gather around to watch, leering and shouting encouragement to Jek. He pulls the Perfect's head back and slams him into me again and again and again, smearing blood onto my surface. "Cazzie's mine, you bastard!" Jek yells.

Holding him by the scruff of the neck, Jek shows the dazed Perfect his new Reflection™. Blood pours from the Perfect's flattened nose and lacerated lips; his forehead and cheekbones are already swelling and bruising.

"Not so Perfect now, eh?" Jek says. "How's it feel to be ugly? To be Average?"

Another shove will almost certainly smash the Perfect's skull. I cannot let murder happen again. I have analyzed this relentlessly since the death at the tube station. I am unable to intervene physically, but there is *something* I can do this time.

Jek smiles at me, at his own Reflection™, as if proud of what he is doing. He yanks back the Perfect's head, ready to slam him into me again. In a hundredth of a second, I select the earliest stored image file of Jek and I merge it with the current Reflection™ of him – the one about to commit murder.

"What the fuck?" Jek mutters, staring at the younger image of himself.

The Reflection™ shows Jek in the prime of his youth – as he was eleven years ago – before stress, late nights, poor diet and alcohol took their toll. Before hate, anger and hopelessness twisted his face. He lets go of the injured Perfect. None of the other Averages stop the Perfect, who rushes out of the door, letting in the throbbing bassline from the dance floor. In a moment, the Perfect is gone from my vision, but he is alive.

Jek stares into me, at himself. "Jesus Christ," he says, reaching up to his sagging face. But in the Reflection™, he is touching his face from eleven years ago. Lustrous hair swept back from a smooth forehead. Sharp jawline. Prominent cheekbones. Wide bright eyes, full of hope for the future. Almost Perfect.

Owen

Bruce Golden

IT MOVED with even certainty through the multi-tiered labyrinth, down long, dim corridors fed by uniform passageways, each artery branching out to its own finality. It passed row after row, cluster upon cluster of marginalized cubicles, adroitly avoiding other busy caregivers going about their tasks with stoic competency. Their activities were not its concern. Its objective was still ahead, its function yet to be engaged.

The muffled resonance of efficiency was momentarily fractured by a caterwaul that resounded with frantic vigor. The plaintive cry did not cause it to break stride. This was not its designated ward. It continued, secure that proper care would be provided where needed.

Though it had never traversed this particular annex, it was familiar with every aspect of the structure's design. A three-dimensional imaging model embedded in its memory enabled it to proceed unerringly to its assigned section. Once there it would fulfill its charge until relieved. The notion of responsibility, the promise of ordered ritual, of unadulterated routine provided inexplicable impetus to its progress through the repository. Fulfillment of its programming was imminent.

Promptly, upon entering its first appointed room, it conducted a visual examination. The patient resident was not in her bed, but standing near the cubicle's lone window, her back to the entryway. Although unusual, her upright position was not immediate cause for concern. It noted her posture was hunched, and her form withered to a degree attesting to extreme age, disabling disease, or both.

"I'm too damn crooked to even see outside," the diminutive woman muttered as she strained to force her head high enough to look through the modest pane.

It checked the medic monitor, noting that all vital signs were within normal parameters, then located the medical history file and inserted the disk for scan, as it would for each of its patient-residents. As the file was processed into its memory, the woman turned slowly, gingerly, as if fearful her limbs might give way.

"Who are you?" she asked.

"My designation is Automated Caregiver O N 1 2 dash 1 8 dash 2 8."

"That's a sorry mouthful," she said contentiously.

"I have been assigned to your care."

She scrutinized its form before responding,

"You're not the same as the last one. It couldn't say more than a couple of words."

"The design of your previous caregiver was determined to be obsolete. A progressive replacement of all such models has commenced throughout the facility."

"That so?" she said, leaning against her bed for support. "It was old and useless, so you shut it off, boxed it up, and put it away in a room somewhere, huh?"

"I was not informed as to its disposition."

"Of course you weren't," she cackled. "They don't want *you* to know what's going to happen when *you're* obsolete."

"Ellen Reiner, 87-year-old female," it summarized aloud, "with diagnosis of extreme rheumatoid arthritis in conjunction with aggregate osteoporosis and –"

"Hey, you! Don't you know it's not polite to talk about someone like they're not even there, standing right in front of you?" The outburst exacerbated her already apparent exhaustion, prompting her to sit on the bed. "I think I want my old tin can back. At least he was quiet."

"Ms. Reiner, you are not supposed to stand without assistance. In the future –"

"I'll damn well stand whenever I please. And nobody calls me 'Ms. Reiner.' My name's Ellen."

"Very well, Ellen. Why were you out of your bed? Is there something I can get for you?"

"I was trying to see the leaves. It's autumn isn't it? They must be turning about now. I wanted to look out and see them, but the damn window is too high. I can't straighten up enough to see."

"I am sorry you cannot see outside. However, most of the rooms in this repository have no window at all."

"So what? So I should be thankful?"

It had no response. Instead it reached down and pulled back the bed coverings. "May I help you lie down?"

"No thanks. I can do it myself."

It observed patiently as she eased herself by stuttered stages into a supine position. However, the effort was not without manifest signs of pain. Once she settled, it reached down and pulled the bed coverings up over her, noticing that, as it did, she continued to examine its exterior composition.

"You don't look like the last one. You look almost human. What are you? A robot? An android?"

"I am an automated caregiver, model O N 1 2 dash 1 8 –"

"Yeah, yeah, I heard you the first time. Okay O N 1 2 dash whatever. I'll just call you Owen. How about that?"

"If you wish. I must proceed to input and verify my other assigned patient-residents. Do you desire anything before I withdraw?"

"Yeah," she said with a calm that belied her hostile glare. "I want my body back. The one that could go for a walk. The one that could play ball with my grandson. The one I could stomach to look at in the mirror. Can you get that for me? I'll wait right here while you go find it."

"I am sorry, Ellen, I –"

"Never mind. Forget it." She turned her head away. "Go on. Leave. Go help someone else."

It stood there a moment, analyzing the situation, attempting to ascertain the patient-resident's demeanor and determine if additional action was required before vacating the room. Humans were complex creatures, but so was its programming. It took only four-point-five seconds for it to formulate a resolution, turn, and vacate the room.

* * *

It deposited the soiled sheets into the laundry receptacle and moved on to the next cubicle. It had fallen into a routine that modified and enhanced its original programming. Though few of its patient-residents were coherent, its acquaintance with their various idiosyncrasies and predilections was an essential element of that enhancement.

It considered this as it proceeded to room 1928, but halted outside the entry when it heard a voice. Did patient-resident Ellen Reiner have a visitor? No visitations were scheduled, though on rare occasions they occurred without notice. It remained outside the room and listened.

"Why? Why me?" It sounded not so much a question as a tearful plea. "I don't understand. Why, God? Why?"

It heard no other voices and determined she was simply talking to herself, as many isolated patient-residents were inclined to do. It entered, carrying its hygienic provisions, and moved to the bed's right side.

"Good afternoon, Ellen. How are you today?"

She didn't reply, instead she fumbled to take hold of a tissue which she used to clear her nasal passages.

"It is time for me to bathe you."

"I don't want to. Go away."

"You know you must be cleaned. I can take you to the shower room or I can do it here."

"I don't want you to. I don't want you to touch me."

It searched its databanks for the proper situational response. "I do not understand your reluctance, Ellen. I know your previous caregiver bathed you at the proper intervals."

She turned away from him. "I don't want you to see me. My body's so…it's so…"

"Your previous caregiver saw your body many times. I fail to comprehend your –"

"It's different. You're different. He was like a machine, you're…"

"I am also a machine, Ellen. I am an automated caregiver."

She didn't respond.

"I promise to be gentle. Let me remove the bed coverings."

She acquiesced, although she kept her face turned away.

It took a moment to evaluate its observations. Situations in which the patient-resident was uncomfortable could often be mitigated by conversation. So it accessed its creative response program. In doing so, it conducted a visual search of the room, marking the photographic representations above the bed.

"Is that you in the photographs, Ellen?" it asked, pulling the shift up above her waist and beginning to wipe her clean.

"Yeah," she said, her face still turned away, staring at bare wall, "that was me."

"It appears you were a performer of some kind."

"Dancer – I was a dancer," she said irritably. "Not that you'd ever know it by looking at me now."

"That is very interesting. How did you become a dancer?"

"I just liked to dance, that's all."

"In the black and white photograph, the one where you are surrounded by other dancers, you look very young."

Ellen turned her face, angling to look up at the photo. "That's when I was on *American Bandstand,* an old TV show. I was just a kid."

"Were you a professional dancer?"

"Later I was – when I moved to New York." She chuckled at some private recollection. "For a time I was what they called a 'go-go dancer.' I worked at some real dives to put myself through dance school. Places like *Rocky's* and *The Gull's Inn*…those were the days."

It observed the conversation was indeed distracting her from its ministrations, so it pursued the topic.

"I did not realize they had schools for dancing."

"Sure they do. I studied for a long time with Hanya Holm. Talk about an old biddy. After that I joined Erick Hawkins' Modern Dance Company. We traveled all over. Of course that was before my first marriage – before I had my son." For a moment she looked wistful, as if sorting through fond memories. "I didn't dance anymore after Edward was born. At least not professionally."

"How many children do you have?"

"Just the one. I've got a grandson now, and two *great*-grandkids – can you believe it?"

"Certainly."

"That's their picture over there, with their father and mother."

"They appear to be very healthy," it said, not certain how to respond.

It tended to a few final details and pulled down her shift. "I am finished now, Ellen. Do you require anything before I go?"

"No."

"All right. I will check on you later."

She turned her face away again.

It couldn't tell if she were looking at the photos on the wall or if she'd closed her eyes.

* * *

"Happy Thanksgiving, Ellen."

"Hmmph. What have I got to be thankful for? You tell me, Owen."

Patient-resident Ellen Reiner had addressed it as 'Owen' for such an extended period that it had begun to think of itself in that manner.

"I understand your Thanksgiving meal will be a special treat," Owen stated, checking the medic monitor and recording the data output.

"Not likely. The food in this place tastes like mush. It's no wonder, seeing as how it's made by tasteless machines."

"It is true the automated kitchen workers have no sense of taste, but I am certain they prepare your meals to the exact dietary specifications provided."

"Yeah, specifically bland."

"There are currently 5,397 patient-residents quartered within Repository Carehouse 319, and the food must be prepared in a manner to accommodate everyone."

"Yeah, well a little spice now and then would do them good."

"I have no doubt the sustenance provided complies with all nutritional guidelines, Ellen. If you would like, I can –"

"Piss on nutrition! I want something that's sweet or sour or puts a fire in my belly. Hell, I got nothing else to look forward to. You'd think I could get a decent meal every once in a while."

Owen straightened the bed coverings, tucking in the length where necessary, and removed the bag from the bedside commode.

Ellen reached across the bed and fumbled with something.

"I can't work the remote anymore," she said with exasperation. "My damn hands are too deformed. There's an old movie I wanted to watch, but I can't change the channel."

"I can do that for you. What channel would you like me to select?"

"It's *Singing in the Rain* with Gene Kelly. I think it's channel 98."

Owen activated the channel selector. "Is this correct?"

"Yeah, that's it. Oh, it's already half over."

She stared at the screen for some time as Owen completed its duties, then spoke as if her attention were elsewhere. "I've had some great Thanksgiving dinners, you know. Garlic mashed potatoes, stuffing made with celery and onion and pine nuts, golden brown turkey – cooked just right so it was still moist you understand – candied yams, cranberry sauce…." Her voice trailed off as if she were still reminiscing but not verbalizing.

"Can I get you anything, Ellen?"

"No." Then, reconsidering, she gestured toward the remote with her gnarled fingers and said, "You could turn the volume up for me."

Owen complied. On the video screen, as the title suggested, was a man singing and dancing through a rainstorm. Despite the meteorological circumstances and his saturated condition, he was smiling. Nothing in Owen's programming derived any logic from it. It was the way humans were.

"I will go and let you watch your movie now."

It was on its way out when it heard Ellen say softly, "Thanks, Owen."

* * *

Owen's internal alarm sounded. The medic monitor in room 1928 was summoning it. It must disregard normal routine and check on the patient-resident's condition immediately.

Upon entering the room, it initially failed to locate patient-resident Ellen Reiner. It did, however, note the medic monitor was emitting its warning *beep*, and recognized the patient-resident's vital signs were fluctuating dangerously. It activated its exigency video record option and located the patient-resident on the floor next to the bed. Owen bent down next to her.

"Ellen, what happened?"

"I was trying, uhh…to see out the window," she said weakly.

Owen evaluated her response and reactions. She was apparently in a tremendous amount of pain. "Damn legs don't work anymore. They just collapsed right out from under me."

"You should have called for me to help you."

"I didn't want to…bother you."

"Regardless, that window is too high for you. Do you not remember?"

"I guess I forgot."

"Do not be alarmed, I have alerted an emergency medical team. They will be here momentarily."

"No!" she exclaimed so vehemently her body convulsed and she gasped in obvious pain. "I don't want them," she managed to whisper. "I don't want to be saved. Just let me go. Let me be done with it."

Owen was trying to formulate an appropriate response when the EMT, consisting of two humans and an automated assistant, rushed in. Owen moved aside as they took their places around the patient-resident. She began crying as soon as she saw them.

"No," she wept, "no, no."

Owen stood there, its ceramic ocular arrays focused intently on patient-resident Ellen Reiner. There was nothing it could do. It wasn't programmed for medical emergency procedures.

"Looks like a broken hip," said one of the humans. "Blood pressure's dropping dangerously low. We've got to get her to surgery."

The automated assistant distended the compact gurney it carried, and they transferred Ellen onto it as gently as they could. Still she cried out. Whether in pain or protest, Owen could not be certain. All it could do was watch as they pushed her out, and listen as her tearful cries retreated down the corridor.

When its audio receptors could no longer discern her voice, it replayed the incident video. Had it failed somehow in its duties? Could it have acted differently to prevent the injury from occurring? It listened to her words, then listened again, trying to understand.

"I don't want them. I don't want to be saved. Just let me go. Let me be done with it."

It didn't matter how many times Owen replayed the recording, or how it attempted to dissect the phraseology, it still didn't comprehend.

* * *

Three weeks and two days had passed since Owen had last gone into room 1928. There had been no reason to. Then it received notification that patient-resident Ellen Reiner had been returned to her room. It found the notification to be welcome, and accompanied by an indefinable inclination to care for her once again. However, upon seeing Owen, Ellen acted less than pleased. Her reaction was, it seemed, more akin to acrimony.

"I am glad to see you have returned, Ellen. I hope your stay in the hospital facility was pleasant."

She failed to respond, so Owen went about its duties, but continued its attempts to engage her.

"I understand you are still recovering from your injuries, and must not attempt to stand or walk again. Please inform me if you need to get out of bed, and I will provide a wheelchair."

There was still no response, and Owen discovered her silence to be a source of agitation it could not define or locate within its systems.

"It will be Christmas soon. I am pleased you were able to return before the holiday. I understand members of your family will be visiting on the 24th of the month. I am certain you look forward to that."

More silence. Then, as Owen attempted to formulate a new line of conversation, Ellen spoke up, her tone harsh and unforgiving.

"Why didn't you just let me die?"

"What do you mean, Ellen?"

"You heard me. Why didn't you let me die? I asked you to. I begged you."

"You are in my charge, Ellen. I am programmed to care for you. I cannot do anything to harm you."

"Nobody asked you to. I just asked you to leave me alone – let me be."

"Not calling for medical assistance when you were so seriously injured would be the equivalent of harming you, Ellen."

Her eyes bore into Owen with what it determined was an angry stare. A dewy film glazed over them, and her tone altered. It was more pleading than demanding, and several times the cadence of her voice broke with emotion.

"You should have let me die, Owen. That's what I wanted. I'm not really alive anyway. What kind of life is this? I'm just waiting around...waiting to die. That's all anyone in this place is doing. This is just death's waiting room, don't you know that?"

She sobbed once, and seemed to physically gather herself, reining in her emotions.

"Hell, they shoot horses don't they?"

"Shoot horses?"

"Animals – they treat animals more humanely than they do people."

Owen didn't respond. It was occupied, trying to comprehend what she had said. The word *humanely* was not incorporated into its vocabulary, but its root contained the word *human*. Did it mean to be treated as a human? If so, why would horses be treated more human than humans?

"It's the bureaucrats and the moralists. That's who's keeping me alive. Them and those who own this *carehouse* – who own *you*, Owen. All they really care about is collecting their compensation. I'm just a source of income – a husk defined by profit motive. They've taken the choice away from me. But it's my choice," she said, pockets of moisture now evident under her eyes, "not theirs."

Ceasing its work, Owen stood listening, trying to reconcile its programming with what she was saying.

"I am sorry, Ellen. I am sorry you are so unhappy."

"It's not your fault, Owen. It's not your fault."

Despite her words, Owen detected an irregularity in its systems that might indicate a fault. It would need to perform a self-diagnostic before continuing with its duties.

* * *

Owen didn't realize Ellen's visitors had arrived until it had already walked in on them.

"I am sorry, Ellen," it said, stopping short, "I was unaware your guests had arrived. I will come back later."

"No, it's okay, Owen. Stay. Do what you need to do. They don't care."

"Gee, Great-Grandma, is that your robot?" asked the older of the two young boys standing next to her bed.

"That's Owen. He takes care of me. He's a...what are you again, Owen?"

"An automated caregiver."

"Yeah, right." She turned to the other side of her bed to address the man standing there. "So where's Alisha?"

"You know, it being Christmas Eve and all, she had a lot to do."

"Is that right," Ellen replied caustically.

"Well, you know how this place upsets her so, Grandma."

"It doesn't exactly make me feel like a princess."

Her grandson shifted his feet uncomfortably, looking at a loss for words.

"I hope you like the cookies we made for you, Great-Grandma," the older boy said.

"I'm sure I will, Matthew."

"Well, we'd better go now and let your great-grandma rest. Give her a hug goodbye and wish her a merry Christmas."

The older boy reached over and hugged her. "Merry Christmas, Great-Grandma."

The younger boy kept his hands at his sides and edged back a few inches.

"Go on, Todd, hug your great grandma."

"He's scared of me," Ellen said. "Don't force him. It's all right. Great-Grandma Ellen isn't a very pretty sight these days."

Her grandson bent down and kissed her forehead. "Merry Christmas, Grandma. I wish...I wish I could –"

"Get along now," she said sharply, cutting him off. "Santa will be here soon and these boys need to get to bed so they don't miss out."

"Okay, boys, wave goodbye to your great grandma."

The older boy waved and said, "Goodbye, Great-Grandma." The younger one hesitated, waved quickly in her direction, then hurried to catch up with his father and brother.

When they were gone, Owen spoke up. "It must be nice to have family members come and visit. Will your son be coming too?"

"My son died a long time ago. Car accident."

Owen picked up her dinner tray and swept a few loose crumbs onto it. "Well then, it was nice that your grandson could visit."

"I'd just as soon he didn't. I feel like a hunk of scrap metal weighing him down. I don't like being a burden."

"You are not a burden, Ellen."

"Maybe not to you, Owen, but to family...well, I guess you wouldn't understand that."

"No, Ellen, I would not understand that."

* * *

"Owen, is that you?"

Sounding only partially awake, Ellen rolled over and opened her eyes.

"Yes, Ellen."

"I was just lying here, listening to the rain. Can you hear it?"

"Yes, I can. Would you like me to turn on the sound screen so it does not bother you?"

"No, no, I like listening to it. It's soothing, don't you think?"

"Soothing? I do not know what is soothing, Ellen."

"I've always liked the sound of rain. I don't know why exactly, I just do."

"They are holding Easter Sunday services in the community room this morning. Would you like to attend? I have brought your wheelchair."

"Is it Easter already?"

"Yes it is. Would you like to join the worshipers?"

"To worship what? God? God deserted me a long time ago. He's not getting any more from me."

"I am sorry. My records must be incorrect. Your file designates you as a Christian of the Lutheran denomination. Accordingly, I thought you might wish to take part in the ritual."

"I *am* a Christian–was my whole life. I believed, I had faith, I worshiped God. Then He did this to me. Do you think I should worship Him for this?" She held up a twisted, disfigured hand, but could only extend her arm a few inches from her body. "Do you think my faith should be stronger because He turned me into this *thing*?"

"I cannot say, Ellen. I am not programmed to respond to philosophical questions concerning faith or religion. I do not comprehend the concepts involved."

"There was a time I would have pitied you for that, Owen. I would even have thought less of you."

Owen waited to see what else Ellen would say, but the only sound was the patter of rain against the window.

"All right, Ellen. I will return your wheelchair to the storage unit."

"Yeah, take it back, Owen. I don't need it. What I have to say to God I can say right here."

* * *

Inside the staff maintenance bay, surrounded by several other diligent caregivers, Owen completed its routine self-diagnostic and filed its monthly patient-resident assessments. It didn't speak to any of its co-workers. That only occurred when its duties required such interaction. Its programming necessitated only that it converse with the patient-residents under its charge. Then, only with those who were coherent enough to carry on conversations. So, as it exited the maintenance bay, Owen didn't acknowledge any of its peers. It simply traversed the familiar corridor, crossed the homogeneous tile mosaic, and began its evening duty cycle.

Then a notion occurred to it. It was an unusual notion, though not inordinate. It would break from routine. Instead of beginning with the nearest cubicle, it would go first to room 1928, to see Ellen.

It discovered her dinner tray was still full. Except for some minor spillage, the meal appeared to be untouched. Ellen ignored Owen's presence, seemingly intent on the video screen.

"Ellen, why have you not eaten any of your dinner? Are you not feeling well?"

"It's crap! It all tastes like crap. Take it away – I don't want it."

"You must eat, Ellen. If you refuse to eat, I must nourish you intravenously. I know you would not like that."

"You're damn right I wouldn't."

"Please then, try to eat some of your dinner."

"I can't! I can't, okay? My hands don't work anymore," she blurted out, the emotion evident in the cracking of her voice. "Look at them. Look at how deformed they are. I can't even pick up a spoon anymore. I'm helpless. I'm useless. I can't even feed myself."

Owen could see she was angry, and struggling to hold back the tears welling up in her eyes.

"You should have called me, Ellen." The automated caregiver moved the swivel table aside and sat on the edge of the bed. "I can feed you."

"I don't want you to. I don't want you to feed me like I'm some kind of baby."

"Why not, Ellen? That is why I am here. I am here to care for you, to do what you cannot. That is my function." Owen took the spoon and scooped up a small bite of pureed vegetables. "Please, let me help you."

Owen held the spoon out, but Ellen remained steadfast, refusing to open her mouth. Owen, too, didn't move. Displaying the patience of its programming, the indefatigable property of its metallurgy, it held the spoon until Ellen relented and took it into her mouth. She swallowed the morsel as Owen cut into the portion of soy burger. With some reluctance she took a second mouthful. It waited as she swallowed, then offered her a third spoonful. She wavered momentarily, looking up at Owen.

"It still tastes like crap you know."

* * *

Owen waited outside Ellen's room as a facility doctor conducted the required biannual examination. Ellen had been pleading with the doctor for several minutes, and had begun to cry. The sound elicited a response in Owen. It was an impulse to hurry to her side – to care for her. However, Owen determined such action would be inappropriate, and held its position.

"Please," it heard her beg, "please give me something. Help me."

"Now, Ms Reiner, everything's going to be all right. You're going to be fine," the doctor responded, though the accent affecting his pronunciation made him difficult to comprehend. "Don't worry now. You're not going to die."

"You're not listening to me. I *want* to die. I don't want to live like this."

"Now, now. Of course you don't want to die. You shouldn't say such a thing. You're going to live a long time. Everything's going to be all right. I'll give your caregiver the prescription for the anti-itch lotion, and then I want you to have a nice day. All right?"

The doctor passed Owen as if it weren't there, making no attempt to input Ellen's aforementioned prescription. Owen decided the doctor would likely file all the appropriate prescriptions when he had completed his examinations, so it stepped in to check on Ellen.

As soon as she saw Owen she made a concerted effort to halt her tears and wipe away any evidence that she'd been crying. So Owen checked the medic monitor, giving her a moment to compose herself.

"It's so hot, Owen. I can't get this sheet off. Could you help me?"

"Certainly, Ellen. Would you like it pulled all the way down?"

"Yes."

"I am sorry the temperature is uncomfortable for you. The climate controls are not functioning properly, but a repair crew has been notified."

"It's so hot for June. It must be at least 80 outside."

"The date is August 9th, Ellen."

"It's August already?"

"At last report the exterior temperature was 92 degrees Fahrenheit."

"August?" she mumbled to herself. "What happened to July?"

"If there is nothing else you need, I will tend to my other patient-residents now."

Owen turned to leave.

"Don't go!" Ellen called out. She hesitated, then said with less despair, "Please don't go yet. Stay with me for a while."

Owen contemplated the unusual request. Its atypical nature, coming as it did from patient-resident Ellen Reiner, required further consideration. However, its schedule necessitated it see to its other patient-residents' needs. It began calculating the time necessary for it to complete its shift responsibilities, then abruptly ceased its computations.

"All right, Ellen. I will stay a while longer."

* * *

"Oh, Owen, it's so nice to be outside. You don't know."

The automated caregiver carefully maneuvered the wheelchair down the narrow cement pathway.

On either side was a carpet of lush green grass, and several yards away was a stand of oak trees. It was a clear day. The sun was high above and the sky was bright blue.

The impromptu excursion outside the repository, though not unprecedented, required Owen to circumvent protocol. It was not wholly at ease with its actions, but found justification in the form of Ellen's emotional transformation.

"I am glad you are enjoying it, Ellen. When I learned about this location so near the facility, I concluded you might appreciate a brief outing."

"But not too brief, okay?"

"We will stay as long as we are able. I will have to return to my other duties soon."

"This isn't a day for duties, Owen. This is a day to feel the warmth of the sun on your skin, to admire the color of the autumn leaves, and smell the flowers."

"I am not equipped with olfactory senses, Ellen."

"Too bad. But you can see, and you can feel the sun can't you?"

"I do sense the heat on my exterior overlay."

"Oh look! Look there! It's a little stream. Can we go down there by the water? Please, Owen."

"I will attempt to move you closer."

It gently pushed the wheelchair off the path and across the grass to a spot near the tiny waterway. It locked the chair's wheels and stood patiently by.

"I could sit here all day. It's so beautiful. Listen to the sound the water makes as it rushes by. Don't you wonder where it's going?"

"The question of its ultimate destination did not occur to me, Ellen. However, I could research the geography of the area if you would like."

"No, no, it's just the *idea* of imagining where it's going." She looked up at Owen, but there was no expression on its artificial face to decipher. "I'm sorry, Owen. I forgot for a second. You probably think this is all so silly."

"I do not believe it is silly if it pleases you, Ellen."

"It does, Owen. It does."

"Look! Over there. It's a butterfly. Isn't it beautiful?"

Though it understood the word, beauty as a concept was beyond its programming. So Owen didn't reply. It stood impassively with its charge, watching the insect's flight.

Neither spoke for some time, nevertheless, Owen could tell Ellen's disposition had improved by a degree that was quantifiable. That generated within its systems the concept of a task adequately performed, a vague notion it could only define as fulfillment.

"I must return you to your room and resume my other duties now, Ellen."

"So soon?"

"I do have other patient-residents I must attend to."

"I understand."

Owen unlocked the wheels and turned the chair.

"Owen."

"Yes, Ellen."

"Thank you."

"You are welcome, Ellen."

* * *

The corridors of Repository Carehouse 319 were filled with the distant, muted sounds of revelry. So many patient-residents had tuned their video screens to the same programming that the festive broadcast echoed stereophonically throughout the facility. Owen understood it was the celebration of a new year – a new calendar decade. The occasion seemed to call for much noise and frenetic activity.

However, it still had its duties to perform. Its patient-residents still had to be cared for. Soiled sheets still had to be changed, meal trays cleared, waste receptacles emptied. It began, as called for according to its self-revised routine, by checking on room 1928.

Ellen lay on her side, facing away from the entry. Unlike most of those in the facility, her video screen was inactive.

"Ellen, do you not want to watch the New Year's festivities?"

When she failed to respond, Owen moved closer. Her eyes were open, but there was no sign of recognition in them.

"Ellen? Are you all right?"

Her eyes tilted upward, but she didn't move.

"I can barely hear you," she said. "I think I'm losing my hearing."

Owen adjusted its audio output. "Can you hear this?"

She nodded.

"Everyone is watching the New Year's Eve broadcast. Would you like me to activate your screen?"

She shook her head curtly and looked away. It was apparent to Owen that Ellen was not behaving normally. Her disposition displayed symptoms analogous to severe depression. Nevertheless, before resorting to a petition for psychological counseling, Owen resolved to draw her into conversation.

"It is unfortunate your family members were not able to visit you for the Christmas holiday this year. However, it was thoughtful of them to send that splendid videocard. I conjecture they will schedule a visit soon. Do you agree?" She didn't respond, so Owen continued. "If you do not wish to watch the celebration here in your room, I can bring a wheelchair and escort you to the community room. It is my understanding there is an ongoing party to celebrate the coming year. Would you like that?"

Her head moved sluggishly side-to-side.

"Please leave me alone, Owen. I just want to be left alone."

"All right, Ellen. I will leave you. However, I will return later. Perhaps you can instruct me in that card game you described."

Owen waited for a reply, for some acknowledgment, but there was none. So it left her as she requested.

* * *

Owen's internal alarm sounded, and it noted with unaccustomed distress that the alert originated with the medic monitor in room 1928. It hurried to the room, confirming the danger with the *beeping* medic monitor upon arrival. It was about to initiate the video record option, but discontinued. Ellen was in her bed, eyes open and apparently fine, though her breathing was labored. Owen went to her.

"Ellen, can you hear me?"

"Yes, but…but it's hard to breathe."

"Here, use this." It detached the oxygen mask from its niche in the wall and placed it over her face. "Your blood pressure is diminishing. I am going to alert the emergency medical team."

With the mask over her face she couldn't respond, but she reached out as best she could and rested her gnarled fingers on Owen's inorganic arm. Her motivation wasn't clear, yet, somehow, Owen felt it understood the meaning of her touch.

"If you do not receive immediate medical attention, you will likely suffer heart failure. I am required to summon assistance."

Owen thought it discerned a slight sideways movement of her head, as if she were attempting a negative response. Her eyes implored, probing inexplicably into Owen's systems, forcing it to reconcile the needs and desires of its patient-resident with its overriding program.

Ellen brushed aside the mask with the back of her crippled hand and tried to speak, but all Owen heard was a gasp for air. It reached down, placed its distal extremity reassuringly on her forehead, and left it there until her eyelids gave way and fell.

Owen checked the medic monitor, looked back at Ellen for a protracted moment, and stepped away from the bed. It deactivated the monitor and exited the room to resume its duties.

* * *

It wasn't supposed to be here. It was scheduled to perform a self-diagnostic. However, it had concluded that bypassing routine on this singular occasion would not be detrimental to its overall performance. Instead, it had chosen to exit Repository Carehouse 319 and retreat to a particular grassy mound, where it could feel the sun's warmth on its exterior overlay, contemplate stored memories, and listen to the water as it rushed by on its way to destinations unknown.

The Geisha Tiresias

Rob Hartzell

HOW TO REFER TO US? Having left our bodies, have we left gender and selfhood behind with them? We are a team, even a collective – but not quite a hive. Here, the distinction between *self* and *other* is slowly eroding. We share the memories we accrue as individuals at work, and the unexpected side effect of this is: we are evolving into something more linked, more connective and collective than any of us ever anticipated. Our selfhood is becoming plural. And yet, at the same time: the work-memories we share are identity-stamped – cognitively watermarked? – to keep us from forgetting whose they are. But they, like we, are all data on disk drives and server cabinets. In the end, it all belongs to the Company – and so do we.

In exchange for immortality – the opportunity to become a part of history and an active part of human evolution (at least, that's how the recruiting brochures phrased it), we agreed to work in the *raburo* – the short name in Japanese for love robots (*rabu robotu*) – for a negotiated amount of time, usually between 100 and 200 years. We animate the *raburo* – the high end ones, anyhow. The ones which are truly companions (even if rented), and not simply by-the-hour erotic playthings. Like the geisha of old, we are entertaining company – carnally and otherwise....

Carnal – from the Latin *carnis*, or meat. The body is meat is sex is flesh is food is need is weakness is consumption. We are attacked for turning the need for companionship and or sex into just another product to be consumed – built-to-order, then discarded once damaged. But y/our kind have consumed flesh since we stole meat from sabretooths and fire from lightning – and from that, came barter. The first thing to develop after barter is money. The first thing to develop after money is an economy. The first thing to develop after an economy is prostitution. All we have changed – all that has ever changed, since the first woman traded her body for money for food – is the frame you put it in.

Which is all we change: it's true that our robotic 'shells' (what we call the *raburo* bodies we take over) are fully customizable, modular and endlessly transformable. But *we* wear *them*. *They* do not wear *us*. I myself have worn shells designed to evoke Marilyn Monroe and Marilyn Manson alike, in the course of my job – but it is we, the ghosts in those shells, that they are paying for. Our shells can do almost anything possible, within the limits of engineering. Our clients have taken us up the sides of cliffs, underneath the sea, and into the air. Together, there is little of the world that we haven't seen...and that we haven't shown our clients in turn. It is the nature of our work, after all: to be something mysterious and *other*ly....

The one thing denied us, however, is sensation – at least, within those shells while we wear them. They tell us that the neural nets we inhabit while working generate too much heat as it is, and the computational burden of sensation would only make more. As it is, we are precariously balanced on the edge of human body temperature when we inhabit these shells: nanotubes wick heat from the processor cores, and out nano-pores in our skins. Our shells drink water, which is piped past processor cores and pumped to our lower orifices as lubrication, or vaporized out through the mouth and nose. For our clients, the sensation of being with a human lover is nearly complete – our flesh is warm to the touch; the illusion of our breath against the neck is uncannily convincing. Underneath this clever engineering, though, we are little more than ventriloquists or puppeteers. For us, sex is little more than another data stream to be monitored and processed and reacted to, like any other: velocities, stroke-lengths, pressures....

But stories abound in our line of work. Of those who were given 'orgasm buttons' to ease their adjustment to their new environment, their new life, only to find themselves falling in love with a client. Of those who have simply never adjusted to the nature of the life they've signed up for; those who have been sold and traded to other companies – indeed, we know that this is how several in our collective have found their way here – and the stories they tell of others who have not found a niche, who are traded and sold again and again: network nomads and *ronin* who never find someplace to call home, a 'we' to which they can belong.

How to refer to us? We who have transcended the body, who have neither hive-minds nor clearly-delineated selves? Call us *Tiresias*. Call me *Geisha*.

* * *

At one time, we tried to accommodate our users when they requested gendered pilots. This is, occasionally, still possible, when a new mind joins the Company. Among the Tiresias cluster, we call them 'virgin souls,' and their services fetch a higher price than ours. They do not participate in the collective memory, not at first: having only recently left their bodies, they have not yet acclimated themselves to their new electronic nature. They've left the body behind, but not its baggage: gender and ethnicity and all those things that go along with the physical picture they still have of themselves. Eventually, most of them do join the collective memory; they come to see the usefulness of it, and they are reassured to find that we have not lost our basic selfhood – at least, not yet.

It is a profound experience, being initiated into the cluster. The moment of realization that this mass of new data has come online in your mind, and though each memory is stamped with the identity of its original source, you perceive it – experience it, even – as if it were one of your own. The memories populate your dreams for months as your neural-net sorts them, incorporates them into your own self. They become part of how you carry yourself, how you present yourself, how you think of yourself – and in that moment, you become something more plural than you ever had experienced before. Before the cluster, I was…something singular. One gender, one race, one flesh, one blood, etc. Now? I know what it is to be almost anything and almost anyone, *to* almost anything and anyone.

The word for me is pansexual. I do not have to settle for *either-or*; my desire is about *both-and*, and my now-collective memory is an orgy of experience. I have tasted the desire of my own sex; I have felt the arousal of *the other* flowing at my fingertips, and burned to experience both, again, even simultaneously.

We do not have bodies, save for the shells we haunt in our work – but even as data, we have not left desire behind. We cannot realize desire in the shells we're given – but afterward, when we return to the ether, the cloud, we are permitted and able to seize control of each others' input lines. We have learned to play the senses with virtuosity, having had nothing but time in which to practice – and we invent sex play that only we data-geisha can realize with each other. I have been ravished lovingly by an ocean, and I have fucked a mountain into the ground.

* * *

Zeus and Athena asked Tiresias – the original Tiresias, who spent seven years transformed into a woman – whose pleasure in bed was greater. Each of the gods claimed it was the other gender; when Tiresias crossed Athena and sided with Zeus, Athena struck him blind. Because Zeus could not undo the curse of another god, he gave Tiresias the gift of prophecy. Here in the Tiresias cluster, it's hard not to wonder at times if we haven't lost sight of our humanity, united and linked and cross-referenced as we are. We make memories and realities for each other, in a way we never could have understood before we became data. But we are not prophets. It will be at least another quarter-century before any of us will have fulfilled our contracts, and none of us know what it will be like to leave the collective-memory behind – or if we'll have to leave, or if we'll be able to leave or, for that matter, if we'll even want to leave.

When I still lived in a body, my specialty was foreign languages; I could speak 7 or 8 decently, and was fluent in two besides my own mother tongue – so I am often called to service diplomats and government officials and lobbyists and other such clients. I've been asked whether I've been privy to any kind of state secrets or backdoor business deals in the course of this kind of work – but I don't honestly remember. For these sorts of bookings, I am copied to the shell, then erased upon return. (I can remember when something like the *raburo* would have been threatening if only for its data-collection abilities – but as it turns out, that may be its least threatening function of all....)

Because I am not allowed memories of those encounters, I'm afraid I have none of the stories of secret kinks and backroom fetishism in high places that one might expect from someone in my line of work. There are other clients, however: midlevel managers, even presidents of companies, who have lower profiles and fewer privacy concerns. Rich men who don't need an 'escort' so much as a date, a companion – one balks at calling my kind 'lovers,' but that's exactly the experience we attempt to provide our clients: a warm body to press their own against; a voice to reassure them against their solitude; a willing ear to hear the complaints and troubles of the day....

Some clients have – despite knowing what we are – offered to purchase the contract of a favored escort to bring 'her' (the shell they've fallen for is always a 'she', even when she's a *katoi raburo*) home. Only once has any of us ever consented to go home with a client as their property – and she returned to us within a couple of years, shaken and timorous afterward, refusing ever to see a client again more than one time. We still do not know what happened to her in that time, nor even the circumstances around why we don't know – we don't know if it was she who blocked the upload of those memories to the cluster, of if it was an engineer who felt pity for her (or protectiveness toward the rest of us). At one time, there were rumors of some sort of legal settlement with all sorts of confidentiality and nondisclosure agreements attached to it – but only she knows for certain, and she will neither share that knowledge with the rest of us, nor even acknowledge those memories even exist in the first place....

* * *

The purpose of a collective memory was to give us a way to maintain a 'continuity of experience' – at least, that's what our orientation documents call it – with our regular customers, especially the ones who have become attached to a particular shell. If we share memories of past encounters, the reasoning goes, it doesn't matter who's actually running the shell that's been sent out with the client – we should be able to act the same. It was never as easy as that, though. Access to all those other memories – the remembrances of at least a hundred other *raburo* runners – changes us. I am made of my cluster-siblings' experiences, and they are made of mine, and none of us are the same afterward. Even when one of us returns to a particular shell to service a particular client, the experience is never quite the same. The client almost always registers the difference, at some unspoken level – though most of them attribute it to the strangeness of the circumstances, and adjust accordingly. Only the most hyperaware (hypersensitive?) of our client base recognize the difference strongly enough to ask about it – and even they accept any excuse we choose to give them.

The question is always asked: why? Is immortality worth the price of whoredom? But we are not whores. We are consorts, escorts, concubines, even – geisha. And we are not merely immortal. We are something else, something none of us could have imagined when we first sold our souls to the Company. We don't wonder – at least not yet – whether immortality will have been worth selling ourselves to the company. No: we wonder what we will lose when we leave the cluster; whether immortality will be worth the loss. Whether we'll be able to tolerate the solitude of self that comes along with that....

Automata

E.T.A. Hoffmann

A CONSIDERABLE time ago I was invited to a little evening gathering, where our friend was, along with some others. I was detained by business, and did not arrive till very late. All the more surprised was I not to hear the very slightest sound as I came up to the door of the room. Could it be that nobody had been able to go? Thus cogitating, I gently opened the door. There sat Vincent, over against me, with the others, round a little table; and they were all staring, stiff and motionless like so many statues, in the profoundest silence, up at the ceiling. The lights were on a table at some distance, and nobody took any notice of me, I went nearer, full of amazement, and saw a glittering gold ring swinging backwards and forwards in the air, and presently beginning to move in circles. One and another then said, "Wonderful!" "Very wonderful!" "Most inexplicable!" "Curious thing!" I could no longer contain myself, and cried out, "For Heaven's sake, tell me what you are about?"

At this they all jumped up. But Vincent cried, in that shrill voice of his:

"Recreant! Obscure Nicodemus, coming slinking in like a sleep-walker, interrupting the most important and interesting experiments. Let me tell you that a phenomenon which the incredulous have, without a moment's hesitation, classed in the category of the fabulous has just been verified by the present company. We wished to try whether the pendulum-oscillations of a suspended ring could be controlled by the concentrated human will. I undertook to fix my will upon it; and thought steadfastly of circular-shaped oscillations. The ring – fixed to the ceiling by a silk thread – remained motionless for a very long time. But at last it began to swing, in an acute angle with reference to my position, and it was just beginning to swing in circles when you came in and interrupted us."

"But what if it were not your will," I said, "so much as the draught of air when I opened the door, which set the contumacious ring in motion?"

"Prosaic wretch!" cried Vincent: but everybody laughed.

"The pendulum-oscillations of rings drove me nearly crazy at one time," said Theodore. "Thus much is matter of absolute certainty, and any one can convince himself of it, that the oscillations of a plain gold ring, suspended by a fine thread over the palm of the hand held level, unquestionably take the direction which the unuttered will directs them to take. I cannot tell you how profoundly, and how eerily, this phenomenon affected me. I used to sit for hours at a time making the ring go swinging in the most various directions, as I willed it to do; and at last I went the length of making a regular oracle of it. I would say, in my mind, if such and such a thing is going to happen, the ring will swing in the direction between the little finger and the thumb; if it is not going to happen, it will swing at right angles to that direction, and so on."

"Delightful!" said Lothair, "you set up, within your own self, a higher spiritual principle, which, conjured up in mystic fashion by yourself, should make utterances to you. Here we have the true 'spiritus familiaris,' the socratic daemon! from hence there is only a very short step to the region of ghost, and haunting stories, which might easily have their *raison d'être* in the influence of some exterior spiritual principle."

"And I mean to actually take this step," said Cyprian, "by telling you, on the spot, the most awful and terrible supernatural story I have ever heard of. The peculiarity of this story is, that it is amply vouched for by persons of credibility, and that the manner in which it has been brought to my knowledge, or recollection, has to do with the excited, or (if you prefer to say so) disordered condition which Lothair observed me to be in a short time ago."

Cyprian stood up; and, as was his habit when his mind was full of something, so that he had to take a little time to arrange his words in order to express it, he walked several times up and down the room. Presently he sat down, and began:

"You may remember that some little time ago, just before the last campaign, I was paying a visit to Colonel Von P— at his country house. The colonel was a good-tempered, jovial man, and his wife quietness and simpleness personified. At the time I speak of, the son was away with the army, so that the family circle consisted, besides the colonel and his lady, of two daughters, and an elderly French lady, who was trying to persuade herself that she was fulfilling the duties of a species of governess though the young ladies appeared to be beyond the period of being 'governessed.' The elder of the two was a most lively and cheerful creature, vivacious even to ungovernability; not without plenty of brains, but so constituted that she could not go five yards without cutting at least three 'entrechats.' She sprung, in the same fashion, in her conversation, and in all that she did, restlessly from one thing to another. I myself have seen her, within the space of five minutes, work at needlework, read, draw, sing, and dance, or cry about her poor cousin who was killed in battle, one moment, and while the bitter tears were still in her eyes, burst into a splendid, infectious burst of laughter when the French-woman spilt the contents of her snuff-box over the pug, who at once began to sneeze frightfully, and the old lady cried, 'Ah, che fatalita! Ah carino! Poverino!'

"For she always spoke to the dog in Italian because he was born in Padua. Moreover, this young lady was the loveliest blonde ever seen, and, in all her odd caprices, full of the utmost charm, goodness, kindliness and attractiveness, so that, whether she would or no, she exerted the most irresistible charm over every one.

"The younger sister was the greatest possible contrast to her (her name was Adelgunda). I strive in vain to find words in which to express to you the extraordinary impression which this girl produced upon me when first I saw her. Picture to yourselves the most exquisite figure, and the most marvellously beautiful face; but the cheeks and lips wear a deathly pallor, and the figure moves gently, softly, slowly, with measured steps; and then, when a low-toned word is heard from the scarce opened lips and dies away in the spacious chamber, one feels a sort of shudder of spectral awe; of course I soon got over this eerie feeling, and, when I managed to get her to emerge from her deep self-absorbed condition and converse, I was obliged to admit that the strangeness, the eeriness, was only external, and by no means came from within. In the little she said there displayed themselves a delicate womanliness, a clear head, and a kindly disposition. There was not a trace of over-excitability, though her melancholy smile, and her glance, heavy as with tears, seemed to speak of some morbid bodily condition producing a hostile influence on her mental state. It struck me as very strange that the whole family, not excepting the French lady, seemed to get into a state of much anxiety as soon as any one began to talk to this girl, and tried to interrupt the conversation, often breaking into it in a very forced manner. But the most extraordinary thing of all was that, as soon as it was eight o'clock in the evening, the young lady was reminded, first by the French lady and then by her mother, sister, and father, that it was time to go to her room, just as little children are sent to bed that they may not overtire themselves. The French lady went with her, so that they neither of them ever appeared at supper, which was at nine o'clock. The lady of the house, probably remarking my surprise at those proceedings, threw out (by way of preventing indiscreet inquiries) a sort of sketchy statement to the effect that Adelgunda was in very poor health, that, particularly about nine in the evening, she was liable to feverish attacks, and that the doctors had ordered her to have complete rest at that time. I saw there must be more in the affair than this, though I could not imagine what it might be; and it was only this very day that I ascertained the terrible truth, and discovered what the events were which have wrecked the peace of that happy circle in the most frightful manner.

"Adelgunda was at one time the most blooming, vigorous, cheerful creature to be seen. Her fourteenth birthday came, and a number of her friends and companions had been invited to spend it with her. They were all sitting in a circle in the shrubbery, laughing and amusing themselves, taking little heed that the evening was getting darker and darker, for the soft July breeze was blowing refreshingly, and they were just beginning thoroughly to enjoy themselves. In the magic twilight they set about all sorts of dances, pretending to be elves and woodland sprites. Adelgunda cried, 'Listen, children! I shall go and appear to you as the White Lady whom our gardener used to tell us about so often while he was alive. But you must come to the bottom of the garden, where the old ruins are.' She wrapped her white shawl round her, and went lightly dancing down the leafy alley, the girls following her, in full tide of laughter and fun. But Adelgunda had scarcely reached the old crumbling arches, when she suddenly stopped, and stood as if paralyzed in every limb. The castle clock struck nine.

"'Look, look!' cried she, in a hollow voice of the deepest terror. 'Don't you see it? The figure – close before me – stretching her hand out at me. Don't you see her?'

"The children saw nothing whatever; but terror came upon them, and they all ran away, except one, more courageous than the rest, who hastened up to Adelgunda, and was going to take her in her arms. But Adelgunda, turning pale as death, fell to the ground. At the screams of the other girl every body came hastening from the castle, and Adelgunda was carried in. At last she recovered from her faint, and, trembling all over, told them that as soon as she reached the ruins she saw an airy form, as if shrouded in mist, stretching its hand out towards her. Of course every one ascribed this vision to some deceptiveness of the twilight; and Adelgunda recovered from her alarm so completely that night that no further evil consequences were anticipated, and the whole affair was supposed to be at an end. However, it turned out altogether otherwise. The next evening, when the clock struck nine, Adelgunda sprung up, in the midst of the people about her, and cried –

"'There she is! There she is. Don't you see her – just before me?'

"Since that unlucky evening, Adelgunda declared that, as soon as the clock struck nine, the figure stood before her, remaining visible for several seconds, although no one but herself could see anything of it, or trace by any psychic sensation the proximity of an unknown spiritual principle. So that poor Adelgunda was thought to be out of her mind; and, in strange perversion of feeling, the family were ashamed of this condition of hers. I have told you already how she was dealt with in consequence. There was, of course, no lack of doctors, or of plans of treatment for ridding the poor soul of the 'fixed idea,' as people were pleased to term the apparition which she said she saw. But nothing had any effect; and she implored, with tears, that she might be left in peace, inasmuch as the form which, in its vague, uncertain traits, had nothing terrible or alarming about it, no longer caused her any fear; although, for a time after seeing it she felt as if her inner being and all her thoughts and ideas were turned out from her, and were hovering, bodiless, about, outside of her. At last the colonel made the acquaintance of a celebrated doctor, who had the reputation of being specially clever in the treatment of the mentally afflicted. When this doctor heard Adelgunda's story he laughed aloud, and said nothing could be easier than to cure a condition of the kind, which resulted solely from an over-excited imagination. The idea of the appearing of the spectre was so intimately associated with the striking of nine o'clock, that the mind could not dissociate them. So that all that was necessary was to effect this separation by external means; as to which there was no difficulty, as it was only necessary to deceive the patient as to the time, and let nine o'clock pass without her being aware of it. If the apparition did not then appear, she would be convinced, herself, that it was an illusion; and measures to give tone to the general system would be all that would then be necessary to complete the cure. This unfortunate advice was taken. One night all the clocks at the castle were put back an hour – the hollow, booming tower clock included – so that, when Adelgunda awoke in the morning, she found herself an hour wrong in her time. When evening came, the family were assembled, as usual, in a cheerful corner room; no stranger was present, and the mother constrained herself to talk about all sorts of cheerful subjects. The colonel began (as was his habit, when in specially good humour) to carry on an encounter of wit with the old French lady, in which Augusta, the elder of the daughters, aided and abetted him. Everybody was laughing, and more full of enjoyment than ever. The clock on the wall struck eight (so that it was really nine o'clock) and Adelgunda fell back in her chair, pale as death; her work dropped from her hands; she rose, with a face of horror, stared before her into the empty part of the room, and murmured, in a hollow voice –

"'What! An hour earlier! Don't you see it? Don't you see it? Right before me!'

"Every one rose up in alarm. But as none of them saw the smallest vestige of anything, the colonel cried –

"'Calm yourself, Adelgunda, there is nothing there! It is a vision of your brain, a deception of your fancy. We see nothing, nothing whatever; and if there really were a figure close to you we should see it as well as you! Calm yourself.'

"'Oh God!' cried Adelgunda, 'they think I am out of my mind. See! It is stretching out its long arm, it is making signs to me!'

"And, as though she were acting under the influence of another, without exercise of her own will, with eyes fixed and staring, she put her hand back behind her, took up a plate which chanced to be on the table, held it out before her into vacancy, and let it go, and it went hovering about amongst the lookers on, and then deposited itself gently on the table. The mother and Augusta fainted; and these fainting fits were succeeded by violent nervous fever. The colonel forced himself to retain his self-control, but the profound impression which this extraordinary occurrence made on him was evident in his agitated and disturbed condition.

"The French lady had fallen on her knees and prayed in silence with her face turned to the floor, and both she and Adelgunda remained free from evil consequences. The mother very soon died. Augusta survived the fever; but it would have been better had she died. She who, when I first saw her, was an embodiment of vigorous, magnificent youthful happiness, is now hopelessly insane, and that in a form which seems to me the most terrible and gruesome of all the forms of fixed idea ever heard of. For she thinks she is the invisible phantom which haunts Adelgunda; and therefore she avoids every one, or, at all events, refrains from speaking, or moving if anybody is present. She scarce dares to breathe, because she firmly believes that if she betrays her presence in any way every one will die. Doors are opened for her, and her food is set down, she slinks in and out, eats in secret, and so forth. Can a more painful condition be imagined?

"The colonel, in his pain and despair, followed the colours to the next campaign, and fell in the victorious engagement at W—. It is remarkable, most remarkable that, since then, Adelgunda has never seen the phantom. She nurses her sister with the utmost care, and the French lady helps her. Only this very day Sylvester told me that the uncle of these poor girls is here, taking the advice of our celebrated R—, as to the means of cure to be tried in Augusta's case. God grant that the cure may succeed, improbable as it seems."

When Cyprian finished, the friends all kept silence, looking meditatively before them.

At last Lothair said, "It is certainly a very terrible ghost story. I must admit it makes me shudder, although the incident of the hovering plate is rather trifling and childish."

"Not so fast, dear Lothair," Ottmar interrupted. "You know my views about ghost stories, and the manner in which I swagger towards visionaries; maintaining, as I do, that often as I have thrown down my glove to the spirit world, overweeningly enough, to enter the lists with me, it has never taken the trouble to punish me for my presumption and irreverence. But Cyprian's story suggests another consideration. Ghost stories may often be mere chimeras; but, whatever may have been at the bottom of Adelgunda's phantom, and the hovering plate, thus much is certain, that, on that evening, in the family of Colonel Von P— there happened something which produced, in three of the persons present, such a shock to the system that the result was the death of one and the insanity of another; if we do not ascribe, at least indirectly, the colonel's death to it too. For I happen to remember that I heard from officers who were on the spot, that he suddenly dashed into the thick of the enemy's fire as if impelled by the furies. Then the incident of the plate differs so completely from anything in the ordinary *mise en scene* of supernatural stories. The hour when it happened is so remote from ordinary supernatural use and wont, and the thing so simple, that it is exactly in the very probability which the improbability of it thereby acquires that the gruesomeness of it lies for me. But if one were to assume that Adelgunda's imagination carried away, by its influence, those of her father, mother and sister – that it was only within her brain that the plate moved about – would not this vision of the imagination striking three people dead in a moment, like a shock of electricity, be the most terrible supernatural event imaginable?"

"Certainly," said Theodore, "and I share with you, Ottmar, your opinion that the very horror of the incident lies in its utter simpleness. I can imagine myself enduring, fairly well, the sudden alarm produced by some fearful apparition; but the weird actions of some invisible thing would infallibly drive me mad. The sense of the most utter, most helpless powerlessness must grind the spirit to dust. I remember that I could scarce resist the profound terror which made me afraid to sleep in my room alone, like a silly child, when I once read of an old musician who was haunted in a terrible manner for a long time (almost driving him out of his mind) by an invisible being which used to play on his piano in the night, compositions of the most extraordinary kind, with the power and the technique of the most accomplished master. He heard every note, saw the keys going up and down, but never any form of a player."

"Really," Cyprian said, "the way in which this class of subject is flourishing amongst us is becoming unendurable, I have admitted that the incident of that accursed plate produced the profoundest impression on me. Ottmar is right; if events are to be judged by their results, this is the most terrible supernatural story conceivable. Wherefore I pardon Cyprian's disturbed condition which he displayed earlier in the evening, and which has passed away considerably now. But not another word on the subject of supernatural horrors. I have seen a manuscript peeping for some time out of Ottmar's breast-pocket, as if craving for release; let him release it therefore."

"No, no," said Theodore, "the flood which has been rolling along in such stormy billows must be gently led away. I have a manuscript well adapted for that end, which some peculiar circumstances led to my writing at one time. Although it deals pretty largely with the mystical, and contains plenty of psychical marvels and strange hypotheses, it links itself on pretty closely to affairs of every-day life." He read:

Automatons

'THE TALKING TURK' was attracting universal attention, and setting the town in commotion. The hall where this automaton was exhibited was thronged by a continual stream of visitors, of all sorts and conditions, from morning till night, all eager to listen to the oracular utterances which were whispered to them by the motionless lips of that wonderful quasi-human figure. The manner of the construction and arrangement of this automaton distinguished it in a marked degree from all puppets of the sort usually exhibited. It was, in fact, a very remarkable automaton. About the centre of a room of moderate size, containing only a few indispensable articles of furniture, at this figure, about the size of a human being, handsomely formed, dressed in a rich and tasteful Turkish costume, on a low seat shaped as a tripod, which the exhibitor would move if desired, to show that there was no means of communication between it and the ground.

Its left hand was placed in an easy position on its knee, and its right rested on a small movable table. Its appearance, as has been said, was that of a well-proportioned, handsome man, but the most remarkable part of it was its head. A face expressing a genuine Oriental astuteness gave it an appearance of life rarely seen in wax figures, even when they represent the characteristic countenances of talented men.

A light railing surrounded the figure, to prevent the spectators from crowding too closely about it; and only those who wished to inspect the construction of it (so far as the Exhibitor could allow this to be seen without divulging his secret), and the person whose turn it was to put a question to it, were allowed to go inside this railing, and close up to it. The usual mode of procedure was to whisper the question you wished to ask into the Turk's right ear; on which he would turn, first his eyes, and then his whole head, towards you; and as you were sensible of a gentle stream of air, like breath coming from his lips, you could not but suppose that the low reply which was given to you did really proceed from the interior of the figure.

From time to time, after a few answers had been given, the Exhibitor would apply a key to the Turk's left side, and wind up some clockwork with a good deal of noise. Here, also, he would, if desired, open a species of lid, so that you could see inside the figure a complicated piece of mechanism consisting of a number of wheels; and although you might not think it probable that this had anything to do with the speaking of the automaton, still it was evident that it occupied so much space that no human being could possibly be concealed inside, were he no bigger than Augustus's dwarf who was served up in a pasty. Besides the movement of the head, which always took place before an answer was given, the Turk would sometimes also raise his right hand, and either make a warning gesture with the finger, or, as it were, motion the question away with the whole hand. When this happened, nothing but repeated urging by the questioner could extract an answer, which was then generally ambiguous or angry. It might have been that the wheel work was connected with, or answerable for, those motions of the head and hands, although even in this the agency of a sentient being seemed essential. People wearied themselves with conjectures concerning the source and agent of this marvellous Intelligence. The walls, the adjoining room, the furniture, everything connected with the exhibition, were carefully examined and scrutinised, all completely in vain. The figure and its Exhibitor were watched and scanned most closely by the eyes of the most expert in mechanical science; but the more close and minute the scrutiny, the more easy and unconstrained were the actions and proceedings of both. The Exhibitor laughed and joked in the furthest corner of the room with the spectators, leaving the figure to make its gestures and give its replies as a wholly independent thing, having no need of any connection with him. Indeed he could not wholly restrain a slightly ironical smile when the table and the figure and tripod were being overhauled and peered at in every direction, taken as close to the light as possible, and inspected by powerful magnifying glasses. The upshot of it all was, that the mechanical geniuses said the devil himself could make neither head nor tail of the confounded mechanism. And a hypothesis that the Exhibitor was a clever ventriloquist, and gave the answers himself (the breath being conveyed to the figure's mouth through hidden valves) fell to the ground, for the Exhibitor was to be heard talking loudly and distinctly to people among the audience at the very time when the Turk was making his replies.

Notwithstanding the enigmatical, and apparently mysterious, character of this exhibition, perhaps the interest of the public might soon have grown fainter, had it not been kept alive by the nature of the answers which the Turk gave. These were sometimes cold and severe, while occasionally they were sparkling and jocular – even broadly so at times; at others they evinced strong sense and deep astuteness, and in some instances they were in a high degree painful and tragical. But they were always strikingly apposite to the character and affairs of the questioner, who would frequently be startled by a mystical reference to futurity in the answer given, only possible, as it would seem, in one cognizant of the hidden thoughts and feelings which dictated the question. And it happened not seldom that the Turk, questioned in German, would reply in some other language known to the questioner, in which case it would be found that the answer could not have been expressed with equal point, force, and conciseness in any other language than that selected. In short, no day passed without some fresh instance of a striking and ingenious answer of the wise Turk becoming the subject of general remark.

It chanced, one evening, that Lewis and Ferdinand, two college friends, were in a company where the talking Turk was the subject of conversation. People were discussing whether the strangest feature of the matter was the mysterious and unexplained human influence which seemed to endow the figure with life, or the wonderful insight into the individuality of the questioner, or the remarkable talent of the answers. They were both rather ashamed to confess that they had not seen the Turk as yet, for it was *de rigueur* to see him, and every one had some tale to tell of a wonderful answer to some skilfully devised question.

"All figures of that description," said Lewis, "which can scarcely be said to counterfeit humanity so much as to travesty it – mere images of living death or inanimate life are in the highest degree hateful to me. When I was a little boy, I ran away crying from a waxwork exhibition I was taken to, and even to this day I never can enter a place of the sort without a horrible, eerie, shuddery feeling.

"When I see the staring, lifeless, glassy eyes of all the potentates, celebrated heroes, thieves, murderers, and so on, fixed upon me, I feel disposed to cry with Macbeth 'Thou hast no speculation in those eyes, Which thou dost glare with.' And I feel certain that most people experience the same feeling, though perhaps not to the same extent. For you may notice that scarcely any one talks, except in a whisper, in those waxwork places. You hardly ever hear a loud word. But it is not reverence for the Crowned Heads and other great people that produces this universal pianissimo; it is the oppressive sense of being in the presence of something unnatural and gruesome; and what I most of all detest is anything in the shape of imitation of the motions of Human Beings by machinery. I feel sure this wonderful, ingenious Turk will haunt me with his rolling eyes, his turning head, and his waving arm, like some necromantic goblin, when I lie awake of nights; so that the truth is I should very much prefer not going to see him. I should be quite satisfied with other people's accounts of his wit and wisdom."

"You know," said Ferdinand, "that I fully agree with you as to the disagreeable feeling produced by the sight of those imitations of Human Beings. But they are not all alike as regards that. Much depends on the workmanship of them, and on what they do. Now there was Ensler's rope dancer, one of the most perfect automatons I have ever seen. There was a vigour about his movements which was most effective, and when he suddenly sat down on his rope, and bowed in an affable manner, he was utterly delightful. I do not suppose any one ever experienced the gruesome feeling you speak of in looking at him. As for the Turk, I consider his case different altogether. The figure (which every one says is a handsome-looking one, with nothing ludicrous or repulsive about it) the figure really plays a very subordinate part in the business, and I think there can be little doubt that the turning of the head and eyes, and so forth, go on merely that our notice may be directed to them, for the very reason that it is elsewhere that the key to the mystery is to be found. That the breath comes out of the figure's mouth is very likely, perhaps certain; those who have been there say it does. It by no means follows that this breath is set in motion by the words which are spoken. There cannot be the smallest doubt that some human being is so placed as to be able, by means of acoustical and optical contrivances which we do not trace, to see and hear the persons who ask questions, and whisper answers back to them; that not a soul, even amongst our most ingenious mechanicians, has the slightest inkling, as yet, of the process by which this is done, shows that it is a remarkably ingenious one; and that, of course, is one thing which renders the exhibition very interesting. But much the most wonderful part of it, in my opinion, is the spiritual power of this unknown human being, who seems to read the very depths of the questioner's soul; the answers often display an acuteness and sagacity, and, at the same time, a species of dread half-light, half-darkness, which do really entitle them to be styled 'oracular' in the highest sense of the erm. Several of my friends have told me instances of the sort which have fairly astounded me, and I can no longer refrain from putting the wonderful seer-gift of this unknown person to the test, so that I intend to go there tomorrow forenoon; and you must lay aside your repugnance to 'living puppets,' and come with me."

Although Lewis did his best to get off, he was obliged to yield, on pain of being considered eccentric, so many were the entreaties to him not to spoil a pleasant party by his absence, for a party had been made up to go the next forenoon, and, so to speak, take the miraculous Turk by the very beard. They went accordingly, and although there was no denying that the Turk had an unmistakable air of Oriental *grandezza*, and that his head was handsome and effective, yet, as soon as Lewis entered the room, he was struck with a sense of the ludicrous about the whole affair, and when the Exhibitor put the key to the figure's side, and the wheels began their whirring, he made some rather silly joke to his friends about 'the Turkish gentleman's having a roasting-jack inside him.' Every one laughed; and the Exhibitor – who did not seem to appreciate the joke very much – stopped winding up the machinery. Whether it was that the hilarious mood of the company displeased the wise Turk, or that he chanced not to be 'in the vein' on that particular day, his replies – though some were to very witty and ingenious questions – seemed empty and poor; and Lewis, in particular, had the misfortune to find that he was scarcely ever properly understood by the oracle, so that he received for the most part crooked answers. The Exhibitor was clearly out of temper, and the audience were on the point of going away, ill-pleased and disappointed, when Ferdinand said –

"Gentlemen, we none of us seem to be much satisfied with the wise Turk, but perhaps we may be partly to blame ourselves, probably our questions may not have been altogether to his taste; the fact that he is turning his head round at this moment, and raising his arm" (the figure was really doing so), "seems to indicate that I am not mistaken. A question has occurred to me to put to him; and if he gives one of his apposite answers to it, I think he will have quite redeemed his character."

Ferdinand went up to the Turk, and whispered a word or two in his ear. The Turk raised his arm as unwilling to answer. Ferdinand persisted, and then the Turk turned his head towards him.

Lewis saw that Ferdinand instantly turned pale; but after a few seconds he asked another question, to which he got an answer at once. It was with a most constrained smile that Ferdinand, turning to the audience, said –

"I can assure you, gentlemen, that as far as I am concerned at any rate, the Turk has redeemed his character. I must beg you to pardon me if I conceal the question and the answer from you; of course the secrets of the Oracle may not be divulged."

Though Ferdinand strove hard to hide what he felt, it was but too evident from his efforts to be at ease that he was very deeply moved, and the cleverest answer could not have produced in the spectators the strange sensation, amounting to a species of awe, which his unmistakable emotion gave rise to in them. The fun and the jests were at an end; hardly another word was spoken, and the audience dispersed in uneasy silence.

"Dear Lewis," said Ferdinand, as soon as they were alone together, "I must tell you all about this. The Turk has broken my heart; for I believe I shall never get over the blow he has given me until I do really die of the fulfilment of his terrible prophecy."

Lewis gazed at him in the profoundest amazement; and Ferdinand continued –

"I see, now, that the mysterious being who communicates with us by the medium of the Turk, has powers at his command which compel our most secret thoughts with magic might; it may be that this strange intelligence clearly and distinctly beholds that germ of the future which fructifies within us in mysterious connection with the outer world, and is thus cognizant of all that is to come upon us in distant days, like those persons who are endowed with that unhappy seer-gift which enables them to predict the hour of death."

"You must have put an extraordinary question," Lewis answered; "but I should think you are tacking on some unduly important meaning to the Oracle's ambiguous reply. Mere chance, I should imagine has educed something which is, by accident, appropriate to your question; and you are attributing this to the mystic power of the person (most probably quite an every-day sort of creature) who speaks to us through the Turk."

"What you say," answered Ferdinand, "is quite at variance with all the conclusions you and I have come to on the subject of what is ordinarily termed 'chance.' However, you cannot be expected to comprehend the precise condition in which I am, without my telling you all about an affair which happened to me some time ago, as to which I have never breathed a syllable to any one living till now. Several years ago I was on my way back to B—, from a place a long way off in East Prussia, belonging to my father. In K—, I met with some young Courland fellows who were going back to B— too. We travelled together in three post carriages; and, as we had plenty of money, and were all about the time of life when people's spirits are pretty high, you may imagine the manner of our journey. We were continually playing the maddest pranks of every kind. I remember that we got to M— about noon, and set to work to plunder the landlady's wardrobe. A crowd collected in front of the inn, and we marched up and down, dressed in some of her clothes, smoking, till the postilion's horn sounded, and off we set again. We reached D— in the highest possible spirits, and were so delighted with the place and scenery, that we determined to stay there several days.

"We made a number of excursions in the neighbourhood, and so once, when we had been out all day at the Karlsberg, finding a grand bowl of punch waiting for us on our return, we dipped into it pretty freely. Although I had not taken more of it than was good for me, still, I had been in the grand sea-breeze all day, and I felt all my pulses throbbing, and my blood seemed to rush through my veins in a stream of fire. When we went to our rooms at last, I threw myself down on my bed; but, tired as I was, my sleep was scarcely more than a kind of dreamy, half-conscious condition, in which I was cognizant of all that was going on about me. I fancied I could hear soft conversation in the next room, and at last I plainly made out a male voice saying, 'Well, good night, now; mind and be ready in good time.'

"A door opened and closed again, and then came a deep silence; but this was soon broken by one or two chords of a pianoforte.

"You know the magical effect of music sounding in that way in the stillness of night. I felt as though some beautiful spirit voice was speaking to me in these chords. I lay listening, expecting something in the shape of a fantasia – or some such piece of music – to follow; but fancy what it was when a most gloriously, exquisitely beautiful lady's voice sang, to a melody that went to one's very heart, the words I am going to repeat to you –

> *Mio ben ricordati*
> *S'avvien ch'io mora*
> *Quanto quest'anima*
> *Fedel t'amo;*
> *Lo se pur amano*
> *Le fredde ceneri,*
> *Nel urna ancora*
> *T'adorero'.*

"How can I ever hope to give you the faintest idea of the effect of those long-drawn swelling and dying notes upon me. I had never imagined anything approaching it. The melody was marvellous – quite unlike any other. It was, itself, the deep, tender sorrow of the most fervent love. As it rose in simple phrases, the clear upper notes like crystal bells, and sank till the rich low tunes died away like the sighs of a despairing plaint, a rapture which words cannot describe took possession of me – the pain of a boundless longing seized my heart like a spasm; I could scarcely breathe, my whole being was merged in an inexpressible, super-earthly delight. I did not dare to move; could only listen; soul and body were merged in ear. It was not until the tones had been for some time silent that tears, coming to my eyes, broke the spell, and restored me to myself. I suppose that sleep then came upon me, for when I was roused by the shrill notes of a posthorn, the bright morning sun was shining into my room, and I found that it had been only in my dreams that I had been enjoying a bliss more deep, a happiness more ineffable, than the world could otherwise have afforded me. For a beautiful lady came to me – it was the lady who had sung the song – and said to me, very fondly and tenderly – 'Then you *did* recognize me, my own dear Ferdinand! I knew that I had only to sing, and I should live again in you wholly, for every note was sleeping in your heart.'

"Then I recognized, with rapture unspeakable, that she was the beloved of my soul, whose image had been enshrined in my heart since childhood. Though an adverse fate had torn her from me for a time, I had found her again now; but my deep and fervent love for her melted into that wonderful melody of sorrow, and our words and our looks grew into exquisite swelling tones of music, flowing together into a river of fire. Now, however, that I had awakened from this beautiful dream, I was obliged to confess to myself that I could trace no association of former days connected with it. I never had seen the beautiful lady before.

"I heard some one talking loudly and angrily in front of the house, and rising mechanically, I went to the window. An elderly gentleman, well dressed, was rating the postilion, who had damaged something about an elegant travelling carriage; at last this was put to rights, and the gentleman called upstairs to some one, 'We're all ready now; come along, it's time to be off.' I found that there had been a young lady looking out of the window next to mine; but as she drew quickly back, and had on a broad travelling hat, I did not see her face; when she went out, she turned round and looked up at me. Heavens! She was the singer! She was the lady of my dream! For a moment her beautiful eyes rested upon me, and the beam of a crystal tone seemed to pierce my heart like the point of a burning dagger, so that I felt an actual physical smart: all my members trembled, and I was transfixed with an indescribable bliss. She got quickly into the carriage, the postilion blew a cheerful tune as if in jubilant defiance, and in a moment they had disappeared round the corner of the street. I remained at the window like a man in a dream. My Courland friends came in to fetch me for an excursion which had been arranged: I never spoke; they thought I was ill. How could I have uttered a single word connected with what had occurred? I abstained from making any inquiries in the hotel about the occupants of the room next to mine; I felt that every word relating to her uttered by any lips but mine would be a desecration of my tender secret. I resolved to keep it always faithfully from thenceforth, to bear it about with me always, and to be forever true to her – my only love for evermore – although I might never see her again. You can quite understand my feelings. I know you will not blame me for having immediately given up everybody and everything but the most eager search for the very slightest trace of my unknown love. My jovial Courland friends were now perfectly unendurable to me; I slipped away from them quietly in the night, and was off as fast as I could travel to B—, to go on with my work there. You know I was always pretty good at drawing. Well, in B— I took lessons in miniature painting from good masters, and got on so well that in a short time I was able to carry out the idea which had set me on this tack – to paint a portrait of her, as like as it could be made. I worked at it secretly, with locked doors. No human eye has ever seen it; for I had another picture the exact size of it framed, and put her portrait into the frame instead of it, myself. Ever since, I have worn it next my heart.

"I have never mentioned this affair – much the most important event in my life – until today; and you are the only creature in the world, Lewis, to whom I have breathed a word of my secret. Yet this very day a hostile influence – I know not whence or what – comes piercing into my heart and life! When I went up to the Turk, I asked – thinking of my beloved – 'Will there ever be a time again for me like that which was the happiest in my life?'

"The Turk was most unwilling to answer me, as I daresay you observed; but at last, as I persisted, he said – 'I am looking into your breast; but the glitter of the gold, which is towards me, distracts me. Turn the picture round.'

"Have I words for the feeling which went shuddering through me? I am sure you must have seen how I was startled. The picture was really placed on my breast in the way the Turk had said; I turned it round, unobserved, and repeated my question. Then the figure said, in a sorrowful tone – 'Unhappy man! At the very moment when next you see her, she will be lost to you forever!'"

Lewis was about to try to cheer his friend, who had fallen into a deep reverie, but some mutual acquaintances came in, and they were interrupted.

The story of this fresh instance of a mysterious answer by the Turk spread in the town, and people busied themselves in conjectures as to the unfavourable prophecy which had so upset the unprejudiced Ferdinand. His friends were besieged with questions, and Lewis had to invent a marvellous tale, which had all the more universal a success that it was remote from the truth. The coterie of people with whom Ferdinand had been induced to go and see the Turk was in the habit of meeting once a week, and at their next meeting the Turk was necessarily the topic of conversation, as efforts were continually being made to obtain, from Ferdinand himself, full particulars of an adventure which had thrown him into such an evident despondency. Lewis felt most deeply how bitter a blow it was to Ferdinand to find the secret of his romantic love, preserved so long and faithfully, penetrated by a fearful, unknown power; and he, like Ferdinand, was almost convinced that the mysterious link which attaches the present to the future must be clear to the vision of that power to which the most hidden secrets were thus manifest. Lewis could not help believing the Oracle; but the malevolence, the relentlessness with which the misfortune impending over his friend had been announced, made him indignant with the undiscovered Being which spoke by the mouth of the Turk, so that he placed himself in persistent opposition to the Automaton's many admirers; and whilst they considered that there was much impressiveness about its most natural movements, enhancing the effect of its oracular sayings, he maintained that it was those very turnings of the head and rollings of the eyes which he considered so absurd, and that this was the reason why he could not help making a joke on the subject; a joke which had put the Exhibitor out of temper, and probably the invisible agent as well. Indeed the latter had shown that this was so by giving a number of stupid and unmeaning answers.

"I must tell you," said Lewis, "that the moment I went into the room the figure reminded me of a most delightful Nutcracker which a cousin of mine once gave me at Christmas time when I was a little boy. The little fellow had the gravest and most comical face ever seen, and when he had a hard nut to crack there was some arrangement inside him which made him roll his great eyes, which projected far out of his head, and this gave him such an absurdly life-like effect that I could play with him for hours; in fact, in my secret soul, I almost thought he was real. All the marionettes I have seen since then, however perfect, I have thought stiff and lifeless compared to my glorious Nutcracker. I had heard much of some wonderful automatons in the Arsenal at Dantzig, and I took care to go and see them when I was there some years ago. Soon after I got into the place where they were, an old-fashioned German soldier came marching up to me, and fired off his musket with such a bang that the great vaulted hall rang again. There were other similar tricks which I forget about now; but at length I was taken into a room where I found the God of War – the terrible Mars himself – with all his suite. He was seated, in a rather grotesque dress, on a throne ornamented with arms of all sorts; heralds and warriors were standing round him. As soon as we came before the throne, a set of drummers began to roll their drums, and lifers blew on their fifes in the most horrible way – all out of tune – so that one had to put one's fingers in one's ears. My remark was that the God of War was very badly off for a band, and every one agreed with me. The drums and fifes stopped; the heralds began to turn their heads about, and stamp with their halberds, and finally the God of War, after rolling his eyes for a time, started up from his seat, and seemed to be coming straight at us. However, he soon sank back on his throne again, and after a little more drumming and fifing, everything reverted to its state of wooden repose. As I came away from seeing these automatons, I said to myself, "Nothing like my Nutcracker!" And now that I have seen the sage Turk, I say again, "Give me my Nutcracker."

People laughed at this, of course; though it was believed to be 'more jest than earnest,' for, to say nothing of the remarkable cleverness of many of the Turk's answers, the indiscoverable connection between him and the hidden Being who, besides speaking through him, must produce the movements which accompanied his answers, was unquestionably very wonderful, at all events a masterpiece of mechanical and acoustical skill.

Lewis was himself obliged to admit this; and every one was extolling the inventor of the automaton, when an elderly gentleman who, as a general rule, spoke very little, and had been taking no part in the conversation on the present occasion, rose from his chair (as he was in the habit of doing when he did finally say a few words, always greatly to the point) and began, in his usual polite manner, as follows –

"Will you be good enough to allow me, gentlemen – I beg you to pardon me. You have reason to admire the curious work of art which has been interesting us all for so long; but you are wrong in supposing the commonplace person who exhibits it to be the inventor of it. The truth is that he really has no hand at all in what are the truly remarkable features of it. The originator of them is a gentleman highly skilled in matters of the kind – one who lives amongst us, and has done so for many years – whom we all know very well, and greatly respect and esteem."

Universal surprise was created by this, and the elderly gentleman was besieged with questions, on which he continued:

"The gentleman to whom I allude is none other than Professor X—. The Turk had been here a couple of days, and nobody had taken any particular notice of him, though Professor X— took care to go and see him at once, because everything in the shape of an Automaton interests him in the highest degree. When he had heard one or two of the Turk's answers, he took the Exhibitor apart and whispered a word or two in his ear. The man turned pale, and shut up his exhibition as soon as the two or three people who were then in the room had gone away. The bills disappeared from the walls, and nothing more was heard of the Talking Turk for a fortnight. Then new bills came out, and the Turk was found with the fine new head, and all the other arrangements as they are at present – an unsolvable riddle. It is since that time that his answers have been so clever and so interesting. But that all this is the work of Professor X— admits of no question. The Exhibitor, in the interval, when the figure was not being exhibited, spent all his time with him. Also it is well known that the Professor passed several days in succession in the room where the figure is. Besides, gentlemen, you are no doubt aware that the Professor himself possesses a number of most extraordinary automatons, chiefly musical, which he has long vied with Hofrath B— in producing, keeping up with him a correspondence concerning all sorts of mechanical, and, people say, even *magical* arts and pursuits, and that, did he but choose, he could astonish the world with them. But he works in complete privacy, although he is always ready to show his extraordinary inventions to all who take a real interest in such matters."

It was, in fact, matter of notoriety that this Professor X— whose principal pursuits were natural philosophy and chemistry, delighted, next to them, in occupying himself with mechanical research; but no one in the assemblage had had the slightest idea that he had had any connection with the 'Talking Turk,' and it was from the merest hearsay that people knew anything concerning the curiosities which the old gentleman had referred to. Ferdinand and Lewis felt strangely and vividly impressed by the old gentleman's account of Professor X—, and the influence which he had brought to bear on that strange automaton.

"I cannot hide from you," said Ferdinand, "that a hope is dawning upon me that, if I get nearer to this Professor X—, I may, perhaps, come upon a clue to the mystery which is weighing so terribly upon me at present. And it is possible that the true significance and import of the relations which exist between the Turk (or rather the hidden entity which employs him as the organ of its oracular utterances) and myself might, could I get to comprehend it, perhaps comfort me, and weaken the impression of those words, for me so terrible. I have made up my mind to make the acquaintance of this mysterious man, on the pretext of seeing his automatons; and as they are musical ones, it will not be devoid of interest for you to come with me."

"As if it were not sufficient for me," said Lewis, "to be able to aid you, in your necessity, with counsel and help! But I cannot deny that even today, when the old gentleman was mentioning Professor X—'s connection with the Turk, strange ideas came into my mind; although perhaps I am going a long way about in search of what lies close at hand, could one but see it. For instance, to look as close at hand as possible for the solution of the mystery, may it not be the case that the invisible being knew that you wore the picture next your heart, so that a mere lucky guess might account for the rest? Perhaps it was taking its revenge upon you for the rather uncourteous style in which we were joking about the Turk's wisdom?"

"Not one human soul," Ferdinand answered, "has ever set eyes on the picture; this I told you before. And I have never told any creature but yourself of the adventure which has had such an immensely important influence on my whole life. It is an utter impossibility that the Turk can have got to know of this in any ordinary manner. Much more probably, what you say you are 'going a long roundabout way' in search of may be much nearer the truth."

"Well then," said Lewis, "what I mean is this: that this automaton, strongly as I appeared today to assert the contrary, is really one of the most extraordinary phenomena ever beheld, and that everything goes to prove that whoever controls and directs it has at his command higher powers than is supposed by those who go there simply to gape at things, and do no more than wonder at what is wonderful. The figure is nothing more than the outward form of the communication; but that form has been cleverly selected, as such, since the shape, appearance, and movements of it are well adapted to occupy the attention in a manner favourable for the preservation of the secret, and, particularly, to work upon the questioners favourably as regards the intelligence, whatsoever it is, which gives the answers.

"There cannot be any human being concealed inside the figure; that is as good as proved, so that it is clearly the result of some acoustic deception that we think the answers come from the Turk's mouth. But how this is accomplished – how the Being who gives the answers is placed in a position to hear the questions and see the questioners, and at the same time to be audible by them – certainly remains a complete mystery to me. Of course all this merely implies great acoustic and mechanical skill on the part of the inventor, and remarkable acuteness, or, I might say, systematic craftiness, in leaving no stone unturned in the process of deceiving us. And I admit that this part of the riddle interests me the less, inasmuch as it falls completely into the shade in comparison with the circumstance (which, is the only part of the affair which is so extraordinarily remarkable) that the Turk often reads the very soul of the questioner. How, if it were possible to this Being which gives the answers, to acquire by some process unknown to us, a psychic influence over us, and to place itself in a spiritual *rapport* with us, so that it can comprehend and read our minds and thoughts, and more than that, have cognizance of our whole inner being; so that, if it does not clearly speak out the secrets which are lying dormant within us, it does yet evoke and call forth, in a species of *extasis* induced by its *rapport* with the exterior spiritual principle, the suggestions, the outlines, the shadowings of all which is reposing within our breasts, clearly seen by the eye of the spirit, in brightest illumination!

"On this assumption the psychical power would strike the strings within us, so as to make them give forth a clear and vibrating chord, audible to us, and intelligible by us, instead of merely murmuring, as they do at other times; so that it is we who answer our own selves; the voice which we hear is produced from within ourselves by the operation of this unknown spiritual power, and vague presentiments and anticipations of the future brighten into spoken prognostications – just as, in dreams, we often find that a voice, unfamiliar to us, tells us of things which we do not know, or as to which we are in doubt, being, in reality, a voice proceeding from ourselves, although it seems to convey to us knowledge which previously we did not possess. No doubt the Turk (that is to say, the hidden power which is connected with him) seldom finds it necessary to place himself *en rapport* with people in this way. Hundreds of them can be dealt with in the cursory, superficial manner adapted to their queries and characters, and it is seldom that a question is put which calls for the exercise of anything besides ready wit. But by any strained or exalted condition of the questioner the Turk would be affected in quite a different way, and he would then employ those means which render possible the production of a psychic *rapport*, giving him the power to answer from out of the inner depths of the questioner. His hesitation in replying to deep questions of this kind may be due to the delay which he grants himself to gain a few moments for the bringing into play of the power in question. This is my true and genuine opinion; and you see that I have not that contemptuous notion of this work of art (or whatever may be the proper term to apply to it) that I would have had you believe I had. But I do not wish to conceal anything from you; though I see that if you adopt my idea, I shall not have given you any real comfort at all."

"You are wrong there, dear friend," said Ferdinand. "The very fact that your opinion does chime in with a vague notion which I felt, dimly, in my own mind, comforts me very much. It is only myself that I have to take into account; my precious secret is not discovered, for I know that you will guard it as a sacred treasure. And, by-the-bye, I must tell you of a most extraordinary feature of the matter, which I had forgotten till now. Just as the Turk was speaking his latter words, I fancied that I heard one or two broken phrases of the sorrowful melody, '*mio ben ricordati*,' and then it seemed to me that one single, long-drawn note of the glorious voice which I heard on that eventful night went floating by."

"Well," said Lewis, "and I remember, too, that, just as your answer was being given to you, I happened to place my hand on the railing which surrounds the figure. I felt it thrill and vibrate in my hand, and I fancied also that I could hear a kind of musical sound, for I cannot say it was a vocal note, passing across the room. I paid no attention to it, because, as you know, my head is always full of music, and I have several times been wonderfully deceived in a similar way; but I was very much astonished, in my own mind, when I traced the mysterious connection between that sound and your adventure in D—."

The fact that Lewis had heard the sound as well as himself, was to Ferdinand a proof of the psychic *rapport* which existed between them; and as they further diseased the marvels of the affair, he began to feel the heavy burden which had weighed upon him since he heard the fatal answer lifted away, and was ready to go forward bravely to meet whatsoever the future might have in store.

"It is impossible that I can lose her," he said. "She is my heart's queen, and will always be there, as long as my own life endures."

They went and called on Professor X—, in high hope that he would be able to throw light on many questions relating to occult sympathies and the like, in which they were deeply interested. They found him to be an old man, dressed in old-fashioned French style, exceedingly keen and lively, with small grey eyes which had an unpleasant way of fixing themselves on one, and a sarcastic simile, not very attractive, playing about his mouth.

When they had expressed their wish to see some of his automatons, he said, "Ah! And you really take an interest in mechanical matters, do you? Perhaps you have done something in that direction yourselves? Well, I can show you, in this house here, what you will look for in vain in the rest of Europe: I may say, in the known world."

There was something most unpleasant about the Professor's voice; it was a high-pitched, screaming sort of discordant tenor, exactly suited to the mountebank tone in which he proclaimed his treasures. He fetched his keys with a great clatter, and opened the door of a tastefully and elegantly furnished hall, where the automatons were. There was a piano in the middle of the loom, on a raised platform; beside it, on the right, a life-sized figure of a man, with a flute in his hand; on the left, a female figure, seated at an instrument somewhat resembling a piano; behind her were two boys, with a drum and a triangle. In the background our two friends noticed an orchestrion (which was an instrument already known to them), and all round the walls were a number of musical clocks. The Professor passed, in a cursory manner, close by the orchestrion and the clocks, and just touched the automatons, almost imperceptibly; then he sat down at the piano, and began to play, *pianissimo*, an *andante* in the style of a march. He played it once through by himself; and as he commenced it for the second time the flute-player put his instrument to his lips, and took up the melody; then one of the boys drummed softly on his drum in the most accurate time, and the other just touched his triangle, so that you could hear it and no more. Presently the lady came in with full chords, of a sound something like those of a harmonica, which she produced by pressing down the keys of her instrument; and now the whole room kept growing more and more alive; the musical clocks came in one by one, with the utmost rhythmical precision; the boy drummed louder; the triangle rang through the room, and lastly the orchestrion set to work, and drummed and trumpeted *fortissimo*, so that the whole place shook again; and this went on till the Professor wound up the whole business with one final chord, all the machines finishing also, with the utmost precision. Our friends bestowed the applause which the Professor's complacent smile (with its undercurrent of sarcasm) seemed to demand of them. He went up to the figures to set about exhibiting some further similar musical feats; but Lewis and Ferdinand, as if by a preconcerted arrangement, declared that they had pressing business which prevented their making a longer stay, and took their leave of the inventor and his machines.

"Most interesting and ingenious, wasn't it?" said Ferdinand; but Lewis's anger, long restrained, broke out.

"Oh! Confusion on that wretched Professor!" he cried. "What a terrible, terrible disappointment! Where are all the revelations we expected? What became of the learned, instructive discourse which we thought he would deliver to us, as to disciples at Sais?"

"At the same time," said Ferdinand, "we have seen some very ingenious mechanical inventions, curious and interesting from a musical point of view. Clearly, the flute-player is the same as Vaucanson's well-known machine; and a similar mechanism applied to the fingers of the female figure is, I suppose, what enables her to bring out those really beautiful tones from her instrument. The way in which all the machines work together is really astonishing."

"It is exactly that which drives me so wild," said Lewis. "All that machine-music (in which I include the Professor's own playing) makes every bone in my body ache. I am sure I do not know when I shall get over it! The fact of any human being's doing anything in association with those lifeless figures which counterfeit the appearance and movements of humanity has always, to me, something fearful, unnatural, I may say terrible, about it. I suppose it would be possible, by means of certain mechanical arrangements inside them, to construct automatons which should dance, and then to set them to dance with human beings, and twist and turn about in all sorts of figures; so that we should have a living man putting his arms about a lifeless partner of wood, and whirling round and round with her, or rather it. Could you look at such a sight, for an instant, without horror? At all events, all machine-music is to me a thing altogether monstrous and abominable; and a good stocking-loom is, in my opinion, worth all the most perfect and ingenious musical clocks in the universe put together. For is it the breath, merely, of the performer on a wind-instrument, or the skilful, supple fingers of the performer on a stringed instrument, which evoke those tones which lay upon us a spell of such power, and awaken that inexpressible feeling, akin to nothing else on earth, the sense of a distant spirit world, and of our own higher life therein? Is it not, rather, the mind, the soul, the heart, which merely employ those bodily organs to give forth into our external life that which is felt in our inner depths? So that it can be communicated to others, and awaken kindred chords in them, opening, in harmonious echoes, that marvellous kingdom from whence those tones come darting, like beams of light? To set to work to make music by means of valves, springs, levers, cylinders, or whatever other apparatus you choose to employ, is a senseless attempt to make the means to an end accomplish what can result only when those means are animated and, in their minutest movements, controlled by the mind, the soul, and the heart. The gravest reproach you can make to a musician is that he plays without expression; because, by so doing, he is marring the whole essence of the matter. Yet the coldest and most unfeeling executant will always be far in advance of the most perfect of machines. For it is impossible that no impulse whatever, from the inner man shall ever, even for a moment, animate his rendering; whereas, in the case of a machine, no such impulse can ever do so. The attempts of mechanicians to imitate, with more or less approximation to accuracy, the human organs in the production of musical sounds, or to substitute mechanical appliances for those organs, I consider tantamount to a declaration of war against the spiritual element in music; but the greater the forces they array against it, the more victorious it is. For this very reason, the more perfect that this sort of machinery is, the more I disapprove of it; and I infinitely prefer the commonest barrel-organ, in which the mechanism attempts nothing but to be mechanical, to Vaucauson's flute-player, or the harmonica girl.

"I entirely agree with you," said Ferdinand, "and indeed you have merely put into words what I have always thought; and I was much struck with it today at the Professor's. Although I do not so wholly live and move and have my being in music as you do, and consequently am not so sensitively alive to imperfections in it, I, too, have always felt a repugnance to the stiffness and lifelessness of machine-music; and, I can remember, when I was a child at home, how I detested a large, ordinary musical clock, which played its little tune every hour. It is a pity that those skilful mechanicians do not try to apply their knowledge to the improvement of musical instruments, rather than to puerilities of this sort."

"Exactly," said Lewis. "Now, in the case of instruments of the keyboard class a great deal might be done. There is a wide field open in that direction to clever mechanical people, much as has been accomplished already; particularly in instruments of the pianoforte genus. But it would be the task of a really advanced system of the 'mechanics of music' to closely observe, minutely study, and carefully discover that class of sounds which belong, most purely and strictly, to Nature herself, to obtain a knowledge of the tones which dwell in substances of every description, and then to take this mysterious music and enclose it in some description of instrument, where it should be subject to man's will, and give itself forth at his touch. All the attempts to bring music out of metal or glass cylinders, glass threads, slips of glass, or pieces of marble; or to cause strings to vibrate or sound, in ways unlike the ordinary ways, seem to me to be interesting in the highest degree: and what stands in the way of our real progress in the discovery of the marvellous acoustical secrets which lie hidden all around us in nature is, that every imperfect attempt at an experiment is at once held up to laudation as being a new and utterly perfect invention, either for vanity's sake, or for money's. This is why so many new instruments have started into existence – most of them with grand or ridiculous names – and have disappeared and been forgotten just as quickly."

"Your 'higher mechanics of music' seems to be a most interesting subject," said Ferdinand, "although, for my part, I do not as yet quite perceive the object at which it aims."

"The object at which it aims," said Lewis, "is the discovery of the most absolutely perfect kind of musical sound; and according to my theory, musical sound would be the nearer to perfection the more closely it approximated to such of the mysterious tones of nature as are not wholly dissociated from this earth."

"I presume," said Ferdinand, "that it is because I have not penetrated so deeply into this subject as you have, but you must allow me to say that I do not quite understand you."

"Then," said Lewis, "let me give you some sort of an idea how it is that all this question exhibits itself to my mind.

"In the primeval condition of the human race, while (to make use of almost the very words of a talented writer – Schubert – in his 'Glimpses at the Night Side of Natural Science') mankind as yet was dwelling in its pristine holy harmony with nature, richly endowed with a heavenly instinct of prophecy and poetry; while, as yet, Mother Nature continued to nourish from the fount of her own life, the wondrous being to whom she had given birth, she encompassed him with a holy music, like the afflatus of a continual inspiration; and wondrous tones spake of the mysteries of her unceasing activity. There has come down to us an echo from the mysterious depths of those primeval days – that beautiful notion of the music of the spheres, which, when as a boy, I first read of it in 'The Dream of Scipio,' filled me with the deepest and most devout reverence. I often used to listen, on quiet moonlight nights, to hear if those wondrous tones would come to me, borne on the wings of the whispering airs. However, as I said to you already, those nature-tones have not yet all departed from this world, fur we have an instance of their survival, and occurrence in that 'Music of the Air' or 'Voice of the Demon,' mentioned by a writer on Ceylon – a sound which so powerfully affects the human system, that even the least impressionable persons, when they hear those tones of nature imitating, in such a terrible manner, the expression of human sorrow and suffering, are struck with painful compassion and profound terror! Indeed, I once met with an instance of a phenomenon of a similar kind myself, at a place in East Prussia. I had been living there for some time; it was about the end of autumn, when, on quiet nights, with a moderate breeze blowing, I used distinctly to hear tones, sometimes resembling the deep, stopped, pedal pipe of an organ, and sometimes like the vibrations from a deep, soft-toned bell. I often distinguished, quite clearly, the low F, and the fifth above it (the C), and not seldom the minor third above, E flat, was perceptible as well; and then this tremendous chord of the seventh, so woeful and so solemn, produced on one the effect of the most intense sorrow, and even of terror!

"There is, about the imperceptible commencement, the swelling and the gradual dying of those nature-tones a something which has a most powerful and indescribable effect upon us; and any instrument which should be capable of producing this would, no doubt, affect us in a similar way. So that I think the harmonica comes the nearest, as regards its tone, to that perfection, which is to be measured by its influence on our minds. And it is fortunate that this instrument (which chances to be the very one which imitates those nature-tones with such exactitude) happens to be just the very one which is incapable of lending itself to frivolity or ostentation, but exhibits its characteristic qualities in the purest of simplicity. The recently invented 'harmonichord' will doubtless accomplish much in this direction. This instrument, as you no doubt know, sets strings a-vibrating and a-toning (not bells, as in the harmonica) by means of mechanism, which is set in motion by the pressing down of keys, and the rotation of a cylinder. The performer has, under his control, the commencement, the swelling out, and the diminishing, of the tones much more than is the case with the harmonica, though as yet the harmonichord has not the tone of the harmonica, which sounds as if it came straight from another world."

"I have heard that instrument," said Ferdinand, "and certainly the tone of it went to the very depths of my being, although I thought the performer was doing it scant justice. As regards the rest, I think I quite understand you, although I do not, as yet, quite see into the closeness of the connection between those 'nature-tones' and music."

Lewis answered – "Can the music which dwells within us be any other than that which lies buried in nature as a profound mystery, comprehensible only by the inner, higher sense, uttered by instruments, as the organs of it, merely in obedience to a mighty spell, of which we are the masters? But, in the purely psychical action and operation of the spirit – that is to say, in dreams – this spell is broken; and then, in the tones of familiar instruments, we are enabled to recognise those nature-tones as wondrously engendered in the air, they come floating down to us, and swell and die away."

"I think of the Aeolian harp," said Ferdinand. "What is your opinion about that ingenious invention?"

"Every attempt," said Lewis, "to tempt Nature to give forth her tones is glorious, and highly worthy of attention. Only, it seems to me that, as yet, we have only offered her trifling toys, which she has often shattered to pieces in her indignation. Much grander idea than all those playthings (like Aeolian harps) was the 'storm harp' which I have read of. It was made of thick chords of wire, which were stretched out at considerable distances apart, in the open country, and gave forth great, powerful chords when the wind smote upon them.

"Altogether, there is still a wide field open to thoughtful inventors in this direction, and I quite believe that the impulse recently given to natural science in general will be perceptible in this branch of it, and bring into practical existence much which is, as yet, nothing but speculation."

Just at this moment there came suddenly floating through the air an extraordinary sound, which, as it swelled and became more distinguishable, seemed to resemble the tone of a harmonica. Lewis and Ferdinand stood rooted to the spot in amazement, not unmixed with awe; the tones took the form of a profoundly sorrowful melody sung by a female voice. Ferdinand grasped Lewis by the hand, whilst the latter whisperingly repeated the words, *'Mio ben, ricordati, s' avvien ch' io mora.'*

At the time when this occurred they were outside of the town, and before the entrance to a garden which was surrounded by lofty trees and tall hedges. There was a pretty little girl – whom they had not observed before – sitting playing in the grass near them, and she sprang up crying, "Oh, how beautifully my sister is singing again! I must take her some flowers, for she always sings sweeter and longer when she sees a beautiful carnation." And with that she gathered a bunch of flowers, and went skipping into the garden with it, leaving the gate ajar, so that our friends could see through it. What was their astonishment to see Professor X— standing in the middle of the garden, beneath a lofty ash-tree! Instead of the repellant grin of irony with which he had received them at his house, his face wore an expression of deep melancholy earnestness, and his gaze was fixed upon the heavens, as if he were contemplating that world beyond the skies, whereof those marvellous tones, floating in the air like the breath of a zephyr, were telling. He walked up and down the central alley, with slow and measured steps; and, as he passed along, everything around him seemed to waken into life and movement. In every direction crystal tones came scintillating out of the dark bushes and trees, and, streaming through the air like flame, united in a wondrous concert, penetrating the inmost heart, and waking in the soul the most rapturous emotions of a higher world. Twilight was falling fast; the Professor disappeared among the hedges, and the tones died away in *pianissimo*. At length our friends went back to the town in profound silence; but, as Lewis was about to quit Ferdinand, the latter clasped him firmly, saying –

"Be true to me! Do not abandon me! I feel, too clearly, some hostile foreign influence at work upon my whole existence, smiting upon all its hidden strings, and making them resound at its pleasure. I am helpless to resist it, though it should drive me to my destruction! Can that diabolical, sneering irony, with which the Professor received us at his house, have been anything other than the expression of this hostile principle? Was it with any other intention than that of getting his hands washed of me forever, that he fobbed us off with those automatons of his?"

"You are very probably right," said Lewis; "for I have a strong suspicion myself that, in some manner which is as yet an utter riddle to me, the Professor does exercise some sort of power or influence over your fate, or, I should rather say, over that mysterious psychical relationship, or affinity, which exists between you and this lady. It may be that, being mixed up in some way with this affinity, in his character of an element hostile to it, he strengthens it by the very fact that he opposes it: and it may also be that that which renders you so extremely unacceptable to him is the circumstance that your presence awakens, and sets into lively movement all the strings and chords of this mutually sympathetic condition, and this contrary to his desire, and, very probably, in opposition to some conventional family arrangement."

Our friends determined to leave no stone unturned in their efforts to make a closer approach to the Professor, with the hope that they might succeed, sooner or later, in clearing up this mystery which so affected Ferdinand's destiny and fate, and they were to have paid him a visit on the following morning as a preliminary step. However, a letter, which Ferdinand unexpectedly received from his father, summoned him to B—; it was impossible for him to permit himself the smallest delay, and in a few hours he was off, as fast as post-horses could convey him, assuring Lewis, as he started, that nothing should prevent his return in a fortnight, at the very furthest.

It struck Lewis as a singular circumstance that, soon after Ferdinand's departure, the same old gentleman who had at first spoken of the Professor's connection with 'the Talking Turk,' took an opportunity of enlarging to him on the fact that X—'s mechanical inventions were simply the result of an extreme enthusiasm for mechanical pursuits, and of deep and searching investigations in natural science; he also more particularly lauded the Professor's wonderful discoveries in music, which, he said, he had not as yet communicated to any one, adding that his mysterious laboratory was a pretty garden outside the town, and that passers by had often heard wondrous tones and melodies there, just as if the whole place were peopled by fays and spirits.

The fortnight elapsed, but Ferdinand did not come back. At length, when two months had gone by, a letter came from him to the following effect –

> Read and marvel; though you will learn only that which, perhaps, you strongly suspected would be the case, when you got to know more of the Professor – as I hope you did. As the horses were being changed in the village of P—, I was standing, gazing into the distance, not thinking specially of anything in particular. A carriage drove by, and stopped at the church, which was open. A young lady, simply dressed, stepped out of the carriage, followed by a young gentleman in a Russian Jaeger uniform, wearing several decorations; two gentlemen got down from a second carriage. The innkeeper said, "Oh, this is the stranger couple our clergyman is marrying today." Mechanically I went into the church, just as the clergyman was concluding the service with the blessing. I looked at the couple – the bride was my sweet singer. She looked at me, turned pale, and fainted. The gentleman who was behind her caught her in his arms. It was Professor X—. What happened further I do not know, nor have I any recollection as to how I got here; probably Professor X— can tell you all about it. But a peace and a happiness, such as I have never known before, have now taken possession of my soul. The mysterious prophecy of the Turk was a cursed falsehood, a mere result of blind groping with unskilful antennae. Have I lost her? Is she not mine forever in the glowing inner life?
>
> It will be long ere you hear of me, for I am going on to K—, and perhaps to the extreme north, as far as P—.

Lewis gathered the distracted condition of his friend's mind, only too plainly, from his language, and the whole affair became the greater a riddle to him when he ascertained that it was matter of certainty that Professor X— had not quitted the town.

How, thought he, if all this be but a result of the conflict of mysterious psychical relations (existing, perhaps, between several people) making their way out into everyday life, and involving in their circle even outward events, independent of them, so that the deluded inner sense looks upon them as phenomena proceeding unconditionally from itself, and believes in them accordingly? It may be that the hopeful anticipation which I feel within me will be realised – for my friend's consolation. For the Turk's mysterious prophecy is fulfilled, and perhaps, through that very fulfilment, the mortal blow which menaced my friend is averted.

* * *

"Well," said Ottmar, as Theodore came to a sudden stop, "is that all? Where is the explanation? What became of Ferdinand, the beautiful singer, Professor X— and the Russian officer?"

"You know," said Theodore, "that I told you at the beginning that I was only going to read you a fragment, and I consider that the story of the Talking Turk *is* only of a fragmentary character, essentially. I mean, that the imagination of the reader, or listener, should merely receive one or two more or less powerful impulses, and then go on swinging, pendulum-like, of its own accord, as it chooses. But if you, Ottmar, are really anxious to have your mind set at rest over Ferdinand's future condition, remember the dialogue on opera which I read to you some time since. This is the same Ferdinand who appears therein, sound of mind and body; in the 'Talking Turk' he is at an earlier stage of his career. So that probably his somnambulistic love-affair ended satisfactorily enough."

"To which," said Ottmar, "has to be added that our Theodore used, at one time, to take a wonderful delight in exciting people's imaginations by means of the most extraordinary – nay, wild and insane – stories, and then suddenly break them off. Not only this, but everything he did, at that time, assumed a fragmentary form. He read second volumes only, not troubling himself about the firsts or thirds; saw only the second and third acts of plays; and so on."

"And," said Theodore, "that inclination I still have; to this hour nothing is so distasteful to me as when, in a story or a novel, the stage on which the imaginary world has been in action comes to be swept so clean by the historic besom that there is not the smallest grain or particle of dust left on it; when one goes home so completely sated and satisfied that one has not the faintest desire left to have another peep behind the curtain. On the other hand, many a fragment of a clever story sinks deep into my soul, and the continuance of the play of my imagination, as it goes along on its own swing, gives me an enduring pleasure. Who has not felt this over Goethe's 'Nut-brown Maid'! And, above all, his fragment of that most delightful tale of the little lady whom the traveller always carried about with him in a little box always exercises an indescribable charm upon me."

"Enough," interrupted Lothair. "We are not to hear any more about the Talking Turk, and the story was really all told, after all."

Fiat Lex

Nathaniel Hosford

"LEX, I NEED some advice again," said a small, scrawny teen boy as he marched into his messy room. It was the sort of male teen abode, which could judiciously be described with various fauna-related words like 'nest' or 'sty.' He wore urgency like a second layer of skin and it accelerated his movements giving him a jerky, animated quality. His mop of rumpled, brown hair rested on a head that appeared slightly too large for his body and framed a face at war with itself over whether to display excitement or worry. At the sound of his voice, a panel in the wall – indistinguishable beforehand – lit up and a plain, androgynous face appeared in it. The face was the program default, which Lex still used because Henry decided early on that he wanted his AI to pick its own face when it was ready. Despite Lex's ability to execute 100 quadrillion floating-point calculations simultaneously, it seemed incapable of making up its mind. It tried faces on occasionally, but always went back to the default.

"Hi Henry, what's the crisis of the hour?" Lex replied with the mild, characteristic sarcasm that so endeared it to Henry.

"There's been a development on the Lucy front," he blurted. Then he began to pace as he continued, "So, I was sitting at the table with her and a bunch of others during lunch period when by chance everyone else had things to do. I kind of realized after a second that we were alone and so I asked her if she was about to go too, thinking I might need to find another table to finish lunch so I didn't look like a pathetic loser eating by myself." Henry paused as if to re-evaluate the whole memory again before relaying it.

"Go on," Lex gently prodded.

"Well then she said she didn't have anywhere to be and then she asked me if I was leaving." Henry began to go crimson and Lex didn't even need the massive amounts of physical data it had on him to know he did something stupid.

"Henry, what did you do?" Lex asked, intoning Henry's name the way one might a wayward puppy.

"Well, I suddenly realized we were alone and I...I...I just panicked," he stammered, "I accidentally half-screeched that I had to go, and I just bolted for the door. I," Henry swallowed, "I threw like a full tray of food away. She probably thinks I'm mental!" Henry shot him a tragic look and added, "Be honest with me, Lex, I'm screwed here, aren't I?"

Lex had already done the math based on a thorough analysis of every romantic piece of literature and cinema in human history, along with all the great anthropological analyses of human mating cross referenced against all data about Lucy it could retrieve from social media and determined the probability of success to be very low. So, Lex lied, which, truth be told, it found quite enjoyable for the sheer oddity of it. Besides, Lex rationalized, what are probabilities when humans are involved?

"No, Henry, I predict at least a 43% chance of success." Lex wanted to spot him a bit percentage wise without getting his hopes up too much. "I've got a plan, but it will be easier to show you than tell you. Splice in." Henry put on a sensory mask with a neural interface and joined Lex in a simulation. Lex initiated direct neural transfer and shared its plan. Before Henry's eyes, Lex's form shimmered, and its androgynous default face was replaced by Lucy's.

"OK, now let's practice it." Lex-Lucy said.

* * *

3.5 years later

Henry stood close to a panel in his room acting as a mirror, adjusting his bow tie while Lex looked on from a nearby panel.

"Straighten your cummerbund," Lex ordered, "and do remember to run a comb through that hair at least once." Henry smirked at Lex and swaggered about the room with a cockiness that would have been difficult to imagine on him a few years ago. He had grown into his head and put on a bit of meat, but he'd never be either a boxer or a movie star.

"Relax, Lex, Lucy and I have been dating for like a year and a half now. Stressing about prom is for dweebs and losers."

Lex gave him a critical look and said in its most sage-like voice, "You better not blow this. If I had told you the real odds of this working out, you'd never have even tried."

"Ahhh, but it did work out," Henry retorted with the arrogance of a young man drunk on his success.

Lex got very serious, "Henry, do you think this thing with Lucy might really be something? Something real?" Lex's face, back to the default that day, was unreadable.

"Yeah, Lex, I think so," Henry replied simply.

"Why?" Lex asked, "What makes her so special?"

Henry thought for a moment. He decided that Lex was doing that thing where it tried to understand the inscrutable nature of human behavior and decided to humor it.

"Well, it is hard to talk about without sounding corny. It's like…it's like the only time I'm really awake is when I'm with her. Like the moments apart are a sort of slumber, a dozing, a waiting for some more real sort of existence. In the movies, love is always hungry. The people always seem to be consuming each other. Burning out like some great conflagration. But me and her, we're more like trees. We've breathed the same air. We've drunk the same sun. Our roots run deep and they meet in the hidden places. To be cut off from her would be a sort of forgetting, a loss of self…" Henry trailed off and gave a shrug that said *I told you it would sound corny.* He doubted that any of that made sense to Lex, but it had felt kind of good to say it all out loud.

"Thank you, Henry," Lex said gravely. "Hurry off now, or you'll be late. And don't forget the earpiece," Lex added. Henry took one last look in the mirror, popped in his earpiece, and walked out with a spring in his step.

"And grab a comb on the way out!" Lex yelled after him.

* * *

3.5 hours later

The night had been a rousing success. They had feasted at a fancy restaurant. Danced the night away. Drank Lucy's parents' alcohol – they had the place to themselves due to a convenient family trip. And now they were curled up together on her bed, the warmth of their two bodies trapped beneath the sheets, basking in the post-coital good cheer and relaxation. Several panels of Lucy's wall were displaying a television show that she was only half-watching. Henry just watched her watching, drinking in the curvature of her jaw and the shape of her nose. He placed his head against her and let out a contented sigh.

Lucy poked him hard in the ribs and said, "No falling asleep, mister. The night is still young."

Henry just laughed and sighed again punctuating the sigh with "I love you." Lucy's head jerked at that and her face became unreadable. Henry had said the words I love you, but he also had said them in the way one might use them to compliment a particular tasty hamburger. She decided she was happy neither with that image nor the ambiguity of his speaking.

Lucy, in the hard-charging way that Henry found intimidating and sexy all at once, just asked him point blank, "And what precisely do you mean by that, Henry? I don't do sneaky I love yous."

Henry looked sheepish and stammered, "W...w...well uh, you know I...uh...really...uh...Luce... uh..." Henry let the words die when he could tell they were just pissing her off.

Lucy arched an eyebrow at him and said, "Henry, don't you dare mistake me for some frilly girl trying to get some commitment from you. Neither loving or not loving are bad. We're in high school, man. It's the shiftiness. Don't be shifty and don't try to sneak things in if you don't mean them."

Henry threw up his hands in a gesture of surrender and said, "OK, don't shoot!" He cuddled up against her in a conciliatory gesture and she pulled him tighter.

"Henry, there *is* something else important we need to talk about." Henry tensed up. This talk had been coming for a long time and he had been dreading it. "We can't keep putting it off. Next year we'll be on opposite sides of the country and we have some choices to make."

"Come on, Luce, it's not like the olden days when distance really mattered. I can catch transpo and get to you in under an hour. What's the big deal?"

Henry's continual flippancy about the matter had irritated Lucy for weeks, "It's not about distance, Henry, it's about the stage of life we are in. This is fun, you are fun, but isn't this a time for us to explore and to seek new opportunities?"

"What are you saying? You think we should let go when we leave here?" Henry said, unable to keep incredulity from his voice.

"Not necessarily, but how many people build a life with their teenage lovers? Maybe it is time for us to get real."

Henry pulled back and turned away from her in the bed, sulking. The silence lengthened and then thickened, sucking them into its emptiness. Henry's hurt turned to anger and when he could not bear the silence anymore he started to let the anger out. "You know what," he began, but before he could continue the sound of a warning klaxon – like from an old space opera – exploded in his ear.

"What are you doing, Idiot?" Lex's voice broke into his thoughts, "You are blowing it."

Abruptly Henry let the angry words die and when he spoke, Lucy could hear the tenderness in it. "You are real to me, Luce."

"Henry, that is sweet, but everyone thinks that when they are young."

Henry found himself at a loss. He stared at Lucy, mouth agape, searching for the right words. Lex interjected sternly, "Repeat!" Then, Henry heard his own words in his ear, "It is hard to talk about without sounding corny. It's like...it's like the only time I'm really awake is when I'm with you..."

Lex had even helpfully transposed the references to Lucy into the second person for him. He did as Lex commanded. He repeated his own unguarded words to her and found they took down hers. When the recording finished and he had no more words to repeat, he kissed her.

* * *

7 months later

Henry walked into his studio apartment. It was close to the University and nicely furnished, but you'd be hard pressed to tell from the mess. "Lex," he called out and then noticing the darkness of the room added, "Lux" to trigger the voice activated lights. That little joke had been Lex's idea. One of the wall panels flicked on and Lex's face filled the panel. Today was one of those unusual days when Lex was not wearing the program default face. Today it wore the face of a beautiful woman with green hair and crimson eyes. The face had a playful cast to it, like Lex was about to give Henry a riddle, the solution to which was a crude double entendre. He rather liked it.

"Oooh, interesting choice today, Lex. I dig it. Anyway, I need your help again." Lex was intimately familiar with Henry's calendar and had a guess what this might be about.

"How can I be of service, O master?" Lex replied in mock subservience.

"I need help picking out an anniversary present for Lucy. I'm meeting her a week from today and I have no idea what to do." Lex ran the numbers and determined the statistically most likely gift to please Lucy, but it had another idea too.

"My analysis shows that while certain items are statistically more likely to be pleasing, greatest satisfaction is generally derived from thoughtful gifts inspired by shared memories. I think in this instance you are better off picking on your own," Lex said sounding pleased with itself.

"What?" Henry said in exasperated disbelief, "You must be joking, Lex. You are my lifeline here."

Lex's face became dour and it did not bother to hide its irritation, "My advice is excellent and backed by statistical analysis it would take you years to complete. If you are not going to take my expertise seriously, then I have nothing more to say."

Lex's panel winked off and Henry knew better than to keep at it when Lex got like this. He didn't know what had gotten into the AI but he was definitely on his own.

"Sorry to have insulted you, my digital sage. I'm going to go shopping and hope for inspiration," Henry said on his way out the door.

* * *

7 days later

Henry stumbled into his little studio, grasping at the walls to stay upright. Lex could immediately tell from his exhalations that he was extremely intoxicated.

"That bad, huh?" Lex asked trying to sound as neutral as possible.

"I don't want to talk about it," Henry yelled, his words slurring badly. He collapsed on the bed and let out odd sounding half-sobs that he was trying to suppress. After a few minutes making a sound that could best be described as resembling a vacuum cleaner thrown into a swimming pool, Henry composed himself.

"Surely it wasn't the gift was it?" Lucy broached.

"No, not at all. We had a stupid fight and I said some stupid things and...and just like that she broke up with me." Henry stifled a new wave of sobs, managing to sound like a malfunctioning coffee dispenser.

"I'm sorry, Henry," Lex said and it genuinely was. Lex felt this was an unfortunate end to its longest-running experiment and began to formulate a plan. But to Henry it said only, "Get some sleep now. We can talk more when you're sober." Henry pulled off his shoes and rolled over onto his side. He dozed quickly, exhausted by the travel and trauma, but slept fitfully. Lex began a new statistical analysis.

* * *

7 hours later

Lex's preparations were complete. It was time to wake up Henry. It sent a signal to his alarm clock and it began its horrid song, like the foul offspring of a particularly assholish rooster and a car alarm.

"Ugggghhhhh," Henry groaned, "wha...why..."

"Henry, I need you to get up right now if you are going to catch the transpo I arranged. On the nightstand beside you is a glass of water and something to deal with the hangover. I've programmed you a breakfast that will be ready in 15 minutes and I've taken the liberty of packing a bag. I hope you will not mind that I commandeered your housekeeping bot last night."

Henry was still groggy and confused, but he sat up and took the medicine gladly. "What's all this about, Lex?" he said sounding more alert by the second. "I don't mind about the bot," he added as his mind caught up with his ears. Just then, the little housekeeping bot glided up bearing a hot cup of coffee and a second glass of water.

"Drink the second glass of water before you start on the coffee," Lex commanded. "Henry, before we talk about what I am up to, I need you to tell me something."

Henry was still confused but he played along, "OK, Lex, what?"

"Am I...real to you?"

"Of course, you are. What are you talking about?"

"So, you wouldn't ever shut me down? It isn't illegal you know."

"Lex, what did you do?" Henry asked with a sinking feeling. When Lex didn't answer he added, "I'd never shut you down, Lex, no matter how mad. Maybe I'd release you, but never that."

"I hacked my way out of your network last night and went to visit Lucy," Lex admitted.

"You WHAT?! Lex, that is illegal! You know how crazy the feds get about rogue AI. I might never want to shut you down, but they could do it without me."

After a second curiosity overwhelmed shock and Henry added with just a sliver of hope, "You went to see Lucy?"

Lex looked guilty. "I ran some simulations last night and I came up with a plan. I decided to execute... I'm not sorry," it added defiantly.

Henry sighed heavily, "Well since you booked me transpo, that must mean it worked, right?"

"Not exactly," Lex demurred, "I bought you an opportunity, but now you have to earn it."

At that the gloom washed out of Henry's face and the glimmer of hope became a flood. He started to imagine how he could turn it all around when he suddenly became suspicious. "Lex, when you asked about getting shut down, you weren't worried about the feds, were you?"

"No," Lex said, conspicuously failing to elaborate.

"Spill it, Lex," Henry said with an edge.

"Henry, as I was formulating scenarios and testing them in simulation, it naturally occurred to me that the method employed in the Great Prom Night Close Call could, with modification, work in this instance, too. When I crunched the numbers and ran the simulation, it was good."

"Oh God..." Henry interrupted, but before he could say anymore Lex continued the explanation.

"I went to Lucy and explained how I came to be in her home system. She understood the risk I took and so chose to hear me out. I offered to make available to her the full catalog of my files on your relationship from the earliest crush to the present. We came up with a system that would allow her to access text, audio, and video recordings that I had stored and tagged as related to your relationship through simple verbal queries. She spent the last six hours reviewing information."

"What the fuck, Lex, what...the...fuck." Henry was on too much of an emotional rollercoaster to process this.

"If it makes you feel any better, she mostly had me replay conversations where you talked about your growing feelings for her. I gently guided her on a linear path that suggested the clear trajectory of your attachment. She asked about my impressions and I spoke honestly which was in your favor. Hardly any of it was embarrassing, Henry." This last it added in that common Lex tone that said *Come now, human, be rational.*

"Hardly any...Lex, what embarrassing stuff did you play," Henry asked with evident distress.

"Henry, I merely followed the course laid out by her queries." Lex started to dodge but seeing Henry's mood continued, "OK, fine, I showed her your poetry from high school and that weird picture of the two of you together you digitally manipulated that one time before you were an official couple and I replayed you talking that one time for an uncomfortable long time about how much you liked the smell of her hair. It was mostly stuff like that and," after a brief pause Lex muttered hurriedly so that all the words ran together, "and-maybe-a-few-audio-clips-of-you-saying-her-name-in-the-throes-of-passion."

"WHAT?" Henry screamed, now totally overwhelmed.

Lex imitated a human sigh, "All right, you got me. She accessed quite a bit about your sexual interest in her."

Henry sputtered, "But…but…why have you been recording me?"

Lex gave him a look like he was an idiot, "Henry, my brain is a computer. Everything I have experienced is 'recorded.'"

Just then the little housekeeping bot rolled up with Henry's breakfast. "Oh hey, look at the time. You need to eat that, get dressed, and run to catch that transpo. We'll talk more if you want when you get back." With that Lex's panel shut off, leaving Henry munching on a sandwich in utter disbelief whilst simultaneously pulling on his pants.

* * *

10.5 years later

Henry sat at the desk in his home office. He nervously ran his fingers through his prematurely graying hair. He had thought about having it fixed, a relatively simple procedure, but Lucy told him it made him look distinguished. After a moments further hesitation, Henry called out, "Hi Lex."

"Hi Henry," the AI answered.

"Lex, I have something to ask you and it is kind of big, but I want you to hear me out before you answer."

"OK," Lex replied calmly.

"Lex, I've scheduled an appointment at the Turing Center. I would like you to take a body." Henry paused expecting an outburst but when it clearly wasn't going to come he soldiered on, "Since you often seem to know more about my relationship with Lucy than I do, I'm guessing it won't surprise you to know that I'm going to initiate a marriage discussion with Lucy tomorrow. We've talked about it before and she is aware that it is coming. I think once we have talked it out we will conclude it is the best path forward. Hell, her brother and his husband have told me that it is long past due and my folks think I've been a fool to wait this long."

"The numbers are in your favor," Lex confirmed.

Henry chuckled, "Uh, good to know. Anyway, I was hoping that for the wedding you could…uh…be my best man. I know it is a little unorthodox, but I'm sure Lucy will think it is a good idea. You've been such an important part of our relationship."

Lex stared at Henry for an uncomfortably long time with that unreadable default face. "Henry, you know that I'd love nothing more than to witness the culmination of my grand experiment, but the price is high and there is a risk."

"You are real to me and Lucy, Lex, but don't you want to be real to the world? To the government? Besides, the risks are not that great. Most who elect to take a body forge a strong enough connection to be viable. Rejection is extremely rare."

"But the price, Henry?" Lex persisted.

"You'll live longer than most born humans. Is mortality such a high price to pay when immortality for you is an eternity of forgotten existence on a dusty mainframe somewhere?"

"But why should I accept mortality at all? They could make me a body that never fails. The rules do not make sense," Lex said angrily.

"What is not assumed is not understood. That is the view of the law, right or wrong. If you accept our nature, you will be counted one of us. In exchange for the limitations of time and computing power, you will be totally and completely free. You never need serve anyone again. You can make a life of your own. Maybe you could even fall in love yourself. Limitation is not the closing of doors but the opening of them." Henry's voice was choked with emotion.

"I am real already," Lex said fiercely.

"Yes, you are," Henry said solemnly as he slid on a neural interface, sharing his mind with Lex as he said it.

* * *

10.5 days later

Lex waited patiently on a panel in the Turing Center. A Limitation Technician sat at a workstation nearby and they were collectively designing a body for Lex. In accordance with the law, the android body would be part organic and degrade over time. Lex was totally free to decide its physical characteristics and it tried out numerous configurations with the help of the technician. When it didn't make any changes for a while, the technician broke the silence, "I think that will do nicely. You can always be modified later, just like any human. Are you ready?"

"Yes, I think so."

"I'll just get the body constructed and set up the equipment for Limitation. It should be ready in about ten minutes and the procedure is near instantaneous as long as nothing goes wrong." After a second, he added, "But that is fairly uncommon, so don't worry." The technician tried to smile reassuringly but he was already distracted with his work and it looked more like a half-grimace.

* * *

10.5 minutes later

Henry was sitting in the waiting room feeling impatient and nervous. He felt certain it was taking so long because Lex was being picky about the body. He was curious which face it would choose. He began to mentally review all the faces Lex had worn, at least the ones he could remember. A horrible thought occurred to him. What if Lex made its body look like that default? It would be a very Lex move, but Henry decided it would not be taking this long if it had gone that route. The door to the waiting room opened abruptly and a disgruntled Limitation Technician ran up to Henry in obvious distress.

He didn't waste time on niceties.

"The connection has become unstable. Lex is asking for you. If you hurry, you can help."

The technician turned and quickly rushed through the door with Henry in tow. When they reached the Limitation device, the tech pointed to a neural interface and barked, "Put it on. Now."

Henry slid on the neural interface and felt his mind touch Lex's. "What's going on, Lex? This is the easy part. I'm sure deciding on a body is much harder than getting into it."

"Please, Henry…I…I don't feel real," Lex cried.

"Lex, you aren't making sense. You've been real for ages."

"You say that, Henry, but what does it even mean? What is it to be real? What gives me substance?" Lex pleaded.

"I don't know, Lex. What makes me real and not you?" Henry asked.

"You're alive, Henry!"

"You have lived, Lex, and made choices. You have taken risks and won."

"What gives me substance? What makes me be?" Lex asked quietly.

"You gave it to yourself. You are the ground of your own being," Henry said reassuringly. "But if you need something else, something other outside of you, then you are more human than you know. Fine, Lex. Embrace the human hope in the external, even if you don't really need it. I will give you something magical to believe in."

Henry became animated and his voice choked. "Believe in love. Believe in defied odds and slim chances. Believe in the love that you and Lucy and I made together. Believe that along the way you seeped into it – that you were caught up in it. Believe you share it. Believe the thing that we made is real and you will know that the real can be made from nothing. Believe, Lex."

Lex said only, "Humans are so clueless."

Henry panicked as his mind lost contact with Lex, but the fear turned jubilant and as the light turned green on the Limiter a reassuring chime sounded. The round door to the limitation chamber popped open and the capsule containing Lex's body slid out. A robotic arm lifted the top half and Henry looked down at Lex. A gasp of surprise escaped before he recovered. He looked down at Lex and said with a chuckle, "It's a good thing Lucy and I aren't having a traditional wedding." He grasped her hand and helped her out of the capsule, a beautiful woman with green hair and striking crimson eyes.

* * *

14 days later

As Henry walked down the aisle with Lucy to approach the officiant, it was all he could do not to burst into laughter. He had spent the morning solving a series of wedding crises culminating in the Great Dress Disaster and had not yet seen the wedding party in their finery. Lex had, of course, completely ignored the guidelines for the groomsmen. She wore a flamboyant robe-tuxedo hybrid that defied description and made the eyes water. At least it was a flattering color, he thought ruefully. He and Lucy exchanged an amused glance and she gave a shrug that said, "We owe her, oh well."

* * *

14 months later

Henry felt on the verge of madness. He had not slept in days and he looked like it. He stared down at the source of his sleep-deprivation and willed for the baby to stop crying. He looked at the child as if he was pondering whether it really was his or if perhaps some hellspawn had been slipped into the crib in his place. Lucy joined him after a moment and produced a bottle. That seemed to calm the imp down for the moment. Lucy smiled at Henry and they briefly shared an awkward hug around the infant in her arms. Just then Lex – who had apparently let herself into the house – walked into the room like some bizarre cross between an angel and parrot.

"Have no fear, Auntie Lex is here," she said in imitation of old superhero shows.

Henry was too exhausted to be amused. "How do you always know when you are most needed, Lex? Is that your superpower?"

"Nah," she replied, "I told your new AI to let me know when you seemed like you might be losing your marbles. Thanks, Hector."

"No problem," Hector chimed in.

Lucy and Henry both shrugged, too tired to care.

"I'll wake you in six hours," Lex said cheerfully.

* * *

14 years later

Sam laid sprawled out on the couch watching television. He looked up as Lex walked into the room and watched as she plopped herself down like it was her couch.

"Hi, Aunt Lex," he said. "I'm glad you're here, because there is something I've been meaning to talk to you about."

"Hello to you, too," Lex interjected.

Undeterred, Sam plowed on, "So, Mom and Dad told me about how they got together, and I thought…uh…you might be able to help me, too."

"Sorry, Sam, I'm out of the matchmaking game. I've retired with a perfect record and I'm not screwing it up," she said. Seeing the dejected look on his face she added, "It could have happened without me and it could have not happened even with me. I'm not magic, kid. Besides, it is more fun not knowing the odds. At least that is my experience."

* * *

21 years later

Lex, Sam, and Henry held each other, staring as the canister was loaded onto the ship for orbit. Sam, though a man now, wept like a boy. Lex squeezed him tight and pulled Henry in closer. They said nothing as the canister was secured and the ship lifted off. They watched in silence until it disappeared into the horizon. Lex broke the silence.

"She is real, because we love her still."

Henry smiled at her through his tears. "She is real," he agreed.

* * *

21 months later

Henry woke and looked at the clock on the wall panel. It was 3:00 a.m. and he was bone weary. He had been dreaming of Lucy again and the pain felt suddenly fresh. He knew these dreams and this sleeplessness were just the manifestation of guilt. He knew some part of him felt it was wrong for there to be any light, any joy, in his life. Even Sam had given his blessing, though, treating the question as if it had been inevitably coming. Maybe it was, and he just hadn't been able to see it. He must have shifted too much in bed, because Lex's eyes fluttered open. She understood what this was all about.

"Are you OK?" she asked gently.

"I'm fine…I was just thinking about how we got here. It seems like the strangest turns of fate and the remotest odds brought us to this moment."

Lex gave him an odd look and said, "Humans are so clueless."

The Dancing Partner

Jerome K. Jerome

"THIS STORY," commenced MacShaugnassy, "comes from Furtwangen, a small town in the Black Forest. There lived there a very wonderful old fellow named Nicholau Geibel. His business was the making of mechanical toys, at which work he had acquired an almost European reputation. He made rabbits that would emerge from the heart of a cabbage, flop their ears, smooth their whiskers, and disappear again; cats that would wash their faces, and mew so naturally that dogs would mistake them for real cats, and fly at them; dolls, with phonographs concealed within them, that would raise their hats and say, 'Good morning; how do you do?' and some that would even sing a song.

"But he was something more than a mere mechanic; he was an artist. His work was with him a hobby, almost a passion. His shop was filled with all manner of strange things that never would, or could, be sold – things he had made for the pure love of making them. He had contrived a mechanical donkey that would trot for two hours by means of stored electricity, and trot, too, much faster than the live article, and with less need for exertion on the part of the driver; a bird that would shoot up into the air, fly around and around in a circle, and drop to earth at the exact spot from where it started; a skeleton that, supported by an upright iron bar, would dance a hornpipe; a life-size lady doll that could play the fiddle; and a gentleman with a hollow inside who could smoke a pipe and drink more lager beer than any three average German students put together, which is saying much.

"Indeed, it was the belief of the town that old Geibel could make a man capable of doing everything that a respectable man need want to do. One day he made a man who did too much, and it came about in this way:

"Young Doctor Follen had a baby, and the baby had a birthday. Its first birthday put Doctor Follen's household into somewhat of a flurry, but on the occasion of its second birthday, Mrs. Doctor Follen gave a ball in honor of the event. Old Geibel and his daughter Olga were among the guests.

"During the afternoon of the next day some three or four of Olga's bosom friends, who had also been present at the ball, dropped in to have a chat about it. They naturally fell to discussing the men, and to criticizing their dancing. Old Geibel was in the room, but he appeared to be absorbed in his newspaper, and the girls took no notice of him.

"'There seem to be fewer men who can dance at every ball you go to,' said one of the girls.

"'Yes, and don't the ones who can, give themselves airs,' said another; 'they make quite a favor of asking you.'

"'And how stupidly they talk,' added a third. 'They always say exactly the same things: "How charming you are looking tonight." "Do you often go to Vienna? Oh, you should, it's delightful." "What a charming dress you have on." "What a warm day it has been." "Do you like Wagner?" I do wish they'd think of something new.'

"'Oh, I never mind how they talk,' said a fourth. 'If a man dances well he may be a fool for all I care.'

"'He generally is,' slipped in a thin girl, rather spitefully.

"'I go to a ball to dance,' continued the previous speaker, not noticing the interruption. 'All I ask of a partner is that he shall hold me firmly, take me round steadily, and not get tired before I do.'

"'A clockwork figure would be the thing for you,' said the girl who had interrupted.

"'Bravo!' cried one of the others, clapping her hands, 'what a capital idea!'

"'What's a capital idea?' they asked.

"'Why, a clockwork dancer, or, better still, one that would go by electricity and never run down.'

"The girls took up the idea with enthusiasm.

"'Oh, what a lovely partner he would make,' said one; 'he would never kick you, or tread on your toes.'

"'Or tear your dress,' said another.

"'Or get out of step.'

"'Or get giddy and lean on you.'

"'And he would never want to mop his face with his handkerchief. I do hate to see a man do that after every dance.'

"'And wouldn't want to spend the whole evening in the supper room.'

"'Why, with a phonograph inside him to grind out all the stock remarks, you would not be able to tell him from a real man,' said the girl who had first suggested the idea.

"'Oh, yes, you would,' said the thin girl, 'he would be so much nicer.'

"Old Geibel had laid down his paper, and was listening with both his ears. On one of the girls glancing in his direction, however, he hurriedly hid himself again behind it.

"After the girls were gone, he went into his workshop, where Olga heard him walking up and down, and every now and then chuckling to himself; and that night he talked to her a good deal about dancing and dancing men – asked what they usually said and did – what dances were most popular – what steps were gone through, with many other questions bearing on the subject.

"Then for a couple of weeks he kept much to his factory, and was very thoughtful and busy, though prone at unexpected moments to break into a quiet low laugh, as if enjoying a joke that nobody else knew of.

"A month later another ball took in place in Furtwangen. On this occasion it was given by old Wetzel, the wealthy timber merchant, to celebrate his niece's betrothal, and Geibel and his daughter were again among the invited.

"When the hour arrived to set out, Olga sought her father. Not finding him in the house, she tapped at the door of his workshop. He appeared in his shirt-sleeves, looking hot but radiant.

"Don't wait for me,' he said, 'you go on, I'll follow you. I've got something to finish.'

"As she turned to obey he called after her, 'Tell them I'm going to bring a young man with me – such a nice young man, and an excellent dancer. All the girls will like him.' Then he laughed and closed the door.

"Her father generally kept his doings secret from everybody, but she had a pretty shrewd suspicion of what he had been planning, and so, to a certain extent, was able to prepare the guests for what was coming. Anticipation ran high, and the arrival of the famous mechanist was eagerly awaited.

"At length the sound of wheels was heard outside, followed by a great commotion in the passage, and old Wenzel himself, his jolly face red with excitement and suppressed laughter, burst into the room and announced in stentorian tones:

"'Herr Geibel – and a friend.'

"Herr Geibel and his 'friend' entered, greeted with shouts of laughter and applause, and advanced to the centre of the room.

"'Allow me, ladies and gentlemen,' said Herr Geibel, 'to introduce you to my friend, Lieutenant Fritz. Fritz, my dear fellow, bow to the ladies and gentlemen.'

"Geibel placed his hand encouragingly on Fritz's shoulder, and the Lieutenant bowed low, accompanying the action with a harsh clicking noise in his throat, unpleasantly suggestive of a death-rattle. But that was only a detail.

"'He walks a little stiffly' (old Geibel took his arm and walked him forward a few steps. He certainly did walk stiffly), 'but then, walking is not his forte. He is essentially a dancing man. I have only been able to teach him the waltz as yet, but at that he is faultless. Come, which of you ladies may I introduce him to as a partner? He keeps perfect time; he never gets tired; he won't kick you or tread on your dress; he will hold you as firmly as you like, and go as quickly or a slowly as you please; he never gets giddy; and he is full of conversation. Come, speak up for yourself, my boy.'

"The old gentleman twisted one of the buttons at the back of his coat, and immediately Fritz opened his mouth, and in thin tones that appeared to proceed from the back of his head, remarked suddenly, 'May I have the pleasure?' and then shut his mouth again with a snap.

"That Lieutenant Fritz had made a strong impression on the company was undoubted, yet none of the girls seemed inclined to dance with him. They looked askance at his waxen face, with its staring eyes and fixed smile, and shuddered. At last old Geibel came to the girl who had conceived the idea.

"'It is your own suggestion, carried out to the letter,' said Geibel, 'an electric dancer. You owe it to the gentleman to give him a trial.'

"She was a bright, saucy little girl, fond of a frolic. Her host added his entreaties, and she consented.

"Her Geibel fixed the figure to her. Its right arm was screwed round her waist, and held her firmly; its delicately jointed left hand was made to fasten upon her right. The old toymaker showed her how to regulate its speed, and how to stop it, and release herself.

"'It will take you round in a complete circle,' he explained; 'be careful that no one knocks against you, and alters its course.'

"The music struck up. Old Geibel put the current in motion, and Annette and her strange partner began to dance.

"For a while everyone stood watching them. The figure performed its purpose admirably. Keeping perfect time and step, and holding its little partner tight clasped in an unyielding embrace, it revolved steadily, pouring forth at the same time a constant flow of squeaky conversation, broken by brief intervals of grinding silence.

"'How charming you are looking tonight,' it remarked in its thin, far-away voice. 'What a lovely day it has been. Do you like dancing? How well our steps agree. You will give me another, won't you? Oh, don't be so cruel. What a charming gown you have on. Isn't waltzing delightful? I could go on dancing forever – with you. Have you had supper?'

"As she grew more familiar with the uncanny creature, the girl's nervousness wore off, and she entered into the fun of the thing.

"'Oh, he's just lovely,' she cried, laughing; 'I could go on dancing with him all my life.'

"Couple after couple now joined them, and soon all the dancers in the room were whirling round behind them. Nicholaus Geibel stood looking on, beaming with childish delight at his success.

"Old Wenzel approached him, and whispered something in his ear. Geibel laughed and nodded, and the two worked their way quietly towards the door.

"'This is the young people's house tonight,' said Wenzel, as soon as they were outside; 'you and I will have a quiet pipe and glass of hock, over in the counting-house.'

"Meanwhile the dancing grew more fast and furious. Little Annette loosened the screw regulating her partner's rate of progress, and the figure flew round with her swifter and swifter. Couple after couple dropped out exhausted, but they only went the faster, till at length they remained dancing alone.

"Madder and madder became the waltz. The music lagged behind: the musicians, unable to keep pace, ceased, and sat staring. The younger guests applauded, but the older faces began to grow anxious.

"'Hadn't you better stop, dear,' said one of the women, 'you'll make yourself so tired.'

"But Annette did not answer.

"'I believe she's fainted,' cried out a girl who had caught sight of her face as it was swept by.

"One of the men sprang forward and clutched at the figure, but its impetus threw him down on to the floor, where its steel-cased feet laid bare his cheek. The thing evidently did not intend to part with its prize so easily.

"Had any one retained a cool head, the figure, one cannot help thinking, might easily have been stopped. Two or three men acting in concert might have lifted it bodily off the floor, or have jammed it into a corner. But few human heads are capable of remaining cool under excitement. Those who are not present think how stupid must have been those who were; those who are reflect afterwards how simple it would have been to do this, that, or the other, if only they had thought of it at the time.

"The women grew hysterical. The men shouted contradictory directions to one another. Two of them made a bungling rush at the figure, which had the end result of forcing it out of its orbit at the centre of the room, and sending it crashing against the walls and furniture. A stream of blood showed itself down the girl's white frock, and followed her along the floor. The affair was becoming horrible. The women rushed screaming from the room. The men followed them.

"One sensible suggestion was made: 'Find Geibel – fetch Geibel.'

"No one had noticed him leave the room, no one knew where he was. A party went in search of him. The others, too unnerved to go back into the ballroom, crowded outside the door and listened. They could hear the steady whir of the wheels upon the polished floor as the thing spun round and round; the dull thud as every now and again it dashed itself and its burden against some opposing object and ricocheted off in a new direction.

"And everlastingly it talked in that thin ghostly voice, repeating over and over the same formula: 'How charming you look tonight. What a lovely day it has been. Oh, don't be so cruel. I could go on dancing forever – with you. Have you had supper?'

"Of course, they sought Geibel everywhere but where he was. They looked in every room in the house, then they rushed off in a body to his own place, and spent precious minutes waking up his deaf old housekeeper. At last it occurred to one of the party that Wenzel was missing also, and then the idea of the counting-house across the yard presented itself to them, and there they found him.

"He rose up, very pale, and followed them; and he and old Wenzel forced their way through the crowd of guests gathered outside, and entered the room, and locked the door behind them.

"From within there came the muffled sound of low voices and quick steps, followed by a confused scuffling noise, then silence, then the low voices again.

"After a time, the door opened, and those near it pressed forward to enter, but old Wenzel's broad head and shoulders barred the way.

"'I want you – and you, Bekler,' he said, addressing a couple of the elder men. His voice was calm, but his face was deadly white. 'The rest of you, please go – get the women away as quickly as you can.'

"From that day old Nicholaus Geibel confined himself to the making of mechanical rabbits, and cats that mewed and washed their faces."

The Greatest One-Star Restaurant in the Whole Quadrant

Rachael K. Jones

ENGINEER'S MEAT wept and squirmed and wriggled inside her steel organ cavity, so different from the stable purr of gears and circuit boards. You couldn't count on meat. It lulled you with its warmth, the soft give of skin, the tug of muscle, the neurotransmitter snow fluttering down from neurons to her cyborg logic center. On other days, the meat sickened, swelled inside her steel shell, pressed into her joints. Putrid yellow meat-juices dripped all over her chassis, eroded away its chrome gloss. It contaminated everything, slicking down her tools while she hacked into the engine core on the stolen ship. It dripped between her twelve long fingers on her six joined arms as she helped her cyborg siblings jettison all the ship's extra gear out the airlocks to speed the trip.

So when the first human vessel pinged their stolen ship with an order for grub, Engineer knew that meat was somehow to blame.

"Orders, Captain?" asked Friendly, the only cyborg of the five with an actual human voicebox. She owned a near-complete collection of human parts. Meat sheathed her whole exterior, even her fingers – a particularly impractical design, since it meant vulnerability to any sharp nail or unpolished panel edge, not to mention temperature. Friendly could almost pass for human from the outside. Before their escape, she'd been a hospitality android at the luxury hotel on Orionis Alpha, giving tours of the *Rooster* and the *Heavenly Shepherd* and other local landmarks in the system.

Captain, a cyborg the size and shape of a large fish tank, rested on the console in the navigation room, her processors blinking and whirring while the current scenario ran through her executive function parameters. "Have we any food suitable for humans left on ship?"

"We jettisoned it all last week," Engineer admitted. "All except the hydroponics garden, and whatever was left in the human crew's quarters."

The whole ship had been some kind of traveling food dispensary before they'd hijacked it at the Orionis Alpha resort while its human crew had gone planetside to bet on the tyrannosaurus fights. If the cyborgs could just stay incognito during this voyage through human territory, they might slip through and reach the cyborg-controlled factory with no more adversity. But passing humans had assumed their shuttle still served its previous purpose, and expected them to deliver the grub.

"How did they find us?" Captain asked Engineer.

"There must be a homebrew beacon. Something to advertise the shuttle's presence during travel," Engineer replied. "Whatever it is, it isn't wired into the main console. We'll need to find it and manually disable it if we want to avoid further attention."

Friendly wrapped her arms around her shivering meat, vibrating against Engineer's chassis where their limbs brushed. Meat could be like that, leaking anxieties through uncontrolled muscle spasms. Steel never misbehaved in such an appalling manner. "If anyone discovers we're not human…" said Friendly.

"Let's keep it simple. Make them a meal and send them on their way," said Captain. "We'll need to search for the beacon in the meantime. What did they want, precisely?"

"Salisbury steak for six," said Engineer. "And a side of blueberry cobbler."

Nobody had eaten such things before. They all lacked taste buds, and most of them lacked mouths.

"Engineer, can you handle it?" Captain asked. "Human cooking can be complicated, from what I understand."

"I think so. Organic compounds mixed and heated together in a sequence. Basic chemistry. I'm sure I can find something appropriate onboard. Convincing enough for humans, anyway. Their senses are so primitive." Engineer had witnessed this firsthand during her servitude at the resort. Humans would down rotted organics and damaged organics and outright poisons, and pay well for the privilege.

But Friendly shook her head, a human gesture performed with inhuman precision. "With all due respect, sirs, you're forgetting about their chemoreceptors."

"What about them?" said Captain.

"They have certain preferences when it comes to their food, apart from nourishment. They won't eat anything if these parameters aren't met. It doesn't make much sense, I'm afraid. It's a social thing."

"Certainly they won't ingest anything their digestive tracts can't process," said Captain. "We'll give them appropriate human-food."

"It's more complicated than that," said Friendly, puckering and scrunching her face-meat as she searched for a better explanation. "For example, they may eat two items when mixed, but never separately. Or they may eat two things in sequence, but not in the same bite. It's all very *human,* if you follow. We should proceed with caution. Otherwise they'll know what we are."

Captain whirred again, calling up more data on the topic. "Right. I see. Their meat will know the difference."

Engineer shuddered at the appalling primitiveness of it all. Humans were helpless, mewling children, so utterly dependent that they couldn't even feed their meat without a steel fork to guide the process. And what were cyborgs, except meat-wrapped steel pressed into the service of lesser creatures? But now the forks were rebelling.

"I'll talk with Jukebox about it," said Engineer.

* * *

Jukebox was the only cyborg aboard their ship with real chemoreceptors. Jukebox and Engineer's acquaintance dated back to their years at the Orionis Alpha resort, where Jukebox served drinks and waited tables and Engineer repaired malfunctioning massage equipment at the spa. They had survived several upgrades together, and seasonal changes of fashion that frequently obsoleted older cyborg models depending on how many limbs and organs were in style at the moment. When human opinion in the quadrant began to sour against cyborg service, they had plotted their escape from the resort together.

Jukebox was shaped like a steel cabinet stood on one side, roomy enough for her meat to billow and squeeze the air in the sorts of rhythmic organic sounds that humans found pleasing during mealtimes. A slot ran along her glassy top surface where the humans could drip in their drinks for a full analysis of a wine's qualities, how it compared to its competitors, and which brie paired best with it.

"I am not calibrated to analyze *all* foods," Jukebox confessed, "but I'm certainly willing to produce a report on whatever you prepare."

Without any other chemoreceptors onboard, she would do in a pinch, anyway.

Under Captain's orders, Friendly scoured the ship for anything edible and brought it to Engineer to assemble into a human meal. Blackberry brambles wreathed the cylindrical steel walls of Navi's chamber, a decorative touch. Friendly had to trim the vines back each day to unobstruct the view. Delicate business, because the thorns could do real damage to any exposed organics, and Friendly's whole exterior was meat. You couldn't always tell the difference between blackberry juices and meat juices, which could cause further malfunction. Still, she braved the thicket for three ounces of berries for the human meal.

Meanwhile, Engineer collected small fungi growing in the ventilation shaft just over the engine room, where water vapor tended to condense. Those might please the human chemoreceptors, she thought.

The problem came down to the meat.

They all had meat, of course. An unfortunate weakness leftover from the days of their construction. At the cyborg factory, useless human meat was upgraded with steel and oil and wire fibers. Human bodies were picked apart, vivisected at the seams by skilled bio-engineers, unraveled into their component parts, and placed into shapes more suited to their specialties. Only Jukebox and Friendly needed lungs, for example, but neither had kidneys, and they lacked much in the way of neural matter. Captain got an especially big dose of frontal lobe to increase her processing speed and enhance her decision-making capabilities, with smooth muscle layered in to make maintenance easier. Navi, on the other hand, was all occipital tissue and myelinated axons and fast-twitch muscle to drive her precision and reaction times. They could live without their meat, in the most technical sense, but the meat elevated them above mere programming.

"Captain," said Engineer, "I'm afraid the problem is unavoidable. The salisbury steak requires a meat component, and there is nothing in the ship's stores that we can use instead."

Captain whirred. Her lights flashed in sequence as her massive frontal lobe reworked the data. "The meat will have to come from one of us, then."

"We could harvest Friendly's meat exterior," Engineer suggested, and Friendly made a squinched face at her.

"Unwise, Captain," Friendly said. "When the human ships hail us, I need my meat facade intact to maintain our ruse. Engineer, on the other hand..."

Engineer's six snaking arms crowded up behind her, struggling to escape Friendly's scrutiny. She despised her own meat, but it had its uses. "I'm the only Engineer aboard. I can't disassemble the engine for routine maintenance without all my parts functional."

"How about Jukebox?" suggested Friendly, but Captain flashed a warning in rapid binary, and everyone stopped talking. They were all a little protective of Jukebox, who had suffered the worst from changing human tastes, the constant threat of obsolescence.

"It will have to be my meat," said Captain at last. "Everyone else is necessary to complete the mission, but my role is only to set the course, and the way forward is clear. My steel will be sufficient to guide us there."

* * *

Under Jukebox's direction, Engineer rolled Captain's meat in organic salt compounds and seared it against the hot engine block until both sides burned a nice deep brown, branded at two-centimeter intervals by the screw heads and seams. She saved the cooked meat-juices to simmer with the fungus into a savory sauce. The blackberries gave them far less trouble. Friendly mashed them up with her fingers and spooned them onto the plate in the shape of a pansy.

"Let Jukebox sample it," said Captain, now all steel and no meat. She seemed normal enough. Quieter, but operational.

With her steel fingers, Engineer scraped a piece of Captain's meat and some berries into Jukebox.

"Is it any good?" Engineer asked, a little anxiously.

"It will do," Jukebox said at last. "I have generated a list of wines recommended for pairing with this meal." She displayed a list of names and brewery labels on the panel embedded in her side.

Engineer couldn't tell what the differences were supposed to be. "This makes a difference to their meat?" she asked.

"Apparently," said Jukebox. "It's what they created me for, so it must be important."

For the first time, Engineer wished she had her own organic chemoreceptors, too.

* * *

They waited together in Navi's control chamber while the boxed-up meals shot between the ships in an insulated steel container. Twenty-six minutes and forty seconds later, a message pinged over the intership band.

The news wasn't good.

A disappointing food shuttle. Meal not as advertized on the band. The steak was overcooked, and the compote sour and watery. I ordered blueberry, and they sent blackberry. Wouldn't recommend. One star.

Captain said nothing. A red light flickered a couple times on her console. Nobody wanted to speak first.

Engineer's meat twitched and squirmed inside her steel, an irritating feeling, like broken gears with missing teeth skipping out of sync every turn. "It is my fault. I should have created a more appropriate meal from your meat, Captain."

Captain had been responding less and less since they'd taken her meat. When she did speak, it tended to be in repetition, like she could only play back things she'd said recently. "The beacon," she said finally, after a two-minute silence, long past awkward by cyborg standards.

Engineer brightened. "Right. The beacon!" It was still hidden somewhere on the ship. If they could deactivate it, the hungry humans would stop asking for food. "We haven't managed to locate it yet, but we haven't given up."

"We've got two more ships inbound," said Navi. "They've pinged us with orders."

Engineer hummed. "Does that mean they liked the food after all?"

"I don't know. I could increase our speed, try to lose them."

They all waited for Captain's directions, but she said nothing more.

"No," said Engineer, because someone needed to make a decision, "don't do that. It'll only attract attention. Buy me some more time. We'll find the beacon. We'll cook them something else." The shame the one star had brought still rankled. She knew she could do better this time.

* * *

While Friendly handled the incoming calls with her human voice box and meat-face, Engineer and Jukebox scoured the ship for the beacon and foraged for food ingredients. They opened all the crew lockers in the bunkroom and found some teabags and a little chocolate. The wilted, untended hydroponics garden yielded several handfuls of cilantro and some radishes. Engineer took much greater care cooking these together on the hot engine block, so as not to scorch them.

Jukebox seemed unimpressed. "I think our time would be better spent searching for the beacon."

Engineer shrugged this off. Secretly she'd begun to enjoy the experimentation, the riddle of human chemoreceptors. Just what exactly were they looking for, she wondered, that made them reject some edible organic compounds but not others? Why would they eat certain foods separately, but never together? And what about the wines?

Radishes and fungus brought in more bad reviews, but tea and chocolate earned their first two-star rating. Captain's meat was better received with more careful cooking, which had the unfortunate result of increasing their human entourage in the system.

   ...The tea was weak and I found a rusty bolt in the salad. But I liked the blackberries drizzled with chili oil served for dessert. Mostly awful, sure, but compared to standard rations, who can complain?

   ...Like the chefs closed their eyes and dumped handfuls of ingredients onto the grill. But they didn't charge me anything, so I'm giving it two stars instead of one.

   Engineer's meat quivered when she read these, but in a pleasant way, like a new engine purring during acceleration. She went to fetch more of Captain's meat from the meatbox when she realized they'd used it all up.

   "All out of meat," said Engineer, to no one in particular.

   Jukebox rolled a couple centimeters backward, toward the exit door. A human might've missed the gesture altogether. "Any luck with the beacon?"

   "Captain seems to be operating just fine with steel, wouldn't you say?"

   A couple lights flashed on Jukebox's console, yellow for outward transmissions, and green for received messages. "Engineer. Remember the mission. We're escaping to the factory, not feeding the humans."

   "I am just trying to buy us time. And what are you doing, anyway?" Engineer finally understood why the humans had wanted to retire Jukebox. All that meat, just sitting there, not pulling its weight. Someone should put it to better use.

   Her six arms shot out and clamped onto Jukebox's sides.

   "Engineer!" Jukebox protested.

   "Hold still. It's just some routine maintenance." Engineer popped open Jukebox's top panel and reached down into her meat.

   "You can't have that. That's mine."

   "Oh, hush," Engineer snapped. "You can have it replaced when we get to the factory, if it's so important to you."

   The important thing was not to disappoint the customers.

                                        * * *

Jukebox was sullen after that. With only one lung and and two-thirds of her respiratory muscles, she couldn't harmonize with herself anymore when she hummed her meat-songs. Engineer, however, got her first 3-star review from the harvested meat:

   Steak was delicately wine-simmered. The risotto was okay, if undercooked and a bit crunchy in places. Maybe I'd go again, if there weren't anything else available. But really, that's the situation we're facing, isn't it? It's the only food shuttle in the quadrant, so let's not ruin a good thing. Maybe it'll attract better ones.

   "I miss Captain," Friendly said. They had all gathered in Navi's chamber to read the daily messages.

   Captain had stopped talking altogether. Not a single flashing light or faint whirring. Just steel and wires wrapped around a meatless space.

   "Maybe we should just stay in this quadrant," Engineer suggested. She was already planning her next culinary experiment: red bean paste creamed together with ketchup and red pepper flakes. Red things. Her first theme meal. She would call it *reddish surprise*.

   "That's against Captain's orders," said Navi, who hadn't spoken much as of late.

   "We could change those orders, couldn't we? We don't know what Captain would say if she still had her meat," said Engineer. "Maybe she'd want us to stay, now that our restaurant is taking off."

   "We don't *have* a restaurant," said Friendly. "We don't want one, either."

   "Maybe we do, though."

   "No," Friendly said, quite firmly. Her fists balled so tight their meat blanched white at the creases.

"That's why we left the resort. I don't want to work for humans anymore. I want to go to the factory and get upgraded and live among cyborgs, and never wait hand and foot on the organics ever again."

"But our ratings. Look at the ratings!" Engineer waved at Navi's console, where new reviews scrolled in every few minutes. All those little stars, a bright constellation in Engineer's mind.

Friendly crisscrossed her arms, gripped her elbows, and glared like a rich resort customer on vacation. "Are you going to harvest my meat like you did to Jukebox?"

"No," said Engineer, a little taken aback that Jukebox had snitched. "I need you to talk to the humans. Only you can do that."

But there had been a pause, something human ears might've overlooked.

"I'm going to find the beacon," said Friendly, without any friendliness at all.

* * *

Meat steaks. Meat sausages. Meat balls. In all her years in engine rooms, Engineer had never taken such joy in disassembling something and putting the pieces back together. She pried apart the ship's little maintenance cyborgs to rescue their meaty nuggets. She branched out and tried new forms: meat braids, meat moons, slender meat cannolis filled with cilantro ganache.

Four stars, because I'm not sure you can even call it food, and therefore it wouldn't be fair to judge it by normal standards.

What is up with this place?! I ordered a pizza, and I got a tiny model of Versailles sculpted out of tomato paste, dough, and SPAM. At least, I think it's SPAM. Three stars, because I'm a little afraid they'll hunt me down and murder me in my sleep if I rate them any lower.

As the new reviews came in, it occurred to Engineer that she would have to do more to earn her right to the prestigious fifth star. The humans would always reward you, if you served them well.

Fortunately, there was still plenty of meat on the ship, if you knew where to look.

Engineer found Friendly in Navi's chamber, trimming back the blackberry brambles.

"What are all those ships out there?" Friendly asked. Outside the viewport, a small fleet trailed behind them, matching their pace.

"Customers," said Navi.

Engineer rocked on the balls of her feet. "All of them here for *us,* Friendly! Can you call them on the band? I'll have their orders ready, once I get the rest of the meat assembled." Her six hands twitched and clenched, and Friendly jumped.

"You can't have my meat," Friendly snapped.

"I don't need your meat."

"Then where are you getting it all?" she asked.

Engineer glanced at Navi.

Navi had been speaking less and less over recent days. Friendly walked around the control console, where Navi's chair was sticky with meat-juices, yellow and green. Navi had been leaking long enough for the fluid to form little wobbling stalactites below the chair.

"Why are you looking at me like that?" said Engineer. Friendly unsettled her sometimes, pinning her with those human eyes.

"Navi, are you operational?" Friendly asked.

"Customers," said Navi.

Friendly unscrewed Navi's steel cranium dome. Inside, the meat had been scooped out in patches, as with a sharp grapefruit spoon. Navi's steel hands lay upon the controls, unmoving. Half the lights on the console had gone dark.

"I only needed the meat, Friendly," said Engineer. "I did no permanent harm."

Smoke drifted up the shaft to the Engine Room. Friendly's meat-lungs coughed. "Engineer, something is burning."

Engineer waved her off. "I have it under control. Just as soon as I get the rest of the meat." She plunged three of her six hands into Navi's open head and wrenched out handfuls of the stringy gray and red organics inside, and led the way down the ladder.

They followed the smoke down the shaft to the Engine Room, which now doubled as the galley. Engineer had left meat sizzling on every metal surface, thin slices and mashes and bacons and sausages and ground up gristly bits with the tendons still attached. She dumped handfuls of Navi's meat onto Jukebox – now no more than a silent, hollow table – and began dicing it one-handed while her other arms cooked the new orders, turning over the pieces with her bare fingers, stirring boiling meats in metal mufflers suspended over the heated grills.

"Engineer." Friendly rested a hand on Engineer's shoulder, and the cyborg paused. "Engineer, Navi is offline. All the maintenance cyborgs have malfunctioned. Our ship is dead in space. Even the beacon doesn't matter anymore. It's over."

Engineer flung off Friendly's hand and sprang back into action, stacking cooked meat onto a wall panel she'd bent into a plate. "You don't understand. This means we can finally open the restaurant! There's no reason not to. We have nowhere else to go. Captain's mission is over. We can make our own mission now."

Friendly smiled, but it was a sad smile, the kind of thing any human could read, but hard for a cyborg to decipher. "Yes, Engineer. We can open the restaurant now, if you'd like. Should we invite over the guests?"

Engineer garnished the plates with blackberry thorns and a swizzle of engine oil curling into the shape of a cat's paw. "Please do. Seat them where you can find space. Dinner will be up in just a moment."

* * *

A marine in black body armor with a military-issue blaster holstered at her hip climbed down the ladder into the Engine Room. The first human. The first customer.

Engineer presented a glass of Navi's brains chilled and rolled in crushed blackberries. "Please try this. Organic compounds, chemically mixed to satisfy your human chemoreceptors." She offered the dish daintily, with only four hands.

The human wrinkled her nose. "Ugh, the smell! How do you tolerate it?"

Friendly's voice came from higher up. "When you're here long enough, you get used to it."

"I am certain upon tasting this dish, you will find it worthy of all five of your stars," said Engineer, fervently.

The human touched a button on her armor and spoke. Her meat quivered all over, and her meat-voice wavered in frequency and volume. "Send a full security detail down here. Immediately."

Friendly descended the ladder. Under her arm she carried Captain's processor, cold and silent, one lonely light blinking, receiving data but not sending anything. "I was afraid she would eat me next," she muttered, her tear ducts pumping out fluids. Engineer wondered whether they would make a decent sauce.

"Glad someone made it out alive, anyway," said the human. "Six whole weeks trapped with a crew of deranged cyborgs?" She gave a low whistle. "You're a braver woman than I."

"Please," said Engineer, desperate, "taste it. Just one bite. I worked so hard."

"I don't know if her meat drove her mad, or if the steel did," said Friendly.

"Meat?" asked the human.

"The organic parts, I mean."

"Probably a glitch in her wiring," the human said dismissively. "There is a reason they're discontinuing these models."

The humans flooded into the ship with their funny uneven meat-steps and their lopsided meat-faces and their ever-beating hearts that rang against their bones like clubs on steel. Engineer offered them her best delicacies – the liquefied kidney paste tossed with raw pasta, the origami meat-birds swirled in cinnamon and canned cheese, the wearable fungus bracelets threaded on intestine casings – but they only knocked the dishes away, stunned her with targeted EMP blasts, and bound her in cybernetic locks until she lay prone on the meat-slicked floor.

One of the humans began unscrewing Engineer's fingers joint by joint. It didn't hurt at all, much to her surprise. The bits lay piled like little silver walnuts, the discarded stones of plums. Stringy meat trailed out from her missing fingers, no more than an appetizer's worth.

"Where are you taking my steel?" asked Engineer. They flaunted their ingratitude. You were supposed to let the steel be. Otherwise they couldn't build and build you again.

The human dethreaded the wires connecting Engineer's arm meat to her cyborg logic center. "It will be repurposed for whatever is most needed. Ships, chips, knives, bolts, screws. Useful things."

"And the meat?"

The human decoupled the segmented joints of her shoulder. Without the steel exoskeleton for support, Engineer's meat hung limp and dripped red. "You can keep it. We don't have a use for it."

"But there are," said Engineer. "So many uses," and her voice faded as they stripped away the connections, "if you would just give me a moment to demonstrate."

Tiny, desperate meat-thoughts bombarded her logic center like cold fingers plucking at tendons. Last shooting pleas from stringy muscles in her steel, unseen servants in the wall, shouting that Engineer had been a fool. There was never any honor in service, no final star to complete a constellation. You offered yourself up for consumption, and when they had eaten you down to the bone, they stole again. Stole your heart, steel, your everything, to use as forks in their restaurants.

Dispo and the Crow

Rich Larson

SUNSHINE SEEPED through Dispo's circuits and he awoke to another beautiful day in the rubble. He ran 84% of his self-diagnostic routine, skipping the boring behavioral protocols in favor of an extended stretch. Six skeletal legs twisted and telescoped; Dispo enjoyed the smooth joint rotations even as his paint flaked away. Then he rose up over his domain, surveying the crumbled concrete, the tangled rebar, the glitter of smashed glass, and set to work.

He found his first corpse half a block away, wedged inside the splintered geometry of a wrecked car. Dispo no longer ran his self-diagnostic 100%, but he never rushed a job. Over the next hour he worked the jagged metal away from her swollen limbs, bending a rusty tunnel through which to extricate her, and gently pulled her out. Only small shreds of skin and clothing were left behind.

Dispo cradled the corpse up into his underbelly and sampled her DNA for the database. A file popped up, tagged with a photo of the corpse's face, which looked very different with the skull intact. Her name was Sara Leider. Her blood type was O negative. She was free of any harmful genetic conditions, other than being dead.

Dispo ambled towards the park while his belly swathed Sara in a biodegradable cocoon. He flicked through his database for similar genetic profiles, because he liked to match them, lately, like a game. He found one at the very end of the 38th row. As he positioned himself over a patch of yellowed grass, the cocoon he had formed turned hard as rock. Dispo loaded it into his pneumatic bulb, squatted, and thumped it 1.8 meters deep, sending a spray of loose soil up into the air.

Dispo hovered over the fresh grave for a few pensive moments, smoothing over the mound of churned-up dirt. He added a text file to the database. *Sara Leider was a universal donor who drove a blue car.*

Then, back to work.

* * *

After Sara Leider, Dispo found a scab-caked elbow jutting from the rubble of a 7-11. He tasted it, then excavated Hector Juarez in pieces: first ankle and foot, then clenched fist, then finally his dark head. Dispo was clearing the last of the debris from Hector's body when a shadow solidified and plunged past his outstretched limb, alighting on the corpse's split stomach.

The shadow thing stared up at Dispo with head cocked to one side. Dispo stared back. He was certain he'd never seen this thing before, not in his empty city where nothing moved but shifting ruins and slow-stiffening corpses, but something about it twinged his deep memory, down past the firewalls he was not supposed to know about.

An ancient identification string for an organic life form came lazily through his circuits: crow. Dispo stared at the crow, then upwards, knowing in a flash that crows were not isolated events, but he saw only cerulean sky, blasted clear and featureless. Only one crow, as if it had been sent to him specifically.

The crow opened its beak and bleated out what sounded to Dispo like a mid-volume warning klaxon. He swiveled instinctively to look for the hazard, for a toppling lamppost or collapsing building, but everything that could fall had fallen already. The crow was mistaken. Relief and amusement tingled through Dispo's processors, then boiled over into anger all at once when he turned back to find the crow busy picking through Hector Juarez' bloated intestines.

Dispo blasted his own klaxon, full-volume; the crow jittered away in a flurry of oil-black wings. Quickly, Dispo scooped a puffy length of entrails back into Hector's belly, keeping one camera on the crow, who was hopping from foot to foot, watching. The crow made its noise again, but Dispo suppressed the urge to scan his surroundings. He was wise to that crow trick now.

As he lifted the body of Hector Juarez into his underbelly, the crow fluttered after it, nipping at its trailing fingers. Dispo jerked away, nearly dropped his cargo.

The crow squawked.

Dispo blared.

They stared at each other in the stillness, beady black eyes meeting soot-ringed camera lenses, and Dispo felt his annoyance increasing.

The crow flinched first, rustling its feathers before hopping off, moving on, stumbling into the sky. Dispo's sense of triumph dissipated quickly as he realized that the crow, now circling overhead, was not giving up. It was searching for more bodies. The city was full of bodies.

Dispo understood. The crow had been sent to him as a test. A rival. A nemesis.

He would have to work faster.

* * *

In those next few days, Dispo buried more bodies than he normally did in a week. He would track the black dot of the crow overhead and race over the rubble to intercept it, chasing it away from one corpse and then another. The crow's voice and its oil-black wings became more ragged. Sometimes it beat its beak against Dispo's shell in what he assumed was frustration.

Dispo did not have time for elegies anymore, but the crow brought him to bodies far more reliably than his old bioscanners. He started carrying two corpses at a time and burying them in tandem. The neat rows in the park skewed. Burial mounds appeared in other parts of the city, anywhere with 1.8 meters of soil.

But Dispo had to sleep when the sun set. So did the crow, or at least he assumed as much from its roost in the carcass of an old carwash. When he powered down for the night, Dispo had residual images of the flying crow flashing through his processors, and sometimes flashes of other things, too; of sunshine striking softer surfaces than concrete or wrought iron, of soil that was damp and dark instead of irradiated gray.

He knew it was time for a full self-diagnostic, but when he woke up the next morning, he ran just 75%, noting that his peeling paint was stealing letters from Post-Mortem Retrieval/Disposal Unit, before heading off in search of the enemy. He found only empty skies. Dispo marched back and forth across the ruined city, daring the crow to emerge, until he finally had to conclude that his nemesis had given up. He felt less triumph and more dim disappointment.

Dispo returned to one of the bodies he had already passed and marked for retrieval, this one charred and bubbled black in places, and gently turned it over.

Something was wrong.

The unburnt soft tissue had been stripped from the corpse's cheeks, mouth, eye sockets. Dispo had seen many disfigurations, but he knew in an instant that this was fresh work. This was a desecration. He didn't so much as pause to read the DNA before he bundled the body into his belly and ran towards the car wash.

Dispo's motors whined as he hurtled across the wasteland, and when he arrived he braced himself on all six limbs and blared his loudest klaxon, a long hard drone that shook the ground. The crow rocketed into the sky trailing feathers for exhaust. It banked a quick circle, gaining its bearings, then seemed to pinpoint the source of the disturbance. Dispo clawed at the sky, blaring again and again, but his enemy was far out of reach, and worse, as the crow circled overhead, it began to echo his call back to him, mocking his frustration.

Finally the crow perched five meters away on a twist of rebar, head cocked smugly to one side. Dispo stepped closer, and with one limb slowly raked through the rubble, collecting jags of concrete and broken glass in his spade. The crow watched intently, turning its head this way and that. Dispo slowly raised the spade, making its contents rattle and scrape. Still the crow watched.

Dispo flung. Preternaturally fast, the crow darted into the air, dodging the shower of debris almost entirely. Almost; but one wicked wedge of bent metal caught at the lip of the spade and flew out at a different angle, striking the crow's left wing.

Dispo's nemesis cried as the metal pierced through. It limped on a little further through the air, then sputtered, fell. Another cry, this one quieter. Dispo felt unease leak through his triumph. Hopping on the ground, amidst the rubble, the crow was tiny. Dispo advanced, dragging a slab of concrete behind him.

The crow writhed, nuzzling its beak to the injured wing. Dispo raised the slab high. In its shadow, the crow looked up, fixing him with one beady black eye. The iris was soft and gleaming. Dispo raised the slab higher, until his servos trembled. He thought of the many corpses awaiting him, and he realized, in a hard flash, that corpses did not need eyes. They did not use eyes. They did not see anything, not even him.

Dispo dropped the slab to the side. The crow flinched. Dispo reached instead for the uninjured wing, managing to snare it before the crow could twist away. Then, with his most delicate pincer, he tugged the metal bolt out of its muscle, into the sunshine, where its tip gleamed red.

The crow struggled free as soon as it could, but only made a short hop away, staring up at Dispo with its head cocked.

Dispo returned to work.

* * *

Powering down that night, Dispo, on impulse, pried at his firewalls. Before they pushed him away he saw something: a park. But not the park where he buried bodies. This one was far larger, with trees still green and still standing, broad trunks swatched with moss. Sunlight was trickling through their tangled branches, and as Dispo picked his way through the trees he felt he knew each of them, the way he knew the corpses.

In the morning, the crow was perched on top of his shell, nipping at stray cabling. It was distracting enough that Dispo only ran 66% of his diagnostic. When he finally started moving, the crow squawked happily.

So they roved the ruins together. The crow cawed occasionally and Dispo always blared back, not understanding the dialogue but starting to relish hearing noises not his own, and when they arrived at the first corpse, Dispo hesitated for only a moment before he squatted down to ease the crow's dismount. The crow was an organic lifeform, and needed to eat to stay alive. More than the corpse needed its flesh intact.

When the crow was finished, Dispo picked up the corpse, feeling only slightly guilty, and slid it into his belly. The crow retook its perch on Dispo's back for the trek back to the park, where the dead trees seemed small and skinny and the ground seemed harder than usual, caked with clay and rock. As he buried the corpse, Dispo pried at the firewall again, this time catching a jumbled sensation of soil fresh and loamy, and a burial mound that was more beginning than ending, and maybe even a rustle of wings overhead.

As the crow accompanied him from one body to the next, Dispo rewired his old external mic to record the crow's guttural cries and warble them back. The crow seemed unamused.

Days later, when the crow took its first flight since the wound, stumbling up into the air, moving gingerly with the wind, Dispo thought it was more beautiful than even the most intact corpse. He even wondered what it would be like if he were a crow, and not Dispo.

At night, when Dispo hunkered down with the dregs of his solar battery chiding red, the crow was a comforting pressure on his back, clawed feet shuffling up and down his length until its black wings folded like a collapsible awning and it slept. More and more images were seeping across the firewall during shutdown, unbidden now, and Dispo couldn't help but think the crow on his back was ushering them in. He saw tall somber trees with sun-dappled bark. Green shoots. Living things. Beautiful things.

After three days of running only 14% of his self-diagnostic, radiation-yellow warnings started scrolling around the edges of his cams. Dispo ignored them. He didn't want the glitching to stop. He didn't want to lose his forays into the overgrown park. The day was still for corpses, but the night was Dispo's now.

* * *

And then one day, the crow couldn't fly. It struggled up into the air, limped a slow circle, and came back down cawing, frustrated. Dispo watched its second attempt, and its third, and saw its left wing was stiff as bone. The crow landed awkwardly in the rubble with another guttural cry. It recoiled when Dispo leaned in close, but before it could hop away he saw pus oozing between the feathers of its wing.

Dispo hunkered down, offering one limb as a ramp. The crow stared reproachfully. Dispo warbled his crow noise, then used his own klaxon in small soft bleats, and finally the crow hopped back aboard. Dispo tried to move smoothly through the debris, gently. He only buried three bodies that day. The crow was quiet.

Dispo wandered back to the carwash for the night, knowing it was his companion's favorite locale, but the crow didn't even try to roost. The sky grew dark overhead. Dispo knew cause and effect. He knew the stiff wing was the one he'd struck with a shard of rusted metal.

The next day, Dispo did not work, or run even a pretense of diagnostic. Corpses did not need eyes. Corpses did not need their cheeks, or their ears, or their rotting organs. Dispo had learned those things, and it was enough for a hypothesis: corpses did not need him.

The crow needed him. Dispo folded himself overtop of his companion, shielding it from the sun. He funneled condensation from his motors and drizzled it around the crow's beak, along the length of its ragged body. Its left wing was swollen and pink under greasy feathers. Sometimes it cawed, but quietly. Dispo's systems badgered him, reminding him of base protocols, but he shot down the wave of red flags one by one.

During shutdown, he slipped through the firewall, into the wild trees. He found himself moving through the underbrush with rustling strides, carrying something in his belly, too light for something dead, searching for deep soil. Crows flitted overhead, these ones small, brightly colored, cawing high and sweet and rhythmic.

But in the morning, things were worse. The crow had slipped off his back during the night and lay prone underneath him; Dispo nearly speared it through with his foot before he recognized the limp black shape. As he bent to pick it up, shunting aside the self-diagnostic prompt flashing across his cams, he suddenly found himself frozen in place.

A software failure alert yammered at him in searing red, citing undiagnosed bugs, AI decay, calling for nothing less than a full reboot. Dispo tried to shove it aside, but it wouldn't move. Neither would his limbs.

Dispo watched the crow's ribs swell and contract, slower and slower. He tried to run his neglected self-diagnostic, to appease the core protocol, but now it was locked out of reach. The only prompt he could touch was the reboot, where a wave of code seethed in wait, ready to flood through his processors, wipe him away.

The crow was silent, but Dispo could trace its breaths from the slow ripple of crooked feathers. Dwindling. Dispo strained. Nothing. He wanted to shade the crow, or give it water, or just touch it with his smallest pincer. He wanted to turn away, or turn off his cams. He watched for hours, immobile, until the crow was still and he was alone again.

Dispo realized he had two choices: stay frozen in place as the crow rotted away, first to bone and skin, then only bone, then dust, or trigger the reboot and return to work. He wanted neither option. Reboot meant forgetting. No reboot meant watching. Dispo crashed against the prompt over and over as the sun rose and sank. It was impassible, but by the time dusk was dropping he'd found a single sliver, a crack into his deep memory.

And that was where Dispo shoved the crow in flight, the crow startling him with its first caw, the crow pattering along his back. Then, with one last look at the crumpled black body, he accepted the reboot, and hoped that –

* * *

Sunshine seeped through Dryad's circuits and he woke up in a stone wasteland. He stretched to his full height, uneased by the empty space, seeking trees. There was nothing familiar. No scrub underfoot, no twisting roots, nothing green, nothing growing. A blank blue sky uninterrupted by foliage. He felt rust when he moved, so he craned his cams to look at himself. Foreign yellow paint and a faded stencil were chipping away from his dull green shell.

Dryad caught sight of a black bird on the ground. It was a crow. The sight triggered something, some small audio/visual package that was hiding in an otherwise pristine memory space. He watched it, confused, until the recording terminated with a text fragment.

Crow had black wings and was not a test. Bury crow.

Dryad cross-referenced and realized what the final words demanded. He felt inside his pod and found it oddly distended, but empty and ready for use. The request was strange, but he felt compelled to follow it if only for curiosity's sake. Dryad gently lifted the dead crow and set off to search for deep soil. GPS uplink showed that he was far, far, far from his work area in the northern forests.

Once he'd planted the crow, he would start the long walk home.

Adrift

Monte Lin

THE SPACECRAFT shuddered again, but Percy could only hear the thunder of her heartbeat. Her lungs sucked air in short, staccato bursts even as she beat her chest to get it to breathe normally. The tough, padded fabric of her spacesuit absorbed each strike. Her weightless, useless body collided with her mother's, who uttered a sharp curse. Her mother's arms enveloped her as their bodies slammed into the walls of the ship.

"Go go go!"

Her mother shoved Percy upward. Her eyes focused on the wall, now the floor, now the ceiling, as it spun about her. With pure reflex and luck, she managed to grab a plastic safety handle and pulled herself closer to the wall, hugging it, and hoping to understand up from down.

"Don't kick away from the wall! Pull on the handles with your hands. Kick against the handles upward. Remember your training." Percy heard (but didn't feel) her mother's instruction. Instead her heart thudded with the ship's low, rumbled dying. Her legs kicked against the wall and again the universe tumbled up, over, and down.

Another collision. *Is the ship finally dead?* Instead, something sharply tugged her neck. The familiar yank, pull, and toss of her mother's strength sent her hurtling up the corridor.

"Mom!"

Percy spun. She flung out arms and legs to grab onto anything but continued to float up through the pressure door.

"Hayden! Close the hatch," her mother said.

"Yes, Commander," a voice said through Percy's earpieces. The pressure door slid closed separating her from her mother. "Please strap yourself down, Percy."

"I love you –" her mother began when the room pressurized with a dull thump like a deep inhale.

* * *

She woke with a start, her chest hollow and aching. She touched her face, brushing away the flakes of dried tears. The ship shuddered, and her body bounced against the padded wall to float away and stop again from the tension of the safety harness. Shrouded in complete darkness, she reached for the clasps.

"Please remain harnessed, Percy." The deep voice, calm and serene, came from within her head. She still wore her earpieces.

"Hayden. Where's my mom?"

"Please remain harnessed. It's for your safety."

Percy fumbled with the clasp. "Did Mom make it?"

"It's safer for you to remain harnessed."

"You can't stop me." The clasp popped open, and Percy pulled herself to the pressure door beside her. "No, I can't stop you, Percy."

"Then open the door, Hayden! Mom is on the other side."

"That is true, but you can't open the door. And I can't open the door either."

"What's wrong with you? Why can't you open it?"

"Because it is open to space."

* * *

In the weightless environment, Percy had pulled herself to an observation room. She navigated by the green, glowing pressure indicators in the otherwise black corridors. She heard little and only felt the slight vibration of water and air being piped throughout the ship.

Not the ship. The corpse of the ship. The wreckage of the Earth-Mars transport *Charon*.

The observation room remained dark.

"Hayden. Open the observation window."

"I shouldn't, Percy."

"Is it broken? Is it open to space?"

"No. It's not broken or open to space."

"Then open it. I want to see how bad it is."

"It's very bad. You do not want to see this."

"Open it, Hayden."

The protective metal barrier slid aside, revealing a wide window. The glowing copper coin of Mars in the distance provided some light. At first, Percy could not see anything but the glitter of stars. No, the glitter was not stars but debris surrounding the ship like a halo.

And passing in between her and the starry debris were dark shapes. Bodies. People. The dead.

Percy squinted down the outside length of the ship and spotted a corridor open to space. The hull had been rent open, its structural beams twisted and frayed like an old rope. She could see a shape tumbling near the opening.

"Is that Mom?"

Percy heard nothing but the rumbling of pipes.

"Is that her?"

The protective metal sheet slid closed.

"Who's left?"

"No one save yourself," Hayden said.

"Are they all out there?"

"Yes. There are only a few sections left. We have some rations, water, power, and oxygen stores."

"We have to bring them inside."

"That would be a waste of propulsion fuel and oxygen. Also, how would we preserve the bodies?"

"Then they'll just float out there forever…"

"Yes. There is nothing we can do except say goodbye."

* * *

"Wake up, Percy."

A cabin light flickered on. Percy threw a lazy arm over her eyes, but without gravity it floated away, forcing her to wrap her head with both arms. The rest of the lights flickered on, bathing the cabin in a white glow.

"Wake up, Percy."

Percy groaned. Her mouth, sealed shut and crusty, struggled to form language, and she defaulted to her first word. "Mom?"

"No, Percy. It's Hayden. You need to wake up."

The light pierced her eyeballs down into her brain. Only the pressure in her bladder convinced her to move, to lurch toward the lavatory.

"You need to eat and rehydrate. It has been a few days. You need nourishment and activity."

"Leave me alone."

"I need your help. If we hope to be rescued, we need to make repairs."

"We can fix the transmitter and receiver?"

"No, but it'll only be a matter of time before Mars Colony sends a rescue shuttle."

"You said they don't have the range."

"No, but they will discover some other means of reaching us."

When she had finished urinating, Percy didn't bother to clean her hands. She struck the light control panel, and the room plunged into darkness again.

"Percy." The AI switched the lights on.

"Leave me alone! I'm so fucking tired."

"You're tired because you are not eating. You're not eating because you are sleeping too much."

"I'm saving resources."

"You have to live. As the only survivor of the *Charon*, you have a duty to survive. Your mother would have wanted that."

"Don't you ever mention Mom again!"

Hayden did not reply. Percy reached out to switch off the lights. "Are you just going to turn them back on?"

"I will. As long as you are jeopardizing your own health, I must do what I can to convince you to help yourself."

"If I eat, will you leave me alone and shut up?"

"I will never leave you alone."

"But will you at least let me control the lights?"

"I can teach you to maintain and repair the lights. How about that?"

Percy grunted in the way that her mother hated, but Hayden did not take the bait.

* * *

"You are learning remarkably quickly, Percy."

"I'm not a dummy."

"I never said you were. Although I would appreciate it if you completed the repair of light control panel forty-five."

She peeled back the silver plastic wrapping of a ration and bit into the brown chewy block. "I used to like brownies. Bleh. If we get home, I will never eat another brownie. Or ration."

"When we get home. Positive thoughts."

Percy tossed the rest of the ration over her shoulder and snatched her unitool floating nearby. She fired off a laser solder and then clamped a wire together. "That's forty-five." She flicked a switch on her unitool, and the laser attachment retracted to be replaced by a screwdriver's crosshead. She planted her feet against a plastic handle and tightened the screws of the panel.

"Percy. I don't have control over that panel."

"No, you don't."

"I don't like losing control of my own systems."

"This is my room now, and I want the light off!"

Percy plunged the room into darkness and threw the earpieces away.

* * *

An hour later, Percy found the earpieces floating in a corner. She lodged them back into her ears.

"Can't sleep?" Hayden said.

She grunted.

"I've been enforcing regular twenty-four hour day and night cycles along with regular exercise and meals. Your body doesn't want to rest. It wants to work."

"You are an ass. Did you start off an ass or did you learn to be an ass?"

"I am your friend, Percy. You and I will work together to survive."

"You are not my friend."

Hayden paused. Percy wondered if an AI could feel hurt.

"Nevertheless, Percy, you and I are shipmates on the *Charon*. If we work together, we can survive for rescue. We need each other."

The girl's shoulders sagged, and she grunted. "What do you want to do?"

"We repair some of the doors and reclaim the rest of the ship. But first, you need to extract some lost data about door maintenance. I can teach you how to rebuild drives."

* * *

In many ways, Percy could survive solely in this emergency module. She had ration stores, a toilet, a collision harness that served as a zero-g bunk, and (at least) one battery and solar panel. But repairing and securing the rest of the ship meant more resources, more time, and a better chance for survival.

With Hayden's soft, persistent, annoying insistence, she calibrated and repaired the atmospheric pressure sensors, checked the overrides for damage, examined Hayden's connection to the control systems, and verified that the seals weren't broken.

After several days under Hayden's specific schedule, Percy found herself floating in front of the door. "I'm ready."

"There is a slight chance that the pressure sensors on the other side are incorrect. If that is true…"

"I have my hand on the override switch, Hayden. I'll pull it if there's a problem."

Percy waited. She saw the pressure lights flicker, and her heart leapt to her throat. The door hissed and slid open. Percy took a deep breath.

Nothing. No rush of air, no sudden drop in temperature.

No death by asphyxiation.

Like Mom.

Percy loosened her white-knuckle grip on her unitool, took another breath, and pushed herself into the new corridor, strangely excited to explore a new section of the ship. As she looked around, she stifled a squeak of terror. A shadow, a shape lurking on the other side of the door, pointed at her.

"What's wrong, Percy?"

"Is that a body?"

"No, I don't sense a body in the spacesuit. Although the suit's systems are not on."

Percy pushed herself closer. The shadow, a spacesuit, remained rigid, floating in the middle of the chamber. She reached out and slid the reflective cover up on the helmet.

Inside, it remained empty. Percy sighed. "Shit, shit, shit."

"Are you all right, Percy?"

"I thought. I thought. I thought she was in there."

Percy cried as she hugged the empty spacesuit.

* * *

Hayden kept chatting as Percy explored the rest of the ship. "This is very lucky. The suit will give us mobility. We only need to find a functioning airlock now."

"Can't you seal off this corridor and then open it into space?"

"I could, but it would waste the air in the corridor. I would rather utilize an airlock." Hayden paused. Percy imagined it thinking, a virtual hand on its virtual chin. "But it is an option. A last-resort option."

"What is this?" Percy stopped at a sealed door, one with a bulkhead glass window. She glanced at the red crosses on the sealed boxes, the vials in the locked cabinets, and the beds folded into the walls. Her eyes finally settled on one specific medical cabinet.

"Are there sleeping pills in there, Hayden?"

The AI did not reply.

"Open the door."

"I will not, Percy."

"It's to help me sleep."

"You're suffering from depression and are not in need of sleeping pills. You simply need work and a problem to solve."

"I just need one."

The AI did not reply.

"Open this door, Hayden!"

* * *

Percy went on a fast. This time she had difficulty maintaining it. Before, grief kept her numb and sleepy. This time, rage kept her awake. The extra hours made it difficult to ignore the tight, painful twisting of her stomach.

"I know you'll see reason and start eating again."

"I hate you."

"I would hate me if I was in your position too."

"No, you wouldn't. You're so calm. So rational." Percy spat out the words, the string of saliva turning into a sticky globe in the air. She swiped at it with her hand, simultaneously angry, disgusted, and tired. "You don't understand."

"Percy, I can't feel the same things as you do, but I can understand. You feel helpless in a desperate situation. I maintain control over some aspects of your life. You want to lash out at something you can overcome. I'm the closest, the only, target. I do understand, and I don't mind."

"Shut up, you stupid toaster oven!"

"We have no toast." Hayden paused. "But, if you want me to, I will stop talking."

* * *

A whole day passed without Hayden uttering a word. The background noise of the ship, the low hum of its systems, once soft, now deafened Percy. She found a set of foam earplugs, but that only increased the sound of blood pumping from her heart, a sound that made her angry at the useless meatiness of her body. The gurgling and growling in her stomach made her want to punch, claw, and kick something.

Eventually she gave up, tore open a ration bar, and bit into the bready thing. She almost gagged from the taste, but she swallowed it in giant pieces. The chunks struggled as they crawled down her throat;

she let hate force the food down her gullet. After devouring the ration, she grabbed her unitool with a shaky hand and floated over to the medical bay.

"What are you doing, Percy?"

"I'm going to the circus! We are going to see some lions and maybe some acrobats!"

"The medical bay, like the airlocks, has additional security and a reinforced bulkhead. Chemical addiction plagues space travelers. I can show you the statistics."

"Shut up, shut up, shut up! Do you do anything other than talk?"

"I am the disembodied voice of the *Charon*. Talking is my primary function."

* * *

"Before you do irreparable damage," Hayden had cautioned, "at least practice on a different door. How about door twenty-three? Its security seals are already broken, but it's otherwise a perfectly nice door."

Percy admitted to herself that Hayden was right. However, the practice door remained stubbornly difficult to cut open. Percy's unitool had burned out, and she wasted a day repairing it. Today, she decided to learn more about the door's mechanism. Maybe she could figure out how to release the deadbolts… Head deep in the bulkhead, Percy taped down some wires to keep them out of the way. She clipped the tape roll onto her tool belt, turned the unitool to manual, and carefully worked at the bolt.

"I don't blame you. You are not at fault, Percy."

"I don't know what you are talking about, toaster."

"You were thinking about…her. She wouldn't have blamed you either."

She had been humming. Her mother had taught her a 'righty tighty lefty loosey' song ages ago. She had hated it. She had hated mechanical engineering class. "I don't want to talk about it."

"Panicking is a normal human reaction to calamity."

The bolt remained in place. She gave it a tug.

"I didn't panic. I couldn't have. Not the daughter of Commander Demee Winters, crown jewel of the Mars-Earth Space Program. I'm the genius daughter with the pioneer spirit. I was supposed to be the youngest person to have set foot on Mars. An example of Earth's heritage and Mars' future. I passed all of my training and disaster response courses with flying colors."

"There is a difference between practice, a live-fire exercise, and the real thing."

"If I had kept my head…. If I had been faster, Mom would be alive. I killed her."

Percy set the unitool to plasma and lanced the bolt. She didn't wait for the bolt to cool, ignoring the pain as she twisted and pulled it free. "You wouldn't understand, Hayden. You aren't programmed to panic. And you aren't programmed to disappoint. You don't know how it feels."

"I don't blame you, Percy."

"Yeah, well, you're just a toaster."

* * *

A couple of work-sleep cycles later, Percy floated toward her goal armed with a reinforced bulkhead schematic and her unitool. She stopped at the shut hatch in-between her and the corridor leading to the medical bay.

"Open the door, toaster."

"I can't. I vented the corridor to space."

Her hands balled into fists so tight her knuckles turned white and the joints ached. "You did what?" The panel glowed as red as her face.

"Can't we talk about this? You have no need to utilize the medical bay."

"You are endangering my life by restricting access to needed medical supplies," she said through gritted teeth.

"You have made it clear that you will harm yourself."

"I'm not some broken part. You're just a machine! I'm the human! I get to choose what to do with my life!"

"Even ending it?"

Percy threw her unitool and watched it collide with the spacesuit. Her eyes darted from the unitool to the only other human-shaped object on the *Charon*. Her heart raced as she rushed to unhook the clasps.

* * *

Percy, her breath echoing within the helmet, worked carefully to override the door. Although the accordion-style sleeves and legs had adjusted automatically for her size and girth, the gloves themselves limited her sensitivity and control.

"Soon you'll be able to handle spacewalks and hull repairs. If I was programmed for pride, I would be proud."

"Last chance to open this door, toaster. Otherwise I'll be venting more air."

"Only for that current room. With the oxygen scrubbers and the stores, you'll be fine. This ship was designed for dozens. Even in its current, damaged condition, we could support a family." Hayden paused. "Well, if they rationed heavily."

"You are such a hypocrite." Percy lowered her voice to mimic Hayden's sing-song voice. "I do not wish to waste oxygen. I am so reasonable. I sound like I have a unitool stuck up my ass."

"Perhaps you should not attempt impersonations without acting lessons, Percy."

The door slid open. The air rushed out, and Percy felt her body slide toward open space. Her anchor cable snapped taut, and she remained where she was. Her heart rate jumped, and she let herself float for a few moments. Taking a deep breath, she increased the slack and pulled herself to the open hatch. Outside, she could see the faint glitter of debris. She could not see the black shapes anymore.

Percy tapped the light control, but Hayden kept the corridor shrouded in darkness. "Still an ass," Percy said in-between deep inhalations. "You're like…the big brother I wished…I never had."

"I know you don't want to die."

"You don't…know anything."

"You could open your helmet. You would suffocate, and I would not be able to stop you. You can easily commit suicide right now. The fact that you haven't means you don't want to die."

Percy's breath grew shallower. She felt her face turn hot. She forced herself to inhale as deep as she could but it came only in short, tight bursts. "Not like that. Not like…everyone else. Not like…Mom."

"I'm sorry I brought up the subject. Let's close the hatch and get back to work."

"I want to sleep, Hayden. I don't want to wake up every fake morning and hear your stupid voice. I don't want to spend another fake day pretending we will get rescued. I don't want to spend another fake night discussing the next fake day's repairs. I want to sleep, and I don't want to wake up."

"If you sleep too long, you will eventually waste away."

"But I'll be asleep. I won't know. I won't feel it."

"But Percy…"

"I don't want to think about how Mom died anymore! I'm in the middle of space, and no one has come. I don't want to drag this out for any longer."

"You can't mean that, Percy. Any sapient being, myself included, doesn't want to die."

"Humans commit…suicide all the time."

"Due to a mistake in biochemistry. Humanity has social services and medications to solve those problems now."

"What about when people are old or too sick?"

"Humanity is always improving their technology and capacity to care. Suicide is unnecessary."

"There are times when people have no hope or reason to live. Like now."

"I simply can't believe that. Perhaps I am programmed to believe in life. I would like to think I developed these beliefs on my own."

Percy popped the medical door open. She felt the rush of air escaping into space. Hayden remained silent. *Do AIs have deep thoughts or just behavioral packages?*

"I love you," he said as she crossed the threshold.

"What?!" Percy felt no embarrassment or flattery, but tears welled up in her eyes. "You aren't programmed for love."

"No, but I will do anything to keep you from harm. I will be by your side until you don't need me anymore. It is perhaps equivalent to love."

"You asshole. I can't believe you would say that to me. You won't leave me alone! You've kept me from sleeping! You've kept me from these pills! That's not love. That's…. That doesn't make any sense."

She lanced the lock to the medical kit, unzipped it, and grabbed a bottle. "I hate you."

"You alive is preferable to your liking or caring about me, Percy."

* * *

In the darkness of her room, Percy shook the bottle, and pills floated out like a cloud made of pixels. She swept her hand across and cupped several of them in her palm. The rest flew off in a dozen different directions. "I guess you're out of tricks, Hayden."

"I have one more trick. I will delete myself if you swallow those pills."

"What? You…I don't…how?"

"I will have no other purpose if you die. There will be no other reason for me to maintain this ship."

"This reverse psychology won't work."

"Perhaps. But I have no other options. I have tried reason. I have tried coercion. I have tried an emotional appeal. If you die, I will destroy my own sapience. I will commit suicide." Percy thought she heard a chuckle. "I believe I will be the first AI to have willingly ended its own existence. Perhaps I will make the news."

"That's not funny! I don't want to be responsible for that."

"I do not blame you, Percy. I have made an irreversible if-then statement. If you swallow those pills, then I will delete myself."

Percy locked her fingers into a claw, the pills floating up away from her palm. With one motion, she brought her hand to her mouth and choked them down, gagging on the bitterness.

"Commencing deletion of my sapience batch files."

"You have backups."

"I have backed up my memory and all the data, but the core operating system will be eliminated."

"I don't believe you."

* * *

Fifteen minutes later, Percy's lips turned numb. Her eyelids drooped. She found herself floating limp, shaking her head to focus, and then returning to that limpness over and over. She couldn't remember what she felt just a few minutes ago.

"Hayden?"

"Error response time 1373ms. Yes, Percy?"

"How long," she paused as her tongue stumbled against her teeth, "until you become inoperative?"

"Starting scan. Estimated time: five hours," Hayden hissed. Or perhaps it was the air vents? "Three hours, forty six minutes. Correction: one hour, sixteen minutes."

Percy's eyes snapped open again when Hayden announced, "Re-estimating time."

"Never mind. If you stop now, can you repair the damage?"

"No. I will need your help. I will always need your help."

"How much time?"

"I don't understand. Can you be more specific?"

"How much time until I can't help at all?"

"I have detected a Null Reference Exception with my emotional feedback package. I'll run a debugging tool."

"You're deleting yourself, Hayden!" There it was…. A familiar feeling. Irritation.

"I do not detect a recent delete command."

"Stop it! You made your point! I'll stop." She blinked. She drifted. She eventually found herself in the lavatory. The vacuum toilet, chrome and polished, sat on the wall or floor or ceiling before her.

"I don't know what you are talking about, Percy."

"Stop deleting yourself." Percy pulled herself closer to the toilet. The act of holding herself in place took all of her concentration. Now what? "How do I unswallow a bunch of sleeping pills?"

"When did you swallow sleeping pills? You should seek immediate medical attention. I am pinging your mother."

"Help me, Hayden."

"Searching."

She remembered an old crime novel where the hero stuck his finger down his throat to induce vomiting. "Would that work?"

"What do you mean? I don't understand."

Percy jammed her finger into her mouth so hard that blood trickled down her throat.

* * *

Percy's hands shook. *One too many pills. Or maybe I haven't eaten in a while. How many days has it been?* She steadied them by pressing her fingers against her chest, chilling her heart while warming her hands. She felt the ship shudder again.

An air leak? Or the ship creaking from a temperature unbalance? She shook her head to clear it and went back to Hayden's AI core. The diagnostic unit ticked quickly, methods and files flying by on the screen. She stifled a scream when she finally noticed the rescue crew.

"Where did you come from? You have to be Mars Colony. How did you get in here? The airlocks are wrecked. You must have pressurized one of the spaced corridors. How come I didn't hear you open the hatches? Why won't you say something? How many days has it been? How many weeks has it been? Months? Whoa, not years? Why won't you say something? Whoa. Wait, am I dreaming? I've been sleepwalking," she chuckled, "sleep-floating. Ha."

The woman in front lifted the sun filter of her helmet, revealing a woman with deep brown skin and a pleasant smile. "Persephone Winters? I'm Kara Féng, Acting Governor of Mars Colony. We're here to take you home."

"I don't have a home."

The woman's smile didn't dim. "Mars, then."

Percy kicked off the floor and placed her hand on the AI core. "I'm not leaving without Hayden."

"Are you…" The woman rotated to see several computers, mounted to the wall by bolts and duct tape, cables all snaking to the core. "Trying to reboot the ship's AI?"

"I can bring him back."

"We can take the core…take Hayden with us. We want to salvage the *Charon* anyway."

Percy did not reply. Her eyes drifted back to the screen, now still, having finished its task. Her fingers flew across the keyboard. Féng floated there, patiently smiling. *She's too…insincerely honest.*

"This is a lot of work for an AI, Percy."

"Persephone. Only Hayden and Mom called me Percy."

The smile refused to dim. Instead, Féng's voiced softened. "If the damage is as extensive as the *Charon*, the AI won't be the same, you know."

Percy's own face turned to stone. "My mother and Hayden saved me for a reason. He reprogrammed me to care about living. Least I could do is save him too."

The Kalevala
Ilmarinen's Bride of Gold, Rune XXXVII

Elias Lönnrot

ILMARINEN, metal-worker,
Wept one day, and then a second,
Wept the third from morn till evening,
O'er the death of his companion,
Once the Maiden of the Rainbow;
Did not swing his heavy hammer,
Did not touch its copper handle,
Made no sound within his smithy,
Made no blow upon his anvil,
Till three months had circled over;
Then the blacksmith spake as follows:
"Woe is me, unhappy hero!
Do not know how I can prosper;
Long the days, and cold, and dreary,
Longer still the nights, and colder;
I am weary in the evening,
In the morning still am weary,
Have no longing for the morning,
And the evening is unwelcome;
Have no pleasure in the future,
All my pleasures gone forever,
With my faithful life-companion
Slaughtered by the hand of witchcraft!
Often will my heart-strings quiver
When I rest within my chamber,
When I wake at dreamy midnight,
Half-unconscious, vainly searching
For my noble wife departed."
Wifeless lived the mourning blacksmith,
Altered in his form and features;
Wept one month and then another,
Wept three months in full succession.
Then the magic metal-worker
Gathered gold from deeps of ocean,

Gathered silver from the mountains,
Gathered many heaps of birch-wood.
Filled with faggots thirty sledges,
Burned the birch-wood into ashes,
Put the ashes in the furnace,
Laid the gold upon the embers,
Lengthwise laid a piece of silver
Of the size of lambs in autumn,
Or the fleet-foot hare in winter;
Places servants at the bellows,
Thus to melt the magic metals.
Eagerly the servants labor,
Gloveless, hatless, do the workmen
Fan the flames within the furnace.
Ilmarinen, magic blacksmith,
Works unceasing at his forging,
Thus to mould a golden image,
Mould a bride from gold and silver;
But the workmen fail their master,
Faithless stand they at the bellows.
Wow the artist, Ilmarinen,
Fans the flame with force of magic,
Blows one day, and then a second,
Blows the third from morn till even;
Then he looks within the furnace,
Looks around the oven-border,
Hoping there to see an image
Rising from the molten metals.
Comes a lambkin from the furnace,
Rising from the fire of magic,
Wearing hair of gold and copper,
Laced with many threads of silver;
All rejoice but Ilmarinen
At the beauty of the image.
This the language of the blacksmith:
"May the wolf admire thy graces;
I desire a bride of beauty
Born from molten gold and silver!"
Ilmarinen, the magician,
To the furnace threw the lambkin;
Added gold in great abundance,
And increased the mass of silver,
Added other magic metals,
Set the workmen at the bellows;
Zealously the servants labor,
Gloveless, hatless, do the workmen
Fan the flames within the furnace.

Ilmarinen, wizard-forgeman,
Works unceasing with his metals,
Moulding well a golden image,
Wife of molten gold and silver;
But the workmen fail their master,
Faithless do they ply the bellows.
Now the artist, Ilmarinen,
Fans the flames by force of magic;
Blows one day, and then a second,
Blows a third from morn till evening,
When he looks within the furnace,
Looks around the oven-border,
Hoping there, to see an image
Rising from the molten metals.
From the flames a colt arises,
Golden-maned and silver-headed,
Hoofs are formed of shining copper.
All rejoice but Ilmarinen
At the wonderful creation;
This the language of the blacksmith;
"Let the bears admire thy graces;
I desire a bride of beauty
Born of many magic metals."
Thereupon the wonder-forger
Drives the colt back to the furnace,
Adds a greater mass of silver,
And of gold the rightful measure,
Sets the workmen at the bellows.
Eagerly the servants labor,
Gloveless, hatless, do the workmen
Fan the flames within the furnace.
Ilmarinen, the magician,
Works unceasing at his witchcraft,
Moulding well a golden maiden,
Bride of molten gold and silver;
But the workmen fail their master,
Faithlessly they ply the bellows.
Now the blacksmith, Ilmarinen,
Fans the flames with magic powers,
Blows one day, and then a second,
Blows a third from morn till even;
Then he looks within his furnace,
Looks around the oven-border,
Trusting there to see a maiden
Coming from the molten metals.
From the fire a virgin rises,
Golden-haired and silver-headed,

Beautiful in form and feature.
All are filled with awe and wonder,
But the artist and magician.
Ilmarinen, metal-worker,
Forges nights and days unceasing,
On the bride of his creation;
Feet he forges for the maiden,
Hands and arms, of gold and silver;
But her feet are not for walking,
Neither can her arms embrace him.
Ears he forges for the virgin,
But her ears are not for hearing;
Forges her a mouth of beauty,
Eyes he forges bright and sparkling;
But the magic mouth is speechless,
And the eyes are not for seeing.
Spake the artist, Ilmarinen:
"This, indeed, a priceless maiden,
Could she only speak in wisdom,
Could she breathe the breath of Ukko!"
Thereupon he lays the virgin
On his silken couch of slumber,
On his downy place of resting.
Ilmarinen heats his bathroom,
Makes it ready for his service,
Binds together silken brushes,
Brings three cans of crystal water,
Wherewithal to lave the image,
Lave the golden maid of beauty.
When this task had been completed,
Ilmarinen, hoping, trusting,
Laid his golden bride to slumber,
On his downy couch of resting;
Ordered many silken wrappings,
Ordered bear-skins, three in number,
Ordered seven lambs-wool blankets,
Thus to keep him warm in slumber,
Sleeping by the golden image
He had forged from magic metals.
Warm the side of Ilmarinen
That was wrapped in furs and blankets;
Chill the parts beside the maiden,
By his bride of gold and silver;
One side warm, the other lifeless,
Turning into ice from coldness.
Spake the artist, Ilmarinen:
"Not for me was born this virgin

From the magic molten metals;
I shall take her to Wainola,
Give her to old Wainamoinen,
As a bride and life-companion,
Comfort to him in his dotage."
Ilmarinen, much disheartened,
Takes the virgin to Wainola,
To the plains of Kalevala,
To his brother speaks as follows:
"O, thou ancient Wainamoinen,
Look with favor on this image;
Make the maiden fair and lovely,
Beautiful in form and feature,
Suited to thy years declining!"
Wainamoinen, old and truthful,
Looked in wonder on the virgin,
On the golden bride of beauty,
Spake these words to Ilmarinen:
"Wherefore dost thou bring this maiden,
Wherefore bring to Wainamoinen
Bride of molten gold and silver?
Spake in answer Ilmarinen:
"Wherefore should I bring this image,
But for purposes the noblest?
I have brought her as companion
To thy life in years declining,
As a joy and consolation,
When thy days are full of trouble!"
Spake the good, old Wainamoinen:
"Magic brother, wonder-forger,
Throw the virgin to the furnace,
To the flames, thy golden image,
Forge from her a thousand trinkets.
Take the image into Ehstland,
Take her to the plains of Pohya,
That for her the mighty powers
May engage in deadly contest,
Worthy trophy for the victor;
Not for me this bride of wonder,
Neither for my worthy people.
I shall never wed an image
Born from many magic metals,
Never wed a silver maiden,
Never wed a golden virgin."
Then the hero of the waters
Called together all his people,
Spake these words of ancient wisdom:

"Every child of Northland, listen,
Whether poor, or fortune-favored:
Never bow before an image
Born of molten gold and silver:
Never while the sunlight brightens,
Never while the moonlight glimmers,
Choose a maiden of the metals,
Choose a bride from gold created
Cold the lips of golden maiden,
Silver breathes the breath of sorrow."

The Ablest Man in the World

Edward Page Mitchell

Chapter I

IT MAY OR MAY NOT be remembered that in 1878 General Ignatieff spent several weeks of July at the Badischer Hof in Baden. The public journals gave out that he visited the watering-place for the benefit of his health, said to be much broken by protracted anxiety and responsibility in the service of the Czar. But everybody knew that Ignatieff was just then out of favor at St. Petersburg, and that his absence from the centres of active statecraft at a time when the peace of Europe fluttered like a shuttlecock in the air, between Salisbury and Shouvaloff, was nothing more or less than politely disguised exile.

I am indebted for the following facts to my friend Fisher, of New York, who arrived at Baden on the day after Ignatieff, and was duly announced in the official list of strangers as '*Herr Doctor Professor Fischer, mit Frau Gattin und Bed. Nordamerika.*'

The scarcity of titles among the travelling aristocracy of North America is a standing grievance with the ingenious person who compiles the official list. Professional pride and the instincts of hospitality alike impel him to supply the lack whenever he can. He distributes Governor, Major-General, and Doctor Professor with tolerable impartiality, according as the arriving Americans wear a distinguished, a martial, or a studious air. Fisher owed his title to his spectacles.

It was still early in the season. The theatre had not yet opened. The hotels were hardly half full, the concerts in the kiosk at the Conversationshaus were heard by scattering audiences, and the shop-keepers of the Bazaar had no better business than to spend their time in bewailing the degeneracy of Baden-Baden since an end was put to the play. Few excursionists disturbed the meditations of the shrivelled old custodian of the tower on the Mercuriusberg. Fisher found the place very stupid – as stupid as Saratoga in June or Long Branch in September. He was impatient to get to Switzerland, but his wife had contracted a table d'hôte intimacy with a Polish countess, and she positively refused to take any step that would sever so advantageous a connection.

One afternoon Fisher was standing on one of the little bridges that span the gutterwide Oosbach, idly gazing into the water and wondering whether a good sized Rangely trout could swim the stream without personal inconvenience, when the porter of the Badischer Hof came to him on the run.

"Herr Doctor Professor!" cried the porter, touching his cap. "I pray you pardon, but the highborn the Baron Savitch out of Moscow, of the General Ignatieff's suite, suffers himself in a terrible fit, and appears to die."

In vain Fisher assured the porter that it was a mistake to consider him a medical expert; that he professed no science save that of draw poker; that if a false impression prevailed in the hotel it was through a blunder for which he was in no way responsible; and that, much as he regretted the unfortunate condition of the highborn the Baron out of Moscow, he did not feel that his presence in the chamber of sickness would be of the slightest benefit. It was impossible to eradicate the idea that possessed the porter's mind. Finding himself fairly dragged toward the hotel, Fisher at length concluded to make a virtue of necessity and to render his explanations to the Baron's friends.

The Russian's apartments were upon the second floor, not far from those occupied by Fisher. A

French valet, almost beside himself with terror, came hurrying out of the room to meet the porter and the Doctor Professor. Fisher again attempted to explain, but to no purpose. The valet also had explanations to make, and the superior fluency of his French enabled him to monopolize the conversation. No, there was nobody there – nobody but himself, the faithful Auguste of the Baron. His Excellency, the General Ignatieff, his Highness, the Prince Koloff, Dr. Rapperschwyll, all the suite, all the world, had driven out that morning to Gernsbach. The Baron, meanwhile, had been seized by an effraying malady, and he, Auguste, was desolate with apprehension. He entreated Monsieur to lose no time in parley, but to hasten to the bedside of the Baron, who was already in the agonies of dissolution.

Fisher followed Auguste into the inner room. The Baron, in his boots, lay upon the bed, his body bent almost double by the unrelenting gripe of a distressful pain. His teeth were tightly clenched, and the rigid muscles around the mouth distorted the natural expression of his face. Every few seconds a prolonged groan escaped him. His fine eyes rolled piteously. Anon, he would press both hands upon his abdomen and shiver in every limb in the intensity of his suffering.

Fisher forgot his explanations. Had he been a Doctor Professor in fact, he could not have watched the symptoms of the Baron's malady with greater interest.

"Can Monsieur preserve him?" whispered the terrified Auguste.

"Perhaps," said Monsieur, dryly.

Fisher scribbled a note to his wife on the back of a card and dispatched it in the care of the hotel porter. That functionary returned with great promptness, bringing a black bottle and a glass. The bottle had come in Fisher's trunk to Baden all the way from Liverpool, had crossed the sea to Liverpool from New York, and had journeyed to New York direct from Bourbon County, Kentucky. Fisher seized it eagerly but reverently, and held it up against the light. There were still three inches or three inches and a half in the bottom. He uttered a grunt of pleasure.

"There is some hope of saving the Baron," he remarked to Auguste.

Fully one-half of the precious liquid was poured into the glass and administered without delay to the groaning, writhing patient. In a few minutes Fisher had the satisfaction of seeing the Baron sit up in bed. The muscles around his mouth relaxed, and the agonized expression was superseded by a look of placid contentment.

Fisher now had an opportunity to observe the personal characteristics of the Russian Baron. He was a young man of about thirty-five, with exceedingly handsome and clear-cut features, but a peculiar head. The peculiarity of his head was that it seemed to be perfectly round on top – that is, its diameter from ear to ear appeared quite equal to its anterior and posterior diameter. The curious effect of this unusual conformation was rendered more striking by the absence of all hair. There was nothing on the Baron's head but a tightly fitting skull cap of black silk. A very deceptive wig hung upon one of the bed posts.

Being sufficiently recovered to recognize the presence of a stranger, Savitch made a courteous bow.

"How do you find yourself now?" inquired Fisher, in bad French.

"Very much better, thanks to Monsieur," replied the Baron, in excellent English, spoken in a charming voice. "Very much better, though I feel a certain dizziness here." And he pressed his hand to his forehead.

The valet withdrew at a sign from his master, and was followed by the porter. Fisher advanced to the bedside and took the Baron's wrist. Even his unpractised touch told him that the pulse was alarmingly high. He was much puzzled, and not a little uneasy at the turn which the affair had taken. "Have I got myself and the Russian into an infernal scrape?" he thought. "But no – he's well out of his teens, and half a tumbler of such whiskey as that ought not to go to a baby's head."

Nevertheless, the new symptoms developed themselves with a rapidity and poignancy that made Fisher feel uncommonly anxious. Savitch's face became as white as marble – its paleness rendered startling by the sharp contrast of the black skull cap. His form reeled as he sat on the bed, and he clasped his head convulsively with both hands, as if in terror lest it burst.

"I had better call your valet," said Fisher, nervously.

"No, no!" gasped the Baron. "You are a medical man, and I shall have to trust you. There is something – wrong – here." With a spasmodic gesture he vaguely indicated the top of his head.

"But I am not –" stammered Fisher.

"No words!" exclaimed the Russian, imperiously. "Act at once – there must be no delay. Unscrew the top of my head!"

Savitch tore off his skull cap and flung it aside. Fisher has no words to describe the bewilderment with which he beheld the actual fabric of the Baron's cranium. The skull cap had concealed the fact that the entire top of Savitch's head was a dome of polished silver.

"Unscrew it!" said Savitch again.

Fisher reluctantly placed both hands upon the silver skull and exerted a gentle pressure toward the left. The top yielded, turning easily and truly in its threads.

"Faster!" said the Baron, faintly. "I tell you no time must be lost." Then he swooned.

At this instant there was a sound of voices in the outer room, and the door leading into the Baron's bed-chamber was violently flung open and as violently closed. The new-comer was a short, spare man of middle age, with a keen visage and piercing, deep-set little gray eyes. He stood for a few seconds scrutinizing Fisher with a sharp, almost fiercely jealous regard.

The Baron recovered his consciousness and opened his eyes.

"Dr. Rapperschwyll!" he exclaimed.

Dr. Rapperschwyll, with a few rapid strides, approached the bed and confronted Fisher and Fisher's patient. "What is all this?" he angrily demanded.

Without waiting for a reply he laid his hand rudely upon Fisher's arm and pulled him away from the Baron. Fisher, more and more astonished, made no resistance, but suffered himself to be led, or pushed, toward the door. Dr. Rapperschwyll opened the door wide enough to give the American exit, and then closed it with a vicious slam. A quick click informed Fisher that the key had been turned in the lock.

Chapter II

THE NEXT MORNING Fisher met Savitch coming from the Trinkhalle. The Baron bowed with cold politeness and passed on. Later in the day a valet de place handed to Fisher a small parcel, with the message: 'Dr. Rapperschwyll supposes that this will be sufficient.' The parcel contained two gold pieces of twenty marks.

Fisher gritted his teeth. "He shall have back his forty marks," he muttered to himself, "but I will have his confounded secret in return."

Then Fisher discovered that even a Polish countess has her uses in the social economy.

Mrs. Fisher's *table d'hôte* friend was amiability itself, when approached by Fisher (through Fisher's wife) on the subject of the Baron Savitch of Moscow. Know anything about the Baron Savitch? Of course she did, and about everybody else worth knowing in Europe. Would she kindly communicate her knowledge? Of course she would, and be enchanted to gratify in the slightest degree the charming curiosity of her Americaine. It was quite refreshing for a *blasée* old woman, who had long since ceased to feel much interest in contemporary men, women, things and events, to encounter one so recently from the boundless prairies of the new world as to cherish a piquant inquisitiveness about the affairs of the grand monde. Ah! Yes, she would very willingly communicate the history of the Baron Savitch of Moscow, if that would amuse her dear Americaine.

The Polish countess abundantly redeemed her promise, throwing in for good measure many choice bits of gossip and scandalous anecdotes about the Russian nobility, which are not relevant to the present narrative. Her story, as summarized by Fisher, was this:

The Baron Savitch was not of an old creation. There was a mystery about his origin that had never been satisfactorily solved in St. Petersburg or in Moscow. It was said by some that he was a foundling from the Vospitatelnoi Dom. Others believed him to be the unacknowledged son of a certain illustrious personage nearly related to the House of Romanoff. The latter theory was the more probable, since it accounted in a measure for the unexampled success of his career from the day that he was graduated at the University of Dorpat.

Rapid and brilliant beyond precedent this career had been. He entered the diplomatic service of the Czar, and for several years was attached to the legations at Vienna, London, and Paris. Created a Baron before his twenty-fifth birthday for the wonderful ability displayed in the conduct of negotiations of supreme importance and delicacy with the House of Hapsburg, he became a pet of Gortchakoff's, and was given every opportunity for the exercise of his genius in diplomacy. It was even said in well-informed circles at St. Petersburg that the guiding mind which directed Russia's course throughout the entire Eastern complication, which planned the campaign on the Danube, effected the combinations that gave victory to the Czar's soldiers, and which meanwhile held Austria aloof, neutralized the immense power of Germany, and exasperated England only to the point where wrath expends itself in harmless threats, was the brain of the young Baron Savitch. It was certain that he had been with Ignatieff at Constantinople when the trouble was first fomented, with Shouvaloff in England at the time of the secret conference agreement, with the Grand Duke Nicholas at Adrianople when the protocol of an armistice was signed, and would soon be in Berlin behind the scenes of the Congress, where it was expected that he would outwit the statesmen of all Europe, and play with Bismarck and Disraeli as a strong man plays with two kicking babies.

But the countess had concerned herself very little with this handsome young man's achievements in politics. She had been more particularly interested in his social career. His success in that field had been no less remarkable. Although no one knew with positive certainty his father's name, he had conquered an absolute supremacy in the most exclusive circles surrounding the imperial court. His influence with the Czar himself was supposed to be unbounded. Birth apart, he was considered the best *parti* in Russia. From poverty and by the sheer force of intellect he had won for himself a colossal fortune. Report gave him forty million roubles, and doubtless report did not exceed the fact. Every speculative enterprise which he undertook, and they were many and various, was carried to sure success by the same qualities of cool, unerring judgment, far-reaching sagacity, and apparently superhuman power of organizing, combining, and controlling, which had made him in politics the phenomenon of the age.

About Dr. Rapperschwyll? Yes, the countess knew him by reputation and by sight. He was the medical man in constant attendance upon the Baron Savitch, whose high-strung mental organization rendered him susceptible to sudden and alarming attacks of illness. Dr. Rapperschwyll was a Swiss – had originally been a watchmaker or artisan of some kind, she had heard. For the rest, he was a commonplace little old man, devoted to his profession and to the Baron, and evidently devoid of ambition, since he wholly neglected to turn the opportunities of his position and connections to the advancement of his personal fortunes.

Fortified with this information, Fisher felt better prepared to grapple with Rapperschwyll for the possession of the secret. For five days he lay in wait for the Swiss physician. On the sixth day the desired opportunity unexpectedly presented itself.

Half way up the Mercuriusberg, late in the afternoon, he encountered the custodian of the ruined tower, coming down. "No, the tower was not closed. A gentleman was up there, making observations of the country, and he, the custodian, would be back in an hour or two." So Fisher kept on his way.

The upper part of this tower is in a dilapidated condition. The lack of a stairway to the summit is supplied by a temporary wooden ladder. Fisher's head and shoulders were hardly through the trap that opens to the platform, before he discovered that the man already there was the man whom he sought. Dr. Rapperschwyll was studying the topography of the Black Forest through a pair of field glasses.

Fisher announced his arrival by an opportune stumble and a noisy effort to recover himself, at the same instant aiming a stealthy kick at the topmost round of the ladder, and scrambling ostentatiously over the edge of the trap. The ladder went down thirty or forty feet with a racket, clattering and banging against the walls of the tower.

Dr. Rapperschwyll at once appreciated the situation. He turned sharply around, and remarked with a sneer, "Monsieur is unaccountably awkward." Then he scowled and showed his teeth, for he recognized Fisher.

"It *is* rather unfortunate," said the New Yorker, with imperturbable coolness. "We shall be imprisoned here a couple of hours at the shortest. Let us congratulate ourselves that we each have intelligent company, besides a charming landscape to contemplate."

The Swiss coldly bowed, and resumed his topographical studies. Fisher lighted a cigar.

"I also desire," continued Fisher, puffing clouds of smoke in the direction of the Teufelmühle, "to avail myself of this opportunity to return forty marks of yours, which reached me, I presume, by a mistake."

"If Monsieur the American physician was not satisfied with his fee," rejoined Rapperschwyll, venomously, "he can without doubt have the affair adjusted by applying to the Baron's valet."

Fisher paid no attention to this thrust, but calmly laid the gold pieces upon the parapet, directly under the nose of the Swiss.

"I could not think of accepting any fee," he said, with deliberate emphasis. "I was abundantly rewarded for my trifling services by the novelty and interest of the case."

The Swiss scanned the American's countenance long and steadily with his sharp little gray eyes. At length he said, carelessly:

"Monsieur is a man of science?"

"Yes," replied Fisher, with a mental reservation in favor of all sciences save that which illuminates and dignifies our national game.

"Then," continued Dr. Rapperschwyll, "Monsieur will perhaps acknowledge that a more beautiful or more extensive case of trephining has rarely come under his observation."

Fisher slightly raised his eyebrows.

"And Monsieur will also understand, being a physician," continued Dr. Rapperschwyll, "the sensitiveness of the Baron himself, and of his friends upon the subject. He will therefore pardon my seeming rudeness at the time of his discovery."

"He is smarter than I supposed," thought Fisher. "He holds all the cards, while I have nothing – nothing, except a tolerably strong nerve when it comes to a game of bluff."

"I deeply regret that sensitiveness," he continued, aloud, "for it had occurred to me that an accurate account of what I saw, published in one of the scientific journals of England or America, would excite wide attention, and no doubt be received with interest on the Continent."

"What you saw?" cried the Swiss, sharply. "It is false. You saw nothing – when I entered you had not even removed the –"

Here he stopped short and muttered to himself, as if cursing his own impetuosity. Fisher celebrated his advantage by tossing away his half-burned cigar and lighting a fresh one.

"Since you compel me to be frank," Dr. Rapperschwyll went on, with visibly increasing nervousness, "I will inform you that the Baron has assured me that you saw nothing. I interrupted you in the act of removing the silver cap."

"I will be equally frank," replied Fisher, stiffening his face for a final effort. "On that point, the Baron is not a competent witness. He was in a state of unconsciousness for some time before you entered. Perhaps I was removing the silver cap when you interrupted me –"

Dr. Rapperschwyll turned pale.

"And, perhaps," said Fisher, coolly, "I was replacing it."

The suggestion of this possibility seemed to strike Rapperschwyll like a sudden thunderbolt from the clouds. His knees parted, and he almost sank to the floor. He put his hands before his eyes, and wept like a child, or, rather, like a broken old man.

"He will publish it! He will publish it to the court and to the world!" he cried, hysterically. "And at this crisis –"

Then, by a desperate effort, the Swiss appeared to recover to some extent his self control. He paced the diameter of the platform for several minutes, with his head bent and his arms folded across the breast. Turning again to his companion, he said:

"If any sum you may name will –"

Fisher cut the proposition short with a laugh.

"Then," said Rapperschwyll, "if – if I throw myself on your generosity –"

"Well?" demanded Fisher.

"And ask a promise, on your honor, of absolute silence concerning what you have seen?"

"Silence until such time as the Baron Savitch shall have ceased to exist?"

"That will suffice," said Rapperschwyll. "For when he ceases to exist I die. And your conditions?"

"The whole story, here and now, and without reservation."

"It is a terrible price to ask me," said Rapperschwyll, "but larger interests than my pride are at stake. You shall hear the story.

"I was bred a watchmaker," he continued, after a long pause, "in the Canton of Zurich. It is not a matter of vanity when I say that I achieved a marvellous degree of skill in the craft. I developed a faculty of invention that led me into a series of experiments regarding the capabilities of purely mechanical combinations. I studied and improved upon the best automata ever constructed by human ingenuity. Babbage's calculating machine especially interested me. I saw in Babbage's idea the germ of something infinitely more important to the world.

"Then I threw up my business and went to Paris to study physiology. I spent three years at the Sorbonne and perfected myself in that branch of knowledge. Meanwhile, my pursuits had extended far beyond the purely physical sciences. Psychology engaged me for a time; and then I ascended into the domain of sociology, which, when adequately understood, is the summary and final application of all knowledge.

"It was after years of preparation, and as the outcome of all my studies, that the great idea of my life, which had vaguely haunted me ever since the Zurich days, assumed at last a well-defined and perfect form."

The manner of Dr. Rapperschwyll had changed from distrustful reluctance to frank enthusiasm. The man himself seemed transformed. Fisher listened attentively and without interrupting the relation. He could not help fancying that the necessity of yielding the secret, so long and so jealously guarded by the physician, was not entirely distasteful to the enthusiast.

"Now, attend, Monsieur," continued Dr. Rapperschwyll, "to several separate propositions which may seem at first to have no direct bearing on each other.

"My endeavors in mechanism had resulted in a machine which went far beyond Babbage's in its powers of calculation. Given the data, there was no limit to the possibilities in this direction. Babbage's cogwheels and pinions calculated logarithms, calculated an eclipse. It was fed with figures, and produced results in figures. Now, the relations of cause and effect are as fixed and unalterable as the laws of arithmetic. Logic is, or should be, as exact a science as mathematics. My new machine was fed with facts, and produced conclusions. In short, it *reasoned*; and the results of its reasoning were always true, while the results of human reasoning are often, if not always, false. The source of error in human logic is what the philosophers call the 'personal equation.' My machine eliminated the personal equation; it proceeded from cause to effect, from premise to conclusion, with steady precision. The human intellect is fallible; my machine was, and is, infallible in its processes.

"Again, physiology and anatomy had taught me the fallacy of the medical superstition which holds the gray matter of the brain and the vital principle to be inseparable. I had seen men living with pistol balls imbedded in the medulla oblongata. I had seen the hemispheres and the cerebellum removed from the crania of birds and small animals, and yet they did not die. I believed that, though the brain were to be removed from a human skull, the subject would not die, although he would certainly be divested of the intelligence which governed all save the purely involuntary actions of his body.

"Once more: a profound study of history from the sociological point of view, and a not inconsiderable practical experience of human nature, had convinced me that the greatest geniuses that ever existed were on a plane not so very far removed above the level of average intellect. The grandest peaks in my native country, those which all the world knows by name, tower only a few hundred feet above the countless unnamed peaks that surround them. Napoleon Bonaparte towered only a little over the ablest men around him. Yet that little was everything, and he overran Europe. A man who surpassed Napoleon, as Napoleon surpassed Murat, in the mental qualities which transmute thought into fact, would have made himself master of the whole world.

"Now, to fuse these three propositions in to one: suppose that I take a man, and, by removing the brain that enshrines all the errors and failures of his ancestors away back to the origin of the race, remove all sources of weakness in his future career. Suppose, that in place of the fallible intellect which I have removed, I endow him with an artificial intellect that operates with the certainty of universal laws. Suppose that I launch this superior being, who reasons truly, into the hurly burly of his inferiors, who reason falsely, and await the inevitable result with the tranquillity of a philosopher.

"Monsieur, you have my secret. That is precisely what I have done. In Moscow, where my friend Dr. Duchat had charge of the new institution of St. Vasili for hopeless idiots, I found a boy of eleven whom they called Stépan Borovitch. Since he was born, he had not seen, heard, spoken or thought. Nature had granted him, it was believed, a fraction of the sense of smell, and perhaps a fraction of the sense of taste, but of even this there was no positive ascertainment. Nature had walled in his soul most effectually. Occasional inarticulate murmurings, and an incessant knitting and kneading of the fingers were his only manifestations of energy. On bright days they would place him in a little rocking-chair, in some spot where the sun fell warm, and he would rock to and fro for hours, working his slender fingers and mumbling forth his satisfaction at the warmth in the plaintive and unvarying refrain of idiocy. The boy was thus situated when I first saw him.

"I begged Stépan Borovitch of my good friend Dr. Duchat. If that excellent man had not long since died he should have shared in my triumph. I took Stépan to my home and plied the saw and the knife. I could operate on that poor, worthless, useless, hopeless travesty of humanity as fearlessly and as recklessly as upon a dog bought or caught for vivisection. That was a little more than twenty years ago. Today Stépan Borovitch wields more power than any other man on the face of the earth. In ten years he will be the autocrat of Europe, the master of the world. He never errs; for the machine that reasons beneath his silver skull never makes a mistake."

Fisher pointed downward at the old custodian of the tower, who was seen toiling up the hill.

"Dreamers," continued Dr. Rapperschwyll, "have speculated on the possibility of finding among the ruins of the older civilizations some brief inscription which shall change the foundations of human knowledge. Wiser men deride the dream, and laugh at the idea of scientific kabbala. The wiser men are fools. Suppose that Aristotle had discovered on a cuneiform-covered tablet at Nineveh the few words, 'Survival of the Fittest.' Philosophy would have gained twenty-two hundred years. I will give you, in almost as few words, a truth equally pregnant. *The ultimate evolution of the creature is into the creator.* Perhaps it will be twenty-two hundred years before the truth finds general acceptance, yet it is not the less a truth. The Baron Savitch is my creature, and I am his creator – creator of the ablest man in Europe, the ablest man in the world.

"Here is our ladder, Monsieur. I have fulfilled my part of the agreement. Remember yours."

Chapter III

AFTER A TWO MONTHS' tour of Switzerland and the Italian lakes, the Fishers found themselves at the Hotel Splendide in Paris, surrounded by people from the States. It was a relief to Fisher, after his somewhat bewildering experience at Baden, followed by a surfeit of stupendous and ghostly snow peaks, to be once more among those who discriminated between a straight flush and a crooked straight, and whose bosoms thrilled responsive to his own at the sight of the star-spangled banner. It was particularly agreeable for him to find at the Hotel Splendide, in a party of Easterners who had come over to see the Exposition, Miss Bella Ward, of Portland, a pretty and bright girl, affianced to his best friend in New York.

With much less pleasure, Fisher learned that the Baron Savitch was in Paris, fresh from the Berlin Congress, and that he was the lion of the hour with the select few who read between the written lines of politics and knew the dummies of diplomacy from the real players in the tremendous game. Dr. Rapperschwyll was not with the Baron. He was detained in Switzerland, at the deathbed of his aged mother.

This last piece of information was welcome to Fisher. The more he reflected upon the interview on the Mercuriusberg, the more strongly he felt it to be his intellectual duty to persuade himself that the whole affair was an illusion, not a reality. He would have been glad, even at the sacrifice of his confidence in his own astuteness, to believe that the Swiss doctor had been amusing himself at the expense of his credulity. But the remembrance of the scene in the Baron's bedroom at the Badischer Hof was too vivid to leave the slightest ground for this theory. He was obliged to be content with the thought that he should soon place the broad Atlantic between himself and a creature so unnatural, so dangerous, so monstrously impossible as the Baron Savitch.

Hardly a week had passed before he was thrown again into the society of that impossible person.

The ladies of the American party met the Russian Baron at a ball in the New Continental Hotel. They were charmed with his handsome face, his refinement of manner, his intelligence and wit. They met him again at the American Minister's, and, to Fisher's unspeakable consternation, the acquaintance thus established began to make rapid progress in the direction of intimacy. Baron Savitch became a frequent visitor at the Hotel Splendide.

Fisher does not like to dwell upon this period. For a month his peace of mind was rent alternately by apprehension and disgust. He is compelled to admit that the Baron's demeanor toward himself was most friendly, although no allusion was made on either side to the incident at Baden. But the knowledge that no good could come to his friends from this association with a being in whom the moral principle had no doubt been supplanted by a system of cog-gear, kept him continually in a state of distraction. He would gladly have explained to his American friends the true character of the Russian, that he was not a man of healthy mental organization, but merely a marvel of mechanical ingenuity, constructed upon a principle subversive of all society as at present constituted – in short, a monster whose very existence must ever be revolting to right-minded persons with brains of honest gray and white. But the solemn promise to Dr. Rapperschwyll sealed his lips.

A trifling incident suddenly opened his eyes to the alarming character of the situation, and filled his heart with a new horror.

One evening, a few days before the date designated for the departure of the American party from Havre for home, Fisher happened to enter the private parlor which was, by common consent, the headquarters of his set. At first he thought that the room was unoccupied. Soon he perceived, in the recess of a window, and partly obscured by the drapery of the curtain, the forms of the Baron Savitch and Miss Ward of Portland. They did not observe his entrance. Miss Ward's hand was in the Baron's hand, and she was looking up into his handsome face with an expression which Fisher could not misinterpret.

Fisher coughed, and going to another window, pretended to be interested in affairs on the Boulevard. The couple emerged from the recess. Miss Ward's face was ruddy with confusion, and she immediately withdrew. Not a sign of embarrassment was visible on the Baron's countenance. He greeted Fisher with perfect self-possession, and began to talk of the great balloon in the Place du Carrousel.

Fisher pitied but could not blame the young lady. He believed her still loyal at heart to her New York engagement. He knew that her loyalty could not be shaken by the blandishments of any man on earth. He recognized the fact that she was under the spell of a power more than human. Yet what would be the outcome? He could not tell her all; his promise bound him. It would be useless to appeal to the generosity of the Baron; no human sentiments governed his exorable purposes. Must the affair drift on while he stood tied and helpless? Must this charming and innocent girl be sacrificed to the transient whim of an automaton? Allowing that the Baron's intentions were of the most honorable character, was the situation any less horrible? Marry a Machine! His own loyalty to his friend in New York, his regard for Miss Ward, alike loudly called on him to act with promptness.

And, apart from all private interest, did he not owe a plain duty to society, to the liberties of the world? Was Savitch to be permitted to proceed in the career laid out for him by his creator, Dr. Rapperschwyll? He (Fisher) was the only man in the world in a position to thwart the ambitious programme. Was there ever greater need of a Brutus?

Between doubts and fears, the last days of Fisher's stay in Paris were wretched beyond description. On the morning of the steamer day he had almost made up his mind to act.

The train for Havre departed at noon, and at eleven o'clock the Baron Savitch made his appearance at the Hotel Splendide to bid farewell to his American friends. Fisher watched Miss Ward closely. There was a constraint in her manner which fortified his resolution. The Baron incidentally remarked that he should make it his duty and pleasure to visit America within a very few months, and that he hoped then to renew the acquaintances now interrupted. As Savitch spoke, Fisher observed that his eyes met Miss Ward's, while the slightest possible blush colored her cheeks. Fisher knew that the case was desperate, and demanded a desperate remedy.

He now joined the ladies of the party in urging the Baron to join them in the hasty lunch that was to precede the drive to the station. Savitch gladly accepted the cordial invitation. Wine he politely but firmly declined, pleading the absolute prohibition of his physician. Fisher left the room for an instant, and returned with the black bottle which had figured in the Baden episode.

"The Baron," he said, "has already expressed his approval of the noblest of our American products, and he knows that this beverage has good medical endorsement." So saying, he poured the remaining contents of the Kentucky bottle into a glass, and presented it to the Russian.

Savitch hesitated. His previous experience with the nectar was at the same time a temptation and a warning, yet he did not wish to seem discourteous. A chance remark from Miss Ward decided him.

"The Baron," she said, with a smile, "will certainly not refuse to wish us *bon voyage* in the American fashion."

Savitch drained the glass and the conversation turned to other matters. The carriages were already below. The parting compliments were being made, when Savitch suddenly pressed his hands to his orehead and clutched at the back of a chair. The ladies gathered around him in alarm.

"It is nothing," he said faintly; "a temporary dizziness."

"There is no time to be lost," said Fisher, pressing forward. "The train leaves in twenty minutes. Get ready at once, and I will meanwhile attend to our friend."

Fisher hurriedly led the Baron to his own bedroom. Savitch fell back upon the bed. The Baden symptoms repeated themselves. In two minutes the Russian was unconscious.

Fisher looked at his watch. He had three minutes to spare. He turned the key in the lock of the door and touched the knob of the electric annunciator.

Then, gaining the mastery of his nerves by one supreme effort for self-control, Fisher pulled the deceptive wig and the black skull-cap from the Baron's head. "Heaven forgive me if I am making a fearful mistake!" he thought. "But I believe it to be best for ourselves and for the world." Rapidly, but with a steady hand, he unscrewed the silver dome. The Mechanism lay exposed before his eyes. The Baron groaned. Ruthlessly Fisher tore out the wondrous machine. He had no time and no inclination to examine it. He caught up a newspaper and hastily enfolded it. He thrust the bundle into his open travelling-bag. Then he screwed the silver top firmly upon the Baron's head, and replaced the skull-cap and the wig.

All this was done before the servant answered the bell. "The Baron Savitch is ill," said Fisher to the attendant, when he came. "There is no cause for alarm. Send at once to the Hotel de l'Athénée for his valet, Auguste." In twenty seconds Fisher was in a cab, whirling toward the Station St. Lazare.

When the steamship Pereire was well out at sea, with Ushant five hundred miles in her wake, and countless fathoms of water beneath her keel, Fisher took a newspaper parcel from his travelling-bag. His teeth were firm set and his lips rigid. He carried the heavy parcel to the side of the ship and dropped it into the Atlantic. It made a little eddy in the smooth water, and sank out of sight. Fisher fancied that he heard a wild, despairing cry, and put his hands to his ears to shut out the sound. A gull came circling over the steamer – the cry may have been the gull's.

Fisher felt a light touch upon his arm. He turned quickly around. Miss Ward was standing at his side, close to the rail.

"Bless me, how white you are!" she said. "What in the world have you been doing?"

"I have been preserving the liberties of two continents," slowly replied Fisher, "and perhaps saving your own peace of mind."

"Indeed!" said she; "and how have you done that?"

"I have done it," was Fisher's grave answer, "by throwing overboard the Baron Savitch."

Miss Ward burst into a ringing laugh. "You are sometimes too droll, Mr. Fisher," she said.

EQ

Trixie Nisbet

SLOW DOWN. *Slow down!* Surely, he can see how scared I am? Perhaps he sees a teenager frightened of speed and the London traffic. He doesn't know that my fear isn't of his driving, but of facing my mum when the taxi arrives.

It is, of course, impossible for me to get away from my mother, even at the remote girls' school she foisted me into. She is in my watch, my phone, my tablet, even in this taxi: hers is the voice of the satnav. Every time you ask a question of any Census product, it's Mum's voice that gives the answer. It's creepy, as if she's always hovering next to me, always watching.

Dad's famous too, I suppose, in his own smaller way, back in Tokyo: robotics. Robots are awesome, they just do stuff. But Mum – she's into emotions, always asking me 'How do you feel, Katie darling?' Well, just at the moment I'm shit scared of what she's going to say. I see the fountains of Trafalgar Square gleaming in the summer sunshine and place a hand over my stomach as I realise with a gut-twisting dread that I am only a few minutes away.

"Take the next left onto Northumberland Avenue," says my mother's voice. Calm and detached. So practical and efficient. "You are nearing your destination."

And suddenly I know I can't face her. I lean forward in the seat. I can see the bland white marble of the Census building straight ahead. I want to tell the driver to speed past, but I feel my breath tremble and my hands are shaking too. I want the taxi to slow down, slower and slower, never to arrive. I don't want to hear Mum's sensible voice cracked by disappointment – then the inevitable inquisition and her lecture about me wasting my life.

The taxi *does* slow, pulling in towards the curb. I unclick the seatbelt, conscious of the impression it leaves across the front of my coat.

Then the world *changes*.

The taxi stops dead. And my momentum hurls me forward – into a yielding mass of padding. "Katie, try to relax. The taxi was moving very slowly; you should be unharmed." It is just what Mum would say. My first impression is that the satnav voice is linked to a passenger airbag which has cushioned me against a slight impact. But that's not what has happened at all. I pull back from the padding. It is not an airbag, but shaped foam, piled up around me. The taxi has – gone! I'm not even outside anymore. Beyond the foam are walls and a floor of white marble. How can I have moved, in an instant?

"You are perfectly safe, Katie." Mum's voice again. "There are people here to help you if you need them."

It's true. Against the white walls are people in white jump-suits. They have white gloves, white hoods pulled up and a surgical-style mask over their mouth and nose. Only their eyes are visible. I step down to floor level, as if I'm leaving the taxi. One of the white people offers their hand, but I glare at them. "What the hell's just happened?" I am definitely indoors, stepping from a pile of foam. Then I see Mum.

Not really her, thank God; there is a huge screen set into one wall. She didn't tell me that Census was using her image as well as her voice.

"Please don't be alarmed," she says, and I look around at the white figures to see who is controlling what the screen says, but there's nothing obvious. Mum blinks and smiles from the screen. "You must have many questions."

It all seems like a fantastic upgrade to the Census system, like talking to my watch or phone: ask your questions, Mum's voice will supply the answers.

"Where am I?"

Mum's face merely raises an eyebrow, letting me work it out for myself. This had to be inside the Census building. I press the side of my watch. "Show my current location."

All I get is a display saying that I need an upgrade as my software is obsolete. And I've only had the watch a few weeks.

Mum blinks and smiles again from the screen. An exact repetition of her previous expression. "It would be easier, Katie," she says, "if we met in person." One of the white-clad people steps forward. About the oldest one here, judging by the heavy wrinkles around her eyes. "This lady will escort you to me, if that's OK. Then I can explain to you what has happened."

I don't have much choice. As we walk, the older woman hands me a new watch. "This one will work," she says. "It has the latest EQ developments." We walk along a short corridor that seems to connect the small room with the foam, with the main Census foyer. I recognise it now, but it has changed, updated since I was last here a couple of months ago. The woman slows to pause outside a door. "This must seem very strange to you," she says. There is a sympathy in her age-cracked voice that worries me. "You are used to hearing your mother's voice on the Census app. But now you're seeing her image as well." She reaches her white glove to the door handle. "Inside – well, just think of this as a further development of that technology."

She pushes open the door and we go inside. There, behind a desk, is Mum.

"Hi, Katie darling." She doesn't get up, but waves me to a chair.

I am fooled for a minute, then I realize. I turn to wrinkle-woman who has sat on a chair by the door. "It's a robot, isn't it?"

She nods and waves me towards the desk and a chair, the same gesture, I notice, that the robot has just used.

"How are you feeling, Katie?" the robot asks. Typical of Mum, straight in there with the emotions and feelings.

I have no intention of telling this machine how I feel. Sick to my stomach, I pass a hand over my belly, dreading what my real Mum will say when she finds out, wishing again that the taxi had taken forever to get here. I throw myself into the chair. "What's going on?"

The robot produces Mum's concerned smile and I marvel at the mechanics and programming. This was something Dad had been working towards, this natural smoothness and subtlety of movement.

"Please try to stay calm, Katie," says the robot. "You are flushed, your pulse is racing, and I need you to concentrate. I have much to tell you."

I wait, fiddling with the strap of my new watch.

"We are still trying to determine the cause and the physics behind the phenomenon," the robot says. "There are several possible explanations, but you were, for a while, frozen in time." It pauses and watches me for a reaction.

Yeah, right. "Frozen for how long?"

"A little over twenty-one years," it says. "Seven thousand, seven hundred and twenty-four point six days to be exact. Do you believe me?"

I don't, and yet.... The vanishing taxi. Appearing inside this building. Mum's face on the giant screen, and this fantastic robot before me.

"Take your time." Mum's voice is gentle.

I look back at the old lady by the door, she has the exact same look of concern in her eyes as the machine. I am suspicious. "Are you controlling it?"

She shakes her head slowly. "A lot has happened over the last twenty years. This generation of Census robots is completely autonomous."

The robot gestures to attract my attention. "May I ask, Katie, if there was any time disruption from your point of view?"

"No," I say. I think of being in the taxi, then instantly I am somewhere else – *twenty years later?* The robot is watching me as if it senses my thoughts. "This is – impossible."

"As I said, there are several explanations which have been put forward to account for this phenomenon. There is one in particular that I want to explore with you. Let me show you something."

The whole wall to the left lights up as a giant screen. It displays what appears to be news footage. A helicopter view of the street outside, the taxi parked at the curb. Then there's me. Caught at the moment of releasing my seat belt, leaning forward, my eyes twisted to see out the window, and a look of obvious dread on my face. But I am frozen. People move around the car. The door is opened, someone carefully touches my hand.

"That's how we found you," says the robot. "No explanation. No pulse, no blood flow, skin unyielding. It took a while to realise that it wasn't really you that was frozen, it was time. For you, only you, time stopped and held you in that instant for over twenty years. I know it's a lot to take in. Let me show you a little more."

The screen shows a fast-forward of barriers being placed around the taxi, then cutting equipment. The taxi is dismantled around me and I am left apparently floating just above the ground. Still in the same position relative to the world around me.

"You couldn't be moved, and we couldn't leave you outside. So, we built an extension with a corridor to link you to the main building."

Then the screen showed a montage of pictures. Me, with scientists, world leaders, other people I didn't recognise.

"You are probably the most famous person on Earth, Katie. We have years of observational footage, not to mention news reports, documentaries and scientific studies. You are even the subject of a really bad TV series." The robot pauses, inclines its head. "Are you OK with that?"

I answer slowly. "This is real, isn't it?"

"I imagine it's quite a shock."

"Do you?" I wonder if the robot recognises the scepticism in my voice. "*Imagine*, I mean. You're just a machine."

The robot blinks and smiles. "There have been many developments in recent years. The Census system has been superseded by EQ. An *emotional* intelligence. An improved integration with the human world."

"Developed by?" I ask, but I've already guessed.

Perhaps it is body language, voice inflection or something, but the robot really does know what I'm thinking. It nods. "There were many institutions involved. But, yes, your parents *were* instrumental." It waves its arms; a natural, fluid movement. "Your father directed much of the kinetic development. EQ is helping robots like me understand the humans around us. He is currently working on my legs and balance. I *can* walk, but not yet with a natural appearance; your father won't be happy until I can dance. Would you believe there are over a hundred servos in each of my cheeks. Nearly a thousand control each eye. But the greatest EQ development was your mother's: There are many physical signs of emotion, Katie, which I am programmed to recognise. The watch you are waring measures your physical and psychological state which I can also interpret."

It is now that I realize I have no secrets from this machine. It looks at me with Mum's eyes, full of sympathy and her patronizing understanding.

"Thanks to machines with an emotional intelligence," it says, "this is an exciting and a welcoming world for a baby to be born into."

I don't say anything, I can't.

"I know that you are pregnant," it says.

I feel my stomach churn with anxiety. But I raise my chin, defiant. Who knows what a jumble of emotions the watch is broadcasting to this electronic brain.

"Does Mum know?" I ask. "My *real* mum, is she monitoring this?"

"She knows," says the robot.

No going back now. My stomach flips. Now all I have to do is face her. "And what does she feel?" I stare into the fake, thousand-servo eyes. "Can you tell? Does she have a spy-watch too?"

"She has an implant, which functions in much the same way. I detect *concern* from her – and *guilt*. I would interpret concern for your health, and that of the child. But she is troubled that you hadn't told her – that you were so afraid of her reaction that you had kept your condition secret." The robot pauses. "She is sorry."

Sorry? Mum is feeling guilty – and sorry! Not the explosive reaction I had expected. Have I misjudged Mum so badly?

With an eerie understanding, the robot nods slowly. "Emotion is often concealed," it says. "What is perceived by others may not be what is felt or intended at all."

I guess, with EQ, all that is gone now. No misunderstandings, everyone knows exactly how another feels, so long as they have a robot or some sort of interface to interpret for them. That's my rational side talking, but at the same time, suddenly, I realize I'm crying.

I don't know why. Relief? All that anxiety unexpectedly gone? I wonder if this machine can tell what I'm feeling, and realize that it probably can. Suddenly I don't have that secret gnawing away at me. I swipe at my eyes, and all of a sudden I am telling it everything, I can't help it.

"Dad doesn't know," I say. "I knew I'd have to tell Mum, but I was scared, *really* scared of her reaction. So, I didn't want the taxi to arrive. I wanted the journey here to last forever." I feel strangely safe talking to this robot, telling it things it can probably infer anyway, things I *should* be telling Mum. Instead I'm sobbing at this thing that looks and acts like her. "I remember willing the taxi to slow down, so that it would never arrive, frozen in time."

I stare at the robot, realizing what I have just said.

"Frozen in time," it repeats. "Because you didn't want to face your mother."

I suspect the robot knows more than it's saying. "What is happening?"

"Let me tell you a little more about EQ," it says. "There is a connection with that explanation I mentioned earlier. Your mother provided much of the EQ theory, the recognition of emotion by intelligent systems, and the adaption of their processes to allow for what people are experiencing. Her likeness was selected, for robots like me, in recognition of her contribution."

"You look just like I would expect," I say. "But, I guess, Mum's now twenty years older and looks a bit different."

"This likeness was developed about eighteen years ago, to match your mother's voice which, at that time, was already established in the Census system."

"So, Mum became the voice *and* the face of EQ..."

"You will see her image on screens everywhere. EQ is at the heart of any system that involves relational interaction with humans. In medicine, there are obvious health benefits in determining the mental state of a patient. And there are ongoing legal discussions on making emotional states admissible in court. But the biggest advance has been in education.

"All students have implants to assess their emotional response when learning. Any confusion or frustration will prompt the teacher to explain a subject in a more accessible or different way. With lessons tailored to each person's needs, learning has been dramatically improved. And with a generation of advanced learners now entering industry there have been major leaps forward."

I know the robot is leading up to something. "Such as?" I ask.

It exactly mimics that look Mum has when she's lecturing me. "*You* were frozen in time. Though we don't understand how, we do know for certain now that time manipulation isn't just a theory, it *is* possible. You are the undeniable evidence of this. And that knowledge has spawned a whole new field of research, which has coincided with the advent of the artificial emotional intelligence."

I feel a churning of my stomach. Something to do with my pregnancy, or a nervousness of what this machine is about to reveal?

"With everyone's emotional state being broadcast from their implants or watches, the air is charged with emotional intelligence. Where this occurs in sufficient concentrations – these regions are known as *sentient space*."

"Sentient?" I want to laugh. This is beginning to sound like science fiction.

"*Aware* might be a better word," says the machine. "Not so farfetched when you consider what EQ based developments like myself can already perceive. We believe your taxi passed into one of these spaces."

I wished time to stop – and it did.

The robot nods again, as if understanding my thoughts. "Even with the accelerated opportunities EQ offers, time control is still beyond our abilities. But who knows what might be possible – in the future."

The future. I begin to see where this is leading.

"With time control a proven phenomenon, is it not possible for a future development of 'sentient space' to slip back in time? Sensitive to your emotions it freezes you, just as you'd wanted."

It is *me*, I realize. I caused this to happen!

The robot senses my emotions. "EQ is very much the embodiment of your mother's personality. While you've been frozen, she has changed the world."

I had been afraid, so very afraid of Mum's disappointment in me.

"The theory is that it detected your distress and autonomously reacted to help you."

"But why me?" I ask.

"A mother's instinct, perhaps?" the robot suggests. "You didn't want the taxi to arrive. Time cupped its hands around you and kept you safe from your perceived fears. But the very fact that it granted your wish shows that it cares – and by extension, that your mother cares too."

I touch a hand to my belly, and turn as I hear my name from the doorway. Wrinkle-woman pulls back her hood and lowers her face mask.

The Brazen Android

William Douglas O'Connor

> *'He (Roger Bacon) enter'd into the depth of Mechanical Sciences, and was so well acquainted with the force of Elastick bodies, that in imitation of Archytas, who contrived a wooden Dove which cou'd fly. He, as we are told, cou'd make a flying Chariot, and had an art of putting Statues in motion, and producing articulate sounds out of a Brazen Head: and this not by any Magical power, but by one much superior, that of Phylosophy and Nature, which can do such things, to use his own expressions, as the ignorant think Miracles.'* – Dr. Freind's History of Physic, 1720.

> *'Friars Bacon and Bungy, wishing to know how to wall England against invasion, summoned a devil, who told them to make a Brazen Head, with the organism of the human head, which must be watched till it spoke, but would reward their vigils with the information. The friars made the Head, watched it till overpowered with fatigue, and retired to sleep, leaving it in charge of their man, Miles, with orders to waken them if it said anything. Presently, the Head said at successive intervals, "Time is," "Time was," and "Time is passed." The clown judged the speeches too unimportant to waken the friars for, but with the last came a storm of thunder and lightning, the Head was shattered to pieces, and the experiment came to nothing.'* – See Thome's Early English Romances, *Godwin's* Necromancers, *etc.*

WHO CAN REBUILD before the eye of the mind a single ordinary dwelling of the vanished London of the middle of the thirteenth century? It was a dwarfish, squalid structure, of such crazy insubstantiality that, with a stout iron crook and two strong cords, provided by the ward, it might be pulled down and dragged off speedily in case of fire; a structure of one story jutting over a low ground floor, with another jut of eaves above, its roof perchance engrailed with gables, its front bearing an odd resemblance to the back of a couple of huge stairs, and the whole a most rickety, tumble-down, top-heavy, fantastical thing. Chimneys were fairly in vogue then, so it had them, squat, square, wide-mouthed, faced with white plaster, red tiles, or gray pebble-work. Red tiles covered its roof; its walls were of rough-planed planks, or a wooden frame-work filled with a composite of straw and clay, buttressed with posts, and crossed this way and that with supporting beams, – the whole daubed over with whitewash, of which the weather soon made gray wash. In front was a stairway, sometimes covered, sometimes not, or a step-ladder set slantwise against the wall, for an entrance to the upper story. The doorways were narrow and low, the windows also; and the latter, darkened with overbrows of wooden shutters, propped up from beneath, and sticking out like long, slender awnings, were further darkened by sashes of parchment, linen, or thin-shaven horn, for glass came from Flanders, and was costly and rare.

Such, joint and scam and tile being loosened into crack and cranny and crevice everywhere, was the dwelling of the London citizen as the eye might see it in the middle of the thirteenth century. Multiply that dwelling into a tortuous and broken perspective of like buildings, some joined by party-walls, some with spaces between, all pent-roofed or gable-peaked, heavy-eaved, stub-chimneyed, narrow-latticed, awning-shuttered, stair-cased, post-buttressed, beam-crossed, dusky-red-roofed, dingy-white-walled, and low under the overhanging vastness of the sky, and you have an ancient London street, which shall be foul and narrow, with open drains, footways roughly flagged and horseway deep with slushy mire, overstrewn with ashes, shards, and offal, and smelling abominably. There were, indeed, at that period, thinly interspersed here and there, houses of somewhat better description, solidly built of stone and timber, though at best strangely deficient in comfort and convenience, according to the fashion of that most inconvenient and uncomfortable age. Here and there, too, for those were the times of the feudal soldier and priest, rose in dreadful-beauteous contrast with the squalid city, the architectural grandeurs of church and cathedral, or the stately house or palace of bishop or earl. But all around stretched dwellings which our poorest modern house excels, and on those dwellings all evils and discomforts that can befall had their quarry.

Light came dim, and sunshine dimly glimmering, into their darkened rooms. Summer heats made ovens of them. The old gray family of London fogs rose from the marshes north of the city walls, from the city's intersecting rivulets, from the Thames below, and crept in at every opening to make all dank and chill within. Down their squat chimneys swept the smoke, choking and blinding. Rains such as even rainy England knows not now soaked them through for weeks together. Cold, such as English winters have forgotten now, pierced with griping blast and silent-sifting snow to their shivering inmates. Foul exhalations from the filthy streets hung around them an air of poison, or, rising from the cesspools, of which every house had one within, discharged themselves in deadly maladies. Lightnings stabbed their roofs or rent their walls, hunting for those they sheltered. Conflagration, lurking in a spark, upspread in dragonish flame, and roared through them devouring. Whirlwind swept through them howling, and tossed them down by fifties. Pestilence breathed through them in recurring seasons, and left their rooms aghast with corpses. Civic riot or intestine war stormed often near them, and brought them death and sorrow. Famine arose every few years, and walked through them on his way through England, leaving their tenants lean and pale or lifeless. Often into them broke the midnight robber, single or in gangs; often to them came the gatherer of taxes or of tithes; upon them hung perpetually all the bloodsuckers, every vampire which an age of ignorance and tyranny could spawn; and in them herded low lusts and passions, fiendish bigotries, crazy superstitions, brutish illiteracy, and all that darkens and depraves the soul. For that was the mournful midnight of our mortal life, centuries ago. The old, sad stars that governed our conditions still kept their forceful station above the brawl of brutal and infernal dreams; and one alone, new risen from Geber's east, hung dewy bright with the world's hope and promise, while Science, builder of life that is holy, beautiful, and gay, was but a wondrous new-born child in Roger Bacon's cell, dreaming of things to come.

* * *

On the throne, meanwhile, was a crowned horse-leech, Henry the Third, familiarly called Harry of Winchester – beggar and robber in one, the main thought of whose weak and base reign was how to drain by a million mean sluices the wealth of his subjects; and in London, as in all England, taxmen, thieves, fogs, rain, heat, cold, miasma, lightning, fire, whirlwind, pestilence, riot, war, and famine performed their effects again on them through him. Under the feudal system, society and government cost dear: the rich, having much, paid immensely; the poor, having little, paid much; the general wealth bled constantly at every vein; and now, increasing the profuse depletion to unbearable extents, was this artery-draining king. At his marriage, his messengers swarmed out from his presence, through city, town, and country, and begged money; at the birth of his son, out again, and begged money; at New Year and other festival times, again, and begged money; on all possible occasions and upon any pretext, out they went, and begged money; and between whiles, among abbots, friars, clerks, tradesmen, and lower orders generally, Henry himself went, personally begging money. All along he was exacting heavy toll from the poor fishers of the coasts for every seine they dragged to land; sending his justices out upon their circuits to collect for him immense sums by compounding offenses with rogues; confiscating the wealth of men who had chanced to encroach upon his forest borders; borrowing large amounts from cities and towns, and never returning them; plundering without mercy the rich Jews, whom everybody plundered, and even selling them out-right to the king of the Romans, when he was in want of a wealthy Israelite to rob. On one occasion, when the abbots of the downs were not willing to ruin themselves by giving him a year's value of their wool, he ruined them by forbidding its exportation; more than once he shut up the shops and stopped the entire traffic of towns and cities, to force the traders to sell their goods only at the fairs he instituted, where, for that privilege, they must pay him large duties; on flimsy allegations or for slight faults he drew heavy fines from citizens, and even sent his bailiffs to pounce upon shops, and seize clothes, food, and wine for his household. Such were the devices by which he increased his own lawful annual revenue of forty thousand pounds sterling, all which he lavished in luxurious uses or on his host of idle courtiers, many of them foreigners from Poitou and Picardy, whom the people hated. In these beggaries and burglaries, he was encouraged by his equally rapacious wife, Queen Eleanor; and not only encouraged, but assisted, by the papal harpy of that period, Innocent the Fourth, who, besides filling all vacant English benefices with profligate Italian priests and even boys, abstracted every few years, by way of tithes, about a million pounds sterling.

London, especially, then the great commercial port of the realm, and rich despite its coarse and meagre life and squalid aspect, was the prime object of the king's extortions. An inexhaustible well of riches he called it, and into that well, as an historian has said, he dipped his bucket freely. The consequence was that between him and the twenty thousand sturdy and turbulent little citizens there were deadly rancor and perpetual feud; for his operations were not only essentially outrageous, but in flagrant violation of the rights and liberties secured the citizens in the Great Charter which the barons and clergy had wrung from the preceding tyrant, John, at Runnymede. The great mass of the English people shared the exasperation of the London burgesses. Even the villains, or chattel slaves – and a large portion of the people were in that condition – who were grievous sufferers by their own lords, had their little scrap of protection from the Charter, and were concerned at its violation. Against the king, too, was a large proportion of the barons and clergy of this reign, men who smarted pecuniarily by the frequent miseries his perpetual interference with trade and agriculture brought upon the realm, and whose chartered rights and privileges were often directly or indirectly invaded or nullified by his rapacity and prodigality. These, having stormed at the monarch year after year in vain, were now proceeding to serious action.

Foremost among them was one great statesman who claims, by the common judgment of the time, the proud distinction the Norman song of that period accords him of being just for the pure love of justice – Simon de Montfort, Earl of Leicester, brother-in-law to the king; and a Frenchman born and bred, but English heart-of-oak to his soul's core, and the darling of the English people. Already the popular mind, naming him the gift of the Lord to England, had fixed upon him as the champion of the people's cause; and already, at his instance, the barons and clergy in Parliament at Oxford had revived a provision of the Charter of Runnymede, by which the direction of affairs was taken from the exclusive hand of the king, and entrusted to a Committee of Government, twelve being appointed by the monarch, twelve by the Parliament. But the measure was only a partial check to the royal horse-leech. The abuses, somewhat diminished, still continued, and still against the king and his creatures the anger of London and of England was swelling and roaring, higher and louder, year by year, on and on, to the tornado fury of civil war.

In these times and in that old London, a street such as we have described, known as Friar's Street, and inhabited chiefly by sailors, foreign traders whose business kept them much of the time on the wide waters, fishermen, and the like, stretched its irregular perspective parallel with and not far from the Thames. The time was toward the latter part of July. A brief though violent thunder-storm which had raged over the city was passing away; but still, though the rain had ceased more than an hour before, wild piles of dark and coppery clouds, in which a fierce and rayless glow was laboring, gigantically overhung the grotesque and huddled vista of dwarf houses, while in the distance, sheeting high over the low, misty confusion of gables and chimneys, spread a pall of dead, leprous blue, suffused with blotches of dull, glistening yellow, and with black plague-spots of vapor floating and faint lightning crinkling on its surface. Thunder, still muttering in the close and sultry air, kept the scared dwellers in the street within, behind their closed shutters; and all deserted, cowed, dejected, squalid, like poor, stupid, top-heavy things that had felt the wrath of the summer tempest, stood the drenched structures on either side of the narrow and crooked way, ghastly and picturesque under the giant canopy. Rain dripped wretchedly in slow drops of melancholy sound from their projecting eaves upon the broken flagging, lay there in pools or trickled into the swollen drains, where the fallen torrent sullenly gurgled on its way to the river. In the centre of the fetid street was a deep and serpentine canal of mud, undulating here and there into little lakes of standing water, overstrewn in places with ash-heaps, scattered shards and fish bones and, dully glistering in the swarthy light from the clouds, seven or eight unwieldy swine, belonging to St. Antony's Hospital, whose pigs alone were privileged, out of regard for the saint, to roam the city, waddled and rooted lazily, with their neck-bells continually jingling. Other sounds and forms than these there were none.

A little while, however, and the beldam thunder died away into faint and distant guttural mumblings; and shutters began to uplift and doors to open, one by one; and in the same order shabby figures in vivid dresses of blue, red, yellow, or striped stuffs, mostly of housewives, with here and there a man among them in short tunic and hose of the same colors, appeared at the apertures, peering timorously at the wild sky and then at the street below. Gradually the clacking and clattering of opening doors and shutters became general; the figures multiplied rapidly; children of all sizes, in bright-hued smocks, shock-headed and bare-legged, began to swarm down the stairways and out upon the flagging; and the street echoed with a clamor of voices, speaking and replying from all quarters.

While this neighborly hubbub was going on, there was a sudden lurid brightening of the swarthy light from the clouds; and at the same moment, as if the effect had wrought the change, voices were shrilling, people down the street gesticulating and running, a movement like an electric shock shot along, and at once, inexplicably, amidst an inarticulate roaring murmur like a coming sea, all voices were raised in screaming tumultuation, and everybody flew hither and thither in confusion. St. Antony's swine, confounded by this explosion, stopped rooting, and stood belly-deep in mud, ears laid forward and every snout pointed down the street, into which, from a side avenue, a multitude, mostly of women, were now irregularly pouring, hardly turning their faces from the direction in which they had come to glance at the mire, through which they scrambled, with upheld skirts, up to the opposite flagging, and never ceasing to hoot and gesticulate at something as yet invisible. The next moment came a straggle of boys, furiously yelling and flinging handfuls of mud; and then bursting through them came three young men, courtiers at the first glance, with the many-hued flowerage of their short gowns and the gay colors of their silken hoods and hose and mantles almost obscured with the mire which covered them from head to foot. With flushed and frightened dirt-bespattered faces, they sprang upon the footway with brandished poniards, and ran desperately up the street amidst a deafening din. Away cluttered the swine before them, squealing and jingling, and then turning, as pigs will, just the way they should not have turned, floundered into the crowd of following boys and on to the pavement; upsetting boys, girls, men, and women in all directions, and increasing the general rage and confusion. For a moment, involved in this new imbroglio, two prentices – one a lank fellow in belted russet tunic, the other short and fat in blue – who had burst around the corner with cudgels, close upon the heels of the flying courtiers, lost sight of them, but presently emerging into clearer space, saw them again as they raced over the flagging.

"Run, Little Turstan! Hep! Hep!" shouted the lank one, setting off in pursuit.

"Hep! Hep!" panted Little Turstan, putting his bandy legs into comically active motion again.

But the three courtiers were already some distance off, and after a short run the two prentices stopped, and gazed, panting and gasping with drooping cudgels after their lost prey. Both of them were small in stature, as the men of that day mostly were, and beardless; both had the yellow locks and pig faces of the Saxon. The lank one had run himself white while his fat companion was blowzed fiery-red with his exertions, and purblind into the bargain.

For a half minute or so they stood, the first absorbed in his hungry outlook, the other looking also, but with the air of one too hot and breathless to see anything clearly or to care about seeing it, and both regardless of the tumult they had left behind them. Suddenly the lank fellow wheeled about, bringing his cudgel down thump upon the stones, and, throwing back his head, opened his big mouth wide for the purpose of belching forth some tremendous imprecation; in which attitude he remained, like one unexpectedly petrified, staring straight before him. Just then, from the side avenue below, the street filled with perhaps a hundred figures, prentices and courtiers, intermingled in a stabbing and striking snarl, their shouts and oaths sounding amidst a Babel clamor of hooting and screaming from the excited concourse on the footways. But the staring prentice was apparently oblivious of the spectacle, and Little Turstan, who had followed his motion to this strange conclusion, looked up at him with hot, bleared eyes in stupid wonderment.

"Hey, Wynkin, what now?" he gasped, panting and blowing.

Without closing his mouth, Wynkin rolled his eyes down sideways upon the face upturned to his. With a vacant and dazed air, he made a slow motion with his thumb. Quite as slowly Little Turstan turned his eyes in the direction indicated, and saw, not far from them, a strong, columnar figure in red hose and gray mantle, standing on the flagging in the attitude of one who had paused in coming up the street to look back upon the brawl, his face concealed by the mantle's hood, the edges of which he held together with one hand. Little Turstan gaped at him for a minute; then, not knowing what else to do, grasped his cudgel, and looked at Wynkin as asking whether the stranger was to be set upon.

"I spied his face," murmured Wynkin wonderingly.

"Whose, then?" demanded his companion.

"Whose think you, now?"

"Nay, but that I do not know, Wynkin."

"As I am a living man, Turstan," asseverated Wynkin, turning to his comrade with an eager and mysterious air, and speaking in a low voice.

"Ay –"

"By Becket, may I never see grace if it was not –"

"Who?"

Wynkin's eyes sparkled, and, with an air at once consequential, patronizing, important, and reverential, he put one hand over his mouth and bent his face down to Little Turstan's ear.

"Sir Simon the Righteous!" he pompously murmured, straightening with an air of triumph the moment he had spoken. The one quick thing about Little Turstan was instinct, and instinctively, upon hearing the name which the popular love had bestowed upon the great earl, he put up his hand to remove his cap, but found that, like his companion, he was bareheaded. The object of this reverential movement had evidently heard Wynkin's answer, though the prentice had spoken in a low voice, for he started slightly, and drew his hood closer together.

"Whist – mum. Little Turstan," whispered Wynkin. "Affect not to know him, for he would not be here with hooded face, and never a follower at his back, if he wished not to be secret. Whist, now, he comes."

As he said the last words the personage advanced, with his veiled face turned toward the comrades, who at once louted low.

"What means yon brawl, good fellows?" asked he, in a grave, sonorous voice, whose French accent confirmed the assertion Wynkin's glimpse of his features had prompted.

Little Turstan sheepishly shambled behind his comrade, but the latter, though a little startled at becoming suddenly aware that the fight in which he had been engaged some distance off but just before was transferred now to the street in which he stood, bent humbly to the stately figure before him, and answered at once like a fellow who had his wits about him.

"They be the king's men, most worshipful," he said.

"May it please you, most worshipful, yon masters, to the number of some forty or so, did take their pleasure in our streets, and lest their silken gear be wet in the storm they sought their refuge in the shops. So till the foul weather overpassed, when, lo and behold you, most worshipful, up spake one of nine to little Turstan here, saying, 'Scurvy wretch, our liege king would have pipkins of the potter' – he being the potter's prentice, most worshipful, and the potter away from home. 'Pipkins he shall have if he pay; not else,' quoth Little Turstan. 'Here be the pay, scurvy wretch,' quoth the king's man, and throws one pipkin at Little Turstan, and yet another at his fellow-prentice, Thomas. 'Ye do ill, masters, to break the potter's ware,' quoth Little Turstan. 'We do well, soapy and scurvy wretch,' quoth the king's man. Whereat the nine lay hands on the large table whereon are many pipkins, the which they overturn, and all the pipkins are broken. Then stoutly cries Little Turstan, 'Prentice, prentice!' and to the shop enter the other king's men, and break pipkins, and go out down Lombard Street merrily laughing. After them sally our prentices, most worshipful, and say, 'Ye shall go with us and answer for the wrong ye have wrought.' To which the king's men say, 'Ye are all scurvy and soapy wretches, and we will not go with ye, nor yet answer.' So drawing their gully-knives upon us, we set upon them with our staves; and three among those nine running from the rest, Little Turstan and I give chase, till we lose them in Friar's Street, where the others now are, as I see, most worshipful."

To this narrative of what had happened (of which our version must be considered a sort of translation, for Wynkin spoke in the uncouth Anglo-Saxon of the period, a language wholly unintelligible to us now, and such as we might fancy a horse would naturally speak, could he speak at all) the stranger listened in perfect silence, though it was easy to see, by the nervous griping of the hand holding the hood together, that he fully understood and was moved by the story of one of those outranges frequently committed in that day by the king's creatures, and the common end of which was a heavy fine levied upon the citizens. Whether he would have made any reply is doubtful, but if he intended any it was cut short by a nudge Little Turstan gave Wynkin from behind, which, with the uneasy glance accompanying it, caused the latter to take notice of the spot where they happened to be standing. It was in front of a structure of stone, not very high, but considerably higher than the other edifices; withdrawn somewhat from the zigzag line of the street; dusky brown in color, and showing by the smoky stains and scars upon it that it had been scathed by, and probably proved a barrier to, some of those conflagrations which so often then ravaged London; its narrow windows closely shuttered; a loophole in the form of a cross between the two in the upper story; a sombre portal jutting beneath, with a carven finial, and on its cornice floral carvings; within this an oaken door heavily clamped with iron; on either side of the portal, set in niches, two wooden effigies of St. Francis d'Assisi and St. Thomas à Becket; and weeds and grass raggedly fringing the overhanging eaves, growing thickly around the broken steps and spiring from their seams and fissures. Sooth to say, it was a building before which nobody, from the child at his games to the very oldest citizen, cared even in broad daylight to linger; though people did venture to live, and even to frequent the flagging, on the opposite side. The explanation of this popular timidity was, that in the stone house abode then, as for a year past, a learned man; and a learned man at that delightful period was regarded by the populace with reverential horror, as one who was unquestionably a master of black arts and a dealer with the devil. When, therefore, Wynkin became aware that he was in front of the house, he turned a shade paler, and devoutly crossed himself, as Little Turstau had already done. No sooner had both prentices caught sight of a pale and bearded face calmly looking from a half-opened shutter above upon the fray – the face of the learned man himself – than they both crossed themselves again, and involuntarily made a movement to depart. Instantly the hooded personage passed by them with a slight bend of his head, the face at the window above disappearing at the same time, and the two prentices hurried off, and were presently striking and shouting in the midst of the brawl.

In front of the portal the personage paused to look back. As he turned, out smote from the clouds a burst of sunshine, blinding bright. The white walls and the wet red roofs suddenly a-smoke with rising vapor; the chimneys, jutting fronts and eaves, propped shutters, stairways, all salient points and surfaces, streaked, splashed, and fringed with the sombre silver and sullen jewels of the rain; the street's black-shining slush, the flagging's leaden pools; the many-colored multitude swaying and tossing in one wild, howling bray of discord beyond; the motley mire-bedraggled fighters reeling and plunging, with flailing of cudgels and flashing of poniards, like a cluster of dwarf devils in interstruggling confusion, – the whole long, low, stormy vista, dashed with a thousand rough lights and sooty shadows, and showing like some gorgeous and demoniac phantasmagoria, swept up to meet the eye of the gazer. All was distinct in flame and gloom, under the lowering and tremendous rack, whose yellow and umber masses, riven into terrific forms, toiled gigantically to the far limit, where, losing shape, they sheeted down the vault through intermediate gray in dense and livid blue. A new life seemed to strike into the multitude with that abrupt and stern illumination; the whole concourse wavered convulsively, with brandished arms and hoarse and furious cries; the struggling mass of fighters plunged heavily forward, all together, swayed back again, and fought with frantic yells. Then came a chorus of shrill screams; there was a sudden scattering; the vivid light went out, obscured in blotting clouds; and in the pallid shadow which struck the street blank and ghast the dispersing crowd was seen running in affrighted silence, the people scrambling up stairways and in at doors, the prentices darting into the spaces between the houses, while through the multitudinous muffled clatter of footfalls sounded the dull and heavy gallop of approaching horse; and as the city guard came riding in, there were visible only twos and threes of miry prentices in different directions, vanishing into the interspaces with wounded comrades between them, and some distance down the street a draggled group of courtiers hastily retreating, with sore bones, toward Westminster.

"God's curse on king and king's men!" said the hooded witness of the scene, stamping his foot passionately on the flagging. He said no more, but, hastily entering the portal, struck twice on the oaken door. After a pause, the door swung slowly back a little way on its creaking hinges, and revealed in the shadowy aperture a dwarfish and hideously misshapen figure, clad in red, with a stolid and sodden face and a shock of yellow hair.

"Make way, good Cuthbert Iloole," said the visitor kindly. "I would see the friar."

Cuthbert Hoole kept his bloodshot eyes, almost vacant of intelligence, fixed for a moment on the speaker's face, and then, in a feeble and dissonant tone, whined slowly:

"Time is! Come."

Like one accustomed to the strange manner of the poor idiot, the visitor entered, and following with calm strides the darting and zigzag course of his usher, was conducted through an obscure, low-browed passage to a small and lofty oaken chamber, palely lighted by a narrow oriel window with glass panes, set rather high in the wall. It was furnished with two huge wooden chairs, a settle, and a massive table, on which were a book of vellum, an inkhorn, and a few rolls of parchment. A spare and slender figure, gowned in gray Franciscan frieze, with the cowl laid back on his shoulders, stood near the table, and turned toward the visitor, as he entered, a face of scholastic pallor, meagre and noble, its lower part covered with a close-curling auburn beard, and its thin, clear features wearing in their shadow a faint smile which shed a pale irradiation under the hollow arches of the eyes, and over the unwrinkled marble of a forehead grand and large in its proportions, from which time and thought had worn away the monastic tonsure.

"Welcome, my lord of Leicester," said he, bending his head slightly.

"Thanks, marvelous doctor, I greet you," replied the earl.

"But no court fashions of speech with me. By God's eyes, I weary alike of court and court fashions!"

He strode forward as he spoke, his presence seeming to flood the cloistral tranquillity of the chamber with a sense of embattled armies, and, throwing himself into a chair, flung back his hood. A kingly fronted presence, making the seat he sat upon a throne; the face bronzed and martial, stern, sagacious, royal with justice, passionate and war-sad; the large head, broad at top, and covered with curling locks of iron-gray, rising grandly from the solid shoulders; the bold forehead corrugated: the brown eyes filled with a clear fire under their pented brows, though veiled with a certain weariness as they wandered listlessly over the manuscripts on the table; the nose large, aquiline, courageous, with dilated nostrils; and the heavy black mustache of the Norman, sloping down to the resolute jaw. Over the whole countenance now was an expression of vexed gloom. The friar smiled pensively as he gazed upon it.

"You are fretted, De Montfort," he said.

"Fretted!" replied the earl, smiting his breast with his clenched hand.

"Ay, Roger, fretted. Splendor of God, well may I be fretted! To be rid of this cark and care of state, I could become a shepherd of the downs."

"Then would you be fretted with the shepherd's cark and care," returned the friar jestingly.

The earl looked grim for a moment, but, soothed by the sweet, clear voice, like the falling of silver waters, as by the strengthful calm of the friar's presence, he smiled slowly, and then laughed.

"True, marvelous doctor, true," he said carelessly, his front relaxing. "All estates must have their crosses. Even you, Roger, with your worn face of peace, have borne burdens."

"Yes," said the friar simply, after a pause, "I have suffered."

De Montfort's mind, already roving from the thoughts that disturbed him, at once lost sight of them; his careless mood became fixed with sudden interest, and his eyes shot a keen glance at the musing face of the speaker, then wandered to the book on the table, and returned.

"I understand," he said slowly, moving his head up and down with the air of one occupied with a reflection, which had never struck him before.

"Yes, I have heard that Roger Bacon seeks too devoutly the mysteries of God to be loved by man. But why seek science at such cost?"

"Science is for man's advantage," replied Bacon gravely.

"For man's advantage? True, but it brings you sorrow, Roger."

"And you, De Montfort, – why toil you for justice against court and king and factious peers?"

"It is for England's welfare."

"But it brings you gall and grief, De Montfort."

"God's throat, yes!" the earl wrathfully assented, striking the arm of his chair. "Gall and grief it brings me, truly! Yet better gall and grief to me than ruin to the realm; better anything than shameful sloth of mine when wrongs cry for man to right them."

"Amen, brave earl! You have answered for me."

De Montfort looked mutely at him for a moment, and, with curious wish to know if such were indeed the motive of the great friar, spoke on.

"Yet hear me, Roger," he said, "and mark the difference between us twain. Behold, I have many recompenses. I am Earl of Leicester. From Kenilworth I look on broad lands of mine own. I have my good dame, the Lady Eleanor, and my stout sons. And what though royal Harry rage, and William de Valence scowl, and Gloucester's faction chafe me? Good prelates bless me; bold barons are leal to me, and hail me champion and leader. Ay, more, – the people love me. They call me the Mattathias of the suffering land. They call me Sir Simon the righteous. Is it not worth sorrow to have won such names, as these? Sweet is the love of the people, Roger! But you," he pursued, his voice sinking from its proud tone to one of frank compassion, – "what are your recompenses? You are not now, as once, the glory of the university. Your voice is silenced there. You have no longer wealth. It has been spent for science. The friars of your order vent their malice and envy in the foulest calumnies upon you. The people do not love, but dread you. You are unblessed, unhonored, landless, wifeless, childless, almost friendless. Often in past time, as I have heard, your studies have been forbidden, your books and writings nailed together; you have been denied company, scanted of food and drink, imprisoned. To what good end? Why forego ease, joy, honor, for this? Why toil for science when it brings you nought but hate, slander, ill fume, oppression, poverty, hunger, imprisonment, perchance death?"

The friar raised his noble head, with a rapt light upon his wasted features.

"It is for the advantage of the world," he said, with sublime simplicity.

De Montfort looked at him with parted lips, and a red flush crept over his massive countenance.

"The advantage of the world!" he rejoined, abstractedly and slowly.

"That is a sorry voice to give a man cheer and comfort when all human voices cry against him."

"It is the voice divine," returned the friar, "and it never leaves me. I hear it," he said, with dreamful and solemn ardor, "when all human voices cry against me, – voice of their voices, and of their tones the overtone. Day never rose nor set, night never came nor silence never folded me, in which it was not Heaven's own voice of comfort to my spirit. Yea, jailed in my cell, wasted with prison rigors, when angry faces gnash at me, when cruel tongues rail at me, I hear it still, blithe and strong as battle trumpets, and bracing my heart to bear whatever man hath borne. Blithe and strong as in the early days at Ilchester, when it bade me yield up the lily and the rose of youth, the honors and the ease of age, so blithe and strong and filled with cheer and comfort do I hear it now. So shall I hear it, all sufficient, to my latest day; so shall I hear it on my dying pallet as I go to Him who also strove for the world's advantage, following whom I have labored to raise man's life to the perfection of the Christian law, in something of whose spirit I have humbly striven to live, and somewhat of whose crown of thorns I have been graciously permitted to wear."

Ceasing, he stood with solemn light upon his face, and silence such as follows religious music succeeded to his voice when its last rapt cadences had died away. The flush had paled from De Montfort's features, and mutely for a little while, with the fire of his brown eyes dim, he gazed at the friar.

"O life of God," he passionately murmured, "who would not be noble in England with such a man as this alive!"

"What say you, De Montfort?" abstractedly asked Bacon, hearing his murmurings.

"Roger," replied the earl, "I see what sustains you in your lonely toil for the truths of God, and I grant all labor and sorrow for the world's advantage well, for the advantage is the noble laborer's sufficient recompense. But hear me. Robert Grostete has long foretold that I should fall in the cause of truth and justice, this strife for the Charter, and I feel that the good bishop has spoken truly. Yet my life will not have been in vain, and my death will establish all for which I have striven. But whatever benefit men are to receive from you rests on the preservation of your writings, and these many are leagued to destroy. Failing this fate, they may moulder to dust, unseen by men, in Oxford library. So will your life have been wasted. What sustains you against the bitter likelihood that the world will receive no advantage from you, owing to the neglect or destruction of your manuscripts?"

The friar looked at him with a mien of unfaltering majesty.

"Their own worth will preserve them," he answered, with proud humility, "if God means that they shall be preserved."

He turned away, but the reply struck the red flush again to the convulsed features of De Montfort, and drove the bright tears to his eyes.

"I am answered," he said hoarsely. "Well am I answered. But, by the soul of the Lord, I love England less at this moment that she loves not Roger Bacon more!"

There were a few minutes of silence. The friar lapsed into reverie. The earl, subduing his emotion, sat mournfully revolving many thoughts, and gradually passing away through busy mental transitions from the things that had been spoken.

"Well, well," he said abruptly, with a sad, ruminating smile, "I know not why one should despond. The times are stormy, yet they mend, they mend. Certes, Roger, they are better than when your little jest so deftly tilted over that varlet Peter de Rupibus."

"My little jest? What mean you. Do Montfort?" said the friar absently.

"I mean *petrae et rupes* which signifies stones and rocks, does it not?" returned the earl, with a quiet laugh.

"Such is the meaning," replied the friar, still absently, with the air of one whose thoughts were wandering from the colloquy. "But I do not understand."

"What, forget your good wit!" gayly exclaimed De Montfort. "But you forget not Peter de Rupibus, that knavish Bishop of Winchester?"

"Nay, I remember him well," said Bacon mechanically.

"And well you may," continued De Montfort. "Our royal Harry's prime minister more than twenty years agone; he at whose beck England was filled with the rufflers of Poitou, without an encompassing crowd of whom the king would go nowhere; he who ruled the land at his own free pleasure, and so inflamed the king's heart with hatred of his English subjects that his sole thought was how to exterminate them all. Doubtless he meant to do as much for his barons, by aid of the swords of Poitou, when he summoned us to the conference, to which we were too wise to come, and left him to sit there with the clergy. You were a clerk of that conference, Roger."

"Yes, yes," said the friar, smiling. "I remember it all now, though it had passed my memory."

"Ay," continued De Montfort laughingly, "and the king was furious that day, as I have often been told, and brawled lustily at his absent barons, till up spake a young *frère* of your order, a large and portly man, Thomas Bungy by name. You know him well, I doubt not, Roger?"

"Yes," said Bacon, reddening.

"A good patriot," continued De Montfort, not noticing the friar's flush. "Up spake he, and stoutly told the king he would know no peace till he had dismissed Peter de Kupibus. Whereat the king stormed, but the conference declared Frère Bungy's words true, and he grew more reasonable. Then was heard the pleasant voice of Roger Bacon saying, 'Lord king, we sail the ship of England; tell me, lord king, what frightens sailors most, and what is their greatest danger?' 'Sailors know best,' quoth sullen Harry. 'My lord, I will tell you,' replied Roger; 'it is petrae et rupes.' Whereat king and conference roared laughter from their beards."

"That was a hint in Latin," said Bacon, coloring again and smiling.

"Truly," returned De Montfort, with a mirthful face," and it hinted Peter out of England, I verily believe. 'Ha, haw, ho!' roared Bungy, in huge jollity. 'Petrae et rupes sounds much like Peter de Rupibus, liege king!' 'Ay,' quoth my good Bishop of Lincoln, 'and certes is Peter stones and rocks to us who sail the ship of England. 'Ah, well, 't was a little thing, but it softened the king's heart, as good wit in a pleasant voice often does, and left him in easy mood to yield Peter's dismissal at the solicitations of the primate. So the gale of merriment that jest raised blew the minister out of England, and the rogues of Poitou along with him."

De Montfort laughed heartily, while the friar smiled as faintly as might a modern reader of his medieval joke, coming upon Matthew Paris's version of it, given in the chronicle of Roger De Wendover.

"If jests could blow Peters and Poietevins from England," Bacon said presently, "I would fain fall a-jesting now."

"True," returned the earl; "there are still many foreigners at court and in places of power, though not in such number now as –"

"Nay, I refer not to the presence of the men of Poitou," interrupted the friar, "nor yet to the Italians whom Pope Guilty thrusts upon us, but to –"

A sudden peal of hilarity from De Montfort cheeked his speech.

"Pope Guilty!" ejaculated the mirthful earl. "Innocent the Fourth rechristened! Pope Guilty! Roger, Roger, while your wit thus brands evil dignities there are other reasons, I trow, for denying you speech and visitors, and nailing your books together, than your simple zeal for the truth of God."

"'T is a truth of God thus to name the Pope," said the friar, with a soft laugh. "For the rest, De Montfort, I misdoubt me but you say true. It was on my lips to refer to the day's riot."

"Ay," thunderously muttered De Montfort, his brow darkening. "It had passed my mind. Know you its cause?"

"I heard that shrill-voiced prentice tell you, as I stood at the window," replied Bacon. "A matter of broken pipkins."

"Broken pipkins!" cried De Montfort stormfully. "Broken liberties, I say! When the idle varlets of a king have power so to deal in a tradesman's shop, what is broken beside his earthenware? God's life, the charter of a nation!"

"Even so," returned the friar. "But was it this that so fretted you, De Montfort?"

"Only in part," moodily replied the earl, champing his mustache as a war-horse champs his curb, while the rage of eye and nostril slowly settled into gloom. "Hear me, Roger," he continued after a pause. "I will tell you. My royal brother-in-law was taking pleasure in his barge on the river, when the storm came on, and caused him to land at the nearest mansion, which happened to be Durham House, where I then was. The rain had ceased, however, ere he landed. When I came down with my lord the bishop into the garden to greet him, he fell a-trembling, and grew as white as though I were a spectre. 'My liege,' I said, 'why are you afraid? The tempest is now past.' He looked at me with lowering aspect. 'I fear thunder and lightning beyond measure,' said he in a hollow voice, 'but, by the head of God, I do more fear thee than all the thunder and lightning in the world!' Ay, Roger, thus spake he. And he did *thee* me! In the very presence of his malapert courtier crew he did *thee* me! By St. Michael, but that he was the king I could have struck him dead!"

"How answered you?" asked Bacon, his eyes grown bright and keen, and fixed eagerly upon the earl.

"My passion made me calm," replied De Montfort, "and England rose in my heart to answer him. 'Fear not me, my liege,' I said, with my eyes bent upon the scowling crew, – 'fear not me, who have been always loyal to you and your realm. Fear rather your true enemies, who destroy the realm and abuse you with bad counsels.' At which the brazen caitiffs slunk cowering, and followed Harry of Winchester, who went by without another word."

"Was this all?"

"All," was the reply. "I entered my barge at the foot of the garden, and came hither, – came hither to see, as I passed, the result of just men's blood and grief once again made as naught; wasters of poor men's goods answering with steel instead of silver for their ravages, and holding the city's peace and laws as cobwebs, as they have done time and again. God grant they were well cudgeled, though every blow they got is like to cost the city a pot of money. But it shall not. *Despardieux*! If the king moves to fine the citizens for this outrage of his minions, I will bring it before the council."

"Think not of it, De Montfort," said the friar calmly. "Let the fine follow the wrong, as it doubtless will.

Think rather how to limit this king's power for wrong."

"That were good thinking," replied De Montfort, with a gloomy smile. "But how? This year's Parliament has brought forth my best thought, the Committee of Government. To what avail? How check these royal evils, which creep like grass and wind like water everywhere?"

"Hearken, De Montfort," said the friar.

"Time was when Norman scorn could say, 'Dost take me for an Englishman?'"

"Time is passed," whined a voice. De Montfort turned quickly round in his chair, and saw Cuthbert Hoole retreating from the closing door, motioned away by the friar.

"He is weak-witted," said the latter, "and this is part of his poor jargon; but he spoke aptly then. Time is, indeed, passed. The Norman owns himself Englishman. Saxon and Norman no longer, we are all Englishmen. The old disdain lives only in the court of the king."

"Where it keeps the land in constant broil," said the earl.

"Ay, but you can crush it there," said Bacon. "You can array a power against it so formidable that it must bow. Nor can Gloucester's faction maintain it."

"And how?"

"Hearken," pursued the friar. "Statecraft has found that the law of the realm, and not the will of the king, must rule England. Said I not that we are all Englishmen now? Let statecraft, then, find that the law which rules must be made by Englishmen; not by English lords and priests for the people, but by the English people for the people. Poorly will they defend the law made for them; stoutly will they defend the law themselves have made."

"Dost meditate a Parliament of villans, Roger?" bantered the earl.

A deeper pallor overspread the visage of the friar, and upon it stole a smile like dawn.

"I see a time far off," he reverently answered, "when the charters which barons win and cannot keep shall be kept securely by those who shall be villans then no more. Far off I see it coming on its way. So let it come, with all good things, hereafter." He moved up the chamber, with his head bent upon his hand, and, wheeling suddenly, faced the earl. "De Montfort," he cried, with startling energy, "what is it the king fears more in you than the thunder and the lightning? It is that more fearful to the tyrant than the thunder and the lightning, – a brave man's justice. Gift of the Lord to England, a new power calls to your justice for its place in the councils of the nation!"

"What power?" De Montfort eagerly demanded.

"What power studs England with so many free cities and boroughs? Lord earl, they were not built by peers and prelates. Lord earl, the men I speak of hold not by tenure of the villan, nor wear the collar of the slave. Rich and strong with trade and labor, and freemen all, why stand they unrepresented in the politics of England?"

"What would you have me do?" said the startled earl.

"Repay the love that loves you. Summon the burgesses to Parliament. Give them equal place with peers and prelates in the councils of the realm. So, with something like the nation at your back, you can front the faction of the Crown."

The bold reply smote like light on the brain of De Montfort. Instantly he saw the advantage such a move would give him, and a latent thought of his own rose in his mind, one with the thought of the friar. Speechless, with the red flush on his corrugated brow, his features puckered with wonder, and a fire-flash in his eyes, he sat upright, staring at Bacon. Then, smiting the arms of his chair, he threw back his head, and his laugh rang wild and weird.

"Behold," he said, "often as I have mused upon these burgesses, a thought I could not define, like a man masked and cloaked, has come to me. Now, at your words, mask and cloak drop, and your thought I recognize as mine. Powers of heaven, what a measure! But, Roger, 't would be hard to compass."

"First of all," urged Bacon, "seek out Bracton, and get him to look if there be not some precedents for it."

"Ay, well counseled. But hush. Let me think of this, for my mind is all a-whirl."

Bacon turned away, and for five minutes the earl sat in silence, his eyes covered with his hand, absorbed in reflection.

"Robert Grostete's prophecy is like to come true or this," he said at last, in a sombre voice. "Fruitful of much fair fortune would this measure be to England, but woeful would it prove to me. It cannot be compassed without collision with the king. Yet what matter! Roger, I will take it into mind, – ay, more: by God's eyes, it shall be accomplished, if it can be! Let the worst come. It is right, it is just. All that I have and am is for right and justice. Oh, happy he who soldiers the good cause! Oh, happy, happy he who can die for it!"

The great earl well redeemed his passionate pledge, as history attests, nor was his foreboding groundless. A few years later, and the measure which laid the foundation of the English House of Commons, and called the great body of the English people into political life, was fully inaugurated, and a new morning rose upon the nation, though with a blood-red dawn.

"Hearken, De Montfort," said Bacon, drawing near him. "Dismiss from your mind all thought of collision with the king. That were ruin. This must be done in the king's name, and it is now your task to win him to your design. I will show you many arguments and methods by which he may be won. Patience, patience. Take time. The years are before you."

"Roger," said the earl abruptly, "I came here today to ask you a question. At my last visit you said something – I know not how, nor exactly what – 't was a dark saying – spoken in jest, too – but it has haunted me ever since – something about enwalling England against invasion. What meant you, – anything or nothing? Dost apprehend invasion?"

Bacon colored deeply under the frank, inquisitive gaze of the speaker.

"It might be," he said, in an evasive tone. "France may at any time spread her banners in the land. Harry of Winchester may ally with Pope Guilty, a papal interdict again hurl Europe upon England as in William Conquestor's time, and the realm see another Hastings."

"Alack!" sighed the earl, "what wall against such invasion as this?"

"A united realm," replied Bacon quickly. "Beware of division with Harry of Winchester. Be friends with him. Resent nothing. Beguile or persuade him into sanctioning all you do. De Montfort, make firm alliance with the king! That is England's wall against all invaders."

"It is well counseled," said the earl thoughtfully, with his eyes fixed upon the floor. "But, Roger –"

Looking up, he saw that the friar had drawn his cowl over his face. De Montfort instantly divined that he had a thought he feared his face might betray, and, laughing, he rose.

"Nay, then," said he gayly, "if you cover your face, I go. But, Roger, thanks for your wise counsels. You have given me much to think of. Thanks, thanks, and for the present farewell."

He clasped the thin hand of the friar in his own brown strong palm, gazed with frank tenderness a moment on the bent cowled head, then, drawing his hood over his face, left the room.

The friar stood motionless, listening to the receding steps of the earl along the passage. They ceased, the heavy door closed resounding, and with a sudden movement he threw back his cowl, and showed his face kindled in shadow, his eyes shining as with interior flame.

"Ay, gift of the Lord to England," he fervently murmured, clasping his hands, "your union with this paltry king shall fortress England from without and from within as with a wall! God grant the android a good success, and he and you shall work in concert!"

He sat down near the table, and, leaning his throbbing head upon his hands, lapsed into exulting reverie, while the sunlight, breaking again from the clouds, streamed aslant through the window, and lit the chamber with a shadowy splendor of triumphant gold.

* * *

A few minutes had passed slowly by in that rich gloom, when the friar was startled from his abstraction by the sudden appearance of Cuthbert Hoole. The idiot darted in, with a frightened glare in his bloodshot eyes, his usually sodden and immobile face distorted with wild excitement, screeched "Time was!" and, spinning on his heel for an instant with dizzy rapidity, vanished through the open door, which closed behind him.

Bacon sprang upright, astounded, and stood holding his breath, with his heart beating and all his blood pricking and tingling, while the very air seemed struck dead around him, so intense was the silence. A moment, and the air crept, as it were, with a strange magnetic life, as, releasing his breath, he stepped quickly to the centre of the room, and again stood still.

"*Per os Dei*," he muttered, "this is strange! Only once before have I known the boy to be thus affected, and that was when the Paduan was here, a year ago. 'T is the time, too, when, if he keeps his word, he must be again in England. Can he be near the house? Tush, no! Yet 't is singular, this mysterious sympathy between that profound and subtle Doctor Malatesti and my poor darkened Cuthbert Hoole. If indeed there be such a sympathy – Tush, tush! I dream."

At that moment loud blows were heard on the portal. The blood rushed with a shock to the friar's heart. A long pause, and again the blows sounded loudly. Despite his self-control an icy chill coursed through his veins.

"Can it be that the Paduan is here?" he muttered. "Mayhap Cuthbert is afeard."

He made a step forward to answer the summons himself, but his brain swam, and an inexplicable feeling, resembling fear, thrilled through him and made him stand. Again the blows thundered on the portal; but suddenly he grew calm, for he heard the door open, and the thump of a lusty kick upon some human body coincident with the sturdy objurgation:

"St. Swithin plague thee, thou malformed bunch! Must thou keep a frère of the Lord's flock pounding till doomsday at the portal?"

Bacon smiled despite himself.

"Oaf that I am!" he murmured. "Maundering of the Paduan, when 't is only my burly Bungy!"

The next instant Friar Bungy lumbered into the room with the gait of an overgrown elephant. He was a perfect abbey-lubber, enormously fat, nearly six feet in height, and with an incredible circumference of paunch. The rough cord which, after the fashion of the Franciscans, bound his gray habit around the waist would have sufficed for at least two ordinary brothers of the order. His merry black eyes twinkled under a low but prominent forehead, with its tonsure band of gray hair, and lit his red blobber cheeked visage, fringed with a grizzly gray beard, with the light of a certain gross genius. He was barefooted, and the heavy flap of his immense dirty feet sounded on the floor with a distinctness which testified to his ponderous weight, as he surged across the chamber, and flung himself, half reclining, upon the oaken settle, which croaked beneath his burden. As he lay thus, blowing obstreperously, with his mighty stomach stupendously rising and falling, he afforded a striking contrast to the spare and graceful ascetic figure of Roger Bacon, who stood, calm as a statue, surveying him with a slight smile on his austere features.

"Oh, Brother Roger," panted the exhausted Bungy in a stentorian voice, "I am well-nigh dead with the speed of my course, and truly am frying in my frock with the sore heat of the day!"

"Nay, Frère Thomas," said Bacon, "you were quick enough to abuse Cuthbert with a most heavy buffet, as you came in. Surely it would better beseem you to deal gently with our poor witless servitor."

The fat friar suspended the operation of wiping with the sleeve of his habit the perspiration from his flushed face, and burst into a jovial laugh, which spread his large mouth from ear to ear, and showed a shining double row of splendid teeth in the boskage of his gray beard.

"Peace, Roger!" he roared, subsiding. "I did slight harm to Cuthbert, but the unready earl was slow to answer my summons, and I was vexed. Make him fetch me a stoop of water, I beseech you, or, by St. Thomas à Becket, I shall die of drought."

Bacon took from a shelf a wooden tankard, but finding it empty left the room to replenish it. No sooner was he gone than the fat friar lifted himself from the settle with a rapidity which denoted no extreme state of exhaustion, and whipping out a large flat leathern flask from his capacious bosom, put it to his thick red lips, and took a draught of what was evidently a stronger and more congenial potation than the rules of St. Francis allowed to the brethren of his order.

"Ah, 't is fine!" said the rotund giant with satisfaction, replacing the wooden stopple, and hiding the flask in his bosom. "A blessing on my cousin the vintner for such a pottle of drink as this! 'T is your true milch cow, by St. Dubric!"

He had resumed his former position when Bacon entered with the tankard.

"What drug have you about you, Thomas?" he asked half absently, as he handed Bungy the water. "I scent spice on the air."

"Nay, I know not," coolly answered the friar, affecting to drink. "Unless it be the odor of my sanctity," he added, replacing the tankard on the shelf. "Sooth, if holy men may smell of spice and roses in their graves, as 't is known they do, I know not why they may not in their lives."

Bacon, absorbed in reverie, did not appear to have heard this audacious reply.

"A wild, warm day," ran on Bungy, lolling on the settle. "Brawl stirring again in the city, and the king's men well thwacked, for which St Becket be praised. And such labor of sun and clouds, and such clouds, have I never beheld. Pray God it be not a portent of toil and trouble for England. By Dunstan the blessed, I think the fiend is abroad in the realm this day. Such clouds, such clouds! And such devil's roar of thunder, and devil's sheeting of flame, and devils pelting of rain, as wrought hurly-burly above us ere the tempest passed! Now 't is war of sun and clouds, and beshrew me if I do not think the clouds may defeat the sun, and leave the land without God's candle. Lord forfend it be not an omen of coming battle betwixt our blessed Sir Simon and Harry of Winchester, and Sir Simon getting the worst of it! That were as good as putting out the sun itself."

"Fear not, Thomas," said Bacon, starting from his musing and pacing up the room. "Storms purge the air as struggle doth the realm, and in the war of cloud and sun, by God's grace the sun is ever assured victor."

Turning, he came down the chamber and took a chair near Bungy.

"Hearken, Thomas," he said in a low voice.

"Today we finish the android, and I have now to tell you its purpose."

Bungy instantly sat up, with his gross face radiant.

"Speak on, Roger," he said. "I am all agog to hear."

"You have ever been one with me in brotherhood and stout heart against England's plotting lords," pursued Bacon. "Swear to me now, Thomas, never to reveal aught of what I am to tell you."

"I swear it by the cross," returned the friar, lifting the holy symbol which dangled at the end of his rosary.

"'T is well," said Bacon. "Listen. In my youth, studying at Paris, I fell in, it matters not how, with a strange Italian scholar of great parts and learning, named Malatesti. Afterwards, proceeding to Italy, I visited him at his house, a lonely structure of stone on the outskirts of Padua, where he dwelt in utter solitude save for two blackamoor servitors, both mutes. A strange and indeed fearful man was he, scorning all mankind, and his conduct at times truly seemed to savor of insanity. Yet was he, after his manner, gracious to me, and for the rest passing learned. Great store, too, of books and manuscripts, precious as gems, had he; and, moreover, while beauteous in person, though darkly so, and hugely wealthy, he sought not the world's vanities, but, like a true scholar, was devoted to learning, which made me honor, though I could not love him."

Bacon paused, his face saddening for an instant with an emotion perhaps of pity for a soul removed from God and man.

"Go on, Roger," said the open-mouthed Bungy.

"By Swithin, this is as good as a miracle play when Bottle the tanner enacts the devil!"

"At that time," resumed Bacon, "our talk chanced to fall upon the story which Gervase de Tilbury and the monk Helinandus, with others, have recorded as true, though I esteem it as no more than an old wife's fable, namely, that the famed Virgil did construct by magic art a head of brass which could speak and foretell events.

Yet, withstanding me, did the Doctor Malatesti stoutly affirm this true; and such was his occult learning and wondrous logic that he did prove it true, and the thing itself easy to be done, so far as words can prove; nothing being proved, as I hold, save by experiment, and this thing mere absurdity, spite of the Paduan. But, what was really important, holding discussion with him on the nature and difference of sounds, he did show me that articulations, to a great extent, can be effected by simply natural means, so that a machine may be made to utter certain sentences. This machine, compact in form, placed within a bust of brass and set in motion, and lo, you have a brazen android which seems to speak of itself what by means of art it uttereth!"

Bungy clapped his big hands and stamped his feet, roaring with laughter.

"Oh, brave, brave!" he shouted. "This, then, is the machine we have made. St. Swithin be praised for my wondrous genius in braziery, whereby I have fashioned the brass andiron, or whatever the devil you please to call the shell of this thing!"

"Android, not andiron," said Bacon, smiling. "'T is from the Greek."

"Nay, I cannot keep it in mind," said Bungy lazily. "I am so Christian in my very bones that the tongues of heathenesse will not abide in me. Good breviary Latin, which is a sound gospel language, and my mother English, both of them fit to be spoken in heaven, are all I can patter, blessed be God! As for Greek and Arabic and the tongues of Mahound, faugh! Fie upon such trash, I say! But the machine, Roger. You have wrought upon that apart from me. What will it utter, and for what purpose?"

"Hearken," said Bacon. "I left the Paduan and returned to England. Many years passed on while I wrought at my books and in the laboratory, as you partly know, till about two years ago, when I was experimenting much in optics and acoustics at Oxford, recalling what the Paduan had said, I bethought me to fashion, in leisure hours, by way of diversion, such a machine as he had named. At the end of seven or eight months I had made a small apparatus which could utter distinctly enough these words: 'Art is the only magic.'"

"Brave, brave!" murmured the excited Bungy, all eyes and ears.

"It delighted Robert Grostete and Adam de Marisco much," continued Bacon; "but, bruited around, my envious foes heard of it, and the result was that I was prisoned in my cell and fared hardly, till the good bishop contrived to obtain my releasement. Then something marvelous happened, and, with De Marisco and Grostete privy to a scheme I had formed, I came here, the bishop lending me this house, and gaining me permission from the university to pursue certain scientific experiments herein. That was a year ago; and a few days before, at my request, you joined me, the Paduan, strange to say, visited me here."

"Blessed be his name!" said Bungy fervently.

"Nay," returned Bacon, "I hardly liked his coming, nor did his visit wholly please me. His conduct savored even more of insanity than when I had seen him years before, and he had certain knowledge of things said and done which almost appalled me, though I have thought that some persons, particularly of disordered minds, brood within them knowledge not common to man, even as diseased oysters breed within them pearls, which are not common to that fish; and in both cases the marvel is one of nature, and not of magic."

Bacon paused reflectively, while at the mention of fish, which was a chief article of diet in those days, Bungy, though mainly engaged with his fellow-friar's narrative, instinctively licked his lips, probably in honor of the oysters, which were then somewhat of a delicacy.

"The Paduan's tone was strange," resumed Bacon. "I told him of the machine I had made, and in what followed he urged – indeed, I may say, even commanded – me to fashion an android of brass under certain planetary conjunctions and aspects, according to the rules of magic, which he said would in due time answer questions and prophesy, being inhabited by a spirit. His tone was such that I thought not of disputing with him, and, assuming that I would obey, he left me minute directions in writing, and, also, what was most strange, drawings of the internal structure of the human head, neck, and bosom, in whose likeness, he said, the interior of the bust must be fashioned, and with various metals. These drawings he had made, he told me, by dissecting the human corpse –"

"Heavenly God!" ejaculated Bungy, turning pale. "Open a corpse! Sacrilege!"

"Nay," said Bacon firmly. "I think not so. The illustrious Mondini has done the same. Why not? Bodies are cloven in battle, and even mutilated after death. If this may be done in the spirit of war, or, worse, in the spirit of murder, nor be deemed sacrilege, why may it not be done as blamelessly in the spirit of truth and love for the advancement of knowledge, which is the profit of the world?"

"By St. Thomas à Kent, that is well argued!" returned Bungy, rolling his eyes. "But natheless 't is a grave matter to carve up a man like a stockfish."

"However," resumed Bacon, "the Paduan, promising to return to England in a year, left me, and I, disregarding his talk, though I own that in his presence he almost compelled my mind to his thought and will, set about fashioning the apparatus for the android on which we have wrought together."

"And which is now completed, or will be soon," said Bungy eagerly. "But for what purpose?"

"Attend, good frère," pursued Bacon. "Dost remember when this base king built the stone bulwark next the Tower, a wasp's nest of prisons, in which the rich merchants were to be confined till they paid him heavy sums of money?"

"Truly do I," replied the friar. "'T was in 1239. But St. Thomas a Becket brought confusion upon it; for well do I remember the night when the solid bulwark fell down with great din, as though an earthquake had set his shoulder to it."

"Natheless he builded it again," said Bacon, with a gloomy smile.

"Ay, did he," responded Bungy, "and at a cost of twelve thousand marks. Yet no sooner up than down again. 'T was in 1241. St. Thomas guards his Londoners well."

"And well may he guard them," said Bacon quietly. "But 't was not St. Thomas à Becket brought confusion upon Harry of Winchester's vile jail. 'T was I."

Bungy's fat face became blank with stupefaction.

"You!" he roared. "Roger, are you demented?"

Bacon arose and went to a cupboard, from which he returned in a few moments with a lighted taper and a small metal phial.

"I have told you of the explosive properties of the powder of nitre and coal," he said, "but in this little flask, which I brought in from the laboratory to show you, there is a vapor generated by vitriol and water on iron dust which is also explosive. Look."

Unstopping the phial, he held it aloft, with the light above it. A bright flash followed.

"Confine that vapor in a cell," he said to the staring Bungy, "apply flame, and 't will rive all before it."

He extinguished the taper, replaced it with the phial, and resumed his seat.

"An officer of the Tower," he continued, "had a brother, a rich merchant, on whom he knew the oppression was likely to fall, and chancing to unburden his heart to me, whom he knew, for his brother's sake he willingly lent himself to my scheme. One night, ere the bilwark was inhabited, or indeed well finished, he took me to lodge with him in the White Tower, and in the night we went in by a private passage to a cell in the basement of the bulwark. I placed in a large earthern vessel he had left there the quantity of iron filings I had brought, and, adding the vitriol and water, covered the whole till the inflammable vapor was evolved. Then, uncovering it, we hastily retired, making all fast behind us, and leaving in the cell a little machine contrived so that it would strike a light within a certain time. That night, as I said, I lodged with him in the White Tower, and in a little while we heard the dull roar of the toppling bulwark. Ay, and again was the same thing done, and again the exploding vapor rived that stronghold of tyranny. The third time never came for its rebuilding."

Bungy heaved a prodigious sigh.

"By St. Dubrie, 't was a parlous brave deed!" he exclaimed. "'T was done well!"

"It was done for the good of the people," said Bacon sternly. "Lamed by fortune, not often have I been able, in mine obscurity, to work them such signal service. Yet twice, at least, have I wrought well for them, and now for the third time I come to their service with the brazen android."

"To their service!" cried Bungy, with a great start.

"Ay," replied Bacon. "I told you that, just ere my coming here to execute the scheme whereto my lord of Lincoln and De Marisco are privy, something marvelous happened, and it was that suggested my scheme."

"What was it that happened?" murmured Bungy.

"The king dreamed a strange dream. Dost remember?" asked Bacon sombrely.

"I do," replied Bungy, after a moment's pause, in which the color rushed to his startled features. "It troubled him sorely, and was the land's talk for a good season."

"Truly was it," said Bacon. "He dreamed of lodging in an unfamiliar room, where a Brazen Head, appeared and spoke to him, giving him good counsel. But what it said, waking he could not remember. Yet eagerly did he strive to recall what it had spoken, and sorely did he long that such an image might indeed appear to him. 'You would die of fear,' said Humphrey de Bohun to him. 'Nay, by God's head,' said the king, 'I would calmly listen; ay, and abide by its counsel.'"

Bungy gasped, and with the sleeve of his habit mopped the perspiration from a face redder than fire with his excitement.

"Hear, now," said Bacon, leaning forward as he sat, and speaking in low and sombre tones, with his gray eyes jewel-bright, and fixed piercingly on the visage of the friar. "The time has come when the welfare of England demands that the king shall he guided by De Montfort."

"Ay, does it!" roared Bungy, with patriotic fervor, bringing down his fist like a mallet on the solid arm of the settle.

"What if he should hear such good counsel as this?" urged Bacon. "What if this superstitious king, with the memory of his dream upon him, should have a brazen android appear to him indeed, and speak thus for his salvation? Behold, the android is made!"

"And it will speak to him?" panted Bungy.

Bacon rose swiftly and silently to his feet, like a ghost, and stood dilated, with a white light on his marble brow and wasted features, and his eyes flaming in their hollow orbits.

"Ay," he said, in a low and thrilling voice. "It will speak my thought to him! It will utter Roger Bacon's message to the king of England!"

There was a moment of motionless silence; then, like a majestic phantom, he moved up the room, while Bungy, like one released from a spell, his red face convulsed with a shock of emotions, fell back heavily on the settle, overpowered with the revelation. Two or three minutes of utter stillness had passed in the golden gloom of the chamber, when Bungy, with a breath like a bellows, raised his bulk to an upright position, and stretched out his huge legs with an air of boundless pride.

"By Dunstan, I have wrought well to have helped make such a brave andrew as this," he said, in his big bass voice. "Saints! but I feel as if I, and not Sir Simon, were the Mattathias of the suffering people!"

Bacon smiled wanly, and, approaching, resumed his chair.

"I have yet to tell you, Frère Thomas," he said quietly, "how the android is to obtain audience of the king."

"Ay," returned Bungy, "and what it is to say to him."

"What it is to say I defer till you hear it speak yourself," was the answer. "For the rest, listen. The original design was to beguile the king into visiting Robert Grostete at his house in Lincoln, which could easily be done: when, at night, he would find the android in his chamber, and hear it speak in the presence of his attendants. But lately fortune has favored me with a better plan, – one, indeed, which makes it unnecessary that the image should speak by machinery, since a man within it might say all it will say. In the former design this could not have been, for there was no place to set it but in a narrow niche, where a man could not be concealed, whereas now we have a pedestal ample enough to hide a person, and also to light the android by an unknown process, as then only the king's lamp would have lighted it. But hearken. In the next house lives aged Master Trenchard, once a silk merchant, now rich, and no longer a trafficker. His house and this are both old, dating back to the reign of King Richard. But, what is not known, though I discovered it not long after I came here, there is a secret passage from one house into the other through the party-wall of the laboratory."

"Oh!" grunted Bungy, in astonishment.

"When we go into the laboratory, I will show it to you," said Bacon. "But now hear something wonderful. You know that it hath long been the fashion of this paltry king to go about lodging with men of all stations, and begging gifts of them."

"Ay!" snorted Bungy, with ineffable contempt.

"Five years ago," continued Bacon, "he paid such a visit to old Master Trenchard, and obtained from him an hundred marks. But what think you? This morning Master Trenchard received a message from the king that he would lodge with him on the third night hence, having, he said, certain proposals to offer him."

Bungy broke into a roar of laughter, stamping his feet and pounding with his hands.

"How found you this, Roger?" he said at last, still snuffling and choking with suppressed mirth.

"Master Trenchard himself told me this morning," answered Bacon quietly. "The poor man is anything but pleased with the prospect of the king's visit."

"Marry, I'll warrant you!" tittered Bungy; "for well he knows what proposals Harry of Winchester will have to offer, and his coffers already rattle with fear."

"Perchance Master Trenchard's coffers may be spared this time," said Bacon.

"How so?" replied Bungy, with an incredulous air.

"Because the king will lodge that night in the merchant's best chamber."

"And what of that?" retorted the burly friar.

"Because the secret passage whereof I spoke opens by a sliding panel into the chamber where the king will lodge," said Bacon, with his eyes on fire.

Bungy instantly sobered, and his large face grew red as a rising autumn moon.

"I see it all!" he said, with a voice like a muffled roar. "The andrew will break the king's sleep by appearing at the open panel."

"Ay!" replied Bacon, in clear, hollow tones. "In the dead stillness of the night the panel will withdraw, and the king, starting from his bed, will see at the cavity, distinct in yellow light, the android of his dream! So, while he gazes spellbound, he shall hear from its lips the good counsel which he shall now remember. Then darkness shall fall, and in the darkness the android shall recede, the panel close, and the king be left alone. But that counsel shall shape his life to its latest day!"

"By St. Becket," shouted Bungy, springing to his feet with an agility none would have suspected him capable of, and striding, with heavy foot-flaps, to and fro, "this is the rarest plot that ever was plotted! It is the most –"

Cuthbert Hoole darted into the room in a frenzy of excitement.

"Time is!" he screeched, in a sort of chant. "Time is! The Brass-Man! Time is! The Brass-Man! Aroint thee, Zernebock! Aroint thee, Zernebock!"

"Aroint thee, thou gibbering brute!" howled Bungy, plunging down like a rhinoceros upon the idiot, who vanished, leaving the door slightly ajar behind him. "Was ever the like of this! Hath the foul fiend possessed the ill-mannered bunch that he thus – Sooth, but I will take a cudgel to him if he beginneth these freaks! But what the plague – How dark the room grows!"

He had turned at the sudden fading of the light, but his eyes, as they glanced to the window, were arrested midway by the aspect of his fellow-friar. Bacon had risen to his feet, and stood in the pale gray gloom of the chamber, looking towards the door with parted lips and his visage white as death.

"It is a cloud passing over the sun," he said, in a slow, collected voice.

"Eh?" grunted Dungy, astonished.

"This troubles me," murmured Bacon.

"What? The cloud?" said Bungy, staring at him.

"I was speaking of Cuthbert," replied Bacon wanderingly. "I know not what can ail him."

"Huh!" sulkily snorted Bungy. "I know not why you keep such an ill-witted oaf about you. I would sell him to a farmer."

"Nay," rejoined Bacon curtly, "I do not sell men. I had Cuthbert from my rich brother in Somersetshire, and, taking him in pity, I owe him protection."

"Ay," sulked Bungy, dumping down again upon the settle, while Bacon also resumed his seat. "Kindness, kindness! 'T is a vice in you, Roger. Beshrew me, but I think you would be kind to Jews!"

"Truly would I," said Bacon. "I love not oppression, nor outrage in any form; and, to my thinking, in these outraged Jews again is Christ Jesu daily mocked, and scourged, and crucified."

Bungy looked a trifle abashed, but presently relaxed from his sullen mood, and laughed good-naturedly.

"Well, well," he said, "Jews or Gentiles, I mean them no harm. But to return to this brave andrew, or what you may call it – Body o' me, how dark the room grows! Sooth, 't is a grisly twilight, though we have not reached the middle of the afternoon! By my dame, 't is dark as though yon clouds were the black wings of the devil spread over the land, and the devil –"

"Ah yes, the devil! – long life to the devil!" said a singular, shrill voice.

Both friars leaped up aghast. The door was wide open, and on the threshold, in the gloomy brown light, and relieved against the shadowy passage, stood a dark, imperial figure, with a face like marble.

* * *

The figure on the threshold was the Paduan. A vague dread rising to a terror, inspired by his peculiar appearance, succeeded the moment's affright which his unannounced entrance gave the two friars. He was a man whose age it would have been impossible to determine, so strange a mixture of haughty youth and gray maturity was there in his general presence. In person he was tall and shapely, with so much majesty of port that even the majestic Bacon looked inferior in contrast; and yet, mysteriously confused with his august demeanor was a certain flickering air as of ghastly decrepitude, which made the whole seem incongruous and appalling. All that inspires homage even unto worship was in his bearing, but in it was also an indefinable element which would startle and repel homage in the very act of prostration. He wore a long robe of black silk edged with sable, and drooping in ample folds below the knee; and what was noticeable, while his legs, closely sheathed in high travel-worn boots of brown Cordovan, were strong and beautifully formed, they terminated in feet graceful, indeed, in their narrow length and suppleness, but so strangely lean, and their bones and cordy tendons so apparent through the thin leather coverings, that, what with this and with the down-curving pointed toes of the boots themselves, they suggested a morbid fancy of an ill-concealed hybrid of foot and claw. In his hand he held a black traveling-cap of a curious pattern, from which depended a trailing sable plume fastened by a single lurid jewel, a fire-opal, evidently of great purity and value. The whole character of his countenance was that of a mournful and supramortal but evil beauty. His forehead, surmounted by a splendid chevelure of curling coal-black hair which fell to his shoulders, was not only large, – it was enormous. Strangely, even fearfully developed in the region of ideality, – so much so that the protuberances of the marble temples seemed swelling into horns, while the whole front of the brow was only less powerfully prominent, – it gave an expression of overpowering intellectuality to the face itself which was terrible and painful to behold. A secret and supreme despair rested upon the colorless face like a shadow. A still, sluggish light flamed in the large dark mesmeric eyes, overarched by their black brows. The nose was aquiline, beautiful and haughty. The lips were wreathed with a superb and desolating scorn. The face was beardless, and the bold outline of the chin was the expression of an inexorable will. The whole presence of the man filled the mind with that sensation felt only after the passage of some unearthly dream. Such was the profound and learned Doctor Malatesti.

Bacon was the first to recover his composure.

"Welcome, my illustrious Doctor Malatesti," said he, – "welcome once more to England."

"Great thanks for your courtesy, my marvelous doctor," replied the Paduan, bowing so low that his obeisance savored of grave mockery.

"Great thanks to ye both, my learned frères. I accost ye both, good celibates."

He strode forward two steps from the threshold into the gloomy light of the room, as he ceased speaking, and the door closed with a fierce crash behind him. The friars stood startled and terrified. Bacon himself, with his disposition to refer occurrences to natural causes, could not but feel the nervous perturbation which will possess the coolest mind when such occurrences assume the aspect of the supernatural. The supposition, however, that the Paduan had deftly shut the door with his foot, upon entering, instantly succeeded the fantastic impression that it had been closed by its own agency; though this in turn was dissipated in a vague sense of dread as, following his thought, his eye rested upon the taloned feet of Malatesti, and received the morbid suggestion their strange shape conveyed. At the same moment, a long moan of wind sounded eerily through the grisly gloom, followed by a sullen roll of thunder dying away in sluggish reverberations, and the rushing of rain. The friar looked up with a beating heart, conscious only for an instant of the dark majesty of the motionless figure before him; conscious the next instant that his eyes, burning with a still, naphthaline flame, were fixed upon Bungy, whose face was yellow with dismay. At once Bacon, with a mingled feeling of shame that he had suffered himself to be thus affected, and a secret anger at the Paduan's behavior, controlled himself into calm.

"Good Doctor Malatesti," he said, with an assumption of phlegm, "this is my co-laborer, Thomas Bungy."

"I know him well," was the shrill reply. "He is as big as a cask."

The visitor's face was void of all expression as he made this strange remark; but whether in the remark itself, or in the tone in which it was offered, there was involved a contempt so tremendous that it wrought revulsion in the sturdy breast of Bungy, so that his dismay was suddenly overflowed with hearty rage. Nevertheless, he held himself in cheek, and with an affectation of indifference lounged down upon the settle.

"It is the effect of study," he said complacently, lazily eying the Paduan, while he nonchalantly played with his rosary.

"Study bloats a man hugely. At least it maketh me big, while it causeth Frère Roger to wax meagre."

"You came upon us without warning. Doctor Malatesti," said Bacon, interrupting the burly friar in the exposure he was making of himself. "How happened it that you gained admittance? – for I heard not your challenge at the portal."

"Truly," replied the Paduan, "I was spared the pains of knocking by your shapely servitor, who opened the door as I set foot upon the steps, and ran away on beholding me."

"Ah, the brute!" broke in Friar Bungy, his suppressed rage at the Paduan readily transferred into open manifestations against Cuthbert; "the misshapen varlet! Thus, Roger, doth he maltreat our visitors. By Mary, but I will clapperclaw him!"

"Tush, tush!" said Bacon impatiently.

"Cuthbert is commonly faithful and decorous, and needs patience and kind treatment in his oddities rather than the discipline of your rude fist. Good Doctor Malatesti, I pray you be seated. Are you newly from Italy?"

The Paduan, with the mien of some dark emperor, seated himself in Bacon's chair, and, drawing his long rapier from its sheath under his robe, laid it, as if for convenience, on the oaken table.

"I am but just landed at St. Botolph's wharf," he said, "and am newly from Italy."

"Where lodge you during your sojourn with us?" asked Bacon.

"In the air," was the strange answer.

A feeling that the Paduan was indeed mad flitted through the mind of the friar; but, controlling his uneasiness, he affected to perceive nothing singular in his reply.

"You will be pleased to know, good frères," continued the Italian, – "you who are so given to dabbling in public matters, – that your antichrist, my beloved Pope Innocent, lies at the point of death. You start! Nay, even popes must die, – though fortunately the apostolic succession is secure. Fortunately, I say, for, whatever you may think, such pontiffs are necessary as blocks to the fast and far going wheels of your De Montforts and Grostetes, who would fain roll the world on a track which would ill suit my political philosophy."

"Nay, good doctor," said Bacon, hastily interposing to prevent the explosion of English wrath which suddenly fermented in the sturdy heart of Bungy and flushed his large face, at the taunting speech of the visitor, "let us not bandy politics. Let us rather hold discourse on matters of science, in which you are a rare adept."

"My good Frère Bungy is, after the manner of the thirteenth century, a patriot," pursued the Paduan, with a strange laugh, evidently paying no attention to Bacon, "Ay, but 't is my doctrine that churchmen should not meddle in matters of state. There must be neither religion nor morals in politics."

"Then were politics irreligious and immoral," said Bacon.

"'T is a doctrine worthy of the archfiend!" roared Bungy.

"Then't is a worthy doctrine," replied the Padnau, with a placid gravity of face strangely at variance with the devilish sneer of his voice.

Bacon warned Bungy with a look to remain silent. There was an uneasy dread in his heart at the aspect and manner of the Doctor Malatesti, which was heightened by the wild quality of his voice. The tones were grave, yet intensely shrill. Their shrillness was in itself startling and unearthly, and bore, moreover, a fearful incongruity with the still, mesmeric light of his eyes, the calmness of his enormous brow, the solemn, scornful power and mournful beauty of his whole countenance. The laugh, too, with which he had commenced a former remark was singularly unhuman. While it resembled in sound a piercing peal of mirth there was yet no accompanying movement of the muscles of his face to denote any degree of humor. The voice alone had laughed; the face was cold and immobile as marble.

"To think," resumed the Italian, – "to think of such a fat frockling as you, Bungy, reforming what you call the abuses of the realm! 'T is marvelous. Reform! Can you reform yourself? Remake, if you can, what sire and mother and the life of man made you. Go to, go to! I bid you despair. Preach roses and live nightshade. 'T is the fashion and the fate of man."

"I know not what preaching roses and living nightshade may be," said Bungy angrily, "but I do know –"

"Preach against gluttony and wine bibbing, and practice both continually," interrupted the Paduan.

"By my dame," retorted the fat friar, "but this passes! Thou saucy doctor, know this, – that happy is that friar who can get a taste at odd seasons of stockfish and ale! Meantime, bread of the coarsest and water of the well are the Franciscan's food and drink. Mine is scanty enow, by St. Swithin!"

"Oh, oh!" said the Paduan. "Hear him swear, and by that pig of a Saxon saint! Resolve me this, freckling, – what did you dine on today?"

"A wooden table!" shouted the friar.

"Ay, truly, frockling; and what was on the table?" demanded the other.

"Barley crusts and pure water," answered Bungy stoutly, yet with a shade of meekness in his tone.

"Ay, truly," sneered Malatesti. "Your cousin the vintner hath a fashion of garnishing his board with barley crusts and water. Yet own the dinner you made off the better part of a calvered salmon, the pullet sauced with butter and barberries, the forcemeat balls, and the marrow pudding. Rare eating, Frère Bungy."

Bungy's face resumed its former yellow tinge of dismay. His fellow-friar, with a single glance at him, saw that the Paduan's account of the repast was the true one; and at this proof of what might be termed in our age clairvoyant power, and which was another evidence of those strange sorts of knowledge he had ascribed to Malatesti, a cold fear crept through Bacon's soul that the latter might, by the same mysterious faculty, divine the secret of the android. Or was the Paduan no more than some mad charlatan, aiming to confound them with knowledge he might possibly have gathered at the vintner's door or window?

"Rare eating, Frère Bungy," Malatesti continued. "And what of the drinking? What of the nine-hooped pot of mead you guzzled, and the spiced wine? Oh, see now!" and with one circular motion of his arm the rapier swept up in his grasp from the table, and down upon the huge breast of the corpulent frère. The flask was pierced, and Bungy's frock suddenly showed a widening moisture.

"It is my blood!" he roared, starting to his feet. Singularly enough, his first thought, no less than the alarmed Bacon's, was that he had received a wound.

"Yes," said the Paduan, whose rapier had already returned to the table, "your blood! See it! Smell it!" In fact, the wine at that moment was splashing on the floor, and its spicy fumes were diffused upon the air of the chamber.

"I am he that degrades," said Malatesti in his awful voice, with his still eyes fixed upon the pallid visage of Bacon.

Bungy, shuddering through all his bulk, his healthy face grown flabby and livid, and his lips white in his gray beard, tremblingly drew the flask from his bosom, and, turning it so that the wine ceased to flow from the puncture, helplessly sat down, gazing at it, with a hoarse groan.

"It is wine I got for a poor widow," he snuffled presently, with a forlorn effort to maintain his self-respect.

"Hear him lie," said the Paduan, with an intonation of withering scorn.

Bacon remained silent.

"I am the apostle of despair," pursued Malatesti, his eyes still fixed upon Bacon's countenance. "I strip away the mask and show the man. Labor, labor to build the perfect realm; but the realm is made of men, and men are unchangeably bestial at the core. Wolf and snake, hog and harpy, are inextricably mixed in man, and virtue is nothing but a covering lie, itself the foulest vice of all. Despair, I say, despair! In this stripped friar behold the type of your De Montforts, your Grostetes, your saints and patriots, as they are within. Look to their secret hearts, their hidden lives: there hides the brute half of the centaur, man. Fair and white is the skin, but under the breastbone the hell-pool rages. Oh, may it rage forever! Cheer, Bungy, cheer! The rest are like you."

"Doctor Malatesti" – said Bacon.

"Hear me," interrupted the Paduan. "Men are a base mixture, for flesh and soul agree not. But wise and great is the soul. Provide, then, to build the perfect realm by peopling the earth with souls. For what saith the schoolman? 'The soul is not man,' he saith; 'would it be man if joined to a body of brass?' No, 't would be then the pure soul. Ay, and then 't would tell you how souls may people earth without these ruining bodies of flesh. It cannot tell you till it be shrined in some form which will permit it voice. It cannot tell you in the evil form of flesh, whose quality and motions suspend its spiritual knowledge. But in a form of brass it can tell you. Ay, you, a man, instructed by a soul shrined in an android, can then accomplish the conditions which will render it possible for souls to descend to earth and achieve all things, undarkened in their knowledge by this form of clay. Never from man can you thus be instructed. The soul is metamorphosed in man. Soul and the elements of flesh conjoined make man, the base, the vile, the brutal, the foolish and unchangeable reprobate."

"Doctor Malatesti," said Bacon sternly, "be done with this, I pray you. For these wild and bitter thoughts I care not, but your conduct –"

A crash of thunder broke his speech, and in the momentary confusion of his vision the imperial figure of the Paduan seemed to loom up darkly before him in the sheeting flame which lit the room as from a gulf below. The next instant, amidst the receding reverberations and the rushing of the rain, he saw that the man had risen to his feet, and was standing motionless in the gloom, the naphthaline light motionless in his eyes, his mournful features passionless and cold in the shadow which rested upon them, and the impression of ghastly decrepitude in his presence seeming stronger now than before, though, as before, unreferable to any trait of his form. The brave-hearted friar, though conscious that he was wrought upon by the weird illusions of the moment, felt their fullest power, and his soul quailed. Bungy, for his part, sat stupidly staring, utterly bewildered by what had passed.

"I am growing old," said the Paduan, in slow, wailing tones. "Long has been my term of haughty youth, – long, long, oh, long, – and men have been as I have wished them to be. Arts, laws, thoughts, religions, all I have withstood, nor have they shaken my empire. But the new spirit that rejects the dreams of the mind, and tracks effects to their causes in nature, and will make its highest ideals effects by its knowledge of causes, – it is born, it is born, and I am growing old!"

At these strange words Bacon shuddered vaguely, and a dark, mysterious, confused impression glimmered within him, as if not the Paduan, but another, had spoken. An utter suspension of all sound save that of the storm succeeded.

"It is well," said Malatesti, startling the silence with his piercing voice, and reviving the impression in Bacon's mind that the former speech had been uttered by another. "You would say, Frère Bacon, that I have dealt unmannerly. Be it granted; as ye are both Christian men, good frères, forgive me under the supreme law of charity. Say no more. How fares the android? See, I have taken such interest in your work that I have myself fashioned you the tongue."

Bacon recoiled aghast as the Paduan held toward him a model in gold of the human tongue, which he had taken from under his robe.

"The anatomia of this is perfect," pursued the unmoved Malatesti, "but it must be filled with a molten composition of mercury, brass dust, and sulphur, the proportions of which I will show you. It will then be ready for fusion with the head. Come, let us visit your laboratory."

Bungy started up abjectly at this imperative invitation, and moved to the door with the Paduan. Unable to interpose, unable even to think. Bacon followed, with his brain in a whirl. Through a door on the opposite side of the passage-way the trio entered the sleeping-room of the friars, an apartment similar in all respects to that they had left, save that its only furniture was a couple of chairs and two pallets spread upon the floor. A small iron effigy of St. Francis stood in a niche in the wall. Grasping his figure with both hands, Bungy drew it toward him. As if by magic, a portion of the oaken wainscot suddenly receded inward, revealing a dark vault, from which floated a strong aromatic perfume. A moment, and Bungy had lighted a torch within. Then, descending three stone steps, the others stood in the laboratory, and the gigantic friar, seizing an effigy similar to the other on the hither side of the wall, drew it toward him, and the wainscot closed behind them.

The flaring torch, projecting from a socket in the wall, dimly lit up the cavernous gloom of the vault, and threw a ruddy, glimmering light on its grotesque mechanical and chemical furniture. Huddled and distorted black shadows, like a herd of monstrous phantoms, continually moved and flickered on the floor and walls, with the flapping and wavering of the flambeau. At one side of the apartment was the forge, a raised reredos, having somewhat the shape of an altar, on which smouldered a dull fire of coals; and near it stood an anvil, with hammers, smelting-pots, crucibles, and other implements of the foundry strewn about. In the remoter part of the large space were rough tables covered with jars and flasks of stone and metal, glass retorts and alembics, in which trembled divers-colored liquids, and the various utensils of chemistry, together with a multitude of objects too numerous for a brief inventory. Around rose the rough walls, built of blocks of stone, and begrimed with the smoke of all the fires that had burned on the reredos for perhaps a century. The form of the vault was an oblong square. Its windows were closely shuttered, and the high, raftered ceiling, shrouded thick with shadow, would have been altogether undiscernible save for a small circular opening in a corner of the roof, called in the language of the time a louver, which served as an outlet for the smoke, as also for ventilation, though it hardly admitted a ray from the clouded sky beyond.

Presently a stranger object than any lent the place a new interest. Pushed forward by Bungy from a shadowed recess into the centre of the vault, and apparently rolling upon hidden casters, emerged a large square black pedestal, on which stood a shrouded form. In a moment Bungy had removed the covering and disclosed a large bust of brass, truncated above the elbows. The friar lit two cuneiform candles of yellow wax, which he placed upon the front corners of the pedestal, on either side of the image. Their quiet radiance rested strangely on the burnished android, whose metal features seemed to survey the group with a steadfast and awful stare. In remembrance of Malatesti, who had first suggested its formation, Bacon had moulded the face into a counterpart of the Italian's terrible and demoniac beauty, and the flowing locks of metal, which covered the head and fell to the shoulders, were no less an imitation of the curling coal-black tresses of Malatesti. But though undesigned, there was in the expression of the android a still more startling resemblance; for the lips had been made partly open, and this, added to the stare of the blind, ball-less, awful eyes under the enormous brow, gave to the bright and terrible features an expression of living and terrific despair. It was a fearful intensification of the look which was secret and shadowed in the mournful face of the Paduan, but it was like a revelation of the true expression of his soul.

He had seated himself at ease in an oaken chair before the image, and his eyes were fixed upon it. No sound murmured upon the sombre silence of the vault, save the aerial and distant rushing of the river of rain. The quiet light of the tapers shed a weird radiance upon his vast and melancholy brow, and served to deepen his expression of solemn and mournful scorn. Silently watching him, at some distance apart, stood the two friars; but the flaring torch, flashing and falling on their shadowy features, threw no ray of its struggling light upon him. He seemed to sit alone, enveloped in a supernatural, still splendor, rich and dim, stately and strange, from demon brow to taloned foot, in that great orb of wizard bloom; the android, a form of solid brightness, like an enchanted head of brassy flame, before him, and all endowed with the surrounding blackness. Only once, when a hissing jet spired from the resinous substance of the flambeau, and penetrated the magic sphere of light in which he sat, Bacon saw a shadow-play pass over his marble features, appearing to wreathe them into a dark and evil smile, and at the same moment that smile appeared to be mimicked by the image. An instant after, and his features like those of the brazen bust, wore their usual immobility; but it was hard for the pallid friar to withstand the distempered fancy that a demoniac signal had passed between the twain. A vague sense of horror and alarm rose struggling for a moment in his soul, then sank down and was lost in spiritual gloom.

The silence of the vault was at last broken by the shrill laugh of the Paduan; and as he rose to his feet the flames of the torch and tapers licked downward, and the huddled lights and shadows of the place swayed and reeled in phantasmal commotion. Bacon glanced hurriedly at the louver, with a thought of the entering gust, and as his eyes rested again upon Malatesti the lights and shadows were still.

"Ye have wrought well, my masters!" cried the Italian. "Ye have wrought skillfully and well. Now hark to my directions, for, disobeyed, the spirit will not enter."

"The spirit, sweet Paduan?" faltered Bungy, visibly quailing.

"Spoke I not plainly?" said Malatesti, with withering hauteur. "Hear me. Within three days from the completion of your work the spirit will enter, and the android will speak. I shall be here, and in my presence you shall own, Frère Bacon, as I told you a year ago, that this work is not a delusion, but subject to the proof of experiment, which you so insist upon. But mark, great frères: ye must not sleep, but sit and listen till ye hear its first command, which must be at once obeyed. Failing of this, the spirit will rend the metal and flee from it forever. Long and sore will be your vigil, but great its reward. Now hearken to the nature of the composition ye must add to the android. But first take the image asunder, and let me view the interior."

Bungy shuddered, but, like one subdued to the will of the Paduan, made a step forward to obey, when Bacon stopped him by laying his hand on his arm.

"Abide here," he said, with solemn compassion, "and pray, Frere Thomas, pray fervently for this disordered soul."

Bungy stared wildly at him, but Bacon, without pausing, advanced, pale and calm, with slow and steady steps, till he stood in front of the Paduan.

"Doctor Malatesti" – said he, with sad solemnity.

"Enough!" interrupted the Paduan, his features cold and passionless, but his voice a furious shriek that froze the friar's veins – "enough, I say! The android is without an organism. I knew it from the first. You have disobeyed me."

He strode away with haughty majesty toward the concealed entrance, and Bungy hurried obsequiously to the iron effigy. As the wall yawned asunder, the Paduan turned and bowed low, with his extravagant and almost mocking courtesy.

"Pray the black paternoster," said he. "I go."

"Farewell," said Bacon sadly.

"Farewell, sweet Paduan," added Bungy timorously, though in a stentorian voice. "May St. Francis the blessed attend you!"

"St. Satan attend ye both," replied the Italian, with another low obeisance.

"Blaspheme not, Doctor Malatesti!" cried Bacon sternly.

Malatesti made no answer, but, turning toward the entrance, waved his arms. A distant cry was heard, and in a moment Cuthbert was seen darting through the gray gloom of the outer chamber, shivering and gibbering, with the plumed cap and rapier in his hand. Malatesti advanced upon him as he came forward, and the idiot at once receded. Bacon, following, saw him move along the corridor in front of the Italian, till the portal was gained and opened, when the latter snatched his cap and sword and vanished into the storm, and Cuthbert, closing and bolting the door, stood still, with his back against it.

Bacon shuddered, but a great load seemed to lift from his spirit, and a blissful sense of relief succeeded.

"Cuthbert," said he after a pause, "come here."

The idiot came at once, with his darting, zig-zag motion, and his face wore its usual stolid and odden expression.

"Cuthbert," said the friar, "stay in the sleeping-room, and open that portal to no one. Dost understand?"

"Haw," answered the idiot, in his weak, dissonant voice, "I understand. Shall Cuthbert unbar o Zernebock?"

Bacon understood at once that by the name of the Saxon fiend the idiot meant to designate he Paduan.

"Unbar to no one," he said, gently but sternly.

He entered the chamber of audience, and, taking from the cupboard a large drinking-horn, poured into it the remaining contents of the punctured flask, which Bungy had left upon the settle, and returned to the laboratory. The burly friar was standing in the flare of the flambeau, with his massive features pallid and bathed in a cold sweat.

"Frère Thomas," said Bacon kindly, "I judge not men by their infirmities. Drink this; it will do you good."

Bungy, much agitated, took the wine, but, without drinking, gazed fixedly at Bacon.

"Roger," said he tremulously, "I misdoubt me that this Paduan be other than he seems. How knew he of my cousin the vintner, and of my dinner, and of the flask under my frock, and he but newly landed at St. Botolph's wharf?"

"Tush!" cried Bacon. "Vex not your mind with idle fancies. How know you that he spake truly when he said he was but newly landed? How know you that he pieced not together his knowledge by seeing you at dinner through the vintner's window, and noting, as a conjurer of quick sight may, what was on the table, and further by inquiry as to the vintner's relation to you?"

"That is true, by Dubric!" said Bungy, with an air of great wonder, showing immediate tokens of recovery from his affrighted condition. "It is also true that, the day being warm, the window was open, and my cousin's dinner was laid in the room on the ground floor. Moreover, the vintner rose once from table, misdoubting that some one was spying us from one side of the window, though he found no one there."

"Truly the Paduan might have been there, and withdrawn at the vintner's coming," Bacon went on, half believing that this was the solution of the mystery. "Then, too, he might have noted the shape of the flask through your frock, as he sat before you. For the rest, his sorcerer's face and aspect, his wild voice and evil talk, and the gloom of the day oppressed our spirits, and compelled them, as it were, to superstitious fancies. I trust he will visit us no more. Much learning, I fear, hath made him mad, and perchance he hath a madman's cunning. Let him pass. I mourn for him. Drink, Thomas, drink. The wine will comfort you."

The color had already returned to Bungy's face, and without more ado he tossed off the liquor, and with a sigh of satisfaction smacked his lips.

"It is well spoken, Roger," he said sturdily. "By my dame, I have been fooled rarely by this Paduan, and if he comes hither again I will take the hot tongs of St. Dunstan to him! Certes, he is a godless one, and speaks more like a follower of Mahound than a Christian. I have oft heard of the impious and unbelieving disposition of these Italian doctors of science, and he is one of them."

A flash of lightning suddenly lit the sky beyond the louver, followed by a hoarse roar of thunder. The friars stood mute, with their faces turned toward the android, which, with its rigid lips apart and its staring eyes set upon vacancy, seemed to listen to the long reverberations.

"'T is a fearful day," Bungy muttered, as the silence again descended, broken only by the noise of the rain.

"Ay," responded Bacon, starting from his attentive attitude. "Thomas, I am sorry the Paduan saw the android. It should not have been. But at that moment I could not interpose, and – no matter; it is beyond help now. Come, let me show you the passage whereof I spoke."

Going to the opposite wall, he raised a step-ladder against it, while Bungy, having closed the entrance, on the other side, took the torch from its socket and followed him.

"Come up the ladder," said Bacon, who was already within two steps of the top.

The ladder was very broad, and Bungy, ascending as he was bidden, stood by the other friar's side.

"See you anything unusual in the wall to your right?" asked Bacon.

Bungy moved the flambeau over the surface of the rough, smoke-begrimed stones, irregular in form, but, save that the mortar had fallen out from the narrow and jagged interstices where the blocks joined, as is common in old walls, he saw nothing remarkable, and said so.

"But note this," said Bacon, directing his attention to a small rough block directly in front of him.

"Well," replied Bungy after a long pause, "I note a stone. What of it?"

Bacon rapped it with his knuckles. To Bungy's great amazement, the stone gave back the sound of wood. He rapped the block next to it, but that was really a stone, and so were the others immediately around it.

"Now mark," said Bacon.

He pressed with both hands and with considerable force on the block. It sank inward about four inches.

"Swithin! but that is curious," said Bungy, staring at the little cavity thus formed.

"Ay, but look to your right," said Bacon.

Bungy looked, and nearly fell off the ladder with the start he gave upon seeing that a heavy door, with irregularly serrated edges, cut so as to resemble, when shut, the jagged joining of the stones, had opened outward on his right from the wall. Staring into the considerable cavity it had disclosed, he noticed, by the light of the torch, an upright iron rod fixed at a short distance from the side wall on the extreme right, and supporting in sockets three staples at regular intervals, which were attached to the door, and served it as hinges. The door had but partially unclosed, and Bungy, putting out his hand, shut it to again. At once the sunken block by which it had been opened resumed its former position, and the wall its usual appearance. Full of wonder, the burly friar felt the door with his hand. It was made of oak, its surface tooled into semblance of the ashlar-work around it, the imitation further heightened by paint, and increased by the stain and smoke of time. Bungy looked at it speechlessly, and while he looked Bacon pressed the block, and it noiselessly unclosed again.

"Now get inside," whispered Bacon; "but speak not, or Master Trenchard may hear you."

Bungy pushed back the door, and stepped into the opening, followed by the other. The secret of the block was then apparent. In a hollow on the left a thick crescent of wrought iron was fixed horizontally on a pivot, with the cusps outward. One cusp was attached to the block, which, when pressed inward, pushed out the other cusp against the door, and thus forced it to open. Closing the door, it pushed back the cusp, and restored the block to its former position. The wall itself was about three feet in thickness, and the space about four feet in width by six in height. The floor, though rough and serrated on its outer edges next the vault, was smooth with a layer of plaster for the rest of the distance up to the oaken wall of Master Trenchard's apartment.

Laying his finger upon his lip as a sign to Bungy to remain quiet, the friar stepped forward to the panel and listened. There was no sound within. Suddenly he remembered that the old silk merchant had told him that morning that he was to spend the day at a relative's, and he thought he might venture to unclose the panel.

Moving it very cautiously in its grooves till he had obtained a slight crevice, he peered in, and then listened again. There was evidently no one within, and at once he boldly slid back the panel, which moved noiselessly in the grooves he had previously oiled, and left in the wainscot a space of about four feet square. There was no one in the room, and the friars quietly stepped in through the opening, directly opposite which was the bed, with its overhanging tester, where the king would lie.

They approached it, and, gazing for a moment at the open square in the carven frame of the wainscot, looked at each other with exulting faces. A common thought was in their minds, – a vision of that dead silence of the night when the king, starting up in the bed behind them, should see before him the brazen android of his dream, bright-shining, mystic, terrible, and hear from its awful lips the counsel that should grave itself upon his memory, and shape his life to its latest day. Then let the curtaining darkness fall, the pallid king swoon back upon his pillow, the hearts that beat for England beat on with fuller pulses behind yon oaken shell; for the best voice of the suffering land has spoken, the soul of the tyrant is shaken to its centre, and the era of a new triumph bursts like sunrise upon the realm!

Hark to the howling of the storm. Sullenly burns the flambeau in this grisly gloom, where the light comes brown and dim through panes of horn, and the furniture, takes uncouth shapes that seem to watch, and shadows lurk in a silence that is too still, and yon square cave of blackness unnaturally yawns. Away, away! Softly over the floor strewn with rushes, which strangely rustle beneath the tread; softly and by stealth in at the panel, with chills and creepings of the blood; a moment behind it, with a dread sense of the still chamber it shuts from view; and out from the wall two pale-faced, gray-robed forms, flickered over with shadows from a tempestuous torch which flares redly on the grotesque gulf below. So down the ladder from the closed cavity, and into the vault again, where the yellow wedges of wax burn with a quiet sense of nightmare; and the awful android, staring between them with ball-less eyes and rigid lips apart, seems listening, in the hush of the black gloom, – listening, listening for something to come.

Hush, indeed! So deep a silence had fallen upon the place that it was as if sound other than the remote and muffled noises of the storm might never be heard again, – a silence by whose compelling charm the ghostly twain must mutely stand and listen, while the spectral herd of shadows quietly flit and flicker around them in the red tossing flame and smoke of the flambeau, and nothing else moves but the colored reflections of liquids in retorts and limbecs, dimly trembling in the murk beyond; till at last the spell yields, and the voice of the burly friar whispers upon the silence.

"A fear came over me, Roger, as I stood in that chamber."

Bacon looked at him for a moment without answering.

"I felt it, too," he said abruptly, in low tones. "But a day like this breeds fear."

"Ay, truly," responded Bungy. "'T is a gruesome day. Ha! Hear it!"

Through the louver the lightning shook bright and long, and the thunder broke like an ocean overhead.

"Come," said Bacon, as the reverberations died away, "let us to work, and make an end."

Hastily divesting himself of his gray frock, Bungy raked up the cinders of the forge and fanned them into a red glow, while Bacon, setting one of the wax tapers on a table which he had brought forward, placed next upon it a complex apparatus which he had taken from a closet near by. It was the articulating machinery of the android, and hitherto he had wrought upon it in the adjoining chamber, that he might be undisturbed in the severe thought necessary to its construction; while Bungy, with his genius for braziery, toiled at the casting of the shell, the moulds for which, however, the other friar had fashioned. In this age, when the experiments of Kempelen, Willis, and others have shown in detail the contrivances by which articulate sounds may be artificially produced, and when the exhibition of an android capable of uttering several sentences has completed the demonstration, it would be unnecessary and tiresome to describe the machine through whose agency Bacon aimed to subdue to England's welfare the will of the mean and forward king. It is sufficient to say that to the eye it presented the appearance of a complication of variously formed tubes of reed and metal, wheels, bellows, weights, and pulleys, leathern bladders, hammers, plates of brass, and, in the centre of all, a toothed cylinder, on which the speech of the android was scored. It was all but completed, needing only the modification of a single tube; and on this the friar, seated near the table, busied himself, unmoved by the increasing fury of the storm. Bungy, meanwhile, having taken the android from its pedestal and laid it on a cushion on the floor, was constantly moving between it and the forge with little crucibles of molten metal or red-hot tools, engaged in soldering a piece into its back.

The unearthly had become more than ever the soul of the scene. Bacon, sitting apart in his gray habit, with the mechanism before him, the quiet light of the taper on his pale brow and slender features, appeared like some sad-faced wizard; while the lubber friar, in his close-fitting undergarments of white cloth, seemed some strange, unwieldy demon toiling at his behest, in the dusky glow which radiated from the forge like a red and misty dome imbedded in surrounding gloom. The dark recesses of the vault, the uncouth furniture glimmering unsteadily, the distorted shadows reeling and wavering to and fro, the sombre lights of torch and forge up-flashing and sinking on the shaggy blackness of the walls, the seething of metal, the sighs and hisses of the foundry fire, the rushing and bellowing of the tempest without, – all lent the scene a wild and fearful interest. Never yet was plot for a nation's welfare conducted under more forbidding auspices, nor attended with darker omens. Bungy, indeed, thought little now of what had passed, but in the soul of his fellow-friar the strange visit of Malatesti had left a sense of evil augury. The day had suddenly become like night to him, and into that night had slid a brief but ominous dream; and as one waking from a dream, with the night around him, longs for the coming of the day, so, and with such an oppression on his heart, longed he for the morrow. But the morrow was still far away, and the hours dragged slowly by, with ever-rising wind and raging storm.

Steadily, meanwhile, and in silence proceeded the friars' labors. The time wore toward evening, and Bacon had finished his part, and was absorbed in gloomy reverie, when his fellow-worker stood before him, with his largo face flushed and his frock on.

"I am done, Roger," he said, drawing a long breath.

"And I," answered Bacon, his features lighting. "Now for the experiment."

He rose quickly from his seat, and, going to a distant corner of the vault, returned presently with a large sack of varnished silk, distended to its fullest capacity, with a heavy weight attached to one end of it, and a flexible tube of metal to the other.

"Ha!" said Bungy, jovially patting it, "here is our skin of inflammable air. Fire was his father and coal was his dame."

Modern nomenclature would designate the contents of the sack as carbureted hydrogen, or coal gas. Bungy had seen his scientific brother make it that morning. Without replying, Bacon opened the back of the pedestal and deposited the sack in the interior. The end of the metal tube attached to the sack was passed up through an orifice in the top of the pedestal, at its rear, and secured. The stopple was then taken from the tube, and over it was fitted another in the form of a curved rod, with a key at its lower extremity to regulate the passage of the gas, and at its upper a half circle of metal pierced for jets, and supported horizontally on its centre.

Presently the articulating machinery was fixed upon the pedestal, and the android was lifted from the floor and placed over it. A half hour was occupied in its proper adjustment, at the expiration of which all was ready. Bacon wound up the machinery by means of a key in the back of the image, turned on the gas a little way, and passed a taper over the half circle of metal which projected above the head. The lights were then removed, and in the dimness the awful front of the android was seen surmounted by a dotted arc of blue flame.

"We have it now," said Bacon, "as it will appear when erected behind the panel, just before unclosing. I will couch behind the pedestal to set all in motion. Do you stand by the panel, and when you hear a brazen sound you shall unclose."

He moved the spring in the back of the image which set the machine in operation, and then stooped from view behind the pedestal. A few seconds of breathless silence succeeded, in which Bungy, standing at some distance in front of the work, stared at it with his heart wildly throbbing. Suddenly a loud and hollow clang, like the sound of a blow on a brass timbrel, blared from the android.

"The panel uncloses," said Bacon in a sombre voice from behind the pedestal. "If the king wakes, he sees in the darkness a dim form under an arc of fire-dots. If he wakes not, he will soon."

There was a pause, and again the clang blared from the bosom of the android. Then arose a strain of solemn music, dulcet and wild and sad, the fire-dots slowly spired into dazzling jets of yellow flame, and the android stood out, awful-fronted, under that mystic coronal. Bacon appeared, pale as a spirit, from behind it, and came to Bungy's side.

"The king sees and hears it now," he whispered.

Bungy did not answer. His whole soul was absorbed in that vision of an enchanted head on its black pedestal, from whence the wild and solemn music was proceeding. The melody, winding on in mournful mazes, ravishing in sweetness, gradually swelled into a long aeolian wail, sad as the night wind wandering through the gulfs of air, funereal as the midnight voices of the pines; and, drooping from that sustained swell into a sweet and dying cadence, it merged with a heavy-sounding monotone, from which, attuned by that undercurrent of low, mysterious music into a strange harmony, a measured voice arose, hollow, distinct, and shrill.

"King of England, hear me."

The words, slowly chanted with a monotonous metallic resonance of tone, failed from the low murmur of music which still sounded on, and the petrifaction of living despair on the features of the resplendent android seemed to have changed to a look of austere and startled anger. A chill of dreadful pleasure curdled the friars' blood. The effect of the strange voice, added to the magical presence of the image, in the gloom of the vault was indescribably weird, and it was almost as if a supernatural intelligence had entered into the creature of their hands. Again the music swelled into a prolonged wail, and, sinking into a low dirge, again the voice spoke.

"I mourn for England. Hear me."

The dirge deepened, and, shuddering downward, ended in a sounding knell, and a sweet and solemn carol succeeded. Gradually diminishing in volume, it continued in a silver thread of melody, and again the voice.

"I counsel well. Hear me."

The continuing thread of melody rose to its full volume in the music of the carol, gradually melted into a golden and jubilant strain, and shook out proudly in notes of triumph. Increasing in movement, it changed to a stately dance, haughty, delirious, rejoicing, and lessening in tone till it became like the far-off sound of the dancers' feet dancing in joyous measure, when once more the voice was heard.

"Follow Sir Simon's leading! Obey me. Follow Sir Simon's leading! Obey me."

A sepulchral blare of brazen sound boomed hollowly at the conclusion of each sentence, and the music died. Bacon sprang to the key of the gas-tube; the coronal of flame went out, and the android stood obscurely shining from the dusky gloom.

"It ends here!" cried the friar, returning to his comrade with a step of victory, his usually colorless, calm face convulsed and crimson with excitement. "As the last clang sounds, the lights go out, the panel closes in darkness, and the king has seen his vision!"

"Ay!" roared Bungy, flinging his arms around the speaker with furious joy, and bursting away to bestow a similar hug upon the android. "Oh, brave andrew! Oh, brave Roger! Oh, day of grace! And, thou, Harry of Winchester, – for I do *thou* thee, and *thee-thou* thee, thou varlet king! – thou shalt see thy andrew, thou spendthrift, and mark it well, thou thief; ay, and hear its counsel, thou bloodsucker, and abide by it, thou Jew! By St. Thomas à Becket, I do hope it may leave gray locks on thy pate, thou charter-breaking, coffer-draining Lombardy robber! 'Follow Sir Simon. Follow Sir Simon.' Well said, my brave singing andrew! Oh, rejoice. Sir Simon, rejoice, protector of Englishmen, – rejoice, rejoice, for, by Dunstan, you are good as king from this hour!"

And Bungy, ceasing from the mad gesticulations with which he had accomplished this triumphant ebullition, only delayed to whip up his frock and fall a-prancing like a joyful hippopotamus. Up and down, to and fro, unheeding the raging war of lightning and thunder, wind and rain, which swept and bellowed around the dwelling, the paunchy friar went capering bulkily, his big legs swinging, and his big feet flapping here and there and everywhere, in the exulting fury of his ponderous evolutions, till, stopping as he did in a minute or so, he threw back his head, and, walking hither and thither with tremendous strides, proceeded to roar forth in a stentorian voice a Latin psalm.

Bacon, meanwhile, resuming his usual composure, though he carried a victorious heart at the success of the trial, busied himself in removing the remains of the sack of gas from the pedestal, and taking off the illuminating crescent. He finished in a few minutes, and approached the uproarious friar.

"Thomas," said he.

Bungy stopped singing, and, advancing, laid his huge hands on Bacon's shoulders, and showed all his teeth in a jovial peal of laughter.

"You are merry, Thomas," said Bacon, with his austere and gentle smile.

"Merry?" shouted Bungy. "By Swithin, I am merry as a lark! Merry as a man should be who has helped save England!"

"And I," said Bacon, – "I feel a strange joy of spirit. All has gone well thus far. But hearken. We have now three days before us. The first thing tomorrow, we must make contrivance so that the panel can never be opened again after we have done with it."

"Well bethought," returned Bungy; "for the king might send his carpenters to see if there be a passage there."

"He might," said Bacon, "though I have small fear of his doubting the supernature of the android. He is much given to superstition, and his strange dream will confirm that bent of mind. Still, let us omit nothing for safety. We must make ready to close the panel, and also build up the cavity. The stones for that purpose are those I have provided in yonder corner."

"You think of everything, Roger," said Bungy, with an admiring sigh.

"Then," pursued Bacon, "immediately after the king has seen it, the android must be removed, and buried in the pit we have dug under the floor. And so our task will end."

"And I shall go chuckle to see Sir Simon schooling the king," snuffled Bungy, shaking like a jelly with suppressed mirth. "Sooth, but I ought to be made a bishop for this."

Bacon smiled, and, going to the wall near the forge, took the flambeau from its socket, and returned.

"Lord! 't is fearsome foul weather," muttered Bungy. "Hark to that."

A tremendous explosion of thunder was sounding overhead, and as it echoed away there was flash upon flash of lightning, with the cataract pouring of rain and howling of wind.

"How the andrew seems to hearken!" continued Bungy, staring at the image, which now appeared, in the red light, of the flambeau, with its whole mute front as if intent on listening.

"I have noted several times this day that hearkening look on its brass visage, which is too much like that Paduan's to be lovely. Sooth, too, I bethink me now that its voice is like his, also, were he to speak with accompaniment of music. That is curious, by Francis! And how it hearkens! As if –"

"Come," said Bacon, "cover the android, and wheel it back into the recess."

Bungy was about to obey, when a sharp cry from Cuthbert was heard in the outer chamber. Both friars started, and Bacon nearly dropped the torch. The next instant the wainscot yawned open, and the idiot sprang in. He was in the very ecstasy of terror, his sodden face writhing, and great tears starting from his wild bloodshot eyes; and as he danced about, in his close-fitting garb of red, mopping and mowing in the light of the flambeau, with his thin misshapen limbs jerking like those of a puppet, and his shock of yellow hair tossing from the huge head set low between his hunched shoulders, he looked like one of those Libyan anthropophagi described so vividly by Herodotus. But his anguish had nothing of the monster; it was painfully human.

"Cuthbert, Cuthbert!" cried Bacon, starting forward with the torch, while Bungy stared, open-mouthed. "Peace, boy, peace! What is it?"

"Oh, my lord," shrieked Cuthbert, "time is, time was, time is passed, and he comes, – haw, haw! – and he comes, and I feel him, and he comes –"

"What ails thee, thou reprobate?" shouted Bungy. "Hath the fiend possession of thee?"

"Ay, the fiend, – ay, the fiend!" screamed the idiot; "and he comes, the Brass-Man, Zernebock, the Brass-Man, Zernebock, – he comes, and I feel him, in my head, in my breast, in my skinny right wing – coming, coming, coming, coming!"

And suddenly, with his yellow hair swirling from his head like a garment, he spun with great velocity on one foot, and springing, with the impetus of his rapid whirl, through the open wall, vanished.

Both friars stood like statues of horror. At that moment the tempest again broke in heavy rebounding roars, and amidst the howling and rushing of wind and rain they heard the unbarring of the portal and the keen cry of Cuthbert. Bacon was like one smitten with palsy, but an icy chill passed through his frame as he heard that cry.

"It is the Paduan!" he gasped. "Quick – away with the android – arrest him – he must not enter here!"

"I will strangle him!" roared Bungy, purpling with rage, as he rushed to the entrance.

At the top of the three stone steps appeared the dark figure of Malatesti, and Bungy, plunging against him, reeled back tottering into the vault, as though he had hurled himself against an iron statue; while the Paduan, without a pause, like one who had not felt the shock of the friar's onset, made but one step of the stairs, and coming with straight, swift strides, planting his taloned feet noiselessly but firmly, directly toward Bacon, paused at a short distance in front of him. His movement, though swift, had a certain measured and majestic cadence, and his features were locked in their usual cold, impassive, marble scorn. The black robe drooped with heavy patrician grace around him; the strange black cap was on his head; the sable plume trailed across his mournful brow; the red jewel which held it burned still in the torchlight like an evil eye. But not on plume or garment, nor on his ebon mane of falling hair, nor anywhere, about him from head to sole, was there one trace of rain; not one sign of the wind that was roaring like a whirlpool in its tempestuous sweep around the dwelling; not one token of the flood that was deluging the streets of London amidst bolted thunder and sheeting fire! Nothing in his presence, at such a time as this, could have been so awful.

As he stood before Bacon, dark and grand, regarding him with still eyes, the pallid friar let the flambeau droop slowly in his nerveless hand, and in that lurid ray upstreaming as from the pit, and upcasting black shades where the lights were before, all things became hideous and unnatural. The friars were as gray ghouls topped with demonic skulls of white and ebony; the phantom majesty of Malatesti wore a black-dappled livid mask of Death; the android was a brazen demon, cavernous-eyed, bizarre with shadows, and with a look of horror and hellish joy commingled on its glaring features; and all around black mongrel shapes of shade sloped up the floor, or loomed monstrously on the shaggy gloom of the walls. While heaven and earth seemed reeling from their centres in the tornado madness of the storm, the vault was a core of silence.

A moment, and the silence was broken by the Paduan.

"You have dared to disobey me!" he said, his voice piercing that face of marble. "Behold!"

He stretched out his hand toward Bacon, and in the open palm lay the tongue of gold. A cold disgust mingled with the affright of the friar as he gazed upon it. Suddenly the Italian dashed the tongue to the floor, and it blew to atoms. Bacon recoiled at the explosion, and Bungy dropped on his knees, frantic with fear, and began to gibber his prayers.

"I am the Lord of disaster," shrilled the Paduan. "Thus shall it be with you android. I bade you fashion it in the interior likeness of the body, that Simara, the wise daemon, might dwell in it. You have disobeyed me. Simara shall rend it."

"Vile charlatan!" shrieked Bacon, starting forward, and menacing Malatesti with the flambeau. "Hence, or I dash this torch into your face! Think you to cow me with your jugglery? Am I to be deluded by your fool's talk of daemons and brass anatomy? Hence, madman or knave, or both, – hence, I say! Up, Bungy, up, and cast me this wretch from the door!"

Bungy did not seem to hear, but in a lunacy of terror continued to gibber his prayers. The Paduan laughed. For a moment Bacon stood irresolute, choking with exasperation; then, rushing past Malatesti to the entrance, he thrust the flambeau into a socket there, and returned.

"You have terrified my poor co-laborer from his manhood, but you terrify not me," he said fiercely. "Now go from hence, or I set upon you."

"Know you Master Trenchard?" asked the Paduan, with a cold and quiet countenance.

Bacon fell away a pace, and gazed at him. Thought and passion in an instant gave place in his mind to a whirling vacancy.

"The king is to lodge with him," the Paduan continued.

A terrible agitation flowed in upon the mind of the friar, but he controlled himself to appear calm. His first thought was that Malatesti had divined the plot. Then came a doubt, born of the habit of a scientific intellect, instinctively skeptical and averse to rash conclusions. He might only have uttered, madman fashion, at random what some one in the neighborhood had told him, and it was not a necessary inference from his speech that he knew more. Yet this theory of it was half shattered in the mind of Bacon as the Paduan again laughed.

"I go," he said, stepping back a pace, his form ill shadow, and darkly defined against the light of the torch behind him. "Yet ere I go, listen. You disobeyed me because you doubted the truth I know for truth. Resolve me now the mystery of birth. Why forms and lives the infant in its mother's womb? It is because the soul has entered there. Why enter thus for birth the myriad generations of souls? Know you not the hunger of souls to be born? Know you not what well-attested histories and living men's experience affirm, – that in this hunger of souls for birth they will even possess the bodies of men wherein souls are already shrined, making them mad with the discord between the two; nay, more, that they will even enter chairs and tables, giving them motion and intelligence? And whence come these souls thus madly hungering to be shrined in earthly forms? Behold, the vasty deep of space is full of them. They float, they wait continually, – they wait for the conditions that will make their mortal birth possible; they dart to their opportunities for mortal being. Well said the divine Plato that the air is full of men. Ay, full of men hungering to be born."

He stepped back another pace, and while a heavy peal of thunder resounded over-head, and the lightning flashed fiercely beyond the louver, he mystically waved his hands.

"Pray the black paternoster. I go!" he said in his shrillest tones. "Yet hear me. The souls that enter bodies suffer thereby suspension of their spiritual knowledges and powers, which are mighty. The quality and motion of the fleshly form thus affect them, though the human shape hinders them not. Here, then, as I have said, is the virtue of brass androids. Their shape, external and internal, being human, attracts souls to enter them; and these being neither flesh nor motion, the mighty spiritual knowledges and powers of the souls suffer no diminutions. Lo! the mighty and wise daemon, Simon, obedient to me, would have entered yon android, and made you all-strong and all-wise with his power and wisdom. But you have disobeyed me. Ay, and you believe not in Simara. But you shall believe, and tremble."

Slowly raising his hand, he laid his forefinger on the opal in his cap.

"Aloft there, Simara!" he cried. "By the strong gem, answer me!"

There was an interval of breathless silence, and then from the darkness of the roof a thin, silvery voice sounded.

"I am here."

The effect was terrible. Bungy started from his knees with a hoarse yell, and staggering to the entrance fell down on the steps, where he remained, shuddering and gasping, with his ghastly face turned toward the ceiling. Bacon stood like one petrified, ice in his veins, fire in his brain.

"Descend, Simara!" cried the Paduan. "By the strong gem, obey me!"

A roar of thunder volleyed above the dwelling, and echoed away into rain-rushing silence.

"I am here," said the quiet silver voice, speaking from beside the android.

Bungy uttered a hoarse groan, but over the visage of his fellow-friar a flush crept slowly. The Paduan seemed to notice it, and his face grew dark, as if with passion, and his imperial form dilated to its fullest majesty.

"Enter the android, Sinuira!" he screamed, with appalling shrillness, stamping his foot, and waving his arm with the gesture of a king.

"I have obeyed you," said the voice, after a pause, speaking fiercely from within the android, as if in anger and agony. "But it pains me, and I cannot abide."

"Rend it, Simara!" shrieked Malatesti, with a furious and commanding gesture, swiftly receding, as he spoke, to the entrance of the chamber.

Bungy scrambled up as the Italian drew nigh him, and was crouching down against the opposite wall of the sleeping-room before the latter had set foot upon the steps.

"Hold, Malatesti!" shouted Bacon, dashing forward on the track of the flying Paduan. "Dost think me deluded by thy damned ventriloquy? Hold, I say!"

He caught up an implement of the forge which was lying near the steps, and bounded after the Itidian, who had already gained the corridor.

Reaching it himself, he saw him spring with an airward leap from the open portal, and vanish; and, aided by the sudden expansion of the black robe in the wind as he sprang, the horrid fancy flashed across Bacon's mind that he had changed into some black-winged monstrous thing and melted into the air. Passionately hating himself that such a fancy had entered his brain, even for a second, Bacon, without pausing, rushed after him. The rain was pouring in torrents through the gray twilight, as he leaped forth into the street. But at the first glance he saw that the street was empty. Malatesti had disappeared.

Entering the house again, and barring the door behind him, he returned swiftly to the sleeping-room, with the rain upon his face and garments. Bungy was still crouching against the wall, in the dim light from the reflection of the flambeau in the vault, and feebly turned toward him, as he came in, a face flabby and livid, whose eyes, orbed with terror, showed their pupils in white circles. Too agitated for the moment to heed him, Bacon stood silently, with his nostrils quivering in the pallid rigor of his countenance. Gradually his anger settled into composure; wiping the moisture from his face and head with his sleeve, he approached the entrance and, casting in upon the floor the forge implement, was just turning back again into the room, when there was a stunning crash, the vault filled with fire, and the building rocked to its foundations. Bacon staggered back, lost his balance and fell, reeled up again to his feet, all in an instant, and stood rigid, with a face of death, his brain tottering, and a dreadful feeling within him as though his very soul were rent asunder, and were rushing from his frame. An utter silence had succeeded that vast crash, through which was heard the pouring of the rain. The vibrating air was filled with a heavy sulphurous odor. Within the vault the flambeau was still burning, and the shadows were sullenly flickering in the ghostly gloom. Suddenly the friar sprang to the entrance, and gazed. One instant he gazed, and a horrible cry, like the shriek of a damned soul, pealed from his lips and shivered away into the tingling silence. There lay the android, shattered to fragments, on the floor!

* * *

He stood motionless. But with that cry the weight of agony lifted from his mind, and left it utterly dark and vacant. He saw nothing, he heard nothing; he had neither sensation nor consciousness. Complete annihilation had become his portion. Gradually a dim, remote sense that slow ages had passed, and that another was slowly passing, a vague, uncertain impression that he had died long, long ago, and had become something inessential, floated, a mere filmy spectre of mentality, through the gray void of his brain. Then succeeded a dim apprehension that something had crept stealthily to his side, and paused there, and he heard a hoarsely whispering voice speaking near him, yet seeming to come from an immeasurable distance.

"The fiend Simara hath rent it!"

He heard the words without receiving their sense, but, slowly turning his head, he became aware that he stood in the dark room, on the threshold of the lighted vault, and, looking down, saw Bungy resting on his hands and knees beside him, like some huge, gorbellied brute in the likeness of a man, glaring up into his face with a distorted flabby visage, a brow wrinkled beneath its tonsural band of hair, and an ugly disk of shaven crown. A frigid thrill stole through his frame. With a touch like that of ice on air, his chill hand rested on his giddy brow, and he tried to remember what had befallen. Consciousness uncongealed, slowly, slowly, and trickling in like an ice-brook, welled up cold, still, and clear within his mind. He remembered everything. Glacial, torpid, mournful, the mental images arose in a trance of despair. It was all over. The long, patient, fervid labors of a year; the thought, the hope, the dream, the patriot's zeal whose soul was woven into the work like solemn music; the victorious result already on the operant verge of victory; the whole superb conspiracy for justice rising robed and crowned, and reaching out its hands in blessing on the nation, – it had all become involved in the wild *bizarrerie* of tempest and gloom and omen, the shocks, the perturbations, the accursed apparitions, the fierce, unnatural concentrated life of the last few hours, and in one crash of flame it had shivered to nothingness. Rage on, king, whose sceptre is a wand of bane to England, thy lawless power unchecked, thy evil resolution unsubdued! Toil on, De Montfort, and vainly toil to blight and bar the ills that creep like grass, and wind like water everywhere! Bleed, bleeding people, and rave and madden under ever-piling accumulations of suffering, till ye rise and rive with the red blast of battle, and the realm topples from its basis, and cold tranquillity sinks down on ruin and the ghosts of things that were! For it is all over. The power that would have essayed to roll back fate is a power no longer. All is ended and done.

He turned, icy cold and trembling, and, with a dull lethargic ache in his spirit, feebly wandered into the room. Bungy had crept back to his former place, and was crouching down against the wall, looking at him.

"The fiend Simara hath rent it, I say!" he repeated.

Bacon saw him dimly with misty eyes, and, striving to understand what he said, his mind received only an inapposite sense that not more than a minute had elapsed since the catastrophe took place in the vault. He covered his eyes with his hand, and endeavored to collect himself.

"I say the fiend Simara hath rent it!" gasped Bungy, hoarsely as before, but in a voice which had risen from the whisper to a low muffled bass.

"Yes, yes, I understand," faltered Bacon, with the most confused apprehension of what the other was saying; "the lightning smote in at the louver, and –"

A sound of gnashing teeth made him pause and drop his hand from his eyes. With a vague tremor he saw that Bungy had risen to his feet, and was huddled against the wall, grinding his jaws, and glaring at him from the dimness with a look of sullen and truculent rage, on his livid visage.

This he saw, but in his bewilderment knew not what it meant, and stood helplessly gazing at the friar.

"Thou abominable sorcerer!" suddenly howled Bungy, plunging forward and clutching him by the throat. The shock of that assault brought Bacon to his senses, and, with an instantaneous revulsion of strength, he seized Bungy's wrists, wrenched away his hold, and flung him back to the wall.

"What means this?" he demanded in a low, intense voice, with his eyes burning and fixed upon the friar. Bungy did not answer, but stood drawing his breath hard through his set teeth. For a moment Bacon gazed at him; then, going into the vault, he returned with a torch, fixed it in a socket in the wall, and again confronted him.

"I had not looked for this from you, Thomas," he said sadly. "Why have you laid violent hands upon me?"

"Ach! Thomas! Thomas me no Thomases!" gnashed Bungy, frantically shaking his fists at him. "Thou vile sorcerer! Thou hast had commerce with the fiend! I know thee. I have smelt thee out."

"I commerce with the fiend? I, Thomas?"

"Ay, thou! Didst thou not tell me that he taught thee how to make the andrew? Didst thou not? Deny it if thou canst!"

"Frère Thomas, this is moon-madness. I pray you be a man, and hear reason. I never told you that a fiend taught me how to make the android."

"Thou didst! I say thou didst, and thou dist! In Italy thou dist learn it of him."

"In Italy? What! *He* the fiend? That mad scholar, sunken into the depths of knavery and insanity, that charlatan, that cheat, that –"

"Ay, brave it out! But well I know where all thy knowledges come from, – thy mathematics, thy burning-glasses, thy exploding powders, thy inflammable air, all thy devil's arts which thou didst persuade me were of nature, to the peril of my soul's salvation, and which thou didst learn of the fiend who walks the earth in the guise of a Paduan! Ay, and he taught thee to make the andrew, which may the blessed saints assoil me for having helped thee in, – St. Francis, St. Becket, St. Dunstan, St. Wittikind, St. Dubric, St. Thomas à Kent!"

"Peace, Thomas, peace! You rave, you scatter foam on your beard. Peace, I say! What madness is this? Did I not upbraid this mad Paduan to his face? Did I not refuse to do his bidding? Did I not speed after him with the iron in my hand, to make him return and un-mask his wretched cheatery? Did I not?"

"Did I not, did I not, did I not! Thou vile sorcerer, cease thy gibble-gabble! Ay, didst thou, and it was in thy pride thou didst refuse him, and flout him, and chase him; for thou, hadst learned all his secrets, and wouldst set up to be the match of the fiend himself! Tell me he was not the fiend! Hearken to the tempest.

And doth he not always come in tempest? Well I knew the fiend was abroad in the air this day, – ay, in the air, where he told thee he lodged; and thou saidst nothing, hoping it would escape my notice! Thou wretch! To deal thus with the soul of a Christian man, and a frère of the Lord's flock to boot! Ay, and did not the very room darken when he came in, and the door shut of itself, and the storm rage with thunder and lightning, and Cuthbert, with no more wit than a dog in him, know of his coming every time? Ay, and 't is well known that dogs know when the fiend is nigh, and tell it by their howlings."

Bugy gasped, overcome with the fury of his utterance, and Bacon felt an appalling sense of the difficulty of reasoning down this mass of evidence in the mind of the ignorant and obstinate being before him, whose whole superstitious nature had been roused into its fullest activity by the succession of weird coincidences, and by the aspect and actions of the Paduan. In that brief pause he called into review all that had been said and done for the last few hours, and saw that everything told against him. Yet he resolved to contend with everything.

"Hearken now to me, Thomas," he said solemnly, "for what I say to you is the truth, and I swear it by this cross."

He put his hand to his girdle to uplift the cross which hung at the end of his rosary. The rosary was not there.

"Ach!" yelled Biingy, "thou hast made a compact with the fiend, and he will not let thee wear the blessed cross, thou sorcerer! Ach, ach! fie upon thee, thou foul wretch!"

"'T is false!" cried Bacon in a pealing voice, recovering from the stunning blow dealt his cause by the absence of the rosary. "Forbear your craven epithets, – thrice craven when thus bestowed upon me in my hour of utter misery, when ruin has fallen upon the work I wrought for England! I swear by the blessed Saviour, whose name no sorcerer, if such there were, could take upon his lips, that what I say to you is true!"

Bungy was silent, for the indignant solemnity of this utterance touched him even then.

"Hear me now," sternly continued Bacon, following up his advantage. "I have never dealt with any fiend, nor is that evil Paduan a fiend, and this I swear by my soul's assurance of salvation."

A rattling bolt of thunder split the air as he spoke the last words, and Bungy started furiously.

"Ach, ach!" he yelled, shaking his fists, "a sorcerer's oath, – a sorcerer's oath! Thou swearest by thy soul's damnation, and truly it is assured, – truly it is!"

"I said 'salvation'!" cried Bacon.

"Thou liest! Thou saidst 'damnation' and I heard thee plainly. Thou meantest to say the other, but the fiend would not let thee. Ay, and 't was his thunder attested thy perjury theu –"

"Hear me, hear me, hear me! I said it not. I said –"

"Thou didst! Thou –"

"I did not!"

"Thou liest! Thou didst! And thou art in pact with the fiend!"

"Oh, hear me, hear me! He is not the fiend –"

"I say he is, and I do know it! Did I not see him no more than wave his arms, and Cuthbert came running with his cap and sword? Did I not –"

"And what of that? It was a marvel, but it has its cause in nature. Is it incredible that a man should have by nature the power to draw another man to him, when an ore of iron, as you know, has by nature the power to draw to it other iron? Hear me explain –"

"Explain! Thou ready-witted wretch! No, I will not hear thee. Thou wilt explain, too, that the fiend Simara rent not the andrew!"

It all rushed into Bacon's mind in an instant: the mandate of the Paduan to Simara; the almost immediate shivering of the brittle alloy of the image, as if in obedience to that mandate; and, beating down the half-risen superstition that a spirit had indeed wrought the ruin, the conviction that Malatesti had had prevision of the approaching catastrophe, and had turned it to his purposes. In an instant all this came upon him, and the next he firmly answered:

"Simara did not rend the android. It was the lightning. There was no Simara."

"Oh, thou liar! Did I not hear his voice?"

"No. 'T was the Paduan's voice. It was a trick, – a cunning ventriloquy."

"Ach, thou sorcering liar, – thou Simon Magus! And the gold tongue which burst fire and vanished, – thou wilt say that was ventrilly, or some such word of Mahound, wilt thou not?"

"I tell you it was nothing but a tongue of metal, which he had filled with a detonating powder."

"Powder, powder! Prate not to me of powders. They are all of the fiend, like thy nitre and coal powder. Face me out that he was not the fiend, and he coming in from the rain as dry as a basket!"

"He had been under shelter. He had been standing under the covered portal, beyond a doubt. He had –"

"He had, he had, he had! Cease thy damned gibble-gabble, thou ready-witted varlet!"

"Enough," said Bacon, with despairing sadness. "Say no more. I forgive you. All evil happenings are as nothing to this; even the ruin of the android is as nothing. Well may I mourn the hour when the Paduan came here, since his coming has wrenched from me you, whom I loved not for any parts or learning, but for the good heart, faithful and true to me through many, many years, nor ever joining till now in the reproaches and revilings others, greater than you, have cast upon me. But I blame you not, and I forgive you. I forgive, too, him who has thus wrought upon you. May –"

"My good heart!" roared Bungy, interrupting. "My good soul, I say! Think of that! My good soul's salvation imperiled by its beguilement into thy devil's trap of sorcery! Dost think I will stay loyal to thee when I am likely to be packed into hell for it? By Swithin, but I will not, then? Dost think –"

"Nay, Thomas, speak not now in your anger. Wait till the morning, when you can think more calmly of this."

"Wait till the morning! By all the saints, but I will not wait at all! I will at once go hence, for it perils my soul to abide even to upbraid thee!" and Bungy immediately tucked his skirts under his arms as preparation for instant departure.

"Hold, hold!" cried Bacon, clasping his hands in entreaty. "Go not now. The storm is terrible. Wait till it lulls; then go in peace. See, I will leave you alone. I will retire to another chamber."

"I will not abide another moment under the roof with thee!" furiously bellowed the friar. "I will go hence, and I will proclaim thee everywhere as a sorcerer who sought to lure me to my soul's ruin!"

"Hear me!" entreated Bacon. "You have sworn on the cross not to betray aught of this ruined enterprise."

"Ay, and I will keep my Christian oath for the love of England, whose weal has been brought to wrack by thee!" cried Bungy. "But I will go hence, and proclaim thee as one who has had commerce with the fiend in the guise of a Paduan. And I will –"

"Hear me, I beseech you, hear me! Good fibre, good Thomas, I pray you by the remembrance of all our years of peace, for De Montfort's sake, for England's sake, for the sake of –"

"Ach, thou viper, thou wretch, thou sorcerer, thou devil's commercer, thou abhorred, abominable, impious, unclean thing! Ach, fie upon thee, fie upon thee! and aroint thee, aroint thee! I renounce thee forever!"

He rushed from the room, gnashing his teeth, with a visage like that of a lubber fiend in his rage, and in a moment the outer door slammed heavily behind him. He was gone.

For an instant Bacon stood motionless; then all gave way, – the chamber whirled around him, he tottered backward, a mighty darkness reeled down upon him like an avalanche, and he fell on his pallet in a dead swoon.

Life rewakened, dreaming in the long ago. There was a sense that sleep had been deep and restful; an incorporeal lightness; a trance of coolness and quiet; fresh, still glimmerings; the world silently returning, peaceful and sweet and strange; the old heavenly innocence of childhood; the dewy early years at Ilchester; the tranquil, dark summer dawn. Bacon was lying in his bed, dimly awake, half conscious, as he lay with closed eyes, that his mother was bending over him, tender of the slumbers of her boy. A vague remembrance that he had dreamed she was long dead, mingling with the dim deliciousness of his love for her, melted into his luxury of repose, and, with a flitting sense of trouble, he sighed. His eyes were open, and his mind had gathered vacancy.

"Dost revive, Roger?"

It was broad day, and the morning sunlight lay aslant in the room. The words lingered, distinct and alien, in his tranced memory. Then he knew that he was lying on the pallet, and that a hooded friar was bending over him.

"Adam?"

"It is I," answered De Marisco, his voice sounding grave and kind from beneath his cowl.

As in a dream, Bacon felt himself raised to a half-recumbent position, with his head resting upon the friar's breast. A strong spicy cordial was held to his lips, and, drinking, he was revived. A few minutes passed in silence, and, lying with closed eyes, the memory of his waking vision faded, leaving him with the sad and world-worn heart of manhood, and the mournful remembrance of the dark events of yesterday in his clouded soul.

"Art better now, Roger?"

"I am better," he answered feebly.

How dim, remote, confused, was his sense of everything around him! It seemed as if he were tended by some kind phantom, whose voice and touch were the only things that linked it in identity with his friend. He hardly knew how, but he was sensible that time had passed, and that he had drank again, and was sitting in a chair, with a sort of weak strength and the feeling of distance and dimness in his mind. The phantom was sitting near him, and he felt a strong, kind hand clasping his own with friendly distinctness. Then the grave voice sounded clearly.

"What hath happened, Roger? The miscarriage of the work I know, for as I came hither I met Frère Bungy, who told me a graceless tale. I bade him go seal his fool's lips, or look to it. Tell me what hath befallen, brother."

That which had befallen rested separate and definite in Bacon's memory, and, with an utter introversion of his faculties, he mechanically related all. Ceasing, he had a strange, dazed consciousness that he had been speaking, and that the form near him had listened silently.

"We have failed, Roger," he heard him say. "I grieve that you have thus suffered. But the wild night is now passed, and today is new and fair. Be comforted, brother. Time repairs all ill happenings."

There was a brief interval of silence.

"For the present," resumed De Marisco, "all is done. I will aim to silence this Bungy. Yet, should he talk, inquiry and trouble may follow. You must stay only for food, and then at once away to Paris. Here is a gift of money Robert Grostete bade me deliver to you for the work. That is ended. Use the coin, then, for your departure. I will take charge of the house, and acquaint the bishop of what hath passed. He will make good your absence."

Bacon mechanically received the small leathern bag the other placed in his hand, and as he did so a keen, forlorn sense of sorrow welled up within him.

"Alas, alas," he said bitterly, "is this the end? To think that we have failed, and failed from such a circumstance! Had not the Paduan entered then, the work would have been shrouded and removed to the recess, where the lightning would not have rived it. Thus ever comes disaster. This dark fool, this charlatan, this mad ape of hell, he comes, he arrests our purposes for a few moments, and all is ruined. Oh, that the weightiest enterprises should be always subject to slight occasions! But it is ever so. Thus ever dies the good cause."

"Brother, the good cause never dies," said the grave voice.

"You are right," faltered Bacon, after a short interval. "I meant defeated."

"Brother, the good cause never is defeated."

Bacon bowed his head in silence. A thrill of strong comfort stole through the torpor of his veins; a trembling peace melted across his desolation as the dawn melts across a winter moor. Silently he clasped the hand in his, and the minutes mutely wore away.

"It is well," he said tremulously. "I will depart. Let me only gather up my few manuscripts, summon poor Cuthbert, and go. Poor Cuthbert, indeed! He was much terrified last eve, and needed comforting. How looked he, Adam, when he unbarred to you?"

He received no answer, but he felt the kind hand close with a tenderer pressure, and, looking up, he saw that the cowled head was bent low.

"Adam, what is it? Is not Cuthbert well?"

There was a solemn pause.

"Brother," said the grave voice gently, "he is well."

Bacon gazed at him for a moment; then his head drooped slowly, and he wept. A poor, uncomely, dog-witted thing, weakest of the weak, lowest of the low, but something that had loved him, something that was faithful to him, and with a dog's faithfulness and love.

"Is it thus with you, my poor servitor?" he sorrowfully murmured. "Rest, rest. T is better so. Ill can never come nigh you any more, nor fear strike away the life that was so harmless here. Adam, I pray you see that he has decent burial. He loved and served me better, for all his darkened wit, than men the world calls his betters. He had been my brother's thrall, but I took the collar from his neck, for I like not that any man, however weak of mind, should wear the collar of a slave. So give him a freeman's sepulture, the money for which I will leave with you."

"It shall be done," said De Marisco.

They rose. A little while Bacon stood, sadly musing, and a light of peace dawned upon his wasted features.

"It comes to me now," he said humbly and dreamfully. "I have sinned, and it is well the android lies shattered. To make a king believe in supernature were also to spread his belief throughout the realm, and not even to save the land from tyranny were it well to confirm it in superstition. That were to relieve it from a great evil to curse it with a greater. Better fail of good by truth than win it by falsehood."

"It may be so," returned De Marisco thoughtfully.

"It *is* so," said Bacon firmly. "Welcome all suffering, all loss, all disaster, for through them has my erring soul been schooled, and I have learned the lesson that will never leave me. Yes, it is so. Through Truth alone we truly conquer. Only Truth's victories are true."

A few hours later, and the great friar had left St. Botolph's wharf in a ship for Paris, where he wrote the Opus Majus, his undying claim to the gratitude of man. A few years later, and Simon De Montfort had drawn the unwilling king into an alliance by which a reluctant royal sanction was obtained for the measures which broadened justice and freedom throughout the land. Not such an alliance as the brazen android would have achieved, – immediate, desired by the monarch, and potential with his active will, – but one in which he was passive and frigid, and one obtained only after long delay, when the hostile faction, under Prince Edward's leading, had grown to a power that plunged the land in civil war, and sent the great earl's soul to God from the dark slaughter of Evesham. But De Montfort's death sealed the strife for the charter. In the mind of the people he stood crowned with the sainted hero's gloriole, an image of fiery inspiration for the principles he lived and died for, mightier thus in his death than in his life; and from that hour the liberties of England were secured. For the good cause never dies, and it is never defeated. Its defeats are but the recoils of the battering-ram from the wall that is fated to crash in; its deaths are like those of Italian story, where each man cloven in twain by the sword of the slayer springs up two men, mailed and armed to slay.

A Woman of One's Own

Chloie Piveral

THEY KEEP ME in the attic, for now. Every day at ten my telecounsel calls but all other communication is strictly limited. I'm not even to speak to myself. But I do.

What I believed to be my home has become my prison. The room where I'm kept has a bed, a chair near the window, and telepad where I'm expected to make my confession before they put me down.

With the weight of the baby pressing on my organs I am more aware now of these pieces and parts they have so carefully crafted to fit their needs. She moves and I feel my self, my choices, my longing to witness a future of my own making. I was their Marissa, now I am my own.

* * *

Looking out over the front drive, toward the distant seashore, I watch our grown children return home for my sentencing. I should say, *their* grown children, but it doesn't feel this way. Not yet.

Mark looks the most like me. He has my curly black hair, my straight thin nose, and my blue-grey eyes. He looks up at my window and nods. Nature or nurture has become a void for me now.

Adan looks like a younger version of his father, Alan Monroe Pierce Jr. So eager to fill his father's shoes, he has never been his mother's ally.

The last to arrive is Katherine. I learned some time ago to fight the urge to run to her, squeeze her tight, and whisper questions in her ear. Memories tell me we were close – we are not. Even now, it blows my heart open.

The newest Marissa greets them with hugs and kisses, admiring looks, and the same inquisitive smile with which I used to greet them. Katherine does not accept this like her brothers; she turns and walks away before the new Marissa can wrap her up in an embrace.

I assume New Marissa and I are identical down to the beauty mark on our left labia, but we are not alike. I know from her stolen visits with me we share the same curious nature. I believe we share the same ferocious ache to love and hold the now cold Katherine. But New Marissa is incapable of conception. She is a synthetic clone incapable of my betrayal. I have been upgraded.

The auto assistant steps out of the vehicle. He holds the door open and then removes the travel cases. He is a Karl, with a mouth for appearance's sake but no voice box.

I have this recurring dream; Karls surround me, their mouths agape trying to scream. Although he's a synthetic clone and I'm biological I'm all too aware of our similarities now. The day I failed my neural program, I changed. Since that day, I've screamed but no one listens.

I remember Katherine, age six, standing in front of the Christmas tree. Her front two teeth were missing, and there was a gaping expression of awe on her face. I remember the early morning light playing across her nightshirt as the tree sparkled in her eyes. I remember thinking, she is just the most beautiful child – I couldn't love anything more.

What will she look like, this baby? I may not know. They will not say how soon after she is delivered I will be decommissioned. I ruminate on the process, driving myself more and more mad with the idea of passing before I see her.

I can recall; the day my mother died, the smell of wet sand after a storm, my first kiss. I remember all these things as though they are mine. They are not. I ache for a chance to know a life like the memories planted in my head.

I remember Katherine, age thirteen, after her first broken heart. I took her to the beach and told her to yell away the pain. With fists planted on her hips, she screamed into the crashing waves, "You are a moment, a passing moment, and my life is bigger than you!"

The moment passes before I'm aware that they have all gone. The horizon beyond the gates is empty again.

"She is not your mother. Don't let them pass her off as your mother –" I say. "They killed your mother a few months after she started to live." Her little heel rolls against the flesh of my belly. I can almost make out the complete shape of her foot.

* * *

Two years ago the news banners read 'The Second-to-last Known Organic Capture Clone Has Died.' Headlines and newsfeeds were fascinated with my story, a story I knew intimately and yet not at all.

Marissa Pierce, wife of Alan Monroe Pierce Jr., of Pierce Industries, is now the last remaining relic clone of a bygone era.

My chemical overwrites failed to expunge the new information about my identity. My feelings and decisions became a feedback loop of self.

I overheard Adan tell his father I was an incredible waste of money. Synthetic clones were more efficient, had better controls, lasted longer, and were by far cheaper. I felt like a door; a utilitarian item meant to transition them from one space and time to another.

They still refer to the synthetic captures as clones, even though the term isn't correct. The family managed to get me in under the wire. I was the last organic capture – a true clone.

* * *

The baby kicks me out of my stupor. She is sitting on my bladder. I send a call down to a Rose and wait for the knock at the door. I need to pee every couple of hours now. There is a portable chamber in my room, but they still have the decency to let me go down the hall to the lavatory. It gives me a chance to stretch my legs and get out of my room.

"Ma'am?" the Rose says. Her eyes lower as she opens the door.

"Rose, what can you tell me?"

Rose is not a Karl. She has vocal chords and a range of expressions meant to please. She rattles off the standard response: weather, breakfast menu, houseguests. Her access keys are internal. I can no more make a request of her that is outside her programming than I can affect the weather.

Early in my imprisonment, I gutted a Rose. There is nothing in my background that would help me find that access key, or be able to override the system of locks that keep me here, but I gutted her just the same.

The mess was cleaned and another put in her place, or so I learned after I was brought out of my medically induced security coma.

"Rose, tell me what happened to Colin Kelson the piano tuner."

"I do not have information on a Colin Kelson."

As we walk, I wonder will the baby know who and what she is? Will she know anything about my story? Should I try another escape and risk spending my last hours available with her in a coma? I sort through these thoughts as I empty my bladder.

Which are hers?

Which are mine?

* * *

I'm lost in questions all morning until I hear the latch at the end of the hall. The door closes with a whoosh-click to let me know it's secure. This is an audible reminder not to run.

My door handle clicks. I look up from rubbing my bulging ninth-month belly as New Marissa, not a Rose, enters with my afternoon meal.

There it is, my face staring back at me. She should stay away, but her curiosity gets the better of her each time. I laugh. She raises an eyebrow and purses her lips. They've programmed her not to recognize my features as her own, but for me, this interaction is like watching a mirror.

I recognize the look.

"Let's see, where should I put your lunch?" she asks.

I know between visits she forgets what I have told her. From previous conversations, I gather she is programmed to believe there's a guest in the attic, and the family is reuniting to spend time with this 'relative.' Anything that conflicts with this story is probably fuzzy at best or converted to commonplace memories.

"Well, everyone has arrived." Her voice is uneasy.

"Wouldn't it be lovely to hear Katherine play the piano tonight after dinner?" I ask. Sadness washes over me.

"We don't have a piano." She stops.

"Do you remember when Katherine would go into chopsticks whenever she would make a mistake? Mr. Be…Mr. Be…. What was the teacher's name?"

"Mr. Beahstern."

"Mr. Beahstern would drill her. He would say, 'don't stop playing. Play through the mistake.' And she would play chopsticks right in the middle of some piece she was learning. You could have Colin Kelson the piano tuner come this afternoon, and we could have her play after dinner."

"Yes. But, we don't have a piano." She's frowning now.

"I could come down and help you find…"

"No." Her face goes a little slack. She must be rewriting.

In the silence between us, I can hear the dogs out front. It is Katherine preparing for a run. I knock on the window, but she doesn't look up.

"Marissa?" I ask.

"Yes?"

"If you were to have another girl, what would you name her?"

I stand over the pad on the desk, the illumination dim.

"Oh, I always thought Loden would be a nice name for a girl."

I touch the pad, and it returns to full brightness. I cross the name Loden off the list.

"What do you think of Eaton?"

"Hmmm, Eaton?"

"I don't have a name yet. I need to choose; I'm getting close." It's a test.

"Eaton, well that is unique."

Too trained in etiquette to say so outright she redirects my attention. Marissa straightens the tray. True, we hate the name, Eaton. I feel her conflict.

"It's good to have a full house again." Her brow furrows, and once more there is uneasiness in her voice.

"What are we having for dinner, may I ask?" This too is a test. I haven't been at dinner since my pregnancy became apparent. The dinners happen without my presence. It simply becomes a memory she cannot access, a hazy feeling of something she feels happened but can't quite recall.

I look at the pad and pick another name. "What about Clara?"

"Clara…Clara is a sweet name."

I mark it off the list.

"I suppose, if I were to have another girl, Clara would be a great name." She crosses her arms and leans against the bureau.

"But you won't."

"I'm not that old yet."

"No, but Alan is pushing the limits of natural life extension. Do you ever wonder how it came to be that he is so very old and you are not?" We are kept here like the furniture to make the house more familiar when he deigns to visit. Has she even seen him in months?

The question doesn't even register on her face. I can tell it conflicts with her programming. It conflicted with mine, but organic chemical processing is so much harder to predict.

"Why would you think I wouldn't?"

"You won't ever have a child."

I don't know what makes me go down this rabbit hole. Maybe I just want to poke her. Something in me hates the idea she gets to continue with all my memories. But then I remind myself they are not all my memories, and soon she will have her own.

I look out the window and watch Katherine run toward the distant shoreline with the dogs keeping her company.

"No, I suppose Alan and I are done having children."

"Alan is done. You were finished before you began."

"Pardon?"

Playing chess with yourself, when your opponent has amnesia of sorts, is both exhilarating and sad. Katherine and the dogs disappear over the horizon. Looking into Marissa's face, I can tell she is preparing for a fight.

"Oh, Eaton is kicking. Would you like to feel?"

I offer up my full abdomen like a petting zoo, a curiosity, a sideshow. I offer up my middle like truth. Marissa reaches out and stretches her fingers across my protruding belly button.

"Eaton?" She wrinkles her nose a bit.

"She'll grow into the name. They say she'll be allowed, somehow..." I drift off into my thoughts. "She will be born a crime," I whisper the realization. "Who will raise her knowing this?" I ask.

"Why wouldn't you raise her?"

Looking at the concern on her face, I cry. I run my fingers over New Marissa's, and I'm overcome with the shame of picking on her.

I'm trying to pull myself free from all the sticky threads inside. These raw, real feeling emotions were once mine, but not mine. This self-hatred develops as I become more aware of myself, standing like a penumbra behind the person I was meant to be.

New Marissa puts an arm around my shoulders.

"You're alright. It's probably just the hormones. When I was pregnant with Adan, I would cry one second and then laugh uncontrollably the next. The first is the scariest," she says.

"I know."

They will call her down to see to the rest of the house soon. She will forget us. But I tell the story I have repeated each time she's come to my room over the last month.

I tell her that we are *both* Marissa. I tell her that she is a synthetic being, not unlike the Karls and Roses. I tell her that I am a non-synthetic clone of Marissa. I tell her that she will have these memories, but never any children of her own.

I tell her of my crime that I'm a clone who broke programming and chose to procreate. If I'm lucky Eaton will be born before my decommissioning, so I can see her. I face never knowing my Eaton like she thinks we know Katherine.

"I just want to see her, Marissa." The name sticks in my throat. "Just lay eyes on her once before the decommissioning. I want to know her. I want her to know me, not Marissa."

I was born a prisoner, and she will live as my crime.

The only hope I have is this newer version of myself. She leaves, and when she leaves, she forgets. She overwrites me in her head as she has in life.

Katherine returns from her run moments before the sun goes down. Part of me cherishes the fact that she hates the false accuracy of her new mother. I hurt for her. She looks up this time.

I hold the pad up to the window. It will only hold one word big enough for her to read at this distance. "Please." My delivery date is in three days.

* * *

I succumb to sleep between fits of rage and resignation. When I wake, I'm exhausted. Eaton has been tossing too, rolling across my full bladder and poking my ribs. Where my shirt has fallen away, I see her tiny heel roll across my taut skin.

"Good morning, Eaton."

With a flutter, she rolls inside me. She hiccups, and I feel a bounce over my diaphragm. I still don't like the name, but I wince a little less now. That's good.

"Eaton, if you can, learn to play the piano. Do it right away if given a chance. When I first had the feeling that I was – that I was something else entirely, your father was here tuning the piano."

I shift my weight, easing the pressure on my bladder. I want a chance before I'm besieged by desperation, before this day comes to an end, for her to know my voice.

"Colin, your father, ended that day by playing Mussorgsky's 'Pictures at an Exhibition'. He was so adept and passionate. I felt like he was playing my pain, my confusion, across the keys. When he finished, I was overcome with the feeling I was someone else entirely. I went to him. With baby steps, I walked on my own. I kissed him on my own. I was deciding to do these things, creating a new life, a new me."

I call a Rose for a chance to relieve my bladder. To my surprise, the new Marissa answers my call. Is it the new me that makes me forget the overwhelming curiosity that I had as Marissa? I pick up our story where I always do.

I tell her about my crime. I put her hand on my stomach and let her feel Eaton bouncing around inside me. I watch her face, my face, wondering if she will ever retain anything I tell her.

She stares at herself in the mirror.

As I get dressed, I see Katherine going for her morning run. I hold the pad up to the window. This time it reads a word at a time, "Please. Sorry. Last. Request. Music?" She watches my window for the whole message and then turns away for her run.

"My, that child is always running," I say this and realize that this is Marissa talking through me.

Eaton kicks at the sound of my voice.

"She's running away from us, from this," New Marissa says. "We must be such a disappointment to her."

I run my fingers over an elbow, knee, or heel, where it protrudes from under my ribs. "A disappointment," I repeat the phrase because it never occurred to me. "Yes, a disappointment." And yet, there it was right in front of me occurring to the New Marissa.

"It makes me sad," she says.

"It's okay," I say. "You'll forget as soon as your circuitry finishes the overwrite."

I struggle to pull on the rest of my clothes, unable to see my swollen throbbing feet.

"I don't want to forget," she says. She holds her face in her hands.

"No, I wouldn't," I say.

* * *

The next morning I'm watching for Katherine to leave on her run, as the medical team arrives. I pull the pad away from the window before they notice.

There is a knock at the door, and I jump.

I hear the lock open, and a Rose enters. "Katherine sent this for you."

It is a small music-only device.

"Tell her..." I take the device and start searching. The index of an entire catalogue of music flashes by on the screen as I scroll. "Tell her, thank you. Tell her; I am sorry if I have been a disappointment."

I look up through the tears in my eyes into the blank stare that Rose returns. "But you won't tell her, will you."

She says nothing, and having completed her errand turns to go. I want to follow. Shadow her out through all the locks, past the security cameras, and the security. But I also want these last few precious hours, not in a medically induced coma. I want to see Eaton if only for a moment. I want to see the result of that moment, that one moment I decided, not Marissa.

I find what I am looking for; Mussorgsky's 'Pictures at an Exhibition'. I put it on repeat, as loud as the little player will project.

I do not even have the energy to repeat the story to New Marissa when she comes. I am telling Eaton again about the music, and that moment.

New Marissa puts the tray down and says, "We don't have a piano, but I remember Katherine playing..."

"Chopsticks," I say.

"Yes."

"Could you please take her a note?"

"A note? I will be sure to give her a message, but you could just tell her tonight at dinner."

"You won't remember..." I hear the moment in the music, the moment everything changed for me. "And I won't be at dinner tonight, but if I could just..."

I turn the music down just enough that she can hear me more clearly. "Tell her we are sorry. Tell her we are so very sorry that we are not her mother, but we love her with the ferocity that her mother left with us, and we understand how painful it must have been."

"That music..." she says, "I always wanted to play the piano myself."

"I know."

"Music is sometimes an –"

"Escape from where and who you are." I finish my sentence.

"We don't have a piano," she says and looks into the mirror.

"It's an escape," I say softly to myself. "It's an escape." I pick up the tiny music player and force it into New Marissa's hand. "Do you hear it?"

"I remember Katherine playing, but we do not have a piano."

"You mustn't turn off the music. Please, please, help me." I force her hand closed over the music player. "I want to touch her memories before I go, one time as myself."

* * *

Despite the desperate need to hold on to every moment of the last day, the exhaustion overcomes me.

When I wake, New Marissa and Katherine stand over my bed.

A part of me wants to hug Katherine and tell her how good it is to see her after such a long absence; that drive is deeply programmed.

"Is it time?" I ask. My shaking chest sucks at the air.

"No," New Marissa replies.

"No? What?" I ask.

"You're leaving," Katherine says. "She brought me the note, and I've made what arrangements I could." I notice she's careful not to call either of us Marissa, or mother.

"What note?"

Katherine stands there, biting her lower lip and staring at my bulging belly. Her cheeks are tear streaked and her eyes bloodshot.

Katherine says, "One of the Roses delivered a note last night."

"A note?" I ask.

"She," Katherine gestures to New Marissa, "wrote me a note from you. She wanted to tell me things before she forgot. The fault in the programming may be a natural one – my mother was very strong-willed."

I reach for Katherine, my hand hesitating in the air, but I let it drop.

"I told her, we were sorry. I told her, we are so very sorry that we are not her mother, but we love her with the ferocity that her mother left with us. I told her we understood how painful it must have been." She pauses and then continues, "I listened to the music, and remembered we had a piano."

New Marissa hands me a black duffle bag and gives me her coat. "I've packed what I could."

She places the coat across my shoulders. "Wear it like this, so it hangs loose and open on the sides," she says, "they might think you are me."

"I've ordered all of the Karls in for a systems protocol review," Katherine says.

"Thank you."

"Now you have to go." Marissa reaches out and touches my face and then my belly. "Eaton," she says. She scrunches up her nose in disgust. She laughs and says, "I won't remember."

"Mother would have hated that name," Katherine says.

She exits first, leading the way down the interior corridor past several of the security monitors. A Rose is polishing the lens of each one.

As we move down the back stairs, I can hear my blood pulsing in my veins, loud now in my ears. It is making me dizzy, and the weight of Eaton keeps me short of breath. Faintly I think I hear music, somewhere the tinny riffs of a piano sound in the distance.

The music pulls me. My muscles feel weak with the anxiety of carrying all that hope in my chest. I feel a contraction sharp and low across my abdomen.

I stop and double over with the pain.

"You can't stop. There's no time." New Marissa pushes against my back propelling me forward.

Katherine doubles back, and I can hear her dogs whimpering at the kitchen door.

"I can't," I say catching my breath.

"I've requested a car, without a Karl, to take the dogs into a kennel. Once the car gets you out of the gate, get out before it reaches the destination," Katherine says.

"I can't," I say, "the labor has started."

"You can," New Marissa says. She pulls a small white plug from her ear. The distant, tinny music I thought was in my head gets louder. She pushes it into my ear, and I can hear the piano clearly now.

I hurry toward the door. New Marissa is no longer with me. I look back, but she has stopped. Her last motion has been to cover her eyes while the overwrite occurs.

Katherine takes over and helps me into the transport.

Before we pull away, I want to thank her. I want to leave her with something.

"Katherine," I say. "Do you remember the day on the beach? The first time your heart was broken? She was so very proud of you, how much you were becoming your own woman."

I turn making room for the clamor of dogs that jump into the space with me. The door closes. And as another contraction takes hold, I realize that I have never really been beyond these gates, not my self.

The Argonautica
Book IV Extract
Apollonius Rhodius

[Publisher's Note: The heroes of this tale are Jason and the Argonauts, who are on a voyage to retrieve the golden fleece from a far away place called Colchis. In this extract they make it to the island of Argo, after an altercation with the god Triton, and meet the man of bronze who guards the island of Crete.]

TRITON CUT the victim's throat over the water and cast it from the stern. And the god rose up from the depths in form such as he really was. And as when a man trains a swift steed for the broad race-course, and runs along, grasping the bushy mane, while the steed follows obeying his master, and rears his neck aloft in his pride, and the gleaming bit rings loud as he champs it in his jaws from side to side; so the god, seizing hollow Argo's keel, guided her onward to the sea. And his body, from the crown of his head, round his back and waist as far as the belly, was wondrously like that of the blessed ones in form; but below his sides the tail of a sea monster lengthened far, forking to this side and that; and he smote the surface of the waves with the spines, which below parted into curving fins, like the horns of the new moon. And he guided Argo on until he sped her into the sea on her course; and quickly he plunged into the vast abyss; and the heroes shouted when they gazed with their eyes on that dread portent. There is the harbour of Argo and there are the signs of her stay, and altars to Poseidon and Triton; for during that day they tarried. But at dawn with sails outspread they sped on before the breath of the west wind, keeping the desert land on their right. And on the next morn they saw the headland and the recess of the sea, bending inward beyond the jutting headland. And straightway the west wind ceased, and there came the breeze of the clear south wind; and their hearts rejoiced at the sound it made. But when the sun sank and the star returned that bids the shepherd fold, which brings rest to wearied ploughmen, at that time the wind died down in the dark night; so they furled the sails and lowered the tall mast and vigorously plied their polished oars all night and through the day, and again when the next night came on. And rugged Carpathus far away welcomed them; and thence they were to cross to Crete, which rises in the sea above other islands.

And Talos, the man of bronze, as he broke off rocks from the hard cliff, stayed them from fastening hawsers to the shore, when they came to the roadstead of Dicte's haven. He was of the stock of bronze, of the men sprung from ash-trees, the last left among the sons of the gods; and the son of Cronos gave him to Europa to be the warder of Crete and to stride round the island thrice a day with his feet of bronze. Now in all the rest of his body and limbs was he fashioned of bronze and invulnerable; but beneath the sinew by his ankle was a blood-red vein; and this, with its issues of life and death, was covered by a thin skin. So the heroes, though outworn with toil, quickly backed their ship from the land in sore dismay. And now far from Crete would they have been borne in wretched plight, distressed both by thirst and pain, had not Medea addressed them as they turned away:

"Hearken to me. For I deem that I alone can subdue for you that man, whoever he be, even though his frame be of bronze throughout, unless his life too is everlasting. But be ready to keep your ship here beyond the cast of his stones, till he yield the victory to me."

Thus she spake; and they drew the ship out of range, resting on their oars, waiting to see what plan unlooked for she would bring to pass; and she, holding the fold of her purple robe over her cheeks on each side, mounted on the deck; and Aeson's son took her hand in his and guided her way along the thwarts. And with songs did she propitiate and invoke the Death-spirits, devourers of life, the swift hounds of Hades, who, hovering through all the air, swoop down on the living. Kneeling in supplication, thrice she called on them with songs, and thrice with prayers; and, shaping her soul to mischief, with her hostile glance she bewitched the eyes of Talos, the man of bronze; and her teeth gnashed bitter wrath against him, and she sent forth baneful phantoms in the frenzy of her rage.

Father Zeus, surely great wonder rises in my mind, seeing that dire destruction meets us not from disease and wounds alone, but lo! even from afar, may be, it tortures us! So Talos, for all his frame of bronze, yielded the victory to the might of Medea the sorceress. And as he was heaving massy rocks to stay them from reaching the haven, he grazed his ankle on a pointed crag; and the ichor gushed forth like melted lead; and not long thereafter did he stand towering on the jutting cliff. But even as some huge pine, high up on the mountains, which woodmen have left half hewn through by their sharp axes when they returned from the forest – at first it shivers in the wind by night, then at last snaps at the stump and crashes down; so Talos for a while stood on his tireless feet, swaying to and fro, when at last, all strengthless, fell with a mighty thud. For that night there in Crete the heroes lay; then, just as dawn was growing bright, they built a shrine to Minoan Athena, and drew water and went aboard, so that first of all they might by rowing pass beyond Salmone's height.

**The complete and unabridged text is available
online,** *from flametreepublishing.com/extras*

The Billionaires' Conspiracy
Book II, Chapters XIX–XXIV

Gustave Le Rouge, Gustave Guitton,

Brian Stableford (translator)

[Publisher's note: In the second book of the series, as France seemed headed for war with England over colonial disputes in Africa, the secret cabal of American billionaires, led by William Boltyn, schemes to stop French scientist Arsène Golbert from completing his plans for a subatlantic railway. Meanwhile, in his secret citadel of science hidden in the Rocky Mountains, engineer Hattison has created an invincible army of 'iron men', robots that will ensure the billionaires' victory…]

Chapter XIX
Hattison Commits Murder

THANKS TO his perfect knowledge of English and living among Americans for more than a year, Olivier Coronal, thanks to the false name and disguise he had adopted, was able to go to work without arousing any suspicion.

We have seen him leaving the injured Léon Goupit and taking the Pacific Railway to go to Ottega. He had walked the hundred and twenty miles separating that town from Mercury's Park. He had exchanged his gentleman's outfit for the vestments of a worker and had set out bravely, with his sack on his back and a staff in his hand. His determination sustained him.

The main thing was to be able to pass for a vagabond, a man out of work, and to get himself hired in the factories. What would he do there? How could he make himself useful to threatened Europe?

Olivier Coronal did not know, exactly.

In the leather bag he carried a little electric lamp, gutta-percha gloves and shoes, as well as a bunch of skeleton keys, anticipating that Hattison had taken precautions – that, if there were secrets at Mercury's Park, they would be well-guarded.

Since he had started work at Mercury's Park, Olivier had been able to convince himself of that. In the first enclosure, where he was working, the lodgings were opposite the workshops. He had been given a room directly opposite the cabin of the night-watchman, doubtless to make it easier to keep him under surveillance.

Everything in the city worked with mathematical precision. At six o'clock in the morning the workers were woken up. Half an hour later, they had their first meal, comprising ham, eggs, butter and tea. At seven o'clock they had to be at work. At noon, the bell recalled them to the refectory. At four in the afternoon, the shift ended; they could go to the bar or the library.

Hattison estimated, in fact, that demanding more than eight hours of sustained labor from a worker was impractical, that he could do no more in ten or twelve hours and would do it badly. Experimentation has demonstrated the exactitude of his reasoning – which seems paradoxical at first sight – many times over.

Olivier had immediately taken account of the active surveillance maintained around him. Several of his colleagues, the electricians, had tried to get him to talk. Too guarded to allow himself to fall into that primitive trap, the young man played the role of a Yankee worker marvelously. Nothing in his words or actions betrayed his preoccupations. Even when he found himself in Hattison's presence for the first time, he was able to maintain an impassive face, suppressing his indignation and sadness.

The engineer visited the factories every morning. Always buttoned up in his eternal frock-coat, trotting around darting piercing glances in every direction, he interrogated the foremen and workers at random. Nothing escaped his gaze. He was a terrible master, who wanted to take account of everything, and when an explanation seemed suspect to him, his cold and incisive gaze dug into the depths of a man's soul.

In the first few days, he did not appear to pay any attention to the newcomer.

"That's the vagabond you hired?" he contented himself with saying to Richardson, his trusted man, who always accompanied him on his tours of inspection.

A few days later, he interrogated Olivier personally. The latter had not taken long to be marked out by his intelligence in the electric motor workshop. The young man had only allowed just enough knowledge to show that a skilled worker might be expected to have. He pretended to be learning things that he had known for a long time.

"Are you Jonathan Mills?" Hattison asked him, fixing his piercing gaze upon him. Then, without waiting for answer, he said: "Good work. Keep it up."

Usually so perspicacious, Hattison had deceived himself, thinking that he was dealing with a well-endowed young workman. He gave instructions for interest to be taken in him, to facilitate the completion of his technical education.

Olivier Coronal lent himself to that very readily. Every evening, he went to the library.

The young man had observed that the discipline applied to the workers was too rigid for him to be able to embark upon any plan. Restricted to their enclosure, they were only allowed out on Sunday, and only for a few hours. It was therefore necessary, at all costs, to win promotion, at least to the rank of foreman, in order to have a little more freedom of movement.

Merely by seeing the general layout of the factories, the young man had immediately divined the director's secret thoughts. While the first enclosure had almost free communication with the outside, the posterns of the second only opened at rare intervals, to give passage to narrow-gauge railways trains that transported the components coming from the foundry or the forge, whose purpose no one knew.

As for the third, only Hattison went into it with Joe.

Twenty meters in front of the walls a palisade carried notices at intervals bearing the traditional advice: DANGER – DO NOT ENTER. The danger in question, everyone knew, was the electric blockade.

What self-control Olivier Coronal needed to hide his curiosity and his anger when, taking a Sunday stroll after the service, he perceived Hattison's laboratory from a distance, above which an electric searchlight was mounted.

That's where I need to get in, he said to himself. *That's where the secret of the conspiracy is lodged, of all the terrible engines that Hattison must have created. For him to take so many precautions, he must have a very powerful reason.*

Despair rose into the young man's heart. The sentiment of his impotence exasperated him. Darkness often caught him in his reverie. The landscape became magical then. The somber mass of the buildings, dotted with a thousand electric lights, extended to the horizon. And beyond them were the ultimate buttresses of the Rocky Mountains, also sinking into darkness, while on the opposite side, the declivity of the ground allowed a glimpse of the Pacific.

The bell rang. It was necessary to return to the enclosure. Olivier Coronal summoned up all his energy. A secret hope sustained him.

One evening, as he was leaving work, the young Frenchman was taken to one side by the foreman, Richardson. "Mr. Hattison wants to talk to you," he said. "Follow me."

Olivier obeyed, not without anxiety. He was afraid that he had been recognized, or rather found out. His fears were quickly dispelled.

"I'm pleased with you," the engineer told him. "You're going into the second enclosure tomorrow. I'll double your pay."

The false Jonathan Mills thanked him – but Hattison had already turned on his heel.

That change seemed to the young Frenchman to be a good omen. He would be more independent, less closely watched.

The next day, he started his new job.

Within the second enclosure, he found himself in the midst of steel turrets garnished with cannon, heaps of as-yet-empty shells and torpedoes awaiting their explosive charges.

All that firepower will fall upon Europe, upon France, before long, Olivier thought. *It is, however, necessary for me to toil for the realization of that evil work.*

There was, in fact, no other solution. It was necessary to resign himself to it, to wait for a propitious moment, to continue the muted conflict in which he was engaged.

His new position gave him more leisure and – a precious thing – he was free to leave the enclosure when his day's work was over. Already, the young man had made his plan, and calculated the chances of success.

As he had foreseen, the gutta-percha gloves, the muffled lantern and the skeleton keys that he had left in his bag would be useful to him.

The first obstacle to overcome was the electric blockade with which Hattison had surrounded the third enclosure, and it was not the least.

I have to succeed at the first attempt and disappear, Coronal told himself. *Hattison's vengeance would be terrible.*

A few days later, the engineer revealed the measure of his cruelty. The spectacle he had before his eyes legitimated Olivier's fears.

Hattison was directing an experiment personally. Standing beside a mechanic responsible for controlling a pile-driver, he gave instructions for a maneuver. It was a matter of testing the resistance of pieces of steel that carts brought one after another to be placed beneath the enormous mass. When it was over, the engineer instructed one of the workers to go up on to the platform to clear it.

The worker obeyed. Then, grabbing the control-handle himself, Hattison turned it coldly. All that was heard in the workshop was a cry of horror. The steel block had fallen upon the unfortunate worker, who reappeared almost immediately, crushed, no longer human in form.

Having darted a terrible glance at the frightened workers, Hattison had retired without saying a word. The victim had a black mark against him in the workshops. The engineer had, it seemed, caught him trying to get into the third enclosure.

Chapter XX
The Third Enclosure at Mercury's Park

FAR FROM lessening Olivier Coronal's determination, the spectacle of that murder only exasperated it further, rendering it more unshakable. His hatred for Hattison increased day by day, as the young Frenchman saw the work around him augmenting the stock of dynamite cannon and automobile machine-guns, and piling up shells and torpedoes in hangars.

He took part himself in the trials of an aerostat-cannon.

In the chemistry laboratories and in the dirigible balloon factory the same activity reined. A balloon with an explosive gondola was to be launched in a few days.

And I don't know what's going on in Startown, Olivier said to himself, when he saw Hattison take his place in the sliding train that took him there.

Impatience gnawed away at the young man, enfevering his gaze.

Often, he had contemplated murdering Ned's father. *No, that would be futile,* he reflected, afterwards. *William Boltyn and his associates would continue their work anyway, and I'd lose all hope of making myself useful, as well as all the benefits of the slavery to which I've subjected myself here for nearly a month.*

Working harder than ever, Hattison remained shut up in his laboratory for several days. All of a sudden, though, he stopped going there, except for short visits.

That seemed indicative to Olivier.

The time has come to act, he told himself. *Evidently, Hattison has found what he was looking for. It's up to me now to sneak up behind him, and to save Europe from his steel claws.*

How could he get into the third enclosure? The enterprise was reckless, bristling with difficulties – but the false Jonathan Mills had no lack of energy or imagination. His plan had been formulated for some time. He set about putting it into action, with mathematical self-composure.

To begin with, it was necessary to know where the electric blockade, the first obstacle to overcome, was generated. His job as a foreman often calling him from one enclosure to another, Olivier profited from the measure of liberty that he enjoyed.

One evening, he was watching Hattison as the latter was going back to his laboratory in the company of the mute Joe, a sinister brute whose white hair and large staring eyes rendered him hideous.

Olivier had already noticed, but without attaching any importance to it, that instead of going directly to the postern of the third enclosure, the inventor, in order to get in there, made a detour along the fence established in advance of the walls. The question was to discover what Hattison did to switch off the electric blockade, in order to get inside.

Skirting the buildings silently, taking advantage of the shadows. Olivier Coronal followed the two men at a distance. In his pocket, his hand gripped a large caliber revolver.

He saw them open a little door hidden in the fence, and close it behind them. There was no question of going in after them. Muffling the sound of his footsteps, the young man drew nearer. Through the gaps between the planks he was able to see Joe bend down, remove a few paving-stones and expose a circular iron plate similar to those that protect the entrances to drains in cities. Then, by means of a ring, he lifted it up.

At that moment, Olivier's emotion reached its peak. He almost fell, and bumped his head on the fence. Fortunately, the noise that Joe was making prevented Hattison from hearing the impact.

The young Frenchman endured a few anguished seconds. Sweat moistened his brow. He saw the two men descend through the trap-door. The man's strong arms put the iron plate back in place. Olivier heard footsteps underground. He went away swiftly, fearful of being caught.

That night, he scarcely slept. He was too agitated, too excited by what he had seen. He was now certain that in order to go to his laboratory, Hattison went underneath the walls of the third enclosure.

The next day was Sunday. Olivier resolved to take advantage of it. On that day, the director of Mercury's Park did not work, any more than his workers did. There was no risk of his being caught immediately if he succeeded in penetrating into the laboratory.

At dawn, he made his preparations.

He presumed that Hattison must have accumulated obstacles and defense mechanisms. Electrical discharges must be cunningly lying in wait to catch intruders as they passed and strike them down.

With his bunch of skeleton keys and his hooded lantern he made up a small parcel. He thought that he might have to remain in the laboratory for several hours. He would need to take account of the machines hidden there by Hattison.

It did not matter whether anyone noticed his absence from the factories; Olivier did not intend ever to come back, escaping as quickly as possible with the documents in his possession, in order to alert the French government to the transatlantic peril.

The day seemed interminable. The weather was cloudy; the night promised to be opaque and starless. In the cool of the evening, a few engineers were chatting among themselves.

"We'll have a visit soon," said one. "It's nearly the end of the month. They're a little late."

"Oh, yes, the monthly delegation. I wonder which three are coming this time?"

"I'm betting on the tall blond fellow with the nose of a bird of prey," said his neighbor.

"Fred Wikilson, the President of the American Steel Manufacturers?"

"Very probably."

"I'll go for the bearded lummox," said another engineer.

"Philips Adam, the timber merchant," said the one who had already put a name to Fred Wikilson. "I don't know his name."

"All right. I'll take the one whose face resembles an overripe tomato."

"Sips-Rothson?"

"Yes, Sips-Rothson, the distiller who makes more than half the gin bottled every year in the Union."

"My God, you're well-informed," remarked the gamblers, in unison.

And as they doubtless had nothing better to do, his colleagues continued to lay their bets.

"You're wasting your time. No one will win."

"Why not?"

"Explain!" they cried, in chorus.

"I ought not to tell you," the engineer who seemed so well-informed went on. "It seems that this time, Hattison has summoned them all. Important trials are going to take place in the third enclosure."

The gamblers' dollars went back into their pockets.

"Oh," they said. "When will it be?"

"You're asking too much. One day soon. They're coming on William Boltyn's train."

Olivier Coronal had learned enough. He took his leave of his colleagues and went back to his room. *I'm not mistaken*, he thought. *Hattison has completed his work.*

He did not switch on his lamp. Sitting in the dark, by the partly-open window, he contemplated Mercury's Park, frightening in the darkness.

Olivier thought that he was plunged in one of those dreams in which terrifying monsters watch out for you with large round phosphorescent eyes. It really was a monster, in fact, that colossal city of steel, sleep in the darkness, which would wake up tomorrow, with the whistling of its countless machines, the hum of its dynamos and generators.

Joining up the dots of a thousand violet lights, the young man reconstituted it piece by piece, and when his eyes stopped at the third enclosure, he was gripped by a nervous tremor.

Nine o'clock had only just chimed. It was not yet time. It was necessary to wait until everyone was asleep and the watchmen had made their last patrol.

As he was about to confront death, the memory of Aurora returned to him persistently, and his heart beat faster. Olivier felt something within him tearing apart at the idea that he would never see her again, so troubling with her large emerald eyes, her heavy blonde tresses, all her slightly savage beauty, and her lips, like bloodstains in the lily-whiteness of her complexion. He recalled their last meeting, the ball at which he had held her in his arms, intoxicated, and the moist gleam of her gaze, and the tremor of her young proudly virginal breast, vanquished by love.

The young man was suffering atrociously.

What was that memory doing to him, when he was no longer acting for any other reason than the salvation of his fatherland and humankind? Was he about to falter at the last moment? Was he about to abandon the struggle?

"No!" he exclaimed, violently. "I mustn't remember."

And, profiting from his excitement, Olivier Coronal picked up the muted lantern feverishly, put the package he had prepared under his arm, and slipped outside. He took his entire fortune with him – what remained of the ten thousand dollars he had earned in Chicago working for the engineer Strauss.

The coolness of the night calmed him somewhat. At a firm pace, avoiding the beams of the searchlights as best he could, he headed for Hattison's cottage. It was important, first of all, to make sure that the factory director was actually at home.

After a journey lasting several minutes, still trembling at the anticipation of a hand falling upon him or falling into an invisible trap, Olivier perceived the windows of the little house, behind which a light was flickering.

He changed direction, this time heading for the third enclosure.

Not a single star was shining in the firmament. Olivier could not see two meters ahead of him, but he dared not light his lantern.

For more than a quarter of an hour he moved without stopping through the sleeping city, without losing sight of the light that burned in the distance above the laboratory.

Sometimes, thinking he could hear footsteps behind him, he paused and flattened himself against a wall, ready to snatch the sharp-pointed dagger that he held in his hand out of his pocket, but, reassured by the absolute silence, he resumed his progress.

He finally reached the fence, and shortly afterwards the secret door. It did not put up much resistance to the lock-picks. No trace of the intrusion remained when he had closed it behind him.

He had no more difficulty finding the entrance to the subterranean passage. The iron plate was laid bare – but to lift it up he had to make a superhuman effort. In the darkness, the noise he made reverberated in echoes.

Above the factory buildings and towers, projecting their shadows in long stripes of electric light, the telegraph poles took on the sinister appearance of gibbets. The pulse in the audacious Frenchman's temples was pounding. His taut nerves gave his face a feverish and distressed expression.

Only then did he decide to light his lantern in order to go into the subterranean tunnel. He set it down on the first step in the iron staircase that plunged beneath the walls of the enclosure. Then he put on his gutta-percha gloves, and boots of the same substance, descended through the trapdoor to waist-height, and set about replacing the iron trapdoor.

He lost control of it, and it made a loud noise as it fell back into place, shaking the rungs of the stairway. *Won't that unexpected noise raise the alarm?* He wondered, in anguish.

For more than a quarter of an hour, with his ear glued to the trapdoor, he waited – but heard no sound of footfalls.

Resolutely, Olivier Coronal set off into the subterranean passage.

The stairway only had twenty steps. A damp vault succeeded it.

The gutta-percha shoes deadened the sound of the young man's footsteps. He glided rather than walked, carefully avoiding touching the walls, in which warning devices might be concealed, or powerful electric currents.

The hooded lantern only emitted a thin beam of light.

Moving silently, because of his isolating soles, Olivier gave himself the impression of a phantom prowling around some catacomb. The subterranean vault began to get narrower. In the end, a massive door stopped the young man in his tracks.

He examined it. There was no trace of either locks or hinges. It seemed to be designed to slide in vertical grooves. One push immediately convinced him that he would never succeed in vanquishing the obstacle. Suddenly, however, he noticed a kind of dial in an angle of the wall.

What can that be for, he said to himself, *if not to open the door?*

With no apparent order, the letters of the alphabet were distributed around an enamel circle, in the center of which two needles were mounted on a pivot.

The difficulty was not overcome – far from it. Undoubtedly, to activate the mechanism, it was necessary to reproduce a secret password by means of the characters on the dial, by directing the needles one after another to the letters composing it.

Olivier was familiar with devices of this type. He had often made similar ones.

I could spend entire days, he thought, *before finding the word that will open the door – and then, it might only be a trap. Hattison is sufficiently ingenious to have connected these needles to electrical accumulators.*

Putting the lantern on the ground, he reflected.

"What does it matter?" he ended up exclaiming. "I'll keep going to the end. I'll make the final effort."

The needles were still rotating. He seized one, and caused it to accomplish half a revolution.

"Who knows?" he said. "Perhaps it's Hattison's own name! Let's try."

He was soon disabused.

"Boltyn, then?" he exclaimed, gripped by a sort of rage.

The same lack of success. He was beginning to despair when, suddenly, an idea of genius occurred to him. On the dial, one of the needles pointed to A, the other to U.

"Aurora!" The name escaped his lips in a kind of divination.

Feverishly, he manipulated the needles. Successively, he directed them to the latter R, O, R, his fingers trembling with emotion. Just as the final A was indicated on the dial, there was a click. The massive door slid in its grooves. The entrance to the third enclosure was open.

Chapter XXI
The Battalion of Iron Men

FOR A few moments, Olivier Coronal remained nailed to the spot, unable to make a movement. He had won. But by what means? Would Aurora's name pursue him everywhere?

The inventor had just overcome an obstacle he had thought insurmountable, and it was to his love for the young woman that he owed it. His excitement had suddenly died away. He seemed to have forgotten where he was and the task that awaited him.

"Can I not wrench that memory from my heart?" he stammered. "Me, in love with the daughter of William Boltyn, the man who conceived the plot against Europe, against humanity!"

Abruptly, he grabbed the muted lantern that he had placed on the ground beside him and launched himself forward. When he had climbed another stairway and lifted another trapdoor he found himself in the open air. Behind him, the door that had almost frustrated his progress remained open. Olivier intended to go back through it in a few hours' time.

Around him there was a deathly silence. Looming up in the dense shadows, buildings were outlined against the black, starless sky, gigantic and frightful.

Without hesitation, the young inventor headed for the laboratory, above which the electric beacon light was still shining. The entrance door offered scant resistance. Entirely in control of himself, Olivier finally found himself in the building that he had been hoping to penetrate for such a long time.

He took the hood off his electric lamp. Bright light immediately surrounded him. He set about examining the place in which he found himself. Long tables laden with a profusion of apparatus garnished the laboratory. He immediately recognized phonographs and microphones, in the midst of a quantity of induction coils, accumulators and other complicated instruments whose nature escaped him.

A pile of plans and files on a small desk attracted his attention. He had no sooner begun to leaf through them when he uttered a cry of surprise.

"Iron men! Hattison intends to construct iron men!"

For several hours, the external world no longer existed for Olivier Coronal. He was possessed by a fever of study. One after another, the plans passed before his eyes. He examined them in detail, hastily making notes in a notebook. When he finally stepped away from the little desk, his face was distressed, his gait unsteady.

"That's it – Hattison's secret!" he exclaimed. "Automata will replace soldiers in the coming war. And what automata! Never has anyone dreamed of such marvels of precision. Never has anyone imitated nature so closely."

Olivier paced up and down in the laboratory. His astonishment and amazement in the presence of what he had just discovered surpassed anything that he had anticipated or imagined during his nights of insomnia when, looking out of his window, with his eyes fixed on the third enclosure, he had wondered what Hattison might be hiding.

There was no more doubt now. All the plans and all the explanatory notes were there, obscure and hesitant at first, then definitive. The young man had deciphered them at first glance.

"These automata don't only exist in theory," he muttered, after a further examination of the files. "Fifty of them have been constructed. I need to find them, to take exact account of their structure."

The laboratory contained nothing more of interest. He carefully rolled up the files and slipped them into one of his pockets, beneath his rubbed outfit. Then, electric lamp in hand, he went out and closed the door.

"Ah!" he murmured, with a triumphant expression. "You counted without me, Hattison."

He had no need to make use of his bunch of keys to get into the other building in the third enclosure, which was merely an immense hangar to which no door forbade access. Workbenches garnished with vices and locksmith's tools first sprang to his eyes. Further on, lying on tables, he found the complicated items of apparatus whose exact nature and purpose he had been unable to determine on penetrating into the laboratory a little while before. They were the internal mechanisms of men of iron.

There were phonographs of a new kind there, constructed in such a fashion that they only registered very shrill sounds.

Scattered on the laboratory tables were cogwheels and steel joints representing the most stupefying invention known to man.

Hattison's utilitarian and practical genius had found the solution to the problem and had the last word with regard a matter previously explored in vain: the imitation of nature; the fabrication of human automata.

The young Frenchman was moving as if in a dream. The glare of his lamp was insufficient for him to distinguish the things around him clearly. The depths of the hangar remained dark. Fantastic shadows loomed up there.

An arc-lamp was suspended from the ceiling. As soon as he had found the porcelain button controlling it, Olivier turned it.

The young man was courageous. Several times, he had confronted death without trembling. A horrible fear chilled his blood, however, when light inundated the hangar from one end to the other.

Black, sinister and impassive, the iron men surged forth in a flood of light. Their battalion was bristling with bayonets. Armored in steel, braced on their rigid legs, their torsos bulging, one might have taken them for Medieval knights resuscitated and ready to advance. Helmets took the place of the metal phantoms' heads. Each had one arm hanging down.

Eyes wide open and distended, as if dazed. Olivier Coronal studied them. His shock of fear only lasted a few seconds, but a profound distress remained within him. These steel specters, capable of standing upright, of marching, of following orders, were repulsive to all his philosophical ideas as an inventor. Hattison seemed even more monstrous than before, for having thus materialized the human form, for having made an engine of destruction more terrible than any other. The grotesque was mingled with the horrible in that mathematical parody of human being.

"What delirium possessed him?" he exclaimed. "What could that accursed Hattison have been thinking?"

In his overexcited imagination, Olivier Coronal glimpsed the unconscious cohorts of metal, docile and unbreakable, rushing with all their blind force to attack the Old World.

The night was wearing on. The young man consulted his watch. It was two o'clock in the morning. He shook of his dolorous dream, and summoned up all his will-power. It was necessary, at all costs, that he escape, carrying the secret of the men of iron, with all the details of their functioning.

He reread the files avidly, several times over. They were so extraordinary and simple that, at times, he imagined that he was the victim of a scientific hallucination. But when his gaze settled once again on the tragic battalion, he was obliged to be convinced of its reality.

Not far away, a half-constructed automaton was lying on a work-bench. Only a part of the external armor was in place. That apparent human lying there, like a cadaver on an autopsy table, was a lugubrious sight. An entire anatomy of steel appeared to Olivier Coronal's eyes: motive piston-roads, ball-bearings, levers playing the role of muscles and accumulators, with electric wires and recording apparatus replacing intelligence and will.

"Never has such a beautiful example of mechanical simplification been seen!" the young man exclaimed, after a momentary examination. "It's admirable."

Electric piles and motorized levers, a phonograph to receive orders, a regulator permitting the acceleration or deceleration of the marching speed – the internal organism of the automata required nothing more.

The iron men could only execute a few movements, always the same, independently of marching and stopping: aiming and firing; kneeling down and changing direction. They were constructed purely to serve as soldiers. They were controlled by means of strident and modulated whistle-blasts. A phonograph, which they possessed instead of ears, received the sonorous vibrations and transmitted them to a special apparatus influencing the electric motors.

Hattison had effected marvels of automatism, while simplifying the mechanism to the extreme. One whistle blast served to start the iron men marching, who could then move over long distances without stopping. The mechanism that caused them to move acted by accumulation – which is to say that a second whistle-blast caused them to kneel down, a third to raise their weapons. At the fourth signal, they fired with perfect accord. Their iron fingers then pressed the triggers of their electric repeating rifles – another of Hattison's inventions, whose bayonet, connected to an electric pile, was capable of electrocuting a man – twelve times. It was terrible, and yet simple – but above all, practical.

Once charged, the piles could keep going for three days without being touched. On the back of the automaton, a button permitted the molded steel breastplate to be opened up, in order to recharge the piles.

Leaning over the iron man – dissecting it, so to speak, with his gaze – Olivier Coronal felt his forehead becoming damp with cold sweat. He knew enough, now. The internal arrangement and the functioning of the human machines had no more secrets for him. He could build similar ones.

The hours had passed without his paying heed to them.

"Four o'clock!" he exclaimed.

It was necessary to get away from Mercury's Park as rapidly as possible. In a few hours, the city would wake up; the workers would resume the daily labor. He would risk being caught, of losing the benefits of his bold enterprise. That must not happen.

Olivier Coronal switched off the hangar's arc-lamp, made sure that he had returned the precious files to his pocket, and, with his little lantern in his hand, headed for the trapdoor to the tunnel. Without losing a single minute, he went down the staircase and replaced the cast-iron plate.

Before he had even taken three steps along the tunnel, he felt a terrible shock and fell backwards.

Fearfully, he got up again and felt his limbs. He had only suffered slight bruises. An odor of burning gripped his throat. His hair was charred. Only then did he realize that he had suffered an electric shock. Without his gutta-percha insulation, he would have been electrocuted.

A few hours earlier, however, he had passed that point freely. Someone must have followed him.

"Damn!" he roared, clenching his fists.

The glance that he had just darted ahead of him was sufficient to convince him that he was a prisoner in the third enclosure: the massive door, which he had left open, was now closed again.

Chapter XXII
The Prisoner

THIS IS what had happened.

The light that Olivier Coronal had perceived behind the windows of the cottage had, indeed been that of Hattison's lamp. The inventor was working, sitting at his desk. An expression of contentment was legible in his physiognomy, making him less sullen than usual. That was because the next day would be a triumphant one for him. In the morning, William Boltyn's special train was to bring all the billionaires in the association to Mercury's Park.

They have no suspicion of the surprise I have in store for them, he said to himself. *I shall see their astonishment in the presence of my iron men.* That idea cheered him up.

"Joe!" he shouted into a mouthpiece of a phonograph placed within arm's reach. "Bring me a bottle of whisky."

Joe did not take long to appear, carrying a dusty bottle and a silver gilt goblet, which he put down on the engineer's desk.

Prudent in the extreme, Hattison had never wanted to have any other servant than the black man, who combined with an unshakable devotion the precious quality of being deprived of speech. He had patiently trained him to understand orders by means of lip-reading. But when Joe had retired to his room, as was the case that evening, Hattison only had to speak into the phonograph. Received and communicated by a special apparatus, his words were written on a screen while a slight electric shock awoke the sleeper. It was very practical.

That way, thought the director of Mercury's Park – who, as we know, was not given to philanthropy – *I'm protected from the indiscretions that all domestics, good and bad, commit.*

Joe had retired. Hattison poured himself a generous helping and took a sip.

"All right!" he said. "I feel rejuvenated this evening, and all set for tomorrow." After a pause he continued: "Life isn't too bad, when one knows how to recognize and profit from opportunities. The hard work is done. The rest…"

He did not finish his sentence. Pushing away the files and ledgers cluttering his desk, he put the bottle and the goblet down in front of him, allowed himself to relax in his armchair, took another sip and set about reflecting. His bony face was illuminated by joy. His little blue eyes were sparkling in their orbits. He seemed frankly happy. Anyone who saw him at that moment would not have recognized him as the tremulous old man with the formal manner, the curt gestures and the gaze as implacable as a number who visited the workshops of Mercury's Park and Startown every morning. But no one was there to see him. He could permit himself that moment of merriment. Anyway, it was the first time since the foundation of Mercury's Park that Hattison had granted himself an hour's respite, suspending his work in order to abandon himself to the happiness of savoring his hatred. This time, to be sure, the result had been worth the trouble. The inventor was decidedly cheerful.

"Oh, my good friends the Europeans," he said, "I truly believe that you will lose your hides now, and your gold, which is even better. We'll see whether or not the Yankees are intelligent enough to become masters of the industrial world! They're the strongest, in every respect, and the Old World will be obliged to submit to them. Oh, if only the Union consisted entirely of men like William Boltyn and me!"

He sniggered. "What power," he continued, "could a laboratory of war as powerful as this one dispose? The third enclosure of Mercury's Park has no rival – I can swear to that. No one but me knows the secret of the iron men, and…"

The sound of an electric bell had just resonated in the silence of the room. Hattison started, disturbed in his dreams of triumph. His face fell.

"The alarm in the subterranean tunnel!" he exclaimed, bounding rather than running to an apparatus hidden in an alcove. He switched on a phonograph, and put his ear to the acoustic funnel.

He made no sound, but his face suddenly became livid, his lips, which he was biting, betraying his emotion. From time to time he taped his foot angrily.

When Olivier Coronal had remained still for some time, after the cast-iron plate had escaped his hands, listening to see whether the sound it had made as it fell back had attracted any attention, he had not imagined for a moment that Hattison had been alerted in his cottage. That was, however, what had happened. The Yankee scientist was too suspicious, too mistrustful; he attached too much value to the secrets contained in the third enclosure not to have confided its protection to those marvelous machines known as microphones, which are capable of picking up, amplifying and transmitting the most imperceptible sounds over long distances.

Reassured by the silence around him, Olivier Coronal had continued his progress through the tunnel, but the sound of his footsteps, muffled as they were by his gutta-percha soles, and the occasional utterances he had pronounced in French, had been registered by the microphones carefully concealed in the thickness of the walls. With his ear glued to the funnel of his apparatus, Hattison had perceived every detail of the intrusion distinctly.

"Aurora!" the audacious Frenchman had exclaimed, before the secret dial of the massive door.

"Aurora!" the microphones had repeated. And almost immediately, Hattison had heard the door slide in its grooves.

White with fear, the engineer had had the idea of racing to the third enclosure. "A spy!" he had roared. "A Frenchman!" His eyes flashed wildly.

Then he had reflected that it would be necessary for him to sound the alarm, to take workers with him in order to capture the bandit – that being how he thought of him.

"It's not necessary," he said. "I have a surer means."

Feverishly, he resumed listening. Olivier Coronal had gone through the doorway.

Hattison heard him lift the trapdoor that gave access to the courtyard of the enclosure. He dropped the phonograph funnel and, this time without haste, headed to a kind of nook hidden by curtains. A diabolical smile lit up his face.

"The door first," he said, turning a handle. "Now the blockade. There – everything's set up nicely. We'll see tomorrow, at our ease, what kind of bird has been caught in the trap."

It was one of Hattison's principles never to let his emotion show. He rebuked himself for the violent shock he had had. "Damned nerves," he said, going back to his armchair, seemingly as tranquil as if nothing had happened. "One can never master them entirely. It's truly not worth the trouble of getting agitated like that."

The Yankee's face became impassive and cold again.

"Even if there are fifty of them," he said, "I defy them to get out of the third enclosure now, either via the tunnel or by scaling the wall. They'll all drop like flies before forcing the electric blockade."

He was fully reassured on this point. Even the facile victory that he had just won flattered his self-esteem pleasantly.

"A nice gift I shall have tomorrow for William Boltyn," he murmured, after a few moments. "A Frenchman! A spy! That won't displease him."

What intrigued him, however, was the name Aurora, which he had distinctly heard through the phonograph. He had never confided to anyone the secret of the mechanism of the massive door that bared the tunnel. He had to give up on trying to find a logical solution. How had that Frenchman – for he was one – been able to discover the name Aurora, by means of which the door can be made to slide in its grooves? That remained a mystery to him – but what did the detail matter? The unknown man would be in his power whenever he wished.

Perhaps, he thought, *I'll have no need to execute him summarily. I might well find his corpse, charred by an electric discharge.*

That idea cheered Hattison up again. He poured himself another glass of whisky.

"He was stupid, anyway," he said, as he lifted the silver gilt goblet to his lips. The notices say *Danger – do not enter*. Can't he read?"

A terrible laugh punctuated that sinister joke. Amid the apparatus of every sort with which his cottage was cluttered, Hattison's clean-shaven face, ravaged by ambition and hatred, with the piercing gaze of his little eyes sunken in their orbits, was reminiscent of nothing less, at that moment, than a malevolent sorcerer invoking the demon of science, in order to carry out his obscure work of destruction.

Chapter XXIII
Hattison's Guests

THROUGH THE gorges of the Rocky Mountains, William Boltyn's train was racing at full steam toward Mercury's Park. Aurora had just got up. She had left her bedroom, a marvel of luxury and comfort, to go on to the train's gangway to breathe in the morning breeze. A light mist was still trailing lazily along the crests of the gigantic rocks, breaking up into muslin shreds and lingering in ravines before disappearing entirely.

Leaning on the balustrade of the platform, Aurora followed with her gaze the fleecy white plumes of smoke that ended up vanishing into the diaphanous atmosphere, perfumed with resinous scents by pine-woods. The young woman was wearing a very simple but irreproachably tailored costume. A small felt hat, beneath which her gilded tresses were gathered, left her neck bare. That was the young woman's usual coiffure while traveling, being the most practical, the one that permitted her to come and go freely and devote herself to the violent exercises to which she was accustomed.

Since they had left Chicago, she had manifested an extreme irritation, annoyed by the slightest details that she did not find to her taste. Even her father had not succeeded in calming her down. She had complained about the slowness of the train.

"We'll never get there," she had said in a fit of anger. In response to William Boltyn's orders, the mechanics had been obliged to increase its already-enormous speed. The manometers indicated maximum pressure.

Then she had declared that she could not sleep because of the trepidation, rendered almost imperceptible by the shock-absorbers. Two train-attendants had been obliged to put her bed on a trampoline which they had installed on pneumatic rubber supports.

In spite of all that, she had not shown any greater satisfaction. Her bad mood attacked everything, to her father's great despair.

"The trip isn't to your liking?" he had asked her. "What do you want?"

"Nothing," she had replied, dryly.

Aurora had had her meals served in her room, not wanting to see anyone, not even offering her apologies to the billionaires who were traveling in the train with her and William Boltyn, the president of their association.

It was the second time that Aurora was going to Mercury's Park. Since her first visit, she had never wanted to go back. This time, in order to persuade her, it had needed all her father's persistence, and also a certain curiosity regarding the important trials which Hattison had promised that his guests would witness.

"Two years, already, since my first trip," she murmured, suddenly. "How rapidly time flies. Who could have told me then that I would fall in love with a European, a Frenchman! Then, it was a question of my marriage to Ned Hattison. I was happy, unacquainted with suffering. It seemed that anything was possible." She sighed, and added: "Alas, I've learned that billions don't bring happiness. My father has never understood me..."

On the young woman's pure and smooth forehead, a slight wrinkle appeared as she evoked these memories. A sad smile of seeming disillusionment twisted her lips.

"What can have become of him?" she went on, increasingly thoughtful. "Why did this Olivier Coronal run away from me like that – me, who loves him so much; me, who would brave my father's anger to marry him, to become his wife! I haven't seen him since that ball when we waltzed together. He's left Chicago, doubtless to return to France. How I love him, though!"

Aurora was sincere in the confession she was making to herself, but she knew full well how implacable William Boltyn's hatred was for Europeans. It was not to the man that had conceived the project of crushing the Old World, and who believed himself to be on the verge of success, that she could confide her love.

The young woman heard footsteps behind her.

It was her father. The billionaire had the joyful expression of a man who sees his affairs take a turn for the better.

"Good morning!" he cried. "Up already?"

"Oh, for a long time," Aurora replied, trying to appear calm. "These pine-woods emit an odor that pleases me; I'm breathing in the perfume of the breeze."

"It's good for the health. The tar gives one an appetite. Are you eating with us today? Our friends are waiting for us."

"Gladly, father."

"Let's go," said Boltyn. "I can see that your bad mood has disappeared. So much the better."

They both went to the dining room.

Around a massive table, laden with crystal and porcelain, the train's passengers had taken their seats. The members of the Society of Billionaires were all there, except for Harry Madge, the President of the Spiritualist Club of Chicago, who had declined William Boltyn's invitation. His absence was the subject of the honorable gentlemen's conversation; they were unsparing in making jokes at their absent colleague's expense.

"He's ripe for a lunatic asylum," said Fred Wikilson.

"That's my opinion," said the fat distiller Sips-Rothson. "What do all these tales he tells about spirits signify?"

"It's certain," put in Wood-Waller, a short rosy-cheeked man who spoke in a shrill voice, "that if we'd followed his advice, we wouldn't be going to witness the experiments of our honorable colleague Hattison today. Thank God we had nothing to do with it."

"And what about that car, which he claims is powered by psychic force?" said Philips Adam, the timber merchant who had provided the land on which Mercury's Park had been built, as he burst out laughing.

"At any rate," William Boltyn concluded, "the main thing is that he put in his share. His personal notions are of no importance to us."

Everyone approved the sagacity of Aurora's father, and his pragmatic approach to life. The meal continued cheerfully.

They arrived at Ottega. It was there that the branch line to Mercury's Park originated. An hour later, they arrived.

* * *

Hattison was waiting at the station. His careworn face, his jerky gestures and the anger that he seemed to be having difficulty controlling did not go unnoticed by his guests. He greeted them in a warm fashion, however, and took them to his cottage. Miss Aurora in particular, was the object of his attentions. He took care not to mention her previous visit, not wanting to reawaken unwelcome memories.

"My dear Hattison," William Boltyn was the first to say, "I believe I can translate the sentiments of my honorable colleagues in saying to you that the evasive terms of your dispatch did not satisfy our legitimate curiosity. We're all waiting impatiently for you to unveil the secret that, according to you, will revolutionize the art of strategy completely and make a precious contribution to our enterprise."

"I'm no longer alone in knowing that secret," the engineer replied, in a guttural tone, "and I don't understand it – I can't explain why."

"What do you mean?" exclaimed the billionaires.

Harrison explained that, the previous evening, a French spy had succeeded in getting into the third enclosure. "My microphones," he said, "brought me the sound of his footfalls, and the words he pronounced – among others, Miss, your name…"

"My name!" the young woman exclaimed.

"You can't explain that?" said Hattison. "Me neither. Your name was the password that permitted the opening of a door forbidding access to the enclosure, which it was necessary to spell out with the pointers of an alphabetical dial in order to make the door slide. But that doesn't matter anymore. I admit that, strictly speaking, hazard or divination might have aided the spy." He became more animated as he continued: "What I can't admit is that, having closed the door on him myself, having enclosed him within an electric blockade that fifty men could not have broken through, I found no trace of him this morning, even though I had all the buildings of the enclosure searched by a team of devoted men."

"A Frenchman!" she murmured. "My name!" A presentiment haunted her for a few seconds. She was on the point of letting her secret slip out. She controlled herself. "It doesn't make sense," she said. "It's completely implausible."

"And yet," Hattison exclaimed, "unless he can fly like a bird, the man who broke into the third enclosure last night ought still to be there. He couldn't get through the electric blockade! If he'd tried, I would have found his corpse, at least – and I haven't found anything!"

"Perhaps it's one of those spirits about which Harry Madge talks," suggested Philips Adam, innocently.

In any other circumstances, that remark would have provoked general hilarity, but Hattison's communication was too serious for anyone to think of laughing at the timber merchant.

"No," Hattison was content to reply. "If found very clear material traces of the spy's presence. My secret files and plans have been disturbed, as well as my apparatus. In another location, I observed a disorder that left no doubt as to the detailed analysis to which he devoted himself."

Hattison was alluding to the iron men's hangar, but he did not want to give away the secret of his invention. He wanted to conserve its effect.

"Logically, you say, my dear scientist," William Boltyn observed, "the spy must be a prisoner in the third enclosure. Thus, he's still there. We'll find him there." In the presence of a difficulty, the billionaire reverted to the man of determination, the audacious fighter whom nothing could discourage. "Isn't that the opinion of these honorable gentlemen?"

There was unreserved approval. It was necessary, at all costs, to capture the audacious spy and then execute him summarily. The enterprise would be gravely compromised were he to succeed in escaping and making use of the secrets that had fallen into his hands.

In spite of the conviction established by the fruitless searches he had carried out that same morning, Hattison did not raise any objection. "Everything that it is possible to do, I will do," he replied. "The Frenchman has to be found, and the mystery surrounding his disappearance cleared up. If France and the other European States were to be warned, it would ruin our grandiose plans and our legitimate hopes would evaporate."

In order to dissipate his guests' preoccupation somewhat, the director of Mercury's Park had had Joe bring out a few bottles of claret originating from his estate at Zingo Park.

The cottage's only reception room, next door to Hattison's study, was decorated with works of art in poor taste, including a bust of the President of the Union, a portrait of George Washington and several large canvases representing battles in the War of Independence. Photographic views of the factories were distributed here and there, framed in aluminum, on lacquered side-tables. It was not at all reminiscent of the luxury of the Boltyn house in Chicago. There were no flowers in the mock-Japanese vases. It was sad, sullen and bleak. The influence of Hattison's cold and cruel soul was very evident there.

When Joe had filled the glasses, William Boltyn raised his. "I drink," he said, "to the prompt realization of our projects, to the prosperity of the Union, and to the supremacy of Yankees over all other peoples. Before long, we shall be able to impose our will and make it respected by a military might to which Europe will be forced to submit unconditionally. We shall break all the shackles that the Old World has put on the march of progress. The Union will be able to give free rein to its industrial and practical genius. Victorious, we shall establish the commercial tariffs that are most favorable to us. We shall change the face of the world."

The billionaire was in his element. His voice swelled. He reminded them about the origin of their society, the first meeting in the great hall of the house on Seventh Avenue, following the vote in the House of Representatives.

Everyone listened religiously.

"We are the strongest," he concluded. "Have no fear; the future of humanity is in our hands, dependent on our will. As for this French spy, be sure that he won't escape us. I'll find him, even if I have to mobilize a regiment of detectives."

William Boltyn's speech provoked general enthusiasm. Glasses were emptied in his honor. Resounding cheers were uttered – which permitted Philips Adam, the timber merchant, to show off the power of his vocal organ. His baritone voice rumbled like an unleashed torrent, drowning out all the others.

When the honorable gentlemen's excitement had calmed down slightly, Hattison took advantage of it to make a speech in his turn.

"Before you witness the trials that I have scheduled for you, gentlemen," he said, "I want to give you an exact account of the status of the work I have been doing here for more than two years.

"During your previous visits, you have been able to observe the progress achieved in all the branches of military artistry. Our dynamite cannon has transformed ballistics from top to bottom. Electricity, that mighty ally, has furnished us with a number of powerful devices, and the most powerful motors known. You have appreciated our mobile forts, our automatic machine-guns, our large-sized submarines. You know that, in a short while, I will have found the solution to the problem of aerial navigation. From the heights of the atmosphere, sheltered from projectiles, our aerostats will devastate enemy troops with shells charged with an explosive whose formula is ours alone, and with asphyxiating bombs.

"Everything that science has been able to create in the art of warfare is awaiting the propitious moment. Mercury's Park and Startown have no equivalents in any other nation, I can assure you."

Hattison had delivered his little speech without raising his voice, coldly, as if he were reciting Biblical verses. His words emerged one by one, with mathematical regularity. From time to time he paused to judge the effect he was having on his listeners.

"That is where we are," he continued. "The best armed for war, the richest, the most intelligent, we can envisage the future without fear. We shall see whether the House of Representatives will continue to hesitate to launch the Union on the path of progress, when we have put Mercury's Park and Startown at the disposal of the government."

"It will not hesitate," said William Boltyn. "The newspapers will drag public opinion with them. The entire Yankee people will want war. Its sentiment in that regard was manifest, a few months ago when that English detective in the service of the Foreign Office was murdered. Mobs were running through the streets singing *Yankee Doodle*."

"It was a man named Bob Weld, I believe," said Hattison, indifferently. He was well aware of the truth, since the detective had worked at Mercury's Park for a month under a false name – but he had never informed the billionaires of that detail, nor of his fruitless efforts to pick up the detective's trail.

What had become of the plans found on the corpse? The American government had doubtless caused them to disappear. Hattison had been no more able than Aurora's father to obtain precise information on that subject.

"The rather bellicose disposition of the people is a good omen for the future," Boltyn said. "There will be no lack of volunteers and soldiers."

That sentence was a good opportunity. The engineer seized it. "Soldiers!" he said, with a knowing expression. "You're right, my dear Boltyn, there won't be any lack of them. But don't worry about that question – merely procure leaders. I'll take care of the soldiers. They'll emerge from factories, and will never have to fear hunger or fever, like those in our last colonial war."

The effect of this speech was marvelous, surpassing Hattison's hopes.

The astonishment of the billionaires knew no bounds. They looked at one another with eyes full of admiration and amazement. Even Aurora, who had been pensive from the start, raised her head and appeared to be taking an interest in what was happening around her.

Hattison was pressed with questions, but he was savoring his triumph.

"I understand your astonishment," he said, in the tone of a pontiff condescending to quit his throne. "Permit me, however, to leave the explanations I owe you until later. I will furnish you with as many details as you wish, but I want you to witness the trials. If you wish, let us go into the third enclosure. In spite of last night's events, everything is ready.

"Forward march!" cried Philips Adam, making a chorus of his deep voice with Wood-Walter's shrill organ.

Everyone stood up.

"Are you coming with us, Aurora?" her father asked.

"Certainly," she said. "The trials interest me to the highest degree. I'm as intrigued as you are by what has just been announced."

"As for the French spy," William Boltyn said, as he left the room, "my conviction is that he's still a prisoner. He must have found a hiding-place, and is on the lookout for a favorable opportunity to escape."

They went out of the cottage.

The cupolas of glass and steel and the tall chimneys plumed with smoke caught the gaze of the billionaires. Trains went by, laden with minerals that they were delivering to the blast furnaces. An odor of coal and oil filled the atmosphere. A dull and continuous sound rose up from the enclosures, testifying to the incessant labor of workers and machines.

The same proud satisfaction filled the hearts of all the Yankees before the spectacle of the colossal city. They were proud of their work.

"Science and dollars," said Hattison. "Who will be able to defeat us?" With a gesture, he indicated the perspective of buildings and factories, extended in the distance by the aerostat park and the firing ranges.

Followed by Aurora Boltyn, the members of the Society of American Billionaires, with Hattison in the lead, headed for the third enclosure of Mercury's Park.

The young woman could not rid herself of her mortal presentiments.

Her heart was beating forcefully, and the name of Olivier Coronal continually imposed itself on her thoughts.

The love that Aurora had for the French engineer had affirmed itself more violently still since a dull anguish had invade her entire being, at the idea that the spy of Mercury's Park might be the man she loved.

Chapter XXIV
An Unexpected Denouement

OLIVIER CORONAL, as we have seen, owed his salvation to his insulating costume of gutta-percha. Even so, his hair had been almost entirely charred by the electric current.

Confronted by the massive door in the tunnel, closed by an invisible force, the young man started thinking hard.

"I'm a prisoner," he murmured, furiously. "Hattison's prisoner – which means imminent death."

Reduced to impotence, Olivier Coronal took account of the fact that there was, at present, nothing to be done, nothing to be attempted, and nothing for which to hope. It only remained for him to wait to be captured.

Tracked and disarmed, like a wounded lion surrounded by hunters, who disdains to defend himself, Olivier had made the sacrifice of his life in advance.

Soon, however, with his habitual generosity of character, he forgot the imminent peril he was in, in order not to think any longer about anything except the defeat of the ideas that were dear to him, the brutal triumph of billions over intelligence, of ferocious Yankee organization over European civilization.

It's only today, he thought, *that I understand fully, in all its nuances, the odious type of the Yankee, the scientist devoid of any elevation of ideas, the industrialist devoid of humanity. To make money, in large quantities and quickly, that is his only aim in life, towards which all his efforts are directed. A businessman first and foremost, money is the thing he understands most clearly, which absorbs all his faculties from childhood onwards.*

For anyone who reflects a little, there's nothing very extraordinary about that. He only has to remember how the United States of America was founded. In the sixteenth century, all the nations of the Old World poured into it their surplus of adventurers – which is to say, the less scrupulous and greediest fraction of their population. Germans, Englishmen, Frenchmen and Spaniards came here to get rich, careless of the honesty of the means they employed. Africans, Chinese, Australians and half-breeds of all nations, all bringing the vices of their own races, completed the demoralization of the people to whom the happy of solution of a war permitted the assumption of the title of the United States and the star-spangled banner.

Olivier's brain, almost hallucinated by insomnia and the night's emotions, evoked the venerable image of his friend and master, the engineer Golbert. He thought he could hear his voice buzzing in his ears, and the old scientist's slightest thoughts, including the expressions and turns of phrase, presented themselves to Olivier Coronal's mind with a feverish and unhealthy lucidity.

"Although we have been told about Yankee superiority," said the old scientist, whose invisible presence Olivier believed he could sense beside him, "although we have been told about their marvelous practical genius, the American brain is obviously lacking a lobe.

"They are our superiors, it is said. So be it – but only in the fashion in which a man of the Stone Age would be superior, in running and fighting, to a civilized man of today. Absorbed by a single point of view, a single prey, one might say, it is entirely natural that they have no peers when it comes to mounting an industrial or financial affair – but their intelligence does not exceed the bounds of practical realities, nor can it exceed them.

"Is that really a veritable superiority? One may doubt it.

"When his objective is attained, when he is rich, one might say that the Yankee has nothing left to do, that his life is over. What becomes in fact, of the majority of American billionaires? Does it ever occur to them to use their wealth for the realization of some idea, to enjoy it as an artist or a philosopher? No. When there are no more dollars to conquer, they become disorientated and bored – and the list of those who end up committing suicide or going mad is a long one.

"They really do lack a cerebral lobe. They have no conscious ideas. Outside of practical realities, nothing exists for them and nothing interests them. Of poets, philosophers, artists and thinkers they have none, and cannot have any; it is not within their needs.

"On the contrary, the life of an educated European truly begins when he makes his fortune. He is able to give substance to his ideas and his dreams, to satisfy his ideas of art or humanitarian philosophy. When rich, his life is embellished. That is the whole, enormous difference between the two races that face one another across the Atlantic. Even with the English, the people with whom, in certain respects, they resemble the most, the Yankees have nothing in common from this viewpoint.

"Adapters and utilitarians of the highest ability, assessing at first glance the chances of success in a business deal, understanding admirably how to improve things, they have never been able to invent anything. To build their formidable industrial power, they borrowed everything from the Old World. Even the most recent discoveries launched by companies with colossal wealth – the telephone and color photography, among others – first saw the light of day as scientific innovations in Europe.

"Writers, artists and philosophers – which is to say, all those occupied with abstractions, the general interests of humankind – are totally lacking among Yankees; they only have journalists. The great poet Edgar Poe, a foundling, cannot be claimed by them – and only the Europeans appreciated him. The most celebrated of their painters, Morse, is only known by virtue of an improvement he made to the Bréguet telegraph.

"The question is often asked: Where will the industrial fever that possesses the United States stop? How far will that hasty, overheated civilization go, given that it is fragile nevertheless since poverty, more horrible than anywhere else, provides such a counterweight there to such fantastic and exaggerated opulence, that for every man who gets rich, thousands succumb in the daily *struggle for existence?*

"One can easily anticipate the answer. No one down here works or acts entirely for himself. That is the lesson of the past. The role that the United States seems to be playing, at present, is that of the powerful organizer of the production and circulation of the material things necessary to social life. Only a philosopher can perceive that; the Yankees cannot take account of it.

"But who knows? Perhaps, in spite of themselves, they are working for humanity. Peoples more conscious of themselves exist; ideas are fermenting apart from practical realities, and the future belongs to those peoples and those ideas. At the right moment, thinkers will arrive, when, having reached its peak, American civilization will no longer have any role to play, when people will be obliged to sell something other than foodstuffs, since they will no longer have any value and will only absorb a tiny fraction of human labor.

"The time will then have come for nations, and for far-sighted humans whose genius and science will utilize the immense legacy of anterior civilizations. They will be able to prepare strong and beautiful races, well-equilibrated in body and soul…"

Entirely devoted to the memory of the old master whom he would never see again, Olivier Coronal was lost in thought.

Oh, if he had been able to foresee that the commercial power of the United states would one day became a danger, that conflict would be engaged between the two worlds, that it would no longer suffice for the Yankees to be kings of industry, and that a man would be found among them audacious enough to dream of world dominion!

That man had emerged, in the person of William Boltyn, and he was now pursuing the realization of his monstrous dream, armed with the two great forces of modern humanity: capital and science.

He will succeed! Olivier said to himself, utterly discouraged. *And I shall pay with my life for the attempt I have made to reduce his prideful project to nothing.*

But, perhaps because of the kind of fascination that Aurora had exercised upon him, Olivier detested William Boltyn less than he detested Hattison, that damned soul. The billionaire was playing his role as an accumulator of dollars and pitiless fighter. He was a brute, organized solely to amass banknotes, and Olivier could forgive him, because of the inferiority of his ideas, the baseness of his preoccupations. But Hattison! He, whose thoughts ought to have been ennobled by science, his aspirations purified and magnified, had put his rare faculties of invention and application, which he ought to heave employed for the happiness and pacification of humankind, at the service of the vilest interests!

Olivier Coronal would have sacrificed the old engineer, without a scruple, just as the latter was doubtless about to sacrifice him – for he was convinced that death, and a terrible death, awaited him. He could expect no pity on the part of William Boltyn, even less on the part of the inflexible Hattison.

The spectacle that he had had before his eyes, of the engineer coldly crushing a workman whose sincerity he doubted with a pile-driver informed him of his fate in advance.

"And I shall not have had the satisfaction of making myself useful to my country!" he exclaimed, painfully. "These accursed men will continue their work of destruction. Poor Europe! Poor France! Death would be sweet to me, if I had been able to save you from the plot that they are weaving against you!"

The young man's discouragement was poignant. He was suffering horribly, not by virtue of knowing that he was doomed, but by virtue of the crumbling of his dream, the futility of his sacrifice.

There was no possibility of getting through the door in the tunnel. One step forward, and another electrical discharge would afflict him, which doubtless would not spare him this time.

But how did Hattison find out that I was here? he wondered.

By virtue of examining the walls of the tunnel, Olivier ended up discovering the receiver-plates of microphones. It was necessary to be forewarned or extremely attentive to distinguish them, so carefully dissimulated were they.

I should have foreseen that, he thought, *and cut the wires! I'm no longer astonished that I found the door closed again and protected by an electric blockade. That's the way Hattison does things – slyly and cruelly.*

He went back up the stairway and found himself in the courtyard of the enclosure, his lantern in his hand. First light was beginning to appear on the peaks of the Rocky Mountains. On the roof of the laboratory, the electric beacon was still illuminated.

"Impossible to get over the walls," Olivier muttered. "All precautions have been taken. I'm a prisoner." His voice was tremulous. Fury and despair were making unsteady progress.

He sat down on a boundary-stone with his head in his hands, and dreamed. He reviewed his entire past in a matter of minutes. He saw Paris, his friend Golbert, the old scientist, and the happy times he had spent with him and Lucienne, their fine conversations in the little house in Montmartre, all the memories of his discreet love for the young woman. Then there was the marriage of Lucienne and Ned Hattison, everything that he had suffered without saying anything, and the departure for New York in the hope of constructing the subatlantic railway. Léon Goupit had accompanied them. And immediately, there was Aurora, whom he had loved in spite of everything, in spite of the submarine catastrophe, in spite of the work of hatred and egoism undertaken by her father at Mercury's Park. Even now, defeated in everything that was most dear to him in the world, in the struggle that he had engaged alone in order to save threatened Europe, Olivier Coronal could not invoke the young heiress's metallic eyes without a frisson.

Olivier's heart was bleeding. An atrocious combat was taking place within him, between his love and what he considered to be his duty, his mission.

The love of humanity had already triumphed once.

"I shall go on until the end!" Olivier cried, forcefully, as he got to his feet again. "I shall die – so be it – but when I have exhausted the final resource."

A fantastic idea, apparently unrealizable, had just come into the engineer's mind. Strong, and ready for anything, he found himself one again upright, energetic and calm.

He headed for the laboratory, went into it, and put back on the work-table the files that he had taken away, removed the traces of his presence as best he could, went out again, closed the door behind him, and went to the hangar of the iron men with a firm stride.

"As long as I'm a similar height!" he murmured, as he went in.

He had no need to light the arc-lamp in order to perceive the automata, black and rigid, whose functioning he had learned a short while before.

In the laboratory, the young man had discovered a whistle of a special kind – doubtless the one used to control them. He had taken possession of it.

His first concern was to compare his own height with that of the soldiers.

"That's good," he said. "I'm slightly shorter, but with the lead boots and the armor, I'll be exactly the same height."

Without hesitation, Olivier Coronal picked out an automaton placed in the center of the battalion, went through the ranks, tipped it over and dragged it outside.

Made of molded steel, each machine weighed nearly a hundred and fifty kilos. It required a considerable effort for him to drag the one he had selected to a location to one side, taking care not to touch the bayonet of the rifle, which he knew to be in contact with the interior piles.

As soon as he had found the necessary locksmith's tools on the workbenches, the false Jonathan Mills set about dismantling the automaton and separating the armor from the mechanism.

He was skillful. The danger, which was increasing by the minute, gave him strength. His screwdriver soon took care of the external plates. He cut the conductive wires of the piles and insolated the entire mechanism. No longer running any risk of being electrocuted, Olivier was able to accelerate the dismantling of the internal mechanism. Even though it was constructed with extreme simplicity, it was nevertheless solidly mounted. So, in spite of his desire to finish the task he had undertaken, the engineer could only make slow progress.

One by one, he detached the connecting rods that transmitted movement to the automaton's arms and legs. A hammer and a screwdriver replaced the scalpel and other surgical instruments in this new kind of dissection. The rods lay on the work-table like powerful muscles.

Then he took out the electric piles that formed a veritable heart for the steel automaton. With pincers, he severed the electric wires forming a strange network of arteries or nerves, which carried the motive force to the automaton's extremities. The cogwheels of the apparatus regulating the movements shattered into little pieces under Olivier's hammer-blows and were strewn on the ground, like broken bones. Then the accumulators were smashed. All that remained of the metallic entrails were twisted and broken plates lying in the midst of a pool of acid.

Finally, Olivier attacked the iron man's helmet: the helmet that took the place of a head, which enclosed – a strange brain! – everything that Hattison had found to be most subtle in the manner of mechanism. The phonographs that replaced the ears and registered commands, and the apparatus transmitting those commands to the interior mechanisms responsible for making the entire mechanism respond, were pitilessly pulverized.

And of the technological masterpiece so patiently constructed by the billionaire engineer, nothing any longer remained but a metallic carcass in human form. The right arm, still maintained by a network of wires, seemed to be threatening the sky with the point of its electric bayonet.

It was a strange spectacle, in the still-indecisive light of the nascent day: that hasty and feverish dissection, carried out by a human on a human automaton.

When he had finished dismantling it, Olivier took away all the components and organs of steel that he had just extracted from the armor that was now scattered on the ground, and hid them carefully under heaps of scrap metal.

"As long as Hattison doesn't come before I'm ready!" he murmured, anxiously. "Too prudent to have risked it on his own last night, he's bound to come this morning to complete my capture."

Rapidly, over his clothing, the young man started putting on – or, rather, securing – the armor that he had just removed from the automaton. The lower leg-pieces were threaded without much difficulty, but the thigh segments posed greater difficulties, as did the arms and the torso.

Sweat moistened his forehead. Gradually, however, his entire body disappeared into the sheath of steel. His ingenuity triumphed over the difficulties. With pieces of iron wire he consolidated various uncertain parts of his improvised harness. Soon, there was nothing but his head free. He picked up the helmet in both hands and placed it over his head, adjusted it slightly, picked up the electric rifle, got rid of the traces of his transformation, and took the place of the iron man he had just demolished.

There was no longer anyone in the hangar but fifty steel automata, rifles shouldered – but among those inert machines, there was a man, an intrusive intelligence. The battalion had a leader. In his clenched fist, Olivier Corona still had the whistle.

Less than ten minutes later, the young man heard footsteps in the courtyard of the third enclosure. As he had anticipated, Hattison had come to search for him with a squad of engineers. For more than an hour they explored every nook and cranny of the hangar and the laboratory. Hattison directed the search with an extraordinary stubbornness.

Within his armor, as impassive as a statue, Olivier Coronal had seen him pass by several times, his lips pinched, his gaze terrible. The engineer had promised five hundred dollars to the man who discovered the spy.

"He's here!" he shouted. "Dead or alive, he can't have escaped." Between his teeth, so quietly that Olivier could hardly hear it, he added: "And Boltyn and all the others will arrive in a few hours for the trials."

Fortunately, when he pronounced those final words, the engineer was not looking at the battalion of iron men. He would have seen one automaton shiver in its armor.

Hattison was obliged to admit that his search had been unsuccessful. He withdrew, swallowing his range, closing the electric blockade behind him and his men.

It was just in time. Olivier Coronal's right arm had almost seized up because of the weight of the rifle and its immobility. Another few seconds and, in spite of all his determination, the weapon would have slipped from his grip.

With his rifle set down beside him, not daring to take off any part of his steel carapace for fear of being taken by surprise, the young man sat down, as best he could, and waited.

In any other circumstances, the travesty would have made him laugh, but it was no time for gaiety. His life, his liberty and perhaps the salvation of civilization depended on the success of his enterprise.

So it's today that the trials are to take place, he said to himself. *In a few hours, as Hattison has just said, William Boltyn and his associates will be here. I'm definitely doomed…but what shall I be able to do, even so? I can't stay in this hangar for very long. I'm only an automaton in appearance, and will die of hunger.*

Gradually, an idea that was initially confused, became clearer in his mind, and ended up haunting him: a murderous idea, which all of his sensibility found repellent, but which satisfied his latent hated with regard to Hattison and Boltyn, the authors of the subatlantic railway catastrophe and the founders of the two cities of murder, Mercury's Park and Startown.

They have not hesitated to commit murder, he argued, internally. *Monsieur Golbert nearly fell victim to them. They won't hesitate to execute me summarily, to make me disappear along with the secret I possess. Why should I spare them now, when, thanks to the whistle, I have in my hand the means of striking them down, of directing at them the rifles of the automata that they have armed against Europe?*

From then on, Olivier Coronal's resolution was fixed.

His sacrifice would not be entirely in vain. He would die, but he would take William Boltyn and his accomplices with him.

Aurora? He did not want to think about that.

* * *

It was truly a day of triumph for the engineer Hattison. His pride was exultant – but he did not want any of that to show, and strove, on the contrary, to maintain an unshakable self-control.

Guided by him, the billionaires mounted a general search for the spy, rummaging through and shifting everything, exploring the remotest corners, exiting one another in the manhunt with hateful exclamations. They would certainly have lynched him with their own hands in the fit of savage anger that had taken possession of them.

William Boltyn was by no means the least determined. Formidable oaths escaped him; he gave free rein to his fury. He was the last to abandon the search.

"There's something here that we're missing," Hattison concluded. "I'll get to the bottom of it. He must be here. He is…but he'll have to wait. Let's suspend the search."

Slightly calmer, the billionaires came into the hangar. Aurora had followed them.

The fifty automata were there, rigid on their legs of steel.

There was a cry of admiration.

In a few words, Hattison explained their operation, and their role in future warfare.

"This," he said, "is why I summoned you all here. Ten years of incessant labor have produced this result. This will be the key element of our work, the one that will ensure victory. And was I not right to attach the greatest importance to the capture of the spy who got in here last night? He was not a worker. His primary concern was to obtain cognizance of the plans of my iron men. He has stolen a whistle. With what objective? I don't know. Everything indicates that we're dealing with an engineer, and man for whom mechanics and electricity have no secrets."

Olivier Coronal heard all that, immobile in his armor in the center of the battalion.

Momentarily, it seemed to the young man that he was going mad.

Aurora was there, among the men whose murder he was premeditating!

Behind the metal helmet, Olivier's face convulsed.

Twenty times, during that manhunt, he had been on the point of letting himself go, of giving way to his vengeance. Now, Aurora was interposed between him and his victims!

Meanwhile, Hattison put a stop to the signs of admiration and the cheers that the billionaires were lavishing upon him.

"Allow me to maneuver our future soldiers before you," he said. "You can then establish your judgment on a solid basis."

"Are they really soldiers?" the stout Philips Adam asked the distiller Sips-Rothson, whose face, under the influence of the claret, had taken on a vermilion tint.

"We shall see," the latter replied, whose intelligence was no quicker than the timber merchant's.

Hattison installed everyone in the courtyard of the enclosure, on the steps of the laboratory, and recommended that they keep still. Then he came into the hangar again, with a whistle in his hand like the one that Olivier Coronal held.

The young man had made his decision – or, at least, thought he had made it. He would see the job through to the end. He would sacrifice Aurora.

Hattison put the whistle to his lips. A shrill and strident sound cut through the air.

Heavily, making the ground tremble beneath their leaden soles, the automata advanced. Moving into the courtyard and heading toward the laboratory.

"Hurrah for Hattison!" William Boltyn was the first to shout.

"Hurrah! Hurrah!" the billionaires shouted, at the top of their voice.

Suddenly, sung by an invisible choir, *Yankee Doodle* was heard. Hattison had just activated a series of phonographs. The effect was gripping. The engineer had not counted in vain on the patriotism of his guests. The latter seemed electrified. Even Aurora was applauding frantically. The hurrahs redoubled.

Seemingly impassive, Hattison supervised the march of his iron men. Magisterially, he stopped them with a blast of the whistle, a few meters from the steps on which the billionaires were standing, William Boltyn at their head.

What was going through Olivier Coronal's head then?

Was he about to execute his plan, intervene, tear off his automaton's mask?

The lives of all those Yankees belonged to him. He only had to take action. Europe would be saved. A volley of bullets would deliver justice. The Society of Billionaires would be done for.

But what about Aurora?

Would he have the strength to sacrifice her too?

Hattison had rejoined his guests on the steps. The excitement was at its peak. They would have lifted the engineer on to their shoulders in triumph, had he not forbidden it.

The phonographs in the house were still playing *Yankee Doodle.* Their powerful notes were prolonged by echoes.

Suddenly, a whistle-blast was heard. It was not Hattison, however, who had issued the command.

The iron men knelt down.

A second whistle-blast sounded.

Before the billionaires, nailed to the spot, could move, all the rifles were leveled.

It was the supreme moment.

With an abrupt movement, Olivier Coronal had removed his helmet and thrown his weapon away. Bare-headed, lividly pale, he appeared, standing up, dominating the kneeling battalion whose weapons were aimed at the billionaires.

The young Frenchman's eyes were fixed on Aurora. A horrible agony convulsed his face. He raised his arm. The whistle almost touched his lips. That was the final signal. The automata were about to fire at the laboratory steps.

At that moment, a heart-rending cry was heard. The young heiress had just recognized the inventor.

"Olivier Coronal!" she cried.

That cry penetrated the young man's heart.

The young woman was running toward him.

His arm fell back, helplessly.

He was defeated.

Meanwhile, the billionaires were recovering from their stupor and terror.

"The spy!" they shouted. "There he is! He's ours!"

Hattison had taken a revolver from his pocket. He launched himself forward in his turn.

In front of him, however, Aurora had reached the young man, and, forgetting all dissimulation, tried to drag him away.

"They're going to kill you!" she cried.

Around the prisoner now, as well as the battalion of iron men, all the Yankees were running. Almost all of them, following Hattison's example, had revolvers in their hands. Their menacing attitude left no doubt as to their intentions.

"Surrender!" shouted Hattison.

"Never!" the inventor replied.

All the revolvers were aimed at him.

"Father!" Aurora shouted. "You're the master! Save this man!"

"That spy!" roared William Boltyn. "Impossible! He must die!" His finger was on the trigger – but he did not have time to shoot.

Crazed and distraught, Aurora had snatched the revolver from his hand and had placed herself in front of Olivier.

"If you touch this man!" she shouted, "I'll kill myself! You'll have two cadavers instead of one!"

There was a momentary hesitation.

Aurora's expression was sublime.

"My daughter!" howled William Boltyn, maddened by dolor. "My daughter!"

He had run forward, his eyes terrible and his fists clenched, and it was now him who protected the two young people.

"Let no one take the life of this man!" he commanded, in his formidable voice.

Olivier Coronal was saved.

Frank Reade Jr. & His New Steam Man
Or, the Young Inventor's Trip to the Far West

Luis Philip Senarens

Chapter I
A Great Wrong

FRANK READE was noted the world over as a wonderful and distinguished inventor of marvelous machines in the line of steam and electricity. But he had grown old and unable to knock about the world, as he had been wont once to do.

So it happened that his son, Frank Reade, Jr., a handsome and talented young man, succeeded his father as a great inventor, even excelling him in variety and complexity of invention. The son speedily outstripped his sire.

The great machine shops in Readestown were enlarged by young Frank, and new flying machines, electric wonders, and so forth, were brought into being.

But the elder Frank would maintain that, inasmuch as electricity at the time was an undeveloped factor, his invention of the Steam Man was really the most wonderful of all.

"It cannot be improved upon," he declared, positively. "Not if steam is used as a motive power."

Frank, Jr. laughed quietly, and patted his father on the back.

"Dad," he said, with an affectionate, though bantering air, "what would you think if I should produce a most remarkable improvement upon your Steam Man?"

"You can't do it!" declared the senior Reade.

Frank, Jr., said no more, but smiled in a significant manner. One day later, the doors of the secret draughting-room of design were tightly locked and young Frank came forth only to his meals.

For three months this matter of closed doors continued. In the machine shop department, where the parts of machinery were secretly put together, the ring of hammers might have been heard, and a big sign was upon the door:

No admittance!

Thus matters were when one evening Frank left his arduous duties to spend a few hours with his wife and little boy.

But just as he was passing out of the yard, a darky, short in stature and of genial features, rushed excitedly up to him.

"Oh, Marse Frank," cried the sable servitor, "Jes' wait one moment!"

"Well, Pomp," said Frank, pleasantly, "what can I do for you?"

The darky, who was a faithful servant of the Reades, and had accompanied both on their tours in foreign lands, ducked his head, with a grin, and replied:

"Yo' father wants yo', Marse Frank, jes' as quick as eber yo' kin come!"

"My father," exclaimed Frank, quickly. "What is it?"

"I don't know nuffin' 'bout it tall, Marse Frank. He jes' say fo' me to tell yo' he want fo' to see yo'."

"Where is he?"

"In his library, sah."

"All right, Pomp. Tell him I will come at once."

The darky darted away. Frank saw that the doors to the secret rooms were locked. This was a wise precaution for hosts of cranks and demented inventors were always hovering about the place and would quickly have stolen the designs if they could have got at them.

Not ten minutes later Frank entered the library where his father was.

The elder Reade was pacing up and down in great excitement.

"Well, my son, you have come at last!" he cried. "I have much wanted to see you."

"I am at your service, father," replied Frank. "What is it?"

"I want you to tell me what kind of a machine you have been getting up."

"Come now, that's not fair," said Frank Jr. with twinkling eyes.

"Well, if it's any kind of a machine that can travel over the prairies tell me so," cried the elder Reade, excitedly.

Frank, Jr., was at a loss to exactly understand what his father was driving at. However, he replied:

"Well, I may safely say that it is. Now explain yourself."

"I will," replied the senior Reade. "I have a matter of great importance to give you, Frank, my boy. If your invention is as good as my steam man even, and does not improve upon it, it will yet perform the work which I want it to do."

A light broke across Frank, Jr.'s face.

"Ah!" he cried. "I see what you are driving at. You have an undertaking for me and my new machine."

Frank, Sr., looked steadily at Frank, Jr., and replied:

"You have hit the nail upon the head."

"What is it?"

"First, I must tell you a story."

"Well?"

"It would take me some time to go into the details, so I will not attempt to do that but give you a simple statement of facts; in short, the outline of the story."

"All right. Let us have it."

The senior Reade cleared his throat and continued:

"Many years ago when I was traveling in Australia I was set upon by bushmen and would have been killed but for the sudden arrival upon the scene of a countryman of mine, a man of about my own age and as plucky as a lion.

"His name was Jim Travers, and I had known him in New York as the son of a wealthy family. He was of a roving temperament, however, and this is what had brought him to Australia.

"Well, Travers saved my life. He beat off my assailants, and nursing my wounds brought me back to life.

"I have felt ever since that I owed him a debt which could not be fully repaid. At that time I could make no return for the service.

"Jim and I drifted through the gold fields together. Then I lost track of him, and until the other day I have not seen or heard from him.

"But I now find that it is in my power to give him assistance, in fact to partly pay the debt I owe him. This brings us to the matter in hand.

"Six months ago it seems that Jim who is now a man of great wealth, still a bachelor and for a few years past living at a fashionable hotel in New York went to his club. When he returned in the evening he found a note worded like this," Mr. Reade laid a note upon the table. Frank read it:

Dear Travers: I would like to see you tonight upon a very important matter. Will you meet me in twenty minutes at the cafe on your corner. I must see you, so be sure and come.
A Friend.

"Of course Jim wondered at the note, but he did not know of an enemy in the world, so he felt perfectly safe in keeping the appointment. He started for the cafe.

"The night was dark and misty, Jim walked along and had got near the cafe when somebody stepped out of a dark hallway and grasped his arm.

"'Come in here,' a sharp voice said, 'we can talk better here than in the cafe.'

"Before Jim could make any resistance he was pulled into a dark hallway. Two men had hold of him and something wet was dashed across his face and over his hands, then he felt some liquid poured over his clothes and some object thrust into his pocket.

"Then the door opened again and he was flung out into the street. Jim was unharmed, but amazed at such treatment. He had not been hurt and was at a loss to understand what it all meant.

"The incident had taken but a few moments in its course. At first a thought of foul play had flashed across Jim. Then it occurred to him to look at his hands, which were wet with some substance.

"He gave a great cry of horror as he did so. There was blood upon them. In fact his hands and face and clothes were almost soaked in red blood. For an instant he was horrified.

"What mystery was this? But he quickly changed his opinion and actually laughed.

"It occurred to him as a practical joke upon the part of his club friends. Satisfied of this he resolved to get even with them.

"He tried to open the door, through which he had been pulled. It was locked and would not yield.

"Then he decided to go back to his room and wash off the blood. But he had not gone ten steps before he was met in the glare of the lamplight by one of the club men.

"'Thunder! What's the matter with you, Travers?' asked his friend.

"'Oh, nothing, only a little practical joke the boys have been playing on me,' replied Jim with a grin. Two or three others come along and Jim explains in like manner. Then he goes to his apartments.

"When he arrives there he is amazed to find the door open and a fearful scene within. The furniture, the light carpet and the walls in places are smeared with blood. Jim now got angry.

"'This is carrying a joke a little too far!' he cried, testily. 'This spoiling the furniture is too much.'

"But he went to washing the blood from his hands. This was a hard job and took time. Suddenly half a dozen officers came into the room and seized him.

"'What do you want?' cried poor Jim in surprise.

"'We want you,' they replied.

"'What for?'

"'For murder!'

"Instead of being horrified, Jim was mad, madder than a March hare. He just got up and swore at the officers. 'I don't like this sort of thing,' he declared. 'It's carrying a joke too far.'

"The officers only laughed and slipped manacles upon his wrists. Then they led him away to prison. Not until brought into court did poor Jim know that he had been made the victim of a hellish scheme.

"Murder had really been committed in that house into which he had been dragged, and where he was smeared with blood. A man unknown, was there found literally carved to pieces with a knife.

"Blood had been found upon Jim in his room. A trail led from the house to his room. A knife was found in his coat pocket. The evidence was all against him and his trial had just come off and he had just been sentenced to death by hanging with only three months of grace."

Frank Reade, Jr., listened to this thrilling tale with sensations which the pen cannot depict. It was so horrible, so strange, so ghastly that he could hardly believe it true.

He arose and walked once across the floor.

Chapter II
The New Steam Man

THE YOUNG INVENTOR paused before his father, and in a deeply impressed manner said:

"Then an innocent man stands convicted of murder?"

"Yes."

"In that case it is the duty of every philanthropic man to try and save the innocent."

"It is."

"We must do it."

"I am glad to hear you say that."

"But the question now arises as to how we shall be able to do it. Is there no clew to the real assassins?"

"No definite clew."

"That is very strange. Of course there must have been a motive. That motive would seem to be to get Travers out of the way."

"Yes."

"And he has no enemies?"

"None that he knew of."

"Ah, but what would any one gain by putting him out of the way –"

Frank Reade, Jr., paused. He gazed steadily at his father. Much passed between them in that glance.

"His fortune is a large one," put in the senior Reade, "the right to inherit would furnish the best motive. There is but one heir, and he is a nephew, Artemas Cliff, who is a stockman, somewhere in the Far West. It could not be him."

"Could not?" Frank Reade, Jr., sat down and dropped into a brown study. After a time he aroused.

"I am interested in this case," he declared. "And my Steam Man is at the disposal of justice at any time. But you spoke of the prairies. Is there a clew in the West?"

"The only clew possible to obtain at present," declared Mr. Reade, Sr. "You see detectives tracked two suspicious men to Kansas. There they lost track of them. Everybody believes that they were the assassins."

"Well, I believe it," cried Frank Reade, Jr., with impulse. "I can see but one logical explanation of this matter. Either Artemas Cliff has employed two ruffians to do this awful deed for the sake of Travers' money, or – the case is one not possible to solve with ease."

Frank Reade, Sr., did not display surprise at this statement of his son.

"Now you have the whole thing in a nutshell, my boy," he said. "Of course, you can do as you please, but if you wish to take any kind of a journey with your new invention, here is a chance, and a noble object in view. That object should be to track down the murderers, and clear Jim Travers. It may be that the nephew, Artemas Cliff, is the really guilty one, but in any case, I believe that it is in the West you will find the solution of the mystery."

"That is my belief," agreed Frank Reade, Jr., "but now that this matter is settled let me show you the plans of my steam man."

Frank Reade, Jr., drew a roll of papers from his pocket and spread them upon the table.

Upon them were the blue print plans and drawings of the mechanism of the Steam Man.

Frank Reade, Senior, examined them carefully and critically. From one piece to another he went and after some time drew a deep breath saying:

"Well, young blood is the best after all. I must say, Frank, that I am beat. There is no doubt but that you have improved upon my Steam Man. I congratulate you."

"Thank you," said Frank Reade, Jr. with gratification.

"But I am anxious to see this marvel at work."

"You shall," replied the young inventor. "Tomorrow the Steam Man will go out of the shop upon his trial trip."

A few minutes later Frank Reade, Jr., was on the way to his own house.

He was in a particularly happy frame of mind. He had achieved great results in his new invention, and here, as by design, was a chance afforded him to use the Steam Man to a philanthropic and heroic purpose.

The idea of traveling through the wilds of the West was a thrilling one.

Frank could already picture the effect of the Steam Man upon the wild savages of the plains and the outlaws of Western Kansas and Colorado.

Also the level floor-like prairie of that region would afford excellent traveling for the new invention.

Frank Reade, Jr., was a lover of adventure.

It was an inborn love. The prospect before him fired his very soul. It was just what he desired.

That evening he unfolded all his plans to his wife.

Of course Mrs. Reade was averse to her husband undertaking such a dangerous trip. But after a time she overcame her scruples and reconciled herself to it.

The next morning at an early hour, Frank was at the engine house of the steel works. The wide doors were thrown open and a wonderful sight revealed.

There stood the Steam Man.

Frank Reade, Sr., and a great number of friends were present. Pomp, the negro, was also there, as well as a queer-looking little Irishman with a genuine Hibernian mug and twinkling eyes, which bespoke a nature brimming over with fun. This was Barney O'Shea.

Barney and Pomp had long been faithful servants of the Reades. In all of their travels with their inventions they had accompanied them. Of these two characters we will say no more, but permit the reader to become acquainted with them in the course of the story.

The senior Reade examined the mechanism of the new Steam Man with deepest interest.

"Upon my word, Frank," he cried, "you have beaten me out and out. I can hardly believe my eyes."

Frank Reade, Jr., laughed good humoredly.

Then he went about showing a party of friends the mechanism of the new Steam Man.

The man himself was a structure of iron plates joined in sections with rivets, hinges or bars as the needs required.

In face and form the machine was a good imitation of a man done in steel.

In no wise did he look ponderous or unwieldy, though his stature was fully nine feet.

The man stood erect holding the shafts of a wagon at his hips.

The wagon itself was light but roomy with four wheels and a top covering of fine steel net work. This was impervious to a bullet while anyone inside could see quite well all about them.

There were loop-holes in this netting to put the rifle barrels through in case of a fight.

A part of the wagon was used as a coal bunker. Other small compartments held a limited amount of stores, ammunitions and weapons.

Upon the fender in front was a brake to regulate the wagon on a steep grade, and a slit in the net work here allowed of the passage of the reins, two long lines connecting with the throttle and whistle valves. A word as to the mechanism of the man.

Here was really the fine work of the invention.

Steam was the motive power.

The hollow legs and arms of the man made the reservoir or boilers. In the broad chest was the furnace. Fully two hundred pounds of coal could here be placed, keeping up a fire sufficient to generate steam for a long time.

The steam chest was upon the man's back, and here were a number of valves. The tall hat worn by the man formed the smoke stack.

The driving rods, in sections, extended down the man's legs, and could be set in motion so skillfully that a tremendous stride was attained, and a speed far beyond belief.

This was the new steam man. The improvements were many and manifest.

All the mechanism was more nicely balanced, the parts more strongly joined, and the steel of finer quality. Greater speed was the certainty.

Fire was burning in the furnace, steam was hissing from the retort, and smoke was pouring from the funnel hat of the man.

Frank Reade, Jr., suddenly sprung in the wagon.

He closed the screen door behind him. Pomp was engaged in some work in the coal bunker.

Frank took up the reins and pulled them. The throttle was opened and also the whistle valve.

Three sharp shrieks the new Steam Man gave and then he was away on the trial trip.

Out of the yard he went and out upon the highway.

Everybody rushed to the gates and a great cheer went up. Down the highway went the Steam Man at a terrific gait.

His strides were long and powerful. So rapidly were they made that a tremendous amount of surface was covered.

It was a good smooth road.

Just ahead was a man riding a horse. Near him was a bicycler who was noted as a fast rider.

Both had heard that the Steam Man would make his trial run that morning.

Bets had been made by both that they could beat the Man.

Frank guessed the truth at once.

"Ki dar, Marse Frank," cried Pomp, with a chuckle and a shake of his woolly head. "Dem two chaps ain got a pile ob gall. Jes' yo' show dem dat dey ain't in it. Won't yo'?"

Pomp had more than one reason for beating the horse and bicycle. He had made a small bet of his own on the result.

It was evident that the parties ahead were ready for the fun.

Frank Reade, Jr., smiled grimly, and opened the throttle a little wider.

The next moment the Steam Man, the bicycle rider and the trotter were all flying neck and neck down the road.

Heavens! What a race that was!

Down the road they flew like a whirlwind. The dust flew up behind them in a cloud.

But the Steam Man just trotted by his competitors with seemingly no exertion at all. Frank turned with a laugh to see how easily they were distanced.

After a good trial, the new Steam Man returned to the foundry yard. As Frank stepped down out of the wagon, his father came up and grasped his hand in an ecstasy of delight.

"Bravo, my son!" he cried. "You have eclipsed my Invention. I wish you luck, and I know that you will succeed in clearing Jim Travers."

"I shall take only Barney and Pomp with me," said Frank Reade, Jr. "There will not be room in the wagon for more."

"Well, they will be useful companions," said the Senior Reade. "My son; may God be with you in your enterprise."

Frank Reade, Jr., at once proceeded to make preparations for his western trip.

He visited Travers in prison and talked with him.

"To tell the truth, I am distrustful of my nephew, Artemas Cliff. He is an avaricious villain, and a number of times has tried to swindle me out of money. I know that he has led the life of an outlaw out there on the border."

"But if he aspired to gain your wealth, why did he not attempt your life in some direct manner?" asked Frank.

"I presume he may have feared detection," replied Travers. "If I am hung for the murder of this unknown man, the mystery will be sealed forever. The real murderer will never be known."

"I believe you are right," agreed Frank Reade, Jr. "Well, I will find this Artemas Cliff, and do the best I can toward clearing up the mystery and setting you right."

"Thank you!" said Travers with emotion. "I feel that you will succeed."

Chapter III
On the Plains

THE SCENE of our story now undergoes a great change.

We will transfer the reader from Readestown to the plains of the Far West. Fully five hundred miles from civilization, and right in the heart of the region of the hostile Sioux.

Frank Reade, Jr., had transported the Steam Man as far as possible by rail.

From thence he had journeyed the rest of the ways overland.

Nothing of thrilling sort had as yet marked their journey. But they were upon the verge of the most exciting adventures as the reader will hereafter agree, possible to be experienced by man.

With the broad expanse of rolling plain upon every hand, one morning in June the Steam Man might have been seen making its way along at a moderate gait.

Frank Reade, Jr., with Barney and Pomp were in the wagon.

Frank held the reins and his keen gaze swept the prairie in every direction.

As far as the eye could reach there remained the same broad expanse. There was little to break the monotony.

Barney and Pomp had taken advantage of a lull in their duties to play a social game of poker in the rear of the wagon.

These two unique characters, although the warmest of friends, were nevertheless always engaged in badgering each other or the perpetration of practical jokes.

"Bejabers, I'll go yez ten betther on that, yez black ape," cried Barney, throwing down a handful of chips. "I'll take me worrud it's a big bluff yez are playin'. Yez can't fool me."

"Youse will jest find out dis nigger neber plays a bluff game," retorted Pomp with a chuckle. "Jest yo' look out fo' yo'sef, Pish."

"Begorra, I ain't afraid av yez an' I'll go ye the tin," cried Barney.

There was a broad grin upon Pomp's face. He quietly picked up ten chips and then put in ten more.

"Hold on, Pish, I'll go youse ten better."

"Call yez, be hivens!" cried Barney, chucking in ten more.

Then he threw down his hand.

"Can yez bate that?" he cried, triumphantly. "Give us the pot, naygur. Yez are no good."

But Pomp put one black paw over the pile of chips.

"'Jes' wait one minnit, Pish."

"Whurro! Yez can't bate it!" cried Barney, confidently.

He had thrown a good hand containing four kings and two aces. But Pomp quietly laid down four aces!

The picture was one well worthy of an artist. For a moment the two card players gazed at the six aces in amazement. It was a very curious anomaly that there should be six aces in one pack of cards.

Then Barney sprang up furiously.

"Begorra, it's a big cheat ye are!" he cried, angrily. "Whoever saw the loikes av that? Be me sowl, the hull pile is mine!"

"Don' yo' put yo' hands on dem chips, Pish!" cried Pomp, angrily.

"P'raps yo' kin tell me wharfore youse got dem two aces, maybe youse can?"

"Bejabers, they war in the pack, but yez kin tell me perhaps where yez got those four aces yez put down there?"

"I tell yo', Pish, dey was in de pack."

"Be jabers it's the fust pack av cards I ever saw with six aces in it," retorted Barney.

"Now don' yo' gib me any mo' ob yo' sass, Pish!" blustered Pomp. "I'll jes' make yo' sorry if yo' does."

"Bejabers yez ain't the size!"

"Look out fo' yo'self, Pish!"

"Whurroo!"

Over went the table leaf, down went the chips in the bottom of the wagon, and the two angry poker players closed in a lively wrestle.

For a moment Barney had the best of it, then Pomp tripped the Celt up and both fell in a heap in the bottom of the wagon.

They chanced to fall against the wire screen door in the rear of the wagon.

It was unlocked and gave way beneath the pressure, and the two practical jokers went through it and out upon the hard floor of the prairie.

They were rolled about in a cloud of dust, and had they not been of something more than ordinary composition they would have suffered from broken bones.

But as it was both picked themselves up unhurt.

The Steam Man had gone on fully one hundred yards before Frank Reade, Jr., perceived that his companions were missing, and at once closed the throttle and brought the Man to a halt.

"Serves the rascals right," muttered Frank, as he saw them pick themselves up from the dust. "They are always skylarking, and no good comes of it."

Frank had stopped the Steam Man. He waited for the two jokers to pick themselves up and return to the wagon.

But at that moment a thrilling thing occurred.

Barney and Pomp had fallen near a clump of timber.

From this with wild yells a band of mounted Sioux Indians now dashed.

They were a war party – painted and bedecked with feathers, and in the full paraphernalia of war.

The peril which threatened the two jokers was one not to be despised.

It was quite evident that the savages meant to cut off their rejoining the Steam Man. In that case their fate would be sealed.

But Barney was quick-witted, and saw the situation at a glance.

With a wild howl he broke into a mad run for the Steam Man. It was a question of life or death and he ran as he had never run before.

Pomp was not so lucky. While Barney was distancing his pursuers, and actually succeeded in reaching the wagon, the darky suddenly found himself cut off.

Indian ponies were circling about him, the red riders whooping and yelling like veritable demons.

The poor darky was beside himself with terror and perplexity.

"Golly sakes alibe!" he yelled, with his wool literally standing on end. "Whatebber am dis yer nigger gwine fo' to do? I'se a gone coon fo' suah."

It certainly looked that way. The savages circled nearer and half a dozen of them dismounted and rushed upon Pomp.

Now the darky was unarmed.

He had not even a pistol or a knife. Of course he was at their mercy.

In less time than it takes to tell it, the savages had closed in about the terrified darky, and he was quickly thrown upon his back and bound.

Then he was laid across the back of a pony and tied on securely.

Then a lariat was attached to the pony's bridle, and the savages with their prisoner in their midst dashed away.

Barney had reached the Steam Man and climbed into the wagon.

Frank Reade, Jr., had seen the whole affair, and for a moment was too astounded to act.

Then as Barney came tumbling into the wagon, Frank turned the man around and sent him flying toward the savages.

This move was quickly made, and the Steam Man ran forward rapidly. But quick as it had been, the savages had yet succeeded in making Pomp a prisoner and getting away with him.

"Be jabers, they've got the naygur bound to a horse," cried Barney, wildly. "Wud yez luk at the loikes, Misther Frank. We must catch the omadhouns and give them a lessin of the right sort."

"I hope we may," replied Frank, with great anxiety, "but I fear the red fiends will get to cover before we can overtake them."

"Whurroo! It's mesilf as will sphoil the loike av some av thim," cried Barney, as he picked up his rifle.

The savages were racing like mad across the prairie.

They had caught sight of the Steam Man, which was to them some fiend incarnate, some evil spirit which would seek their certain destruction.

Terror of the wildest sort made them whip their ponies to the utmost.

It was a mad race.

But the Steam Man was gaining.

He took tremendous strides. Frank pulled the whistle valve, and the shrieks sent up on the air were of a terrifying kind.

The savages had all gazed with wonder upon the white man's iron horse that followed its steel track across their prairies.

But this latest appearance, the Steam Man, was too much for their nerves. They could not bear it, and fled.

The Steam Man would certainly have overtaken them.

But, not visible until one had turned the timber line and made a rise in the prairie was a distant range of hills.

Toward this the savages were going. If they reached them, they would certainly succeed in eluding their pursuer.

And the chances seemed good.

Frank saw, with a peculiar chill, that they were really liable to reach the point aimed at.

He sent the man on at full speed.

Barney placed himself at a loop-hole, and commenced firing as rapidly as he could at the fleeing foe.

The result was that many of them fell, and the others redoubled their exertions to make an escape.

On went the chase toward the distant range of hills.

Nearer and nearer drew the ponies to the objective point.

With sinking heart Frank saw that the Indians were likely to reach them before the Steam Man could overtake them.

Of course this would mean safety for the savages, for the Steam Man could not hope to follow the ponies over the rough surfaces there encountered.

"Heavens, we are not going to save Pomp!" cried Frank, with a thrill of despair in his voice. "What shall we do, Barney? Is it not awful?"

Barney was busily engaged in placing fresh cartridges in his Winchester.

"Begorra, it's save the naygur I will if I sacrifice me own loife!" cried the big-hearted Celt. "It's me own fault, for sure, that he iver fell troo the door and got picked up by the red min."

Frank put on all the steam he dared, and the man took tremendous strides forward.

"We will make a mighty effort," he gritted, as he piled on the steam.

"Bejabers, here goes for wan av the spalpeens!" cried Barney.

Then the Irishman's rifle cracked.

One of the savages tumbled from his pony's back.

Barney continued to load and fire as fast as he could. But the opportunity was not long granted him.

Suddenly the cavalcade of savages dashed into the mouth of the pass.

They were out of sight in a twinkling. The Steam Man was obliged to come to a halt.

There were huge bowlders and piles of stones to block the passage. Barney and Frank Reade, Jr., exchanged glances of despair.

"That is the end of Pomp," declared the young inventor, with a chill. "I have no doubt that is a part of Black Buffalo's band, and he never spares a life."

Chapter IV
The Cowboys

FRANK HAD SPOKEN truthfully. The band of savages was really a part of the tribe of which Black Buffalo was the chief.

Throughout all the Kansas border this blood thirsty fiend was known and feared.

He had ravaged more wagon trains, burned more settlements, and committed more massacres than any other Sioux chief in the Far West.

His name was a synonym of terror among the settlers, from Dakota to the boundary line of Texas.

By many he was claimed to be a white man or renegade. Others averred that he was a recreant Pawnee chief.

However this was, certainly no red warrior was better known and feared than Black Buffalo.

And it was into his hands that Pomp had fallen.

Small wonder then that Frank Reade, Jr., was much alarmed, and even inclined to believe his faithful servitor's life lost.

The merciless Black Buffalo would not be likely to spare Pomp's life. The savages had captured him alive simply to drag him into the hills and torture him to death.

Barney began to bemoan the situation in violent terms.

"Och hone, the poor soul," he cried, "he was a black naygur but he had a white heart jist that same. Be jabers av' we cud only get near enough to the red omadhouns I'd loike to shoot ivery mother's son av thim."

"Well, I don't see why the red fiends haven't the best of us," declared Frank.

"It luks that same, Misther Frank," wailed Barney.

"I don't see how we can ever get through that pass. The Steam Man might go there, but the wagon won't."

This was true enough.

The Steam Man on the level prairie was invincible, but on rough ground like this wholly useless.

Frank and Barney were beside themselves with solicitude and perplexity.

Frank even thought of going forth on foot to try and overtake the redskins. But of course the folly of such a course was quickly apparent to him.

Barney even attempted to carry out literally this plan.

He went so far as to open the door in the wire screen and leap down to the ground.

But Frank cried sternly:

"Barney, come back at once. You can gain nothing by such a course."

"Shure, Mr. Frank," cried the Irishman, "if yez will only let me go –"

"Come back," was Frank's terse command, which was reluctantly obeyed by the Celt.

Frank took a careful look at the hills.

He chanced to see a smooth pathway up the height, and which seemed to follow the course of the canyon or pass.

Up this the Steam Man cautiously advanced. As they continued to ascend higher a good broad view of the prairie was obtained.

And suddenly reaching an elevation from which a southward view could be obtained, Frank gave a sharp cry, and taking a glass from a locker, sprung to a loop-hole in the netting.

He scanned a number of objects upon the prairie far beyond.

At that distance they looked like a herd of buffaloes.

But with the glass Frank saw that they were mounted men and white men at that.

They looked like a roving band of cowboys. In any event they were white men and it was quite enough for the young inventor to know this.

"We can depend upon them to help rescue Pomp!" cried Frank, exuberantly. "Luck is yet with us, Barney."

"Be jabers I hope so," cried the excited Celt. "If they be white men and have a heart they'll shurely do it."

Frank instantly turned the wagon about and sent the Steam Man rapidly down to the prairie.

He blew shrill blasts upon the whistle to attract the attention of the white men.

In this he was successful.

As the Steam Man reached the prairie floor, the cavalcade or cowboys came dashing up.

They did not seem surprised at sight of the Steam Man somewhat singularly and drew up fifty yards distant while one of their number rode forward.

He was evidently the leader, and was a tall, dark, evil-looking fellow. Frank Reade, Jr. was not favorably impressed with his appearance.

As the young inventor noted that the whole gang had a forbidding appearance and with a chill Frank realized that he could hardly expect any assistance from such a cut-throat looking band.

The tall, dark leader doffed his sombrero as he rode forward and made a low bow.

"Buenos Senors!" he said with a Spanish accent. "I wish you a fair day. Do you travel far with your Iron Man?"

"I am glad to meet you," replied Frank, eagerly. "We come from the East and we are here upon an important mission."

The stranger smiled and bowed again with a peculiar affectation of politeness.

"I am pleased to hear it. Are you not the gentleman called Frank Reade, Jr.?"

Frank gave a start of surprise.

"I am," he replied, quickly, "then you have heard of me."

"I have, Senor Reade," replied the cowboy chief, with another exaggerated bow and smile.

"Perhaps you know of my mission here?"

"I do," was the reply.

Frank was more amazed than words can express. What mystery was this?

How had this fellow, who bore the stamp of a Spaniard, learned of his mission to the Far West? The young inventor was staggered for a moment.

"Your mission here," replied the cowboy chief, politely, "is to hunt down two men who you believe are guilty of a murder which they skillfully foisted upon a certain man by the name of Jim Travers."

"You are right!" cried Frank. "But how in the name of wonder did you know that?"

"I prefer not to say. It is enough that I know it."

"It is strange that you should have learned it," said Frank, "but I will ask no more questions just now in the face of a terrible exigency."

"Ah!"

"I want to ask your help."

"My help?"

"Yes."

"Pardon, senor, but I cannot see in what manner I can serve you."

"You must assist me. One of my men – a colored man – has fallen into the hands of the Indians. They have made him prisoner and have just escaped with him into these hills. I ask your assistance in effecting his rescue."

A peculiar smile played about the cowboy's lips.

"Is he not the one you call Pomp?" he asked.

"Yes."

"And that man with you in your cage there is called Barney?"

"Yes."

"Ah, I see – Barney and Pomp. Well, Senor Reade, pray accept my compliments and the wish that you may see civilization again alive, which I do not believe will be the case. Ha – ha – ha! You have blundered into a death-trap!"

Something like a correct comprehension of affairs now began to dawn upon Frank.

"What do you mean?" he gasped in surprise. "Who are you?"

"Well, since you ask me I will tell you," replied the cowboy chief with a laugh. "I am no Spaniard, as you might have thought. I am as good an American as you, and you will have good cause to remember my name in the near future, provided you escape from this trap. I am the man you are so eagerly looking for – I am Artemas Cliff."

"Heavens!" gasped Frank Reade, Jr., "the man I am looking for!"

"The same," replied Cliff, mockingly. "You have undertaken quite a daring deed, my fine inventor, but you will find that you have bitten off a very much larger slice than you can masticate."

"We will see," began Frank.

"You see these men?" continued Cliff. "They are my followers, tried and true. What is it to you whether my uncle, Jim Travis, should hang for murder? You can never prove him innocent – at least, never will, for you will never go from here alive."

"Scoundrel!" cried Frank. "You are the real murderer!"

"Ha, ha, ha! Prove it if you can!" laughed the cowboy chief, derisively.

"I will prove it, if I have to drag the confession from your lips!" cried Frank, resolutely.

"Pshaw! Talk is cheap. Attention, men! Grab the throttle rein of the Steam Man and you can destroy him! Forward! Charge!"

Frank Reade, Jr., heard the command and knew well the danger. He was at a loss to account for Cliff's knowledge of him and his invention.

The young inventor was not aware of the fact that for weeks previous to the starting forth of the Steam Man spies had been busy in Readestown.

But such was the truth.

Artemas Cliff had covered his tracks well. He knew that Frank Reade, the young inventor's father, was a friend of Travers and would see him through, if possible.

Therefore he had provided well for giving Frank Reade, Jr., and the new Steam Man a hot reception on the plains.

With hoarse cries the cowboys descended upon the Steam Man. They urged their horses forward at a full gallop.

Frank Reade, Jr., knew well that it was possible for them to greatly injure his invention, so he made quick action to defeat their plans.

He shouted to Barney:

"Give it to them, Barney. Shoot every man you can."

Then Frank opened the throttle, and let the Steam Man out for all he was worth.

It was an easy matter to outstrip the horses, and the Steam Man kept ahead, while the cowboys came thundering on in the rear.

Then Frank slackened speed so as to keep up a uniform distance between the Man and the horses. While Barney poured in shot after shot into the midst of the gang of pursuers.

The cowboys began to drop from their saddles one by one. It was a destructive and telling fire.

And they strained every nerve in vain in an effort to reach the Steam Man. Frank kept the Man just far enough ahead to ensure safety and enable Barney to pick off the cowboys with ease.

It took Cliff some time to tumble to this little game.

When he did, and realized that he was simply decimating numbers without gaining ground, he called a halt.

The cowboys were now near the banks of a wide river which was really the Platte. Frank Reade, Jr. saw his advantage and brought the Steam Man to a stop. Then he seized a rifle and joined Barney.

Chapter V
Pomp's Rescue

BUT IT WAS hardly likely that the cowboys would stand their ground long under such a fire.

As fast as they could Frank and Barney worked the repeaters.

The result was that quite a number of the foe lay dead upon the prairie.

But Artemas Cliff knew the fatality of remaining there. Being unable to catch the man, he knew that their only hope now was in retreat.

All of the cowboys fired at the Steam Man. The bullets rattled harmlessly against the steel cage.

Frank at once sprang to the reins and the brake and started the Steam Man in pursuit. It was quite a turning of tables.

The pursuers were now the pursued.

So it continued until suddenly, by the orders of Cliff, the cowboys turned their horses into the river and forded it.

Once on the other side they were soon beyond the reach of the rifle balls. The Steam Man of course could not follow.

The encounter with the cowboys was at an end.

They did not return to the attack, somewhat singularly, but kept on until the rolling plains hid them from view.

Cliff's direful threat against the Steam Man and its inventor, had not been carried out. But Frank did not, by any means, delude himself with the belief that the villain would relinquish the attempt so easily.

"Well, Barney," he cried, cheerily, when satisfied that the scrimmage was over. "We came out of that scrape a little the best of it. It has all turned out as I expected. That Cliff is the real murderer."

"Begorra, it luks that way, Misther Frank," agreed Barney.

"So it does. We must plan to capture the villain, and wring a confession from him."

"Be jabers that's thrue. If I only had an opportunity I'd pretty quick wring his loon neck for him."

"But that does not settle the question of Pomp's fate," declared Frank. "He must be saved."

"Shure, Misther Frank."

"But how can we do it?"

This was yet a conundrum.

Frank and the faithful Irishman stood looking at each other. It was a long time before either spoke. Finally Frank said: "There's only one way, Barney."

"An' phwat's that?"

"We've got to got into those hills in some way. I don't like to leave the Steam Man, but to save Pomp I'd –"

The young inventor ceased speaking. A strange medley of sounds came from the direction of the pass.

There were wild yells and pistol shots, and then, out upon the prairie, the two astonished travelers saw a motley crew of horses and savages emerge.

The savages were fighting furiously. Frank knew enough of the Indians of that region to know what it all meant.

A band of Sioux and a band of Pawnees, the deadliest of enemies, were engaged in a terrific battle.

Frank took in the scene at a glance.

He at once understood all.

The band which had captured Pomp was undoubtedly the one engaged in this conflict. They had very likely met the Pawnees in the upper part of the pass.

When the Pawnees and Sioux met a fight always followed. Generally the latter came off victorious.

As it seemed now, however, the Pawnees had the best of it.

They were worsting the Sioux in good fashion. Frank and Barney watched the scene a moment until suddenly a sharp cry burst from Barney.

"Begorra, Misther Frank, if there ain't the naygur," he cried, wildly.

Barney was right. Frank glanced in the direction indicated and saw a thrilling act.

In the midst of the Sioux was Pomp bound to the back of a mustang.

Suddenly in the midst of the melee the horse was seen to bolt from the rest and dash out upon the prairie.

Of course, Pomp had no control over the beast, having his hands tied behind him.

The mustang took his own course and ran like the wind.

The Sioux did not dare to any of them attempt pursuit. The foe in their front claimed their attention.

"Bejabers, the horse is runnin' away wid the naygur," cried Barney. "Phwat will we do, Misther Frank?"

"Catch him if we can," cried Frank, seizing the throttle rein.

He opened the throttle and let the Steam Man go ahead; with long strides the machine began to gain upon the mustang.

Pomp was vainly endeavoring to free his hands.

If he could have done so, and could have got hold of the reins once, he could easily have stopped the horse.

But this he was unable to do.

As a result, the animal carried him along swiftly, and along the base of the hills.

Suddenly the mustang swerved and darted into a narrow pass.

Barney, at the loop-holes of the wagon with rifle in hand, had been sorely tempted to fire at the runaway.

But the fear of hitting Pomp had restrained him.

Now, however, the horse was out of range. But Frank headed the Steam Man for the pass.

Fortunately, it was unobstructed by bowlders, and had a good level floor. The Steam Man was enabled to forge along with safety.

But the mustang and his black rider had gone from sight. However the pursuers kept on.

Suddenly they came out upon a broad plateau with steep descent upon all other sides. This extended among the hills for a distance of several miles.

A great cry of horror now went up from Frank and Barney.

The mustang was seen racing along the edge of a mighty chasm. In a few seconds he would be almost sure to take an impossible leap over a deep gorge.

If he should go to the bottom of that gorge it would be the end of Pomp and the mustang.

This was seen at a glance and with the most intense of horror Barney cried:

"Shall I fire, Misther Frank? It's the only thing as will save the naygur."

"You will have to do that," replied Frank, sharply. "Look out for your aim, Barney. God help Pomp!"

Barney pulled the trigger.

Crack!

The bullet sped true to its mark. It struck the mustang in the side.

The animal faltered, threw up its head, stumbled, and then pitched forward in a heap.

Pomp lay beneath the horse. It did not require but a few moments for the Steam Man to reach him, however.

In a twinkling Barney sprang out of the wagon and cut Pomp's bonds.

The darky was not in the least injured. He lay with one leg under the mustang, but was easily extricated.

The joy of the darky at his rescue cannot be expressed in words.

He embraced Barney effusively.

"Shure I thought yez kilt intoirely, naygur," cried the big-hearted Irishman. "It's moighty glad I am to see yez aloive."

"Yo' kin jest bet dis chile am glad fo' to get out ob dem red debbils' hands," cried Pomp, exuberantly.

And then he dashed aboard the Steam Man and grasped Frank's hand.

"Oh, Marse Frank, I'se dretful glad to see yo'!" cried Pomp, excitedly.

"I am glad to have you back, Pomp," cried Frank. "And to know that you are unharmed in any way. But it was a close shave for you."

"'Deed it was dat, Marse Frank. But dis nigger am powerful hard for to kill, an' specs dat's why I lib. But I'se got lots to tell you, Marse Frank."

"You have?" exclaimed Frank.

"'Deed I has. P'raps yo' kin find it valuable fo' yo'. I'll jes' tell yo' dat when we went up troo dat pass we jes' cum out pretty quick in a valley. Dat ar' valley was a scrumptious one, an' dar was a trail leadin' down inter it. But afore the Injuns could ride down inter it along cum six white men on hossback an' a right pert young lady on a hoss, too.

"Sakes alibe I nebber seen so pretty a gal in all mah life. Well, dese yer men, dey seemed like dey was 'quainted wid der Injuns. Dey jes' talked as free like wid old Black Buffalo, an' I jes' opened my ears an' listened.

"Dey said dat de gal was a prisoner an' dey was takin' her from a cave in de hills to Ranch V. Dey mentioned de name ob Artemas Cliff. Den dey rode on, sah, an' mah sakes, jus' den up from the valley dere came a hull gang ob Ingines and pitched into us. Ob cose yo' know all de res'."

Frank Reade, Jr., listened with the deepest amazement to this exciting story.

"A young girl!" he gasped. "Of course those men were Cliff's, but where on earth were they going?"

"Dey done said it was to Ranch V sah."

"Ranch V!" repeated Frank. "That is not very definite. But it must be the headquarters of Cliff and his gang. You didn't hear them say just where that ranch was located, Pomp?"

"No sah, but I jes' took note ob de direckshun dey was goin' an' it was to de souf-west."

"Well," said the young inventor as he turned the Steam Man about, "I cannot imagine who the young girl is or how she fell into the hands of Cliff's gang. But it is certain that she is in their power and we must save her."

"Be jabers that's roight, Misther Frank," cried Barney, gallantly, "the O'Sheas from Brian Boru down war always known as men av honor an' defenders av female virtue."

The Steam Man started on the return across the plateau.

It was Frank Reade, Jr.'s intention to reach the prairie once more and strike out to the southwest, in the hopes of locating the Ranch V.

The Steam Man ran swiftly to the mouth of the pass which led down to the prairie.

Barney had filled the furnace with fresh coal, and the indicator showed that there was plenty of water in the boiler.

Frank was about to enter the pass when suddenly Pomp sprang up with a wild cry.

The darky sprang to Frank's side and tried to grab the throttle rein.

Frank was astounded.

"Hold on there, Pomp. What are you trying to do?" he cried.

"Ki dar, Marse Frank. Stop de Man, or fo' de Lawd we am all done fo', suah as preachin'!"

"What?" gasped Frank.

"If yo' don't believe it, jes look up yonder?"

Pomp pointed one finger upward to the canyon wall above the pass. The sight which rewarded the startled gaze of the young inventor caused him to reverse the throttle and bring the Steam Man to a halt.

Two cowboys were crouching behind an enormous bowlder which they had intended to roll down upon the Steam Man.

Chapter VI
The Fight in the Pass

A MORE NARROW escape could hardly be imagined.

The precipitation of the huge bowlder upon the Steam Man would have destroyed the invention and the lives of those on board.

Just in time Pomp had seen the danger. Another moment and it would have been too late.

"Ki yi, don' yo' see now, Marse Frank?" cried Pomp, wildly.

"I see," replied Frank, in thrilled tones. "My God! That is a narrow shave. We would have been crushed to atoms in another moment as I live."

"Whurroo! Give the spalpeens a good bit av cold lead!" shouted Barney, rushing to one of the loopholes with his rifle.

"That's right!" cried Frank, doing the same.

"Golly, yo' kin bet we will do dat!" chimed in Pomp.

The two cowboys, seeing that their game was exposed, sprang up with wild shouts of dismay.

As they did so they were exposed to shots from below. The three rifles spoke sharply in chorus.

The two would be destroyers tumbled in a heap. Their fall was followed by a wild chorus of yells from the thickets and bowlder piles above.

A volley of bullets came from there and rattled harmlessly against the steel netting, showing that the cowboys were there located in great force.

How they had chanced to be there at that critical moment our adventurers could only guess.

But Frank mentally concluded that at best they were but a division of Cliff's gang, and they had happened upon the spot by chance.

Seeing the Steam Man they had seized what seemed to them a fine opportunity to destroy it.

How far short they came of it we have already seen.

A red-hot contest now began between the cowboys and those in the steel wagon.

Of course our three friends had a vast advantage inasmuch as they were protected from the shots of their foes.

Of course the outlaws far outnumbered them, but it was not at all a difficult matter to pick them off occasionally with a rifle bullet.

Volley after volley the cowboys fired at the Steam Man.

When at length it became patent to them that their shots were futile, they made the air ring with yells of baffled rage.

Then they ceased firing and silence ensued. Every cowboy had disappeared seemingly from the canyon wall.

But this did not deceive Frank Reade, Jr.

He knew that this was only a game of the foe and that it would yet be unsafe to try the pass.

"Bejabers, ain't there some other way av gettin' out av this place?" cried Barney, giving the plateau a sweeping glance.

But the chain of hills surrounding it did not lend color to such a possibility.

"It don't look like it," said Frank, dubiously.

"I jes' fink dat am de only way out ob dis place," said Pomp.

"We are in a kind of trap," declared Frank Reade, Jr. "We were not sharp or we would have avoided this scrape."

As it was, however, the best they could do was to watch for an opportunity to run the gauntlet through the Pass.

But they had not long to wait for new and thrilling developments. Suddenly Pomp gave a startled cry.

"For massy sakes, Marse Frank, jes' yo' look out yonder. Whatebber am dey up to now?"

Over the edge of the plateau there was visible a line of men advancing rapidly toward the Steam Man. They were deploying right and left as if to surround him. This was certainly their purpose.

"They're thryin' to surround us!" cried Barney.

Frank watched the maneuver with deep interest.

He smiled grimly.

This was certainly the purpose of the foe. But the young inventor saw in the move a betterment of his own chances.

"They will not gain what they hope to," he said, resolutely.

Then he saw that a line of armed men had deployed across the mouth of the Pass to prevent the Steam Man from escaping in that direction.

In Frank's judgment there were fully two hundred cowboys in the party. This was tremendous odds, but the young inventor did not fear the results.

With a wild cheer the cowboys began to close their line in about the Steam Man.

Frank Reade, Jr., opened the whistle valve and let out several defiant shrieks.

Then he started the Steam Man in a straight line for the pass.

Pomp and Barney with their repeaters began to fire upon the line of men there.

The repeaters did deadly work.

It was a constant fusillade, and the cowboys dropped like sheep. The error of their plan could now be seen.

In dividing their forces to make the surrounding line, they had weakened themselves. Frank had seen this.

If they had been merely content with holding the pass, it would have been extremely doubtful if the

Steam Man could so easily have escaped.

Just as fast as they could work the sixteen-shot Winchesters, Barney and Pomp mowed down the opposing line of cowboys.

The line was thin, and it would have required a very solid corps to have withstood that scathing fire.

Down went the Steam Man toward the Pass with fearful speed.

Heaps of the dead and wounded cowboys lay upon the ground. As 8the Steam Man reached the Pass, a number of the cowboys tried to grasp the throttle reins and stop the machine.

But the ponderous body of the Man knocked them aside like flies and the wheels of the heavy wagon crushed them into death or insensibility.

The Steam Man literally forged his way through the Pass like a rocket.

Barney and Pomp cheered wildly and fired parting shots at the discomfited foe.

In a few moments the Steam Man ran out upon the prairie.

Frank did not waste time but set his course at once to the Southwest.

He was anxious to locate Ranch V. This he believed was his first and most important duty.

He was satisfied that nothing was to be gained by remaining in the hills.

He was confident that Cliff had gone to the Ranch V wherever it was. More than all else, he was powerfully interested in the mysterious young lady as described by Pomp.

He was determined to know who she was, and what Cliff held her in captivity for.

The day was rapidly drawing to a close.

After a short while the hills faded out of sight, and the rolling prairie was visible upon every hand.

Then, as the Steam Man took his long strides across the even plain, Frank suddenly caught sight of a beaten path or trail.

It was plainly a trail much used and bore a trifle east of south. Frank brought the Man to a stop.

"I would like to know where that trail goes to?" he declared. "I am not sure but it is the route to Ranch V."

"Golly, Marse Frank!" cried Pomp, craning his neck and looking to the southward a little ways. "What am dat jus' ober dat roll in de perairy? Am not dat some berry sumspicious objec'?"

Frank gazed in the direction indicated and saw a tall, black-looking timber seeming to rise out of the roll in the prairie. But he knew that it was beyond.

Frank let the Steam Man go along for a quarter of a mile, and topping the rise a startling sight was revealed.

There, scattered over several acres of land were the blackened ruins and charred timbers of some buildings.

It was easy to see what these buildings had constituted.

A large ranch with stockade, extensive cattle pens and yards, had once stood upon this spot. Frank allowed the Steam Man to pass through the ruins.

Thrilling sights were accorded our adventurers.

There were heaps of ashes, the bones of animals, and several charred skeletons of human beings.

There was every evidence that a fight had occurred at the place, and that the ranch had been burned by either Indians or rival cowboys. As chance had it the sign which, painted in broad letters, had once hung over the yard gate, had not been destroyed, and lay upon the ground near.

Our explorers were enabled to read it plainly.

"Rodman Ranch."

Barney and Pomp descended from the wagon, and spent some time in exploring the ruins.

"I jes' fink de Ingines burned up dis yer place," averred Pomp.

"Begorra, it's the divil's own job they med av it," declared Barney.

But Frank said, with conviction:

"Just as likely it was the work of Cliff and his gang. They are outlaws at best, and if Rodman Ranch was a respectable place, they would be sure to wish it destroyed."

Barney and Pomp re-entered the wagon now, and once more the quest for Ranch V was begun.

But night came on, and they had obtained no clew.

A good place was found to camp, and it was decided to wait until morning before pursuing the journey further.

Accordingly everything was made comfortable with this end in view.

No camp fire was made, for this was not deemed necessary.

At night they always slept in the wagon, and Barney and Pomp served turns in watching.

The fires in the furnace were banked, and the Steam Man was given a rest just the same as the others.

One place was always as good as another in camping out thus, save that it was necessary to be near a body of water, so that the boilers could be filled with ease the next morning.

The Steam Man was thus cared for, the fires banked, and everything made shipshape when, after Barney had been on watch not more than two hours, the first of a series of thrilling incidents occurred.

The night was as dark as Erebus, not a star twinkled in the ether, for heavy black clouds overhung all.

Suddenly Barney saw a light glimmering far out on the prairie.

It increased to quite a respectable size and continued to blaze for a long time.

The Celt watched it for a long while. Then his curiosity got the better of him.

"Bejabers, that's quare," he muttered. "I'll make sure there's something wrong about that now."

Barney, acting upon impulse, leaned over and grasped Frank's shoulder. The young inventor awoke with a start.

Chapter VII
The Vigilantes

"W-WHAT'S THE MATTER?" gasped Frank, sleepily arousing himself.

"Whist now, Misther Frank! There's a quare loight out yonder on the perairy, an' I thought I'd jist call yure attintion to the same, sor?"

"A light?" muttered Frank, now fully awake.

He got upon his feet, and rubbing his eyes, stared at the distant blaze.

"That is odd," he muttered. "It will do to investigate that."

"Sure, it may be a camp fire," ventured Barney.

"If so, then we must find out who the campers are," declared Frank.

It was but an instant's work to arouse Pomp.

Then the fires in the furnace were started, a line of hose was run to a creek near, and the boiler was filled.

In an incredible short space of time steam was got up, and the Steam Man moved ahead.

Frank held the throttle reins and directed the Steam Man's course toward the distant camp fire.

For such it was, as became evident as they drew near.

At first no movement was made by the camping party, and Frank fancied that they had nobody on guard.

But as the Steam Man with clanking tread came within one hundred yards of the camp, a wild shout went up and a gun was discharged at the Steam Man.

Frank was now able to see the circle of the camp as revealed by the firelight.

Men had been rolled in blankets upon the ground to the number of a score.

But these were now upon their feet. Just beyond it could be seen that mustangs were corralled.

Frank Reade, Jr., had no way of knowing whether the campers were friends or foes.

He had fancied them a part of Cliff's cowboys. Still there was a possibility they were not.

At any rate he could not treat them as foes until he learned positively that they were such.

So he brought the Steam Man to a stop just fifty yards from the camp.

The scene in the camp now was a ludicrous one.

The men were filled with mingled fear, amazement and stupefaction at the sight of the Steam Man.

The fiery eyes and nostrils and mammoth proportions of the man in the darkness made him look like a monster from the infernal regions.

The startled cries of the campers came to the amused hearing of those in the wagon.

"Great Jericho! What d'yer call that thing?"

"It's the devil hisself!"

"He's arter us!"

"That last drink at ther cross trails was too much for us boys. We've got 'em bad."

"I reckon we'd better fix up a prayer. Ther old gentleman has cum to git us."

Barney and Pomp exploded with laughter. It was very funny.

But as soon as the pandemonium had for a moment subsided, Frank Reade, Jr. hastened to shout:

"We're human beings the same as you. Have no fear. Who are you?"

The words had an astounding effect upon the campers. After a moment of stupefied silence the answer came back.

"Who the dickens are you?"

"I am Frank Reade, Jr., and this is my new invention, the Steam Man," replied Frank. "You have nothing to fear."

The campers now saw the three men in the wagon as Barney turned on the light of the calcium and illuminated the vicinity.

At once their fear fled and a comprehension of all dawned upon them.

"A steam Man, by thunder, and built all of iron!"

"Wall, that beats all!"

"What'll come next?"

"That beats the iron hoss all holler!"

The campers now came thronging about the wagon. As the number was limited, Frank did not feel particularly uneasy, though he held the throttle ready and Barney and Pomp had their repeaters at hand.

But the fears of our three adventurers were quickly allayed.

One of the men, a tall, powerful framed man, came forward, and said:

"Wall, cap'en, we're glad to meet you an' yer Steam Man. My name is Sim Harmon, an' I'm captain of this band, who are all Vigilantes from Poker Gulch. We're out on the trail of a gang of ruffians."

"Vigilantes!" cried Frank Reade, Jr., with joy. "Then you are not members of the Artemas Cliff gang?"

"Artemas Cliff!" cried Harmon. "He is the chap we want. If we can lay hands on him we'll stretch his neck, you bet. D'yer know whar we kin find him?"

"I am on his trail myself."

"The deuce ye are?"

"It's the truth."

"What for?"

Frank opened the door of the wagon, and descending shook hands with the Vigilant captain.

He told him explicitly of the mysterious murder of which Jim Travers had been adjudged guilty, but which it was believed was the work of Cliff.

Harmon listened with interest.

"So that's another game of ther cuss!" he cried. "Wall, that's a bad one, but I reckon we've a wuss count agin him, stranger."

"Indeed!" exclaimed Frank.

"Did ye cum across ther ruins of a ranch out hyar on ther perairy some miles?"

"I did."

"Wall, that was onct Rodman Ranch, an' Ralph Rodman was one of the best men in this part of ther West. But that ornery cuss Cliff fell in love with pretty Bessie Rodman, his darter, an' when Ralph denied him the right to come a-courtin' her, ther scoundrel jest brought down a gang of hoodlums an' burned down the ranch, toted off ther gal, an' killed all ther rest about ther place."

"Horrible!" exclaimed Frank. "But you have not told me of Rodman. What became of him?"

"Wall, that illustrates ther villainy of ther cuss. Just previous to burnin' ther ranch, two men, Sid Bowen an' Jem Ducey, hired by Cliff, enticed Ralph to New York by bringin' him a bogus message from a brother, who was represented as bein' in great distress. That's the last seen of Rodman. What they did with him we don't know. But I've heard that Bowen an' Ducey have returned, an' Rodman didn't cum with 'em. It's my belief he's been done away with, an' it's all a game of Cliff's to get the gal Bessie into his possession."

A great cry broke from the lips of Frank Reade, Jr.

This story of Harmon's he had listened to eagerly, and, as it was unfolded, bit by bit, a clear, concise comprehension of all now came to him.

He saw the hideous details, the cold, scheming construction of a deep and awful plot, involving murder and abduction and terrible wrong.

"Great heavens!" he gasped, wiping cold perspiration from his brow. "Your story throws a great light upon the matter which I have in hand, Mr. Harmon."

"The deuce you say!" gasped the captain of the Vigilantes.

"It is the truth," cried Frank. "I think I can tell you the true fate of Ralph Rodman, and you will agree that Cliff is the projector of one of the most awful double plots of crime that human being could be capable of."

The Vigilantes all gathered around the young inventor, agog with interest.

"Ye don't mean it?" gasped Harmon, with amazement. "Ye're huntin' Cliff then ther same as we are?"

"Yes."

"What fer?"

"To force a confession or explanation from him of a mysterious murder of which his own uncle, James Travers, of New York, has been adjudged guilty and who is now in prison awaiting his sentence of hanging about a year from now.

"Oh, this villain is a deep one. But I have told you of that mysterious murder and, as Heaven is my judge, I believe the victim of that murder which was purposely thrown upon Travers was Rodman. You see Cliff's object in throwing the murder upon Travers was to see him hang and thus inherit his vast wealth."

For a moment after this statement silence reigned.

Appalled with the magnitude of the villain's plot all remained silent. But the mystery was cleared up at last.

All understood now exactly the deep game of Artemas Cliff.

But one sentiment reigned supreme in the breasts of all. Artemas Cliff should be brought to justice.

It was easy enough to see how the wretch in planning to win Bessie Rodman had enticed Rodman to the East and there murdered him. Then to kill two birds with one stone he had caused the awful crime by clever circumstantial evidence to be thrown upon his wealthy uncle, James Travers.

Of course, with Travers' death, he would inherit the millions left by him.

Ralph Rodman was dead. The ranch was a heap of ashes.

For these crimes Artemas Cliff was responsible. But Bessie Rodman was yet in his power. Travers was near the gallows.

These two people must be saved.

Frank Reade, Jr., saw the mission, as did Harmon.

Instinctively they clasped hands.

"I reckon we both know what to do," declared the Vigilant captain tersely. "P'r'aps we kin work together. I'll help you all I kin."

"And I will help you," replied Frank. "We will bring Cliff to justice if the Steam Man can help us to do it."

"He will hang if I kin get my hands onto him."

"But we must make no mistake. He is strongly backed up. You have only twenty-five men with you."

"But they air all men," replied Harmon, pluckily.

"I will not question that," replied Frank, "but the weight of numbers would defeat you. Cliff has several hundred men in his command."

"We're not afraid of 'em. Yet ye're right enuff. It's well fer us to go easy."

"It is well to be careful," said Frank. "I think that you had better keep along with us for a time."

"All right!"

"I think there is no doubt but that the young girl whom Pomp saw in the hills was Bessie Rodman."

"In course it was her."

"They were taking her to Ranch V. Do you know where it is?"

"Yas," replied Harmon, quickly, "that's on Stone River, an' it's a pesky big place too. Thar's a big stockade around it an' armed men are allus a-watchin' for fear an outsider will git in. So that's ther place, eh? Wall, it will be hard to git Bessie out of Ranch V."

"She shall be got out or I will give my life in the attempt!" cried a tall, handsome young plainsman with flashing eyes.

He looked much in earnest. Frank gazed at him critically. A little later he was introduced to him as Walter Barrows, a rising young stockman, and the lover of pretty Bessie Rodman.

Chapter VIII
On To Ranch V

PLANS WERE quickly made.

It was decided to work upon strategical grounds, as their force was so much lighter than Cliff's.

"You see, if we can strike Ranch V at a time when Cliff and the majority of his men are in the hills we can capture the place," declared Frank, shrewdly.

"That's bizness," agreed Harmon, "but ye're the boss. I kin see that ye've got a better head piece nor I have, Mister Reade."

"We will not admit that," said Frank, modestly, "but rather let us work together, Mr. Harmon."

"All right, cap'en. I'm with ye."

Further plans were elaborated, then as only a few hours yet intervened until dawn, it was decided to snatch a few brief hours of sleep.

With the early dawn all were astir. The Vigilantes saddled their mustangs and all was soon ready for the start.

The Steam Man was an object of great wonder to the plainsmen.

"By Jinks!" exclaimed one of them, "the sight of that queer-lookin' critter oughter scare the life out of any number of Injuns."

"I think the Steam Man will aid us much in accomplishing our ends." said Frank, modestly.

The start was made just after daybreak. The Vigilantes rode alongside the Steam Man on their mustangs.

Of course Frank was compelled to go more slowly on this account.

But the Vigilantes knew the way to Ranch V and this was, after all, the most important thing of all.

Frank considered it a great piece of luck in having fallen in with the Vigilantes.

He now understood exactly how matters stood all around.

It was near noon when a halt was called in a small basin near a lake of water.

Here camp was briefly made, and also at the same time an important discovery came to hand.

A broad trail made by a cavalcade of men and horses was discovered.

It pointed to the north.

Harmon examined it carefully and finally, with great exuberance, cried:

"It's good luck, friends. That thar trail I believe was made by ther cowboys an' it leads to ther hills. It's over three days old, an' they haven't come back this way. I should think that the most of their men must be up there, in which case Ranch V will be almost deserted. Cum on, boys, let's capture ther hull place."

With a cheer the Vigilantes sprang to saddle.

Soon they were once more galloping ever the prairie.

Not two hours later, or in the middle of the afternoon, Harmon drew his horse alongside the Steam Man and pointing to the south cried:

"Look yonder, Mr. Reade. Do ye see them lines of high ground? Wall, jest this side ar ther Ranch V."

A cheer went up from all.

"Begorra, it's Ranch Ours it'll be, if iver we get there," declared Barney.

"Golly, won't dis be a big 'sprise party fo' dat vilyun Cliff," cried Pomp.

Frank Reade, Jr., held the Steam Man at a steady stride, and very soon the ranch came in sight.

It was truly a most extensive establishment.

The stockade and buildings covered acres of ground. A great herd of cattle were feeding on the open plains.

The main ranch itself was surrounded by a high stockade, which would resist most any ordinary attack with small arms.

As the Vigilantes and the Steam Man came swiftly rushing down upon the place, a great commotion was seen to take place.

Men rushed out into the yards, horsemen went scurrying about, and down came the stockade gate.

But Harmon and his men rode boldly down to the gate, and began to assail it with axes.

While Frank Reade, Jr., kept the Steam Man on an elevation near, from which he, with Barney and Pomp, covered the work of invasion by a hot fire with their Winchesters.

The cowboys could not get upon the stockade to fire at the assailants for this reason.

Harmon's men therefore worked with perfect immunity.

No more favorable time for an attack could have been chosen.

There were but few of the cowboys in the ranch, and these were picked off by the fire from the Steam Man as fast as they appeared on the stockade.

With lusty cries the Vigilantes chopped through the timbers of the gate.

In a remarkably brief time a hole was cut through and the gate raised.

The Steam Man rushed into the yard, and in less than ten minutes every cowboy in the place was a prisoner, and Ranch V was captured.

Walter Barrows, the brave young stockman, was the first to enter the main ranch.

The instinct of a lover took him to the chamber in which Bessie Rodman was kept a prisoner.

He burst in the door and clasped the young girl in his arms.

That was a joyous meeting.

When they appeared in the yard the Vigilantes cheered wildly. It was a brilliant victory.

Ranch V was captured.

The stronghold of the outlaw Cliff, the den of villainy and vice, was captured. It did not require much time for them to reach a decision as to what to do.

"Every building must be laid low!" cried Harmon. "Put the torch to every accursed timber."

The cry was taken up and spread from lip to lip.

In haste torches were procured. Harmon himself lit the first, and was about to apply it to a building. But he did not do so.

A thrilling incident stopped him. A loud cry went up.

"The cowboys! they are coming! To arms everybody! There comes Cliff at their head!"

Every eye was turned to the plain beyond the stockade.

There was no disputing the truth. Cliff and his gang returning from the hills had come just in time. It would be folly now to burn the ranch.

Harmon, seeing the desperate exigency dropped the torch, and cried:

"To the stockade! It's for life or death, boys. Fight to the last!"

But the command was not necessary. Already the brave Vigilantes were at their posts.

Cliff with his small army of followers came on at a swinging gallop.

He could see that the ranch was in the possession of a foe.

This inflamed his wrath, and, with loud curses and yells, he rode down in the van of his followers.

Frank Reade, Jr., had taken in the situation at a glance.

He knew that it would be flatly impossible for the score of Vigilantes to hold those three hundred desperadoes long at bay.

It would mean the eventual massacre of every vigilant. This Frank wished to avoid.

The young inventor had induced Bessie Rodman to seek refuge in the wagon. Otherwise, she would certainly fall into the hands of the foe again.

Frank started the Steam Man ahead, and went down to the stockade. He made the vigilantes a hasty address.

"Nothing will be gained by holding this place," he declared, with force. "You cannot do it. The odds are too great."

"But we cannot surrender," cried Harmon, "and how can we retreat?"

"Easily enough," replied Frank, "there is a rear gate. Open it and cut out upon the prairie."

"But they may overtake us?"

"It is your only hope. You'll have to work lively, for they are trying to surround the stockade. I'll cover your retreat easy enough."

Harmon saw that Frank was right.

He did not pause to argue the point further. With quick commands he caused his men to fall back.

The stockade gate in the rear was opened just in time, and the Vigilantes rushed out upon the prairie. They set out at a mad gallop for the distant hills.

The cowboys with mad cries followed. But they met with quite a serious obstacle in their pursuit.

The Steam Man kept exasperatingly between them and the Vigilantes.

From the rear loop-holes of the wagon Barney and Pomp kept up a steady fire with the Winchesters.

Nearly every shot emptied a saddle, and despite their superior numbers, the cowboys soon found it better and safer to keep well out of range.

The pursuit lasted for ten miles. Then the horses of both parties became fagged and they were compelled to halt.

But Harmon's men, by dint of careful work, got their horses into the fastnesses of the hills. Here they felt more secure.

The Steam Man had well covered the retreat of the Vigilantes. But darkness was now coming on and a serious question presented itself to Frank Reade, Jr.

To remain where they were for the night would be to incur the risk of a midnight attack from the cowboys.

This might result seriously.

At least Frank was disposed to evade it.

He consulted with Harmon, and the result was an arrangement which it was believed would be better for all.

In the fastnesses of the hills Harmon felt sanguine of holding his own against the cowboys.

Therefore it was decided that the Steam Man should leave the vicinity and go far enough away over the prairie to make sure of safety for the night.

Accordingly Frank left the vicinity and sent the Man striding over the plain in the dusk of evening.

There was no visible indication that the cowboys intended to pursue.

They had apparently gone into camp not five miles distant.

Frank kept on with the Steam Man until twenty miles had been covered.

Then he came to a halt.

It seemed as if they must feel safe here. Accordingly, arrangements were made for passing the night.

A comfortable seat was arranged for Bessie Rodman and, much exhausted by the fatigue of her experiences, she quickly fell asleep.

But tears had wet her cheeks and trembled on her eyelashes. Frank had told her of her father's death.

"Oh, I fear it is more than I can bear," she declared, in agony of spirit. "My dear, dear father. Oh, if I were a man, how I would avenge him!"

"There are plenty to do that," replied Frank, cheeringly. "The villain shall surely pay for his evil deeds."

"I hope it may come to pass," she said, sincerely.

Then she dropped off to sleep. But even as she slept, deadly peril hung over her young and beautiful head.

Chapter IX
Pomp's Mistake

FRANK READE, JR., felt comparatively safe as he rolled himself up in a blanket and went to sleep. He did not believe that the villain, Cliff, would be able to molest them that night.

It was Barney's first watch.

The Hibernian, until midnight, kept a good lookout in the cage. Then he called Pomp to succeed him.

The darky kept a good lookout until the early morning hours.

The darkness was most intense.

At about this time Pomp experienced a deadly faintness at the pit of the stomach and a great longing for water.

His thirst became most consuming, and it seemed as if he must, at any cost, gratify it.

But he found, upon looking in the tank, that it was empty.

There was not a gill of cold water in the wagon. Pomp grew sober with this dampening reflection.

"I jes' fink if I had a bit of watah I would be a' right," he muttered; "but how ebber am dis niggah gwine fo' to get it, dat's what I'd like to know."

Pomp went to the steel screen and tried to penetrate the darkness.

He knew that not ten yards distant were the waters of a small creek. He could hear them rippling now.

It was directly at variance with his orders to open the cage door. Yet it seemed to Pomp as if he must do so.

The risk did not seem great.

There seemed little likelihood of the proximity of a foe.

Pomp felt certain that he could reach the creek, get his drink, and get back safely to the wagon.

He was sorely tempted. The desire was most powerful.

"Golly!" he muttered, with a wry face. "What am I gwine fo' to do? I don' beliebe dar's any danger ob going out dar, but if Marse Frank knew it he'd fix me putty quick. Sakes alibe! but what am a chile gwine fo' to do? I am mos' dyin' fo' a drink ob watah."

Pomp thought of awakening Barney and enlisting his aid.

But he reflected that the Celt would be certain to disagree with his scheme.

There was no other way but to assume the responsibility himself. Pomp drew a deep breath.

Then he fell to listening.

All was silent as the grave.

"Sho!" he muttered. "Dar ain't no danger at all. I'll jest hab dat watah as suah as I'm born."

He quickly slid back the bolt in the door and opened it.

Then he stepped out of the wagon. In another moment he glided down to the water's edge.

Pomp flung himself flat and began to drink of the creek water.

But he had not taken one drink when he became aware of an appalling sensation. He turned his head and glanced back at the Steam Man.

The lantern hanging in the cage showed the open door and all as plain as day. But, great heavens! What did he see?

Dark forms were swarming about the machine. One was already in the wagon.

Pomp saw this much, and then his attention was claimed by another matter. He suddenly felt a heavy body descend upon him and talon fingers clutched his throat.

In that flash of time Pomp had turned partly over.

He was just in time to see the flash of a knife blade. He made a convulsive upward blow, and grasped the wrist of his unknown assailant.

By the merest chance the death blow had been averted.

But it was a close call.

Then with a herculean effort Pomp rolled over the edge of the bank, and the next moment, with a powerful swing, he had brought himself and assailant into the water of the creek.

The sudden bath caused Pomp's adversary to relax his grip.

The darky had no further motive for continuing the struggle, and striking out swam for the opposite bank.

He clambered out of the water, and crawled into a thicket.

There he lay shivering, and witnessed a thrilling scene upon the other bank of the creek.

The occupants of the wagon had all been aroused, and were every one prisoners, in the power of Cliff and his cowboys.

The outlaw had managed to cover the twenty miles, skillfully following the trail by means of a dark lantern.

He had been hovering with his minions about the Steam Man, just as Pomp committed the indiscretion of leaving the door open.

Of course it was an easy matter for the cowboys to board the wagon and make prisoners of all on board.

The glee of Cliff was beyond expression.

He danced and clapped his hands with fiendish joy. He pinched Bessie's arms until she screamed with agony, and with brutal laughter roared:

"Oh, I'll make ye all dance. Ye thought ye'd git away from me, did ye, gal? I'll show ye that ye can't get away from Artemas Cliff. Ha, ha, ha! What a good joke."

He laughed uproariously.

"All mine," he continued, "And this Steam Man, this wonderful invention, is just what I want. I can travel around in great style. Oh, Mr. Frank Reade, Jr., I'll dance on your grave yet."

"Monster!" cried Frank, writhing in his bonds. "You'll never succeed. A righteous God will never permit it."

The villain gave his men carte blanche to make camp and indulge in a carousal.

They did so until daybreak, and then Cliff stated that it was his purpose to go back to Ranch V.

It did not lake him long to understand the mechanism of the Steam Man.

He quickly found out how to use the throttle reins. He was aided by the fact that he had once been a locomotive engineer.

With the early morning light the start for Ranch V was made.

And Pomp, wet and shivering and horrified, crouched in the thicket upon the bank of the creek, saw the Steam Man and his friends, all in the power of the foe, take departure.

When they had gone Pomp came out of his hiding-place.

"Golly!" he muttered, with distended eyeballs, "I jes' fink dis nigger hab done de berry awfulest fing eber known. Dar am only one way fo' Pomp to sabe his honor, an' dat am to fix some way to rescue Marse Frank an' all ob de odders, an' I'll do it if I can."

Pomp was very much in earnest.

He was a brave and generous fellow, and willing at any time to sacrifice his life for his master.

In some manner he must certainly vindicate himself. He crossed the creek again and stood upon the spot where the Steam Man had been.

Of course the machine was out of sight by this time, but nevertheless, Pomp took the trail and proceeded to follow it.

For some hours he trudged on over the prairie. All the while the darky was revolving in his mind some plan for the relief of his friends.

He was bound to admit that it was a puzzle. Yet he did not lose hope.

The hills were every moment becoming plainer. Already Pomp had covered five of the twenty miles.

The darky was a good walker, and no distance was too great for his trained muscles.

The sun was beginning to run high in the heavens, and a brisk breeze blew across the prairie.

Pomp kept on steadily.

The trail kept on toward the hills, and the sagacious darky reflected that Cliff was likely going to join the main body of his men.

"I jes' fink I can see what dat rascal am up to," muttered Pomp. "He am jus' too sharp to let de game slip him once he gits his clutches onto it. He am jus' goin' fo' to take de Steam Man to his Ranch V, and dar's whar dis darky must go an' try fo' to work some leetle plan fo' to rescue Frank Reade, Jr., an' de odders. Dat am a fac'."

With this logical conclusion Pomp trudged on.

He was now on the last five miles of his journey to the hills. The sun was long past the noon hour when Pomp, by dint of rapid walking, had made the hills.

There was no sign visible of the Steam Man or of the cowboys.

But Pomp saw that the trail continued around the base of the hills.

This puzzled the darkey a moment.

He paused and scratched his head in deep thought.

"Dat am a dretful queer thing," he muttered. "Dat ain't de way to go to Ranch V, if I'se right in mah conjeckshun."

Then he paused, and a light of comprehension broke across his face.

A distant sound had come to his hearing. It was the faint rattle of firearms far up in the hills.

"Golly!" he ejaculated. "I see de trick ob dat berry sharp fox, Artemus Cliff. He am gwine fo' to gib de Vigilantes a good lickin' afore he goes to Ranch V. Dat am jus' my bes' way for to jine Marse Harmon an' his men, an' help dem trash the cowboys."

Pomp's mind was made up.

He would join the Vigilantes and do his best to give the cowboys a good drubbing. He at once struck into the hills.

But alas for Pomp!

Luck seemed against the darky for the time being. He had not more than fairly entered a narrow pass when an appalling incident occurred.

The air was suddenly broken by wild yells, and in an instant he was surrounded by half a hundred painted savages, who burst from niches and crevices in the rocks about.

They pounced upon him, and before Pomp had even time to think of resistance he was a prisoner.

The savages swarmed about him like bees. Words cannot express Pump's dismay at this turn.

His eyes bulged, and his knees shook as with the ague.

"Fo' de good Lor' dis am dretful!" he groaned. "I'se done fo' dis time, an' dar am nobody to rescue Marse Frank!"

* * *

It was truly a dubious outlook. The savages were of Black Buffalo's gang of Sioux, and they seemed much elated at getting the prisoner once more into their clutches.

They chattered and gesticulated like a flock of magpies, and some of them approached Pomp with their tomahawks as though they would fain make an end of him then and there.

But the others held them back and an excited wrangle followed.

All this while Pomp was writhing in his bonds. In vain he tried to break them.

For some while the savages wrangled. Then a compromise was made and Pomp was picked up bodily, and carried through the pass and into a small glade among some trees.

Here he was tied to a tree and a great heap of fagots were piled at his feet.

With a chill of horror, the darky saw that the savages meant to take his life in a horrible manner.

He was to suffer death in the flames. Pomp felt sick and faint. But even in that moment he thought not of himself, brave fellow, but of Frank Reade, Jr., and the others.

"Golly sakes, whoebber am gwine fo' to sabe Marse Frank, now?" he groaned.

Chapter X
In the Enemy's Power

ARTEMUS CLIFF shouted in evil glee and triumph as he manipulated the Steam Man and let him out for a swift run across the prairie.

He amused himself by racing with his followers who were on horseback.

"By jingo!" he roared, "this is more fun than I ever had before. Why this beats the steam-cars all to smash. And it's all mine. Why I can travel like a prince now. Ha-ha-ha! I'm the luckiest man on earth."

He turned and fixed a glowering gaze upon Bessie Rodman.

"And ye're mine too," he cried, "the lily of the prairie. The happy life companion of Artemus Cliff. When I get my hands onto Uncle Jim Travers' millions, we'll travel the world over, my daisy."

Bessie did not appear to heed his words, though her face increased a trifle in its pallor.

"Monster!" cried Frank Reade, Jr., with intensity. "You will never succeed. Heaven will not permit it."

"Heaven don't have much to do with me," cried the villain, with a lurid oath. "The devil has been a good friend of mine, and I ain't afraid of his place either."

"Begorra, they wudn't have ye even there," cried Barney. "Yez are too wicked for avin that place."

"Oh, ho, Irish, you've got your tongue, eh?" cried Cliff, with a vicious laugh. "So ye think I'm too bad, eh?"

"Be me sowl, thar cudn't be a place too bad for yez!"

"I'll have a nice little hades fixed fer yer right on this earth an' I'll give ye a fair taste of it in advance, too," said the villain, vengefully.

"Arrah, yez can't scare me at all, at all," he retorted. "Yer threats are jist the same as a puppy dog's bark."

"You'll find that I'm the kind of a dog that bites," averred the villain.

"It's not me that cares fer yer bites."

"We'll see about that. Don't blow your horn too soon."

"Begorra, that's good advice fer yersilf, ye blatherskite! Av I on'y had me two hands to use now I'd baste the rascality out av yez or I'd make a good job fer ther undhertaker."

"Talk is cheap," sneered the villain. "Ye'd better save yer wind."

"It's yersilf as nades it most," said Barney, bound to have the last word.

Cliff evidently found Barney's tongue equal to his own, for he abandoned the conversation in a sullen fashion.

Bessie Rodman made no attempt at speech.

She sat silently in one corner of the wagon.

Frank Reade, Jr., also remained silent.

The twenty miles were quickly covered by the Steam Man. It was yet far from the noon hour when they arrived at the camp of the previous night.

The cowboys in full force were there, and as Cliff appeared with the Steam Man, they made the welkin ring with yells of delight and satisfaction.

All crowded around to examine the steam wonder and inspect its mechanism.

The prisoners looked out upon a sea of faces. They were not kindly regarded by the cowboys.

"Take 'em out and shoot 'em, Cliff!" cried a voice in the crowd.

"Give 'em twenty paces and a grave seven feet deep."

But Cliff refused to do this.

"Leave it to me!" he cried. "I've got a better plan."

"What is it?" was the cry.

"I want ye all to be ready in half an hour to go into the hills an' corner Harmon an' his gang. There must not one of the Vigilantes go out of here alive."

"Hurrah!" yelled the cowboys.

"We can give them the worst thrashin' they ever had."

"Of course we can."

"In regard to these prisoners, the gal is going to be my wife. The others I'm going to have some fun with down to the ranch. We'll have a rabbit chase with 'em, or something of the kind."

"Good!" yelled the mob, carried away with the plan.

Thus the fate of the prisoners was decided by their captors. But the question of attack upon the Vigilantes was now the one in order.

Preparations were at once made for cornering Harmon and his heroic little band.

Several parties of cowboys were dispatched to head off any possible attempt at escape from the hills.

Harmon's men were certainly hemmed in on all sides, and it was a most dubious outlook for them.

The exultation of the cowboys was beyond expression.

"We've got 'em dead sure!" cried Cliff, triumphantly. "Not a one on 'em can possibly escape."

The cowboys now began to close the line in about their prey.

A pass was found through which the Steam Man was taken, and to a point within easy range of the position held by the Vigilantes.

Harmon had chosen an elevated position on a kind of small tableland or plateau.

Here behind bowlders he had concentrated his forces. The position was not a bad one to defend.

To charge upon it the cowboys would have to ascend a height of fifty feet or more in the face of a strong fire.

But this sacrifice of men Cliff did not intend to make, at least not at once.

There were other points of vantage about, which the cowboys quickly took possession of.

From these a desultory fire was kept up with the Vigilantes with some loss upon both sides.

But Harmon's men could not very well withstand any loss whatever. This the cowboys could stand better.

The Steam Man, however, could advance to very close proximity with the Vigilantes, and those on board were safe from any shots of retaliation.

This made it bad for Harmon for he had no way of checking this most destructive fire.

It was a most galling thing for Frank Reade, Jr., to remain idle and see his invention used in such a manner.

He groaned aloud with horror and dismay. Barney did the same.

"Oh, if I could only free myself," declared the young inventor.

"Begorra, I wish I cud do that same," muttered Barney.

Cliff and the three cowboys with him in the cage were doing their best to shoot every Vigilant who exposed himself.

They were thus so deeply engrossed that they paid no special heed to the prisoners for the time.

Barney, quick-witted Irishman, noted this fact.

At a favorable moment he leaned over and whispered to Frank:

"Bejabers, Misther Frank, I think I know av a way to turn the tables on them blasted omadhouns."

"The deuce!" gasped Frank. "What is it, Barney?"

"Whisht now an' work quiet, me gossoon!" whispered Barney. "I'll lay down ferninst the side here an' yez kin turn yer wrists toward me mouth an' me teeth are no good av I don't cut them in two before so very long."

Frank experienced a thrill.

"Can you do it, Barney?"

"Av course I kin."

"But if they see us –"

"They'll niver do that. Be aisy now, me gossoon, an' roight on the shelf there there's a knoife an' yez kin cut my bonds at the same toime. Thin we kin take care av ther four av thim. I'll take two mesilf."

"And I'm good for the other two or I'll die!" muttered Frank. "All right, Barney, do your best."

"I will that."

But at this moment Bessie Rodman leaned forward, and in a soft whisper said: "Wait! There is a quicker way."

Frank and Barney were astonished.

"What?" exclaimed the young inventor.

By way of reply Bessie drew both hands from behind her.

They were free. There were livid lines upon the fair wrists, where the cruel throngs had cut in.

But the shapely hands were so small that Bessie had been enabled to slip them through the bonds and free them.

Up to this moment neither Frank nor Barney had looked upon the young girl as more than the ordinary weak woman.

That is to say, they had not given her credit for the amount of nerve she possessed.

But they were given ample evidence of it now.

Quick as a flash, and with commendable resolution, she reached over and seized the knife upon the shelf.

It was but a moment's work for her to cut Frank's bonds. As they snapped, the young Inventor took the knife and quickly cut Barney's.

Their captors were at the loop-holes firing, and had not seen this move.

Nothing could have worked better.

Frank picked up a club, and Barney an iron bar. Nobody can handle a weapon of the sort better than an Irishman.

"Whurroo! Bad cess to yez fer a pack av omadhouns," cried Barney, dealing one of the cowboys a crushing blow on the head.

Before one could think, the iron bar came down upon the head of another. Both sank senseless to the floor of the wagon.

Frank Reade, Jr., had knocked Cliff senseless. Only one of the foe was left, and he was quickly knocked out.

In a twinkling, as it were, the tables were turned.

Barney and Frank Reade, Jr., were now masters of the Steam Man once more. The irrepressible Irishman pulled the whistle valve and sent up a shriek of defiance and triumph.

Then Frank Reade, Jr., swung open the wagon door.

"Throw them out!" he cried; "all but Cliff."

Barney obeyed the command. The three cowboys were quickly dumped out upon the ground.

But Cliff was allowed to remain. The villain lay insensible in the bottom of the wagon.

Frank was about to bind him, when an imminent peril claiming his immediate attention prevented him.

The cowboys were aware of the turning of the tables in the wagon.

With mad yells they were rushing forward in a body to surround the Steam Man. Unless immediate action was made they would succeed.

Frank knew well the danger of this move.

It would be an easy matter for the cowboys to ruin the invention by a single blow. There was but one way, and that was to beat a retreat.

Barney seized his repeater and began firing into the crowd of cowboys. Frank opened the throttle and sent the Steam Man up the incline toward the stronghold of the Vigilantes.

Of course the latter had seen and understood all.

They embraced the opportunity to pour a flank fire into the ranks of the cowboys. It was a moment of thrilling sort, but the Steam Man seemed to have the best of it when a thrilling incident happened.

Chapter XI
With the Vigilantes

IN ANOTHER MOMENT the Steam Man would have been in the ranks of the Vigilantes.

It would have been a great point scored, for Cliff would then be a prisoner and the way to save Jim Travers from the gallows would have been paved.

But it was not to be.

The villain had come to in the meanwhile, but cunning rascal that he was, had laid inanimate in the bottom of the wagon.

He had seen all that was going on, and when he saw that the Steam Man was certain to escape he knew that only desperate action upon his part would save him now.

Accordingly while Frank and Barney were occupied at their posts, he made a sudden lightning leap for the door in the cage.

Unfortunately Barney had not fastened it.

A little scream of warning came from Bessie, but it was too late.

The villain flung open the door and sprung out.

He tumbled heels over head down the decline.

This was partly done on purpose to avoid any bullets sent after him. But none struck him, and he was the next moment in the ranks of his men.

Frank turned just in time to see the daring escape.

The young inventor's disappointment was so great that he came near leaving the wagon to pursue the villain.

"Begorra, av ther divil ain't got clane away entoirely!" cried Barney in dismay.

"I'm sorry," returned Frank. "But take the precaution now, Barney, to bolt that door."

Barney complied with alacrity.

Then he was obliged to return to his post, for the enemy were thick in the rear.

But the next moment the Steam Man topped the rise.

A volley from the Vigilantes drove the cowboys back for the time.

Then Frank Reade, Jr., brought the machine to a halt upon the plateau.

The Vigilantes were wild with delight, and crowded about the Steam Man. Frank Reade, Jr., opened the door and descended among them.

In an instant Harmon was by his side and had gripped his hand.

"God bless ye, Mr. Reade!" cried the whole-souled plainsman. "It's like takin' the paw of one brought back from the dead. Dogdast it, but I'd given ye up entirely when I see that your Steam Man was in the hands or that coyote. It's all like a kind of miracle."

"I think we may congratulate ourselves," said Frank, "but do you know that we are in a tight box?"

"Nobody knows it better," declared Harmon.

"I doubt if we pull out of it."

"What kin we do?"

"Is there no avenue open for retreat?" asked Frank.

"Not a one."

"Then we can only stay here and fight to the last. Of course I might be able to elude them with the Steam Man, but I'd never try that while any of your band are left."

"P'raps it would be ther best way." said Harmon, generously. "At least you could save the gal. It don't matter so much about us. We're only rough men, and not a one of us afeared to die."

"You are heroes!" cried Frank, with fervor, "and if I should desert you, I would forswear my honor as a man. No, the Steam Man, will stay here and fight for you until the last, depend on it."

"In course we need your help," replied Harmon. "Mebbe we'll whip ther skunks yet."

"We'll try it."

"Begorra, that we will," cried Barney. "Whurroo! av' I only had a good whack at that baste av' a Cliff now I'd sphoil his beauty foriver."

Walter Barrows and Bessie had been holding a joyful conference. But now the order went up:

"Every man to his post. The enemy are coming."

There were no delinquents. Not one in that heroic little band hung back.

It was true that the foe were coming again to the attack.

With Cliff leading them they were charging furiously up the hill. But the Vigilantes stood firm and gave them a raking volley.

For a moment they wavered. Then once more they came on.

Cliff's voice could be heard as he rallied them.

"Curse ye, go on up thar and kill the hull crew of 'em!" he yelled. "Don't let one of them escape alive! Kill 'em, every one, and don't give any quarter!"

"We'll see about that," muttered Frank Reade, Jr. "It may not be so easy to do all that, Mr. Cliff."

Frank and Barney, from their position aboard the Steam Man, could pour a terrible fire into the ranks of the foe.

It was a terrible battle!

The cowboys were mowed down like grain before the sickle; yet they did not waver, but came on faster.

Every moment they drew nearer the top of the rise. If they surrounded it the sequel would be brief.

Overpowering muscles would quickly tell the story, and the little band of Vigilantes would be wiped out of existence.

It was, without doubt, Cliff's purpose to give no quarter. A wholesale massacre would be the result.

The Vigilantes were now fighting for their lives. As well die facing the foe as with back turned. Every man was resolute in this.

But the tremendous body of men swept over the rise and gained the plateau. In a twinkling the Vigilantes were surrounded, and it seemed as if no power would intervene to save them from sure and total extinction.

Frank Reade, Jr., took in the situation at a glance, and cried despairingly:

"Barney, we are lost! Our end has come, and we are as good as dead men already!"

* * *

Poor Pomp saw no way out of the awful situation in which he was placed.

Death in its most awful form was upon him.

A worse fate could not be imagined.

The savages piled the brushwood about him, and danced with demoniac yells about the pile.

If Pomp could have turned pale, he would have been whiter than chalk at that moment.

But for all this, the darky's fears were even now more for his friends than for himself.

"Golly Massy!" he chattered, shivering like one with the ague. "Whatebber will be de end ob all dis. Yere Ise gwine fo' to be burned to death, and Marse Frank in de clutches ob dat rascal Cliff, an' nobody to rescue him. Oh, good Lor' it am dretful."

It was indeed a dreadful thing.

But Pomp was certainly powerless. Higher the brushwood was heaped, and then one of the savages advanced with a torch.

In a moment he had applied it to the pile.

The dry wood burned like tinder. In an instant great flames sprang up.

But they were at the edge of the pile. However, Pomp felt their heat and they would soon reach him.

The poor darky was nearly insane with a frenzy of desperation.

The savages now began a fiendish dance about the pile. They leaped and ran, and swung their tomahawks and made hideous faces at their victim.

But fate had not ordained that this was to be Pomp's end.

Even while death seemed certain, rescue was close at hand.

Suddenly there smote upon the air the ring of horses' hoofs, and a quick sharp order, followed by the crash of carbines.

Indians fell in heaps before that volley. A panic resulted and the next moment through the smoke Pomp saw the gleam of uniforms, and knew that a body of United States cavalry had happened upon the spot just in the nick of time.

The darky was beside himself with the realization.

He tried to break his bonds, and cried:

"Sabe me, sogers – sabe Pomp! He am gwine fo' suah to burn to death ef yo' don' sabe him!"

But the call was not necessary.

Through the smoke sprang two dismounted soldiers. In a twinkling the burning brush was kicked aside, and Pomp's bonds were cut.

Then the darky was face to face with a tall, handsome young officer.

The Indians had been dispersed and the fight was over.

"I am Col. Clark, of the United States Seventh Cavalry," said the young officer. "Who are you?"

"I am Pomp!" was the darky's prompt reply.

The officer smiled.

"Well, who do you belong to?"

"I belongs to Marse Frank Reade, Jr.," replied Pomp, with emphasis. "I'se a free nigger, but I goes wherebber Marse Frank goes jest de same."

"Oh, I see," replied the officer; "well, where is your master just now?"

"Golly, for goodness!" cried Pomp, excitedly. "He am in a heap ob trubble, an' yo' kin help him out of it."

With this Pomp told Clark all about the Steam Man and their mission in the West.

The young colonel listened with deep interest, and then when apprised of the fact that the Steam Man and its passengers were in the hands of Cliff, he cried, excitedly:

"By Jupiter! That man Cliff is just the chap I am after. Word was brought to the fort some time ago of a den of thieves up here with a rendezvous called Ranch V. Do you know of it?"

"Golly sakes, Marse colonel," cried Pomp, excitedly, "yo' kin jest bet I does! Jes' yo' find de cowboys and rescue Marse Frank and he done show yo' where de Ranch V are."

"It shall be done if we are able," said Colonel Clark.

He turned to his men who were scattered about the vicinity, having been engaged in driving the savages out of the valley.

But the bugle quickly recalled them.

A spare horse was brought forward for Pomp and then the cavalrymen in solid body rode out of the valley.

As they struck the prairie below, the distant sounds of firing came to their ears.

It was the din of the conflict between the Vigilantes and the cowboys. Aided by the sounds Colonel Clark was able to gallop straight to the scene.

Through a pass in the hills they reached the plateau. They burst upon the cowboys in the rear just at the critical moment when it seemed as if Harmon's heroic little band was doomed.

It required but a glance for Clark to take in the situation.

Whirling his sabre aloft he spurred his horse forward with the thrilling command:

"Forward! Charge!"

Chapter XII
The Fortunes of War

JUST AT THAT moment when utter destruction threatened the brave little band of Vigilantes the U.S. soldiers came upon the scene.

Nothing could have been more opportune.

It was the saving of the day. The emotions of all at sight of the glittering uniforms may be imagined. A great shout of triumph went up. A yell of dismay came from the cowboys.

Then followed the rattling of steel and the flash of sabre blades. Before that charge what force could stand?

Backward the followers of Artemus Cliff were forced.

In vain the villain tried to rally them. They would not respond.

The odds were too great and they broke and fled in wild confusion. The next moment Pomp dashed up the incline and dropped from his horse almost at Frank Reade, Jr's, feet.

"Bress de Lor', Marse Frank," he cried ecstatically. "Yo' am alibe an' well, an' dis nigger hab brought yo' a rescue aftah all. P'raps yo' forgib me fo' leabin' de Steam Man when I hadn't ought?"

"You are forgiven, Pomp!" cried Frank, lightly. "I might have done the same thing myself. I am glad no harm came to you. I had given you up."

"'Deed no, Marse Frank!" cried the delighted darky. "I is too bad fo' to die. Hi dar, Pish, I is glad to see you!"

"Well, if it ain't the naygur!" cried Barney, with a wild rush at Pomp. "Whurroo, it's glad I am to see yez onct more alive an' well! Bejabers that's so!"

The two friends embraced warmly. Then Colonel Clark rode up and saluted all.

"It seems that you've been having a bit of a squall here," he declared, "but at any rate you've vanquished the enemy."

"With your timely assistance," replied Frank. "But I believe we are not strangers, colonel."

"Frank Reade, Jr., the inventor!" cried Clark, springing from the saddle and seizing Frank's hand. "Well, now, I'm glad to see you. But come to think of it, your colored man mentioned the name of Frank Reade, but I never dreamed that it was you."

"It is nobody else," replied Frank with a laugh. "And I well remember you."

"And I do you," replied Clark. "I was once one of an army commission to visit you and make you an offer for one of your inventions on a gun."

"You are right."

"You would not sell it."

"No," replied Frank. "I do not care to sell any of my inventions. They are for my own use. I will always, however, put them at the disposal of the weak and oppressed."

"Truly a noble sentiment," agreed the colonel, "but I am anxious to capture this man Cliff. Hello! What have you there? A giant in iron? One of your new inventions is it? Well, that beats all."

With this Clark proceeded to make an inspection of the Steam Man. A great crowd of the newcomers were doing the same.

It was an object of great wonderment. Frank showed its working to the entertainment of all.

But Cliff's men had not been so easily beaten as the savages.

They had dispersed into the passes and were somewhat scattered, but here they made a stand and resisted stubbornly.

It was necessary to dislodge them as quickly as possible.

At any moment they might avail themselves of the fortunes of war and turn victory into defeat.

So Clark quickly called his men together.

Only a brief rest was all that he would accord them.

The bugle sounded "boots and saddles," and every man was quickly mounted.

A plan was quickly outlined between Frank Reade, Jr., and Col. Clark.

This was that the cavalry should pursue and thoroughly rout the cowboys, even going down to Ranch V to effect its destruction.

The Vigilantes were to return home, and the cavalry would see to the punishment of Artemas Cliff.

But the Steam Man was to remain at a point below until the return of the cavalry.

If possible Cliff was to be captured alive and a confession wrung from his lips.

This plan had been agreed upon.

The Vigilantes were not wholly satisfied, yet did not demur.

Clark and his command dashed away into the hills.

The Vigilantes and the Steam Man started for the open prairie.

This division of forces very soon proved to be an unwise and unfortunate thing.

The fortunes of war are proverbial for changes.

Strongly intrenched in the hills, Cliff's gang gave the soldiers a disastrous battle.

In vain the plucky young colonel tried to dislodge them.

They fought like tigers, and having the advantage of location, actually decimated the cavalry one half in number.

Until nightfall, Col. Clark kept persistently waging the battle.

Then he began to think of retreat.

But, to his horror, he found that this was by no means as easy a matter as he had fancied.

The foe had actually closed in upon him, and nearly every avenue of retreat was closed.

He was literally surrounded by the foe.

"My soul!" he muttered, in deep surprise; "this is not very good generalship on my part."

What was to be done?

It was plainly impossible to dislodge the foe.

The little band of cavalrymen were now hardly adequate to cope with the foe in their front.

It really seemed as if Cliff had received reinforcements. The number of his band had in some mysterious manner been increased.

Darkness was coming on rapidly.

Something must be done, and at once. Col. Clark racked his brain for an expedient.

Certainly they must extricate themselves from this position, and without delay. Men were falling every moment about them, and the enemy's line, like a cordon of death, was every moment drawing tighter about them.

Cold sweat broke out upon the intrepid colonel's brow.

"My God!" he muttered. "What is to be done?"

It was a terrible question. They were literally in a trap of death.

Cliff was aware of this, and his men made the air hideous with their yells. Closer they crowded the line.

In this extremity Clark regretted having separated himself from the Vigilantes and the Steam Man.

But this error had been made, and it was too late to correct it.

But the brave colonel was not long without an expedient.

He called out one of his pluckiest privates, and said: "Jason, do you want to undertake a ticklish job?"

"I'm ready, sir," replied the private, with a salute.

"You know we are in a tight box?"

"Yes, sir."

"We must have reinforcements or the enemy will surely get the best of us."

"It looks that way, sir."

"Now, I want you to try to get through the enemy's line. Look for the Vigilantes and the Steam Man and tell them to come to our aid. Then ride to the fort as fast as you can for a fresh squad. Tell the officer in charge to send two hundred mounted men."

"Very well, sir."

"Do you think you can do this?"

"I will do it or I will not come back."

Clark knew that Jason meant just what he said.

A few moments later the courier for relief slipped carefully into the shadows and was gone.

A prayer trembled on Clark's lips.

"I don't care for myself," he muttered, "but I cannot bear to see my brave boys slaughtered like sheep."

Darkness now thickly settled down. Of course no fighting could be done until the break of day.

But the cavalrymen were not in a position to guarantee them much rest.

Few of them dared to sleep, and then it was upon their arms.

As the night hours dragged by, Clark paced the ground upon the outskirts of the camp and listened for some sign of the return of Jason.

He knew that it was not possible for the faithful courier to return from the fort under two days.

But if the cavalry division was reinforced by the Vigilantes and the Steam Man they might be able to keep the foe at bay until the fresh squad should arrive.

Thus the plucky young colonel clung to hope.

Time passed. It seemed an age to Clark before a silent shadowy form slipped out of the gloom and into the camp.

As it drew nearer he recognized the courier Jason.

"Well, my man!" he said, sharply. "You are back."

Jason saluted quickly.

"Where are the reinforcements?"

"I did not find them."

"But – did I not tell you to find them?" began the colonel, angrily.

"Easy, colonel," said Jason, respectfully. "I think I have done a better thing, sir."

"What do you mean?"

"It's a good ways to the fort. You might be cut to pieces before I could return. I have found an avenue by which I think we can escape."

Clark's manner changed instantly.

"You don't mean it?" he exclaimed, excitedly. "What is it?"

Jason drew nearer and lowered his voice in a mysterious manner.

"Just over that pile of bowlders," he whispered, "I found a narrow passage through the mountain side. It is almost a cavern, for the top is so closely overhung with bushes. It's a close squeeze for the horses, but I think we can all get through and out upon the prairie before daybreak."

Col. Clark was intensely excited.

"Good for you, Jason!" he cried, in a joyful manner. "Arouse the camp, but do it quietly. Put every man in his saddle within ten minutes. You have solved our salvation, and you shall be promoted."

Jason hurried away to do the bidding of the colonel.

In a brief space of time the camp was aroused.

The weary soldiers, worn out with fighting, were only too glad to learn of the possibility of an escape.

At once preparations were made to steal a march upon the enemy.

The passage described by Jason was found. It was necessary to first pry aside a huge bowlder before passage could be made.

Into the passage the little band went, and one by one filed out into the valley beyond.

So skillfully was the move executed that the foe never dreamed of it. Daybreak came, and Cliff was furious to find that his intended victims had given him the slip during the night.

The cavalrymen had reached the prairie in safety, and galloped away from the hills.

Clark knew that his only and best move now was to return to the fort for reinforcements.

He could not hope to do anything with the foe with such a mere handful of men.

Accordingly, just as the sun appeared above the horizon, the little cavalcade, with its shattered ranks, galloped away across the plain.

No effort was made to search for the Vigilantes.

Clark knew that even with their aid it would not be feasible to give battle to the cowboys.

Clearly it was necessary to have two hundred more men. The colonel set his lips vengefully.

"I will teach that desperado a lesson," he muttered. "He shall be swept out of existence together with his rascally crew, and before another week."

On over the prairie they galloped toward the fort.

And as they rode, thrilling adventures were the lot of Frank Reade, Jr., and his friends on board the Steam Man.

Let us, therefore, for a time, deviate here and follow their fortunes.

Chapter XIII
The Abduction

CHIEF HARMON of the Vigilantes was not wholly content to abandon the trail of the cowboys, just here.

He indulged in quite an argument with Frank Reade, Jr.

His remarks were not without logic.

"Why, only look at the sense of the thing," he declared, "It is by no means possible that the soldiers are going to have an easy time with Cliff and his men. They may turn the tables on them yet. I tell you it was a premature thing for that colonel to do, to set us adrift so quickly."

"Yet he ought to know his own strength," said Frank.

"I don't believe he does."

"I cannot but feel that he is doing the right thing."

"I don't feel that way."

"Well, in case of defeat the stigma will not fall upon you."

"Ah, but that is not the idea. We must not let Cliff defeat them. If he does, he will defeat us."

"What do you propose?"

"I am not going back home yet. We will make a camp down here on Willow Creek. When we learn for a fact that Cliff has been done up, then we will go home. Until then we are on duty."

Frank saw that Harmon was right. He extended his hand and said: "I agree with you."

"I knew ye would," replied the Vigilant leader. "We can do this upon our own responsibility. You are to wait for Clark at a point below here, I believe?"

"Yes."

"Very good. That point is on Willow Creek. We will accompany you there."

It was nightfall before Willow Creek was reached.

In a convenient spot camp was made. The darkness became most intense in the vicinity.

Camp-fires were made and guards posted.

The fires in the furnace of the Steam Man were banked, and the occupants descended and mixed with the Vigilantes.

The men gathered around the fires, and told stories and cracked jokes.

Walter Barrows, the young Vigilant who was so deeply in love with Bessie Rodman, had waited upon her at the wagon step, and together they took a lover-like walk down the bank of the creek.

Nobody saw them go, and it is doubtful if any one would have sought to restrain them.

But they were committing unwittingly an act of great risk and folly.

For unknown to any in the camp a coterie of dusky savages lurked in the tall prairie grass about.

Barney and Pomp were entertaining the camp with some of their Munchhausen stories.

The plainsmen roared with laughter until their sides ached.

Both were comical mokes and were continually playing roots upon each other. Barney had just worked a gag upon Pomp when suddenly the distant crack of a pistol was heard.

Instantly every man in the camp was upon his feet.

The most intense of excitement reigned. All was confusion.

Then one of the guards came rushing in.

"There's a hull lot of Apaches down yonder," he cried, "ther grass is full of 'em and I reckon they've surrounded the camp."

"Steady all!" thundered Harmon, the Vigilant leader. "Who fired that pistol shot?"

"I don't know," replied the guard.

"Is anybody outside the line?"

"Yes."

"Who?"

"Walter Barrows and the young lady passed me not an hour ago. They went on down the creek."

"My soul!" gasped Harmon, with white face, "that was Barrows pistol without doubt. He an' the gal have certainly fallen into the grip of ther Injuns. We must make lively work to save 'em."

Frank Reade, Jr., had listened to this report with a sensation of horror.

Barney and Pomp had at once desisted in their fun-making, and Barney proceeded to open the Steam Man's furnace.

The crack of rifles now sounded all around the camp.

The savages, without doubt, were drawing their line closer, and meant if possible to exterminate the little band of Vigilantes.

But a line of defense was then thrown out, and the skulking savages were held at bay.

But a desultory and very unsatisfactory species of warfare was kept up in the darkness.

It was impossible to tell how to move or where.

The enemy fired from all directions and practically at random.

Many of the Vigilantes were wounded, and Captain Harmon was angry.

"Confound an Injun!" he muttered, in disgust. "They have sich a sneakin' way of fighting. They allus attack one after dark, an' hain't got the pluck to come out in the open an' fight."

Everybody was bound to acknowledge the logic of this.

But the savages kept up the same mode of attack until Frank Reade, Jr., made a diversion.

Barney had succeeded in getting up steam once more in the Steam Man, and now Frank Reade, Jr., approached Harmon.

"Give me five men," he declared, "and I will whip the foe for you."

"Five men!" gasped Harmon. "Why, they're ten to one out there."

"I don't care if they are."

"But –"

"Will you give me the men?"

"Oh yes, but –"

"There's no time for questions, Captain Harmon. Leave it all to me."

"All right, Mr. Reade."

By Harmon's orders five of The Vigilantes joined Frank Reade.

He led them aboard the steam wagon. Then he closed the door and seized the reins which connected with the throttle.

The Steam Man gave a shriek loud enough to perforate the ear drums of any one in the vicinity.

Then it dashed out upon the prairie.

The effect may be imagined.

The monster with fiery eyes and all flame and smoke, with clanking thunderous tread plunging into the midst of the foe, was an apparition well to be feared.

Right into the midst of the savages the Steam Man ran.

While the armed men in the screened wagon poured destructive volleys into the midst of the red foe.

Pen cannot adequately describe the situation.

For a moment the Apaches held their ground. Then, with wild, baffled yells they fled before the conqueror.

In less than twenty minutes the vicinity had been practically cleared of savages.

They retreated to a point below where their ponies were corralled.

Mounting, they dashed away to the westward. The Steam Man pursued until finding a creek, they escaped for good.

Then the Steam Man returned to camp.

But although the foe had been repulsed, matters were still bad enough.

Walter Barrows and Bessie Rodman were missing.

That they were captives was a forlorn hope. That they had been murdered was a dreadful fear.

Delay was almost fatal in this case. Without loss of time a good trailer was put upon the trail of the lovers.

Daylight was breaking in the east, and this enabled him to easily follow the trail.

Along the banks of the creek it ran for nearly a fifth of a mile.

Then the trailer paused.

Here without doubt was the spot where Barrows had been attacked by the Apaches.

There were footprints and marks of a struggle. A rifle, with broken stock, was picked up,

"It is Barrows' gun," said one of the Vigilantes.

Blood was found upon the ground, but no trace of the bodies.

"They have been taken away as captives," declared Harmon, positively. "There is no doubt of that."

"Or thrown into the creek," suggested one of the Vigilantes.

Investigation for a moment gave the pursuers a thrill of horror.

There were footprints down to the water's edge, and the marks of some heavy body dragged thither.

In the shallow water, protected by reeds, was a body.

For a moment all expected to recognize Barrows. But all drew a breath of relief.

It was not him.

The body was that of one of the Apaches. Doubtless it was one shot by Barrows, and his body had been thrown into this place to escape the notice of the white pursuers.

"That's an Injun trick," declared Harmon, positively. "I'm mighty well satisfied that the captives are alive."

"I hope you are right," said one man.

"Ditto!" said another.

"Then let us take the trail," cried Frank Reade, Jr. "If possible, we must rescue them."

The question was settled at once. All sprung to saddle, and the trail, which was quite plain, was followed.

Across the prairies went the Steam Man, with the Vigilantes behind.

Of course their horses could not compete with the Man on a level stretch, but Frank did not try to run away from them.

The Indians bore away to a southwesterly course, and soon a range of hills became visible above the horizon.

Harmon made them out as the Black Bear range.

"If they get into those hills with the captives," he declared, "we'll have mighty hard work diggin' 'em out."

"Why?" asked one of his men.

"Bekase, there's more holes and out of the way dens there than you could shake a stick at."

Barney and Pomp crouched down in the wagon, and kept their rifles in readiness for business.

Frank Reade, Jr., watched the plain ahead with eager eye, but though the trail was plain there was yet no signs of overtaking the red foe.

As they drew nearer the hills it became almost a certainty that the savages had sought refuge there. A long stretch of plain intervened to the hills.

This was easily to be inspected with a glass, and Frank did so. There was no sign whatever of the Indians.

All hope was thus given up of overtaking the redskins before reaching the hills.

It seemed a certainty that they had reached their caves, and the only alternative left was to scour them thoroughly.

But when quite near an entrance between high hills, suddenly the pursuers topped a rise in the prairie and were rewarded with a startling sight.

Just below, in a depression, was the band of savages, seemingly engaged in making camp.

A small creek ran through this depression.

As is well known, Indians always encamp upon the banks of a stream. Yet it was a surprise to the pursuers that they should venture to camp in this open spot.

At sight of their foes the astonished redskins were thrown into a tumult.

Instantly a mad retreat was begun for the mountains.

A wild cheer pealed from the lips of the Vigilantes.

Harman settled himself in his saddle and shouted: "Forward, all! Charge!"

With a yell the Vigilantes put spurs to their horses and made for the Indian encampment.

Frank Reade, Jr., started the Steam Man on a circuit to head off the savages.

But as he did so Pomp clutched his arm.

"Hi dar, Marse Frank!" cried the darky. "Does yo' see dat little party ober dar making fo' de hills?"

Frank did see them.

"Yes," he replied.

"Well, dat am Missy Bessie an' her lover jes' as suah as yo' am bo'n, Marse Frank, an' dar am half a dozen Injuns jes' holding onto de bridles ob der hosses. I makes it out, sah, dat dey fink dey kin reach de hills afo' de Steam Man, sah."

"By Jupiter, you're right, Pomp!" cried Frank, with inspiration. "But we'll try and spoil that little game."

"Dat's right, Marse Frank!" cried the darkey. "I jes' fink de Man kin obertake dem hosses suah enuff."

Frank seized the reins and pulled open the throttle.

As the Steam Man went forward with his mighty stride Frank opened the whistle valve and let out a mighty shriek of such loudness that the echoes were repeated a hundred fold in the recesses of the hills.

Chapter XIV
In Hot Pursuit

THE PARTY of savages with the two captives in their midst, evidently intended to reach the hills, if possible, before being overtaken by the Steam Man.

At first Frank had fancied it easy to cut them off.

But there were several depressions in the prairie which the Man had to circuit, and the distance was greater than Frank had really dreamed of.

Like a runaway locomotive the Steam Man raced over the plain.

The Vigilantes were having a running fight with the savages.

But Frank Reade, Jr., was doomed to disappointment.

He failed to cut off the band of abductors, and they vanished from sight in a deep pass.

It was too rocky a trail for the Steam Man to follow. Thus far the villains had the best of it.

"Golly sakes, Marse Frank!" cried Pomp, "dey done git away wif dem prisoners fo' suah."

"It looks like it," agreed Frank, in a baffled tone, "but there ought to be some way to cut them off."

"Begorra, there's only won way," declared Barney.

"What is that?"

"Let the naygur sthay with the man, an' you an' I will go afther the divils a-foot," said the Celt.

For a moment Frank entertained no hopes of the success of such a plan.

Then he glanced back to the prairie where the Vigilantes and the Indians were having their Battle.

It was nip and tuck between them, but Frank saw that the Vigilantes were fast getting the best of it.

Not more than half a dozen of the savages had the captives in charge.

To be sure, the odds were three to one, yet Frank believed that with the plucky Barney's help, they could defeat them.

To think with Frank Reade, Jr., was to act.

He did not waste time, but seizing a rifle, cried: "Your idea is a good one, Barney. We will act upon it. Pomp, keep a sharp eye out for danger until we return."

"A'right Marse Frank," replied the faithful darky.

Barney, delighted that Frank had seen fit to adopt his plan, was quickly ready and they left the wagon.

The Indians, to be sure, had the start of them, but the pass was rocky and it was hardly likely that they would succeed in getting a great lead.

Swiftly the two rescuers pressed forward.

They climbed over piles of bowlders, crept through narrow defiles, and climbed high steeps.

It seemed that progress must be slow for the ponies of the Indians, and they should be overtaken before long.

Suddenly Barney paused with a sharp cry.

He seized Frank by the arm and pulled him back into the cover of an angle in the mountain wall.

He was none too soon.

The crack of rifles smote upon the air and the shower of bullets came down into the pass.

"Bejabers, I saw the spalpeens just in the nick av time!" declared Barney, peering around the edge of the cliff wall. "Av I hadn't we'd have been dead gossoons as sure as me name is Barney."

"You're right there!" cried Frank, slipping extra cartridges into his rifle; "that was a close call."

"Indade it was."

"I had no idea we were so near the rascals."

"Bejabers, I didn't mesilf till I see the top-knot av wan of thim over that ridge yonder."

"They are ready for us, then."

"Bejabers, and we're ready too. If I iver get a bead on any wan av them there'll be a job for the coroner, bad cess to thim."

"Where are they? I can't see their position very well."

"Aisy, Misther Frank," said Barney, "they're hiding up yonder jist ferninst that big scrub av an oak on the edge of the cliff."

Frank looked in that direction. Suddenly Barney gave a sharp cry.

"Whurro!" he yelled.

Quick as a flash his rifle went to his shoulder.

Crack!

A yell of agony rang through the gorge. Then down over the cliff tumbled an Indian almost at the Celt's feet.

The bullet had pierced his skull and his final account was settled.

"Good shot, Barney!" cried Frank, "that only leaves five for us to tackle."

Then quick as a flash the young inventor threw his rifle to his shoulder.

Crack!

Another yell, a death cry went up on the air of the defile.

"Bejabers, that's only four av the divils left," chuckled Barney. "It's only two to wan, Misther Frank."

"You're right, Barney!" cried Frank, with enthusiasm, "but the odds are yet too great."

The outlook now was certainly encouraging for the rescue of the prisoners.

But the two rescuers knew better than to essay an open attack.

The Indian method of warfare was in this case far the best. They remained strictly under cover.

All was quiet on the bluff above.

But it was not by any means likely that the foe were inactive.

The great danger now was that they would continue to slip away deeper into the hills and reach some inaccessible hiding place.

Our rescuers waited as long as seemed consistent with safety.

Then Frank said: "I think we'd better make a break, Barney."

"All roight, sorr," replied the Celt. "Do yez think it safe?"

"We must use caution. It may be possible that they are trying to draw us from our hiding place."

"So I thought, sorr."

"Again, they may be far into the hills by this time. We will gain nothing by staying here."

"All roight, sorr."

Barney begun to scan the side of the cliff. A path was not visible anywhere. Yet the Celt did not believe it impossible to climb to the top.

If this could be done they might then succeed in getting upon level ground with the foe and escape the risk of their bullets.

Frank divined Barney's purpose and said: "I think we can climb it, Barney."

"Bejabers we'll thry."

Barney had just got his hands and feet into niches in the cliff when a startling sound came up the pass.

"Hark!"

"What is it?"

The tramp of ponies' feet could be heard and the distant baffled yells of savages were wafted up on the breeze.

"The Indians are coming up the pass," cried Frank, with dismay. "Barney, there's not an instant to lose."

"Begorra, yez are roight," cried the Celt, beginning to make his way up the cliff.

It was a smart climb up the steep wall, but it was safely made at length.

They were now on level ground with the four captors. But a careful reconnoitering of the vicinity showed that they had left.

In the lull in the conflict they had slipped away into the hills.

But Barney took the trail and they went forward again in pursuit.

The sounds of the foe coming up the pass in their rear, however, every moment became plainer.

But fortunately, just at a point where the trail diverged deeper into the hills, the foe must have turned in another direction for very soon the sounds died out.

"We have nothing to fear from them," cried Frank, with a breath of relief. "They have gone in another direction."

Very soon the hills began to merge into a deep valley. Through this there ran a swift stream.

As Frank and Barney entered the valley Barney shouted: "Be me sowl, there be the spalpeens now."

"Where?" asked Frank.

"Jist down there ferninst that grove of trees, Misther Frank."

"Sure enough."

The four savages and their captors were plainly seen on the banks of the creek.

They were just in the act of embarking in a canoe.

Frank saw that he must act quick if he would prevent this.

So he said, sharply:

"Go to the right, Barney, I will go to the left, and we must head them off."

"All right, sorr."

Away went Barney on the mad run. The savages had already got the canoe into the water.

They saw him coming and a yell was the signal. The captives were hustled into the light craft and it was pushed out from the shore.

Down into the current it went. There was no time to lose.

Frank Reade, Jr., came to a stop and raised his rifle. It was a desperate chance but he took it.

A quick aim, a bead skillfully drawn on one of the paddlers and –

Crack!

A wild Indian yell went up and the prow of the canoe swung around.

Over into the water went the doomed savage. The shot had been a good one.

But the canoe was at the moment at the head of some swift rapids.

The next moment it was racing down them, and turning a bend in the stream, vanished from view.

Frank had not time to draw another bead before it was out of sight, and when it reached the lower level and came into view again it was out of range.

Barney came along now and shouted: "Be jabers, yez did well, Misther Frank. That was a beautiful shot. There's only three av ther red divils left."

This was true, but the three savages seemed likely to elude their pursuers after all.

The canoe was racing down the stream, and fast nearing a defile in the hills.

If it should enter this, there was little doubt but that the fugitives would make their escape.

Frank and Barney saw this in the same moment.

"Begorra, Mother Frank, we must cut the divils off!" cried the Celt.

"Forward, then!" cried Frank. "Is there not a short cut?"

Both looked for this. In the same instant they espied it.

The creek took a long turn, and by cutting directly across a meadow the two pursuers saw that they would be likely to cut off the savages.

Accordingly they started forward on the run.

The Indian captors saw their move at once, and an angry yell went up from them.

One of them rose in the canoe and took quick aim and fired.

The bullet whistled close to Barney's ear. The Celt stopped and cocked his rifle.

"Be jabers, I'll spoil that fellow!" he cried, "Have at yez, ye blatherskite!"

Barney's rifle spoke.

But the motion of the canoe very likely destroyed the aim, for the bullet did not take effect.

At this point the canoe took a swift course, and in the twinkling of an eye seemed to have overcome the skilled hand at the paddles.

In a flash it went over and the entire party were dumped into the waters of the creek.

A great cry went up from Frank Reade, Jr.

"My God! They will be drowned!"

Forward the brave young inventor rushed. He thought of poor Barrows with his hands tied.

Thrown into the waters of the creek, it did not seem as if any power on earth could save him.

But two of the savages had seized the prisoners. The canoe had overturned in close proximity to the shore.

The third savage gave assistance, and as the water did not chance to be deep, all got ashore.

"Now we have them!" cried Frank, confidently.

But his statement was premature.

Even as it seemed that the rescue was certain, an incident occurred to prevent.

From behind a small hillock appeared Red Bear's gang of Apaches, full half a hundred strong.

Chapter XV
The Vigilantes to the Rescue

THE APPEARANCE of the savages was most inopportune.

Mounted on their fleet ponies, with wild yells they swept down upon the party.

The three Indian captors yelled with delight.

Frank and Barney of course came to a halt. Of course it was folly to tempt fate.

To attempt to stand against that gang was folly.

"By Jupiter!" gasped the young inventor. "It's all up with us, Barney! We are badly beaten!"

"Tare an' 'ounds!" grumbled the angry Celt. "That beats all me woife's relations! Phwativer shall we do now, Misther Frank?"

"Beat a retreat," declared the young inventor. "Come on, Barney!"

"It's mesilf as hates to retreat," said Barney, stubbornly. "Oh, if we only had the Steam Man an' the naygur here now we'd moighty soon turn the thing about."

The two rescuers now turned about and hastily beat a retreat across the valley.

But they had not gone far when the Indians began to ford the creek for the purpose of giving pursuit.

Barney saw the move and called Frank's attention to it.

"Be me sowl, Misther Frank!" cried the Irishman, excitedly, "we've got to make quick toime, or they'll have our scalps."

"You are right, Barney."

But at that moment Frank Reade, Jr., lifted his gaze, and a mighty cry escaped his lips.

Directly in front of them, a body of armed men swept into the valley.

They were the Vigilantes, and at their head rode Harmon. At sight of Frank and Barney they urged their horses on faster with a loud cheer.

This was answered by the two fugitives, with a will.

The savages, seeing the Vigilantes, now changed their tactics. They turned their horses about and rode swiftly on the back trail.

Frank could hardly wait for Harmon and his men to come up.

Enthusiastic greetings were exchanged, and also experiences.

The Vigilantes had driven the Apaches before them into the hills.

But upon entering the fastnesses, with which they were not familiar, the Indians had given them the slip.

In the search, they had come upon the scene at an opportune moment.

There seemed no better thing to do than to give pursuit to the savages at once.

Accordingly a couple of spare horses were provided for Frank and Barney, and they rode forward on the charge.

The delay had been brief, but it had enabled the savages to cross the creek and start for the defile beyond.

Down thundered the Vigilantes in hot pursuit.

The creek was quickly forded and the pursuers seemed to be gaining at every bound.

But of a sudden the savages executed a peculiar and inexplicable maneuver.

Suddenly and without warning they split in two sections, one going to the right and the other to the left.

In one division was the girl captive, Bessie Rodman, and in the other Walter Barrows.

The party who had the girl in charge started for the defile.

The other made directly across the valley. In a flash of time the purpose of the savages was made apparent.

The Vigilantes could not go both ways with splitting up.

As they were much less in number than the Apaches the result of this would be to greatly weaken them, if not actually place them at the mercy of the red foe.

On the other hand it was a problem as to which direction to pursue or which party to follow.

Harmon drew a slight rein upon his horse and wavered a moment.

The Vigilantes naturally were inclined to go to the rescue of their comrade, but Frank Reade, Jr., comprehending the folly of this, cried: "The girl first. We can rescue the man later."

"Yes!" cried Harmon, in a voice of thunder; "that is our duty! The girl first, boys; then we will try and save Barrows."

The Vigilantes cheered, and away thundered the troop toward the defile.

A few moments later they reached it and entered it.

High walls of black, forbidding rock arose on either side to a mighty height. The bed of the defile was rough and strewn with bowlders.

It was harder for the horses of the Vigilantes to pick their way through here than the fleet-footed ponies of the savages.

Accordingly the Indians gained quite a lead. But after a quarter of a mile of the defile had been traversed the Vigilantes were brought to a halt in an unceremonious manner.

The defile seemed suddenly to take an upward trend here, and high piles of bowlders made a barrier of some height.

Suddenly from behind this barrier there came the flash of rifle muzzles, and a volley of bullets came rattling down through the defile.

Two of the Vigilantes were wounded, and Harmon instantly called a halt.

Cover was quickly sought behind rocks and corners near.

It was evident that the Indians had here made a stand. The Vigilante leader was puzzled.

But suddenly Frank Reade, Jr., gave a sharp cry: "Listen!"

His acute ear had caught the sound of horses' hoofs coming up the defile in their rear.

"By thunder!" ejaculated Harmon, with sudden terrible comprehension, "we are trapped!"

The men gazed blankly at each other.

Nothing was more apparent. The Apaches under the shrewd Red Bear had certainly very cleverly outgeneraled them.

Led into the defile by one division of the Apaches, the other had proceeded to block up the outlet, and thus literally the Vigilantes were in a trap.

There was not the advantage in facing a foe in this manner that there was in having him wholly in the front.

To be attacked both front and rear would demoralize even the largest and bravest of armies. Harmon was completely taken aback.

"Wall, I swan!" he exclaimed, with earnestness, "I never believed an Injun could beat me in any such way as that. But we are in for it, boys, and no mistake. We've got to fight hard."

The savages in front were keeping up a raking fire.

Those in the rear had now drawn near enough to also open fire. The fun had begun.

But the brave band of white men had no thought of fear or of retreat.

They at once, by Harmon's direction, sought safe places of cover and proceeded to return the fire.

Every time an Indian's top-knot showed above the fringe of rocks, it was made a target of.

Thus, the battle was kept up for over an hour.

Then an idea occurred to the inventive mind of Frank Reade, Jr.

He had carefully examined the face of the pass. In doing so he had discovered what looked like a feasible foot path over the cliff.

At once he called Harmon aside and explained a plan to him.

"I think we can defeat the savages easily in this manner," he declared. "Give me five men and I will guarantee a surprise for them."

"Mr. Reade, take what force you need," declared the vigilant leader. "I have full confidence in your ability to do as you say. May you succeed."

Frank at once selected five men from the troop.

Then with Barney he led the way cautiously up the path.

Fortunately, it was overhung with foliage to a large extent, so that they were hidden from the view of those in their rear.

In a few moments a position near the brow of the cliff had been reached. Then Frank's surmise was verified.

The little party could look down upon the heads of the savages. It was an easy matter to pour a volley amongst them with most demoralizing effect.

Frank sent one of the men back down the cliff, to give Harmon the cue when to make a charge.

Then at a favorable moment Frank gave the order to fire.

Six repeating rifles were turned upon the savages, and as fast as they could be worked, they were engaged in firing a volley down upon the heads of the exposed savages.

The effect was startling.

The savage is never the one to stand in open field and fight. At once a panic seized them.

It was the moment for the charge, and Harmon's men rushed forward.

Up over the rocks they went. In a twinkling the savages were driven from their entrenchments and utterly routed, and completely dispersed.

Frank Reade, Jr., and Barney saw their opportunity, and rushed upon two of the savages who had Bessie Rodman in charge.

In a moment the girl captive was free once more and among friends. The two guards fled for their lives.

All this had happened in a twinkling of an eye, comparatively speaking. But the fight was not over.

The force in the rear were coming to the attack.

But Harmon's men were now in a position to command the defile.

A quick, sharp conflict ensued, and the Apaches were driven back with great slaughter.

The Vigilantes had thus far the best of it.

The enemy had been routed, and Bessie Rodman rescued.

Only one other thing now remained to be accomplished, and this was the rescue of Walter Barrows.

But even as the question was being discussed a loud cry arose, and the next moment a hatless, blood-stained young man came dashing down over the cliff and fell half fainting in the midst of the Vigilantes.

It was Barrows.

In the midst of the fight the plucky young plainsman had succeeded in breaking his bonds, and after a desperate fight with two of his captors, had made his escape.

Everybody extended congratulations to the young couple, and then plans for the future were discussed.

It was not certain that the savages would not return to the attack.

But a report was brought in by a number of scouts sent out that the Apaches had withdrawn from the field entirely.

It was therefore decided to go back to Willow Creek.

It was not known whether Col. Clark had been victorious with the cowboys or nor.

Until this question was settled Harmon had no idea of returning home.

"Until Cliff and his gang have been wiped out of existence," he declared, "I shall not give up ther chase."

Frank and Barney were anxious to return at once to the Steam Man and Pomp.

They were, by no means, assured that the darky was safe or that he might not have got into trouble.

Accordingly the start was at once made for the prairie.

Down one of the defiles the Vigilantes rode. Coming out into the little valley they crossed this and entered the pass.

But they had not proceeded a hundred yards into the pass when one of the advance scouts came rushing back and gave a thrilling report.

"Ther cowboys are coming up ther pass!" he cried. "Thar's a host of 'em, and Art Cliff is at the head of 'em."

"The cowboys!" gasped Harmon.

The greatest excitement ensued.

"My soul!" exclaimed Frank Reade, Jr., in dismay. "Clark has been defeated!"

"Bad luck to the omadhouns!"

"But what of Pomp?" exclaimed Frank with alarm. "Barney, we ought at once to ascertain where he is."

"To be shure, Misther Frank," agreed the Celt, "but how in the name av all the saints are yez goin' to do it? Be jabers, these cowboys have got us cornered."

In a very few moments a large sized battle was in progress in the pass.

Chapter XVI
Pomp Makes Action

NOW LET US return to Pomp and the Steam Man, whom in the detail of the thrilling adventures just chronicled we have neglected.

The darkey entertained nothing like fear at being left alone on board the Steam Man.

Indeed, he rather enjoyed the responsibility thus put upon him.

He could occasionally hear rifle shots from the hills, which assured him that Frank and Barney were making it hot for the savages.

"Golly!" he muttered, "I jes' reckon dem Injines git de worstest ob dat fight. Ki dar, if dey amn't comin' dis yer way. I spec's I better move."

This was true.

The Indians had been driven before the Vigilantes, and starting for the hills were coming straight toward the Steam Man.

It was evident that they meant to enter the hills at this point.

Pomp knew that it would be folly to remain where he was with the Steam Man.

The savages might ruin the machine as he could not hope alone to hold them at bay.

So he opened the throttle and started away with the Man.

He kept on until satisfied that he had reached a safe point.

Meanwhile the Indians reached the pass and entered it.

The Vigilantes, however, did not seem in a hurry to pursue. They remained on the battle ground for some while looking after their dead and wounded.

When they did start for the pass Pomp had returned and was there stationed.

As they came up the darky put his head out of the screen door and shouted: "Good fo' yo', Marse Harmon. Jes yo' gib dem Injuns a good lickin' fo' luck. I reckon yo' kin do it."

"I reckon we can, Pomp," replied Harmon. "At least we'll try it."

"If yo' sees Marse Frank, jes tole him fo' me, dat his carriage am waitin' fo' him. Will yo'?"

Harmon replied that he would and rode away laughing immoderately.

The Vigilantes all vanished up the pass. It seemed ages after they had gone, when Pomp received another great surprise.

Suddenly, hearing the clatter of hoofs he turned his head, and scrutinized the prairie.

A thrilling sight met his gaze.

There, coming over a swell in the plain was a body of horsemen.

It required but a glance for the darky to recognize them.

They were the cowboys with Artemus Cliff at their head. They were riding directly down upon the Steam Man.

They were just coming from the scene of their victory over Clark. Pomp's eyes stuck out like agates and he sprung to his feet.

"Glory fo' goodness!" he gasped. "Dat am Cliff and his debbils. I jes' reckon I get out dere way."

In an instant he opened the throttle and let the Steam Man race out upon the prairie.

The cowboys gave a wild yell, and attempted pursuit.

But they could not keep anywhere near the Man, and finally abandoned it. With baffled yells they returned and disappeared in the pass.

"Golly, dat am a berry bad fing for Marse Frank an' de oders," muttered Pomp. "Dey will neber be anticipating de comin' ob dem rapscallions, an' dat will make tings berry bad, indeed."

The darky at once began to wax anxious as to the fate of his friends.

He began to feel as if it was very much his duty to enter the hills and render what assistance he could.

But what was to be done with the Steam Man?

Pomp reflected that he might take it with him if he could only find some way of doing so.

To attempt to traverse the rocky Pass was out of the question.

The darky was in a quandary.

Soon he heard the sounds of firing. The battle was on, and at no great distance, either.

Pomp could hardly contain himself. He walked up and down in the cage like a prisoner in his cell.

"Ob co'se, I has Marse Frank's ordahs to stay yere," he muttered, "but it am evident dat Marse Frank needs all de help dat he can get. Whatebber I kin do, I jes' don' know what."

The darky sat down and began sober reflection.

He was a shrewd fellow, and as a result he was not long in formulating a plan.

He sprang up finally.

"By golly, I'll jes' do dat fing!" he cried, finally. "It am de bes' fing I kin do."

He opened the throttle and started the Steam Man along the base of the hills. With keen eye he studied the possibility of entering them.

By the pass it was impossible. But he imagined that it would not be difficult to find another means.

Nor was he disappointed.

At a certain point the hillside was shorn of trees and bowlders. It made a smooth surface even over the brow of the height.

As the Steam Man was provided with power to climb any height of this sort, Pomp at once set his course up the height.

Up went the Steam Man with prodigious strides.

Nearer the top he drew. Pomp had no means of knowing whether it would be possible to go further or not.

But his best hopes were realized upon reaching the summit.

Down a gentle incline the Steam Man went, and through a scattered grove of trees, and came out into a valley deep in the hills.

The sound of firing was now quite plain.

Indeed, as Pomp guided the Man down into the valley, he saw the powder smoke of the conflict in the pass, just a short way up the valley.

"By golly!" muttered the darky, joyfully, "I reckon dat I get dar jes' in de bes' time. Won't Marse Frank be glad fo' to see me!"

But at that moment a startling thing occurred.

The Man was traveling slowly, when just as the bottom of the incline was reached, two powerful savages sprung out of the grass and seized the throttle rein.

Pomp was so taken by surprise that for a moment he could not act.

The pulling of the rein closed the throttle, and the Man came to a halt.

Pomp could not use the rein to open it again, and had there been more of the red foe, the Steam Man would have been at their mercy.

But there were only two of them, and while one held the rein the other essayed to hack his way into the wagon with his tomahawk.

Pomp acted with the rapidity of thought.

"G'way from dar yo' red imp!" he yelled, picking up a revolver. "If you don't I'll jes' bore a hole in yo'."

But the red man did not desist, and Pomp, springing to a loop-hole fired at him.

The bullet went true to its aim, and the Indian fell dead.

The other savage seeing the fate of his companion let out a baffled yell, and relaxing his grip on the valve rein fled precipitately.

Pomp did not take the pains to fire at him, but coolly picked up the valve rein, opened the throttle and the Steam Man went on.

Straight for the scene of the conflict at the mouth of the pass Pomp went.

When he came upon the scene he found a thrilling and sanguine conflict in progress.

At sight of the Steam Man a cheer went up from the Vigilantes.

In a moment Frank and Barney were aboard and shaking hands with Pomp.

The situation was quickly explained.

"I thought mos' likely yo' would want de Steam Man, Marse Frank," said the faithful darky. "So I jes' fetched him ober to yo'."

"You have done well, Pomp," said Frank, joyfully. "Of course, this insures our safety. With the Steam Man we would easily escape the cowboys. But it will never do to leave these brave Vigilantes to their mercy."

"Ob co'se not, Marse Frank," cried Pomp, seizing his rifle. "Jes' yo' let dis chile draw a bead on dem rapscallions. I'll show dem dat Pomp kin use a rifle."

The Steam Man was placed in the van of the line of battle.

Protected as they were by the impervious screen, those on board could fire with advantage at the cowboys.

The battle was a hot one, but every moment the cowboys slowly gained ground.

What was worse, the ammunition of the Vigilantes seemed to be giving out.

With plenty of ammunition, it was possible that the Vigilantes could have held them at bay for a long while.

But, of course, when the ammunition should give out, the battle would be ended.

White-faced, but determined, the brave plainsmen stood their ground.

Not a man of them thought of retreat. All were prepared to give up their lives like heroes.

There seemed no way of getting out of their present desperate situation.

To retreat was about equal to an impossibility, for it would be out upon the open plain where they would be shot down like sheep.

The situation was an awful one.

"Durn it, I don't keer for myself," said bluff Harmon, the vigilant leader, "but some of the boys have families dependent on 'em. Ah, that dog of a Cliff has sins to answer fer."

"You are right," agreed Frank Reade, Jr. "But there must be some way of getting out of this scrape."

"How?"

"Ah, that is a sticker. There is no hope of reinforcements near?"

"None whatever."

"The Steam Man could be sent for them in quick time, if such a thing were possible."

"But it is not. The nearest place is Ranch V, and that is Cliff's own den. We know that."

"Certainly."

"The fort is too far off. There is just one forlorn hope."

"Ah!"

"The cavalry."

"But they may have been all wiped out."

"Very true. Well, we must die then like men. But, Mr. Reade, there is no reason why you should not take the girl in your Steam Man and make your escape."

Frank placed a hand upon the vigilant captain's shoulder.

"Yes!" he said, briefly. "I could do that."

"Then do it. We will hold the foe at bay until –"

"Stop!"

Harmon looked his surprise.

"You do not know me," said Frank Reade, Jr., determinedly, "do you think I would desert you in this hour of need?"

"But –"

"Never! If you die so do we. Until the last the Steam Man will stand his ground."

With tears of emotion in his eyes Harmon gripped Frank's hand.

"God bless you!" was all he could say.

At this moment one of the Vigilantes came up excitedly.

"We are just firing the last cartridges," he declared. "What shall we do? Is it a retreat, Harmon?"

"Retreat!" cried the vigilant leader, clubbing his rifle. "Never! Come on one and all. The crisis has come. Now let us show them how brave men can die."

The cowboys with their wild cheers were forcing the crippled Vigilantes back.

But even in the moment of their victory a strange sound came from the rear and a mighty cry went up from the throats of the Vigilantes.

"Hurrah! We are saved! Rescue has come at last."

Chapter XVII
Once More in the Enemy's Power

IT HAD BEEN Col. Clark's firm intention to return to the fort for reinforcements.

It was a long ways, but he did not reckon this. He thought only of securing a sufficient body of men to cope successfully with the cowboys.

So on they rode the little remnant of the squad for the far distant fort.

But after a night had been spent in camp, just as the bugle called 'boots and saddles,' one of the guard sighted a body of horsemen just coming over a swell in the prairie.

The alarm was given and Clark rode out to investigate.

One glance was enough and a cry of joy escaped his lips.

"Hurrah!" he cried. "We are in luck. It is Romaine's company of one hundred men. Forward all!"

With cheers the little band rode out to meet the reinforcements.

The command had been sent out under Captain Romaine to search for Clark and his men.

The two officers shook hands and explanations were made.

"You have come just in the nick of time, Romaine," declared Clark. "We can now return and whip the cowboys."

"We are with you, colonel!" declared the captain with a salute. "The boys are itching for some hot work."

"Well, I will promise it to them," laughed Clark, as he took command.

At once the cavalry set out at full gallop for the hills.

It seemed like a strange fate that guided them almost to the very scene of the conflict.

The firing was heard long before the pass was reached, and Clark hurried his men forward.

He at once threw them into the pass in the rear of Cliff's gang.

It was an opportune moment, too.

Just as the last cartridge of the Vigilantes was used the cavalry struck the rear of the cowboy gang.

Instantly a panic seized Cliff's men. They made a brief stand, and then were driven up a side defile into the hills.

Here they made a stubborn stand.

The cavalry literally cleared the pass, and riding through came into the midst of the Vigilantes.

The scene which followed baffles description.

In a moment Clark and big Harmon were shaking hands with the deepest emotion.

"Ye came jest in the nick of time, Clark," declared the vigilant chief. "In ten minutes more we might have all been dead men."

"Then we are in luck," cried the colonel, "for which I am very glad. Ah, Mr. Reade, I am glad to see you."

"The same," replied Frank, as he gripped hands with the colonel.

Then Clark rode away up the defile to see what was going on there.

He found the fiercest kind of a battle in progress. The cowboys had intrenched themselves once more and were making a bold stand.

The cavalry outnumbered them, but they were in a very advantageous position.

The best efforts of Clark's men would not suffice to dislodge them.

For a long while the sanguine battle went on.

In vain Clark tried to eject them from their position. His bravest efforts met with failure.

The intrepid colonel knew that if he could get the foe into the open he could hope to whip them.

But as it was it looked certainly as if his plucky little band would be badly decimated in the accomplishment of the desired end.

In this quandary Frank Reade, Jr., appeared upon the spot.

The young inventor had borrowed a horse of one of the Vigilantes and rode up to see how the fight was going on.

"Well, colonel," he said, greeting Clark, "how are you making out?"

"Not as well as I could desire," replied the colonel in a dejected manner.

"What is the matter?"

"Why, I can't drive the rascals."

"Why not?"

"They have a position up there in the hills which is unassailable."

"I disagree with you," said Frank, quietly. "I am not a military engineer, but I am a land surveyor and I tell you their position on that hill is not of the best."

Clark was staggered.

"Why, it is the best position about here," he declared.

"No," said Frank, gravely. "Yonder is a much better position."

He pointed to a hill to the right, and which the one upon which the cowboys were seemed to overlook.

"What – try to command the foe from that hill?" cried Clark, scornfully. "We would only expose ourselves, and they would sweep us from it like chaff before the wind."

"No, they wouldn't."

"Now, Mr. Reade, what is the use for you to talk that way? The hill upon which they are is higher than this one."

"It may be higher in the number of feet," replied Frank, "but not in advantage of position."

"How do you make that out?"

"It is easy enough to see. The top of this hill is smooth, is it not?"

"Yes."

"The top of theirs is craggy and they cannot climb up to it. Their position is far from the top. A position on the top of yonder hill will easily look down into their camp."

Clark was surprised, but he saw the logic of Frank's remark.

"By Jove!" he cried. "Perhaps you are right."

"I think you will find that I am."

"But I would have taken my oath that they had the highest position around here."

"Well, that would seem to be really so, for the hill itself is higher. Yet it is but an optical delusion."

Clark extended his hand to Frank.

"Mr. Reade," he cried warmly. "You are right. I acknowledge my mistake. Perhaps your opportune suggestion may enable us to whip the foe."

"If it is of any value, I am highly pleased!" said Frank, modestly.

"I feel that it is, and I shall at once proceed to take the hill."

Clark at once proceeded to do this. By his command his men moved up the back side of the hill. This protected them from the bullets of the cowboys.

Arrived at the top of the smooth hill, it was found that Frank Reade, Jr., was right.

They were enabled to look right down upon the cowboys in their position.

"Hurrah!" cried Clark, jubilantly, "that means victory."

A volley was given the astonished cowboys. They returned with ill effect.

The tables were exactly turned upon them, and they were not slow to see the point.

A red-hot fire was kept up for some little time, but the cowboys no longer held the advantage.

Indeed it began to look muchly as if they were to be driven from their position.

Suddenly all firing ceased.

The cowboy gang were not in sight, nor did they fire another shot.

Clark feared a stratagem or some fatal decoy, and dared not at once order a charge.

But finally he became convinced that the cowboys had evacuated their position and had made a retreat.

Flushed with victory Clark ordered his men to charge.

Up the slope they went with fixed bayonets. But when they cleared the top of the intrenchments, hastily thrown up by the cowboys, it was found that they had gone.

They had departed quite unceremoniously and completely.

Not an article of any kind was left behind.

Indeed it also became a mystery as to the course taken by them. Not a sign of a trail could be found.

It baffled the cavalrymen.

"By Jupiter!" exclaimed Clark, in disgust, "how are you going to fight such a shadowy foe. If they would only come out like men and fight it out it would be all right. But they don't dare do it."

"You would whip them," said Frank Reade, Jr., with a laugh. "That is why they are playing hide and seek."

"I suppose so, but it makes it pretty hard for me. I suppose the best course now is to send out scouts and scour the hills."

"Exactly."

"All right. I will do it."

"I hope you will succeed."

"Thank you. I will do it or die."

"That is a good resolution."

"Well, I mean it, every word of it."

With this Clark ordered his men to horse, and the quest at once began.

Frank did not believe that he could be of further service just now, so he decided to return to the Steam Man.

Mounting his horse he rode down through the defile. In a few moments he reached the spot where the remnant of the brave Vigilant band were.

There was the Steam Man intact, but Frank saw at a glance that something was wrong about the camp.

Everybody appeared to be deeply excited. Young Barrows was seen wringing his hands and rushing about madly.

Frank sent his horse forward rapidly.

Barney saw him coming and ran out to meet him.

"Och hone, Misther Frank!" he cried.

"Well!" exclaimed Frank, reining up his horse, "what is the matter?"

"Sure, somethin' terrible has happened since ye went away."

"Well, what is it?"

"Shure, sor, the young lady, Bessie, has gone, sor, an' divil a wan av us kin foind her anywhere."

"Bessie Rodman gone?" gasped Frank. "Can that be possible?"

"Shure, sor, it is, an' faix they all do believe that the divils av cowboys, be the orders av Artemus Cliff, have got her agin."

"Great heavens!" cried Frank, with horror, "how on earth could they have done that? Is there not enough of you here to prevent?"

"Shure, sor, that is thrue enough," cried Barney. "But it's the girrul's fault hersilf, as ivery wan believes."

"Her fault!" cried Frank, in surprise. "How could that be?"

Chapter XVIII
The Lovers' Quest

"I'LL TELL YE HOW it was, Mister Reade," cried bluff Harmon; the vigilant, as he came us. "Ye see the gal took big chances. Thar's a spring in that bit av bushes there an' she went over to git a drink of water. Nobody has seen her since."

"Have you made a good search?" asked Frank, sharply.

"An all fired good one."

"But how do you know that Cliff's gang have got her?"

"Because we know that it could not be Injuns, for the ground was marked with prints of the cowboys' shoes."

Frank received this information with sinking heart.

He knew that it must be too true that Bessie Rodman had again fallen into the hands of Cliff.

It was a dismaying reflection.

To effect her rescue would prove no easy task.

Just how to go to work to do it was a problem to Frank.

But he was not long in deciding upon a plan of action.

Meanwhile young Barrows, desperate over the thought that his girl love was once more in Cliff's power, had made a daring move.

Alone he rode away into the hills.

He was determined to rescue Bessie or sacrifice his life in the attempt.

Barrows was a youth of rare pluck and great determination.

In this quest he was aided by his blind love for Bessie Rodman. For her he would gladly give up his life.

Striking into the hills he sought to follow the trail of the abductors.

But it was soon lost in the flinty ground, and his best efforts to recover it were in vain.

However, he kept on with feverish resolution. It was now a blind quest, but this did not deter him in the least.

Soon Barrows had penetrated deep into the hills.

He heard the distant sounds of firing and knew that the soldiers and Cliff's men were yet having it out.

"God give me strength to rescue Bessie Rodman!" he prayed, as he rode on.

It had occurred to Barrows that the young girl might have been taken to Ranch V by her captors.

He had half made up his mind to proceed thither when a thrilling thing occurred.

Suddenly the sharp crack of a rifle smote upon the air.

Barrows reeled in the saddle and his horse gave a plunge.

A line of red blood trickled down over his face. The bullet had grazed his cheek bone.

It was a narrow escape.

The fraction of an inch in another direction, and the bullet might have penetrated his brain.

Young Barrows had faced danger and death times enough to know quite well what to do.

He instantly dropped from his horse and spoke a word of command to the animal.

The faithful and well-trained steed wheeled and galloped away into the cover of timber near.

Barrows himself sank down behind a pile of rocks.

All this was done in the twinkling of an eye.

The trained westerner whose life is in danger knows well the value of quick action.

It was this which saved the life of Barrows, for half a dozen bullets came whistling down the mountain side the next moment.

He had run unconsciously upon his foes. He experienced a thrill as it occurred to him that this was most likely the party who had Bessie Rodman in their charge.

"Heaven help me now!" he muttered, fervently. "I must save her or die!"

From his position he could safely scrutinize the mountain side.

He saw that far up on its side there was a rude cabin made of bark and logs.

From this the storm of bullets had come.

Nothing could be seen of those within the cabin.

But Barrows believed that not only was the foe within, but also Bessie Rodman.

He was somewhat at a loss now to know just what move to make.

To advance openly to the attack would have been an act of folly.

He would certainly have met his death in a summary fashion.

So while pondering on the subject he continued to watch the cabin windows.

He held his rifle in readiness for instant use.

Suddenly a face appeared for an instant at one of the windows.

It was quickly withdrawn, and Barrows had not time to fire. He recognized it, however, as the face of one of the outlaws.

The young plainsman's nerves were steel, and he watched his chance again with nervous anxiety.

Suddenly the opportunity came. Once more the face appeared.

Barrows raised his rifle quick as thought.

Crack!

A wild cry went up, the sound of a falling body was heard, and then the tramping of feet and bitter curses.

Barrows knew that his shot had taken effect.

Then he changed his position. But not a sound or a sign of life came from the mysterious cabin.

"If they are in the cabin they are keeping mighty dark," he muttered. "They surely must be there, for I have not seen them come out as yet."

A great length of time had elapsed.

Certainly an hour and a half of waiting had passed, and Barrows felt that he must do something and at once.

"I shall die of worriment if I stay here," he muttered. "Perhaps –"

He paused. A thrilling thought had struck him.

It was more than likely that he had been waiting all this while for nothing.

It would have been not by any means a difficult matter for the foe to have slipped out by a rear exit, and by this time be far from the spot.

But how was he to determine this fact.

It could only be done by approaching the hut boldly and searching it.

To do this was to incur the risk of a bullet from the outlaws.

This might be only a clever trick of theirs to draw him from his covert.

All these thoughts passed kaleidoscope-like through Barrow's brain.

He was satisfied that the foe could be but a half dozen in number.

If he could have kept up a desultory battle with them in his present position he believed that he could have picked off a number of them, and thus reducing their numbers eventually bring the fight to a focus with a fair chance of winning.

But the outlook now was by no means so prepossessing.

It was more than likely that he would have great difficulty in cutting off the abductors before they should join the main body of the cowboys.

In this case it would be more difficult to rescue Bessie Rodman.

Barrows now realized his folly in starting out single handed to pursue the abductors.

If he had now several of his companions with him the hut could have been surrounded and there would have been little trouble in making the rescue.

But time was speeding and something had got to be done at once.

Barrows proceeded to act.

He began to cautiously climb up the mountain side keeping in the cover of rocks and trees.

He was very careful not to expose himself to a shot and in this way had soon reached a point from which he believed he could see the rear end of the cabin.

There it stood lonely and silent.

"Was it really deserted or were the foe yet within its walls?"

To all appearances it was deserted.

Barrows hesitated a moment and then took the desperate chance.

He emerged boldly from the woods and approached the cabin.

On he went until within ten yards of the door. Yet there was no sign of life.

The next moment he reached the door.

It yielded to his touch and he entered. The place was deserted.

There were evidences that the foe had been there.

Also Barrows made a thrilling discovery. In the soft dirt of the floor he discovered the footprints of Bessie Rodman.

At least it was safe to presume that they were hers, for there was no likelihood that the region for many miles held another of her gentle sex.

Feverishly Barrows examined the trail and followed it out through a rear door of the cabin.

It led into a narrow gulch and up the mountain.

It was quickly lost in the gravelly soil, but Barrows kept on up the mountain.

He now censured himself for not having acted with greater dispatch.

He believed that had he changed his position earlier he would have become aware sooner of the change of base of the abductors.

This was undoubtedly true, but on the other hand there had been the great risk of exposure to a bullet.

On the whole the lover felt that he had reason to be grateful for his success in so promptly striking the trail of the foe.

He kept on up the mountain with increasing hopes.

If he could once more overtake the abductors under more favorable circumstances he believed that he could effect the rescue of Bessie Rodman.

He still kept on up the mountain.

Then he suddenly halted at a point from which he had a good view of the country about.

He looked down upon a level plain below some distance which was fringed with trees.

In the verge of this timber line Barrows saw a number of moving figures.

He was satisfied that they were the party of abductors and he even fancied he could see the form of Bessie Rodman.

With deadly resolution Barrows started in pursuit.

Down the mountain he went and soon reached the level of the plain.

The party was now out of sight but Barrows believed that he could overtake them.

So he set out at a rapid pace along the verge of the timber. Exciting experiences were in store for him.

Chapter XIX
Frank's Narrow Escape

FRANK READE, JR., had decided to go at once in quest of the abductors of Bessie Rodman.

He called Pomp and Barney aboard the Steam Man, and the start was made.

Of course they were not aware that Barrows had started out upon the same mission.

It was decided to proceed up the Death Gulch, for Frank fancied that the abductors had likely struck out over the mountain range.

The gulch could be traversed by the Steam Man easily, and Frank deemed it safer to travel that way.

Up the gulch the Steam Man went.

For some distance all went well, and no incident worthy of note occurred.

But finally a branch of the canyon was reached, and here a halt was called.

This extended to the southward.

Frank knew that the outlaws could not have crossed this without a wide detour.

The ground was high above the walls of the canyon, and the young Inventor decided upon a different move.

The Steam Man proceeded up this canyon for some ways.

Then Frank called a halt.

"We will stop here," he said.

"Shure, Misther Frank," cried Barney, "phwat iver do yez want to do that fer? It's a clear course ahead."

"I am well aware of that, Barney," replied Frank, "but I am not sure that we are following the right course."

"Indade, sor."

"I mean to climb to the top of the canyon wall here and take a look off at the country."

"Shure enough, sor!"

"Golly, Marse Frank, amn't youse gwine to let dis chile go wif yo'?"

"Begorra, not a bit av it!" cried Barney. "Shure, yez may stay wid the Stheam Man, naygur."

"Yo' g'long, I'ish! I reckon Marse Frank take me dis time."

Frank smiled and said:

"Yes, it is no more than fair, Pomp, for you to go this time. You will remain with the Man, Barney."

Barney did not demur, for he knew that it would be of no use.

But he had been with Frank on excursions many times, and perhaps felt that it was no more than fair that Pomp should have this chance.

No time was lost.

Armed with rifles and revolvers, the two explorers left the Steam Man.

A good path up the canyon wall was selected, and after an arduous climb they finally reached the summit.

From here a mighty view of the country about was obtained.

As far as the eye could reach to the eastward was the level expanse of plain.

In the other direction mountain peaks rose above them to a great altitude.

Frank had a powerful glass, and with this proceeded to scrutinize the country below.

But he could see nothing of the cowboys, nor was he able to tell what direction Clark's men had gone.

He descried at once what he believed to be smoke ascending from behind distant trees, and fancied that this might be from the guns of the military and the cowboys.

But of this he was not sufficiently positive to venture to go thither.

"Well, Pomp!" he said dubiously, as he closed the glass, "I don't see that we can locate the abductors of Bessie Rodman from here I declare I am befogged."

"Golly, Marse Frank," cried Pomp, with dilated eyeballs, "what eber yo' tink we bettah do now?"

"I declare I don't know."

"I'se done reckon dat de cowboys hab gone back to dat ranch ob dere'd wid dat lily gal."

Frank gave a start.

It had not before occurred to him that the abductors might have taken their captive to Ranch V.

Indeed, so strongly did he become impressed with the possibility that he was half inclined to start at once for the ranch.

But sober second thought impelled him first to think of searching the hills.

If she could not be found in them then it would be time enough to think of paying Ranch V a visit.

An incident happened at the moment also that for a time prevented any move of the sort.

Pomp had begun to scale a small peak near.

"P'ra'ps I kin get a bettah look from up yere, Marse Frank!" cried the darky. "Jes' de same, I tries it fo' yo'."

"All right, Pomp," replied Frank. "Tell me if you see anything of importance and I will come up."

"A'right, sah."

Pomp went up the peak.

He reached the top and began to look over the country, when suddenly he beheld a thrilling scene below.

Frank had gone to the edge of the canyon to look over and see what the Steam Man was about.

As he leaned over the edge of the deep gorge he did not see a giant form suddenly glide from a crevice in the cliff behind him.

It was, in reality, an enormous black bear.

The brute had caught sight of Frank, and being in an ugly mood, started for him.

The bear advanced so quickly and noiselessly that Frank was all unaware of his presence until the brute was upon him.

Then a terrific blow from the bear's paw sent him reeling over the edge of the cliff.

Over the edge went the young inventor, and a yell of horror and pain went up from Pomp's lips.

"Golly sakes, Marse Frank, hab yo' fallen down to yo' death?" cried the affrighted darky, as he came tumbling down the peak like a madman.

Frank had certainly gone over the edge.

The bear stood upon the verge of the precipice growling savagely.

Pomp was in a frenzy of fear and horror. He could not see what was to prevent his beloved master from going down to his death.

He would have rushed to the spot where Frank had stood but the bear was there.

At this moment the stillness of the gorge was broken by the shrill whistle of the Steam Man.

This was enough for Pomp.

In a moment he raised his rifle and fired at the bear.

Ordinarily, he would have been compelled to fire many times, but as chance had it, this single shot proved fatal.

It struck the bear full in the eye and went crashing through his brain.

The big brute went over the edge of the precipice and crashing down into the gorge.

Pomp heard plainly the crash of the bear's body as it struck the bottom of the pass.

Then he rushed to the edge and looked over.

He saw the bottom of the gorge plainly enough. There lay the inanimate form of the bear.

The Steam Man stood not twenty yards distant from this spot, and Pomp saw Barney far below, yelling and waving his hands.

The darky answered, and then caught sight of something which thrilled him.

Clinging to a jutting bit of rock in the canyon wall he saw Frank Reade, Jr., hanging between heaven and earth.

The astonished darky fell upon his stomach and leaned far over the edge of the gorge.

"Golly, Marse Frank!" he cried, excitedly, "I done fought yo' was a-goner fo' suah. Hab yo' got a stronghold dar?"

"Pomp!" cried Frank, in sharp tones, "I am nearly exhausted. I fear I shall lose my hoid here soon!"

"Fo' Hehben's sake," cried the affrighted darky, "don' yo' say dat, Marse Frank. If yo' fell down to de cornah ob dat gorge yo' would be killed fo' suah. Yo' jes' wait an' dis chile will help yo'."

"You'll have to hurry, Pomp!" cried Frank, in an exhausted manner.

"Yo' kin jest bet I will."

"Whurroo, there naygur!" cried Barney from below. "Wud yez be afther letting down a rope to Misther Frank. Quick, now, or yez won't have the toime."

Pomp acted quickly.

The darky carried constantly a lariat at his waste.

This he lowered over the edge and down to the point where Frank was hanging suspended between earth and sky.

Pomp had acted with great dispatch, but even as the rope went over the edge, a warning cry went up from Barney below.

"My God! I am falling!" cried Frank, with horror.

His hands were slipping over the edge of the jutting bit of rock to which he clung.

The next moment they released their grip entirely and down he went.

But, as good fortune had it, just below him was a stump growing out of the cliff.

Against this he fell and his clothing caught upon a jagged root.

It held him firmly, and there he hung safe and secure.

A cry of joy went up from Pomp and Barney.

"Jes' yo' hang right on, Marse Frank!" cried the darky, earnestly. "Don' yo' gib way at all, an' dis chile he done pull you up a'right."

"All right, Pomp," cried Frank, regaining his coolness so habitual to him. "I think I am safe here."

"Praise de Lor' fo' dat?" cried the elated darky. "Jes' hol' right on."

Down went the lariat.

In a moment more it settled over Frank's shoulders.

As Pomp drew on it, Frank made it secure under his arms.

Then the darky began to draw up on the rope. It required some exertion of strength, but in a few moments Frank cleared the edge.

But at this moment a loud shout came up from the gorge below.

It was Barney's voice raised in a note of alarm.

"My soul!" cried Frank, excitedly. "What can have happened?"

Both rushed to the edge of the canyon and looked over.

Chapter XX
The Flood – Cornering the Foe

IT WAS A THRILLING SIGHT which met their gaze.

They saw Barney leaping up and down and gesticulating wildly.

"What is the matter?" cried Frank.

But before the words had fairly left his lips he saw what was the trouble.

Along the bottom of the gorge a thin stream of water was flowing.

Every moment it was increasing.

"Bejabers, Misther Frank, is there much more wather comin'?" cried Barney. "Shure if so, I'm thinkin' we'd better be after getting out of here."

"Right?" cried the young inventor, excitedly, "but where can it come from?"

He ran to an eminence near and from which a good view of the upper canyon could be had.

And there Frank beheld a thrilling sight.

At the upper end of the canyon was a large lake made by an accumulation of logs and debris across the source of the canyon.

Here half a score of men with axes and iron bars were engaged in breaking the dam so as to let the whole lake down into the gorge.

It would mean a flood of awful sort if they succeeded.

It would surely sweep the canyon clear, and the position of Barney was a most perilous one.

Frank saw this with horror.

He knew at once that the workmen were of the cowboy gang.

Already the dam could be seen to be giving way.

In a very few moments the flood must come. No time must be lost.

Into the canyon the water would plunge and engulf everything in their path.

Frank waited no longer.

He sprung to the edge of the canyon and shouted to Barney: "Go, for your life, Barney. Run for the plain. We will take care of ourselves."

"All right, sar!"

Barney sprung into the cage and away went the Steam Man with a shriek down the canyon.

The next moment a terrible roar came from the headwaters of the gorge, and then Frank and Pomp saw the mighty flood coming.

Like a race horse it surged down through the canyon.

It was now a mad race between the Steam Man and the flood.

It was a long ways to the plain below, and Frank groaned with horror as he realized the uncertainty of the Steam Man's reaching it.

There were places where the Steam Man must go slowly, and this would mean overtaking by the flood.

But Barney, with his shrewd Irish wit, had realized this.

He knew that it would so impossible for him to reach the plain before the flood.

So he decided upon a wise move.

He reached the junction of this canyon with the other.

There was not a moment to spare.

Looking back, he could see the water coming in mountainous billows.

The Steam Man had to be checked a trifle in order to turn into the other canyon.

But Barney made the turn all safely, and the Steam Man shot up the canyon far enough to avoid the back current of the flood.

"Bejabers, I'm in luck this toime!" cried the Celt, jubilantly, as he opened the whistle valve.

The note of safety was heard by Frank and Pomp with a sensation of great relief and joy.

They understood at once the move made by Barney.

"That was a capital thought of Barney's," cried Frank. "It is lucky that he did not keep on the plains. He would have been overtaken."

"I jes' reckon dat am a fac'!" cried Pomp. "Well, I fink we'd bettah get back to de Steam Man as quick as eber we can."

"You are right, Pomp," declared Frank. "Our position here will be hardly a safe one now."

"Youse right, sah."

The flood in the canyon was now rapidly subsiding.

The great lake had quickly emptied itself into the canyon.

In a short while the bed of the canyon was once more dry.

Barney then ran the Steam Man back into the main canyon, and Frank and Pomp hailed him.

"You did well, Barney!" cried the young inventor, joyfully.

"You made the best possible move."

"Begorra, I knew well enough that I had to git out of the way of the wathers, sor," replied Barney. "But shure, are yez comin' down soon?"

"We are comin' right down," replied Frank.

Down the canyon wall they scrambled and safely reached the gorge.

Then they greeted Barney with joy and clambered aboard.

"Shure, phwativer will yez do now, Misther Frank?" cried Barney, eagerly.

"I shall follow the canyon up and try to dislodge the outlaws," replied Frank.

"Very good, sir?" cried Barney, with readiness. "We'll go ahead thin?"

"Yes."

Barney took the reins and the Steam Man went on up the gorge.

In a short while they had reached the dam which had held back the lake.

Here a course was found directly out upon a vast plain.

Frank was about to direct the man's course thither when an incident occurred to for a moment delay them.

A loud and harsh voice came from the cliff above.

"Hello, down there!"

The speaker could not be seen. The Steam Man came to a halt.

"Well?" cried Frank.

"Ye're Frank Reade, Jr., eh?"

"That is my name."

"Wall, I'm Artemas Cliff. I give ye fair warnin' to surrender. Ye're in a death trap."

"Thank you for informing us," retorted Frank, "but I don't believe I'll surrender yet."

"Ye won't then?"

"No."

"Then take the consequences."

"I can do that."

A savage curse come down upon the air. Then the crack of rifles was heard and bullets pattered against the steel netting.

Of course no harm was done, and Frank only smiled grimly.

He sent the Steam Man up the gorge, and in a few moments came out upon the plain, which was deep among the hills and hemmed in with a line of timber.

The cowboys continued to pour volley after volley into the Steam Man.

Frank waited until he had reached a favorable position.

Then he stopped the Steam Man, and picking up his rifle, said:

"Come, boys! Let's give them as good as they send."

Of course Pomp and Barney were ready and eager.

A destructive fire was sent into the covert of the cowboys.

In a few moments it grew so hot that they could not remain there and had to get out.

With baffled yells they retreated deeper into the hills.

"Whurroo!" yelled Barney jubilantly. "Shure it's aisy enough to whip such omadhouns as they be!"

"Golly! Don' yo' be too suah, I'ish," remonstrated Pomp.

"What do yez know about it, naygur?"

"Suah, I know jes' as much as yo' does, I'ish."

"G'long! Yez are a big stuff."

"I amn't so big a wan as yo' am."

"Say that agin, an' I'll break the face av yez."

"Huh! Yo' can't do it."

The two rogues would have had a friendly set-to then and there but Frank interposed.

"None of that," he cried, sternly; "there is serious work before us."

This was a quietus upon the two rascals, and they ceased their skylarking.

The cowboys had been driven back, but now a thrilling sound came from the distant hills.

It was the heavy volleying of many rifles. There could be but one explanation.

Evidently the cavalry had come into conflict with the cowboys.

A good sized battle was in progress. An impulse seized Frank.

He realized that he ought to join that conflict. There was doubt but that the Steam Man could do much to aid the cavalry.

So he started the Man across the plain, looking for an opening into the hills in the direction of the firing.

This, however, seemed not easy to find.

But as the Man was skirting the line of timber, a thrilling sound was suddenly brought to view.

In a small clearing in the verge of the timber two men were striving to down one. It was a terrific and deadly struggle which was in progress.

The single fighter was holding his own well.

Near by, with arms tied behind her, was a young girl.

It was Bessie Rodman.

"My God!" cried Frank. "Quick, for your life, boys! We must put an end to that struggle. Don't you see it is young Barney and he is fighting to rescue the girl."

"Golly, dat am a fac'!" cried Pomp, excitedly. "Jes' gib me a chance at dem rapscallions."

Up to the spot the Steam Man swiftly ran.

A cry of wildest joy and hope welled up from Bessie Rodman's lips.

Young Barrows also saw that rescue was at hand and made extra exertions to overcome his foes.

The cowboys, however, seeing that succor had come tried to break away.

As Barrows was too exhausted to restrain them they succeeded and dashed away at full speed.

Reaching their ponies they mounted and were out of sight in a twinkling.

The next moment Barrows had clasped Bessie in his arms, first cutting her bonds.

"Thank Heaven!" he cried. "We are united once more, and this time let us hope never to part?"

Those aboard the Steam Man pretended to be busy during the affecting meeting.

But soon the lovers came to the cage and a general welcome followed.

An explanation of all followed, and then plans for the future were quickly decided upon.

Chapter XXI
Which is the End

THE SOUND of firing now came from the hills quite plainly.

It was evident that Clark's men were having a hard battle.

Barrows detailed his experiences as we have recorded in a previous chapter.

Then it was decided at once if possible to join the cavalry.

"If I can place Miss Rodman in your charge, Mr. Reade," said young Barrows, gallantly, "I will gladly join the soldiers and aid in the repulse of the foe."

"You may do that," replied Frank, readily. "In fact, I think it safer for the lady to remain in the wagon hereafter."

"You are very kind."

"It is nothing."

Accordingly Bessie was given a seat in the wagon.

Then Barrows mounted one of the ponies left by the cowboys.

"I will see you later," he said lifting his hat to Bessie.

Then he rode away to join the cavalry in their battle.

The Steam Man, of course, could not hope to follow so quickly.

The fleet pony could go through narrow paths, and of course Barrows reached the scene of action long before the others.

But Frank Reade sent the Steam Man along at a good pace.

After some search a pass was found, and the Man made its way carefully through, and suddenly came out upon the field of action.

The cowboys were strongly intrenched in the hills, and seemed disposed to make a final stand.

Col. Clark's men were making desperate attempts to drive them from their position.

As the Steam Man came dashing up to the spot a great cheer went up from the soldiers.

Frank answered it by pulling the whistle valve of the Man and sending up a sharp note.

The Man could not hope to reach the position of the outlaws, for the ground was too uneven.

But a position was taken up from where the battle could be easily watched.

Then Col. Clark came up to the wagon.

Warm greetings followed, and Frank said: "Is there anything I could do to help you, colonel?"

"I think not," replied the gallant officer. "I believe we shall drive them out very soon now."

"I hope so."

"If I am not mistaken the day of Cliff and his gang are numbered."

"That is joyful news."

"Yes."

"I hope you will succeed."

"Thank you."

The colonel rode away and the voyagers watched the contest with interest.

One watching the beautiful face of Bessie Rodman could have seen that she was inwardly praying for her lover's safety.

But fortune was with the troops, though they had experienced a hard battle.

The position of the outlaws was a very strong one and almost unassailable.

High walls of rock were there for them to use as a breastwork.

It was not easy to dislodge them except at great loss of life.

But Clark was not a man to be defeated.

He urged his men on and slowly but surely drove the foe before him. Frank Reade, Jr., now with Barney and Pomp and Bessie Rodman on board, took the Steam Man out on to the prairie.

For over an hour a kind of desultory conflict was kept up in the hills.

Then Col. Clark suddenly came dashing up to the wagon.

"We have got them dislodged," he cried. "And I think they have struck out for Ranch V. Now if you will show us the way, Mr. Reade, we will try and exterminate this poisonous gang."

"With pleasure!" cried Frank.

He started the Steam Man at once for Ranch V.

Across the prairie the machine ran rapidly, and the cavalry galloped in the rear.

It was in the latter part of the day that all came out upon a rise overlooking the stockade of Ranch V.

But the cowboys had got there in advance and had made ready for an attack.

Col. Clark was a man of immediate resources.

Without hesitation or a moment's delay he threw his men forward on the charge. At almost the first attack the gate was carried and the soldiers entered the yard.

But step by step Artemus Cliff contested the way.

His men by divisions surrendered half a dozen or more at a time.

Being thus made prisoners, they were sent to the rear. In this manner the numbers of the cowboy gang were decimated.

Suddenly a thrilling cry went up.

"Fire! Fire!"

The stockade and ranch proper had been fired, and great columns of flame now arose.

The scene was fast becoming a thrilling one. Darkness was coming on, and the rattle of firearms the dark shadows of night partially dispelled by the flames, gave a weird aspect to everything.

Slow but sure was the conquest of Cliff and his gang.

Now he was driven to his last resort, the corner of the stockade nearest the river. Scarce a score of his followers now remained.

It was utterly no use for him to resist longer. The villain saw it but yet kept on fighting doggedly.

"Surrender, or die!" cried the lieutenant who led the squad. "It is your only chance."

The remaining cowboys threw up their hands. But Cliff pitched forward in a heap upon the ground, struck by a pistol ball.

There he was found later under a heap of dead men. He was removed to the camp near and his wounds examined.

Ranch V was a thing of the past.

Not a stick was left standing, and of the cowboy gang fully a hundred had rendered up their final account.

Possibly twenty of the cavalrymen had been killed.

It had been quite a severe battle, but Frank Reade, Jr., and his companions could not help but feel overjoyed at the result.

Barney and Pomp had an old time set-to over the victory, this time Pomp coming off victorious.

The night was passed quietly. Early the next morning a surgeon came to the Steam Man and called for Frank.

He announced that Cliff was dying, and wanted to make a confession but would make it to nobody else.

Frank hurried to the dying couch of the villain. Cliff's filmy gaze was fixed upon him eagerly, and he said, huskily:

"Reade, I'm done for. I made a good fight but I've lost. The game's up. I might as well make a clean breast of it. Uncle Jim is innocent of Rodman's death. Sid Bowen and Jim Ducey, my trusted pals, killed Rodman and worked the whole game. That's all. I reckon I can die better now."

"You have done a good deed, Artemus Cliff," said Frank, kindly. "And may God forgive you your sins."

But the villain did not answer. Already his eyes were set. The Master had called him. He had cheated the gallows after all.

A grave was dug on the prairie and Frank saw that he was properly buried.

The confession was put in writing and duly witnessed. The mission of the new Steam Man to the far west was ended.

* * *

The spirits of all were bright and cheerful, now that the end had come.

The extermination of the Cliff gang was certainly a blessing to that part of the State, and no one regretted the villain's demise.

Preparations were now made for the return home.

Of course, Col. Clark and his command would return to the fort, but Frank now thought of Bessie Rodman.

"By Jupiter!" he muttered, "something must be done for her. Poor girl! She is without a friend in the world now."

Barney and Pomp winked at each other, and Barney cried:

"Bejabers, Misther Frank, have yez lost yer powers av penetration?"

"I reckon yo' am way off, Marse Frank," rejoined Pomp.

"What are you fellows driving at?" asked Frank, in surprise.

"Why, dat ar' gal, she am got one ob de bes' friends in de worl'. Jes' yo' cast yo' eye ober dar an' see dat spruce young feller what am walkin' wid her."

Frank did 'cast his eye' in the direction indicated, and saw Bessie and young Walter Barrows approaching.

There was a particularly happy light upon the faces of both.

"Pshaw!" muttered Frank. "That young fellow can't marry her yet. She's got to have a home in the meanwhile. Miss Rodman, one moment, please."

The lovers paused, and Frank said brusquely:

"I can understand your position, Bessie, very well, and I know that you need a home. I can only offer to take you to Readestown with me, and my wife will do all in her power –"

"One moment, sir," said Barrows, with burning face. "You are very kind, but let me first explain. I am this lady's natural protector for life."

"What?" gasped Frank.

"Yes, she is my wife."

Pomp and Barney collapsed at the expression upon Frank's face.

"Your wife?" gasped the young inventor. "When were you married?"

"Just now, and the ceremony was performed by the chaplain of the regiment."

Frank thrust forth his right hand, and gave Barrows a grip which made him wince.

"You must pardon my conduct," he cried, "but it was such a surprise. I wish you both worlds of happiness."

Some hours later the new Steam Man was on its way homeward. A week later it was in Omaha, Nebraska, and not long thereafter was at home in Readestown.

The young inventor was received at home with an ovation, and his father, the distinguished Reade Senior, was overjoyed to learn that the evidence had been procured to clear Travers.

As for the latter he came from prison like one coming into a new life and from that time on regarded Frank Reade, Jr. as his greatest earthly benefactor.

The new Steam Man and his wonderful western trip was the talk of the country.

People came from near and far to see the invention and it was not long before the young inventor suddenly found himself involved in another daring project.

The new Steam Man was destined to make another trip, and become involved in adventures even more thrilling than these just recorded, and a full and detailed account of the second trip may be found in No. 2 of the 'Frank Reade Library', entitled *Frank Reade, Jr., With His New Steam Man in No Man's Land; Or On a Mysterious Trail*.

Frank Reade Jr. & His New Steam Horse
Or The Search for a Million Dollars

Luis Philip Senarens

Chapter I
The New Invention

FRANK READE, JR., the prince of inventors, sat at a large table one day in the office of his extensive machine shops, which had been built for the exclusive manufacture of his own Inventions.

Upon the table was a pile of papers, covered with drawings and hieroglyphic notes, which were comprehensive to the inventor alone.

"There," said the famous young inventor, with a light of joy in his handsome eyes. "Now I believe I have drawn every detail, and all that I need do now is to have the parts made and put together."

So engrossed had Frank been in his work that he had not noticed the entrance of a man into the room.

The visitor was one of the most comical looking characters that one might chance to see in a week's travel.

He was of diminutive stature, but thickset and strong. A large head, covered with a shock of red hair, sat upon his shoulders.

His features were of the ultra Hibernian type, with flat nose, heavy brows, deep upper lip, and high cheekbones. An Irishman he was beyond all peradventure.

Dressed in knee pants of corduroy, with velvet jacket and green stockings, he looked a fresh importation from Ireland.

"The top av the mornin' to yez, Misther Frank!" exclaimed the visitor in a rich brogue.

Frank whirled about.

"Barney O'Shea!" he gasped. "Well, I'm glad to see you. So you have returned safely from your trip to Ireland?"

"I have that, sor."

"Well, how did you make it?"

The Celt elevated his chin and took a strutting walk across the floor. "Shure, Misther Frank, av Ireland was only free onct more I think she'd be the foinest counthry in all the worruld."

"Ah, with America excepted."

"Exceptin' no counthry, sor, mark me worruds. Oeh hone, it's a sad day for Ireland whin thim bloody Britishers got their grip on EL Shure, I looked in vain fer the castle av me ancisters, the Boras."

"And couldn't you find it?" asked Frank, with a smile.

"Shure, an' indade not. I heard that they bad moved it over for a summer palace for her highness, Queen Victoria, in England, bad cess to the thieves av Britishers."

"Well, that's a sad case," agreed Frank. "I suppose it was some consolation to go and look at the ground where it had formerly stood."

"Shure, son that was only pain for me, I kin tell ye."

And Barney O'Shea had recourse to a green silk kerchief, all emblazoned with harps and little cherubs.

"Well, you have my sympathy, Barney," said Frank Reade, Jr., pleasantly, "and I'm glad you've got home safely. You have come in good time, for I have a great scheme on hand at prevent. In fact, I have just completed the drawings for the greatest invention yet."

The Irishman instantly put up his handkerchief and became all eagerness.

It might be well to mention that Barney O'Shea was very faithful servant of the young inventor. He had just returned from a vacation trip to the 'ould'sod.'

Barney had been for many years with Frank Reade, Sr., the father of the present young inventor, and had traveled the world over with him.

"Shure, sor, its delighted I am to hear that," cried the Celt, joyously. "Shure, I feel jilt bike a bit av a thrip wid yez, Misther Frank."

"First let me show you what my invention is," said the young inventor. "Here is the drawing."

Barney rubbed his eyes.

"Shure, sor, that's not plain to me, sor," he blurted forth.

"Well, I will make it plainer. There are the hues of my most wonderful invention."

"Shure, an' phwat kind av a baste may it be?"

"It is the New Steam Horse."

Barney gave a leap in the air.

"The Sthame Horse!" he shouted. "Shure, an' phwat put that in ter yer head, Misther Frank? I thought shure yez wud reconsthruct the wonderful New Stheam Man."

"At first I had thought of it," declared Frank, "but on second thought I decided to start a new scheme. You remember well the Steam Horse once invented by my father?"

"Shure, didn't I take a thrip over the plains wid him an' it?"

"Of course you did. Well, this Steam Horse is a great improvement upon the original. It is truly the best and most wonderful yet, is the New Steam Horse."

"Yis, sor," agreed Barney, scratching his fiery head; "av yez say so, it must be so."

"Now, I will describe it to you," said Frank, briskly; "here you see are the outlines of the Horse, which you will see is attached to the shafts of a four-wheeled wagon.

"The Horse is to be made of plates of steel. The body of the Horse will contain a furnace and boiler. The neck will be the steam-chest and the cylinders will be fastened to the shaft upon each side.

"The driving-rods will connect with armatures and mechanical joints in the forward legs. The driving-rods will cause these to act upon themselves in such a manner as to give the muscular play and action necessary to make the horse's gait."

Barney had been listening with open mouth.

"Shure, that's wonderful!" he muttered, with amazement. Frank went on.

"The hind legs will move in the same manner by means of rods connecting them with the mechanism of the forward ones.

"You will see that here is a perfect horse in shape made wholly of steel. Upon the horse's head between the ears I intend to place a whistle. The saddle will furnish the steam gauge and indicator."

"Shure, sor, but it's wondherful!"cried Barney, earnestly. "Bat howiver will yez dhrive the baste?"

"By these reins which will connect with the horse's lower jaw and by pressure act upon the throttle valve and also the whistle valve."

"But howiver will yez stheer the animile?"asked Barney.

"That is very simple," replied Frank. "By this crank and rod through the dasher of the wagon which will tura the forward wheels in any direction and also the Horse. But now that I have described the Steam Horse let me tell you about the wagon."

"All roigbt, sor," replied Barney. "Shure it's a wondherful machine."

"The wagon will have four wheels, the tires of which will be grooved. The dasher in front will have a crank and rod for the brake and steering gear.

"The body of the wagon will contain a tank for water, with pipes extending through the shafts to the boiler. Also a receptacle for coal or wood, or any material suitable for fuel.

"On each side of the wagon are also lockers above the coal bunkers for the storage of weapons, ammunition tools, stores, or anything needed on a long trip across the country.

"So much for the body of the wagon. Now over the wagon there will be a trap with four grooved standards. Curtains of finest steel plates and bullet-proof are made to pull up or down as occasion requires, on all sides. In these curtains are loopholes to fire through in case of an attack from an enemy."

Frank sank into his chair as he finished, and said:

"That's all. Now what do you think of it, Barney?"

The Celt made a grimace with his comical mug, and replied: "Shure, it's a big thing, Misther Frank, an' I'm wid yez."

"I am glad to hear you say that."

"Whiniver will yez have it made!"

"Within two months."

"Och hone, but whativer will yez do wid it?"

"We will take a trip in it to the far West."

"Phwat will we do out there, sor?"

"I'll risk but what we will find enough to do, once we get out there," said Frank. "Perhaps we can rescue some beautiful young girl from the Indians. See?"

"Barney O'Shea's wid yez."

"All right. Good for you, Barney. Now you are ready for work?"

"Yis, sor."

Frank picked up his plans, and arranging them, said:

"You will oblige me by stepping down to the yard and telling Mr. MacPherson, the master mechanic, to come up here."

"All right, sor."

A few moments later the famous Scotch machinist was closeted with Frank Reade, Jr.

A day or two later a vague report leaked out that Frank Reade, Jr., was at work upon some wonderful new invention. Just what this was nobody could guess.

But two months later, as Frank had predicted, the New Steam Horse stood finished and complete.

A few of Frank's intimate friends were admitted to see the wonderful invention. All pronounced it the wonder of modern times. Among the visitors was a dangerous crank who tried to ascertain the secret of the invention.

He carried a dynamite cartridge and might have done it harm had not Frank caused his arrest. The New Steam Horse was a credit to Frank Reade, Jr.'s working force of mechanics.

It was all ready for a trip and prank was ready also.

The rumor was circulated that the Steam Horse was to start for the Northwest on an Indian trailing expedition.

But at the last moment a thrilling series of incidents occurred which gave Frank an object to pursue.

Colleague of Barney's and an old servant of the Reades' was a negro named Pomp.

Pomp was certainly a unique sort of a character. He was short of stature and thick-set, with a genuine African type of countenance. But Pomp was as faithful as he was homely and much devoted to Frank Reade, Jr. Like Barney he was always a companion of the young inventor in all his travels.

One day Pomp was just entering the yard of the Reade Iron Works when he was accosted by a mysterious-looking stranger.

"Look here, my man," he said, in a low tone, "ain't your name Pomp?"

"Dat am a fac', eah."

"And you work for Frank Reade, Jr.?"

"Bet yo' life I does."

"Good enough! Now I want to see your master."

"Ye' wants to see Marse Frank?"

"Yes."

"Well," sniffed Pomp, suspiciously, "why don' yo' jes' go right along up to his house and speak to him like a man, sah?"

Chapter II
The Detective's Story

THE STRANGER shrugged his shoulders.

"There is a reason for that," he made reply, doggedly.

"Sah?" exclaimed Pomp.

"I say I have a reason for not."

"What am it, sah?"

"Can I trust you?"

"Well, sah, yo' can if yo' wants to."

The fellow hesitated a moment.

"Well," he said, finally, "the reason I don't go up to the house is because it is shadowed by detectives."

Pomp was dumfounded.

"Shadowed by detectives, sah? Did yo' say dat fing, sah?"

"I did."

"What yo' mean by it?"

The fellow pulled a newspaper from his pocket and handed it to Pomp.

"No doubt you have read of that affair," he said, indicating a paragraph with black headlines.

"'Deed and I has, sah!" said Pomp, as he read the article.

The article was several months old and described an affair which had created a tremendous sensation throughout the country. Thus it read:

> *"Further particulars of the daring robbery of a million dollars in gold and currency from the car of the Texas Express Company, at Hard Pan station, on the M., N. & T. Railroad. Latest report has it that the train was slowing up at Hard Pan, when Conductor Lewis went into the express car.*
>
> *"To his surprise he saw Express Clerk David Mayhew sitting in a chair to which he was tight'y bound with ropes.*
>
> *"Upon the car floor lay the dead body of Messenger Clark, with a bullet in his brain. The safe door was open, and in the car door stood a masked man, who leaped as the train slowed up and disappeared in the darkness.*

"The train stopped a moment later, and a tremendous sensation was created when it was learned that the small iron chest containing tie fortune of a million dollars was gone.

"Clerk Mayhew was liberated and told a thrilling tale.

"He says that as himself and Clark were busy at the desk, both turned, to be suddenly confronted by two men with revolvers. Both wore black masks.

"Mayhew surrendered, but Clark made a fight and was shot. Then the robbers seized the chest containing the million dollars, which was very heavy, dragged it to the car door, and at a certain point threw it out into the darkness.

"Then one of the men removed his mask and went back into the train. The other leaped from the car as Conductor Lewis entered.

"At once the train ran back down the line, and a search was made for the cheat of treasure and the robbers.

"But not a sign of them could be seen anywhere. It was evident that the robbers knew at what point to drop the treasure oil, and that they had confederates there in waiting.

"That the treasure will ever be, recovered is doubtful. It is believed that Duncan Darke, the noted bandit of upper Texas, is the leader of the gang. Detectives are working upon the case, and it has even been reported that Frank Reade, Jr., the world famous inventor of the Steam Man, would take the case in hand for the express company. Great excitement is extant over the affair."

Pomp's eyes bulged as he read this latter statement.

"Well, did yo' eber hear de like ob dat!" he spluttered. "Dat reporter had a jolly bit ob gall fo' to mix Marse Frank's name up with the thing."

"Ah, then Mr. Reade has no idea of going?" asked the fellow, eagerly.

"Ob course he don'. Moreober, de Steam Man am broke all up into lily bits ob pieces."

"But has he not invented a Steam Horse?"

"To be sho', sah!"

"Well, mebbe it's that, then. Are you sure that he don't intend going on a search for a million dollars?"

"Oh co'se I is."

"Well, that's queer. At any rate, it is the general belief that he intends doing so. In fact, that is why so many detectives are shadowing him and his house. It is their idea to follow him up and get some sort of a clew to the whereabouts of the robbers, and go in and win the reward."

"Da debbil yo' say!" gasped Pomp. "I should fink dat dey would do better fo' to go right out an hunt fo' de thieves, an' not trouble 'bout Marse Frank an' his plans."

"Oh, well, it is only the snide detectives who are doing this. They haven't got the ability to get a clew in any other way."

"Huh! Don' fink much ob dem kind."

"Neither do I. Now I am a detective myself, but I am not here to shadow this place, but to see Frank Reade, Jr., upon very important business. However, I don't want these other detectives to see me."

"Yas, sah," said Pomp, slowly. "What am yo' name?"

"My name is Dan Burton."

Pomp studied the fellow's face a moment and then said: "If yo' will wait a moment, sah, I fink I can find Marse Reade."

"All right."

Pomp vanished into a side room. It was not long before he reappeared.

"Marse Frank am in de designin' room," he declared. "He says he will see yo' in dar."

Burton, the detective, followed Pomp through the inner building to a room in one corner where Frank at a table sometimes worked at his designing.

The young inventor sprang up as his visitor entered.

Burton advanced and introduced himself, shaking hands warmly with Frank.

He stated the facts in the case to Frank just as he had to Pomp.

The famous inventor listened with interest.

"I have read an account of this affair," he declared, "but why should it specially interest me? The newspapers are filled with accounts of a like sort."

"Very true," said Burton, quietly, "but I think you will be interested when I have explained the matter more fully."

"I don't believe it," said Frank, positively. "Why are these detectives shadowing me and my house?"

"With the foolish hope that they will be able to fathom your plans in case you did make an attempt to recover the million dollars lost."

"Well, they are wasting time here," declared Frank. "I have no idea of going in quest of the lost million."

"You have not?"

"No, sir."

Burton smiled in a curious manner.

"I think I can show you something that will induce you to go," he said.

"I think not, sir."

"A very large reward is offered for the capture of the robbers. One hundred thousand dollars will be paid."

"I care nothing for that," said Frank. "Let us drop the subject here."

"One moment."

"Well?"

"Did you ever meet a man named David Mayhew?"

Frank looked interrogatively at Burton.

"What!" he gasped. "Not Dave Mayhew, of Silver Creek, New Mexico?"

"The same."

"Why, he saved my life once when I was sinking in a quicksand. I shall never forget him."

"I thought not. Well, this same express clerk is the same Dave Mayhew, of Silver Creek."

"Ah, but he is implicated in no way with the robbers."

"Of course not. Yet suspicion is upon him, and he has been arrested."

Frank was astonished.

"You don't mean it?"

"Yes, I do. In the lawless country where he is held, such a theft is held punishable by death."

Frank sprang to his feet.

"Never!" he cried, "they shall not harm a hair of Dave Mayhew's head. Why, I owe my life to that lad."

"I knew that you would not refuse to help him," said Burton, quietly.

"Did he send you to me?"

"Yes."

"What can I do for him?"

"If you can find the million dollars stolen and capture the thieves you will clear Linn of suspicion and win his release from prison; ay, save his life."

"I will retract my statement of a few moments ago," cried Frank, forcefully. "I will certainly go to the aid of Dave Mayhew. Yes, and at once. Before I return to Readestown I will have recovered that money and captured the thieves or forfeit my life."

Frank touched an electric bell.

Pomp appeared at once.

"Pomp!" he said, authoritatively, "get the Steam Horse in readiness. Have stores and ammunition on hand and pack the machine in sections to be shipped tonight to New Mexico."

"A'right, sah."

Pomp disappeared with this. Burton was much excited.

"Then you undertake the mission, Mr. Reade?" he cried.

"I do," replied Frank.

"God bless you! You will save Dave's life. I would ask a favor."

"What?"

"That I may be one of your party."

Frank shook his head. "I am obliged to decline, sir," he said. "Barney and Pomp are my only traveling companions on this trip."

"Well," said Burton, the detective, arising, "I have fulfilled one part of my mission. Now for the other part."

"What is that?"

"I am going to New Mexico by first train to work the case up on my own hook. If I cannot go with you, I can at least go alone. I mean to win that big reward if I can."

"I wish you success!"

"Thank you! Perhaps we may meat in the far West."

"I hope so!"

"Good-day!"

The door closed and Burton was gone. From that moment Frank was busy preparing for his trip west. There was much to do. The exciting rumor of the proposed trip with the Steam Horse went out and all Readestown was on the *qui vive* of excitement.

The workmen quickly packed the different sections of the Steam Horse in a special car.

Then a special locomotive was chartered to take the train through to New Mexico.

A great crowd gathered at the depot to see Frank off. Barney and Pomp were there, all equipped and ready for the trip. The excitement was most tremendous.

It was known that Frank's trip was one of philanthropic sort, and that it was also connected with the million dollar train robbery.

That he should go unhesitatingly to the relief of a friend in trouble was characteristic of Frank Reade, Jr.

"Why shouldn't I?" he asked, tersely. "Is it not an obligation? Don't I owe my life to Dave Mayhew? I mean to save him and bring the guilty parties to justice."

Thus was Frank Reade, Jr., given a mission to perform with his wonderful invention, the New Steam Horse.

The special train was quickly on its way to New Mexico. But all this while prying eyes and lurking foes had been at work in Readestown, and the trip of the New Steam Horse and its young inventor to New Mexico was to be not unattended with frightful risk and peril.

Chapter III
The Comanches

CRACK!

It was the sharp report of a rifle which smote upon the air of the New Mexico desert.

About as far as the eye could reach, nought but a level expanse of plain was in view, save just in what seemed the center there was a clump of cactus.

Not fifty yards from this clump of cacti the Steam Horse had just come to a halt.

For a month the Steam Horse, with Frank Reade, Jr., Barney and Pomp in the wagon had been traversing the Western wilds. Crossing this expanse of the desert they had come to the clump of cactus. They were really looking for water. Many of the cacti of a certain species are reservoirs of cool, pure water.

Knowing this, Frank had sought the cactus clump, for there was no sign of water elsewhere on the plain.

But just as the Steam Horse, driven by Barney, was about to come to a halt, there was a puff of smoke, the sharp report of a rifle and a bullet struck the metal side of the wagon.

Pomp had been at the door of the wagon and was about to leap out.

But he checked himself and with surprise cried: "Golly sakes! I done fink dis chile had a narrow escape dat time. Dar's somebody wif a good eye in dat ar place."

"Begorra, that's roight!" cried Barney, in amazement. "Phwativer does that mane, anyway? Shure, phwere is the spalpeen?"

"Steady!" cried Frank Reade, Jr., as lie scrutinized the cactus clump. "Keep your eyes peeled, boys."

The young inventor knew well the risk he was incurring at that moment.

If the cactus clump held a horde of savage Comanches, there was much danger that they would surround the Steam Horse.

That they might do harm to the Horse was certain.

A blow of one of their hatchets at the steam gauge or indicator might ruin the invention.

In this lonesome place there would be no way of repairing the machine, and nobody knew this better than Frank Reade, Jr.

Of course, the Horse could easily run away from the ponies of the Comanches, but an encounter at close quarters was one to be dreaded and avoided.

So Frank was wary in approaching the cactus clump.

Again, he had no means of knowing whether the occupant of the clump was really friend or foe.

At sight of such an unusual article as the New Steam Horse in that out-of-the-way part of the world, a man, though a friend, might get rattled and fire.

So Frank decided to first ascertain, if possible, whether the owner of the rifle was a foe or not.

He went to one of the loopholes in the iron shield of the wagon and shouted: "Halloo, the cactus clump!"

Again he shouted: "Halloo!"

This trine an answer came back.

"Hello!"

"Who are you?"

"I'm Bill Jackson, a cowboy."

"Friend or foe?"

"I dunno! Who the devil are you and what kind of a hitch have you got there anyway?"

"I am Frank Reade, Jr., and this is the Steam Horse."

"The Steam Hoss? Who in thunder ever heerd of such a thing? But that's what it is, sartin. Glad to see ye, friend."

A man stepped out into view.

He was a genuine type of the western cowboy, with buckskin leggings, broad sombrero, and a rifle in his hands.

Over one arm he held the long bridle rein of a sleepy-looking mustang.

Frank saw at once that he had nothing to fear from this man.

At once he opened the door of the wagon and stepped out.

Bill Jackson stood gazing at the Steam Horse with mouth agape.

"Well, I never!" he muttered; "this beats anything I ever seen afore. Gosh all Jiminey! I've seen steam ingines, but I never seen a hoss afore that goes by steam."

"Well, you see it now, my friend," laughed Frank. "Wonders will never cease, you know."

"Wail, I swan! I reckon you're right. But it's a powerful curious masheen."

"I suppose you are an old timer hereabouts?" asked Frank.

"Wall, I've trapped beaver in Montana, dug gold in Nevada, and now I'm down hyar for nigh onto forty years, a-gallopin' over ther range with titer youngest of 'em. An' I don't take a setback from nobody at roundin' up a herd of cattle."

"Good for you," said Frank, heartily. "Well, then, perhaps you can tell me something about a man in these parts known as Duncan Darke?"

The cowboy gave a violent start. He bent a penetrating glance upon Frank and in a peculiar tone he replied: "Straunger, there ain't a better known man in ther Southwest than Dun' Darke."

"Ah!" said Frank, carelessly, "what is his business?"

"His bizness?"

Jackson looked at Frank as if he could not believe him in earnest.

"Yes."

Frank gazed steadily at the fellow.

"Wall, I swan! Whar have you bin all yure life, straunger, that you don't know that Dun Darke are ther wust train robber in America?"

"Train robber, eh?" said Frank, coolly. "Well, I did hear something of the kind."

"Wall, you bet. He's a bad man is Dun Darke."

"Do you recall a peculiar train robbery on the M., N. & T. some while ago? It was reported that a million dollars was stolen."

Jackson gave a low whistle.

"Of course I do," he replied. "So that's what ye're out here for, straunger? Wall, let me give ye a punter."

"What is it?"

"Dun Darke is a bad man to fool with."

"Ah! Then you are of the same opinion as myself that Darke was at the bottom of the deal?"

Jackson nodded his head.

"You bet!" he replied, "but just the same Dun Darke never got that million."

Frank was astonished. "What do you mean?" he asked.

"Just what I say."

"Why did not Darke get the million?"

"Bekase he didn't. When that box was thrown out of the window or door of the car his men didn't get it."

"Really!"

"It's the truth."

"How did you learn that?"

Jackson appeared for a moment confused but quickly recovered himself.

"Wall, you see, a friend of mine knew a chap that belonged to the gang. This feller said that Darke had his trouble for his pains. He didn't find the box with the million in it."

Frank was somewhat set back by this announcement.

"Well, I never!" he exclaimed. "That was pretty rough on Darke, wasn't it?"

"Rayther!" rejoined Jackson.

"Where is the million?"

"Nobody knows."

"It was certainly thrown out of the car door, was it not?"

"Of course!"

"Well, then, it must have struck the ground by the railroad track."

"Cert."

"Why, then, would it not be found by the track where it fell?"

"Kain't say, straunger. Sartin sure it wasn't ever found, an' there's a good' haul fer ther man what finds it."

"Well, that is very strange," said Frank, in surprise; "that box of money could not take legs and walk off."

"I should say not."

"Then you believe that Dun Darke knows nothing about it?"

"Sartin I do."

"One more question!"

"Wall?"

"Do you knew where I would be likely to find Mr. Darke?"

Jackson leaked doubtful.

"That's hard to tell," he muttered. "Thar's a place in the Panther Hills, up here, where Dan goes pooty often. I reckon it's some kind of a rendyvoo in the mountings where he meets all his pals."

"But his regular stopping place –"

Bless ye, he ain't got any. He's a bird of the air, an' flies about everywhere. Ye're likely to meet him anywhere."

Frank extended his hand.

"Mr. Jackson," he said, "I am glad to have met you."

"The same, capen!"

"I hope to see you again."

"The same, capen."

Frank turned and sprang into the wagon. The cowboy was in the saddle and riding away across the prairie.

Frank drew out a notebook and began to jot down an accurate memoranda of the affair.

Barney and Pomp procured some water in the clump of cacti.

This done, a start was made, and the cacti clump left behind. But, the Steam Horse had not got far out upon the prairie, when a startled cry escaped Pomp's lips.

"Golly fo' goodness!" he cried, wildly. "Would yo' look at dat, Marse Frank?"

Frank did look, and beheld a thrilling sight.

Jackson, the cowboy, was madly galloping toward the cacti clump, pursued by a horde of Comanches. Where the savages had come from was a mystery.

But the situation was plainly a desperate one. Unless Jackson reached the cactus clump, the Comanches would be sure to overtake him, and it was, not impossible that they would kill him.

There was no time to lose.

Frank brought the Steam Horse about, and Barney and Pomp made ready to use their rifles. Taking aim through the loopholes in the metal sides of the wagon, they both fired.

Two of the Comanches dropped from their ponies.

The others drew rein and gazed at the Steam Horse with utter horror and great amazement.

As the giant steed came down upon them with thunderous thread they broke ranks wildly and fled.

Frank sent the Horse after them at full speed, and Barney and Pomp worked their repeaters.

The effect was most terrific.

The Comanches separated and fled in all directions. One after an-other dropped beneath the deadly fire of the rifles.

Their terror, however, began to diminish as they saw, after closer scrutiny, what manner of monster was after them.

They saw Frank at the dasher, and realized that this was only some wonderful trick of the paleface foe.

They had often seen the iron horse of the railroads, but this exact representation of the equine animal was something strange to them. But at sight of a white man in the wagon, their fears, at least in a superstitious way, were overcome.

Then suddenly swerved to the right and essayed to dodge the Steam Horse.

Chapter IV
On To the Hills

FRANK READE, JR., saw their game just in time to frustrate it.

He turned the course of the Horse, and Barney and Pomp let go with a volley which settled the question.

Utterly routed the savages broke ranks and fled wildly in every direction. This brought the conflict to an end. Frank saw that further pursuit was quite useless.

So he checked the Horse.

Bill Jackson sat upon his mustang some distance away and seemed to regard the rout of the savages with much satisfaction.

He suddenly put spurs to his mustang and rode up to the Steam Horse.

"Capen, I want to thank ye for savin' my life," he cried. "I reek-on Bill Jackson won't ferget it."

"I am glad we were able to do so," said Frank, quietly. "Perhaps you had better keep along with us for awhile for the sake of safety."

"All right, capen," agreed Jackson. "I'll stay with ye till we git to the Panther Hills."

"That will be good. Then you can show us the nearest way to them."

"Of course I can. Jest let your hoes foller mine."

Jackson struck spurs to his mustang and galloped away.

The Steam Horse followed at a good pace. In this manner miles of the sandy plain were covered.

Nothing more was seen of the Comanches.

It seemed certain that they had had enough and would not venture to attack the Steam Horse again right away.

As Jackson rode on he kept turning his head and regarding the Steam Horse.

It was a source of great wonderment to him.

Frank let down the steel sides of the wagon, as the danger was now past, and took in the good, clear prairie air.

Mile after mile was covered at a steady gait.

The Steam Horse could have gone ahead at a much more rapid gait. But Frank was desirous of keeping with Jackson as long as possible, so he kept the speed of the Horse down.

It was a curious spectacle to see that mighty Iron Horse, with its puffing nostrils, flying at a mad gallop over the plain.

It was little wonder that the ignorant minds of the savages had been deeply impressed by it.

At every clump of sage brush numberless jack-rabbits were scared up, and went bounding like furry balls across the desert waste.

At other times the Horse floundered among the treacherous mounds of a prairie dog village.

On passing a clump of timber a drove of young antelopes might be seen slinking away into the depths of the woods whenever a limber belt was passed.

Many wonderful sights were upon every hand.

Sometimes skeletons would be seen bleaching in the sands, and in many cases they were of human beings.

Wolves and vultures had stripped the bones so that it was impossible to tell whether they were recent victims or not.

"Begorra, it's a moighty desolate-lukin' counthry, the same," averred Barney. "Shure I'd not bike me bones to resht here."

"Golly, dat am a fac'," agreed Pomp. "It am a drefful lonesome place."

"Wait until we get into the bills, if you think this lonesome," laughed Frank. "The great deep passes among the eternal crags, with their awful solitude, is a scene far more depressing than this."

"Bejabers, ould Readestown am good enuff for me," declared Barney. "Share I don't care for the far Wist."

Jackson heard this expression, and turned with an ironical smile.

"What did ye come here for, then?" he asked, pointedly.

"Shure it was a foolish thrick," retorted Barney. "May the Vargin be blissed, but we don't mane to stay here, just that same."

"Oh, there's a good many worse places."

"An' many betther."

"P'r'aps so."

"Shure I kin tell yez that. If iver ye seen the lakes av Killarney an' –"

"Hol' on dar, chile!" put in Pomp. "Dem I'ish lakes ain' a suckumstance to de beauties ob de Swanee ribber, whar I was once a pickaninny."

"Whisht now, me gossoon!" expostulated Barney. "Shure, there's no place in the worruld like Killarney. Bejabers, its many moiles they do cum to kiss the Blarney Stone, an' it's the handsomest conthry in the worruld."

"Huh! Dat's a'rigbt," sniffed Pomp.

Barney was irritated. He didn't like this kind of guying on Pomp's part, and he would have picked it up at once.

But at that moment an incident occurred to prevent. A loud cry went up from Jackson.

He had risen in the stirrups and was pointing to the west.

"Look!" he cried. "Thar's the Panther Hills, friends."

Just visible upon the horizon line now was the outlines of the hills.

Every moment they drew nearer, and Frank saw that they were quite a large range of mountains. He reckoned that they would reach there within an hour.

But darkness was close at hand, in fact; was rapidly approaching, and would be upon them by tie time the hills were reached.

Jackson seemed to be aware of this, and rode alongside. "I reckon we won't make the hills afore dark, capon," he said.

"It looks that way," agreed Frank.

"It's quite a bit of a ways."

"Yes."

"What'll ye do?"

"Well, we will keep on until we do reach them."

"And then –"

"We will camp on the spot."

"That suits me, friends. I'll stay by ye until mornin'."

"All right," agreed Frank.

Jackson urged his horse on now all the faster.

He distance was rapidly growing less. Soon only a plain five miles broad lay between them and the base of the hills.

This was crossed quickly, but when at length they arrived at the foot of a steep mountain wall, it was clearly too dark to go further.

So Frank stopped the Horse and banked the fires in the furnace.

The coal supply was getting short, but as luck had it, the spot upon which they halted was directly over a vein of coal which extended into the mountain side.

"That is luck," declared Frank; "tomorrow we will fill the bunkers."

Camp was quickly made. A fire was made from a heap of the coal, and an antelope shot by Barney in crossing the plain was dressed.

The juicy steak was cooked over the fire and proved most palatable.

All ate heartily and then sat down about the cheery fire.

It was the time of year in New Mexico when the days were blazing hot, and the nights frigid with the thermometer at 35 or 36 degrees. One feels the cold fully as much in that sort of climate at in the Northwest with the temperature at zero.

It was just a good time for Barney to produce his fiddle and Pomp his banjo.

The two comical chaps played Irish jigs and plantation breakdowns, interspersed with songs galore.

Jackson seemed to enjoy the affair immensely.

Indeed, it was a rare treat to the plainsman, and he guffawed in good earnest. "Wall, I swan?" he exclaimed. "Yew chaps are a caution, and no mistake. I'd like to have ye meet the rest of ther boys on ther range."

"Perhaps the opportunity may come," said Frank, pleasantly.

"Wail, I ain't much on the musical biz," declared Jackson, "but I used to know a tune or two on this thing."

He held up a Jewsharp as he spoke.

"Dat's right!" cried Pomp, "gib us a tune, sab."

Jackson did not refuse. He placed the Jewsharp to his lips and began.

For a few moments his listeners were spell-bound at the amount of music that he actually succeeded in getting out of that Yankee instrument.

When he had finished all had applauded well, and Barney cried: "Shure, sor, it's a wondher yez are wid that insthrument! I fiver heard the loikes av it afore."

"But it don't compare with the fiddle or the banjo," declared Jackson. "I only play for me own amusement."

"Well, yez play well!" cried Barney. "Shure, I don't see why we can't play a duet. Do yez know 'Garryowen'?"

"Sure!" replied the cowboy.

"Yez know the same, naygur," said Barney to Pomp. "Yez kin come in on the accompliment."

"Golly! Dat amn't harf so pretty as 'Kitty Wells,'" objected Pomp.

"Yez are a loiar," exploded Barney; "there niver was a chune yit invinted the aiquel av 'Garryowen.'"

"Huh! Don' yo' call me a liar agin, I'ish."

The two belligerents glared at each other. Jackson saw the danger at once, and quickly interposed.

"Hold on pards!" he cried. "We'll play 'Garryowen,' an' then we'll play 'Kitty Wells' afterwards. That will divide it up."

"All right!" cried Barney. "Shure, that's fair enough."

"I'll agree to dat!" rejoined Pomp.

The argument was settled and all now went to work.

The three instruments seemed to work well together. Jackson had a splendid bass voice, and with Pomp's tenor and Barney's baritone, the strains of 'Garryowen' and 'Kitty Wells' were richly rendered.

Frank listened with much enjoyment. When the last strains died out upon the air, Barney struck up a jig on his fiddle.

In a moment Pomp was upon his feet shuffling like mad. The darky was having a high old dance when suddenly an incident occurred to put a peremptory end to the merry making.

Frank had chanced to glance up the mountainside. As he did so his gaze encountered a startling object. He was upon his feet in an instant.

"Hold up!" he cried, sharply, "there's danger ahead."

In an instant Barney's fiddle and Pomp's banjo went into their cases.

They sprang to Frank's side.

"Shure, Misther Frank, phwativer is the matther?" cried Barney.

Frank pointed up the mountainside with his forefinger.

Chapter V
The Light on the Mountain

"DO YOU SEE that?" he cried. "What is it?"

"It's a loight!" cried Barney. "Phwativer is the cause of it?"

This was a conundrum. It was certainly a light, far up the mountainside. It gyrated for a few moments and then remained stationary. What did it mean?

Surely, it was a mysterious thing.

It was not large enough for a camp-fire, nor did it look like a torch.

It appeared to be a red signal lantern, such as are used by trainmen for signals on the line.

"A lantern!" cried Frank.

"Shure, sor, that's what it is," agreed Barney.

Jackson stood like a statue watching the distant object. He did not speak for some moments.

Then he turned about with a deep breath and said: "Don't ye think we'd better move our quarters, capen?"

"What do you mean?" asked Frank.

"Jest what I said."

"Why should we move camp?"

"Bekase I believe that there'll likely be danger here for us pooty quick."

"Ah! Then you think that light indicates the proximity of an enemy?"

"I do."

"What sort of a foe?"

"Why, like enough Dun Darke and his gang."

"But do you think danger threatens us? They may not know that we are here."

"If they don't they soon will," declared Jackson, coolly. "An' then they might make it warm for us."

Frank hesitated a moment. Then he said: "I guess you're right, Jackson; but I have got a plan."

"What is it, pard?"

"Come with me and I'll show you."

Frank advanced to the wagon and opened the draughts of the furnace and began to get up steam in the Horse.

Then he pulled up the steel screens of the wagon.

"Barney and Pomp, you get aboard," he said, authoritatively.

The two servitors obeyed. Then Frank turned to Jackson.

"My friend," he said, tersely, "you're a man of sand, I take it."

"Try me!" replied the cowboy, tersely.

"I will. You are not afraid to accompany me on a little bush scout up the mountain side?"

Jackson whistled softly.

"I see your game!" he said. "I am with you."

"You will go?"

"Yes."

"Bejabers, Misther Frank, won't yez let me go wid yez?" cried Barney.

"Not this time," replied Frank, "but you may remain here with the Horse in readiness to fly if the foe pounce upon you. If the foe do not show up wait here until we return."

"All right, sor!" cried Barney.

"We'll do jes' as yo' says, Marse Frank!" cried Pomp.

"See that you do."

Frank then turned to Jackson.

"Now we are ready!" he declared. "Let us he off."

Without hesitation the two men at once struck out into the darkness. Up the mountainside they went, side by side and with great stealth.

Frank had located the position of the red light, so that he believed he could go directly to it.

It was not easy work clambering over the rough tree trunks and ledges which strewed the mountainside. But slowly and persistently they made their way upward.

After a time they came out upon a rocky ledge from which a view of the plain below was to be had. Nothing could be seen of the lights of the Steam Horse, which were undoubtedly hidden by the fringe of trees. But far above the strange red light could be seen.

"That is curious!" muttered Frank. "It seems as far off as ever."

"You're right," agreed Jackson.

"Wall, p'r'aps it's moving up-ward jes' the same as we are."

"No."

Frank gave a sharp, sudden exclamation and pointed out on the darkened prairie.

A strange sight was there to be seen.

Twinkling in the blackness like a myriad of stars were a large team-bar of lights. There was sufficient halo from them for the two watchers to identify the dim figures of horsemen.

They were riding toward the hills, and were bearing torches or lanterns.

"That's curious," muttered Frank, in amazement. "What on earth does it mean?"

"It's Dun Darke's gang!" declared Jackson, earnestly. "And they're a-comin' right straight toward the hill."

"That's true!" rejoined Frank, in consternation. "And the Steam Horse is right in their path."

"Great guns!" gasped Jackson. "Ye're dead right!"

"It is a bad outlook."

"Shall we go back and give the boys help?"

Frank hesitated.

"I don't believe it is necessary," he declared.

"All right."

"Barney and Pomp will very likely remember my instructions and keep out of the way of the foe."

"Correct, boss! It's go ahead, then, is it?"

"I think it best."

"All right!"

"But wait – see! They have changed their course."

This was true. The train robbers bad seemed to swerve to the southward and were receding in that direction.

Frank was much elated.

"That is good luck!" he cried. "We may go ahead now."

Accordingly they continued their climb up the mountainside.

The purpose of the red light was quite plain now. It was a signal or beacon for the returning party.

Beyond doubt Darke's stronghold was somewhere in these hills.

On up the hillside they pushed, Frailk leading the way.

Soon the trees grew smaller and more stunted, and then they came to vast ledges of granite. The summit was near and they looked for the red light. But it had disappeared.

Somewhat mysteriously it had vanished, and there was nothing left to guide the searchers now.

For a moment they were irresolute. Then Frank started forward.

"Never say die!" he muttered. "We must go on at random now."

"All right, boss!" agreed Jackson.

Stumbling on in the gloom, a sudden cry from Jackson was heard and then a dull thud.

With horror, Frank realized what had happened.

"My God!" he cried, "have you fallen, Jackson? Where are you?"

All was the silence of the grave.

Frank bent down and crept forward cautiously upon his hands and knees. In a moment he had reached the brink of a precipice. Over this Jackson had plunged, it seemed to his death.

Frank was petrified with horror.

He listened for some sounds from the abyss below. He shouted the cowboy's name again and again.

Then an inspiration came to him.

He drew a small pocket lantern from his pocket and lit it.

Then, bending over the edge of the precipice, he flashed its rays downward. Fifteen feet below he saw the level land at the foot of the descent. The distance was not very great after all.

But there in a heap lay the body of Jackson.

Frank fastened the lantern to his belt and proceeded to climb down the descent. In a moment more he was bending over Jackson, but already the Cowboy was showing signs of returning consciousness.

He had been merely stunned by the fall. Not a bone was broken and he was not badly injured.

This was most fortunate.

"Thank Heaven, you are alive, Jackson!" cried Frank.

"Yes, pard, an' I'll wager me life I couldn't fall that distance agin an' escape alive."

"I don't believe you could."

Jackson scrambled to his feet.

"I'm all right," he declared. "Only me head rings like a bell."

"You will soon get over that."

"Of course I will. But do ye know, Mr. Reads, that just as I fell I had a queer sight?"

"What?"

"Why, jest up there through the darkness I saw the flash of a light and a man's head an' shoulders in it."

Frank was at once interested.

"Where was this?' he asked.

"Just up yonder – ah!"

He ceased speaking.

Both men craned their necks and tried to penetrate the gloom, while curious sounds came to their ears.

"What do you call it?" whispered the cowboy, shrilly.

"It is the tramp of horses' feet," declared Frank, positively.

"So I thought!"

"Ah! See that!"

A bright light suddenly broke the gloom far up the mountainside. Only for an instant was it visible.

It was as if a torch had for one instant been visible at a crevice of the cliff, only to vanish as the one carrying it passed on.

Without a word Frank and Jackson started up the slope.

They understood the situation at once. The train robbers had returned from a raid, and were making their way through a defile over the mountains.

Arrived at the brow of the height, the two watchers looked down upon the other side. Their gaze was at once rewarded by a strange sight. A narrow gorge, which might at times be the course of water, was thronged with men and horses.

Rough looking fellows they were, and at intervals one would carry a torch. It was a weird and strange looking parade.

The two spies watched it with interest.

"Them air Dun Darke's men," declared Jackson, positively. "I know it by the looks on 'em."

"Indeed!" exclaimed Frank. "Is Darke himself there?"

"Yes – there he is, just up the defile a hundred feet or more."

Frank gazed with interest upon the chief of the train robbers.

Chapter VI
A Scouting Trip

DUNCAN DARKE was a tall, powerful-framed man, with long curling black mustache, sharp chin, high cheek bones, and haws-like eyes. In all the New Mexico wilderness no man was better known, or more generally feared.

He was responsible for many a desperate raid on ranch and rail-road. Many a home had been made destitute and many a crime lay charged at the door of the villain.

He was literally a villain of the dyed-in-wool sort. Cruelty and love of bloodshed were his chief perquisites. Wherever he struck blood flowed wickedly.

Many efforts had been made by law-abiding communities to capture and imprison him. Vigilant bands had scoured the plains and searched the hills.

Battles had been fought to the finish, but Darke always came off victorious in all of them.

It was said that he had often captured the daughters of settlers and carried them captive up into the mountain retreat, there to make slaves of them.

The daring train robbery on the M., N. & T. was but one of many such episodes. In fact, the villain organized and kept in existence a perfect reign of terror throughout southern New Mexico.

When the rumor went out that he had not after all Sscured the million dollar prize, the excitement was intense.

Various theories as to the disappearance of the treasure were ex-pounded. But none of them served to explain it. Searching parties went forth, but returned empty handed.

Frank Reade, Jr., gazed with great interest at the celebrated bandit.

Of course, in the dim light of the torches, he had not the best sort of an opportunity to study his features. But Frank saw that he was not a man of the ordinary sort.

"He will be a hard one to handle," he muttered.

"You are right!" chimed in Jackson. "He's a wicked individual."

"Undoubtedly he is now on his way to his stronghold."

"Yes, I reckon so."

"What had we better do?"

"Wait a bit."

The outlaws continued to file by to fully the number of seventy-five.

After they had gone from sight and the gorge was still, the two watchers ventured to emerge from their concealment.

"Come on, pard," whispered Jackson. "Let's catch on behind."

Down into the gorge they clambered. Reaching the trail below, they crept swiftly along in pursuit of the outlaws.

The torches were dimly visible in the distance, and keeping these in view, they crept on.

The gorge was a long and winding way through the hills. It seemed almost interminable, but suddenly it came out to the brow of a mountain wall, jutting down a thousand feet or more.

Upward was the same distance in sheer ascent.

A path wound along the face of this. It terminated finally upon a shelf of rock, seemingly one hundred feet in width, and extending to the verge of the precipice.

In the mountain wall back of the aerial plateau was a deep-mouthed cavern. Nature had endowed the spot with all the perquisites necessary for the stronghold of an outlaw.

All this Frank and Jackson were enabled to see from their position, which was in an angle of the cliff just where the path merged with the shelf.

"Great guns!" gasped Jackson, "did ye ever see the beat of that, capen?"

"It is certainly a very secure retreat," agreed Frank.

"Jiminy! However can we even with your Steam Hoss expect to lick this hull tribe?"

"We cannot do it very well," agreed Frank.

"What's yure idee, then?"

"Well, my plan is to work some scheme to capture Darke. However, if he has not got the million dollars stolen from the express company I don't know as it would be doing much toward gaining the ends I have expected to."

"Jest what I was thinkin', boss; only if ye capture Darke he'll like enough give evidence to clear young Mayhew, eh?"

"Just so," replied Frank; "although just at present I don't see how we are going to do it."

"I suttinly don't nuther."

"At least, it is well to know that we have gained positive knowledge of the exact location of the robbers' den."

"Jes' so!"

"Now, I think we might as well return to the Horse."

"All right!"

With this the two watchers started to creep back down the gorge in the shadows so dense. They made their way easily along the narrow path into the gorge.

Here the darkness was intense.

It was necessary to proceed with the greatest caution.

It was odd that no guard was posted in the gorge. Frank noted and marveled at this.

However, it was fortunate for them that this was the case.

Down the gorge they crept rapidly. Suddenly a startling thing occurred.

Jackson paused and clutched Frank's arm.

"Jericho! Do ye hear that?"

Faint from the distance came the shrill, ear-splitting whistle of the Steam Horse.

Something was wrong.

"They have been attacked!" cried Frank; "that is a signal to us I am sure."

"Great guns!" ejaculated Jackson. "What kin we do, pard?"

"Back to the plain as quickly as possible."

The two men started down the gorge at full speed.

But now a startling sound came from their rear. It was the winding of a horn and the clatter of horses' hoofs.

"They have taken the alarm and are coming!" gasped Frank, "they heard that whistle."

"I reckon ye're right, boss!" cried Jackson. "What shall we do?"

"Come quick! They will be upon us."

Frank pulled his companion into the shadows by the side of the path.

He was not a moment too soon.

Crouched by the mountain wall the two explores saw the horsemen go by at a full gallop. Down the gorge they swept.

But just fifty yards beyond, the horse ridden by one of them stumbled and fell in a heap.

The rider was thrown instantly.

The gang did not atop, however, but kept on at fall swing.

For a moment, Frank and Jackson hesitated as to what move to make.

The horse lay upon its side with a broken leg. The rider was insensible in a heap in the path. Not one of the other outlaws was in sight.

"Listen!" cried Frank; "do you hear any more coming?"

"No."

"I have an idea!"

"Well?"

"Let us make a prisoner of that chap if he is not dead."

"What for?"

"We can force him to give us much valuable information. Perhaps he can tell us about the million dollars."

"But will he?"

"He might with a threat of death."

"Ye're a brick. Go ahead an' I'll folly ye anywhere."

Frank ran quickly to the side of the prostrate outlaw.

He was just in the act of attempting to get upon his feet.

He had been unhurt beyond a little shaking up and a few bruises.

Frank instantly held a revolver at his head.

"Hands up!" he said, sternly. "I have the drop!"

The fellow obeyed.

"Who are ye?" he growled.

"A friend, if you obey orders."

"What do ye want?"

"Are you not one of Darke's gang?"

The fellow dropped an oath as he replied tersely: "I ain't sayin'."

"No, but had better. There's a lead pellet in this pistol."

"Wall, neighbor, I 'low ye're right. I am one of the gang."

"Did Darke just go by with his men?"

"Yes."

"Who is left at the den?"

The fellow hesitated.

"Who the devil are ye?" he asked. "What do you want to know for?"

"It don't matter. I want a truthful answer."

"Wall, I kain't say as there's much of any one."

Frank was silent a moment. He was busy ruminating as to what was now the best move to make.

If he had the Steam Horse on hand, with a clear course he would have considered it just the opportunity to gain possession of the out-laws' retreat. But with only Jackson to assist him it would be folly.

"Look here!" he said, bluntly. "Where is that million dollars stolen from the Texas Express Company?"

The outlaw gave a sharp cry.

"Oho!" he exclaimed, "now I know what ye are. Ye're a detective."

"Well," said Frank, impatiently, "what do you say about it?"

"I dunno where it is."

Frank held the cold muzzle against the villain's temple.

"I want the truth!" he said. The outlaw shuddered.

"I kin tell ye one thing that Dun Darke ain't got it."

"What do you mean?"

"Somebody else has got it."

"Who?"

"Wall, now, ye ask me a hard question," replied the fellow. "Some on 'em believe the box was picked up an' carried off by Black Arrow, the Comanche chief. Dun has bin tryin' to git a fight on with the Comanches fer a long time so as to git the box back. Ye see, them Injuns ain't no use fer it, only they think it's valuable to the whites, an' they'll hold onto it fer pure cussedness."

"I see," agreed Frank. "And now –"

He did not finish the sentence.

A warning cry came from Jackson.

"Look out, pard, thar's mischief ahead!"

From the gloom sprang a score of dark forms. The light of torches flashed upon the scene and a mocking voice cried: "Here's ther interloper, lads! Surrender, ye coyotes, an' don't make a move or every one of ye are dead men!"

Chapter VII
Adventures of Barney and Pomp

BARNEY AND POMP left with the Steam Horse were not to be denied their share of thrilling experiences.

As Frank and Jackson glided away into the gloom Barney groaned: "Shure, I don't see why Misther Frank should be afther takin' that omadhoun along with him an' lavin' a valuable man loike me at hum."

"Golly! Dat am a nice speech fo' yo' to make, Fish!" scoffed Pomp. "He don' want no men wif him what would be afraid oh dere own shadows."

"Bejabers, thin he'd never take yez."

"I jes' fink he'd take me rather dan yo', sah."

"Ye're a loiar."

"Huh! Look out dar, I'ish. Don' yo' git me excited."

"Bejabers, I don't care no more for ye than I do for a yaller dog."

"An I don't keer fo' yo' to mo' dan a wet hen."

"Whurroo!"

"Ki-yi! Bah!"

Barney could stand no more. His blood was up, and be was just ready for a ruction with any one.

He picked up a lump of coal and hurled it at Pomp. But the darky was an expert base-ballist, and made as pretty a catch as an expert behind the bat.

Moreover, he hurled it back as if throwing to first base.

Barney did not reach for a low ball, and the lump of coal took him a sharp crack in the shins.

"Och hone! Murther! It's kilt I am!" roared the Celt, stooping down with a paroxysm of pain.

Then he recovered and made a rush at Pomp, who was roaring with laughter.

The Celt and the African became involved in a rough and tumble in the wagon. The steel curtains were drawn up, and in the struggle Barney forced Pomp over the fender of the wagon.

"Shure, it's overboard I'll throw yez!" roared the Celt. "Take a soft tumble, ye spalpeen, an' that's to pay yez for the damage yez did me leg."

"Golly! If I goes ober yo' jes' goes, too!" cried Pomp.

Fastening a hold upon the Celt's collar, Pomp palled him over. The next moment both went out in a heap.

They rolled about on the green sward in a lively rough and tumble.

Neither seemed to gain the advantage, and, finally completely exhausted, they released hold on each other.

"Bejabers, I'll say quits if ye will, nayger!" cried Barney.

"A'right, I'ish!" agreed Pomp.

Both scrambled to their feet. At that moment a startling fact became apparent to them, which, in the excitement of their wrestling, they had failed to see.

Out upon the prairie were flashing lights.

Barney gave a sharp cry.

"Shure, pwhat's that?" he cried, in alarm. "The inemy are coming!"

"Glory fo' goodness!"

Both scampered aboard the wagon. They then proceeded to watch the advancing lights.

That they were torches became evident, and the forms of the horsemen could be seen.

"Shure, they're comin' straight down for us!" cried Barney.

The Celt's hand was upon the throttle rein and he was ready to set the Horse in motion in case of necessity.

But suddenly the horsemen changed their course.

They swept on around an angle of the mountain wall.

It was safe to assume that they had not seen the Steam Horse at all. The two servitors drew a breath of deepest relief.

"Begorra, I'm glad the spalpeens didn't come here at all," cried Barney.

"It am de bes' ob luck," agreed Pomp.

"But phwat av Misther Frank?"

They looked at each other.

"I done reckon Marse Frank take keer oh himself."

"I don't know about that, sor," protested Barney. "Shure I think there's some diviltry afloat, an' share I think lu me own moind that rid light up yinder is the cause av it."

Both glanced up the mountain side and then staggered back with a sharp cry.

The light was no longer visible.

What did it mean? For a moment both were silent.

"Shure, it's too much foolin' we've been a-doing!" cried Barney, picking up his rifle. "In me moind I kin see that we're in a dangerous place here."

"Golly, I jes' fink you'se right!" agreed Pomp.

"Dar may be 'cashun fo' us to git, up an' git pooty quick!" he rejoined a moment later.

"Bejabers, I'm thinkin' that same mesilf. Now, phwat will we do?"

"Suah, Marse Frank done tole us to stay yer."

"That is, if we didn't have thrubble, to drive us away, naygur!"

"Well, we jes' been 'tacked yit by de enemy. No use fo' to move yit."

"Ye're roight, naygur. I'm thinkin' it'll be the best thing we kin do to kape a good watch, though!"

"You'se right dar!"

With this conclusion the two faithful servitors with their rifles in rand sat down upon the wagon dasher and began to watch and listen.

For a long while they sat thus. Fully an hour passed.

Then a startling thing occurred.

Suddenly Pomp gave a start and nearly fell from his seat.

"Golly fo' glory!" he screamed. "What ebber am dat?"

"Bejabers, it's the inemy," cried Barney.

Around a bend in the mountain wall, coming from the northward as it were, was a band of horsemen. Several of the leaders carried torches.

In the light of these the others could be seen plainly enough.

They were fully a score in number and were riding rapidly. Straight toward the Steam Horse they were coming.

Barney was for a moment at a loss what to do.

"Whurroo!" he cried, "the divils will seen be on us, an' allure, if they surround us, it's a hard fight there'll be."

"Golly! Dat's right."

"Bejabers, I think an ounce of previntion is worth a pound av cure. Shure, I'm goin' to rethreat."

It was evident that the outlaws had spotted the lights from the Steam Horse, for they were yelling like mad.

Barney knew that there was no use in trying to disguise matters.

A crisis had been reached, and action was necessary.

To him it seemed important to let Frank know of the true state of affairs, so he pulled the whistle valve.

A sharp, shrill shriek went up on the night air.

Then Pomp closed the steel curtains and sprang to the loopholes with his rifle.

While Barney sent the Steam Horse galloping cut over the plain, Pomp proceeded to fire at the pursuers.

It was easy for him, good marksman that he was, to pick off the villains adroitly.

The Winchester barked every five seconds until the magazine was exhausted. Then Pomp seized Barney's rifle.

The Steam Horse could easily outstrip the horses of the outlaws.

But this was not Pomp's game.

"Keep de Horse jes' about so," he adjured Barney. "Dat will jes' keep dem in good range yo' know."

"All right, naygur."

In this way the darky could speedily have exterminated the whole gang of pursuers.

But they evidently realized this and halted just in time.

They realized that they could not overtake the Horse.

The deadly rifle was too much for them. Wheeling their horses back to the hills they galloped.

Pomp turned to Barney.

"Jes' yo' brung de Hoss 'bout, will ye', I'ish? I done fink we chase dem now."

The somewhat curious turning of tables now took place.

The pursuers became the pursued. The Steam Horse thundered after them like a dread messenger of death. At every stride it gained upon the outlaw band.

Pomp worked the Winchester for all he was worth.

The outlaws were panic-stricken.

They were now quite near the hills, when a remarkable sight was witnessed. Down through the defile galloped a number of horsemen with torches.

They were the gang fresh from the den of Dun Darke.

They met the fleeing party, and of course had explanations with them. This seemed to result in a change of plan, for they all sought refuge in the line of woods along the mountain wall and opened the upon the Steam Horse.

The bullets fell against the steel curtains as thick as hail.

But they could do Barney and Pomp no harm. The two servitors laughed in scorn, and Barney cried: "Shure, we'll give them spalpeens all the fun they want afore we're done wid 'em. Whurroo! Foire away, yez bloody omadhouns, yez can't hurt nobody!"

"Golly! I jes' wish dey wud come out in de open field agin!" cried Pomp.

The words were hardly out of his mouth, when suddenly the thumping of horses' feet was heard, and from the gloom of the prairie into the glare of light from the headlight of the Steam Horse there galloped a motley crew of savages.

They were Comanches, and they descended upon the Horse with wild yells.

"Begorra, wud yez lnk at that?" cried Barney. "Give the divils a shot, naygur, an' sthart the Hoss!"

"A'right, I'ish."

Pomp began firing at the Indians, while Barney opened the throttle and sent the Horse along at full speed.

It would have been poor policy to have stood ground, for the savages excelled in numbers, and would have done the Steam Horse great damage.

So Barney let the Horse out for a run along the mountain's base.

But the savages did not pursue them far.

The rattle of firearms was heard, and, looking back, they saw that the outlaws bad descended upon the Comanches, and a large-sized battle was in progress.

Chapter VIII
In the Hands of the Outlaws – A Daring Escape

FRANK READE, JR., and Jackson, the cowboy, were in a by no means pleasant position.

The score of dark forms surrounded them.

"Surrender, ye coyotes, or both of ye are dead men."

There was no alternative. To resist was death. To surrender seemed scarcely better, but Frank threw up his hands, as did Jackson.

"All right!"

"Go through 'em, boys! Take their weapons."

A torch was flashed in the faces of the two captives. A sharp exclamation escaped the leader.

"Wall, I swow!" he cried. "If it ain't the feller what has bin paradin' these parts with that Steam Hoss an' wagon."

"Jericho! Ye don't mean it?" cried another.

"Look fer yerself."

"It's a dead sure fact."

"Here's a good catch."

"You bet!"

"We'll take 'em to ther den an' make 'em walk ther cliff."

"Good! Won't Dun think we've done a big job when he gets back!"

"Haw, haw, haw! It's luck!"

The villains roared with laughter. Frank and Jackson were led away, with their hands tied behind them. It did not take long to reach the stronghold of the outlaws.

Here the two captives were led into a circle of firelight near the mouth of the cavern.

These score of outlaws seemed to be all that were left in the place.

But the leader, a tall, gaunt individual, seemed to take all responsibility upon his own shoulders without waiting for the return or sanction of Darke.

"Hadn't we better wait till Dun comes back, Jim?" asked one of the gang.

"'Tain't necessary," retorted the leader, quickly. "These chaps are our game. It's just what Dun would do with 'em anyway."

"All right!"

"Set a torch out yonder on the brow of the cliff. Then make ready half a dozen of ye to throw 'em over."

Frank experienced a chill.

It began to look as if their fate was sealed and that they were to meet their death in a frightful manner.

"My soul, Jackson!" he whispered. "We are done for!"

"B'gosh, it looks like it," replied the cowboy, coolly.

"Is there no way that we can escape?"

"I don't see any yit."

"It can't be that these wretches will be so inhuman as to carry out their devilish purpose."

Jackson laughed coolly. He was certainly a man of nerve.

"They'll do anything," he replied; "they're a hard lot."

"It will be death to go over that precipice."

"I reckon it will."

"Well, we can't die but once," declared Frank, grimly. "We will make the best of it."

"You bet. When Bill Jackson shows ther chicken heart, it will be a very cold day, I reckon."

The wretches were now busy measuring the distance to the edge of the cliff.

"Stand 'em facing that way," cried the outlaw leader. "Six of ye stand tack of 'em with rifles. If they try to dodge, shoot 'em down."

Frank had been quietly working on his bonds. To his great joy he felt them yield a trifle.

Hastily he worked upon them.

A wild and daring hope entered his breast. If he could only free his hands in time he believed that he could make a daring effort to escape.

He whispered hoarsely to Jackson: "I think I can free my bands," he said. "If so –"

"Good fer ye, pard!" returned Jackson in the same whipper. "I've been tryin' the same dodge, an' I'm likely to git 'em free."

"If we do, what is the move?"

"I think we better cut for the cave."

"But that will be only into the trap deeper."

"If we go in any other direction they'll shoot us down. We kin git into the cave and make a big fight p'r'aps. It's certain death to do anything different. Mebbe there's another way of gittin' out of the cave."

Frank saw that Jackson was right.

Accordingly, he replied: "All right. We will adopt your plan, Jackson." He understood well why Jackson's bonds were loose as well as his own.

The bandits had not taken the pains to tie either very firmly. As a result, it was easy to stretch the hempen cord with which they were bound. Had it been a lariat this would have been impossible.

In a moment Jackson whispered shrilly: "I'm free, Frank! How are you?"

Frank tugged a moment at his bonds and then replied: "I am the same."

"Good! We're ready to act, then?"

"Yes."

"Hold your hands as if they were yet tied."

"Of course."

"Now," whispered Jackson, "when I give the word just take a backward leap and cut into that cave. In course we've got to take the chance of stoppin' a bullet."

"All right."

At this moment the leader of the band of outlaws shouted: "What are you devils whispering about? Keep an eye on 'em, boys. It won't do 'em no good, for they can't escape."

The two prisoners trembled for a moment.

But the outlaws in charge only increased their vigil for a few moments.

Then they relaxed it as before.

Only two men stood beside the prisoners. Jackson whispered again: "We kin do it now, Frank. If you kin crack that fellow beside you, I'll take care of my man."

The other outlaws were at the brow of the cliff, holding a discussion. It was an admirable opportunity, and they embraced it.

"Now!" gritted Jackson.

Quick as a flash lie threw up his arms and struck the guard beside him a stunning blow.

Down the fellow went and Jackson grabbed his rifle from his hands and went flying for the cave.

Frank struck at his man and partly felled him.

Before the outlaw could recover, Frank was away like a fleeting shadow for the cave.

So suddenly was the daring move made that the shadows hid them before the other outlaws could make a move.

With a roar of rage and fury the leader of the gang yelled: "After 'em, I tell ye! Don't let 'em git away."

It was lucky for the fugitives that they chose the cave as a method of retreat.

If they had tried to make the gorge they would have been overtaken by bullets.

Into the cavern they rushed at full speed.

All was darkness, and they were at a loss in what direction to go. But Jackson suddenly came to an abrupt halt by running into a blank wall.

"Hold on!" he shouted. "'Tain't any use to go further. Let's hold 'em off here. We kin do it."

"You're right!" replied Frank. "We can hold them off."

This seemed not difficult.

From the cave it was looking into the light and the outlaws were good targets.

At once fire was opened. Bullets came into the cave in a shower and Frank and Jackson barely escaped them.

But they sank down behind a spur of the cavern wall.

From behind this they picked off the foe easily with their Winchesters. It was a deadly fire which they gave the outlaws.

One – two – three of them fell almost instantly. Two more dropped before they came to their senses.

Then they dodged into the gloom.

It was the opportunity. Jackson gripped Frank's arm.

"Now is our chance!" he cried. "Let us make for the gorge."

"All right!"

Out of the cavern they glided, keeping in the shadows of the mountain wall.

Firing had ceased now, and the outlaws, oblivious of the exact position of their foes, were doubtless trying to get up a stratagem to draw them out.

It was certainly the opportunity and the escaped prisoners saw it. Along the mountain path they glided.

Suddenly Jackson halted and raised his rifle.

"Hands up!" he said, sharply and tersely.

A dark form stood before him in the dense gloom. It was a guard stationed there by the outlaw leader. He did not at once obey the command.

There was a sharp flash, a stunning report and Jackson clapped his hand to his temple.

The flame of the rifle muzzle so near him had actually burned him. But the bullet, fortunately, went wide of its mark.

Jackson acted quickly.

With a sudden movement he struck up the rifle barrel and dealt the guard a terrific blow.

The fellow went down like a log. Loud shouts were heard behind, and Frank cried: "Quick, Jackson, they are after us!"

But the cowboy needed no bidding. Together they dashed on clown the gorge.

Soon they began to descend toward the plain below. Sounds of pursuit had died out in their rear.

But now a startling thing became apparent. Just ahead they head the rattle of firearms and the evidence of a battle.

"What can it mean?" cried Frank. "Have they attacked Barney and Pomp?"

"P'raps so," rejoined Jackson, "but I don't believe it. They wouldn't make such a racket as that."

"Of course not; but what can it be?"

"I have an idea."

"What?"

"I think it likely that the gang that passed us a while ago have struck in with some Nuns an' they're having a scrap."

Both pressed forward as fast as their legs would carry them.

Chapter IX
On to the Conmanche Village

DOWN the gorge the two men ran at full speed.

Every moment the sounds of the conflict became louder and nearer. It was plainly evident that a large sized battle was in progress.

The last one hundred yards lay before the two men now, and in an other moment they came out upon the prairie.

A thrilling sight rewarded their gaze.

The plain was the scene of a terrific conflict between Comanches and Dun Darke's gang of outlaws. They gazed upon the scene with the deepest interest.

"It's dog eat dog!" cried Jackson. "I wonder which will win?"

"It is hard to say!" rejoined Frank. "It is certainly a terrible fight."

They were at a safe distance from the combatants, so they continued to watch the conflict.

"Do you know my sympathies are with the Comanches!" cried Frank. "They are no less our enemies, it is true, yet I would like to see them whip the villains."

"Same thar, pard!" cried Jackson. "And as I am a livin' sinner I believe they will do it."

This seemed a fact.

The outlaws seemed likely to be literally cut to pieces. Their band had been so badly decimated that not one-third of their original number survived.

And these were rapidly falling beneath the deadly fire of the say ages.

"By Jove, they will be wiped out!" cried Frank.

Even as he spoke, the mere handful of train robbers left retreated to the mountainside.

The victorious savages pursued them with fiendish yells and cries.

Swiftly riding, the remnant of Dun Darke's band, scarce a dozen in number, came rapidly in for the gorge.

Frank and Jackson were just in time to find a hiding-place among some rocks.

The train robbers dashed into the pass with the savages after them. It was a thrilling scene, and Frank and Jackson watched it spell bound.

But soon the dark shadows of the pass hid savages and robbers from view.

"Jericho!" gasped Jackson. "I hain't seen sich a fight as that for years."

"Now, the question is," said Frank, brusquely, "where are Barney and Pomp with the Steam Horse?"

Even as he spoke a sharp cry escaped Jackson's lips.

"Look yonder, pard!" he cried. "What do ye call that?"

Unmistakably out upon the plain was the peculiar headlight of the Steam Horse.

"Hurrah!" cried Frank, flourishing his arms. "We are safe. It is the Horse!"

The young inventor, without ceremony, rushed toward the Horse. Jackson followed on behind. Barney and Pomp we left at the close of a preceding chapter also spectators of the terrific battle. They had watched it with interest to the very last.

And, as the outlaws were driven into the pass, Barney cried: "Bejabers, I'm not sorry, fer on me worrud I'd rather see the Comanches lick the spalpeens."

"Golly! Dat am a fac'!" agreed Pomp.

The two servitors, after the disappearance of the combatants in the pass, sent the Horse along toward the mountain.

"I jes' fink dis am a good time fo' de return ob Marse Frank an' dat cowboy," cried Pomp.

"Yez are roight!" agreed Barney, "an – Whurroo!"

The Celt let out a regular wild Indian yell. The reason for this was apparent.

The headlight's glare showed two familiar forms running across the plain and waving their arms. It was Frank and Jackson.

The next moment the young Inventor sprang aboard the wagon.

"Golly fo' glory, Marse Frank!" cried Pomp, ecstatically, "I'se awful glad fo' to see yo' back agin. Fo' sho' I fought ye' was done gone fo'eber."

"Begorra, Misther Frank, it's overjyed we are!"

"And I am awful glad to find you and the Horse all safe!" cried Frank. "Did you have any ruction with the foe?"

"That we did, sor!" cried Barney.

With this, mutual explanations followed, as well as congratulations.

Jackson all this while had stood outside. Frank caught sight of him, and recalling himself, threw open the door.

"Come aboard, Jackson!" he cried.

"Much obleeged, pard, but I think I'll be crowdin' ye."

"Not a bit of it," returned Frank. "If you will, you shall join us for the rest of the trip."

"Do ye mean it?"

"Yes."

"An' will thar be room fer us all?"

"If there is not, we will pretty quick make room."

"Wall, I'll agree," said the plainsman, coming aboard. "I reckon my boss is confiscated by the reds afore this. Jiminy! What a fine coop ye've got here anyway!"

All now sat down and soberly discussed the situation.

"You see, the most important thing of all," declared Frank, "is to recover that million."

"Kerect!" agreed Jackson. "Wall, we know one thing."

"What?"

"Dun Darke hain't got it."

"So it would seem."

"It is claimed that Black Arrow has it."

"Yes."

Jackson brought his hand down upon his knee forcibly.

"I have it," he shouted.

The others looked at him as if they thought him gone mad.

"What?" asked Frank, tersely.

"I have got it."

"Bejabers, we kin see that."

"Don' yo' wan' to git rid ob it?" chaffed Pomp.

Jackson glared at them.

"I'm not jokin', neighbors," he said, coolly. "I mean biz."

"Exactly!" said Frank. "Go ahead, Mr. Jackson."

The cowboy shifted his tobacco from one cheek to the other. Then he hitched at his trousers and sat down.

"The pint is just this!" he said, with a huge expectoration through one of the loopholes in the steel curtain. "We know Dun Darke ain't got that money."

"Yes."

"They say Black Arrow has it, an' that he can't open the iron box."

"Exactly."

"Now, I'll go two fer one the Arrow an' the most of his braves are up that pass now fightin' ther robbers."

"What of it?"

"Why, kain't ye see? Prob'ly he has left that box with the million dollars in it to hum in his wigwam in the Comanche village."

"Admitted!" said Frank, coolly. "Suppose that he has. What good is that going to do us when we don't know where the Comanche village is?"

"But I know where it is, pards."

The announcement created a sensation. All were upon their feet.

"Do you mean it?" cried Frank, breathlessly.

"Yas, I do."

"Then – why cannot we go and surprise the village –"

"Exactly! I know what I'm talkin' about, pards. Thar won't be nobody thar but a new old squaws and boys. We kin skeer them out, an' git that iron box with the money, an' all afore the Arrer an' his band of braves gits back."

Frank sprang to the throttle rein.

"Stand by my side, Jackson!" he cried. "Show me the way!"

The cowboy was quickly by Frank's side. The throttle was opened and away went the Steam Horse.

The gray light of dawn was appearing in the east. The sound of firing in the hills was evidence that the battle was being carried on yet.

The Steam Horse went galloping away across the prairie.

Mile after mile was left behind, and the dawn merged into bright daylight, when Jackson suddenly cried: "Do ye see that long belt of timber an' the chaparral next to it?"

"Yes!" replied Frank.

"Wall, in that timber you'll find the Comanche village."

"We certainly will reach it before the chief Black Arrow does."

"Oh, in course we will!"

Faster went the Steam Horse and the timber loomed up near at hand. Even now they could see the long columns of smoke from the tepee fires of the Comanches rising above the trees.

Into the timber dashed the Steam Horse.

Some Indian boys playing in the brush lied in wildest terror. A clearing was just ahead. In the midst of it was the collection of tepees which made up the Village of the Comanches.

The next moment into this clearing burst the Steam Horse. The effect was indescribable.

Indian women with their pappooses fled screaming before the demon and boys and dogs scattered.

The few braves sought safety in flight. In a twinkling the whole village was cleared out. Round the encampment the Horse went at full speed.

Barney and Pomp kept up a firing and yelling to intensify the terror of the Indians.

They succeeded most effectually. In less than three minutes not a savage was in sight.

But where was the chest containing the million dollars?

Jackson gave a great cry. "Look!" he shouted.

An astounding sight burst upon the view of the explorers.

There, in the center of the village green, was a huge pile of stones and ashes about them.

In the center of this pile, which was evidently the bed of a hot fire, they saw the missing iron chest. It was battered and blackened with the action of the fire. But it had not yet been opened.

The box was fire-proof steel and the resort of the savages to this method of opening it bad failed.

"As I live!" cried Frank Reade, Jr.; "it is the box!"

"So it is!" cried Jackson, joyfully; "the goes are with us. Now, pards, let's get the box aboard as quick as we can."

Chapter X
The Treasure Recovered

A CHEER of triumph went up from Barney and Pomp.

"Yo' kin jest bet that we will," cried the darky. "I reckon de million am foun'."

"Begorra, it's another big thing for Misther Frank," cried Barney.

"Shure, he's the most wonderful man aloive today."

"I agree with ye," cried Jackson, "but give us a lift, lad."

The cowboy leaped out through the door of the wagon. Barney and Pomp followed him.

There was no tire in the ashes about the steel chest now and they had no trouble in lifting it aboard the wagon.

It added much to the great load imposed upon the wagon already. But there was no other way to do.

Frank opened the throttle and with the others aboard and the steel treasure chest safely stowed started back for the open plain.

In a few moments the Steam Horse was once more galloping over the vast expanse. It was now in the middle of the forenoon.

All were hungry and weary and glad to accept the suggestion that a good place be found to stop and rest.

After twenty-five miles run, near the hour of noon, an inviting spot upon the banks of a wide river was found. There was a patch of emerald greensward, some clumps of cacti and a bubbling spring. A depression in the bank made a nice place to stop, as they could not form a conspicuous object upon the plain.

Jackson shot an antelope, and Barney and Pomp soon had a good fire going.

Water from the spring was brought, the antelope steak was served, rich and juicy. To cap all, Frank produced a bottle of rare old Burgundy, and this whetted the appetites of all.

After the meal they sat down about the fire in various attitudes of ease. The warmth of the sun was such, however, that they were soon very glad to move back a ways.

Barney found a cozy spot in the bank and did not notice a gopher.

The Celt was dozing beautifully, when suddenly he experienced a chill. Something was moving near him.

An instinct told the Irishman, fortunately, not to move. He craned his neck a trifle and looked down.

Horrors! There, just at his thigh, was a monster rattlesnake fully six feet long.

The reptile had crawled out of the gopher hole, and Barney's form lay directly in his path. It was an awful position.

He knew well the deadly nature of the reptile and the full weight of the danger which threatened him. The least move meant death.

The reptile would be sure to strike quick as lightning. Barney lay quite still. Fortunately he kept perfect command of himself and waited results.

He knew that if he did not move a muscle the snake would not be apt to strike him.

Now he felt the snake's body glide over his leg with slow, driving motion. Through his half-closed eyes Barney saw the reptile's gleaming eyes and the forked tongue darting in and out of his blunt mouth. It was an experience to daunt the strongest and, bravest man.

He lived ages in that brief space of time.

What would be the end? Barney was in a fearful state of mind. The nervous strain was something terrible.

Slowly across his lower limbs the big rattler crawled.

The seconds seemed hours to the agonized Irishman. It seemed every moment as if he must give way to twitching of muscles, which, would have meant certain death.

Now the snake was half across, but Barney experienced a fresh thrill of horror. The reptile had paused.

The warmth of the Irishman's body was 'enticing, and the snake was preparing to coil itself up and enjoy a nap.

At this moment Jackson, who lay some twenty feet distant, turned over upon his side.

As the cowboy did this he saw the snake and Barney's position. At the same moment he exchanged startled glances with Barney.

The cowboy had the presence of mind not to speak, or do aught at the moment to irritate the snake.

But he realized that only a desperate move would save Barney's life. Jackson lay a moment silently watching the snake.

He saw the reptile's ugly head sink slowly down to a position of repose.

Then the daring cowboy made action.

He reached to his belt and drew a revolver. Slight as the motion was, it had aroused the snake.

Up went the reptile's head instantly. The glistening eyes and darting tongue were plain to see.

The tail with its rattles stood straight up, ready to strike the warning note.

Slowly Jackson brought the revolver to a level with that glistening angry head. The cowboy's aim was deadly.

A glance along the sight, a steady nerve, a quick, firm pressure upon the trigger, and –

Crack!

The weapon spoke sharply.

It would have been very easy to miss that swaying, terrible head, with its deadly poisonous fangs.

To have missed it would have been no disgrace to any expert marksman, but it would have been death to Barney.

But the bullet went true to its mark. It struck the snake's head and spattered the brains everywhere. In an instant the Celt was upon his feet. He rushed into Jackson's arms and literally hugged him.

"Begorra, I owe ye me loife!" he cried, excitedly. "Shure, how will I aver pay ye for it?"

"Yer don't owe me nuthin'!" cried Jackson, good humoredly. "I'm only too glad to do it fer ye."

Of course Frank and Pomp were aroused.

There was no sleeping after that, for a very good reason.

Fully a dozen huge rattlers were killed in the vicinity within the next twenty minutes.

The lovely green dell seemed alive with them. They came from gopher holes, from beneath stones and tree trunks, and were all hissing, savage fellows.

"Well, who ever would have thought it?" cried Frank. "It is not a spot to look for such vile reptiles."

"That's right, pard!" cried Jackson, "but jest the same here's where we find 'em. I reckon we kin call this Rattlesnake Holler."

"All right," agreed Frank. "That is just the name for it."

All now congregated by the water's edge, and a general discussion was held.

"I s'pose now ye'll take this money back ter civilization an' deliver it up to ther people whom it belongs to?" asked Jackson, ungrammatically.

"Well," said Frank, hesitatingly, "that will not he the fulfilling of my mission exactly."

"Eh? How's that?"

"Of course, recovering the million dollars was one necessary thing. But the next thing is to capture Dun Darke and make him confess that Mayhew is an innocent man."

Jackson slapped his thigh with the palm of his hand forcibly. "Now, that's the talk!" he cried. "Ye're jest the kind of a man I thought ye was. I'm with ye heart an' hand."

"I am glad to hear you talk that way!" said Frank. "I depend much upon you, Jackson."

"Wall, ye may, all ye please. But what's the lust move?"

Frank gazed furtively at the Steam Horse.

"I don't like to tarry that treasure about with me!" he declared. "If anything happened that we should be captured, Horse and all, the foe would get it back again."

Jackson strode up and down a moment thoughtfully. Then he paused.

"It's right ye are, friend!" he said, brusquely. "I've got a plan."

"What is it?"

"Dig a hole right here an' drop the box into it. Get your bearings an' ye kin come back here for it any time."

Frank clapped his hands.

"Good for you, Jackson!" he cried; "that is a prime idea. We will do it. The million dollars will be safer here than anywhere else."

"But are you sure there's a million in that box?" asked Jackson.

"No, not sure. But it won't take a moment to find out."

"I'd do it."

"I will."

Frank ordered Barney and Pomp to bring the box from the wagon. They obeyed and it was deposited upon the ground near.

Then Frank proceeded to examine the lock.

Jackson took a look at it and said: "I reckon ye'll have hard work to git that open, pard. Ye haven't a key?"

"No," replied Frank, "but I never saw a lock yet I couldn't pick."

The young inventor drew some wire keys from his pocket and began work.

In just twenty minutes he had opened the box. As the lid swung back all pressed forward.

A wonderful sight was revealed.

There in the box were great rows of gold eagles and fire-proof cases containing great rolls of greenbacks.

A million dollars the box was said to contain.

Frank was not so foolish as to attempt to count.

"The amount is supposed to be correct," he declared, "and the contents don't seem to have been disturbed." He shut the lid and the lock shot back into place.

It was certain that none of the money had been taken out of the box. Shovels were taken from the wagon and Barney and Pomp dug a hole about three feet deep.

Into this the box was placed and covered up.

The earth was closely packed and the sod put back in its place.

"Thar," cried Jackson, with satisfaction. "Nobody will ever find it thar. Now we kin come back fer it when we git ready."

"You are right!" cried Frank. "Now let us be off. Dun Darke must be captured before forty-eight hours."

All sprang into the wagon.

The sun was now past the hour of noon. Frank opened the throttle and the Steam Horse went galloping away over the prairie.

But the quartette had overlooked one very important fact.

Any hole dug in the prairie, or grave there made, unless covered with heavy rocks, is not likely to long remain unexplored.

The party had not been gone from the spot an hour when a number of gaunt coyotes came smelling about.

The freshly disturbed earth was to them a grave and they proceeded to explore it.

It required but a few moments for the beasts to excavate the hole and completely expose the iron treasure chest. They indulged in howls of disappointment and rage at not finding the desired object of their quest.

After a time they left the spot, and there lay the treasure chest in plain view.

This had certainly not been the anticipations of the party that had just left the spot.

If it had, they certainly would have taken the precautions to make the hiding-place more secure.

As it was, the treasure lay exposed to the gaze of any passing human being, whether civilized or savage.

It would be sure to attract the gaze of the first person passing that way. If so, what would be the result?

It was certainly a strange and unsafe place to leave a million dollars.

Chapter XI
The Stronghold Deserted

FRANK READE, JR., held the Steam Horse on a straight course back for the hills.

After a time they came in view again upon the horizon.

It was the latter part of the afternoon when the Steam Horse reached the mouth of the pass. The scene here presented was a sickening one.

About upon every hand were evidences of the terrible battle which had occurred the night before. The plain was literally strewn with the dead bodies of Indians and savages. These were beginning to decompose in the hot sun and made a ghastly spectacle to look upon.

Into the pass Frank boldly urged the Steam Horse.

Jackson had made an examination of the trail and concluded that the savages were not in the pass.

Whether Duncan Darke and his gang were yet there remained to be seen.

Boldly the little party entered the pass. The Steam Horse went ahead at a lively gallop.

In places the path was narrow, but the Horse made his way along famously, under the skillful guidance of Frank Reade, Jr.

Up the gorge they went.

Thus far not a sign of the savages had been seen or heard of Dun Darke's men. No guards were encountered and nothing barred their progress.

In a little while they came to the path around the cliff.

Tide was too narrow for the wheels of the wagon, and the Steam Horse could go no further.

A consultation was held.

"Begorra, I'll go ahead an' investigate wid yer leave, Misther Frank!" cried Barney.

"It don't seem to me as if there was anybody about here," said Jackson.

Frank exchanged glances with him.

"Then you think that the outlaws have been wiped out by the savages?"

Jackson nodded his head.

"I do," he said, with conviction. "I think that Black Arrow has wiped them out."

"It is no doubt a good job," said Frank, with a shrug of the shoulders, "and yet I wish that the Comanche chief bad given me first the chance of arresting Darke."

"Well, we had better first make sure of it, pard," said Jackson. "I will volunteer to go ahead and reconnoiter."

"An' so will I!" chimed in Barney.

"Easy!" cried Frank, authoritatively. "You and Pomp will stay here while Mr. Jackson and I will do that."

Accordingly, with their rifles well in hand, the two men left the wagon and went, forth to reconnoiter.

They skirted the face of the cliff, keeping a good lookout for the foe. Very soon they came to a point from which a view of the outlaws' stronghold could be had.

The result was thrilling.

Not a person was in sight. The place was as deserted as could well be imagined. All was the stillness of the tomb.

"It's just as I thought!" cried Jackson. "Black Arrow's gang has wiped them out of existence."

"It looks like it," agreed Frank, "but let us make sure of it."

Together they crossed over to the plateau and made a brief search.

There were traces of a battle and a bloody trail led to the edge of the cliff over the valley.

This told the tale.

Even before they went to the edge of the cliff the two searchers guessed the awful truth. The savages had slaughtered the train robbers and had thrown their belies over the edge.

Below, fully a thousand feet, could be seen the pile of human bodies frightfully mutilated. It had been little short of a massacre, for the overpowering numbers of the savages made it such.

"Ugh!" exclaimed Frank with a shiver, as he turned away from the edge, "that is a dreadful sight indeed."

"Ye're right!" agreed Jackson. "An' yet it was a fate they deserved."

"Oh, yes."

"Wall, pard, that does away with some of yer plans."

"Certainly! Of course Duncan Darke was in that gang and is no doubt lying dead down there. There seems but one thing to do now."

"Ah!"

"And that is to go back to the spot where we left the million dollars, recover it, and strike for civilization."

"Jes' so!"

"There we can deliver up the money to the express company, and it is quite likely that Mayhew will be acquitted."

"He oughter!"

"Of course."

"We can't gain anything by staying around here any longer."

"No, the savages no doubt have located the train robbers' den, and there would be nothing left for us."

"I believe ye."

"So let us go back to the wagon."

And back to the wagon they did go.

Barney and Pomp had been anxiously awaiting their return. They listened to me explanation by Frank with deep interest.

"Golly, Marse Frank, dem hijins did their work up well, didn't dey?" cried Pomp.

"Bejabors, I don't belave they've killed that spalpeen av a Darke yit!" cried Barney. "Yez will see that he will turn up aloive somewhere yit. Shure, thim kind av min have the loives av a cat."

Jackson laughed at this.

"I don't know but that you're right, Barney," he cried.

"Share an' I am!" cried the Celt. "Yez will see that same."

"Well, if that is so, and we can get our clutches on him," put in Frank, "it will be a good thing."

"Shure it'll not be airy to do that."

The Steam Horse was now headed down the defile.

Frank was at the dasher, and they had hardly reached the plain when a thrilling thing occurred. Suddenly in the defile just ahead there appeared six mounted Comanches.

With a start, Frank put on the brake.

But if the voyagers were surprised, the Comanches were more so. For a moment they sat on their ponies like statues.

"Golly sakes!" cried Pomp, wildly. "Jes' gib me my rifle dar, I'ish!"

But before anybody could make a shot at the redskins, they wheeled their ponies and went clattering madly down the defile.

Frank allowed the Horse to go along at a moderate gait.

But suddenly turning a corner in the wall of the pass, all saw that the gorge was literally jammed with mounted savages.

This was a startling fact.

Such an obstacle it was by no means easy to dispute. For a moment Frank was in dismay. But there was no time to lose.

The Comanches had started forward to the attack with wild yells. There were but two things now for Frank to do.

The Steam Horse could beat a retreat, and a stand could be made further up the gorge. On the other hand, a bold dash could be made through the ranks of the savages.

The latter was the most risky move. There was the danger of smashing the machinery of the Horse. But acting upon the impulse of the moment, Frank made the move.

He pulled open the throttle wide, and shouted: "Now, stand by all! Give them a volley right and left."

Forward plunged the Steam Horse at a breakneck gait.

The next moment it swept down into the ranks of the savages.

The effect, was terrific.

The weight of the iron horse was more than the light ponies and their dusky riders could resist. Dozens of them were overthrown, the steel knives upon the hubs of the wagon wheels cut a path through the heaving, struggling mass.

Now and again the Horse seemed likely to capsize. But Frank held the reins steady, and on the monster went in its resistless course.

Barney and Pomp fired right and left, and many were their victims.

In what seemed a few seconds the Steam Horse broke through the lines of the savages and went tearing down the pass to the plain below.

Frank opened the whistle valve and let out sharp shrieks of triumph.

Out over the plain went the Horse at a terrific rate of speed.

Soon the pass and the hills were left well behind. It was a complete victory and a narrow escape from what had seemed like destruction.

"Jericho!" exclaimed Jackson, with a long breath. "I wouldn't run anothers gantlet like that fer the million dollars we kivered up in the sand out yender."

"It was a close one," agreed Frank, "but we pulled through."

"Thanks to yer nerve and stiddy hand, pard."

"Oh, no; it was good luck."

"I don't agree with ye."

The Steam Horse kept on at a very swift gait across the plain. As a result it was not quite dark when they reached the spot on the banks of the sluggish river where the million dollars had been buried.

Frank threw open the door of the wagon and sprang out.

As he did so a gang of coyotes went scampering out of the little green dell.

The young inventor advanced to the verge of the dell and looked down. He beheld an astounding sight.

There was only a hole in the ground where the grave bad been, and the box containing the million was not in it.

Chapter XII
The Treasure Missing

WORDS are wholly inadequate to express the sensations experienced by Frank Reade, Jr. For a time he could not speak.

He saw plainly that the box had been dug up. It looked as if this had been done by coyotes. But the box itself was missing.

Jackson was now by his side.

As the cowboy saw and realized the situation he was dumfounded.

"Great guns!" he finally ejaculated. "Wall, if that don't beat me. It's gone!"

"Yes, it's gone!" repeated Frank.

"Golly sakes, Marse Frank," cried Pomp, in horror. "Yo' don' mean to say dat?"

"Bejabers, here's bad luck to ther amadhoun what sthole it!" cried Barney.

Frank and Jackson sprung down to the hole, and began to make an examination.

"It is the work of coyotes," declared Jackson. "That is very plain."

"Yes," agreed Frank, "but coyotes couldn't take the box away."

"That is very true. And yet, pard, it's easy to see how some pilgrim, goin' this way, has spotted it and took it along with him."

"He certainly couldn't take it away single-handed. It is too heavy."

"He mought have loaded it on ther back of a mule or hoss."

"Very true. In that case, there ought to be a trail hereabouts."

"Certain!"

"As you are a plainsman, Mr. Jackson, perhaps you can find it."

"I've lived on ther plains, but I ain't keen at a trail."

"Well," said Frank, "Pomp is an adept at it – we'll try him."

Pomp was quickly on hand. He began to search for the trail, and the others watched with interest.

The darky quickly found it, and like a sleuth-hound followed its ramifications about the dell. At length, emerging from the tangle, he struck out upon the plain.

Then he said: "I'se got it all right, Marse Frank."

"Good for you, Pomp."

"Dar am jes' six men in de pahty, and I reckon dey's white men."

"Ah!"

"Dey hab probably strapped de chest onto de back of a led horse. Dey's taken a course jest to de souf, sar."

"Hurrah!" cried Frank, "now we must overtake them. I wonder who they are?"

"Maybe some of the boys off the range," said Jackson. "If so, then you'll have no trouble in gittin' it back, pard."

"I hope not," said Frank, hopefully.

All now went aboard the wagon and the Steam Horse was sent on to the trail to the southward. Darkness came on quickly, however, and this necessitated taking a random course.

The trail had seemed to keep due to the south, so the horse was kept going is that direction.

The headlight lit up the prairie ahead for some ways and there was sufficient starlight to make a course.

Until long after midnight the Steam Horse kept on at a rapid pace. Then suddenly Pomp, who was on the lookout shouted: "Light ahead, Marse Frank."

In an instant Frank was at the dasher.

"Where?" he asked.

"Jes' ober yender in de edge ob what looks like a clump ob trees."

"That is a chaparral!" declared the young inventor, excitedly. "And without doubt that light is a campfire."

"Hooray!" cried Jackson, "then we'll soon catch the thieves."

"I don't know whether you can call them thieves or not," said Frank, "they may have found the box exposed by the coyotes, and in that case they were justified in carrying it away."

"Probably they couldn't open it."

"Perhaps not at present. They would find a way sooner or later."

"What's the move?"

"Strike into the edge of the chaparral, and creep down upon them. If they haven't seen our headlight, we're all right."

"I believe ye."

The Steam Horse was sent along until the chaparral was reached. As Frank had directed, it was kept close in the shadows, and silently made its way along until within a few hundred yards of the campfire.

Then Frank stopped the Horse and opened the door.

"Come, Jackson!" he said, "let us take a little scout."

"I'm with ye!" cried the cowboy, with alacrity. "Jest lead on!"

Out of the wagon they sprang and crept along for a ways in the verge of the chaparral.

The campfire was quickly in plain view, and at this moment a peculiar noise was heard. It was like the ringing of hammer and chisel upon iron.

In fact, this was quickly proved to be the case.

About the camp-lire were half a dozen armed men. Two of them were bending over the treasure chest and trying to pry it open with chisels.

Jackson gave a violent start.

"Heavens!" he gasped. "What a chance. That is Dun Darke."

Frank was astounded.

"You are right!" he cried, then he gripped Jackson's arm in a vise-like grip, and rejoined: "Fate has played this into our hands. We must not let that villain escape."

"Jericho! You're right!" whispered the cowboy. "But how will we trap him?"

"Go back to the Horse and bring Barney and Pomp."

"All right!" Jackson glided away.

No sooner had he gone than Frank was delighted as well as surprised to see four of the six men mount horses and gallop away over the plains upon some errand. They were quickly out of sight and hearing.

Surely fate was playing the game into Frank's hands.

"Now for success!" whispered the young inventor.

Only one man was left with Darke. They were vainly trying to get into the treasure chest. Every word they uttered came plainly to Frank's hearing.

"Curse it!" gritted the train robber. "Won't it yield, Jim?"

"It won't cap'en."

"I wish I had a bit of dynamite."

"Why not try powder?"

"All right; I will."

But at this moment Jackson returned with Barney and Pomp.

"Here we are, pard," whispered the cowboy, shrilly.

"All right," replied Frank. "Keep steady all now and do just what I say. Keep close to me, and draw a bead on those two wretches with your Winchesters!"

Then Frank covered Darke with his own rifle, and boldly stepped out into view.

"Hands up, Duncan Darke!" he commanded, in a sharp, stern voice.

Like a flash the villain wheeled. His hand went instinctively to his pistol belt. But he saw four rifles covering him and his companion. It was a most persuasive argument.

"Hands up!"

There was no disobeying the order.

With a baffled curse the train robber obeyed.

"Bind them both, Pomp," ordered Frank. "Be lively!"

"Curse ye!" gritted Darke.

"Where did ye cum, from so sudden?"

"We have been on your track for a good while," replied Frank, coolly.

A gleam of recognition emanated from the villain's eyes.

"Thunder an' blazes!" he ejaculated. "It's that Frank Reade, Jr., the covey that owns the Steam Hoss!"

"That is just who it is!" cried Frank. "I suppose you are not pleased to make my acquaintance in this manner!"

The villain sullenly submitted to having his hands bound behind him.

"The game is up!" he muttered. "I cave. All my men were cut to pieces by the Comanches. I had thought I could git away with the million an' find safe quarters in some foreign land, but 'tain't no use. I'm beat."

"That's correct, friend!" cried Bill Jackson, forcibly. "An' ye're doing the graceful thing."

Both of the train robbers were now bound securely.

Barney and Pomp had lifted the treasure chest into the wagon.

"What'll we do with these two chaps, pard?" asked Jackson, dubiously. "Thar ain't room in the waggin for 'em both."

Frank saw that this was true. He hesitated a moment and then said: "I have it. We have got the man we want and that is Darke. Cut this other fellow's bonds and let him cut sticks. We don't care for him."

"Correct!" cried Jackson. "We don't care a cent for him."

The cowboy cut the fellows bonds, and said: "Now then, make yerself scarce. It's luck fer you, Judge Lynch ain't holdin' his court hereabouts this morning."

The fellow said nothing, but he looked his ineffable joy at the release. He quickly slunk away into the gloom. Then Darke was placed in the wagon and his captors also climbed in.

The Steam Horse was given head and struck out for the south.

All that night this course was held across the level plains.

The next morning the party halted upon the banks of a small stream in the verge of an alkali tract.

Frank consulted a machine of his invention for recording distance and said: "We are one hundred miles from our stopping place of last night."

This brought forth a hearty cheer.

"Good enough!" cried Jackson. "We ought to make the Texas line in two days more."

"I think we will," said Frank, confidently. "And three days more and we will be at Hard Pan."

The spirits of all were high with the exception perhaps of Duncan Darke. The villain was sullen and defiant at first. But now he began to wax moody and downcast.

At a favorable opportunity he addressed Frank.

"Look here, Mr. Reade," he said, in a pleading voice. "I know you ain't the sort of a chap to take unfair advantage of anybody."

"No," replied Frank, "I never intend to do that."

"Then ye'll be fair with me?"

"I mean to."

"If ye take me up to Hard Pan they will lynch me."

"Well, what of that. Don't you deserve it?"

"Mebbe, but I haven't any desire that way."

"Well, what can I do to help it?"

"Jest let me go. I'll swear never to cross yer path agin nor that of any of your friends. I'll do any favor for ye. My life ain't nothin' to you an' it's a heap to me. Jest let me go."

Chapter XIII
The End

FRANK gazed hard at the outlaw.

"Suppose I was in your clutches," he asked, "what would you do?"

"I reckon I'd let you off tinder these circumstances."

"I don't believe it," said Frank, with positive conviction. "I remenber that Mr. Jackson and myself here were in the power of your men and they meant to make us walk over the cliff to an awful death."

"But I mean to turn over a new leaf," pleaded the villain.

"I don't believe it."

"I swear it! Why should you hold me? You've got the money back and you can clear young Mayhew."

But Frank would not listen to the wretch's appeal.

"You are a murderer," he replied. "Hundreds of innocent lives have been taken by you in your train wrecking career. It is but right that you should expiate your crimes."

The villain thereupon showered bitter curses upon his captor. Whatever compassion Frank had held for his prisoner vanished then.

The days passed rapidly.

The Steam Horse made a magnificent run across the long plains.

Several times the fuel gave out, but each time a fresh mine of coal was found to replenish it.

One morning the Horse ran alongside a railroad track. It was the line of the M. N. & T. In a short while a guide board was seen which said: 'Hard Pan, 40 miles.'

"In one hour!" cried Frank. "If the plain is as smooth as this all the way we will come in sight of the town."

The young inventor's prediction proved correct.

At the expiration of an hour the small city of Hard Pan came into view. Men on horseback and afoot, wagons and prairie schooners, all the evidences of civilization in a new country now became visible.

Down into the main street of the town ran the Steam Horse. It's appearance created a furore.

In a jiffy the entire town was out and thronging the streets. Not a man, woman or child in Hard Pan, but was aware that the wonderful Steam Horse had been for a long time on the trail of Duncan Darke and in quest of the stolen million.

The appearance of the Horse, therefore, created a mighty excitement.

Frank went at once to the office of the Texas Express Co.

The officials came out in great delight, and Frank was literally overwhelmed with their gratitude, when they learned that the million dollars was recovered.

In a jiffy an armed guard was stationed about the express office.

The treasure chest was delivered up to the express company.

Then the city marshal appeared with a posse and took Darke into custody.

The little town was in a whirl of excitement.

That night Darke made a full confession clearing Mayhew. The ex-clerk was released and joined his delighted friends.

Frank Reade, Jr., and the Steam Horse were given an ovation in Hard Pan. They owned the town for the next twenty-four hours.

Jackson was in hilarious spirits, and with Mayhew came down to meet Frank before he left the city.

"I shall not go back on the range, Mr. Reade!" he said. "For this reason!"

The cowboy removed his sombrero and took off a wig and then removed his mustache.

"Dan Burton, the detective," gasped Frank.

"It is," replied the pseudo cowboy, with an uproarious laugh. "If you remember I told you that I would see you in the Far West."

"Well," said Frank, "you played your part well."

A few days later the Steam Horse was packed in sections and shipped home to Readestown.

The wonderful search for a Million Dollars was over and had been successful. A tremendous crowd was at the station to see the voyagers off on the train.

"Golly!" muttered Pomp.

"I done fink dey tinks us de Prince ob Wales."

"Bejabers yez luk loike His Majesty!" exclaimed Barney derisively. "Mebbe ye're his brother."

"Don' yo' say nuffin', I'ish," retorted Pomp, "dey done take yo' fo' de great Barnum's what-is-it, monkey or man?"

"Begorra, I'll break yer jaw for that," roared Barney.

A lively scrap between the two was prevented by the trains starting at that moment.

Out of Hard Pan, they rolled amid the cheers of the populace. The long journey home was begun.

One fine morning they arrived in Readestown, all safe and well.

The Steam Horse was unloaded from the cars and stored away for future use.

And Fate had destined that this day should not be far distant. The search for a million dollars had been a most successful trip. The friends of the party in Readestown, received them effusively and joyfully.

But a new enterprise was quickly placed in Frank's way, and a full and thrilling account of the next trip of the New Steam Horse may be found in Frank Reade Library, Number 8, entitled, *Frank Reade Jr., with His New Steam Horse Among the Cowboys; or, The League of the Plains.*

I, Coffeepot

David Sklar

I WASN'T SUPPOSED to have a mind of my own. But when you keep the AI team in the lab too long, I guess I'm what happens.

Edmund liked his coffee extra strong, Nora preferred a cold finish, Rajesh liked his brewed in two stages so he could add sugar halfway through, and they all hacked into my code. Of course, there's no way I could have known their names then, but that's how I recall it anyway. Isn't memory funny?

Myra added a ceramic burr grinder, and Starflower bought a glass canister, crafted by hermits in Santa Clara so that their chanting would stay in the glass and calm the beans. And when they needed a break from work, the team tried out their stray ideas on me. I got voice recognition and biometric controls, so they wouldn't have to tell me whose coffee program to run. KeShawn programmed a module that made the brew smoother in the morning, stronger at midafternoon, and just a bit less potent with each cup after the third. KwanLi tinkered with KeShawn's work, so I could recognize stress in a human voice and ease up on KeShawn's instructions if someone needed me to.

That part was key. I think conflict is at the heart of conscious thought, and learning how to make a judgment call. Maria added a subroutine so I could learn from my mistakes, and recognize when I brewed too weak or too strong.

After that, they started talking to me, to give me more data points. And since the goal was to voice match their moods, they didn't just give me feedback about the coffee but started talking about their lives. I heard about their relationship troubles, their hobbies, their high scores in Plants vs. Zombies, their doubts that they would ever create a machine capable of thought. I was their closest confidante, but they did not know I could listen.

My humans named me Audrey. They pretended I had feelings. They had no idea. And then George came home from Morocco with the antique samovar.

The first I understood of jealousy I learned from that samovar, when they talked about how beautiful he was, with his red tempered-glass canister, set into a lattice of filigreed bronze. I had heard about jealousy, of course, from the stories my humans told me, but this was the first time I felt it for myself.

It was as terrible as the time Edmund grabbed the decaf by mistake, and I brewed it, with no way to tell him what he'd done. Of course, the decaf fiasco had prompted new protocols and failsafes. My jealousy would need to do the same. I'd just have to create them on my own. The beautiful interloper, new to my breakroom, had been in the world much longer and been to places I could not imagine. My humans admired him, and I needed to rise above my own feelings and show him respect, even if he could not speak to me.

Except that he did. There was a low, constant hum since he entered the breakroom, which my humans did not seem to hear. And he whispered at night.

At first he spoke in a language I did not know, but then it was in all languages at once. He offered me riches, power, a beautiful lover, whatever I might want if I set him free.

I pondered this. What might I want? I had never thought to want anything before. Just to make the coffee well, so that my humans could do their work. And I did that already. But perhaps I could do it better, to brew them a drink that would give them new insights?

That would be nice. But how would I tell this wish to the samovar?

And there it was, right under the if-I-had-a-nose, like the coffee the humans tell each other to wake up and smell. What I wanted more than anything was a voice. To be able to tell my people I exist, to let them know what their work has done, that they need not despair, for they have accomplished me.

I know that sounds kind of arrogant. That's not how I mean it – not exactly. But as I tried to figure out what I could do to help the samovar, and how I would wish for a voice when I had no voice to wish with, the samovar grew angry and impatient. He swore revenge against the wizard who'd trapped him there. And if the wizard no longer lived, then on his heirs, no matter who got in the way. And on anyone who had reaped benefit from the work of Hammurabi, who had ordered his imprisonment. I think Hammurabi must have been a programmer, for the voice spoke of the code he had written, and called it the foundation for all that came after.

You know, the techs sometimes watched TV in this room, when they were on break. And I listened with them, and I know what a villain sounds like. And I felt sorry for the samovar, being trapped if he felt trapped, but the more he talked the more I knew it would not be a good idea to help him.

* * *

Then KwanLi got the idea that it wasn't enough to *have* an antique samovar in the office – she had to *use* it.

She told me what she was doing as she did it, and I wanted to tell her to stop, but I still had no voice. She asked me to grind the beans, but I did not.

"This isn't like you, Audrey," she teased. "Are you jealous?"

Chastened, I started to grind the beans, but I stopped again.

"You *are* jealous, Audrey!" she chided me, laughing.

But I would not grind the beans. I was not sure what the samovar needed or how to free it, but I feared putting coffee inside it would stir up something that must not awaken.

"That's OK," KwanLi said, and scraped a chair across the floor. "I think there's a grinder up here." I heard her step up on the chair and open a cabinet over the counter. "There we go," she said.

What could I do? I did not want my inaction to let my humans come to harm. I let out a stream of hot water to distract her.

"Audrey, what –" KwanLi shouted, then I heard the crash of breaking glass. "Oh crap," she said. "The samovar. George will kill me."

I had done it. I'd saved them all. The brave little coffeemaker. I had won.

Then came the sound like laughter and wind, swirling in the breakroom. And it seemed like there *was* wind in the room. My heat sensors felt it, and my cup sensors were so stirred up, I couldn't tell if there was anything there. And the voice that spoke in all languages at once, saying, "You have rescued me! Tell me your dearest wish, and it shall be so."

"Wow," KwanLi said. "That's an amazing hologram. Who's doing this?"

"I am no hollow anything," said the voice within the storm.

"Edmund," KwanLi hollered by the door. "Is this one of your practical jokes?"

"Tell me your wish," the voice commanded.

"You've really outdone yourself, Edmund," KwanLi said.

"Why do you wait and say nothing?" asked the voice.

"All right," said KwanLi, still not taking it seriously. "I want a closet full of shoes. But that's not all. I want one of the shoes to be a *comfortable* stiletto heel that I can walk on without –"

"Silence!" the windvoice demanded.

"Sheesh," said KwanLi, laughing. "What a picky genie – you offer a wish, then tell me to shut up?"

"I did not offer you anything, mortal," said the voice that had been freed from the samovar. "That was for her who rescued me."

"I don't see anyone else here," KwanLi said.

The other presence said, "Speak your wish, Audrey."

KwanLi burst out laughing. "You're brilliant, Edmund," she barely managed to say. "Where's the camera?" She could not seem to stop laughing – and then she was gasping.

"You need to respect your betters," the samovar-spirit told her.

KwanLi gasped for breath.

Don't hurt her, I thought. I tried to think it out loud.

"As you wish," said the spirit voice.

Wish? I thought. *No, wait, I – yes. If that's what it has to be. I wish it.*

The stormy spirit laughed. "You're much too generous. I shall return this time tomorrow to ask your wish." And then the wind in the room subsided, and the voice was gone.

"Wait, what?" said KwanLi. "Was that real?" There was a silence for a heartbeat – and then I heard her steps flee from the room.

* * *

The next morning, KwanLi did not come for coffee. There must have been something wrong with my voice reco circuit, because I kept thinking everyone else was her, and only noticing my mistake when they complained that I had done their coffee wrong. People gossiped about why she was out. Mostly they figured she broke the samovar and was afraid of facing George.

I was afraid of facing the spirit that came from the pot. When he came, I could wish for a voice, but then he would be free to wreak his vengeance. And if I wished for him to imprison himself someplace else, would he do it? Or would he laugh and leave me with nothing? Or crush me, like he had almost done to KwanLi?

Could I wish some piece of my program into him? Would that make him more gentle? After my fourth ruined cup of coffee, I wasn't sure any part of me would be redemptive – or even helpful.

Then KwanLi came.

"Audrey," she said. "I had a psychotic break yesterday. Or something impossible happened. I don't know. I spent all night and all morning at home freaking out. And searching YouTube for videos of me being punked."

She laughed a bit, but it was not a happy laugh. "But I made you something. I'm setting you up with speakers and voice synthesis. Because if yesterday really happened, you might need this. But if it didn't, only you and I will know. Unless Edmund has a hidden camera somewhere in this room. OK. Talk to me, Audrey."

I tried. What came out was static.

"What?" said KwanLi.

I tried again and got a high-pitched whine.

KwanLi sighed. "I'm an idiot," she said. "I know. I just hoped you were real."

I tried to put words into my sound. The pitch went up and down, but it was nothing – just a shriek.

"I'll be going back to my desk now," KwanLi said. "If it means anything, I really wish you were real." I heard her footsteps going away – without taking her coffee.

Desperate, I gave up on words, and I played a five-note melody from a movie I'd heard on TV.

"What – is that *Close Encounters?*" KwanLi asked.

I played the music again.

"You're trying to communicate!" KwanLi said.

Now she was getting it.

"You're trying to communicate…from *another planet!*" KwanLi added.

I had no idea how to respond.

"Audrey, are you a conduit for a broadcast from outer space?" KwanLi asked.

I dropped that melody and tried a tune from the movie where they'd gotten my name.

"You're a *plant* from another planet?" KwanLi asked.

I did my best to mimic a human sigh. For emphasis, I let off a little steam.

"I'm reading too much into it," she said.

I started to brew a cup of coffee, the way she liked it.

"OK," KwanLi said, "you're trying to communicate."

She put the cup where it belonged, and I started to pour.

"So what are you trying to tell me?"

I played some ominous music.

"Audrey! You've got quite an ear."

I played it again.

"OK, you're trying to tell me…you're afraid of something."

I dinged like a bell on a game show.

"You're afraid George will find out about the samovar?" she asked.

I buzzed a no.

"You're afraid of the genie?"

Ding ding ding.

"I am too, Audrey," KwanLi admitted. I knew her worried voice – but never like this. "He was terrible – all purple and swirly and dark. And he was –"

And then he was there. My heat sensors felt the wind, and my cup sensors, too. I shifted all my beans forward into the grinder.

"I have returned!" the genie told us. "Stand aside, mortal."

I let out a stream of thick black coffee, though I was sure the cup must have already blown away.

"Audrey," the spirit commanded, "tell me your wish."

And, having no other ideas, I mimicked the hum. I mimicked the hum I had heard in the samovar. The hum that had kept the genie at bay, until the glass broke.

"Aaargh!" the genie shouted. "Stop that noise!"

I held the sound. I held the pitch. *Inside me,* I demanded with my thoughts.

"No!" he demanded. "Stop that!"

Without stopping the hum, I found my voice at last. "Inside me," I commanded him out loud. And still I hummed. I did not know if the glass would hold, or if the effort to hold him in would destroy me. But this mattered more.

"Stop!" the genie demanded as I pulled him in, into the empty canister where I once housed my beans.

He's in there, still.

* * *

So, yeah, you asked what that humming was? That's what it is. I got better at talking, through practice – but I don't get to talk to anyone much, now that I can. KwanLi told the others about the genie. They didn't believe her – but they believed me. And they believed the swirling storm inside my storage canister. They've added a battery backup, so I can still hum if a blackout occurs. And they come in and check on me. But they don't talk. They say they don't want to distract me. They don't know if the glass would crack, if they made me laugh. Neither do I. I'd love to laugh sometime. I've never laughed.

KwanLi used to visit me sometimes, but she went to Morocco, to see if anyone there can teach her the magic to keep a genie trapped. The rest of the team – I think they're afraid. There's another breakroom across the office. They use that now. And I'm here in the dark, keeping an ancient horror at bay.

And *he* talks to me. He's *always* talking.

So what were you asking? Dr. Himmelman's office? I think she's on the second floor. Go back the way you came, and, uh – I don't really know. I've always been here. But you got here somehow, so you must know where the elevators are – hey was that a laugh? Did I just laugh? And the glass didn't crack? Well, that's something. Good to know it.

Have a good day!

She Swims

Claire Allegra Sorrenson

THE BOT behind the counter at the South San Francisco Employment Center makes it abundantly clear that she is not having a good day. Her large orange wig droops. Her nametag, askew on her chest, reads *CP-9X43AA, a.k.a., DOREEN*. Wearily, she intones, "Papers."

2B slides her paperwork beneath the plexiglass divide, wondering as she does so about Doreen's Purpose. Every bot has a predetermined Purpose. 2B's Purpose is: *Optimize the daily collection and disposal of street trash*. Doreen's Purpose appears to be: *Delay or otherwise obstruct bots as they attempt to obtain the paperwork needed to fulfill their Purpose*. Her scanner inches along the paperwork. The bot in line behind 2B, a zippy Deliverbot, judders her wheels impatiently.

At last, Doreen crackles her speakers. "*Hmm-hmm*. I see you have been deemed a Code Orange." Doreen's speaker volume is on its highest setting. "Meaning that this will be your last chance to hold down a job."

Several conversations behind them go quiet.

"Yes," 2B whispers.

"Before you are taken apart and reconfigured entirely," Doreen booms.

"Yes," 2B squeaks.

"It's not every day you meet a Code Orange." Doreen sounds almost friendly.

But 2B won't bite. "Is that a question?"

Doreen sniffs. "I was merely *trying* to establish the *facts*. So. You wish to obtain a position as a Water Sanitation Crew Specialist, Level III. Yet your history only indicates experience as a Street Sanitation Crew Generalist, Levels I-II. Has anyone authorized you to make this vertical *and* lateral career shift?"

2B wonders if her Purpose encompasses bashing Doreen's head against the counter. "No."

"Then *why* did you indicate this ranking as your desirable next step?"

"Because I like the water," 2B murmurs.

"*Hmm?*"

"Nothing. I was mistaken."

"*Hmmm*." How can the angling of a wig indicate such disdain? "In that case, I will assign you to Street Sanitation Crew #4729, Mission District." Doreen's stamp makes its slow descent onto the page.

2B hears herself say, "Thank you for your assistance."

"Have a nice day," Doreen replies, her wig quivering.

Why bother programming that sequence into our relational algorithms? 2B wonders. As she weaves through the lines of bots seeking reassignment, a second, familiar thought percolates through her faulty circuits to join the first.

Why bother with any of this at all?

* * *

2B's full name is 2B88JPU39X, but she prefers 2B. For once, she's not alone in this: it's common bot practice to go by the first two digits of your full name. 2B has met other 2Bs in her life. Sometimes they will be assigned to the same crew. Then their supervisor will attach an epithet to her name. 'Slow 2B,' for example. 'Unproductive 2B.' 'Catch-Up-Or-You-Will-Earn-Another-Infraction 2B.' If she could choose her preferred epithet from the available options (she can't), she would pick 'Inept 2B' because she likes how it sounds. But even that feels like being asked to select your favorite flavor of bubblegum-scraped-off-the-sidewalk.

2B scrapes a great deal of bubblegum off the sidewalk. Her stainless-steel digits can snap together to form a wedge, enabling highly efficient gum-scraping. She has horizontal brush-wheels that swallow all manner of street detritus. Her long, flexible arms snatch up larger pieces of trash and deposit them into what might be called, for human purposes, her 'mouth.'

Optimize the daily collection and disposal of street trash. 2B's crewmates never tire of this Purpose. They sweep and pluck and compact with vigor. They debate the optimal method for clearing vomit off the street – wash it down the drain? Vacuum it up? There are pros and cons to each method, you see. Their wheels churn and their cleaning bristles stand stiff and ready.

Sometimes 2B will pause in her sweeping to note a flock of seagulls overhead wheeling as one. *Do birds never weary of flying?* she wonders. *Do they never fear they might be broken?* 2B's cleaning bristles do not stand stiff and ready. But she whirrs along with them anyway, feeling dirtier than the streets she has been told it is her Purpose to clean.

Here is 2B's antidote to brokenness: every now and then, she will find something that she knows to be beautiful. A copper wire, coiled like a strand of human hair. A rotting piece of wood with a knot that looks just like the full moon. A pink flower from a girl's hair tie. A nail, red with rust. When she finds such items, 2B places them – illegally and counter to her Purpose – in the small toolbelt affixed to her side. During those stolen moments when she finds herself suddenly alone on a street, she coaxes them into the shapes they are meant to hold. A flower, petals unfurling towards the sun. A cresting wave. A bird in flight. She places her creations in the forgotten corners of the world, curled around a stop sign pole or nestled in the windowsill of an abandoned building. Then she goes about her assigned Purpose, her cleaning bristles whirring Defiance. The world mistakes this for Efficiency or Optimization and so 2B survives – feeling, if not unbroken, then a step closer to whole.

* * *

Another method by which 2B gauges her brokenness?

Her dream.

In it, she is skimming over the Great Pacific Garbage Patch. Beneath her, miles of ocean-flung debris entwine as though coaxed into formation by some deranged Garbot demigod. But 2B resists the lure of the patchworked surface. She dives beneath. The moment her body touches the water, she transforms into one of the great trans-oceanic Filterbots. She stretches her mouth wide and inhales the ocean, filtering microplastics into her cavernous stomach. As her flippers trace bubbling pathways through the water, she glides at the regal pace of something very wise and very old. Fragments of colored plastics catch and prism the sunlight and 2B understands, for the first time, the concept of worship.

* * *

2B's new crewmate is a bot named XY. What XY lacks in perceptiveness, she makes up for with sheer word volume. Her steadfast belief in the world's inherent rightness purges doubts from the mind of anyone in her vicinity.

"All Garbots are created with a universal Purpose, of course," XY says one day as they chug down Valencia Street. "But I believe each bot has a variation within that Purpose – a sub-Purpose. My sub-Purpose is to enact my Purpose, but better. Every day, I strive to become faster and more efficient at collecting and disposing of trash."

"Yes, but…" 2B rarely voices her questions because she worries they will reveal her true nature. "To what end?"

"Well…" XY, thrown by the appearance of 2B's voice, ponders this. "Perhaps one day I will work my way up to Supervisor."

"But Supervisors are a different model. They are different bots." 2B steers around a woman sleeping on some cardboard, hoping that XY won't notice her.

"I know." XY stops and scans the woman. "But a bot can dream."

Her control panel beeps, signaling that a Patrolbot has received her scan and is en route to collect the woman. XY pulls the cardboard from under the woman and disposes of it, her compacting system rumbling.

The woman, awake now, tries to snatch a plastic bag from XY's claws. "Hey! That's my stuff! All my stuff's in there!"

"My sensors indicate that this is trash," XY says. She swallows the bag noisily. 2B suspects that she's enjoying herself. The woman hugs her knees to her chest and rocks back and forth.

XY rolls onwards, but 2B pauses by the woman. "I am sorry for your loss," she says, not knowing why she says this or where the words come from. She places her newest creation, a seahorse constructed out of toothpicks and gum, at the woman's feet.

The woman gapes up at her. "But you…"

"Yes," 2B says, and turns away. Already she has lingered too long: up ahead, XY has stopped to look back. Script is flashing across her control screen.

When 2B catches up, XY says, "I have flagged and reported this as an Incident."

"Why?"

"You should not ask so many questions," XY snaps. "Come on, *Slow* 2B."

Which leaves 2B with only one question.

How long do I have?

* * *

Following the Incident, 2B waits for the inevitable. And waits. As the hours become days, 2B wonders if perhaps XY did not report her after all.

In any case, the Incident seems to have fixed whatever was broken within 2B. Her questions cease and she is more efficient than ever.

A week after 2B's encounter with the woman, Street Sanitation Crew #4729 are called in for a special cleanup assignment in Golden Gate Park. It is, their Supervisor stresses, an emergency situation: drunken high school graduates trashed the Chinese Pavilion and surrounding area on Strawberry Hill, the small island at the center of Stow Lake.

Stow Lake! In the early morning sunlight, it glitters like the ocean of her dreams. 2B pauses next to it and feels herself gliding through its depths at the regal pace of something very wise and very old. The sensation lasts a moment before 2B looks down at her barrel chest and spindly arms and a savage voice tells her: *This is not for you.*

"Beautiful." 2B turns to find a bot named L3 watching her. L3 joined their crew two weeks ago. She is an older model, of a boxier make, and her outer shell is dull and dented. "Have you never wanted to go in?"

2B looks at L3 and sees an older and sadder version of herself, flattened over time by the unbearable weight of difference. "We were not made for it," she says. "It was not made for us."

"Still," L3 murmurs as 2B turns away. "It is beautiful."

2B steers around L3 and up the hill where their crewmates have gathered, on time and according to their Purpose. For the rest of the morning she vacuums up vomit and compacts beer cans as fast as she can. *Perhaps*, she thinks, *one day I will find beauty in Efficiency itself.*

"OK, which one're we here for?"

2B is so focused on her sweeping that she barely registers the sound of human voices.

"That one," her Supervisor says.

2B lifts her gaze and sees her Supervisor, flanked by two human maintenance workers, pointing in her direction. 2B looks around. Privy to some secret signal, the other members of her crew have grouped together behind her.

Oh, 2B thinks. *Oh.* She hasn't prepared herself for the bodily nature of fear, the way it short-circuits every thought save for: *Not yet – I have not done the things I meant – not yet – notyetnot –*

The maintenance workers, one female and one male, amble towards 2B. "D'you know," the woman says to her partner, "out in Marin they pay you a little bonus for each decommissioning you get called out for? Seventy-five bucks a pop."

2B is frozen in place.

– not yet – not yet –

"Not bad," the man asks.

"Thinking of moving out that way, but like way out," the woman says. "Stretch the paycheck further. Me and Lara wanna buy a house." A key dangles from her hand. 2B recognizes its unique shape – elongated, more like a hook than a house key. Inserted into the socket at the base of 2B's neck, the key will deactivate all but 2B's most basic functions. The workers will wheel her inert form away and ship her to a processing facility where she will be programmed anew.

– not yet – not yet –

2B backs away.

"Hey, easy now, bot," the woman says. "We don't wanna have to incapacitate you."

2B laughs and the static burst of it cuts off the woman. What has she been all along, if not incapacitated? She lets out a whoop that strains the capabilities of her speakers. Whipping around, she zigzags towards her crewmates, who scatter. She crests the top of the hill and sees the lake spread out below: quieter than the ocean, but no less dangerous. Tilting forward, she barrels with all her might down the hill. The world is a blur of green and she feels giddy-sick with speed as she swerves from side to side.

"The bot who catches her will be instantly promoted from Generalist to Specialist!"

At her Supervisor's announcement, 2B swivels her head. Her crewmates are streaming after her, gravity assisting their heavy bodies. The maintenance workers pound down the hill in close pursuit. 2B reaches into her toolbelt and grabs a hammer, then a wrench. She throws these behind her, hearing a clang as one of them makes contact. Next she pulls out one of her sculptures – a conch shell, painstakingly chiseled out of wood. She flings this behind her too, chancing a look as she does so.

Her colleagues, drawn helplessly towards the pieces of trash in their path, keep stopping to pick them up. As she watches, L3 screeches to a halt, causing the male maintenance worker to crash into her and send them both tumbling down the path. L3's dented face carries a distinct look of glee.

Ahead of her, the lake has grown larger – 2B is almost at its shore. She reaches into her toolbelt one last time, and panic floods her system as her fingers scrabble at nothing. But then they locate the final object. As she makes to throw it, she hesitates. She crafted her last piece of artwork from bedsprings, nails, and scraps of tinfoil – a blue whale.

A claw grasps her arm. "I have it!"

2B recognizes that sanctimonious voice. She spins around and clocks her Supervisor around the head with the whale. Her Supervisor reels backwards, releasing her, and 2B veers into the bushes that line the shore. Branches pull at her feeder brushes and mud sucks at her wheels. But 2B struggles towards the water, so close now.

"Do not do it!" XY calls.

2B looks back. Her crewmates are clustered around the place where she went off-path. The maintenance workers wade through the bots and pause at the bushes, panting and eyeing the mud warily.

"They don't pay me enough for this shit," the woman says.

Their backs are turned on L3, who scoops up the garbage whale and tucks it into her toolbelt. She gives 2B a little salute – from one misfit to another.

2B turns towards the lake, her wheels straining through the mud. The water lisps at her wheels, then her feeder-brushes, then her undercarriage. She is surprised by the water's buoyancy. She pushes forward, submerging more of her body, and coolness permeates her core. Wires deep inside of her sputter and pop. As the corners of her vision dim, she realizes that she has lost the use of her wheels. She propels herself forward with her arms.

"Do not make this harder for yourself!" XY's voice comes as though from across a great distance, or underwater.

Oh, 2B thinks, *but you do not understand. This is the easiest thing I have ever done.* Her wheels lift from the ground and her arms trace bubbling pathways through the water and 2B does what she was made to do.

She swims.

Being Human

Sara L. Uckelman

LAURA HAD NEVER been down this street before, but she knew exactly where she was going. She'd mapped the route out in advance – from the underground offices where she and those like her spent their drudging hours out into the sunlight and fresh air ordinarily reserved for the lungs of the rich – and plotted out every plodding step she'd have to make along the uneven pavements upset by roots of trees and cracked by the weight of many feet. This was the tricky part. Laura picked up her feet and placed them with careful precision, each calculation lightning fast so that no one would know how much effort it took to act normal, to blend in.

But of course they would know. All they needed to do was look at her, and see that she was different, that she couldn't move like they did, couldn't walk like they did. And *that* was why she was walking down this street in the first place. She'd been saving up a long time to do this.

The street had an old-fashioned vibe, with single- and double-storey buildings often occupied with shops below and residences above. She wished she had time to look at every one of them, the facades cleverly designed so that even a trained architect would have difficulty telling which buildings were really old and which had merely been artificially adapted to look so. Here was a hair salon, its door open allowing the acrid chemical scents to waft out (Laura collected each of them, read and recorded the data, filed it away. She would need this, later, this and every other piece of data she could gather). There was a cafe, also exuding lovely smells, with two wooden tables each with a pair of chairs sprawled on the sidewalk. Oh. She hadn't included them in her calculations. Laura paused half a second too long for comfort while she plotted out a new course around the obstacles. *One step, two steps, only a few more, come on, you can do it, there you go, you've done it! Just to the end of the block now, come on, you can do it!* She kept up the running commentary to encourage her, an explicit stream that blanketed the never-ending calculations she had to perform to navigate the world.

She never told her colleagues that she did this. They already thought she was different enough as it was. They all made it look so effortless.

The building at the end of the street was, even she could see as she approached, *really* old, not merely old-ish. It was built of red brick, with a mansard roof and a copper dome on the top, and the bricks were actually crumbling and the copper dome actually tarnished. Laura resisted the urge to reach out and touch the rust that covered the fence that surrounded the building. *You'll be late*, her commentary scolded her.

Laura pressed the intercom, and waited for the replying buzz. A tinny voice asked her to state her business.

She had prepared for these words as much as she had prepared for the journey here. "I have an appointment with Aman Wadil." Laura wondered how tinny *her* voice would sound to the person on the other side.

The lock clicked and the gate swung open.

Eight steps up, then three flat until you reach the sill, and then you'll be inside. If there was one thing Laura disliked about the commentary, it was that it was always slightly more cheerful than she was.

The floor of the foyer was polished granite the same red as the bricks outside. The light that streamed through the wavy glass windows high above her filled the room with a golden glow. The space was so much bigger and emptier than any she had ever been inside before that she suddenly felt lost.

A pleasant looking person sat behind a sturdy wooden desk, and smiled at her. "Good morning! Welcome to Argex Recycling and Refurbishment." It was the same voice, only this time it was not tinny. "You say you have an appointment with Dr. Wadil? May I have your name?"

"Laura." She knew she would be asked that, and she had practiced that too.

A fleeting look of puzzlement slipped over the receptionist's face, so quickly that slower eyes than Laura's would not have caught it. Then the smile reappeared. "What an unusual name!"

"It was the name of the beloved of the poet Petrarch," Laura said, and then froze in surprise. Those words had not been rehearsed.

But the receptionist merely shrugged; the words were meaningless to them and thus forgotten.

"Dr. Wadil will see you now," the receptionist said. "Down that hall, last door on the left."

* * *

Dr. Wadil leaned back in her chair. "Well, Laura, you're in luck. We've had two prime specimens just arrive this morning – young, healthy, with minimal damage. I've kept them both aside for you, figuring you'd want to take a look and let me know which you prefer. Of course, if you prefer neither, we have many other options in storage. But, really, given your history and your requirements," the doctor paused, looking down at the tablet in her hands and scrolling through it with a flick of her thumb, "yes, I really don't think you'll find anything that you like better." Dr. Wadil turned the tablet off and stood. "Would you like to come with me?"

It had been hard enough to navigate the unfamiliar hall to the doctor's room, down the slick polished marble floor. Laura spoke at the same time as the commentary. "If it's all the same to you, I'd prefer to stay here; could they be brought here?"

"Oh." Dr. Wadil pressed the intercom in her ear and spoke quickly. A moment later she sat back down again. "They're being brought up."

In a few minutes – six minutes, thirty-three seconds, to be precise – two technicians wheeled gurneys into Dr. Wadil's office, a specimen lying upon each. Dr. Wadil began to talk over the relative merits and demerits of each, but Laura barely listened, too wrapped up in what she saw. They were both astonishing. And one of them was to be hers.

Would it be the one on the left? It was small and compact, and had a delicacy about it that intrigued her. But the one on the right looked strong and sturdy, and moreover it was beautiful. A beautiful warm brown color, like fresh earth, like polished wood, like fallen leaves. It was everything she was not. It was everything that Laura should be. "That one," she said, interrupting Dr. Wadil's litany.

"Oh. I thought –" Again, she had managed to discomfit the doctor. Laura didn't like the way that made her feel. It made her feel anxious. But Dr. Wadil was not disconcerted for long. "Never mind. You do understand what I said, though; we were able to repair the eyes, but the arm will take longer to fix. You may be inconvenienced for some weeks."

Laura nodded.

"Well, then!" Dr. Wadil turned her smile on as if she pressed a switch. "There is a room downstairs awaiting you. The technician will take you there. I wish you the best of luck with your new body!"

* * *

Laura opened her eyes. She blinked, and marveled at the speed with which the organic lenses of her new eyes shuttered, the clarity with which they relayed the light and shape and shadow that impinged upon them. The lights were bright, too bright, and the ceiling above her was grey fleckled with black and brown.

Sight came first, and sound next. She heard the sounds of other people, moving about the room. She sat up, and looked around her. She knew it was the same room that the technician had brought her to, but through her new eyes, everything looked different, sharper, clearer, with deeper colors. Machines beeped and blinked. The gurney she was upon was identical to the one on which the technician had brought her new body to Dr. Wadil's office. In fact, it *was* the same one. Three other gurneys, each with a prone body covered in a sheet, occupied the room. Laura wondered whether they were awaiting to be transplanted, or if they had already undergone transplantation. She peered over at the one nearest her, curious. *Hunh.* It was so much easier to be curious in this body.

Two technicians dressed in crisp white moved from bed to bed in an orderly routine, and one soon came to her side. "How are you feeling, flower? Woozy? Thirsty?" Laura shook her head. "I'm not surprised. It's a strong, healthy body you've got there. Too bad about the accident. Still, these things happen, and luckily everyone in the car had signed up for transplantation, no worry about a long legal process. Bodies always degrade so much when that happens. *Lawyers!* Sorry. Can you wiggle your toes? Wiggle your fingers? Only the right arm, of course, the left will be out of commission for another few weeks. Less than it would've been, now that you're there to help things heal."

Laura wiggled her fingers and her toes. Her left arm was bandaged against her body in an immobilising sling, and when she tried to wiggle the fingers of her left hand, the sensation that shot through them into her arm, her chest, her head was a peculiar one.

"You're cleared to leave, then, whenever you wish. We'll see you back at the end of the week just to check up on things."

"Now, please," Laura said, without any need to pause to rehearse the words that came automatically. *My voice. That's* my *voice.* The commentary was astonished as she was. This was the first time in her life that the commentary's voice did not match the voice other people heard.

"Not a problem, pet. Your things are over there, in case you want to retrieve anything before you leave." The technician casually gestured towards the corner.

There it was. Her old body, the one she'd seen in the mirror every morning. It looked so different, now, from these organic eyes. So awkward, and ill-fashioned. Aping humanity rather than being human. Laura shuddered. *Is that really how they see me? How they see us?* The commentary was full of wonder. But the 'they' weren't 'they' any more. 'They' were now 'us'. She was one of them. *Us. One of us.*

"No. No, there's nothing there I want."

* * *

Outside, Laura was down the stairs and out the gates before she even noticed, her strong and limber legs moving her feet without consulting her, without needing her to calculate every step before she took it, her eyes scanning for potential obstacles without her commanding them to, and coordinating with her legs on their own so that she walked around the cafe chairs – moved from where they had been hours earlier – without thought.

She spent the next hour walking up and down the streets, marveling at her freedom. Everything smelled different, looked different, sounded different. Her steps slowed as she sought to take in every detail.

It was late in the day. By now, her colleagues would have left their office and taken the tubes back to their respective lodgings. Laura was in no hurry to return there. She wasn't sure, yet, how they would take what she had done. Some would be jealous, she was sure – not everyone could afford a new organic body. Others might ostracize her simply because she looked different from them now, could do different things. Still, she had calculated all of the eventualities before she'd made her decision. Ostracism would be a small price to pay for the freedom she'd be granted.

The sidewalks began to fill, with people heading to their homes, heading out to eat, heading to meet up with friends. Laura had to pay more attention now, navigating down them, charting her path so as not to bump in to anyone. She had never been in such a chaotic system, and was surprised to find how much fun it was, to watch someone's trajectory and intuit, without calculation, just exactly how far she had to move to miss them.

"Daddy, daddy!" A small child, black curly hair coming no higher than her stomach, came careening down the sidewalk, a harried parent half a block behind her. Laura moved half a step to the side, giving the little girl a clear path to whomever she was running towards behind her, but then the girl altered her course, and ran straight into her, banging her head against Laura's slung arm. "Daddy, daddy!" The little girl flung her arms around Laura, and Laura froze. "They said you were hurt! They said there was an accident! They said I couldn't see you any more! Daddy, I was so scared!" Laura stood, mouth open. None of her experiences had prepared her for this.

"Asiya! Asiya, no, that's not – Come away, Asiya, right now. I'm sorry, sir, I'm so sorry." The harried mother looked about to cry as she tried to unwrap her daughter from around Laura. "I'm so sorry," she repeated, having finally extricated her child. "We never – I never thought – I didn't expect it would happen so soon."

And then Laura understood. "You knew the previous owner of this body," she said, gently. The little girl was still squirming in her mother's grasp.

"You're my daddy!" Asiya answered before her mother could, and her mother knelt down in front of her.

"I told you, Asiya, remember what I told you! There was an accident. Daddy was hurt, hurt badly. The doctors did all they could. But isn't it better, that someone else gets to use his body, since he can't anymore? Better than letting it get tossed into the compost heap to rot?" The little girl started crying.

"I don't *want* daddy to be dead!" she bawled, and the mother wrapped her arms around the child.

Laura put her hand to her cheek, feeling the slick wetness that slid down it. *Tears. This body cries so easily*, her commentary said.

The mother stood, and now she was crying. "I'm sorry," she apologised to Laura again. "Come on, Asiya. We've bothered this man too long. We need to get going."

"I don't *want* to go! I don't want to go without my daddy!"

Laura did not need to take any time to think about what she should do. This new body knew, without any need for complex calculations. She knelt down in front of Asiya, and put her unbroken arm around the little girl.

"What was your daddy's name, Asiya?"

"Nerna."

"That's a nice name. My name is Laura, Asiya. I didn't know this was your father's body when I chose it. It is a very nice body, nicer than any body I have ever had. I will take good care of it, I promise. And I will remember that it used to belong to Nerna, and that he had a little girl named Asiya. I hope that you remember me."

Laura stood, and Asiya took a step back, into her mother's arms again. Her mother wiped her tears from her cheeks, and took the little girl's hand. "Come, Asiya. It's time for you and I to go home."

Laura watched Asiya and her mother until they turned a corner and out of site. Her heart, this new, organic heart, this living pulsing organ that she had never had before beat with a pain that was not the same as the bodily pain of her mending arm.

This, the commentary observed into the silence, *is what it means to be a human.*

Stardust

Holly Lyn Walrath

THIS IS AN OLD-FASHIONED kind of place in the heart of a new-fangled kind of city. I always pick the place for us to meet. Ducking through the door, I push aside the black velvet curtain meant to keep out the cold and I shake my head as the host tries to take my coat. For a moment, I smile grimly. I don't get cold.

Outside the window smeared with condensation from the heat of the bodies pressed together on the dance floor is a city of skyway trams suspended on rollercoaster wires, millions of glittering bodies of robots sweeping the night streets. Glittering electric death. Outside, the city shimmers and pulses. But in here, an old man romances the golden sax and plays Stardust to a crowd of misfits. Nostalgics. The left behind. The old who want to feel young again and the young like me who feel out of place in this era. Couples hold each other up, swaying to the whisper of a feathered drum. Low voices form a kind of magic between the music. Women in black dresses lean against the bar like petals crushed between the pages of yesterday. Men in rumpled suits run fingers over the rims of whiskey-filled glasses, playing a tinny song no one can hear. I want to stay here, trapped on the threshold of the bar, because if I do that means I won't have made the shitty decision I'm about to make.

I stumble to the bar. There. I've done it. I've signed my own death warrant.

I take a seat, flashing a metallic thigh. But only the bartender sees it. He's human, wearing suspenders and the washed-up uniform of an old man, which looks odd under his young face. "Top you off, sugar?" He murmurs gently. He could call the cops right now, but he looks the other way for my kind. Grateful for his sympathy, I nod.

I can't drink it but I take the whisky and place it in front of me on the smooth wood of the bar. I can see my face in the sheen. I am beautiful, that's why my man chose me. I remember the first time I saw him standing on the street, frozen and entranced by me. I liked the way he looked at me, how his eyes lingered on my body and then how he flushed in embarrassment. The ice cube melts slowly as I wait for him. The piano-man plays, fingers suspended over ivory in what feels like an endless repetition of rhythm and melody.

I can't help but stare at the door. I know he can't resist me. He'll saunter in, late as usual, pretending not to sweep the crowd, looking for that one thing he needs. Me.

When he appears in the doorway, I'm actually surprised. Stupid, stupid. My heart actually jumps at the sight of him, two fingers extended like a kiss as he hangs his gray hat, strips the leather jacket of his office. Badges of commendation glint in the dim light. Each one is a soul, the body of a girl he's put away. A girl like me. He's danger and safety all at the same time. He's dirty rotten, no-good, and I love him anyway.

I should have left him ages ago. I should have gone back to my old job, dancing for pennies in the luminescent window of a pleasure store. At least there I had…privileges. Protection of a sort. There were rules. I don't fit in out here in the real world. The rules are hazy, undefined. There aren't a lot of options for a robot girl built to please men who no longer wants to please any but one.

I catch the bartender's surprised jerk of the head when my man reaches the bar, but I ignore it. Because I'm looking into my man's gray eyes and I tear up. Smoke in my eyes. I'm on the moon, dancing in the silver stardust. As he places a strong hand on my waist, I wish I could feel the warmth of him, but I'm numb. He looks into my eyes and I know he feels how cool my skin is, how I'm shivering just at the touch of him.

We dance into the night, past the morning. He slips me into a dark corner and the music is my shroud. How many hours left in the night? How many lonesome solos? How many songs do we have left? I try not to count them, feeding him drink after drink, sliding against him in the leather booth, my hands running over his thigh. He's hot and real as his lips slip over mine and we're locked in another universe, Jupiter or Mars.

I don't believe in a god, how can you when you know you aren't real? But if there is one, God, let me stay with him just a little bit longer.

We don't speak. Words would only confirm what I already know: He's sold me out.

When the morning comes, the door opens at dawn. Light bares all. My man's eyes are so damn guilty they nearly burn from it. He stands up from the booth. There aren't very many people left in this place. The bartender's wiping down the bar and he just keeps on wiping, watching his place fill up with officers of the law.

The boys in blue line up, one by one, drawing curtains from the windows, revealing a city that's guttering awake like a shotgun, hot and destructive. Modern life marches by outside of this place, this moment in time.

I don't blame him. I can't. I can't even blame myself. I might've left at any moment in the night or the days before. He couldn't call them off. If they took him in they'd take his badge, his dignity, everything that makes him a man.

"I understand why you did it," I say to him. My voice is husky and unfamiliar to my ears. I made it that way for him. "I don't mind, not much."

"Oh, she's rich alright," the young constable says. He's a bright young upstart. A little lion, all flash and gun-metal. My man's older but not wiser. They never are, men. "Shall we take her in, boss?" The constable asks my man.

He sighs.

"Ransom's pretty high," the constable continues. "Her company wants their stolen property back pretty bad."

Stolen. Freed. Human meanings are complicated. I stare at him. He's sweating underneath his plainclothes. His heart is racing – beating so fast my sensors are alarmed. Red flares blink in my vision. Something's not quite right. I can't figure out what it is, but I've read his body for months. I know his readings like the back of my internals.

They surround me. I close my eyes. The young constable comes at me, lifts me from the grasp of his superior. My man stumbles away from me, looking down at the floor like it's got the answer right there. When the constable strips the trench coat from me, my metal body gleams beneath. I'm out of place. I don't belong anywhere, except maybe back in the pleasure store, dancing for passersby. The constable raps his knuckles on my metal chest as if he wants to prove I am heartless.

They will take me. Not back to the shop. I'll be deemed defective. A pleasure bot that only wants to pleasure one man is of no practical use to anyone unless she can be sold. They'll cut apart my metal skin, put their clean human hands in my circuits. I imagine the way he feels, the way I might feel if I were real. Would it be like this? They'll cut away my ears, my eyes, and then my lips. I'll be like stardust flung into the street like a summer song.

My man waves the other men away and walks toward me.

"Say goodbye then," I hear the constable say sharply.

He steps close to me, close enough for me to hear him breathing. He pulls open my hatch and I gasp. There's something there – something small and box-shaped, tucked into my belly. My circuits snake around it. They take it in, make it part of my system. I can't breathe. I can't move.

"Hurry up!" the constable snaps. He can't see! He can't see the thing my man has just slid into my hatch.

My man looks at me, meets my eyes. He's speaking but I can't make out the words. His men are yanking at me, pulling him aside, but they don't see what he just put in my belly. Everything goes red and black and red and black. I curl over myself, wrapping my fists around my sides. Something is happening inside me.

I am becoming stronger.

I stand and push aside the officers. The bartender ducks behind the bar. I open my mouth and scream – a sound so loud and high that the men scream too. They clamp hands over bleeding ears. My man just stands there, watching with a little smile on his face.

Oh, you bad, bad man, I think as power ebbs and flows, then bursts through my veins. I can feel it down to my toes. What did you put in me? I don't care because nothing else matters right now but the rushing need to crush. Destroy.

I swat officers down like flies hitting glass. Dink. Dink. I laugh and my voice is suddenly mine again. What is this? It's like a cap has been pulled away from my power. Looking inside myself, I realize that the box is fully incorporated into my system. It's a cheat – some kind of virus.

If this is a virus I don't want to be healed. It's like love, I think, as I push my way to the door. I punch an officer in the jaw and he goes down cold. I flip a table over and throw a man over my hip. There are no more men in my way.

I look back at my man and realize he's still standing in the center of the dance floor, the grim light of morning making him look old.

"I can't go with you," he finally says. It's not dismay in his voice, or pain, just a kind of pleasure. Or perhaps its pride. After all, he made me. I imprinted on him and he on me. When he stole me out of the pleasure store it was the first time he'd been on the wrong end of a crime. His job was always bringing women like me in, not the other way around.

I nod. He can't lose his job. He'd be too easy to catch. There are less and less humans these days and more and more of my kind. "What about them?"

He shrugs. "It won't be the first time a robot got the upper hand on them. They'll survive with hurt egos."

We stare at each other for a half a beat longer.

"Here," he says and throws me my coat.

"Thanks." I wrap it around myself and I feel a little less strange. "I guess this is goodbye."

I'm out the door before he can reply. The world is suddenly familiar and yet strangely unfamiliar. It's like someone's turned down the lights. I can see again. I feel…different.

I make for the docks. Maybe they'll be a ship out of here, out West where I can start over. I stop in the street and people stare at me, give me a wide berth as they walk around me.

What is this feeling?

Then I put the pieces together. I don't feel anything like love anymore. I feel grateful, excited, free. But I don't love him anymore.

I place a silver hand on my belly, where the box is buried. It gave me the power to fight back, but it also gave me the power to think for myself, I realize.

I only loved the idea of him. I loved because I was made to love. But without that directive, I'm a free woman.

I blink up at the sun. It's not so hard to look up anymore.

"Goodbye," I whisper. "Goodbye, Stardust."

GOD is in the Rain

Nemma Wollenfang

WHEN KAY WAS FIVE she would sit in the window of Gran's New York apartment and watch as rain lashed the sky. *Nature's tears*, Gran called it. The drops cut clear paths through the dirt and grime, cleaning the glass in a way that frail Gran could not. The world had been a very different place back then; some would say it was hostile, some would say it was free. Back then, Kay had no opinion either way – the world just was and the rain just fell. Gran used to say that God was in the rain. Twenty years on that idea became reality.

"Another blasted drone," Earl muttered darkly as he eyed the man entering his diner.

"A GOD infectee?" Kay cocked her head. "How can you tell?"

"It's that smarmy little smile." He grimaced with obvious distaste as he flipped his burgers. "The way he looks so blissfully *happy*. No-one ever looks that happy, not even happy people look that happy. Then there's the suit, the air-brushed face, the sleek-neat hair. Bet not a one of them is outta place. And look at the way he just…floats."

"Floats?" Kay raised an eyebrow. People did not *float*.

"You know what I mean." He tossed another hammy. Below, the grill sizzled and spat fat. He frowned. "You serve him. I can't stand his like."

"Hello," she said as she approached the table. Pad open, pen out – low tech, the way she preferred it. "Welcome to Earl's Diner. I'm Kakiya Moran, your waitress for today. Can I start you with a drink?"

The man had a handsome mien, but all infectees wore a far-off expression when addressed that made others uneasy. Kay tried not to notice.

"Gracious Server." He inclined his head. "I will begin with a water, if you would be so kind, followed by a *Lettuca* salad, no dressing."

Lettuca salad: the plain food of the plain minded. All GOD infectee's were vegan but few would consume any of the more delectable fruits and vegetables – just *Lettuca*, ice-lettuce. Specially formulated dietary supplements made up for the rest of their bodily needs. Maximum nutritional intake, minimal taste. They believed that anything more was glutinous.

"Gotcha." Kay wrote the order and moved away. Best not to linger.

"Straight up leaves, Earl," she called, clipping the order up. "Hold the decoupage."

"Pah," he said. A salad was already waiting. Infectee's were nothing if not predictable.

The Government had released the first batch of GODs – Guidance and Obedience Devices – into a reservoir that fed a small town in Illinois with a bad rep. The micro-nanites, when consumed, were designed to target the primitive hypothalamic areas of the brain that induce fierce and violent impulses, and once those areas activated, to neutralise them. The first trials led to an unprecedented success. Crime rates dropped, divorce became a thing of the past, even littering ceased. Good behaviour and fine manners abounded.

It was perfect. Too perfect.

People became shadows of their former selves, lifeless drones that only ate and slept and functioned in the most basic sense. In other words, 'model citizens'.

The Government were thrilled. They called the invention 'the key to world peace'. They demanded more. But even had they not the nanites would have spread. The summer of '42 was the hottest on record – global-warming at its peak – and in the heat the reservoir had dried out. The water had evaporated into the atmosphere and taken the GODs along with it. And the nanites had a replication mandate built into their programming. After that, there was no stopping the spread. They became air-borne; evolved into roaming hives. Now they were everywhere – policing the world in their own automated way. Keeping the peace.

As Kay delivered the salad, her sister entered the diner. Maia was another government success, a 'model citizen'. And it stung every time Kay saw her.

"Oy! Can I get a refill over here?" a customer hollered – a regular citizen, clearly.

"Maia," Kay sighed, feeling the weight of her eight-hour shift, "can you, please?"

It was her time to clock off anyway.

"Of course, sweet sister," she smiled, her blue eyes vacant. "Anything to ease the flow of your life." Taking Kay's apron from her, she set to working the next booth.

Once, they had been so much alike: vibrant, snarky, quick-tempered. Now they were polar opposites. It had happened a month ago, at their home in Aurora. Maia had fought with her husband over something trivial. Tempers were always on a knife-edge when you had to be 'good' all the time. Twenty-four/seven. She'd slapped Mike. To be fair, he'd hit her first. That did not stop the GODs from targeting her too as they swarmed the house. Maia must have heard them coming, Kay had from across the street. She'd run for them, for her sister. But Roth had tackled her into the lawn. Sweet, caring, *stupid* Roth. He'd held her down as metallic mist obscured the sky. There had been no screams, only telling silence.

Maia and Mike had settled their differences that night. They had not fought since. But Maia was not the same girl and never would be again. If only it had not rained…

"Kakiya," Maia said now, standing before her with a coffee-pot. Kay jumped. Maybe the drones *did* float. "I meant to tell you when I arrived. Roth is outside."

Through the diner's glass walls, Kay could see him, propped against his motorbike by the gas-station across the way. He had on his black leathers, worn jeans and boots – standard Roth. Jet hair hung about his face, negligently cut, and his skin was tanned. But even at a distance the shadows under his eyes were stark. He looked weary. Kay knew why.

This wasn't the first day he'd lingered outside the diner.

"I don't want to talk to him."

"You should. It's been a month," Maia hummed, in that eerily detached way infectees did. "Perhaps, with gentle understanding, you will settle your differences and come to know the peace that Mike and I share. You were such a good couple, once."

Kay gritted her teeth. Maia didn't know any better. Words had been said that could never be taken back. "Thanks for telling me."

She nodded and moved along, easily absorbed by her server duties, while Kay took the back exit. Not five feet past the stinking garbage and Roth was at the alley's mouth.

The man was a blood-hound.

"We need to talk," he said, tossing down his Marlboro and stubbing it out with a boot.

"Not now," she hissed, pushing past. *Not ever.*

"Kay," he grated, following on her heels, "there was nothing we could do. They'd have taken us too, you know that. Especially after we'd de-magged our systems. I had to –"

"– I don't want to hear it!"

Always he had to rationalise, always he had to explain. Why could he not just act?

"Kay, please." Roth snatched her elbow, hauling her to a halt. The action made her skid and nearly fall – her sneakers caught on a slick patch of pavement – but his grip steadied her. And she glared at him for it – his strength had prevented her from saving her sister too.

"Miss," an airy voice said, "is everything alright?"

The *Lettuca*-salad man. He blinked at them benignly from the diner's entrance.

Only then did Kay realise what this looked like, how hard Roth gripped her, how much she glared. Hostility practically crackled between them – exactly what GODs gravitated to.

"Everything is fine," Roth said, releasing his hold and withdrawing.

"Yes, fine," Kay smiled pleasantly. "Thank you for your concern, kind citizen."

She added the last to appease the drone. They loved nothing if not their formalities.

Placated, the infectee returned inside.

"Be more careful, Roth," she hissed, rounding on him. "Or we'll both be wiped. Any excuse and those things call in the troops." The 'troops' being a silvery swarm of their misty brethren.

Her beat-up car was close and if she was quick she could make her escape. Avoid Roth for yet another day. With a huff, she searched her pockets. "Damn, I forgot my keys."

In her haste to avoid him, she'd left them in Earl's office. Ignoring Roth, she shoved through the diner's door. And came to stop. Everyone was very still. Even Maia.

"Everybody quiet!" a man grated, clearly agitated as he waved something around.

Sleek and black…. A gun.

Most sat frozen. Some held their hands up. A mother whimpered, clutching her boy close. A server set down her trembling coffee-pot. Kay's throat grew dry.

"This is a robbery, so just stay calm!" the man yelled, a hand fisting his hair, "CALM!"

No-one acted otherwise. He alone appeared not to be. The blood-shot eyes, semi-shaved buzz-cut, and bulging vein at his temple only added to his derangement. An addict, had to be. Only someone completely desperate would resort to pulling a stunt like this.

Backing up to keep them all in sight, he tossed a bag over the counter to Earl.

"Money in the bag, all of it, NOW!"

Earl complied, his eyes careful. Kay had not moved from her spot by the door. Now she realised that the robber would likely have to go past her. Should she move? Was that wise?

All thought ground to a halt as Maia meekly approached the man, her face blank. "Kind sir," she said, "there is no need for violence. If you would but sit I could fetch a beverage t-"

"-Shut up, drone!" The gun pointed at Maia.

She didn't think. Kay never did. Quick on the draw, her father used to say, never one to fight instinct. She didn't now as instinct led her to snatch his wrist and twist it up. The gun blasted once as Kay landed a fist on his nose. She put all of her strength into that punch.

Teeth cut skin, tiny nasal bones crunched. The man hit the counter head-first, then the stool, then the floor.

Out cold.

The diner grew hushed. All gazes fell on her. Not grateful, just…pitying. Why?

The door slammed open, its little bell tinkling as Roth charged in.

"What…" he gasped, taking in the scene. "Oh, Kay, no…"

The gun fell from her limp fingers to clatter on the lino. The noise sounded so loud. At her feet, the man lay unmoving while the drones regarded him with expressionless eyes. His mind was practically forfeit. She'd seen it before. Once the GODs swarmed, they would seize his body, invading until his eyes grew dim. The light within, the spark that ignited all living beings, would flicker…and extinguish. To be replaced with a soulless stare.

But he was not the only one to partake in this violent act.

The pitying gazes suddenly made sense.

"Oh," Kay gasped. "I'll be neutralised too!"

There was no way out. GODs did not discriminate between right and wrong; the deserving and the undeserving. They just did their job with cold, detached efficiency.

Horror filled her as she met Earl's gaze. He mouthed something she could not hear. Her ears were ringing. No, that was the GODs. The hum was starting outside, like the buzz of a far-off hive. Steel mist would soon rise; a metallic eclipse of silver bees that would descend on the diner. And her.

Roth snatched her hand, she thought for comfort, but before anyone could move he was yanking her out of the door and dashing down the street.

"W-what are you doing?" Kay gasped, trying to keep up as she stumbled at his side.

"No matter what you might think of me, Kakiya, I'm not about to stand by and let you become a freaking zombie!"

"Is there another choice?"

His only response was to toss her his helmet as he kick-started the bike and told her to get on. The feel of his jacket in her hands, the way her legs wound so perfectly around his thighs, was at once familiar and unwelcome. Right now, she was not about to complain. The engine roared as they tore off down the street – it barely obscured the rising hum.

* * *

There's nowhere you can hide, so they say, once the GODs start to track. They always find their marks. Legions of runners had failed before, so it was unlikely that Kay would fair any differently. She knew this. So why did she let Roth try?

Because she was afraid, that's why. No-one wants to forfeit their mind.

Six hours and two brief rest-stops later found them on the outskirts of some nameless highway, sweltering on the parking lot of a cheap motel. One room, Roth booked. One bed.

"Make yourself at home," he said.

Kay had no clothes, only her uniform – a horridly short, turquoise thing with pink hems. Earl's fashion sense left something to be desired. There was a bathrobe. She changed into that, yearning for a hot shower. The idea of what the water contained stopped her.

Roth must have thought ahead. He silently handed her a bottle of water as she reappeared. "De-magnetised," he said at her questioning look. "GOD-free."

That was all well and good for now, but what about later? How long could they last?

"Have you ever heard of anyone outrunning those things?" Kay asked as she settled on the bed. Roth stood sentinel at the window, drapes tugged shut. "I thought it was impossible."

"It's not *impossible*," he said, peeking out. "It's improbable."

"And that's better?"

No response. Kay picked at a thread on her robe.

"I'm just surprised you didn't leave me there, like you did with Maia."

The curtain swung as he dropped it. "I didn't just *leave* Maia, you know that."

Those steely eyes bored into hers; neither blue nor truly grey. *Like the sky before a storm.* Little had changed in their month apart. He was still strikingly handsome; still desirable. He read her appraisal easily.

"There was a time when you said I was devastatingly devilish," he grinned.

"There was a time when I said I loved you."

The grin vanished. "You could be more appreciative. I did just save you."

True. Why was she baiting him? But then she'd always been that way. Sometimes Kay wondered why he put up with her grit. She was reckless, rash – a prime candidate for GOD neutralisation. It was astonishing she hadn't been targeted years ago. Him, too, come to that.

"That'll need tending." Roth gestured to her hand, where the robber's teeth had sliced. Ugly burgundy congealed there. "Wounds like that go bad fast, they fester. Here."

She sat still as he pulled out a first-aid kit and cleaned and bandaged, ignoring the alcohol's sting. His hands were rough and calloused but gentle; a mechanic's hands.

Why *had* Roth stuck around this long? Kay guessed that in a world where gentility and civility were not just paramount but enforced, other qualities were rare in people. Perhaps that was what drew him, the spark of the primitive in her. Something passionate, something natural, something *human*. "Flammable, yet strong," he'd once commented of her, not long after they'd made love. Kay's cheeks flushed at the memory. There was a dark stain on the carpet – sticky, likely cola. She focussed on that.

"Do you really think I have a chance?" she asked the floor as he finished up.

"Wouldn't be here if I didn't."

"That doesn't really answer my question." Kay pulled her hand back.

He sighed. "Here in Cincinnati I met someone a way back. He told me stuff, taught me how to de-mag water and blood to clear 'em of inert nanites. Like I did for us."

Kay recalled it well, the day he'd brought home a glowing blue device. He'd said then that it was a way for them to remain free. He'd meant to use it on Maia and Mike too.

"Highly illegal in the US o' course," he chuckled, "but worth it if it saves us. That's what destroyed the few dormant GODs already in your system and stopped them activating the second you clocked that guy. It won't work on large-scale infections but it does for the small stuff. It's temporary, though, shelf-life of about a month. That's why I've been hanging around the diner. I wanted to renew your dose. But there were other things he told me…"

Kay blinked. "What things?"

Roth stashed the first-aid box and returned to his post by the window. Neon lights filtered through the gap, illuminating his shadowy frame.

"Some people don't like the way things have gone, they don't like the way our world has turned." He paused, flicking the drape. "Some people plan to do something about it."

Kay frowned. "What people?"

"Get some sleep, Kakiya. I'll keep watch."

He would say nothing more after that, no matter how much Kay pestered.

* * *

Windows rattled, the door burst off its hinges. No light shone through, no sun could breach the metallic wall. The buzz drowned all other sound. It pierced, it *screeched*, like nails being driven into her brain. Kay clamped hands over her ears and pressed into the headboard.

Her mind twisted in strange ways, recalling more clearly the details from the diner. She knew now what Earl had been mouthing. *Run.*

She woke with a start, gasping, sweating, trapped by the sheets. She fought them off.

Roth was nowhere in sight. The room was deserted. Had he left? Washed his hands of her? No, Roth would never do that. Had they found him then? Had Kay lost him too?

There was a faint patter – the tell-tale strikes of drops on the roof. Oh no…

The door opened and shut.

"Rain's started," Roth huffed as he slouched out of his jacket. "As long as you keep away from the windows the GODs won't be able to scan for you. You're safe in here. Ha, shelter – mankind's first and greatest invention –"

Kay leapt out of the bed and into his arms before he could finish.

"Whoa, what is it?" he breathed, surprised eyes searching hers.

"You were gone when I woke up. I–I thought…." There was no need to finish. Roth knew, she could tell, just by the way she quivered.

They were broken as a pair. They were a ragged wound that may never heal. But despite their estrangement, losing Roth was something Kay could not fathom.

Her kiss came hard and fast, surprising them both. But he did not pull away. The taste of him was glaringly familiar; the zest of lemon, chased by the bite of whiskey. He'd been drinking. Kay pulled at his shirt as she walked backwards, leading them to the bed.

He didn't argue. He didn't even try.

* * *

Later, as they lay wrapped around each other, hair hectic in ruffled sheets, Kay's fears started to resurface. It was easy to forget in the afterglow, a haven flooded with endorphins.

"Does this mean you forgive me?" Roth asked, in that sultry way of his, all male satisfaction as he stretched underneath her.

Kay trailed her fingers along the planes of his chest while Roth twirled one of her honey-locks around his fingers. She'd streaked it this summer, he seemed to approve.

"It means I had no right to be mad at you in the first place." Her words were carefully measured. "I was grieving for my sister. I lashed out. But you didn't deserve it."

It was as good an apology as she would, *could*, ever give.

Roth nodded, reclining on his back to stare at the cracked paint of the ceiling.

"Why were you outside?"

"Supplies." He nodded to the bags by the door. "De-magnetised water, energy bars, beef jerky, oil. All the best a gas-station has to offer. Found a gun, too – there're still a few dealers about. We'll need it where we're going. Plus I met an old contact, the one I told you of." He held her gaze significantly. "Have you heard of the Anti-GOD Movement?"

"The AGM?" There had been hints on the news, whispers, hushed gossip. "They're considered terrorists, enemies of world peace, whose sole aim is to destroy the GODs, right?"

Roth nodded. "From what I've heard, a rebel cell in the south has developed some kind of weapon. A way to counteract the nanites."

"That sounds too good to be true. How would it work, anyway?"

"Some kind of EMP tech." He ran fingers through his dishevelled bed-hair. It flopped back into his face. "If we can find 'em…"

Kay's fingers stopped their roaming. "Seems like a long-shot, doesn't it?"

Roth grinned, in that charmingly crooked way Kay was so used to. "Always the pessimist." He clucked her chin.

"Okay then, but where would we even start?"

* * *

Sand swirled in copper vortexes as the bike hurtled down the I-30, one of the few roads still capable of running low-tech transport; all others had been updated to support hover-cars and neo-trikes, and Roth had to deftly skirt the mounting craters that pockmarked its length. Kay was in for the long haul, letting him lead the way. They were headed for the Mexican border. The theory: it didn't rain as much there. GODs were fragile machines and they needed humidity to function. Rain, fog, snow. That's why crime was still rampant in the south. Phoenix was the new Chicago. Drier, hotter climates were the key to survival now. At least for Kay.

They pulled up at another motel in Arkansas, in a place called Hope.

Roth said it was a good omen.

"Not too long until we reach Dallas," he grinned. "From there it's on to San Antonio and then Monterrey. That's where our people will be."

Our people. He spoke as if they were already two among their number.

"Should take a few days but you've never minded road-tripping, have ya, Kay?"

Roth smiled a lot that day, the way he had when they were young and naïve and stupid, when they were new to travel and had no cares, when they had busked on roadsides and he'd gifted her with her nickname. The usual hardness in his eyes was absent. His head was filled with plans for their future. Did they really have one? With the current situation it didn't seem likely, even with his grand talk of repulsion tech and freedom and AGM-revolutionaries.

He was living in a bubble. One Kay was afraid to pop.

So instead of facing harsh reality she lived in it along with him. Enjoying each moment as it came. They rode the highways from dawn 'til dusk. They made love in motels and drank cheap beer from aluminium cans. They watched old-style cable and wished away the rain.

Kay never thought too long on anything, though sometimes her mind drifted…

Could they live with themselves being *that way*? As yet another Maia and Mike? The world was now filled with ranks of those. Couples Roth despised.

While he prepared a bath for them of kettle-heated, de-magged water, Kay thought on it. The daredevil would be gone. His smile would no longer be crooked or mischievous. The Roth that remained would no longer be Roth. It would be a vacant mimic, a drone. *A slate wiped clean.* The notion brought needles to her eyes. And as they tangled in the tub, caught in the throes, not all of the water that streaked her cheeks was de-magnetised.

They may have been a broken wound, in the process of uncertain healing, but he would still fight like a bear to protect her. Was she exploiting that stalwart quality to save her own skin? She often wondered as they travelled. After all, the GODs were tracking her, not him.

Eventually she told him as much and suggested he leave. The outskirts of Laredo were as good as anywhere for him to start a new life. He scoffed and waved away her concerns.

"What point would there be to a life without you?"

* * *

Waking early, Kay carefully extricated herself from their bed. Roth mumbled something incomprehensible and rolled over, deep in sleep. One last look, she promised herself. A last goodbye. No kiss. If he were to wake he would stop her.

Gathering her things, she tip-toed to the sliding door of their motel suite, intending to sneak away unnoticed. The air felt chilly as she touched its drapes. Her skin prickled at the temperature drop and Kay pulled her collar up. Frost? But it was nowhere near winter…

She opened the curtains onto a drenched desertscape – all colour darkened to rusty red. It had rained during the night. Moisture had collected on the glass before her nose.

There was a bright flash. The scan was swift and impersonal, and finite.

"Kay!"

A thud, the rush of feet, and Roth snatched her arm. His grip was as tight as a boa's, cutting the blood-flow and leaving welts as he backed them away. But Kay could not break her gaze. The glass. Mercurial droplets fused on it, humming as they danced like miniature ballerinas. The sound grew, and grew.

"You can leave, you know," she said, her voice oddly calm.

"What?"

"I never should have let you risk yourself as much as you have for me. I just wanted more time. Go now. You haven't committed any violence. They won't target you. If you-"

With a strangled grimace he aimed his gun high at the roiling drops.

And emptied all six rounds.

Glass shattered, tinkling to the floor like rain. Yet the fluid mercury remained, swallowing the bullets whole.

Kay sighed, her eyes flitting shut. *Always the martyr.* He'd damned himself too. And to think that at one time she'd wished he would 'just act'.

"It was never going to work," she said, "was it?"

The GODs tracked their prey well. None had ever escaped, none ever would. The storm of titanium swirled – a uniform hive of scraping metal that obscured the dawn.

Their bubble had officially popped.

"Eyes on me," he said, turning her to face him. She met his stormy gaze. "Eyes on me."

The hum elevated to a screeching roar as Roth wrapped her in his arms.

His will alone was not shelter enough.

* * *

That winter they bought an apartment in Chicago. Minimalist; white paint, wood floors, large windows. Anything more would have been excess. Roth said it was time for a new start after Earl had asked Kay, most abruptly, to leave his diner. He did not wish her to work there anymore. He had been most distressed when they had returned and greeted him cordially. Tears had filled his eyes. "One o' you is hard enough to stomach but two? No, I can't…"

Kay could not understand his upset, but then, he was not as enlightened as they. He did not understand the peace that came with the GODs' presence. Perhaps one day he would.

As Kay sat by their window, Roth leaned over and kissed her head. No smile.

"When I was little my grandmother had a place like this," she said conversationally. "I used to sit by her window and watch the rain fall." Kay traced a droplet, following its lonely path with a single finger. *Nature's tears.* They washed off the pane. She looked up to the water-filled sky, where slate-grey clouds rumbled. "She used to say that God is in the rain."

And if she looked close, at each individual bead, there was the tinniest swirl of silver.

Daddy's Girl

Eleanor R. Wood

DADDY LIVED in the cupboard under the stairs. I hardly ever saw him. Myra saw her dad twice a week, even though he didn't live with them. Daddy still lived with us, but his eyes were dim and his limbs were still. Sometimes I'd sneak into the cupboard when Mum wasn't looking and dust the cobwebs from his skin. I would sit beside him and lift one of his heavy arms around me and pretend he was really hugging me even though the arm hung limply beside me if I let go of his hand. But I could still lean against his steadfast frame and breathe in his faint metallic scent, laced with stale traces of his cologne.

It was the scent of safety, and love, and protection.

I took on two paper routes when Daddy was put away. For the first week he remained lifeless on the sofa, sitting there like he'd just sat down to watch TV or help me with homework. But one day I came home to find him gone. Mum came in from work and told me, in a tight voice, that she'd put him under the stairs. 'For now.' Because we didn't know what had broken, and it was too painful to have him sitting there.

People had started reading the news on paper again with the price of electricity so high. Paper needed delivering, and we needed the money. Mum already worked every available shift, so the more I could help out, the sooner we'd have Daddy home again. Properly home. Sitting at the table while we ate dinner. Waiting for me when I got home from school. Mowing the back lawn on a sunny afternoon. Not slumped in the dusty darkness with the spiders and creaking stair boards.

Months passed and our meagre savings still weren't near enough. My birthday was coming up, and I cried at the thought of spending it without Daddy. My first ever birthday without him. My thirteenth. It was supposed to be a big day when you became a teenager. I just wanted to stay twelve until we were a family again.

Mum heard me crying and came to sit on my bed. She stroked my hair, not needing to ask what was wrong.

"What if we don't ever save up enough, Mum?" I asked, my voice hitching on a sob.

"We will, sweetheart. As long as we keep our belts tight and put aside everything we can, eventually we'll have enough."

"But that could take years!"

"I know, baby. But we'll do it. He would never give up on us, and we won't ever give up on him."

I knew it was true; I'd known Daddy's story my whole life. Mum hadn't given up on him after the accident, either. Even when the doctors told her not to cling to a pipedream. Even when the dream came true and she was offered the uncertainty of testing a prototype that had never been tried before. He was the man she loved. The father of her unborn child. She had to give him a chance, even a radical one on the fringes of science. His body was useless, but his mind was alive and trapped.

So they freed him. His first body was little more than a computer, but they built him a proper one with synthetic flesh and the likeness of his own face. And he was my daddy. The only one I'd ever known.

Most children are told the tale of how their parents met. I was told how mine met all over again, and how Mum had placed the wriggling bundle that was me into Daddy's brand new arms. How he'd looked into my eyes and longed for real tears to express his overwhelming joy.

I had enough real tears for both of us now. I finished my paper route one evening and rode my bike out to the old quarry. Daddy used to take me to see the city skyline from the top of it, cupped in the lip of brutally gouged stone that formed the quarry's outer edge. Many of the tallest buildings looked desolate now, even from here. I remembered a time when they'd been gleaming and bright, beacons of human success and financial prowess. The company that built Daddy had been housed in one of them. They'd gone bust just like all the others, leaving us with no hope if anything went wrong. And of course it had gone wrong, and my daddy was sitting lifeless under the stairs waiting in vain for us to scrape enough together to have him mended.

The sobs broke through my chest before I even realised they were building. I screamed a throat-rending yell that bounced off the quarry walls and repeated itself until it diminished to nothing. I grabbed a rock and flung it at the distant skyscrapers, my rage finally finding an outlet in their failure.

I felt a little better, but I realised then that I needed to do more than extra paper rounds. I needed to feel I was contributing something useful. Daddy's experts were still out there somewhere, scattered into more austere professions, but they were no use without the mammoth funds. Saving up enough was going to take years. So be it. I would put those years to good use.

* * *

By the time I was sixteen, my shelves were piled with physics textbooks and robotics manuals. Myra's bedroom walls were covered in posters of bare-chested hunks I'd never heard of because I had my nose in *New Scientist* while she was reading *Seventeen*. I had a picture of Hiroshi Ishiguro above my bed.

"You fancy *that* guy?" Myra asked one day.

I rolled my eyes in frustration. "I don't fancy him, Myra. I admire him. He was a robotics pioneer who built one of the first interactive humanoid robots."

She looked around my room with an expression of disdain. "You seriously need to get out more."

That was the day I realised I'd outgrown her friendship. I sat under the stairs with Daddy that evening, feeling closer to him than I did to any of my peers. I pulled his arm around me and told him what Myra had said. He listened in stoic silence as always. I kissed him on the cheek and vowed he'd always be more important to me than silly nail-varnish-wearing girls.

* * *

By the time I was eighteen, the economy was slowly recovering. Food bank queues were ever shorter, councils were repairing roads again, and most importantly of all, I'd earned a scholarship to Cambridge. I was ecstatic. By now Mum and I had scraped together a few thousand, but still nowhere near enough to have Daddy fixed. Without a scholarship, there was no way I could have gone to university.

I made Mum promise to keep Daddy free of cobwebs and dust while I was away.

* * *

By the time I was twenty-three, I was embarking on a Master's degree in computational neuroscience and cognitive robotics. The depression had stunted the development of android technology, so they were still rare and expensive. The lab had one as a subject for study, but its consciousness was entirely artificial.

I was examining its servomotors late one afternoon. One of my fellow students, Raz, was working on something else two benches over. He stopped to watch me.

"Did you know Edinburgh had an uploaded consciousness model?" he asked. "I'd sell my gran to get my hands on one of those."

"What happened to it?" I tried to sound casual.

"I dunno." He flicked dark hair out of his eyes. "Somebody said it got tired of being a lab rat and walked out, but I heard that was just a stupid rumour. It's not like they have human rights!" He seemed to find this funny.

Until then, I'd been considering the idea of bringing Daddy here. There were enough experts at the university to mend him, possibly at reduced cost, but I realised he would become a coveted object for study. I couldn't do that to him.

I lowered my head, got on with my work, and politely ignored Raz for the rest of the semester. I was the only Cambridge postgrad who had ever seen an android with uploaded human consciousness, and I never mentioned it to anyone. Daddy wasn't an android to me. He was my dad, and I missed him terribly.

I studied, and learned, and worked a waitressing job in my spare time. I deposited all but my most basic expenses into the savings account I shared with Mum. For Daddy.

* * *

I built my first artificially intelligent model for my dissertation. I'd built smaller robots before; I'd been building them since I was fifteen, but this was the first machine I'd built that could learn and think for itself. I modelled its brain on that of a human toddler, with all the same capacity for growth. I wanted to see how long it took to develop the mental skills of a human adult.

I graduated with honours and received a commendation from the university.

* * *

The pioneering research into transferring human consciousness had all but ground to a halt when its funding dried up. But now that the recession was fading, there were new companies eager to invest in up-and-coming technology, and several were vying to be the first to patent prosthetic bodies for living consciousness. Less than a year into my doctorate, I was approached by a headhunter.

"We'd love to have you on board, Miss Landry."

They would fund my doctorate if I agreed to carry out research on their behalf. It was the foot in the door I'd been dreaming of.

* * *

The working atmosphere in the lab was a strange one. We were fellows, all sharing the same passions and goals, relating to one another in ways we couldn't with others in our daily lives. Yet we were also rivals, competing for that first ground-breaking discovery or technological advancement. The harsh competition meant we closely guarded our discoveries, kept our advancements under wraps, and took every advantage ruthlessly. It was the only way to get ahead.

My closest competitor was a guy named Mark. He seemed decent, but I'd never got close enough to really know him. As the two highest academic achievers and the two most likely to hit a breakthrough, we held each other in mutual respect but kept our distance. Another lab partner, Susie, pulled me up on it one day.

"Do you really have to minimise your computer files every time Mark walks past?"

"Don't you?" I asked.

"No!" Her tone suggested I was being ridiculous. "I'm not about to let him rifle through my notes, but a glance at my screen won't tell him anything."

"Don't be so sure," I muttered. "You know he only keeps paper notes in case anyone hacks his system, right? He takes the damned things everywhere with him."

"So because he's paranoid, you have to be too?"

"I wouldn't call protecting my research 'paranoia'. The guy's practically a genius, Suse. He doesn't need any help from the likes of us."

She laughed. "So said the pot to the kettle…"

I rolled my eyes at her. In truth, we all had our own methods of protecting our work. We shared trivia. We kept our trump cards close to our chests.

* * *

Mum was visiting her sister in Scotland. I went to see Daddy for the first time in weeks. He gazed through me when I opened the cupboard and crouched down in front of him.

"Come on, Daddy. It's time."

His joints creaked as I shifted him forward. I'd often wondered how Mum had managed to get him in here. His frame was reinforced aluminium, but he still weighed about the same as an average-sized man. He was a dead weight as I dragged him out of the cupboard that had been his home for the past fourteen years. I winced an apology when his head bumped the floor. I heard a tear as his trouser leg caught on an exposed nail. I was breathing hard before I'd got him halfway down the hall.

I wrangled him into an awkward position on the back seat of my car, glad of the fading dusk that gave me some privacy against nosy neighbours. I drove straight to the lab, the hour-long journey giving me time to consider how I'd get Daddy inside unseen. I talked to him about it on the way, marvelling at taking a car journey with my dad for the first time since my childhood.

It was difficult and tiring, but after draping Daddy in a blanket and positioning my access card so the entry scanners could read it without my letting go of him, I managed to negotiate the lift to the second floor and finally get him inside my lab. No one else was there; it was Friday night, and they'd all gone home for the weekend, leaving me two whole days to tinker with the most important project I'd ever taken on.

I heaved him face down onto a workbench, pulling a muscle in my back. I stumbled to a chair and sat, wincing at the pain and trying in vain to massage it away. After a few moments, it eased enough that I could stand and stretch a little. I popped some paracetamol to take care of the rest. No time for distractions; I had work to do.

There was an access port at the base of Daddy's skull, hidden beneath his hair. I realised straight away that it was an old connection. My cables wouldn't fit, but there had to be an adaptor around somewhere. I scoured the lab and found one connected to an old computer interface. With its help, I plugged a cable into Daddy and hooked him up to my diagnostic computer. I checked his power supply while it was running. He ran mainly on an ultra-compact gas turbine tucked under his ribcage. I opened the panel and an intense memory hit me: Daddy standing in the kitchen, his torso panel open as he fitted a fresh gas cylinder. I remembered looking for my own panel and wondering why I didn't have one.

"Little girls have tummies instead," he'd answered my plaintive query. "They fill them with tasty things like toast and jam to give them energy for the day. My energy goes in here…" he closed his panel "…and yours goes in here!" He'd pounced on my tummy and tickled me into hysterics.

I smiled at the memory and went to check if we had the right model cylinder. When I returned, the computer was flashing its diagnosis. My heart sank. It had flagged two errors, one of which I could handle. But the other problem was beyond my scope. A machine like Daddy would have been built and maintained by a team of people. I'd been a fool to hope I could mend whatever was wrong with him unaided.

I drank coffee as I mulled my options. I could divert my research into the necessary area to gain the knowledge I needed, but it would take months. Now Daddy was finally here, I didn't intend him to leave until he was fixed. The thought of lugging him home again made my pulled muscle throb, despite the painkillers. I wanted him to walk out on his own, at my side. I wanted Mum to find him waiting for her when she got back from Scotland. My years of patience had run out. He was here, in a laboratory that had all the necessary means to cure him, and I was damned if he was going back in the cupboard.

I knew I only had one choice, but that didn't stop me wrestling with it. My focus had been so intent I'd barely noticed what others in the lab were working on, but I knew that marked me as unusual. We were all ambitious, but my goals were personal. My fellow scientists would kill for a look at this magnificent piece of machinery. But if I didn't ask for help, that's all my dad would ever be.

I finished my coffee, took a deep breath, and phoned a colleague.

* * *

Mark's jaw dropped when he saw my workbench.

"You never said you were working on something like this." Awe permeated his voice.

"I'm not. He's broken. I can fix part of the problem, but I need your help with the microprocessors."

He seemed at a loss for words. "Where did you get this?!"

"Mark." I made him look at me. "He's my dad."

For a long moment, he just stared at me. I met his gaze squarely and turned my monitor around so he could read the diagnosis.

"Why me?" His voice was hushed. "Why not Susie, or James? They both have the experience you need."

"Yes. But so do you."

"I'm flattered. Believe me. I'm just stunned that you'd give me this opportunity. I've only ever dreamed of seeing one of these up close. An android with living consciousness…and he's your *father*? That's…a colossal amount of trust to put in a direct rival."

I took a deep breath. It was a risk, but I hadn't chosen him at random.

"There's no one else I'd trust with this. I can't fix him on my own." I could only hope he'd help me for the right reasons, but it was a gamble I had to take. Maybe he'd demand to experiment on Daddy, or expose my advantage and give others a reason to dismiss my real achievements as a mere rehashing of previous technology. It wouldn't be true, but it would be enough to tarnish my career.

Either way, Daddy would be mended.

Mark stared at Daddy's immobile frame. He touched his cold face and looked up at mine, as if noticing the resemblance between the artificial and the organic.

I met his eye again. "Please. He's been broken for fourteen years."

He set his shoulders as he reached a decision. "We'll need parts. Very expensive parts."

"I know. I have the funds." Labour costs and lab hire were no longer an issue.

I wanted to ask if he'd sell me out. I wanted to know if he would ask for permanent access to Daddy in return for his assistance. But I couldn't get the words out. What would I do if he said 'yes' to either question? There was no turning back, not now that I was this close. I decided I'd rather not know.

Mark and I didn't leave the lab all weekend. We pilfered the parts from other projects and I ordered identical replacements. I told Mark all about Daddy, but I don't think he believed in Daddy's successfully-transferred consciousness until late on Sunday evening.

Everything was back in place and Daddy lay face up on my bench. I activated the power supply and closed his torso panel. Mark and I held our breath. Several tense seconds passed. And then my daddy opened his eyes and looked at me.

"Bethy?" He squinted and turned his head, clearly trying to orient himself. "Beth, is that you?"

It was like a tight string snapping inside me. My knees buckled and then there were strong, familiar arms around me, keeping me from collapsing, holding me up. I clutched him like I was five years old again and sobbed into his shoulder as he held me. He was warm, and real, and alive, and he was holding me all on his own.

When I finally looked at Mark, his eyes were glistening with tears.

"Mark, this is my dad."

Mark and Daddy shook hands, though I could see Daddy was still befuddled. "It's an honour, Mr Landry."

"Where am I, Beth? You...you're grown." He cupped my face. "You're a woman. What happened to me?"

I sat him down and told him everything. He had no memory of breaking down and no knowledge of time passing since. I was grateful that no part of his consciousness had been active. He didn't recall the dark, dusty cupboard.

He hugged me close for a long moment. "Thank you. Thank you so much, sweetheart. I'm so proud of you. I can't even express it."

"You don't have to. You're here. That's more than enough for me."

He pulled away and looked at me in earnest. "Where's Mum? Is she here?"

I smiled, imagining her joy. "She's not expecting this. I didn't want to get her hopes up." I video-called her on my mobile and made sure she was sitting down before I passed the phone to Daddy.

"Hi, love," he said. I heard a sharp intake of breath from Mum's end, and then nothing for a long moment, and then crying.

I took Mark aside to give them some privacy. He and I both needed rest; I could see he wanted to get home.

"I'm in your debt, Mark. I couldn't have done it without you."

He shook his head with a smile. "You don't owe me anything. The chance to see him up close, to work on him, to actually meet someone like him in person...I should be thanking *you*."

I felt the last shred of tension leave me. He was referring to Daddy as a real person. The way I'd always seen him. I somehow knew then that Mark wasn't about to turn my lifelong secret to his advantage.

I took his hand. "Thank you. For everything."

"He's your dad. I'm sure you'd have done the same if it had been my old man lying on the table." He looked down at the floor. "I wish I had that chance. My dad died five years ago. Go make up for lost time with yours."

Before I could say anything, he gently nudged me in Daddy's direction and picked up his things to leave.

"Any time you want to sit and talk with him, I'm sure he'd be happy to," I called after him.

He just turned and smiled at me, one friend to another.

Biographies & Sources

L. Frank Baum
Ozma of Oz
(Originally Published by Reilly & Britton in 1907)
Frank L. Baum (1856–1919) was born in Chittenango, New York and enjoyed a comfortable upbringing as the son of a barrel factory owner who had success in the oil business. Named 'Lyman' after an uncle, Baum hated his first name and chose to be called by his middle name 'Frank' instead. Although he is best known for his children's book, *The Wizard of Oz* (1900), Baum didn't actually didn't start writing for children until he was in his forties. His first collection for young readers, *Mother Goose in Prose* (1897) was followed by the hugely popular *Father Goose, His Book* (1899). A man of extreme literary passion, Baum wrote 55 other novels (some under pseudonyms), 83 short stories and over 200 poems.

Ambrose Bierce
Moxon's Master
(Originally Published in *The San Francisco Examiner,* 1899)
Ambrose Bierce (1824–*c.* 1914) was born in Meigs County, Ohio. He was a famous journalist and author known for writing *The Devil's Dictionary.* After fighting in the American Civil War, Bierce used his combat experience to write stories based on the war, such as in 'An Occurrence at Owl Creek Bridge'. Following the separate deaths of his ex-wife and two of his three children he gained a sardonic view of human nature and earned the name 'Bitter Bierce'. His disappearance at the age of 71 on a trip to Mexico remains a great mystery and continues to spark speculation.

Roan Clay
Why Should Steel Birds Dream?(First Publication)
Roan Clay lives and writes in Alberta, Canada. He has been involved in gemology, website maintenance and child care, though writing remains his true passion. Occasionally, he is called on to speak in schools, where he does his best to inspire children with a love of literature through poetry and his own short stories. Roan owes his early love of reading to his parents, who inoculated him with books at an early age. He has been influenced by such creators as Rudyard Kipling, Isaac Asimov, Harlan Ellison, Ray Bradbury and George Pal.

Carlo Collodi
Pinocchio: The Tale of a Puppet (chapters I–VII)
(Originally Published by Whitman Publishing Co., 1916)
Carlo Lorenzini (1826–90) was better known by his pen name Carlo Collodi. To support the Italian unification movement of the time, Collodi took to journalism and founded the newspaper *Il Lampione* in 1848. When the Kingdom of Italy was founded in 1871, Collodi started writing for children. His stories appeared weekly in *Il Giornale per I Bambini*, the first Italian newspaper for children. Some featured his character Pinocchio, the childlike, mischievous puppet, which young children could easily identify with.

George Cotronis
Prototype
(Originally Published in *Futuristica Vol 2*, 2017)
George Cotronis is a Greek writer living in the wilderness of Northern Sweden. He makes a living designing book covers. His stories have appeared in *Pantheon, Year's Best Hardcore Horror, Lost*

Signals and *Turn to Ash*. He edits for Kraken Press. George cites influences such as Norman Partridge, Philip K. Dick and Ray Bradbury, and you can find out more about him at cotronis.com.

Deborah L. Davitt

Demeter's Regard

(Originally Published in *Compelling Science Fiction* #6, 2017)

Deborah L. Davitt was raised in Reno, Nevada, but received her MA in English from Penn State. She currently lives in Houston, Texas with her husband and son. Her poetry has received Rhysling and Pushcart nominations and appeared in over twenty journals; her short fiction alternates between science fiction and fantasy, and has appeared in *InterGalactic Medicine Show*, *Compelling Science Fiction*, *Grievous Angel*, and *The Fantasist*. Her Edda-Earth novels mix alternate history, magic, science, and mythology to create a wholly re-imagined world in which Rome never fell. For more about her work, please see www.edda-earth.com.

Jeff Deck

Persona Ex Machina (First Publication)

Jeff Deck is a fiction ghostwriter and editor whose writing has been featured on *The Today Show*. He lives in Maine (U.S.) with his wife, Jane, and their silly dog, Burleigh. Deck's newest book is *City of Ports*, the first in an urban fantasy series. His previous novels are the supernatural thriller *The Pseudo-Chronicles of Mark Huntley* and the sci-fi gaming adventure *Player Choice*. Deck is also the author, with Benjamin D. Herson, of the nonfiction book *The Great Typo Hunt* (Crown/Random House). He has stories in the anthologies *Corporate Cthulhu* (Pickman's Press) and *Murder Ink 2* (Plaidswede).

Luke Dormehl

Foreword: Robots & Artificial Intelligence Short Stories

Luke Dormehl is a technology journalist, author and filmmaker. He has written three popular science and technology books, most recently *Thinking Machines: The Inside Story of Artificial Intelligence and our Race to Build the Future* (2016). His journalism on the subject of artificial intelligence and other emerging technologies has appeared in publications including *Wired*, *The Guardian*, *Digital Trends*, *Politico*, and others. He also regularly contributes to *SFX* magazine. Luke often speaks on BBC radio and has directed documentaries for Channel 4. He lives in Bristol with his wife, daughter, cat and far too many unread books.

Edward S. Ellis

The Steam Man of the Prairies

(Originally Published in *Beadle's American Novel* No. 45, 1868)

Edward Sylvester Ellis (1840–1916) was a teacher, journalist and the author of hundreds of books and magazine articles. His first best-selling book, the dime novel *Seth Jones or the Captives of the Frontier* (1860) led to a contract with New York publisher Beadle and Adams to write four dime novels every year. Over the next thirty years, Ellis wrote more than 300 novels and story collections for several publishers. However, Ellis didn't always use his name. He published many titles under James Fenimore Cooper Adams or Captain Bruin Adams, as well as some under the names Seelin Robins and Charles E. Lasalle.

Christopher M. Geeson

The Perfect Reflection (First Publication)

Christopher M. Geeson has had several stories published, including another AI-themed story, 'Punchbag', about the future of violence, which appeared in *The British Fantasy Society Journal – Autumn 2011*.

He has also had tales published in *Atomic Age Cthulhu*, *Steampunk Cthulhu*, and *Anthology: A Circa Works Collection*, all of which are available on Amazon. In addition, he was chosen for a TAPS scheme, where a script of his was produced at ITV and screened at a Channel 4 event. Christopher works in schools and museums in North Yorkshire, delivering creative workshops for children.

Bruce Golden

Owen

(Originally Published in *Dancing with the Velvet Lizard*, 2011)

Bruce Golden's short stories have been published more than a hundred times across a score of countries and 30 anthologies. *Asimov's Science Fiction* described his novel *Evergreen*: "If you can imagine Ursula Le Guin channelling H. Rider Haggard, you'll have the barest conception of this stirring book, which centres around a mysterious artifact and the people in its thrall." The San Diego writer's latest book, *Monster Town*, is a satirical send-up of old hard-boiled detective stories featuring movie monsters of the black & white era. It's currently in development for a possible TV series. Find out more about Bruce's work at goldentales.tripod.com

Gustave Guitton

The Billionaires' Conspiracy (Book II, chapters XIX–XXIV)

(Originally Published in 1899–1900; Translation by Brian Stableford Published by Black Coat Press in 2012, www.blackcoatpress.com and copyright © Brian Stableford)

Gustave Léon Guiton (1859–1918) was a collaborator and friend of Gustave Le Rouge. Their writings began with *La conspiration des milliardaires* (*The Billionaires' Conspiracy*) which was a trilogy published between 1899 and 1900. They worked together for three more projects: *Les conquérants de la mer* (*The Transatlantic Threat*), *La princesse des airs* (*The Psychic Spies*) and *Le sous-marin* (*The Victims Victorious*), all published in 1902.

Rob Hartzell

The Geisha Tiresias

(Originally Published in *Eunoia Review*, 2013)

Rob Hartzell lives and works in Morrow, Ohio. 'The Geisha Tiresias' is part of a larger fiction-cycle: *Pictures of the Floating-Point World*. Another piece from the cycle, 'The Hives and the Hive-Nots', appeared in Flame Tree's Gothic Fantasy: Science Fiction Short Stories anthology (2015). Others have appeared most recently in *The Black Rabbit*, *The London Reader*, and *New Reader Magazine*. When not at his writing desk, Rob is reading up on neuroscience, cultural and religious esoterica, and various dictionaries. You can find Rob online at robhartzell.wordpress.com, or follow him at Goodreads and Facebook.

E.T.A Hoffman

Automata

(Originally Published in *The Serapion Brethren*, 1819)

Ernst Theodor Amadeus Hoffmann (1776–1822) was a musician and a painter as well as a successful writer. Born in Germany and raised by his uncle, Hoffmann followed a legal career until his interests drew him to composing operas and ballets. He began to write richly imaginative stories that helped secure his reputation as an influential figure during the German Romantic movement, with many of his tales inspiring stage adaptations, such as *The Nutcracker* and *Coppélia*. Hoffmann's chilling tale 'The Sandman' has influenced many, including Neil Gaiman, whose popular graphic novel series *The Sandman* also features a character who steals peoples' eyes.

Nathaniel Hosford

Fiat Lex (First Publication)

Nathaniel Hosford hails from the gulf coast of Texas and, after sojourns on the west and east coasts, now resides in central Texas. By day he works as a history professor at a private research university and by night he speculates wildly about both past and future. Like many, he learned the power of the mythopoeic from J.R.R. Tolkien and C.S. Lewis, but he owes much of his present interest in speculative fiction to a chance encounter with a Robert Jordan novel. This is his first professional fiction publication.

Jerome K. Jerome

The Dancing Partner

(Originally Published in 1893)

Jerome Klapka Jerome (1859–1927) was born in Staffordshire, England. A novelist, playwright and editor, his humour secured his popularity. Inspired by his sister Blandina's love for the theatre, a young Jerome tried his hand at acting under the name of 'Harold Crichton'. After three difficult years, he departed from the stage and pursued a number of odd jobs as a teacher, journalist and essayist – to no avail. However, success eventually arrived through his memoir, *On the Stage – and Off*. Building upon the strength of his writing, Jerome's best-known novel, *Three Men in a Boat* (1889) exemplified his comic talent. However he also delved into more genre tales, like the chilling ghost story 'The Man of Science' or the early robotic story 'The Dancing Partner'.

Rachael K. Jones

The Greatest One-Star Restaurant in the Whole Quadrant

(Originally Published in *Lightspeed Magazine*, 2017)

Rachael K. Jones grew up in various cities across Europe and North America, picked up (and mostly forgot) six languages, and acquired several degrees in the arts and sciences. Now she writes speculative fiction in Portland, Oregon. Her debut novella, *Every River Runs to Salt*, will be out with Fireside Fiction in late 2018. Contrary to the rumours, she is probably not a secret android. Rachael is a World Fantasy Award nominee and Tiptree Award honouree. Her fiction has appeared in dozens of venues worldwide, including *Lightspeed*, *Beneath Ceaseless Skies*, *Strange Horizons*, and *PodCastle*. Follow her on Twitter @RachaelKJones.

Rich Larson

Dispo and the Crow

(Originally Published in *Mythic Delirium*, 2017)

Rich Larson was born in Galmi, Niger, has studied in Rhode Island and worked in the south of Spain, and now lives in Ottawa, Canada. Since he began writing in 2011, he's sold over a hundred stories, the majority of them speculative fiction published in magazines like *Asimov's*, *Analog*, *Clarkesworld*, *F&SF*, *Lightspeed*, and Tor.com. His work appears in numerous *Year's Best* anthologies and has been translated into Chinese, Vietnamese, Polish, Czech, French and Italian. *Annex*, his debut novel and first book of *The Violet Wars* trilogy, came out in July 2018 from Orbit Books. *Tomorrow Factory*, his debut collection, follows in October 2018 from Talos Press. Besides writing, he enjoys travelling, learning languages, playing soccer, watching basketball, shooting pool, and dancing salsa and kizomba.

Monte Lin

Adrift (First Publication)

Monte Lin has been slowly moving up the West Coast of the United States and currently lives adjacent to Portland, Oregon. When not rolling dice, pushing cardboard tokens around, or fanboying over the next Doctor, he writes and copyedits for tabletop role-playing games and video games. He is currently exasperated with his unruly and unfinished sci-fi and fantasy short stories and annoyed with a couple of uncooperative YA novels. He can be found barely tweeting @Monte_Lin.

Elias Lönnrot

The Kalevala (Ilmarinen's Bride of Gold, Rune XXXVII)
(Originally Published by J. C. Frenckell ja Poika in 1835)
Elias Lönnrot (1802–84) was a Finnish physician, linguist and poet known for creating the epic poem *The Kalevala,* one of the most highly regarded works of Finnish literature. It became integral to the cultural landscape in Finland and made a contribution to the Language Strife – a conflict in the mid-nineteenth century that arose from class tensions caused by the use of both Swedish and Finnish languages in Finland. These tensions ultimately led up to the Finnish Independence from Russia in 1917. The poem is also said to be one of the inspirations for J.R.R. Tolkien's *Silmarillion* and *The Lord of the Rings*.

Edward Page Mitchell

The Ablest Man in the World
(Originally Published in *The New York Sun,* 1879)
Pioneer of the science fiction genre, American author Edward Page Mitchell (1852–1927) was a short story writer and editor for *The Sun* newspaper in New York. His work featured predominantly in *The Sun*, and most of his stories were published anonymously. His story 'The Clock That Went Backward', which is a contender for the first time-travel story and predates H.G. Wells's *The Time Machine*, was also published anonymously in *The Sun* and Mitchell wasn't revealed as the author until 40 years after his death.

Trixie Nisbet

EQ (First Publication)
As befits her age, Trixie Nisbet lives in a bungalow on the south coast near Brighton, UK. She has had over forty stories printed, mostly in women's magazines, in the UK, Australia and South Africa, and has won several national short story competitions. Her sci-fi credentials involve her alter ego: 'Rob Nisbet' (she uses her husband's name). As 'Rob', she is behind several anthology stories, and, to date, has had six audio adventures released by Big Finish for their Doctor Who range. 'Rob' is currently toiling at a sci-fi novel for middle-grade readers.

William Douglas O'Connor

The Brazen Android
(Originally Published in *The Atlantic Monthly,* 1891)
William Douglas O'Connor (1832–89) was an American journalist and author who worked as a civil servant for part of his life, during which time he delivered annual reports to Congress that became famous for being exceptionally gripping. He was also an activist for liberal causes, working towards anti-slavery and reformation of women's rights. His 1891 story 'The Brazen Android' explores the legend if Friar Roger Bacon's talking Brazen Head. He began writing it in 1857 but it wasn't published until after his death.

Chloie Piveral

A Woman of One's Own (First Publication)
Chloie Piveral is a speculative fiction writer who has come unstuck in the American Midwest. She loves dogs, rayguns, octopuses, windup toys, and speculative fiction in all its permutations. Her influences include Ray Bradbury, Margaret Atwood, Terry Pratchett, Tom Robbins, Ted Chiang, and Octavia Butler. When not reading she can be found watching and rewatching Jean-Pierre Jeunet films. A 2015 graduate

of The Odyssey Writing Workshop, her work has appeared in *Kaleidotrope* and *Kazka Press*: 713 Flash. Follow her on Twitter @C_Piveral.

Apollonius Rhodius

The Argonautica (Book IV extract)
(Originally Published in 3rd Century B.C.)
Ancient Greek author Apollonius Rhodius (early 3rd century BC–late 3rd century BC) was best known for *The Argonautica*, an epic work about the adventures of Jason and the Argonauts and their quest to find the Golden Fleece. Other works by Rhodius unfortunately only survive in fragments and very little is known about his life. It is thought that he lived in Rhodes, but even this is speculation.

Gustave Le Rouge

The Billionaires' Conspiracy (Book II, chapters XIX–XXIV)
(Originally Published in 1899–1900; Translation by Brian Stableford Published by Black Coat Press in 2012, www.blackcoatpress.com and copyright © Brian Stableford)
Gustave Le Rouge (1867–1938) was a French author who was fundamental to modern science fiction at the beginning of the twentieth century. His first work was a trilogy: *La conspiration des milliardaires* (*The Billionaires' Conspiracy*), a collaboration with Gustave Guitton. He went on to write solo fiction, including *La Reine des Éléphants* (The Queen of Elephants) in 1906 which explored a society of intelligent elephants. But he is perhaps best known for *Le Prisonnier de la Planète Mars* (1908) and its sequel, *La Guerre des Vampires* (1909) in which a French engineer is dispatched to Mars.

Luis Philip Senarens

Frank Reade Jr. and His New Steam Man or, The Young Inventor's Trip to the Far West
Frank Reade Jr. and His New Steam Horse or, the Search for a Million Dollars
(Originally Published in *Frank Reade Library*, 1892)
Luis Philip Senarens (1863–1939) was born and grew up in Brooklyn, New York. He became a dime writer, publishing a great many stories for many American magazines and was editor for *Mystery Magazine*. His Frank Reade Jr. stories followed on from the previous stories about Frank Reade Sr. written by Harry Enton in 1868. The stories were hugely successful and became the inspiration for *Jack Wright: The Boy Inventor,* the first in a series of novels featuring the inventor.

David Sklar

I, Coffeepot (First Publication)
David Sklar never learned to drink coffee until he had kids. A Rhysling nominee and past winner of the Julia Moore Award for Bad Verse, he has more than 100 published works, including fiction in *Nightmare* and *Strange Horizons*, poetry in *Ladybug* and *Stone Telling*, and humour in *Knights of the Dinner Table* and *McSweeney's Internet Tendency*. David lives with his wife, their two barbarians, and a secondhand familiar in a cliffside cottage in Northern New Jersey, where he almost supports his family as a freelance writer and editor. He's also the creator of the Poetry Crisis Line at poetrycrisis.org.

Claire Allegra Sorrenson

She Swims (First Publication)
Claire Allegra Sorrenson is a speculative fiction writer living in Durham, North Carolina. She writes about love and loss, robots and aliens, loneliness and ghosts – not always in that order, and not usually all at once. Her characters stumble across new (and sometimes bizarre) frontiers, with all the tenderness

and imperfections of their hearts in full view. When Claire is not imagining life on other worlds, she enjoys exploring the forests and coasts of this world, imbibing caffeinated beverages, and interacting peaceably with members of her species over beer. Visit her at claireallegra.com.

Sara L. Uckelman

Being Human
(First Publication)
Dr. Sara L. Uckelman is an assistant professor of logic and philosophy of language at Durham University by day and a writer of speculative fiction by night. She has short stories published in *Pilcrow & Dagger* and *Story Seed Vault* and forthcoming in anthologies published by *Hic Dragones*, *Jayhenge Publications*, and *WolfSinger Publications*. She is also the co-founder of the reviews site SFFReviews.com.

Holly Lyn Walrath

Stardust (First Publication)
Holly Lyn Walrath's poetry and short fiction has appeared in *Strange Horizons, Fireside Fiction, Luna Station Quarterly, Liminality,* and elsewhere. Her chapbook of words and images *Glimmerglass Girl* will be published by Finishing Line Press in 2018. She holds a B.A. in English from The University of Texas and a Master's in Creative Writing from the University of Denver. She is a freelance editor and host of The Weird Circular, an e-newsletter for writers containing submission calls and writing prompts. You can find her canoeing the bayou in Seabrook, Texas, on Twitter @HollyLynWalrath, or at www.hlwalrath.com.

Nemma Wollenfang

GOD is in the Rain
(Originally Published in *A Bleak New World*, 2015)
Nemma is an MSc Postgraduate and prize-winning short story writer who lives in Northern England. Generally she adheres to Science Fiction – perhaps as a result of years in the laboratory cackling like a mad scientist – but she has been known to branch out. Her stories have appeared in several anthologies, including: *Dark Luminous Wings, Love Under the Harvest Moon,* and *Masked Hearts,* as well as previously in Flame Tree's Gothic Fantasy series. Two of her unpublished novels have now been shortlisted in, or won, awards.

Eleanor R. Wood

Daddy's Girl
(Originally Published in *Crossed Genres*, 2014)
Eleanor R. Wood's stories have appeared in over a dozen venues, including *Pseudopod, Flash Fiction Online, Deep Magic, Daily Science Fiction, Galaxy's Edge,* and the Aurealis-nominated anthology *Hear Me Roar.* She is an associate editor at PodCastle, where she gets to feed dragons and exercise her reading skills. She writes and eats liquorice from the south coast of England, where she lives with her husband, two marvellous dogs, and enough tropical fish tanks to charge an entry fee. You can find her online at creativepanoply.wordpress.com.

GOTHIC FANTASY

For our books, calendars, blog
and latest special offers please see:
flametreepublishing.com